S0-AGU-481

PRAISE FOR THE HARDCOVER EDITION

"[A] faithful translation—accompanied by striking black-and-white illustrations, evocative of shadow theatre, by Andrea Dezsö....[T]he Grimms are spare, spinning the tales into beautifully wrought short stories."—Francesca Wade, *Times Literary Supplement*

"This new translation...allows those without German expertise a chance to re-experience familiar stories in all their original Hemingwayesque terseness."—Michael Dirda, *Washington Post*

"[T]he new Zipes translation of the first edition, with all its notes and annotations, is a must, a treasure for anyone with a serious interest in fairy tales, the motifs of which linger perpetually in the collective mind."—Carmel Bird, *Sydney Morning Herald*

"Thoroughly engaging, Zipes' translations into colloquial American English breathe life into these stories. Award-winning artist Andrea Dezsö's cut-paper black and white illustrations capture the essence of this strange and enchanting world that will entice fans of mystical realms and those interested in better understanding the Grimms' enduring influence on literature."—Barbara Basbanes Richter, *Fine Books & Collections*

"[M]agnificent...what makes this newly released original volume especially enchanting are the breathtaking illustrations by Romanian-born artist Andrea Dezsö."
—Maria Popova, *Brain Pickings*

"The new book, published by Princeton University Press, offers a fascinating insight into how the collection has changed with the times."—Nick Enoch, *Mail Online*

"Think you know fairy tales? Be prepared for a nasty shock."—Andrew Donaldson, *Rand Daily Mail*

"Zipes has produced the inaugural English translation of the two original volumes in a gutsy, robust style—warts-and-all."—Marguerite Johnson, *The Conversation*

"A far more unsettling, exhilarating, oral and adult encounter than you might expect of 'fairy stories.'"—Arifa Akbar, *Independent*

"Jack Zipes's new translation of the original two volumes of the Grimm Brothers' fairy tales is a revelation....I know I'll be going back to this book, time and again in the years to come."—Benjamin Read, *Books To Look For*

"[A]ccepted as probably the world's greatest authority on the Grimms and fairy tales in general, Zipes is well qualified to redress the common perception of the brothers' published works."—Kevin Murphy, *Magonia*

"Zipes puts forth expert and readable analysis and thoughts on the Grimms, and provides an excellent critical starting point to foster interest in the brothers' history and continuing legacy."—Sam Harby, *Nudge Books*

"It's one thing to read Zipes's erudite commentary on the tales, and quite another to discover these differences for oneself in the reading experience, and thus I encourage folklorists, fairy-tale scholars, and lay readers alike to peruse the pages of the first edition of the Grimms' tales. The illustrations by Andrea Dezsö—stark, simple, and beautiful—are an additional treat."—Jeana Jorgensen, *Journal of Folklore Research*

"A massive and brilliant accomplishment—the first English translation of the original Grimm brothers' fairy tales. The plain telling is that much more forceful for its simplicity and directness, particularly in scenes of naked self-concern and brutality. Hate, spite, love, magic, all self-evident, heartbreaking, delightful. I will return to this book over and over, no doubt about it."—Donna Jo Napoli, author of *The Wager*

"This complete, unexpurgated, and insightfully annotated English-language edition of the Grimms' tales keeps readers anchored in the timeless world of the fairy tale. It will be treasured by all lovers of stories. Irresistible and unputdownable."—Shelley Frisch, translator of *Kafka: The Years of Insight*

"Jack Zipes's translations of the 156 tales in this significant edition are truly exquisite." —Ulrich C. Knoepflmacher, author of *Ventures into Childland: Victorians, Fairy Tales, and Femininity*

"Zipes, who edited and translated the new collection, has done splendid work, first in arguing for the early tales' significance....Zipes' most important achievement, though, is simply putting the complete, uncensored tales before readers to judge for themselves....*The Original Folk and Fairy Tales*—beautifully illustrated by Andrea Dezsö, by the way—isn't the Disneyfied version of the Brothers Grimm that we all grew up with. But for readers whose tastes lean more to, say, Tim Burton, wading into the collection might feel like stumbling into an agreeably dark and Gothic forest."—Doug Childers, *Richmond Times-Dispatch*

"Who wouldn't want to read a story called *The Singing Bone*? 156 fables—their collected works—newly translated but easily just as creepy and weird."—*Globe and Mail*

"Zipes's translation of the first edition of the collection by the Brothers Grimm is a wonderful addition to the material available in English."—Rowan Williams, *New Statesman*

"As nature, admittedly sharp in tooth, claw and thorn, intended."—James Kidd, *South China Morning Post*

"With Disney's adaptation of Stephen Sondheim's fairy tale mash-up musical *Into the Woods* finding a wide, wide-smiling reception at the box office, it's the perfect time to consider the source: Jacob and Wilhelm Grimm's dark and stormy tales....Andrea Dezsö's illustrations—black-and-white, woodcut-like silhouettes—add the right note of eerie timelessness to these wondrous, wondrously strange yarns."—Steven Rea, *Philadelphia Inquirer*

THE ORIGINAL FOLK
AND FAIRY TALES OF
THE BROTHERS GRIMM

THE COMPLETE FIRST EDITION

The Original Folk & Fairy Tales OF THE BROTHERS GRIMM

TRANSLATED & EDITED BY
JACK ZIPES

ILLUSTRATED BY
ANDREA DEZSÖ

JACOB AND WILHELM GRIMM

PRINCETON UNIVERSITY PRESS

Princeton and Oxford

Copyright © 2014 by Princeton University Press
Illustrations copyright © Andrea Dezsö 2014
Published by Princeton University Press, 41 William Street, Princeton, New Jersey 08540
In the United Kingdom: Princeton University Press, 6 Oxford Street, Woodstock, Oxfordshire
OX20 1TR

press.princeton.edu

Cover illustration and design © Andrea Dezsö.

Seventh printing, first paperback printing, 2016

Paperback ISBN: 978-0-691-17322-1

The Library of Congress has cataloged the cloth edition of this book as follows:

Grimm, Jacob, 1785–1863.
[Kinder- und Hausmärchen. English. 2015]
The Original Folk and Fairy Tales of the Brothers Grimm : the Complete First Edition / [Jacob
Grimm, Wilhelm Grimm ; translated by] Jack Zipes ; [illustrated by Andrea Dezsö].
    pages cm
Includes bibliographical references and index.
ISBN 978-0-691-16059-7 (hardback : acid-free paper) 1. Fairy tales—Germany. 2. Tales—
Germany. 3. Folklore—Germany. I. Grimm, Wilhelm, 1786–1859. II. Zipes, Jack, 1937–
III. Dezsö, Andrea. IV. Title.
GR166.G54313 2015
398.20943—dc23
        2014004127

British Library Cataloging-in-Publication Data is available

This book has been composed in Garamond Premier Pro

Printed on acid-free paper. ∞

Printed in Canada

10 9 8 7

For Bianca Lazzaro and Carmine Donzelli,
whose friendship has sparked my life and
my interest in folk and fairy tales

CONTENTS

Volume II

FIGURES

ACKNOWLEDGMENTS

Over the past forty years or so I had often wondered why nobody had ever translated the first edition of the Grimms' *Kinder- und Hausmärchen* (1812/15) into English, and it was not until 2012, the bicentenary of these two volumes, that I decided, if nobody was going to undertake this "task," I would do it—and do it out of pleasure and to share the unusual tales the Grimms collected as young men when they had not fully realized what a treasure they had uncovered. Their tales are, in fact, a treasure that belongs not only to Germany but also to many other countries in the world.

In sharing this treasure I have been most fortunate to have the understanding of the editorial staff at Princeton University Press, wonderful editors, who have supported my work in the fields of folklore and fairytale studies during the past ten years. So, I want to take this opportunity to thank them all for their assistance. In particular, I want to express my gratitude to the two editors in charge of *The Original Folk and Fairy Tales of the Brothers Grimm*, namely, Alison MacKeen and Anne Savarese, who shepherded the manuscript through the first stages of approval. Their advice has been invaluable. In addition, there are not words enough to thank Sara Lerner, with whom I have worked on a few occasions. She is one of the most thorough, attentive, and keen production editors I have ever encountered. Jennifer Harris, who copyedited the entire book, improved the manuscript immensely, and I relied greatly on her advice.

Maria Lindenfeldar and Jason Alejandro have played key roles in creating the art design for the book and have guided me wisely in selecting the images for the tales. Last but not least, I want to thank Andrea Dezsö for contributing her extraordinary illustrations that reveal many of the hidden meanings of the tales.

INTRODUCTION: REDISCOVERING THE ORIGINAL TALES OF THE BROTHERS GRIMM

JACK ZIPES

Just a little over two hundred years ago, in December of 1812, Jacob and Wilhelm Grimm published the first volume of their *Kinder- und Hausmärchen* (*Children's and Household Tales*), followed by a second volume in 1815. Little did the Grimms realize at that time that their tales would become the most famous "fairy tales" in the world and that the bicentennial of these two extraordinary books would be celebrated in conferences and ceremonies worldwide between 2012 and 2015. Ironically, few people today are familiar with the original tales of the first edition, for the Grimms went on to publish six more editions and made immense changes in them so that the final 1857 edition has relatively little in common with the first edition. From 1812 to 1857 the Brothers deleted numerous tales from the first edition, replaced them with new or different versions, added over fifty tales, withdrew the footnotes and published them in a separate volume, revised the prefaces and introductions, added illustrations in a separate small edition directed more at children and families, and embellished the tales so that they became polished artistic "gems."

All these editorial changes to the tales in the first edition of 1812/15 should not lead us to believe that the tales were crude, needed improvement, and do not deserve our attention. On the contrary. I would argue that the first edition is just as important, if not more important than the final seventh edition of 1857, especially if one wants to grasp the original intentions of the Grimms and the overall significance of their accomplishments. In fact, many of the tales in the first edition are more fabulous and baffling than those refined versions in the final edition, for they retain the pungent and naïve flavor of the oral tradition. They are stunning narratives precisely because they are so blunt and unpretentious. Moreover, the Grimms had not yet "vaccinated" or censored them with their sentimental Christianity and puritanical ideology. In fact, the Brothers endeavored to keep their hands off the tales, so to speak, and reproduce them more or less as they heard them or received them. That is, the tales were not their own in the first place. Though they gradually made them their own, these stories retained other voices and still do. They originated through the storytelling of various friends and anonymous sources and were often taken from print materials. Then they were edited for publication by the Grimms, who wanted to retain their ancient and contemporary voices as much as possible.

It was not until the second edition of 1819 that there was a clear editorial change of policy that led to the refinement of the tales, especially by Wilhelm, who became the major editor from 1816 onward. The break in policy was not a sudden one; rather, it was gradual, and Jacob was always of the opinion that the tales should not be altered very much and tried to resist embellishment. But he was occupied by so many other projects that he did not object vociferously to Wilhelm's changes as long as his brother preserved what he felt to be the essence of the tales. However, Wilhelm could not control his desire to make the tales more artistic to appeal to middle-class reading audiences. The result is that the essence of the tales is more vivid in the two volumes of the first edition, for it is here that the

Grimms made the greatest effort to respect the voices of the original storytellers or collectors.

It is important to remember that the Grimms did not travel about the land themselves to collect the tales from peasants, as many contemporary readers have come to believe. They were brilliant philologists and scholars who did most of their work at desks. They depended on many different informants from diverse social classes to provide them with oral tales or literary tales that were rooted in oral traditions. Although they did at times leave their home—for example, to find and write down tales from several young women in Kassel and Münster and from some lower-class people in the surrounding villages—they collected their tales and variants primarily from educated friends and colleagues or from books. At first, they did not greatly alter the tales that they received because they were young and inexperienced and did not have enough material from other collectors to make comparisons. And, indeed, this is why the first edition of 1812/15 is so appealing and unique: the unknown tales in this edition are formed by multiple and diverse voices that speak to us more frankly than the tales of the so-called definitive 1857 edition, which had been heavily edited by Wilhelm over forty years. These first-edition Grimms' tales have a beguiling honesty and an unusual perspective on human behavior and culture, and it is time we know more about their history.

Little-Known History about the Quest of the Brothers Grimm

In the past twenty-five years, scholars of folklore, conversant in German and familiar with the biographies and collecting practices of the Brothers Grimm, have made great progress in exposing false notions about their works and have also added immensely to our knowledge and understanding of how the Grimms shaped the folk and fairy tales that they collected. However, the general English-speaking public is not fully aware of all the facts and how important it is to know just how drastically the Grimms began changing their tales after the publication of the first edition of the *Kinder- und Hausmärchen*, which included scholarly annotations as well as an appendix with notes about the beliefs of children. Moreover, most people do not know how the Grimms more or less "stumbled" onto folk-lore and accidentally became world famous as the foremost collectors of folk and fairy tales.

Jacob (1785–1863) and Wilhelm Grimm (1786–1859) did not demonstrate a particular interest in folk or fairy tales during their youth in the small towns of Hanau and Steinau in Hesse, where they spent their childhood. Certainly, they were familiar with them, but they were schooled in a traditional classical manner that included learning Greek and Latin. In fact, there were few if any books of folk or fairy tales for children to read in those days, and there is no evidence that they were exposed to any of them. Their father, Philip Wilhelm Grimm, a prominent district magistrate in Hanau, provided them with private tutors so that they could pursue a classical education, but he died suddenly in 1796 and left his large family in difficult pecuniary circumstances. Their mother had to depend on financial aid from relatives to support Jacob, Wilhelm, and their three younger brothers (Carl, Ferdinand, and Ludwig) and a sister (Lotte). Socially disadvantaged, the Grimms sought to compensate for their "handicap" by demonstrating unusual talents and distinguishing themselves in their studies at school.

In 1798 the Brothers were sent to attend the Lyzeum in the nearby city of Kassel, where they proved themselves to be precocious and ambitious students. They prepared to study law at the University of Marburg and hoped eventually to find secure employment as civil servants so that they could help support their family. Philology and folklore were not on their minds or on their agenda. They intended to follow diligently in their father's footsteps. In the end, however, their paths diverged, and neither of the brothers became a lawyer or magistrate.

While studying at the University of Marburg from 1802 to 1806, the Grimms were inspired and mentored by Friedrich Carl von Savigny, a young professor of jurisprudence, who opened their eyes to the historical, philological, and philosophical aspects of law as well as literature. It was Savigny's historical approach to jurisprudence, his belief in the organic connection of all cultural creations of the *Volk* (understood as an entire ethnic group) and to the historical development of this *Volk*, that drew the attention of the Grimms. Savigny stressed that the present could only be fully grasped and appreciated by studying the past. And he insisted that the legal system had to be studied through an interdisciplinary method if the relationship between laws, customs, beliefs, and values were to be fully grasped.. For Savigny—and also for the Grimms—culture was originally the common property of *all* members of a *Volk*. The Germanic culture had become academically divided over the years into different disciplines such as religion, law, literature, and so on, and its cohesion could be restored only through historical investigation. The Brothers eventually came to believe that language rather than law was the ultimate bond that united the German people and were thus drawn to the study of old German literature—though they remained in agreement with Savigny's methods and desire to create a stronger legal sense of justice and community among the German people.

The Grimms had always been voracious readers of all kinds of literature and had digested popular courtly romances in their teens. During their university years they turned more and more to a serious study of medieval and ancient literature. Since literature and philology were not yet fully recognized fields at German universities, however, they set their sights on becoming librarians and independent scholars of German literature. They began collecting old books, tracts, calendars, newspapers, and manuscripts, wrote about medieval literature, and even debated with formidable professors and researchers of old Germanic and Nordic texts by writing contentious essays and editing scholarly collections of ancient sagas and legends. They made a brotherly pact to remain and work together for the rest of their lives, and together they cultivated a passion for recovering the "true" nature of the German people through their so-called natural *Poesie*, the term that the Grimms often used to describe the formidable ancient Germanic and Nordic literature. Yet these were difficult times, and their plans to gain recognition and respect through their academic work were not easily realized.

By 1805 the entire family had moved to Kassel, and the Brothers were constantly plagued by money problems and concerns about the future of their siblings. Their situation was further aggravated by the rampant Napoleonic Wars. Jacob interrupted his studies to serve the Hessian War

Commission in 1806. Meanwhile, Wilhelm fortunately passed his law exams, enabling him to become a civil servant and to find work as a librarian in the royal library in Kassel with a meager salary. In 1807 Jacob lost his position with the War Commission when the French occupied the city, but he was then hired as a librarian for the new King Jérome, Napoleon's brother, who now ruled Westphalia. Amid all the upheavals, their mother died in 1808, and Jacob, only twenty-three, and Wilhelm, twenty-two, became fully responsible for their brothers and sister. Yet, despite the loss of their mother and difficult personal and financial circumstances from 1805 to 1812, the Brothers managed to prove themselves as innovative scholars in the new field of German philology and literature.

Thanks to Savigny, who remained a good friend and mentor for the rest of their lives, the Grimms made two acquaintances who were to change their lives: in 1803 they met Clemens Brentano, one of the most gifted German romantic poets at that time, and in 1806, Achim von Arnim, one of the foremost German romantic novelists. These encounters had a profound impact on their lives, for Brentano and Arnim had already begun collecting old songs, tales, and manuscripts and shared the Grimms' interest in reviving ancient and medieval German literature. In the fall of 1805 Arnim and Brentano published the first volume of *Des Knaben Wunderhorn* (*The Boy's Wonder Horn*), a collection of old German folk songs, and they wanted to continue publishing more songs and folk tales in additional volumes. Since they were aware of the Grimms' remarkable talents as scholars of old German literature, they requested help from them in 1807, and the Brothers made a major contribution to the final two volumes of *Des Knaben Wunderhorn*, published in 1808. At the same time, Brentano enlisted them to help him collect folk tales, fables, and other stories for a new project that was to focus on fairy tales. The Grimms responded by gathering *all kinds* of folk tales from ancient books, not just fairy tales, and by recruiting friends and acquaintances in and around Kassel to tell them tales or to record tales from acquaintances. In this initial phase the Grimms were unable to devote all their energies to their research and did not have a clear idea about the profound significance of collecting folk tales. However, the more they began gathering tales, the more they became totally devoted to uncovering the "natural poetry" (*Naturpoesie*) of the German people, and all their research was geared toward exploring the epics, sagas, and tales that contained what they thought were essential truths about the German cultural heritage. Underlying their work was a pronounced romantic urge to excavate and preserve German cultural contributions made by the common people before the stories became extinct. In this respect their focus on collecting what they thought were "Germanic" tales was a gesture of protest against French occupation and a gesture of solidarity with those people who wanted to forge a unified German nation. It should also be noted, however, that most of their tales were regional and emanated largely from Hesse and Westphalia. There was no such thing as a German nation at that time.

What fascinated or compelled the Grimms to concentrate on ancient German literature was a belief that the most natural and pure forms of culture—those that held communities together like the close-knit ones in Hesse and northern Germany—were linguistic and were to be located in the past. Moreover, in their opinion, "modern" literature, even though it might be remarkably rich, was artificial and thus could not express the genuine essence of *Volk* culture that emanated organically from people's experiences and bound the people together. In their letters, essays, and books, written between 1806 and 1812, the Brothers began to formulate their views about the origins of literature based on tales, legends, myths, and pagan beliefs, or what was once oral art and to a certain extent continued to be a precious art form. The purpose of their collecting folk songs, tales, proverbs, legends, anecdotes, and documents was to write a history of old German *Poesie* and to demonstrate how *Kunstpoesie* ("cultivated literature") evolved out of traditional folk material and myths and how *Kunstpoesie* had gradually forced *Naturpoesie* (tales, legends, fables, anecdotes, and so on) to recede during the Renaissance and take refuge among the folk in oral traditions. Very early in their careers, the Brothers saw their task as literary historians who were to preserve the pure sources of modern German literature and to reveal the debt or connection of literate culture to the oral tradition. For them the tales were second nature, and their profound significance deserved recognition. As they state in the "Preface" to the 1812 volume:

Wherever the tales still exist, they continue to live in such a way that nobody ponders whether they are good or bad, poetic or crude. People know them and love them because they have simply absorbed them in a habitual way. And they take pleasure in them without having any reason. This is exactly why the custom of storytelling is so marvelous, and it is just what this poetic art has in common with everything eternal: people are obliged to be disposed toward it despite the objections of others. Incidentally, it is easy to observe that the custom of storytelling has stuck only where poetry has enjoyed a lively reception and where the imagination has not yet been obliterated by the perversities of life. In that same regard we don't want to praise the tales or even defend them against a contrary opinion: their mere *existence* suffices to defend them. That which has managed to provide so much pleasure time and again and has moved people and taught them something carries its own necessity in itself and has certainly emanated from that eternal source that moistens all life, and even if it were only a single drop that a folded leaf embraces, it will nevertheless glitter in the early dawn.

As their research and correspondence expanded, they also became more aware of how widespread oral storytelling was throughout Europe and of how the cultures of these other European countries at once resembled and differed from their own.

By 1809 the Grimms had amassed about fifty-four tales, legends, animal stories, and other kinds of narratives, and they sent the texts to Brentano, who was living in the Ölenberg Monastery in Alsace. He had told them that he would probably adapt them freely, and that they could also make use of the tales as they wished. Consequently, before they sent him these tales, they copied them. Brentano was not particularly impressed by the tales he received, and never made use of them, though, fortunately, he left them in the monastery. I say fortunately because the Grimms destroyed their texts after using them in their first edition of *Kinder- und Hausmärchen* in 1812. The handwritten texts that the Grimms had sent to Brentano, now referred to as the Ölenberg Manuscript by scholars, were discovered only much later, in 1920, and have provided researchers with important information about the Grimms' editing process.[1] All the tales of the Ölenberg Manuscript, most of them written down by Jacob, were very rough and often fragments. Sometimes they were skeletons of stories. For the most part, however, the raw stories were transformed in their first edition of 1812 by the Brothers into complete tales with clear transitions that corresponded to the Grimms' philological and poetical concept of the genuine, dialect folk tale. In addition they often retained fragments and nonsensical ditties that they considered valuable for comprehending folk beliefs and customs. The two models they kept in mind were "The Juniper Tree" and "The Fisherman and His Wife," two tales written down in Hamburg and Pomeranian dialect by the painter Philipp Otto Runge and sent to them by Achim von Arnim, who had published "The Juniper Tree" in 1808 in his short-lived weekly, *Zeitung für Einsiedler*. The Grimms edited these tales slightly and published them in dialect from the first edition to the last. It should be noted, however, that the Grimms' editing in 1812 was relatively moderate compared to Wilhelm's editing in later editions of their tales.

In 1812, Arnim, perhaps Brentano's closest friend at that time, visited the Grimms in Kassel. At that point, he was aware that Brentano was not about to do anything with their texts, and he also knew that the Grimms had spent an enormous amount of time collecting all sorts of tales, legends, anecdotes, and animal stories, even more than they had sent to Brentano. So he encouraged the Grimms to publish their own collection, which would represent their ideal of "natural poetry," and he provided them with the contact to the publisher Georg Andreas Reimer in Berlin. Thanks to Arnim's advice and intervention, the Brothers spent the rest of the year organizing and editing eighty-six tales for publication in volume one of the first edition of 1812.

Although the Grimms had not entirely formalized their concept while they worked on the publication of the first edition, their editorial principles could already be seen in their previous works and were clearly stated in the preface to the first volume of 1812:

We have tried to grasp and interpret these tales as purely as possible. In many of them one will find that the narrative is interrupted by rhymes and verses that even possess clear alliteration at times but are never sung during the telling of a tale, and these are precisely the oldest and best tales. No incident has been added or embellished and changed, for we would have shied away from expanding tales already so rich in and of themselves with their own analogies and similarities. They cannot be invented. In this regard no collection like this one has yet to appear in Germany.

Of course, this statement is only relatively true. The Grimms edited the tales that were not their tales and were compelled to make changes because many of the narratives were rough and incomplete. Yet, fidelity to the words and essential features of the tales was a guiding principle, and in the first edition, they refrained from embellishment and making major alterations in substance and plot.

This first volume of 1812 was only fairly well received by friends and critics. Some thought that the stories were too crude, were not shaped enough to appeal to children, and were weighed down by the scholarly notes. Other writers wondered why the Grimms were wasting their time on such trivial stories, and they also felt that there should at least be some illustrations, as did the Grimms themselves. Also, the Brothers entered into a debate with Arnim, who believed that they were too idealistic and too negative in their critique of literary tales and modern literature. Nevertheless, the Brothers were not deterred from following their original philological and poetical strategy of remaining faithful to the etymology of words and language. Even though, as I have already pointed out, there were some differences between Jacob and Wilhelm, who later favored more drastic poetical editing of the collected tales, they largely held to their original goal of salvaging relics from the past. Just how important this goal was can be seen in their debate and correspondence with Arnim between 1812 and 1815, when the second volume of the first edition appeared. In fact their disagreement had actually begun earlier, as can be seen in a very long letter of October 29, 1810, that Jacob had written to Arnim:

> Contrary to your viewpoint, I am firmly convinced that all the tales in our collection without exception had already been told with all their particulars centuries ago. Many beautiful things were only gradually left out. In this sense all the tales have long since been fixed, while they

continue to move around in endless variations. That is, they do not fix themselves. Such variations are similar to the manifold dialects that should not suffer any violation either.[2]

Then, in another letter, written on January 28, 1813, Jacob wrote in support of Wilhelm's views:

The difference between children's and household tales and the reproach we have received for using this combination in our title is more hairsplitting than true. Otherwise one would literally have to bring the children out of the house where they have belonged forever and confine them in a room. Have children's tales really been conceived and invented for children? I don't believe this at all just as I don't affirm the general question, whether we must set up something specific at all for them. What we possess in publicized and traditional teachings and precepts is accepted by old and young, and what children do not grasp about them, all that glides away from their minds, they will do so when they are ready to learn it. This is the case with all true teachings that ignite and illuminate everything that was already present and known, not teaching that brings both wood and fire with it.[3]

Though the Grimms made it clear in the preface to the second volume of the first edition of *Kinder- und Hausmärchen*, published in 1815, that they would follow the agenda of their first volume, they also explained the important difference they made between a book for children and an educational primer (*Erziehungsbuch*):

In publishing our collection we wanted to do more than just perform a service for the history of *Poesie*. We intended at the same time to enable *Poesie* itself, which is alive in the collection, to have an effect: it was to give pleasure to anyone who could take pleasure in it, and therefore, our collection was also to become an intrinsic educational primer. Some people have complained about this latter intention and asserted that there are things here and there [in our collection] that cause embarrassment and are unsuitable for children or offensive (such as the references to certain incidents and conditions, and they also think children should not hear about the devil and anything evil). Accordingly, parents should not offer the collection to children. In individual cases this concern may be correct, and thus one can easily choose which tales are to be read. On the whole it is certainly not necessary. Nothing can better defend us than nature itself, which has let certain flowers and leaves grow in a particular color and shape. People who do not find them beneficial, suitable for their special needs, which cannot be known, can easily walk right by them. But they cannot demand that the flowers and leaves be colored and cut in another way.[4]

Though mindful of the educational value of their collection, the Grimms shied away from making their tales moralistic or overly didactic. They viewed the morality in the tales as naïve and organic, and readers, young and old, could intuit lessons from them spontaneously because of their essential poetry. As André Jolles has demonstrated in his book *Einfache Formen*, the Grimms responded to the paradoxical morality of the miraculous in fairy tales. Jolles writes that the basic foundation of the fairy tale derives from the paradox that the miraculous is not miraculous in the fairy tale; rather it is natural, self-evident, a matter of course. "The miraculous is here the only possible guarantee that the immorality of reality has stopped."[5] The readers' interpretations of fairy tales are natural because of the profound if not divine nature of the tales, and in this sense, the Grimms envisioned themselves as moral cultivators or tillers of the soil; they viewed their collection as an educational primer of ethics, values, and customs that would grow on readers, who would themselves grow by reading these living relics of the past. Here it should be pointed out that the Grimms tales are not strictly speaking "fairy tales," and they never used that term, which, in German, would be *Feenmärchen*. Their collection is a much more diverse and includes animal tales, legends, tall tales, nonsense stories, fables, anecdotes, and, of course, magic tales (*Zaubermärchen*), which are clearly related to the great European tradition of fairy tales that can be traced back to ancient Greece and Rome. It is because their collection had such deep roots and a broad European heritage that the Grimms firmly believed that reading these tales would serve as an education for young and old alike. In some ways their book was intended to be part of the European civilizing process, and to a certain extent, the formative body of their tales, which have been translated into 150 languages, has become an international educational primer.

After the publication of the second volume in 1815, however, the Grimms were somewhat disappointed by the critical reception. They were convinced that reviewers and readers were misunderstanding the purpose of their collection. Although they did not abandon their basic notions about the "pure" origins and significance of folk tales when they published the second edition in 1819, there are significant indications that they had been influenced by their critics to make the tales more accessible to a general public and more considerate of children as readers and listeners of the stories. Altogether, there had been 156 tales published in the two volumes of the first edition, intended primarily for scholars and educated readers, and the number grew to 170 in the second edition of 1819 without the extensive scholarly notes, which appeared later in a separate volume in 1822. Wilhelm did most if not all of the editing and often made changes to downplay overt cruelty, eliminated tales that might be offensive to middle-class taste, replaced tales with more interesting variants, added some Christian homilies, and stylized them to evoke their folk poetry and original virtues. Yet, despite these changes, it was clear that the Grimms continued to place great emphasis on the philological significance of the collection that was to make a major contribution to understanding the origins and evolution of language and storytelling.

Restituting the Significance of the Unknown Tales of the First Edition

As I have already stated, most readers of the Grimms' tales throughout the world are familiar mainly with the seventh edition of *Kinder- und Hausmärchen* published in 1857, considered the standard if not definitive edition. Most people are not even aware of the fact that there were seven editions that Wilhelm, for the most part, kept amending and changing after 1815. Nor are most readers aware that there was a smaller edition of fifty tales intended more for children and families and published ten times from 1825 to 1858. Some contemporary critics have reprimanded the Grimms or even denigrated their work because they kept transforming oral tales into literary stories and often appealed to Christian and puritanical standards. In fact, several scholars have accused the Grimms of lying to their readers and making it seem that the tales in their collection were from the mouths of peasants and represented an authentic folk tradition.

Though there is some truth to these claims, they are misleading and disregard the fact that the Grimms were transparent about their editorial principles and never purposely deceived their readers. If anything, their romantic idealism and devotion to the German people led them to exaggerate the "genuine" folk qualities of the tales. In this regard, the Grimms were very much a part of the romantic movement in Germany. Ironically, the contradictions in their method of collecting and shaping the corpus of their tales—that is, the seven editions that they kept altering—stem from their profound belief that their tales were like gems, thousands of years old and part of a vast Indo-European oral tradition. Wilhelm, sometimes with the aid of Jacob, chiseled and honed their tales, often comparing multiple versions of the same tale type to make their tales glisten and to uncover their deep-rooted philological significance. It did not matter who their informants were because they regarded them only as mediators of the treasures of ancient storytelling of ordinary people. What mattered was that their informants took the tales seriously and made every effort to preserve the simple orality and naïve morality of the tales. As I have mentioned before, the Grimms envisaged themselves—and their collaborators—as moral cultivators of these tales, or tillers of the soil. Their mission was to excavate them, study them, sort them carefully, and to keep shaping them so that they remained artistically and philologically resilient and retained their primal essence.

In the first edition of 1812/1815 the Brothers relied on all sorts of people who either told folk tales to them that they recorded or correspondents who wrote them down as they themselves had heard them and sent written copies to the Grimms; they also relied on their research and discoveries in ancient manuscripts and books. There was a group of middle-class young women in Kassel consisting of Marie, Jeanette, and Amalie Hassenpflug and Lisette, Johanna, Gretchen, Mimi, and Dortchen Wild, and other members of these families, who provided over twenty stories. These young women often gathered in social circles and recited the tales, or in other places such as gardens or homes, where the Brothers recorded them. The young women were well-educated and had either read or heard the tales from their nannies and servants. Nearby, in Allendorf, Friederike Mannel, a minister's daughter, was a talented storyteller and writer who sent several unusual tales to Wilhelm. In another nearby city, Treysa, the teacher and later pastor Friedrich Siebert provided eight important tales that he had collected in the region, as did the pastor Georg August Friedrich Goldmann in Hannover. Then there were the members of the aristocratic von Haxthausen family in Münster: August, Ludowine, and Anna along with Jenny von Droste-Hülshof, who contributed approximately sixty stories, some of which they heard from peasants or soldiers. Sometimes the tales were told and written down in the local dialect and printed in dialect. The Grimms visited the Haxthausens and recorded many of the tales that stemmed from people who lived on August von Haxthausen's estate Bökerhof in Westphalia.

However, the most consummate storyteller was Dorothea Viehmann, a tailor's wife, who lived in the village of Niederzwehren outside Kassel and told them about forty tales. She was the mother of six children, and since the family was poor, she sold vegetables at a market in Kassel and would go to the Grimms' home for a few hours of storytelling on market days. The Grimms portrayed her as the exemplary peasant storyteller. Though there has been a debate about her status as a "peasant," it is quite clear that she belonged to the lower classes and had a much different perspective on life than the young women of Kassel or the aristocrats of Münster. Another important contributor was the retired soldier Johann Friedrich Krause, who exchanged seven tales for some leggings. He told several stories that involved discharged soldiers who upset kings or heroes and gained revenge after being mistreated. Aside from collecting oral tales, many of the Grimms' narratives were taken from books dating back to the sixteenth century and were adapted. The Grimms were familiar with all the major

European collections of folk and fairy tales. They knew the Italian works of Giovan Francesco Straparola and Giambattista Basile and the French collections of Charles Perrault, Mme Catherine d'Aulnoy, and Mlle de la Force. They were also aware of recent German anthologies of folk and fairy tales by Benedikte Naubert, Johann Gustav Büsching, Otmar, Adalbert Grimm (no relation), the anonymous *Feen-Mähchen*, and other collections. Moreover, they transcribed tales from such authors as Johannes Praetorius (*Der abentheurliche Glücks-Topf*, 1668), Johann Karl August Musäus (*Volksmährchen der Deutschen*, 1782), and other authors and collectors. Consequently, the first edition of *Kinder- und Hausmärchen* is an unusual mix of diverse voices and tales conveyed by peasants, craftsmen, ministers, teachers, middle-class women, and aristocrats. As Heinz Rölleke, the foremost German scholar of the Grimms' tales, has explained in his important book, *Es war einmal . . . Die wahren Märchen der Brüder Grimm und wer sie ihnen erzählte* (*Once Upon a Time . . . The True Tales of the Brothers Grimm and Who Told Them to Them*, 2011),[6] the tales in the first edition tend to be more raw and stamped by an "authentically" oral tradition than the tales published in later editions because the Grimms did not make vast changes at the beginning of their work. These tales are fascinating because they bear the imprint of their informants and are largely unknown to the general public. To grasp the historical significance of these first-edition tales, it is important to know something about the background of the informants and sources as well as the sociocultural context in which they were gathered. Yet it is somewhat difficult to gain this knowledge because the Grimms and other collectors at the beginning of the nineteenth century did not pay much attention to the storytellers and the social context of the storytelling. They were more interested in the tales per se, and the tradition of the tales. Clearly, the oral tradition of storytelling was strong and deep in all social classes, but very few historians or scholars of the eighteenth and early nineteenth centuries wrote in detail about how and why the tales were transmitted and about the lives of the storytellers. It was only in the latter part of the nineteenth century that researchers began providing and recording information about the informants, storytellers, and sources. Nevertheless, there are some clues in the Grimms' tales themselves and their styles that provide background information about the views of the tellers of the tales and the sociohistorical context.

Here it is important to stress that the tales of the first edition are often about "wounded" young people, and many of them were told to illustrate ongoing conflicts that continue to exist in our present day. For instance, the tales frequently depict the disputes that young protagonists have with their parents; children brutally treated and abandoned; soldiers in need; young women persecuted; sibling rivalry; exploitation and oppression of young people; dangerous predators; spiteful kings and queens abusing their power; and Death punishing greedy people and rewarding a virtuous boy. While many of these tales were a few hundred years old before they were gathered and told by the Grimms' informants, they bear the personal and peculiar marks of the storytellers themselves, who kept them in their memory for a purpose. Despite the unusually different styles of each of the tales—and eleven were told and written down in the local dialect—they are all notable because of their terse and frank qualities. As I have already stressed, these tales were not told for children, nor can they be considered truly children's tales, though children heard them, and some perhaps read them. If anything, they are *about* children, as can be seen in "How Some Children Played at Slaughtering," "Death and the Goose Boy," or "The Stubborn Child." The beginning of "Good Bowling and Card Playing" is indicative of the spirit and perspective of many tales: "Now, there was a young man from a poor family who thought to himself, 'Why not risk my life? I've got nothing to lose and a lot to win. What's there to think about?'"

Throughout all the tales of the first edition, there is what I call an "underdog" perspective. That is, there is almost always a clear hostility toward abusive kings, cannibals, witches, giants, and nasty people and animals. There is always a clear sympathy for innocent and simple-minded protagonists, male and female, little people, and helpless but courageous animals. Kings often renege on their promises or abuse and exploit their subjects, including their daughters, and they are either exposed, dethroned, or killed. The majority of the protagonists are innocents. Some are aristocrats, but most are farmers, tailors, servants, smiths, fishermen, soldiers, shoemakers, spinners, poor children, and little animals. Innocence is never enough by itself to be rewarded. Innocence is always tested, and the protagonists must prove their integrity and demonstrate virtues such as kindness to be worthy of a reward, whether it be wealth, marriage, bliss, or peace. There are a number of tales in the first edition in which young men are called simpletons, such as "Simple Hans," "The Simpleton," and "The Poor Miller's Apprentice." Inevitably, these bumpkins turn out to be much smarter than they appear, have a great deal of courage, and use their wits to overcome oppression. They achieve their goals through humility and kindness. This is also true of the tales about persecuted young women, such as "The Three Little Men in the Forest," "Maiden without Hands," "The Robber Bridegroom," "Princess Mouseskin," and "The Clever Farmer's Daughter." Though patriarchal notions flourish in most of the tales, there are subversive tendencies that can be seen in the resistance of young women, who are not satisfied with their positions in life.

The Grimms' tales that are not their own enable other voices to be heard. Indeed, whether folk or fairy tale, the miraculous makes self-evident what is wrong in the "real" world. There is a wide spectrum of tale types and genres in the first edition of 1812/15—fables, legends, jokes, farces, animal stories, and anecdotes—that are connected to events of the times and the personal experiences of the tellers. The descriptions are bare; the dialogues, curt; and the action, swift. The storytellers get to the point quickly, and there is generally a fulfillment of social justice or naïve morality at the end. What is justly fulfilled in all these tales was certainly lacking at the time they were told and is still lacking today.

Some of these tales in the first edition were printed in the following six editions of *Kinder- und Hausmärchen*, but in much different versions and often with different titles. Others were deleted or were placed in the scholarly notes. It is difficult to explain why the Grimms made all these deletions and changes because the reasons were different or unknown. For instance, tales like "How Children Played at Slaughtering" and "The Children of Famine" were omitted because they were gruesome. "Bluebeard," "Puss in Boots," and "Okerlo" were not reprinted because they stemmed from the French literary tradition. The same is true for "Simple Hans" because of its Italian origins. Some tales like "Good Bowling and Card Playing," "Herr Fix-It-Up," "Prince Swan," and "The Devil in the Green

Coat" among many others were simply replaced by other stories in later editions because the Grimms found versions that they preferred or combined different versions. The changes made by the Grimms indicated their ideological and artistic preferences. For instance, in the 1812/1815 edition of "Little Snow White" and "Hansel and Gretel" the wicked stepmother is actually a biological mother, and these characters were changed to become stepmothers in 1819 clearly because the Grimms held motherhood sacred. In the first edition "Rapunzel" is a very short provocative tale in which the young girl gets pregnant. The 1819 version is longer, much more sentimental, and without a hint of pregnancy. Here are two examples of how Wilhelm changed the tales to accord with middle-class notions of taste, decorum, and style. The contrasts between the different versions are clear. The second version of "The Frog King," which was called "The Frog Prince," was deleted in all the following editions.

THE FROG KING, OR IRON HENRY (1812)

Once upon a time there was a princess who went out into the forest and sat down at the edge of a cool well. She had a golden ball that was her favorite plaything. She threw it up high and caught it in the air and was delighted by all this. One time the ball flew up very high, and as she stretched out her hand and bent her fingers to catch it again, the ball hit the ground near her and rolled and rolled until it fell right into the water.

The princess was horrified, and when she went to look for the ball, she found the well was so deep that she couldn't see the bottom. So she began to weep miserably and to lament: "Oh, if only I had my ball again! I'd give anything—my clothes, my jewels, my pearls and anything else in the world—to get my ball back!"

As she sat there grieving, a frog stuck its head out of the water and said: "Why are you weeping so miserably?"

THE FROG PRINCE (1815)

Once upon a time there was a king who had three daughters, and in his courtyard there was a well with beautiful clear water. On a hot summer's day the eldest daughter went down to the well and scooped out a glass full of water. However, when she looked at it and held it up to the sun, she saw that the water was murky. She found this very unusual and wanted to scoop out another glass when a frog stirred in the water, stuck its head up high, and finally jumped on to the edge of the well, where he spoke:

"If you'll be my sweetheart, my dear,
I'll give you water clearer than clear."

"Oh, who'd ever want to be a nasty frog's sweetheart?" she cried out and ran away.

Then she told her sisters that there was an odd frog down at the well that made the water murky. The second sister became curious, and so she went down to the well and scooped a glass of water for herself, but it was just as murky as her sister's glass so that she wasn't able to drink it. Once again, however, the frog was on the edge of the well and said:

"If you'll be my sweetheart, my dear,
I'll give you water clearer than clear."

"Do you think that would suit me?" the princess replied and ran away.

Finally, the third sister went, and things were no better. But when the frog spoke,

"If you'll be my sweetheart, my dear,
I'll give you water clearer than clear,"

she replied, "Yes, why not? I'll be your sweetheart. Get me some clean water."

However, she thought, "That won't do any harm. I can speak to him just as I please. A dumb frog can never become my sweetheart."

THE FROG KING, OR IRON HENRY (1857)

In olden times, when wishing still helped, there lived a king whose daughters were all beautiful, but the youngest was so beautiful that the sun itself, which had seen many things, was always filled with amazement each time it cast its rays upon her face. Now, there was a great dark forest near the king's castle, and in this forest, beneath an old linden tree, was a well. Whenever the days were very hot, the king's daughter would go into this forest and sit down by the edge of the cool well. If she became bored, she would take her golden ball, throw it into the air, and catch it. More than anything else she loved playing with this ball.

One day it so happened that the ball did not fall back into the princess's little hand as she reached out to catch it. Instead, it bounced right by her and rolled straight into the water. The princess followed it with her eyes, but the ball disappeared, and the well was deep, so very deep that she could not see the bottom. She began to cry, and she cried louder and louder, for there was nothing that could comfort her. As she sat there, grieving over her loss, a voice called out to her, "What's the matter, princess? Your eyes could move even a stone to pity."

RAPUNZEL (1812)

One day, a young prince went riding through the forest and came upon the tower. He looked up and saw beautiful Rapunzel at the window. When he heard her singing with such a sweet voice, he fell completely in love with her. However, since there were no doors in the tower and no ladder could ever reach her high window, he fell into despair. Nevertheless, he went into the forest every day until one time he saw the fairy who called out:

"Rapunzel, Rapunzel,
let down your hair."

As a result, he now knew what kind of ladder he needed to climb up into the tower. He took careful note of the words he had to say, and the next day at dusk, he went to the tower and called out:

"Rapunzel, Rapunzel,
let down your hair."

So she let her hair drop, and when her braids were at the bottom of the tower, he tied them around him, and she pulled him up. At first, Rapunzel was terribly afraid, but soon the young prince pleased her so much that she agreed to see him every day and pull him up into the tower. Thus, for a while they had a merry time and enjoyed each other's company. The fairy didn't become aware of this until, one day, Rapunzel began talking and said to her, "Tell me, Mother Gothel, why are my clothes becoming too tight? They don't fit me anymore."

"Oh, you godless child!" the fairy replied. "What's this I hear?"

RAPUNZEL (1857)

A few years later a king's son happened to be riding through the forest and passed by the tower. Suddenly, he heard a song so lovely that he stopped to listen. It was Rapunzel, who passed the time in her solitude by letting her sweet voice resound in the forest. The prince wanted to climb up to her, and he looked for a door but could not find one. So he rode home. However, the song had touched his heart so deeply that he rode out into the forest every day and listened. One time, as he was standing behind a tree, he saw the sorceress approach and heard her call out:

"Rapunzel, Rapunzel,
let down your hair."

Then Rapunzel let down her braids, and the sorceress climbed up to her.

"If that's the ladder one needs to get up there, I'm also going to try my luck," the prince declared.

The next day, as it began to get dark, he went to the tower and called out:

"Rapunzel, Rapunzel,
let down your hair."

All at once the hair dropped down, and the prince climbed up. When he entered the tower, Rapunzel was at first terribly afraid, for she had never laid eyes on a man before. However, the prince began to talk to her in a friendly way and told her that her song had touched his heart so deeply that he had not been able to rest until he had seen her. Rapunzel then lost her fear, and when he asked her whether she would have him for her husband, and she saw that he was young and handsome, she thought, "He'll certainly love me better than old Mother Gothel." So she said yes and placed her hand in his.

"I want to go with you very much," she said, "but I don't know how I can get down. Every time you come, you must bring a skein of silk with you, and I'll weave it into a ladder. When it's finished, then I'll climb down, and you can take me away on your horse."

They agreed that until then he would come to her every evening, for the old woman came during the day. Meanwhile, the sorceress did not notice anything until one day Rapunzel blurted out, "Mother Gothel, how is it that you're much heavier than the prince? When I pull him up, he's here in a second."

"Ah, you godless child!" exclaimed the corceress. "What's this I hear? I thought I had made sure that you had no contact with the outside world, but you've deceived me."

The florid descriptions, smooth transitions, and explanations are characteristic of most of the tales in the 1857 edition. Wilhelm embellished and elaborated the tales with good intentions—to enhance their value as part of an educational primer. So, in the case of "Rapunzel," he demonized a fairy by changing her into a sorceress and minimized gender and class struggle. Though the Grimms were politically "liberal" for their times, they shied away from printing tales that were too radical in depicting resistance to patriarchal authority and opposition to monarchs. This may be the reason why they eliminated tales like "The Tablecloth, the Knapsack, the Cannon, and the Horn," in which a common man defeats a king and takes his daughter for his wife. On the other hand, the Grimms were very much disposed toward presenting the underdog in positive ways and toward publishing animal tales in which the weak almost always triumph over the strong who abuse their power. This can be seen in a major group of animal tales in the first edition, such as "The Wolf and the Seven Kids," "The Sparrow and His Four Children," "Old Sultan," "Loyal Godfather Sparrow," "The Fox and the Geese," "The Wren and the Bear," and "The Faithful Animals." In many tales the protagonists who respect animals, birds, and fish and are kind to them are later helped by them. There is a strong bond between humans and talking animals in the Grimms' collection. In general the Brothers show a predilection for collecting tales that focus on the cooperation of brothers, brothers and sisters, and humans and animals who work to overcome evil. It is striking how much this theme of cooperation among underdogs who work together to attain justice is central to the narratives in the first edition and often reinforced in the later editions of *Kinder- und Hausmärchen*. Unfortunately, many of the best tales in the first edition were excluded or shunned in later editions.

In many respects the unknown original tales in the present republication of the first edition read like startling "new" tales that are closer to traditional oral storytelling than the final collection of 210 tales in the 1857 edition. This is not to minimize or discredit the changes that the Grimms made but to insist that the history of the Grimms' tales needs to be known to fully comprehend the accomplishments of the Grimms as folklorists. In every edition of their tales, they began with "The Frog King," also known as "The Frog Prince," and ended with "The Golden Key." The reason they did this is, in my opinion, because "The Frog King"—and there are two different versions in the first edition—is an optimistic tale about miraculous regeneration, love, and loyalty and signals to readers that the tales in the collection will bring hope to readers and listeners despite the conflicts filled with blood and gore. The final tale, "The Golden Key," is highly significant because it leaves readers in suspense and indicates that tales are mysterious treasures. We just need the right key to discover and appreciate them. In this respect, however, the tales that are to be rediscovered and will become known are never the end of our quest to understand the mysteries of life, only the beginning. And so it is with the unknown original tales of the Brothers Grimm. They are only the beginning.

Notes

1. See Franz Schultz, *Die Märchen der Brüder Grimm in der Urform* (Frankfurt am Main: Frankfurter Bibliophilen-Gesellschaft, 1924); Joseph Lefftz, "Die Märchenhandschrift der Brüder Grimm im Kloster Ölenberg," *Elsassland* 4 (1924): 361–65; Joseph Lefftz, ed., *Märchen der Brüder Grimm. Urfassung nach der Originalhandschrift der Abtei Ölenberg im Elsaß* (Heidelberg: Schriften der Elsaß-Lothringischen

Wissenschaft, 1927); and Heinz Rölleke, ed., *Die älteste Märchensammlung der Brüder Grimm. Synopse der handschriftlichen Urfassung von 1810 und der Erstdrucke von 1812* (Cologny-Geneva: Fondation Martin Bodmer, 1975).

2. Reinhold Steig and Herman Grimm, eds., *Achim von Arnim und die ihm nahe standen*, vol. 3 (Stuttgart: J. G. Cotta'schen Buchhandlung, 1904): 237.

3. Ibid., 269.

4. *Kinder- und Hausmärchen gesammelt durch die Brüder Grimm* [1812/1815, Erstausgabe], ed. Ulrike Marquardt and Heinz Rölleke, vol. 2. (Göttingen: Vandenhoeck & Ruprecht, 1986): viii–ix.

5. André Jolles, *Einfache Formen: Legende/Sage/Mythe/Spruch Kasus/Memorabile, Märchen/Witz*. (Darmstadt: Wissenschaftliche Buchgesellschaft, 1958): 243. Reprint of the 1930 edition.

6. See Heinz Rölleke, ed., *Es war einmal . . . Die wahren Märchen der Brüder Grimm und wer sie ihnen erzählte*, illustr. Albert Schindehütte (Frankfurt am Main: Eichorn, 2011).

NOTE ON THE TEXT
AND TRANSLATION

The present translation is based on *Kinder- und Haus-Märchen. Gesammelt durch die Brüder Grimm*, 2 vols., Berlin: Realschulbuchandlung, 1812/15. With the exception of the commentary on children's beliefs, the evidence for the *Kindermärchen*, and the scholarly notes, my translation is the first complete English translation of the Grimms' first edition. Those readers who know German and are interested in the complete German commentary and notes can readily obtain them in any reliable German reprint of the first edition. As for the scholarly notes to the tales, I have provided a thorough summary of each note to indicate sources, and I have also translated the variants of tales that I thought were important. These notes reveal, in my opinion, how knowledgeable and erudite the Grimms were at a very young age.

I have endeavored to capture the tone and style of the different tales by translating them into a basic contemporary American idiom. My main objective was to render the frank and blunt qualities of the tales in a succinct American English. Eleven of the tales were published in different German dialects, and since it is practically impossible to match these dialects in American English, I did my best to reproduce the brusque manner of the narratives. As I have emphasized in my introduction, the Grimms' tales, though diverse and not their own, share an innocent and naïve morality that pervades their works. It is this quality that I have tried to communicate in my translation.

VOLUME I

PREFACE TO VOLUME I

When a storm, or some other catastrophe sent from the heavens, levels an entire crop, we are relieved to find that a small patch, protected by tiny hedges or bushes, has been spared and that some solitary stalks remain standing. When the sun shines once again and favors them, they will continue to grow alone and unnoticed. No sickle will cut them down too early so they can be stashed in a large silo, but late in the summer, when they are ripe and fully grown, some poor and pious hands will come searching for them. Ear upon ear will be carefully bound in bundles, inspected, and attended to as whole sheaths. Then they will be brought home and serve as the staple food for the entire winter. Perhaps they will be the only seed for the future.

This is how it seemed to us when we began examining the richness of German literature in earlier times and then saw that nothing much had been preserved from that richness. Even the recollection of that treasure had been lost, and only folk songs and those innocent household tales are all that has remained. The places by the stove, the hearth in the kitchen, stone stairs leading to the attic, holidays still celebrated, pastures and woods in quiet seclusion, and above all the undisturbed imagination have been the hedges that have protected the tales and have allowed them to be transmitted from one generation to another.

Now that we have reexamined our collection of tales, we'd like to offer our present reflections. In the beginning we thought that a great deal had perished, and only the tales that we knew already were the ones that had remained, and that variants, as is usually the case, were also told by other people. But on the lookout for everything that really *was still there* from these poetic stories (*Poesie*), we also wanted to get to know these other versions, and it turned out, however, that there was much more new material than we had realized. Even though we were not able to make inquiries at places very far from us, our collection grew from year to year, so that, after approximately six years have flown by, it now seems rich to us. At the same time we realize that we may be missing a great deal, but we are pleased by the thought that we possess the most and the best tales. Aside from a few exceptions that we have noted, almost everything has been collected from oral traditions in Hesse and Main and in the Kinzig regions of the Duchy of Hanau, where we grew up, and that is why pleasant memories are attached to each and every tale. Few books like ours have originated with such pleasure, and we would like to express our gratitude publicly once again to everyone who has participated in our work.

It was perhaps just the right time to record these tales since those people who should be preserving them are becoming more and more scarce. (Of course, those who still know them know a great deal, but people die away, while the tales persist.) Indeed, the custom of storytelling is on the wane just like all the familiar places in homes and gardens are succumbing to an empty splendor that resembles that smile when one speaks of these tales, a smile that appears lavish and yet does not cost very much. Wherever the tales still exist, they continue to live in such a way that nobody ponders whether they are good or bad, poetic or crude. People know them and love them because they have simply absorbed them in a habitual way. And they take pleasure in them without having any reason. This is exactly why the custom of storytelling is so marvelous, and it is just what this poetic art has in common with everything eternal: people are obliged to be disposed toward it despite the objections of others. Incidentally, it is easy to observe that the custom of storytelling has stuck only where poetry has enjoyed a lively reception and where the imagination has not yet been obliterated by the perversities of life. In that same regard we don't want to praise the tales or even defend them against a contrary opinion: their mere *existence*

suffices to protect them. That which has managed to provide so much pleasure time and again and has moved people and taught them something carries its own necessity in itself and has certainly emanated from that eternal
source that moistens all life, and even if it were only a single drop that a
folded leaf embraces, it will nevertheless glitter in the early dawn.

The same purity runs through these tales that brings out the wonderful
and blessed qualities of children. The tales have the same sky blue, flawless,
shining eyes (in which small children love so much to see themselves[1]) that
no longer grow while the other parts of their bodies are still tender, weak,
and too awkward to be put to use on the earth. Most of the situations in the
tales are so ordinary that many readers will have encountered them, but like
all actual things in life, they continually appear new and moving. Parents
have no more food, and, in desperation, they must cast their children from
their home. Or a harsh stepmother lets her stepchildren suffer[2] and would
like to see them perish. Then there are some siblings abandoned in the
desolate forest. The wind terrifies them, and they are afraid of the wild animals; yet, they faithfully support each other. The little brother knows how
to find his way back home, or if he is transformed into an animal through
magic, the little sister guides him in the forest and gathers foliage and moss
for his bed, or she silently sits and sews a shirt for him made out of star
flowers that destroy the magic spell. The entire cast of characters in this
world is precisely determined: kings, princes, faithful servants, and honest tradesmen—especially fishermen, millers, colliers, and herdsmen, who
are closest to nature—make their appearance. All other things are alien
and unknown to this world. Also, similar to the myths that speak about
a golden age, all of nature in these tales is vibrant; sun, moon, and stars
are approachable; they give gifts and let themselves be woven into gowns.
Dwarfs work in the mountains and search for metals. Mermaids sleep in
the water. Birds (the doves are the most beloved and the most helpful),
plants, and stones, speak and know how to express their sympathy. Even
blood cries out and says things, and this is how the tales already exercise
their rights where later storytelling strives to speak through metaphors.
This innocent familiarity of the greatest and the smallest has an indescrib-
able endearing quality to it, and we tend to prefer the conversation of the

stars with a poor deserted child in the forest than the sound of the music in the spheres. Everything beautiful is golden and strewn with pearls. Even golden people live here. But misfortune is a dark power, a monstrous, cannibalistic giant, who is, however, vanquished, because a good woman, who happily knows how to avert disaster, stands ready to help. And this type of narrative always ends by opening the possibility for enduring happiness. Evil is also not anything small or close to home, and not the worst; otherwise one could grow accustomed to it. Rather it is something terrible, dark, and absolutely separate so that one cannot get near it. The punishment of evil is equally dreadful: snakes and poisonous reptiles devour their victims, or an evil individual must dance to death in red-hot iron shoes. There is much that also carries its own meaning within itself: a mother gets her real child back in her arms after she manages to cause the changeling, which the elves had substituted for own child, to laugh. Similarly, the life of a child begins with a smile and continues in joy, and as the child smiles in its sleep, angels talk to the baby. A quarter of an hour each day is exempt from the power of magic when the human form steps forth freely as though no power can completely enshroud us. Every day affords individual people moments when they can shake off everything that is false and can view things from their perspective. On the other hand, the magic spell is also never completely vanquished. A swan's wing remains instead of an arm, and when a tear is shed, an eye is lost with it. Or worldly intelligence is humbled, and the fool, mocked and neglected by everyone, gains happiness only because of his pure heart. These features form the basis that enables the tales to readily provide a good lesson or a use for the present. It was neither their purpose to instruct nor were they invented for that reason, but a lesson grows out of them just as a good fruit grows from a healthy blossom without the involvement of mankind. It is in this that all genuine poetry proves its worth because it can never be without some connection to life. It rises from life and returns to it just as clouds return to their place of birth after they have watered the earth.

This is how the essence of these tales seems to us—naturally they resemble all folk tales and legends in their outward appearance. They are never set and change from region to region and from one teller to another; they faithfully preserve the same source. In this regard they distinguish themselves from the original *local folk legends*, which are tied to real places or heroes of history, and which we have not included here, even though we have collected many and are thinking of publishing them some other time. We have sometimes provided several versions of one and the same tale because of their pleasant and unique variations. Those tales that are less important have been included in the notes. In general, however, we have collected the tales as faithfully as we could. It is also clear that these tales were constantly reproduced anew as time went on. This is exactly the reason why their origins must be very old. Some of them have left traces in Fischart and Rollenhagen[3] that we have noted and that prove and indicate the tales are almost three hundred years old, but it is beyond any doubt that they are even older than that even if lack of evidence makes direct proof impossible. The only, but certain, evidence can be derived from the connection with the great heroic epics and the indigenous animal fables, but this is naturally not the place to go into detail, and anyway, we have said some things about this in the notes.

Given that these tales are so close to the earliest and simplest forms of life, this closeness can account for its general dissemination, for there is not a single group of people that can completely do without such *Poesie*. Even the Negroes of West Africa delight their children with stories, and Strabo[4] expressly says the same thing about the Greeks. (Similar attestation can be found among others at the end, and this proves how highly such tales were esteemed by those who understood the value of a voice speaking directly to the heart.) There is another highly remarkable phenomenon that can be explained from all this, and it pertains to the great diffusion of the German tales. In this case they don't merely equal the heroic stories of Siegfried the dragon slayer, but they even surpass them because we find these tales and exactly the same kinds spread throughout Europe, thus revealing an affinity among the noblest peoples. In the north we are familiar only with the Danish heroic ballads that contain much relevant material primarily in songs that are not entirely appropriate for children because they are meant to be sung. However, here, too, the boundary can hardly be designated with exactitude when it comes to the more serious historical legend, and there are to be sure points of overlap. England possesses the Tabart collection of tales,[5] which is not very rich, but what treasures of oral tales must still exist in Wales, Scotland, and Ireland! Just in its *Mabinogion*[6] (now in print) Wales has a true treasure. In a similar way, Norway, Sweden, and Denmark have remained rich sources. Much less so, perhaps, the southern countries. We know nothing about Spain, but a passage from Cervantes leaves no doubt about the existence and telling of tales.[7] France has certainly much more now than what Charles Perrault provided.[8] But he treated them still as children's tales (not like his inferior imitators Aulnoy and Murat[9]). He produced only nine. Of course, they belong to the best known tales, which are also among the most beautiful. His merit consists in his decision not to add anything to the tales and to leave the tales unchanged, discounting some small details. His style of depiction deserves only praise for being as simple as possible. Indeed, the French language in its present state of cultivation curls together almost by itself into epigrammatic remarks and finely honed dialogue, and this makes it nothing but more difficult to be naïve and direct—that is, in fact to be without any pretentiousness—while telling children's tales. (Just see the conversations between *Riquet à la houpe* and the dumb princess as well as the end of *Petit Poucet*.) In addition they are sometimes unnecessarily long and wordy. An analysis that is about to be published maintains that Perrault (born 1633, died 1703) was the first one to invent these tales, and it was through him they first reached the people. This study even asserts that Perrault's "Tom Thumb" is an intentional imitation of Homer that wants to make Ulysses' predicament when threatened by Polyphemus understandable to children. Johanneau had a better view of this matter.[10] Older Italian collections are richer than all the others. First in Straparola's *Nights*,[11] which contains many good things, then especially in Basile's *Pentamerone*,[12] a collection that is as well known and beloved in Italy as it is seldom and unknown in Germany. Written in Neapolitan dialect, it is in every regard a superb book. The contents are almost perfect and without false additions. The style is overflowing with good words and sayings. To translate it in a lively manner would require someone like Fischart[13] and others from his era. Meanwhile, we have been thinking about translating it into German in the second volume of the present collection in which everything else that is provided by foreign sources will find a place.

We have tried to grasp and interpret these tales as purely as possible. In many of them one will find that the narrative is interrupted by rhymes and verses that even possess clear alliteration at times but are never sung during the telling of a tale, and these are precisely the oldest and best tales. No incident has been added or embellished and changed, for we would have shied away from expanding tales already so rich in and of themselves with their own analogies and similarities. They cannot be invented. In this regard no collection like this one has yet to appear in Germany. The tales have almost always been used as stuff to create longer stories, which have been arbitrarily expanded and changed depending on their value. They have always been ripped from the hands of children even though they belonged to them, and nothing was given back to them in return. Even those people who thought about the children could not restrain themselves from mixing in mannerisms of contemporary writing. Diligence in collecting has almost always been lacking. Just a few, noted by chance, were immediately published.[14] Had we been so fortunate to be able to tell the tales in a very particular dialect, they would have undoubtedly gained a great deal. Here we have a case where all the accomplishments of education, refinement, and artistic command of language ruin everything, and where one feels that a purified literary language, as elegant as it may be for everything else, brighter and more transparent, has here, however, become more tasteless and cannot get to the heart of the matter.

We offer this book to well-meaning hands and thereby think chiefly of the blessed power that lies in these hands. We wish they will not allow these tiny morsels of poetry to be kept entirely hidden from poor and modest readers.

Kassel, October 18, 1812

Notes

1. Fischart, Gargantua 129b, 131b. (The Grimms cite Johann Baptist Fischart's translation of François Rabelais's *Gargantua*, which was published in German under the title *Affentheurlich Naupengeheurliche Geschichtklitterung*, 1575. JZ)

2. This kind of relationship occurs often here and is no doubt the first cloud that appears on the blue skies of a child and squeezes out the first tears that adults don't see, but that the angels count. Even flowers have received their names from this relationship. The tricolored violet is called "Little Stepmother" because there is a slender little green leaf beneath each yellow leaf that supports it. They are the chairs that the mother gives to her own cheerful children. The two stepchildren must stand above, mournful in dark violet, and they have no chairs.

3. The references are to Johann Baptist Fischart (ca. 1546–91), author of *Affentheurlich Naupengeheurliche Geschichtklitterung* (1575), and Georg Rollenhagen (1542–1609), author of *Foschmeuseler* (1595). JZ

4. Strabo (64 BC–AD 24), Greek philosopher, historian, and geographer. JZ

5. Benjamin Tabart (ca. 1767–1833) published an important series of fairy tales called *Popular Tales* (1804) in four volumes as well as inexpensive chapbooks. JZ

6. The *Mabinogion* is a collection of eleven medieval Welsh tales with folk-tale and fairy-tale motifs. They are connected to the Arthurian legends and became available to the Grimms at the beginning of the nineteenth century. JZ

7. —y aquellas (cosas) que à ti te deven parecer profecias, non son sino palabras de consejas, ocuentos de viejas, como acquellos des cavallo sin cabeça, y de la varilla de virtudes, con que se entretienen al fuego las diltatadas noches del invierno. Colloq. Entre cip. Y Berg. (Mistakes in the Spanish appear in the original. JZ)

8. Charles Perrault (1628–1703), author of the famous collection of fairy tales *Histoires ou Contes du temps passé* (1697). JZ

9. The references are to Mme Marie-Catherine d'Aulnoy (ca. 1650–1705), who published several books of fairy tales including two volumes, *Contes de fées* (1698), and Henriette Julie de Murat (1670–1716), author of *Contes de fées* (1698). JZ

10. The reference is to the French philologist Éloi Johanneau (1770–1851). JZ

11. Giovan Francesco Straparola (ca. 1480–1558), author of *Le piacevoli notti*, 2 vols. (1550–53). JZ

12. Giambattista Basile (1575–1632), author of *Il Pentamerone* (1634–36), also known as *Lo cunto de li cunti* (*The Tale of Tales*). JZ

13. Given the language of his day and his admirable memory, what a much better book of folk tales he could have produced if he had recognized the value of a true, unadulterated recording in a different way.

14. *Musäus* und *Naubert* made use of what we have called local legends. The much more esteemed *Otmar* made use only of those kinds of legends. An Efurt collection of 1787 is poor; only half of a *Leipzig* collection of 1799 belongs here, even though it is not all that bad. Among all these collections, the one from *Braunschweig* of 1801 is the richest, although its tone is wrong. There was nothing for us to take from the latest *Büsching* collection, and it should be expressly noted that a collection called

Kindermärchen (Children's Tales) was published a few years ago by *A. L. Grimm* in Heidelberg with whom we are related by name only; it was not done very well and has absolutely nothing in common with us and with our work.

The recently published *Wintermärchen* (Winter Tales) by Father Jahn (Jena at Voigt 1813) only has a new title and actually appeared ten years ago.

There is also a Leipzig collection with tales written by someone with the name Peter Kling and all in the same manner. Only the sixth tale and part of the fifth are of value; the others have no substance and, apart from a few details, are hollow inventions.

We ask those who possibly have the opportunity and the inclination to help us to improve particular parts of this book to amend the fragments, and especially to collect new and unusual animal tales. We would be most grateful to receive such information, which would be best sent to the publisher or to bookstores in Göttingen, Kassel, and Marburg.

[The authors and books referred to by the Grimms are

Büsching, Johann Gustav Gottlieb. *Volks-Sagen, Märchen und Legenden*. Leipzig: 1812.

Feen-Mährchen zur Unterhaltung der Freunde und Freundinnen der Feenwelt. Braunschweig: 1801.

Gottschalck, Kaspar Friedrich (Otmar). *Die Sagen und Volksmährchen der Deutschen*. Halle: Hemmerde und Schwetschke, 1814.

Grimm, Albert Ludwig. *Kindermährchen*. Heidelberg: Morhr und Zimmer, 1808.

Kling, Peter. *Das Mährleinbuch für meine lieben Nachbarsleute*. 2 vols. Leipzig: Weygand, 1799.

Musäus, Johann Karl August. *Volksmährchen der Deutschen*. 5 vols. Gotha: 1782–87.

Naubert, Benedikte. Neue Volksmährchen der Deutschen. Leipzig: Weygand, 1789–92.

JZ]

I

THE FROG KING, OR IRON HENRY

Once upon a time there was a princess who went out into the forest and sat down at the edge of a cool well. She had a golden ball that was her favorite plaything. She threw it up high and caught it in the air and was delighted by all this. One time the ball flew up very high, and as she stretched out her hand and bent her fingers to catch it again, the ball hit the ground near her and rolled and rolled until it fell right into the water.

The princess was horrified, and when she went to look for the ball, she found the well was so deep that she couldn't see the bottom. So she began to weep miserably and to lament: "Oh, if only I had my ball again! I'd give anything—my clothes, my jewels, my pearls and anything else in the world—to get my ball back!"

As she sat there grieving, a frog stuck its head out of the water and said: "Why are you weeping so miserably?"

"Oh," she said, "you nasty frog, you can't help me! My golden ball has fallen into the water."

"Well, I don't want your pearls, your jewels, and your clothes," the frog responded. "But if you will accept me as your companion and let me sit next to you and let me eat from your little golden plate and sleep in your little bed and promise to love and cherish me, I'll fetch your ball for you."

The princess thought, "what nonsense the simple-minded frog is blabbering! He's got to remain in his water. But perhaps he can get me my ball. So I'll say yes to him." And she said, "Yes, fair enough, but first fetch me the golden ball. I promise you everything."

The frog dipped his head beneath the water and dived down. It didn't take long before he came back to the surface with the ball in his mouth. He threw it onto the ground, and when the princess caught sight of the ball again, she quickly ran over to it, picked it up, and was so delighted to have the ball in her hands again that she thought of nothing else but to rush back home with it. The frog called after her: "Wait, princess, take me with you the way you promised!"

But she didn't pay any attention to him.

The next day the princess sat at the table and heard something coming up the marble steps, *splish, splash! splish, splash!* Soon thereafter it knocked at the door and cried out: "Princess, youngest daughter, open up!"

She ran to the door and opened it, and there was the frog whom she had forgotten. Horrified, she quickly slammed the door shut and sat down back at the table. But the king saw that her heart was thumping and said, "Why are you afraid?"

"There's a nasty frog outside," she replied. "He retrieved my golden ball from the water, and I promised him that he could be my companion. But I never believed at all he could get out of the water. Now he's standing outside in front of the door and wants to come inside."

As she said this, there was a knock at the door, and the frog cried out:

"Princess, youngest daughter,
Open up!
Don't you remember, what you said
down by the well's cool water?
Princess, youngest daughter,
Open up!"

The king said: "You must keep your promise no matter what you said. Go and open the door for the frog."

She obeyed, and the frog hopped inside and followed her at her heels until they came to her chair, and when she sat down again, he cried out: "Lift me up to the chair beside you."

The princess didn't want to do this, but the king ordered her to do it. When the frog was up at the table, he said: "Now push your little golden plate nearer to me so we can eat together."

The princess had to do this as well, and after he had eaten until he was full, he said: "Now I'm tired and want to sleep. Bring me upstairs to your little room. Get your little bed ready so that we can lie down in it."

The princess became terrified when she heard this, for she was afraid of the cold frog. She didn't dare to touch him, and now he was to lie in her bed next to her. She began to weep and didn't want to comply with his wishes at all. But the king became angry and ordered her to do what she had promised, or she'd be held in disgrace. Nothing helped. She had to do what her father wanted, but she was bitterly angry in her heart. So she picked up the frog with two fingers, carried him upstairs into her room, lay down in her bed, and instead of setting him down next to her, she threw him *crash!* against the wall. "Now you'll leave me in peace, you nasty frog!"

But the frog didn't fall down dead. Instead, when he fell down on the bed, he became a handsome young prince. Well, now indeed he did become her dear companion, and she cherished him as she had promised, and in their delight they fell asleep together.

The next morning a splendid coach arrived drawn by eight horses with feathers and glistening gold harnesses. The prince's Faithful Henry accompanied them. He had been so distressed when he had learned his master had been turned into a frog that he had ordered three iron bands to be wrapped around his heart to keep it from bursting from grief. When the prince got into the coach with the princess, his faithful servant took his place at the back so they could return to the prince's realm. And after they had traveled some distance, the prince heard a loud cracking noise behind him. So, he turned around and cried out: "Henry, the coach is breaking!"

"No, my lord, it's really nothing
but the band around my heart,
which nearly came apart
when you turned into a frog and your fortune fell
and you were made to live in that dreadful well."

Two more times the prince heard the cracking noise and thought the coach was breaking, but the noise was only the sound of the bands springing from Faithful Henry's heart because his master had been released from the spell and was happy.

2

THE COMPANIONSHIP OF THE CAT AND MOUSE

A cat and a mouse wanted to live together, and so they set up a common household. They also prepared for the winter and bought a little jar of fat, but since they didn't know of a better and safer place to put it, they stuck it under the altar in the church, where it was supposed to stay until they needed it.

Now, it was not long before the cat felt a craving for the fat and went to the mouse and said, "Listen, little mouse, my cousin has asked me to be godfather for her child. She gave birth to a baby boy, white with brown spots. I'm to hold him at the christening. Would you mind letting me go out today and taking care of the house by yourself?"

"No, no," answered the mouse. "Go there, and when you get something good to eat, think of me. I sure would like a little drop of that sweet, red christening wine."

But the cat went straight to the church and licked up the skin off the top of the fat. Then he strolled around the city and didn't return home until evening.

"You must have enjoyed yourself very much," the mouse said. "What name did they give the child?"

"*Skin-Off,*" the cat answered.

"Skin-Off? That's a strange name. I've never heard of it before."

Soon thereafter the cat felt another craving and went to the mouse and said: "I've been asked to be godfather once more. The child has a white ring around his body. I can't refuse. You must do me a favor and look after the house."

The mouse consented, and the cat went and ate up half the jar of fat. When he returned home, the mouse asked, "What name was this godchild given?"

"*Half-Gone.*"

"Half-Gone! You don't say! I've never heard of such a name. I'm sure it's not on the list of proper baptismal names."

Now the cat couldn't stop thinking about the jar of fat.

"I've been asked to be godfather again for a third time. This child's all black and has white paws. Aside from that there's not a white hair on his body. That only happens once every few years. You'll let me go, won't you?"

"Skin-Off, Half-Gone," the mouse said. "Those are really curious names. I'm beginning to wonder about them. Even so, go ahead."

The mouse cleaned the house and put it in order. Meanwhile the cat ate up the rest of the fat in the jar and came home stout and stuffed late at night.

"What's the name of the third child?"

"*All-Gone.*"

"All-Gone! Hey now! That's the most suspicious of all the names," said the mouse. "All-Gone! What's it supposed to mean? I've never seen it in print!"

Upon saying that, the mouse shook her head and went to sleep.

Nobody called upon the cat to become godfather for the fourth time. However, soon winter came, and there was nothing more to be found outside. So the mouse said to the cat, "Come, let's go to our supply that we stuck beneath the altar in the church."

But when they arrived there, the jar was completely empty.

"Oh!" said the mouse. "Now I know what's happened! It's as clear as day. You ate it all up when you went to serve as godfather. First the skin, then half, then . . ."

"Shut up!" yelled the cat. "One more word, and I'll eat you up!"

"All gone" was already on the tip of the poor mouse's tongue. No sooner did she say it than the cat jumped on her and swallowed her in one gulp.

3

THE VIRGIN MARY'S CHILD

A poor woodcutter and his wife lived at the edge of a large forest with their only child, a three-year-old little girl. They were so poor that they couldn't afford daily meals anymore and didn't know how they would provide food for their daughter. One morning the woodcutter, who was distressed by all this, went into the forest to work. As he began chopping wood, a tall, beautiful woman suddenly appeared before him. She was wearing a crown of shining stars on her head, and she said to him, "I am the Virgin Mary, mother of the Christ Child. Since you are poor and needy, bring me your child. I'll take her with me and be her mother and look after her."

The woodcutter obeyed her. He fetched his child and gave her to the Virgin Mary, who took her up to heaven. Once there everything went well for the girl: she ate only cake and drank sweet milk. Her clothes were made of gold, and the little angels played with her. One day, about the time the girl had turned fourteen, the Virgin Mary had to go on a long journey. Before she went away, she summoned the girl and said, "Dear child, I am trusting you with the keys to the thirteen doors of the kingdom of heaven. You may open twelve of the doors and look at all the marvelous things inside, but I forbid you to open the thirteenth door that this little key unlocks."

The maiden promised to obey her commands, and after the Virgin Mary had departed, she opened a new room every day and looked into the rooms of the heavenly realm. In each one of them, there was an apostle in dazzling light. Never in her life had she seen such splendor and glory. When she had finished opening the twelve doors, the forbidden door was the only one left. For a long time she resisted her curiosity, but finally she was overcome by it and opened the thirteenth door as well. And as the door sprang open, she saw the Holy Trinity sitting in fire and splendor. Then she touched the flames a little bit with her finger, and the finger turned golden. Quickly she slammed the door shut and ran away. Her heart started pounding and wouldn't stop.

A few days later the Virgin Mary returned from her journey and asked the maiden to return the keys of heaven to her. When the girl handed her the bunch of keys, the Virgin looked into her eyes and said, "Didn't you also open the thirteenth door?"

"No," she answered.

Then the Virgin Mary put her hand on the maiden's heart and could feel it pounding and pounding. Now she knew the girl had disobeyed her command and had opened the door. Once again she asked, "Are you sure you didn't open the door?"

"I'm sure," the maiden denied doing it for a second time.

When the Virgin Mary glanced at the finger that had become golden from touching the heavenly fire, she knew the maiden was guilty and said: "You've disobeyed me and lied. You're no longer worthy to stay in heaven."

All at once the girl sank into a deep sleep, and when she awoke, she was lying on the earth beneath a tall tree surrounded by thick bushes so that she was completely encircled. Her mouth was also locked so that she couldn't utter one word. Since the tree was hollow, she could sit inside during the rain and storms, and it was also where she slept. Roots and wild berries were her only food, and she went out looking for them as far as she could walk. In the autumn she gathered roots and leaves and carried them into the hollow tree. When snow and ice came, she sat inside the tree. Before long her clothes became tattered, and one piece after the other fell off her body. So she sat there completely covered by leaves. As soon as the sun began to shine again, she went out and sat in front of the tree. Her long hair covered her on all sides like a cloak.

One day during springtime she was sitting in front of the tree when someone forced his way through the bushes. It was the king, who had been hunting in the forest and had lost his way, and he was amazed to find such a beautiful maiden sitting alone in this desolate spot. So he asked her whether she would like to come with him to his castle. However, she couldn't answer. Instead, she merely nodded a little with her head. Then the king lifted her up onto his horse and brought her to the castle. Soon he became so fond of her that he made her his wife.

After a year had passed, the queen gave birth to a beautiful son. During the night, however, the Virgin Mary appeared before her and said, "If you'll tell me the truth and say that you unlocked the forbidden door, I'll give you back the power of speech, without which you really can't enjoy life. If you are stubborn and won't confess, I shall take your baby away with me."

But the queen remained stubborn and denied that she had opened the forbidden door. So the Virgin Mary took the little child and disappeared with him. The next morning, when the baby was no longer there, a rumor began circulating among the people that the queen was an ogress and had eaten her own child.

Then another year passed, and the queen gave birth to another son. Once more the Virgin Mary appeared before her and asked her to tell the truth, otherwise she would also lose the second child. But the queen persisted in denying that she had opened the forbidden door. So the Virgin Mary took the child away with her. The next morning, when this baby was also missing, the king's councilors said openly that the queen was an ogress, and they demanded that she be executed for her godless deeds. However, the king ordered them to keep quiet and refused to believe them because he loved his wife so much.

In the third year the queen gave birth to a princess, and the Virgin Mary appeared before her once more and took her to heaven, where she showed her how her two oldest children were playing with a globe of the earth. Thereupon, the Virgin Mary asked the queen once more to confess her mistake and stop lying. However, the queen wouldn't budge and continued to stand by her story. So the Virgin Mary left her and took away her third child, too.

Now the king could no longer restrain his councilors, who continued to claim that the queen was an ogress. They were certain, and since she couldn't speak, she couldn't defend herself. Consequently, she was condemned to die at the stake.

As she stood tied to the stake, and the fire began to burn all around her, her heart was moved, and she thought to herself: "Oh, before I die, I'd like to confess to the Virgin Mary that I opened the forbidden door in heaven. I've been so wicked by denying it all this time!"

And just as she was thinking all this to herself, heaven opened up right then and there, and the Virgin Mary descended with the two little sons at either side and the daughter in her arms. The fire was extinguished by itself, and the Virgin Mary stepped forward to the queen and said: "Since you want to speak the truth, your guilt is forgiven." Then she handed the queen her children, opened her mouth so that she could speak from then on, and bestowed happiness on her for the rest of her life.

4

GOOD BOWLING AND CARD PLAYING

Once upon a time there was an old king who had the most beautiful daughter in the world. One day he announced: "Whoever can keep watch in my old castle for three nights can have the princess for his bride."

Now, there was a young man from a poor family who thought to himself, "Why not risk my life? I've got nothing to lose, and a lot to win. What's there to think about?"

So he appeared before the king and offered to keep watch in the castle for three nights.

"You may request three things to take with you into the castle, but they have to be lifeless objects," the king said.

"Well, I'd like to take a carpenter's bench with a knife, a lathe, and fire."

All of these things were carried into the castle for him. When it turned dark, he himself went inside. At first everything was quiet. He built a fire, placed the carpenter's bench with the knife next to it, and sat down at the lathe. Toward midnight, however, a rumbling could be heard, first softly, then more loudly: "*Bif! Baf! Hehe! Holla ho!*"

It became more dreadful, and then it was somewhat quiet. Finally, a leg came down the chimney and stood right before him.

"Hey, there!" the young man cried out. "How about some more? One is too little."

The noise began once again. Another leg fell down the chimney and then another and another, until there were nine.

"That's enough now. I've got enough for bowling, but there are no balls. Out with them!"

There was a tremendous uproar, and two skulls fell down the chimney. He put them in the lathe and turned them until they were smooth. "Now they'll roll much better!"

Then he did the same with the legs and set them up like bowling pins.

"Hey, now I can have some fun!"

Suddenly two large black cats appeared and strode around the fire. "Meow! Meow!" they screeched. "We're freezing! We're freezing!"

"You fools! What are you screaming about? Sit down by the fire and warm yourselves."

After the cats had warmed themselves, they said, "Good fellow, we want to play a round of cards."

"All right," he replied, "but show me your paws. You've got such long claws that I've got to give them a good clipping before we begin."

Upon saying this, he grabbed them by the scruffs of their necks and lifted them to the carpenter's bench. There he fastened them to the vise and beat them to death. Afterward he carried them outside and threw them into a pond that lay across from the castle. Just as he returned to the castle and wanted to settle down and warm himself by the fire, many black cats and dogs came out of every nook and cranny, more and more, so that he couldn't hide himself. They screamed, stamped on the fire, and kicked it about so that the fire went out. So he grabbed his carving knife and yelled, "Get out of here, you riffraff!"

And he began swinging the knife. Most of the cats and dogs ran away. The others were killed, and he carried them out and threw them into the pond. Then he went back inside to the fire and blew the sparks so that the fire began again and he could warm himself.

After he had warmed himself, he was tired and lay down on a large bed that stood in a corner. Just as he wanted to fall asleep, the bed began to stir and raced around the entire castle.

"That's fine with me. Just keep it up!"

So the bed drove around as though six horses were pulling it over stairs and landings: "*Bing bang!*"

It turned upside down, from top to bottom, and he was beneath it. So he flung the blankets and pillows into the air and jumped off.

"Anyone who wants a ride can have one!"

Then he lay down next to the fire until dawn.

In the morning the king arrived, and when he saw the young man lying asleep, he thought he was dead and said, "What a shame."

But when the young man heard these words, he awoke, and as soon as he saw the king, he stood up. Then the king asked him how things had gone during the night.

"Quite well. One night's gone by smoothly, the other two will go by as well."

Indeed, the other nights were just like the first. But he already knew what to do, and so on the fourth day, he was rewarded with the king's beautiful daughter.

5
THE WOLF AND THE SEVEN KIDS

A goat had seven young kids, whom she loved very much and carefully protected from the wolf. One day, when she had to go and fetch some food, she called them all together and said, "Dear children, I must go out to find some food. So be on your guard against the wolf and don't let him inside. Pay close attention because he often disguises himself, but you can recognize him right away by his gruff voice and black paws. Protect yourselves. If he gets into the house, he'll eat you all up."

Upon saying this, the goat went on her way, but it was not long before the wolf arrived at the door and called out, "Open up, dear children. I'm your mother and have brought you some beautiful things."

But the seven kids said: "You're not our mother. She has a lovely, soft voice, and yours is gruff. You're the wolf, and we're not going to open the door."

The wolf went away to a shopkeeper and bought a big piece of chalk, which he ate, and it made his voice soft. Then he returned to the house door of the seven kids and called out with a soft voice: "Dear children, let me in. I'm your mother, and I've brought something for each of you."

But the wolf had put his paw on the windowsill, and when the children saw it, they said, "You're not our mother. She doesn't have a black paw like yours. You're the wolf. We're not going to open the door for you!"

So the wolf ran to a baker and said, "Baker, put some dough on my paws for me."

And after that was done, the wolf went to the miller and said, "Sprinkle some white flour on my paws."

The miller said no.

"If you don't do it, I'll eat you up!"

So the miller had to do it.

Now the wolf went once again to the house door of the seven kids and said, "Dear children, let me in. I'm your mother, and I've brought something for each of you."

The seven kids wanted to see the paws first, and when they saw that they were snow white and heard the wolf speak so softly, they thought he was their mother and opened the door. Once the wolf entered, however, they recognized him and quickly hid themselves as best they could. The first kid slid under the table, the second hid in the bed, the third in the oven, the fourth in the kitchen, the fifth in the cupboard, the sixth under the large washbasin, and the seventh in the clock case. However, the wolf found them all and swallowed them, except for the youngest in the clock case, who remained alive.

When the wolf had satisfied his craving, he went off. Shortly thereafter, the mother goat came home, and oh, what a terrible sight! The wolf had been there and had devoured her dear children! She thought they were all dead, but then the youngest jumped out of the clock case and told her how everything had happened.

In the meantime, the wolf, who was stuffed, had gone to a green meadow, where he had lain himself down in the sun and had fallen into a deep sleep. The old goat thought she still might be able to save her children. Therefore, she said to the youngest kid: "Take the scissors, needle, and thread and follow me."

After she left the house, she found the wolf lying on the ground in the meadow and snoring.

"There's that nasty wolf!" she said and inspected him from all sides. "There he is after eating my six children for supper. Give me the scissors! Oh, if only they're still alive inside him!"

Then she cut his belly open, and the six kids that had been swallowed whole by the gluttonous wolf jumped out and were unscathed. Immediately she ordered them to gather large and heavy stones and to bring them to her. Then she filled his stomach with them, and the kids sewed him up again and hid behind a hedge.

When the wolf had finished sleeping, he felt that his stomach was very heavy and said: "It's rumbling and tumbling in my belly! It's rumbling and tumbling in my belly! And I've only eaten six kids!"

He thought he had better have a drink of fresh water to help himself, and he looked for a well, but when he leaned over, he couldn't stand straight because of the stones and fell into the water. When the seven kids saw this, they came running and danced joyfully around the well.

6

THE NIGHTINGALE AND THE BLINDWORM

Once upon a time there lived a nightingale and a blindworm, each with one eye. For a long time they lived together peacefully and harmoniously in a house. However, one day the nightingale was invited to a wedding, and she said to the blindworm, "I've been invited to a wedding and don't particularly want to go with one eye. Would you be so kind as to lend me yours? I'll bring it back to you tomorrow."

The blindworm gave her the eye out of the kindness of her heart. But when the nightingale came home the following day, she liked having two eyes in her head and being able to see on both sides. So she refused to return the borrowed eye to the blindworm. Then the blindworm swore that she would avenge herself on the nightingale's children and the children of her children.

"Well," replied the nightingale, "see if you can find me.

I'll build my nest in the linden, so high, so high, so high.
You'll never be able to find it, no matter how hard you try."

Ever since that time all the nightingales have had two eyes, and all the blindworms, none. But wherever the nightingale builds her nest, a blindworm lives beneath it in the bushes and constantly tries to crawl up the tree, pierce the eggs of her enemy, and drink them up.

7
THE STOLEN PENNIES

One day a father was sitting at the table with his wife and children and a good friend who was visiting him, and they were having their noonday meal. As they were sitting there, the clock struck twelve, and the visitor saw the door open, and a pale child dressed in snow-white clothes entered. He didn't look around or say anything but went silently into the next room. Shortly thereafter he returned and went away just as quietly as he had entered. On the second and third day the child came again. Finally, the visitor asked the father who the beautiful child was that entered the room every day at noon. The father answered that he knew nothing about him. He hadn't seen anything.

The next day as the clock struck noon, the child entered again, and the visitor pointed the child out to the father, but he didn't see the boy. Neither did the mother nor the children. The visitor stood up, went to the door, opened it a little, and looked inside. There he saw the pale child sitting on the floor, digging and rummaging in the cracks of the boards. However, as soon as the child noticed the visitor, he disappeared. Now the visitor told the family what he had seen and gave an exact description of the boy. The mother was then able to recognize the child and said, "Alas, it's my own dear child who died four weeks ago."

Then they ripped up the boards of the floor and found two pennies that the boy had received from his mother at one time to give to a poor man, but the child had thought, "You can buy yourself a biscuit for that." Therefore, he had kept the pennies and had hidden them in the cracks of the floor. This is why he hadn't been able to rest in his grave and had come back every day at noon to look for the pennies. So the parents gave the money to a poor man, and after that the little child was never seen again.

8
THE HAND WITH THE KNIFE

There once was a little girl who had three brothers, and the boys meant the world to her mother. Yet the little girl was always neglected, treated badly, and forced to go out early in the morning every day to dig up peat from the dry ground on the heath, which they used for making fires and cooking. To top it all off, she was given an old, blunt shovel to perform this nasty work.

But the little girl had an admirer who was an elf and lived in a hill near her mother's house. Whenever she went by the hill, he would stretch out his hand from the rocky slope and offer her a knife that had miraculous powers and could cut through anything. She used this knife to cut out the peat and would finish her work quickly. Then she would return home happily with the necessary load, and when she walked by the rocky slope, she would knock twice, and the hand would reach out and take back the knife.

When the mother noticed how swiftly and easily she came back home with the peat, she told the girl's brothers that there must be someone helping her; otherwise, it would be impossible for her to complete the work so fast. So the brothers crept after her and watched her receive the magic knife. They overtook her and forced her to give it to them. Then they returned to the rocky slope, knocked the way she had always done, and when the good elf stretched out his hand, they cut it off with his very own knife. The bloody arm drew back, and since the elf believed that his beloved had betrayed him, he was never seen after that.

9

THE TWELVE BROTHERS

Once upon a time there was a king who had twelve children, all boys. Moreover, he didn't want to have a daughter and said to his wife: "If you give birth to our thirteenth child, and it's a girl, I shall have the twelve boys killed. However, if it's a boy, then they'll all remain alive and stay together."

The queen thought of talking him out of this, but the king refused to hear anything more about this topic.

"If everything turns out like I said, they must die. I'd rather chop off their heads myself than let a girl be among them."

The queen was sad about this because she loved her sons with all her heart and didn't know how she could save them. Finally, she went to the

youngest, who was her favorite, and revealed to him what the king had decided.

"Dearest child," she said, "go into the forest with your eleven brothers. Stay there, and don't come home. One of you should keep watch on a tree and look over here toward the tower. If I give birth to a little son, I'll raise a white flag on top of the tower. However, if it's a little daughter, I'll raise a red flag. If you all see that it's red, then save yourselves. Flee into the wide world, and may our dear Lord protect you. I'll get up every night and pray that you won't freeze in the winter and are able to warm yourselves by a fire and that when it's hot in the summer, you can rest in a cool forest and sleep."

After she gave her blessing to her sons, they went out into the forest, where they frequently looked toward the tower. One of them had to sit on top of a high tree and constantly keep watch. Soon a flag was hoisted, but it wasn't a white one. It was a blood-red flag that foreshadowed their doom. As soon as the brothers caught sight of it, they all became angry and cried out: "Why should we lose our lives because of a girl?"

Then they all swore to remain in the middle of the forest and to keep on their guard, and if a maiden were to appear, they would kill her without mercy.

Soon after this they searched for a cave where the forest was the darkest, and that's where they began to live. Every morning eleven of the brothers went off to hunt. One of them had to remain home, cook, and keep house. Whenever they encountered a maiden, she was treated without mercy and lost her life. This is how they lived for many years.

In the meantime their little sister grew up and was the only child left at home. One day there was a large amount of washing to do, and among the clothes there were twelve shirts for boys.

"Whose shirts are these?" the princess asked the washerwoman. "They're much too small for my father."

It was then that the washerwoman told her that she had once had twelve brothers, but they had mysteriously gone away. Nobody knew where because the king had wanted to have them killed, and the twelve shirts belonged to the twelve brothers. The little sister was astonished that she had never heard of her twelve brothers, and during the afternoon as the clothes were drying and she was sitting in the meadow, she recalled the words of the washerwoman. After giving considerable thought to what she had heard, she stood up, took the twelve shirts, and went into the forest where her brothers were living.

The little sister made her way straight to the cave that served as her brothers' dwelling. Eleven of them were out hunting, and only one of them who had to cook was at home. When he caught sight of the maiden, he composed himself and drew his sword.

"Kneel down! Your red blood will flow this very second!"

But the maiden pleaded: "Dear sir, let me live. I'll stay with you and serve you honestly. I'll cook and keep house."

She spoke these words to the youngest brother, and he took pity on her because of her beauty and spared her life. Later, when his eleven brothers returned home and were astonished to find a maiden alive in their cave, he said to them: "Dear brothers, this girl came to our cave, and when I wanted to cut her to pieces, she pleaded for her life so much and said that she would serve us faithfully and keep house that I spared her life."

The others thought that this would be a great benefit to them because now all twelve of them could go hunting, and they were satisfied with this arrangement. Then the maiden showed them the twelve shirts and told them that she was their sister. Indeed, they were all very happy about this and were glad that they hadn't killed her.

Now the little sister took over all the household chores, and when the brothers went out hunting, she gathered wood and herbs, kept the fire going, made up the beds nice and white and clean, and did everything with zeal and without getting tired.

One day, when she was finished with all the work, she took a walk in the woods and came to a place where there were twelve large beautiful white lilies. Since they pleased her so much, she plucked all twelve of them. No sooner did she do this than an old woman stood before her.

"Oh, my daughter," she said, "why didn't you let the twelve budding flowers just stand there? They're your twelve brothers. Now they've been changed into ravens and are lost forever."

The little sister began to weep and said, "Isn't there any way that I can save them?"

"No, there isn't any way in the world except one that's so difficult you won't be able to rescue them. You must spend the next twelve years without speaking. If you say one single word, even if there's only an hour left, everything will be in vain, and your brothers will die that very moment."

Well, the little sister responded by climbing a tall tree in the forest, where she took a place. She wanted to sit there twelve years without saying a word to free her brothers. But it so happened that a king was out riding and hunting in the forest, and as he rode by the tree, his dog stood still and barked. So the king stopped, looked up, and was very amazed by the princess's beauty. He called to her and asked her whether she wanted to become his wife. However, she remained silent and only nodded a bit with her head. So the king himself dismounted, helped her down from the tree, and lifted her up before him onto his horse. Then he brought her home to his castle. Meanwhile the princess did not utter one word, and the king thought that she was mute. They would have lived happily with one another if it hadn't been for the king's mother, who began to slander the young queen in front of her son.

"She's a common beggar that you've dug up from nowhere, and she's doing the most disgraceful things behind your back!"

Since the young queen couldn't defend herself, the king was led astray and finally believed what his mother said. So, he sentenced his wife to death, and a enormous fire was built in the courtyard, where she was to be burned to death.

Soon the queen was standing in the flames that grazed the fringes of her dress. One minute was left before the twelve years of her silence would be completed. There was a noise in the air, and twelve ravens swooped down into the courtyard. As soon as they touched the ground, they became twelve handsome princes who instantly put out the fire's flames and led their sister to safety. Then she spoke once again and told the king how everything had happened and how she had to save her twelve brothers. Indeed, they were all pleased that everything turned out so well.

Now they had to decide what they should to with the evil mother-in-law. Well, they stuck her into a barrel full of boiling oil and poisonous snakes, and she died a ghastly death.

10

RIFFRAFF

The rooster said to the hen, "The nuts are ripe. Let's go up the hill and for once eat our fill of nuts before the squirrel hauls them all away."

"Yes," responded the hen. "Let's go and have a good time together."

So they went up the hill, and since it was such a bright day, they stayed till evening. Now, I don't know whether it was because they had stuffed themselves too much, or whether they had become too high and mighty, but they didn't want to return home on foot. So the rooster had to build a small carriage made out of nut shells. When it was finished, the hen got in and said to the rooster, "Now you can just harness yourself to it."

"No," said the rooster. "You have some nerve! I'd rather go home by foot than let myself be harnessed to this carriage. No, that wasn't part of our bargain. I'd gladly be coachman and sit on the box, but I refuse to pull the carriage!"

As they were quarreling, a duck came by quacking and pouted, "You thieves! Who said you could come up on my nut hill? Just you wait! You'll pay for this!"

She charged at the rooster with a wide-open beak, but the rooster was on his toes and threw himself at the duck's body nice and hard. Then he dug his spurs into her so violently that the duck begged for mercy and willingly let herself be harnessed to the carriage as punishment. Now the rooster sat down on the box as coachman, and off they went in a gallop.

"Duck, run as fast as you can!" cried the rooster.

After they had gone some distance, they encountered two travelers on foot, a needle and a pin, who called and asked them to stop. They said it would soon be very dark, and they wouldn't be able to go one step farther. Besides, the road was dirty. So they asked if they could have a ride. They had been at the tailor's tavern outside the town gate and had had one beer too many, which made them late as well.

Since they were thin and didn't take up much room, the rooster let them both get in, but they had to promise not to step on his or the hen's feet. Later that evening they came to an inn, and since they didn't want to travel any farther, and since the duck was not walking well but swayed from side to side, they decided to stop there. At first the innkeeper raised a lot of objections and said his inn was already full. Moreover, he thought they were not a very distinguished-looking group. However, they used some sweet talk and offered him the egg that the hen had laid along the way and told him that he could also keep the duck, who laid an egg a day. So finally he relented and said they could spend the night. Now they ordered some good hot food and had a merry time of it.

Early the next morning, as the sun was rising and everyone was asleep, the rooster woke the hen, fetched the egg, pecked it open, and together they devoured it. After throwing the shells on the hearth, they went to the needle, who was still asleep, grabbed him by the head, and stuck him into the innkeeper's easy chair. Then they stuck the pin into the innkeeper's towel. Finally, without much ado, they flew away over the heath.

The duck, who liked to sleep in the open air and had spent the night in the yard, heard the flapping of their wings. So she roused herself, found a brook, and swam away. That went much faster than being harnessed to a carriage. A few hours later the innkeeper got out of bed, washed himself, and took the towel to dry himself. However, the pin scratched his face, leaving a red mark from ear to ear. Then he went into the kitchen and wanted to light his pipe. But, as he leaned over the hearth, the eggshells popped into his eyes.

"Everything's attacking my head this morning," he said, and went to sit down in his easy chair to settle his bad mood, but he jumped up immediately and screamed, "Oww!" The needle had stuck him worse than the pin and not in the head. Now he was completely angry and suspected the guests who had arrived so late the night before. But when he went looking for them, they were gone. Then he swore he would never again let riffraff stay at his inn, especially when they eat so much, pay nothing, and play mean tricks on top of it all.

II

LITTLE BROTHER AND LITTLE SISTER

A little brother took his little sister by the hand and said, "Ever since our mother died, we've not had one moment of happiness. Our stepmother beats us every day, and when we come near her, she kicks us away with her foot. We get nothing but hard crusts of bread, just leftovers for food, and the dog under the table is better off. At least he gets a good chunk of meat to eat every now and then. Lord have mercy on us, if our mother only knew! Come, let's go off together into the wide world."

So they went away and came to a large forest, where they were so sad and so tired that they crept into a hollow tree and just wanted to die from hunger. Then they both fell asleep. When they woke the next morning, the sun was already high in the sky and warmed the hollow tree with its rays.

"Little sister," said the little brother after a while, "I'm thirsty. If only I knew where to find a spring, I'd go and have a drink right away. Listen, I think I hear one trickling."

"What good will that do?" the little sister answered. "Why do you want to drink when we just want to die from hunger?"

The little brother kept quiet and climbed out of the hollow tree, and since he always held his sister's hand tightly, she had to climb out with him.

Now, their evil stepmother was a witch, and when she had noticed that the two children had left, she followed them and caused a clear little stream near the tree to trickle from some rocks and form a spring. The trickling spring was intended to lure the children and make their mouths water. But whoever drank from the spring would be changed into a little fawn.

The little brother soon came to the spring with his sister, and when he saw the glittering water trickle over the stones into the spring, his thirst became even greater, and he wanted to drink some of the water. However, the little sister was fearful. She thought she heard the spring speak to her as it trickled: "Whoever drinks me will be changed into a fawn! Whoever drinks me will be changed into a fawn!" So, she begged her little brother not to drink the water.

"I don't hear anything," said the little brother. "I just hear how lovely the water is trickling. Let me go!"

Upon saying this he lay down on the ground, leaned over, and drank, and as soon as he felt the first drop of water on his lips, he was changed into a little fawn sitting beside the spring.

The little sister wept and wept. However, the witch was angry that she hadn't been able to lure the little sister to drink the water as well. After the girl wept for three days, she stood up, gathered some bulrushes, and wove them into a soft rope. Then she attached it to the little fawn and led him with her. She looked for a cave, and when she found one, she carried moss and foliage inside and made a soft bed for him. The next morning she went out with the fawn to a place with tender grass, and there she gathered the most beautiful grass, which he ate out of her hand. The fawn was delighted and romped about on the hills. In the evening when the little sister was tired, she laid her head on the back of the fawn. It was her pillow, and this is how she fell asleep. If only her brother could have retained his human form, it would have been a wonderful life.

For many years they lived like this in the forest. Then one day the king went out on a hunt, and when he became lost, he stumbled upon the maiden with the little animal in the forest and was amazed by her beauty. He lifted her up onto his horse and took her with him, while the fawn, attached by the rope, ran along side. At the royal court the maiden was treated with honor. Beautiful young women had to serve her, but she herself was more beautiful than any of the other ladies. She never let the fawn out of her sight, and she tended him with care. Shortly after her arrival the queen mother died, and the king wed the sister, and they lived together in great joy.

However, the stepmother had heard about the good fortune of the poor little sister. She had thought that the maiden had long since been torn to pieces by wild beasts, but they had never done anything to her. Indeed, the maiden was now the queen of the realm. The witch was so angry about this that she could only think of some way she might ruin the queen's happiness.

When the queen gave birth to a handsome prince the next year and the king was out hunting, the witch appeared in the form of a chambermaid and entered the room where the queen was recovering from the birth.

"The bath has been prepared for you," she said. "It will do you good and strengthen you. Come, before the water becomes too cold."

The witch led the queen into the bathroom and locked the door behind her. Inside there was a brutally hot fire, and the beautiful queen was suffocated to death.

Now the witch had a daughter of her own, and she endowed her with the outward shape of the queen and laid her in bed in place of the queen. In the evening when the king returned home. he didn't realize that he had a false wife. But in the night—and the nurse saw this—the real queen appeared in the room. She went to the cradle, lifted the child to her breast, and suckled him. Then she plumped up his tiny mattress, laid the baby in the cradle again, and covered him. After this, she went into the corner, where the fawn slept, and stroked his back. This was how she came and went every night without saying a word.

One time, however, she entered again and said:

"How's my child? How's my fawn?
Twice more I'll come, then I'll be gone."

Then she did what she had usually done the other nights. Meanwhile, the nurse woke the king and told him secretly what had occurred. So the next night the king kept watch, and he, too, saw how the queen came, and he clearly heard her words.

"How's my child? How's my fawn?
Once more I'll come, then I'll be gone."

However, he didn't dare to speak to her. The following night he kept watch again, and the queen said:

"How's my child? How's my fawn?
There's no more time. Soon I'll be gone."

The king could no longer restrain himself. He sprang forth and embraced her, and as soon as he touched her, she was restored to life, rosy red and well. The false queen was led into the forest, where the wild beasts devoured her. The evil stepmother was burned at the stake, and as the fire consumed her, the fawn was transformed, and brother and sister were once again together and lived happily until the end of their days.

12

RAPUNZEL

Once upon a time there lived a husband and wife who had been wishing for a child many years, but it had all been in vain. Finally, the woman became pregnant.

Now, in the back of their house the couple had a small window that overlooked a fairy's garden filled with all kinds of flowers and herbs. But nobody ever dared to enter it.

One day, however, when the wife was standing at the window and looking down into the garden, she noticed a bed of wonderful rapunzel. She had a great craving to eat some of the lettuce, and yet she knew that she couldn't get any. So she began to waste away and looked wretched. Her husband eventually became horrified and asked what was ailing her.

"If I don't get any of that rapunzel from the garden behind our house, I shall have to die."

Her husband loved her very much and thought, "No matter what it costs, you're going to get her some rapunzel."

So one evening he quickly climbed over the high wall into the garden, grabbed a handful of rapunzel, and brought the lettuce to his wife. Then she immediately made a salad and ate it with great zest. However, the rapunzel tasted so good to her, so very good, that her craving for it became three times greater by the next day. Her husband knew that if she was ever to be satisfied, he had to climb into the garden once more. And so he went over the wall into the garden but was extremely terrified when he stood face-to-face with the fairy, who angrily berated him for daring to come into the garden and stealing her rapunzel.

He excused himself as best he could by explaining that his wife was pregnant and that it had become too dangerous to deny her the rapunzel.

"All right," the fairy finally spoke. "I shall permit you to take as much rapunzel as you like, but only if you give me the child that your wife is carrying."

In his fear the man agreed to everything, and when his wife gave birth, the fairy appeared at once, named the baby girl Rapunzel, and took her away.

Rapunzel grew to be the most beautiful child under the sun. But when she turned twelve, the fairy locked her in a very high tower that had neither doors nor stairs, only a little window high above. Whenever the fairy wanted to enter the tower, she would stand below and call out:

"Rapunzel, Rapunzel,
let down your hair."

Rapunzel had radiant hair, as fine as spun gold. Each time she heard the fairy's voice, she unpinned her braids and wound them around a hook on the window. Then she let her hair drop twenty yards, and the fairy would climb up on it.

One day a young prince went riding through the forest and came upon the tower. He looked up and saw beautiful Rapunzel at the window. When he heard her singing with such a sweet voice, he fell completely in love with her. However, since there were no doors in the tower and no ladder could ever reach her high window, he fell into despair. Nevertheless, he went into the forest every day until one time he saw the fairy, who called out:

"Rapunzel, Rapunzel,
let down your hair."

As a result, he now knew what kind of ladder he needed to climb up into the tower. He took careful note of the words he had to say, and the next day at dusk, he went to the tower and called out:

"Rapunzel, Rapunzel,
let down your hair."

So she let her hair drop, and when her braids were at the bottom of the tower, he tied them around him, and she pulled him up. At first Rapunzel was terribly afraid, but soon the young prince pleased her so much that she agreed to see him every day and pull him up into the tower. Thus, for a while they had a merry time and enjoyed each other's company. The fairy didn't become aware of this until, one day, Rapunzel began talking and said to her, "Tell me, Mother Gothel, why are my clothes becoming too tight? They don't fit me any more."

"Oh, you godless child!" the fairy replied. "What's this I hear?"

And she immediately realized that she had been betrayed and became furious. Then she grabbed Rapunzel's beautiful hair, wrapped it around her left hand a few times, picked up a pair of scissors with her right hand, and *snip, snap*, the hair was cut off. Afterward the fairy banished Rapunzel to a desolate land, where she had to live in great misery. In the course of time she gave birth to twins, a boy and a girl.

On the same day that the fairy had banished Rapunzel, she fastened the braids that she had cut off to the hook on the window, and that evening, when the prince came and called out

"Rapunzel, Rapunzel,
let down your hair,"

she let the braids down. But when the prince climbed up into the tower, he was astonished to find the fairy instead of Rapunzel.

"Do you know what, you villain?" the angry fairy said. "Rapunzel is lost to you forever!"

In his despair the prince threw himself from the tower. He escaped with his life, but he lost both eyes. Sadly he wandered around in the forest, eating nothing but grass and roots, and did nothing but weep. Some years later, he made his way to the desolate land where Rapunzel was leading a wretched existence with her children. When he heard her voice, it sounded familiar at first, and then he immediately recognized it. She recognized him, too, and embraced him. Two of her tears fell upon his eyes. Then his eyes became clear again, and he could see as usual.

THE THREE LITTLE MEN IN THE FOREST

There was a man whose wife died, and he was undecided whether he wanted to marry again. Finally, he took off one of his boots that had a hole in the sole and said to his daughter, his only child: "Take this boot and carry it up to the loft, where you'll find a large nail. Hang the boot on the nail. Then fetch some water, and pour the water into the boot. If it holds the water, I'll get married again. But if it leaks, I'll let things remain as they are."

The maiden did as she was told. The water drew the hole together, and the boot became full to the brim. The father checked to see for himself whether this was true. Then he said: "Well, now I've got to take a wife."

So he went and courted a widow who brought a daughter from her first husband with her into the house. When she saw that her stepdaughter was beautiful and that everyone was fond of her, and that her own daughter was ugly, she scolded the stepdaughter whenever she could and only thought of how she might torment her.

One day, in the middle of winter, when the snow was high, the stepmother sewed her a dress made of paper, and when it was finished, she called her stepdaughter to her and said, "I've got a craving to eat strawberries. So put on this dress, go into the forest, and fetch me a basket of strawberries. And don't you dare return home until the basket is full."

The maiden wept bitter tears and said, "Strawberries don't grow in winter, and even if they were there, they'd be covered by the snow. How am I supposed to find them? It's so cold outside that my breath will freeze. How can I go out in a paper dress? The wind will blow right through the dress, and the thorns will tear it off my body."

"Don't say one more word!" the stepmother replied. "Get going and look for the strawberries."

In her jealous heart she thought that the maiden would freeze outside and never return. That's why she had made the thin paper dress. Since the maiden was obedient, she put on the paper dress and went out into the forest. There was nothing but snow, not even a blade of green grass. So she kept going, and when she reached the middle of the forest, she saw a small cottage, and three little men were looking out the window. She wished them a good day, and since she greeted them so politely, they asked her what she was looking for in the forest dressed in such a thin paper dress when it was wintertime.

"Oh," she answered, "I'm supposed to look for strawberries, and I'm not allowed to return home until I've gathered a basketful."

The three little men responded: "Go behind our house and clear the snow away. The strawberries have been protected there and have grown. You'll find enough to fill your basket."

The maiden thanked them and did as she was told. While she cleared away the snow and gathered the strawberries, the three little men began talking among themselves.

"Since she's been so polite to us and is so beautiful, what gifts should we grant her?"

"I'll make sure that she becomes even more beautiful than she is. This is my gift," one of the little men said.

"Each time she speaks, golden coins will fall out of her mouth. That will be my gift," said another one of the little men.

"I'll grant her a king who will come and take her for his wife," the third little man said.

When the maiden came back to them, they bestowed their gifts on her, and when she wanted to thank them, golden coins fell out of her mouth. Then she went home, and the stepmother was astonished by the strawberries that she had brought with her and was even more astonished when she saw the coins that fell from the girl's mouth. Shortly thereafter, a king came, took the maiden with him, and made her his wife.

Now the mother thought about how she might provide her daughter with the same great fortune. So she sewed her a splendid fur coat and told her to go into the forest and ask the little men for a gift. But the men saw that she had a wicked heart, and instead of giving her good gifts, they gave her bad ones. The first wished that she would freeze in her fur coat as if it were made of paper. The second wished that she would grow uglier with each passing day. The third wished that she would die a miserable death.

The girl returned home shivering, as if her fur coat had been made of paper, and she told her mother what she had encountered, and when her mother saw that the curses of the three men were starting to take effect, she thought only of avenging herself. So she went to her stepdaughter, who was now the queen, and pretended to be friendly and charming. Consequently, she was welcomed and given her own apartment.

Shortly thereafter the queen gave birth to a prince, and one night, when she was alone and sick and weak, the wicked stepmother lifted her out of the bed with the help of her daughter, and they carried the queen outside to a river and threw her into it. The next morning they told the king that the queen had died during the night.

The following night the kitchen boy saw a duck swimming through the drain into the kitchen, and it asked:

"Are all my guests now sound asleep?"

Then the kitchen boy answered:

"Yes, indeed, you can't hear a peep."
"How about that baby of mine?"
"He's asleep and doing just fine."

Then the duck assumed the shape of the queen, went upstairs, suckled and nursed the baby, plumped up his little bed, covered him, and returned to the drain, where she swam away as a duck. This happened the next night too, and on the third night, she said to the kitchen boy, "Go and tell the king to take his sword and swing it three times over my head on the threshold."

The kitchen boy ran and told the king, and when he swung the sword three times, his wife appeared before him alive and well. The duplicity of the stepmother and her daughter was now clear as day, and they were cast into the forest to be devoured by wild animals.

14

NASTY FLAX SPINNING

In olden times there lived a king who loved flax spinning more than anything else, and his daughters had to spin the entire day. If he didn't hear the wheels humming, he became angry. One time he had to take a trip, and before he said his farewell, he gave a large casket of flax to the queen and said: "All this must be spun by the time I return."

The princesses became distressed and wept.

"If we are to spin all of that flax, we'll have to sit the entire day, and we won't be able to get up at all."

But the queen replied: "Console yourselves. I'll certainly help you."

Now there were three especially ugly spinsters in the realm. The first had such a huge lower lip that it hung beneath her chin. The second had an index finger on her right hand that was so thick and wide that one could make three other fingers out of it. The third had a thick and wide flat foot that was as large as a kitchen board. The queen summoned the three spinsters to the castle, and on the day that the king was supposed to return home, she sat them down next to one another in her room, gave each of them a spinning wheel, and ordered them to spin. Moreover, she told each of them what to answer when the king questioned them. As soon as the king arrived, he heard the humming of the wheels from a distance and was so glad that he intended to praise his daughters. However, upon entering the room and seeing the horrible spinsters sitting there, he was at first startled. Then he stepped toward them and asked the first woman how she got the hideously large lower lip.

"From licking, from licking!"

Then he asked the second where she got her thick finger from.

"From turning the thread, from turning the thread and twining it!"

As she said this, she let the thread run around her finger a couple of times. Finally, he asked the third one where she got her flat foot from.

"From stamping, from stamping!"

When the king heard all this, he commanded the queen and the princesses never ever to touch a spinning wheel again, and this is how they rid themselves of their agony.

15

HANSEL AND GRETEL

A poor woodcutter lived on the edge of a large forest. He didn't have a bite to eat and barely provided the daily bread for his wife and two children,

Hansel and Gretel. It reached a point when he couldn't even provide that anymore. Indeed, he didn't know how to solve this predicament.

One night as he was tossing and turning in bed because of his worries, his wife said to him, "Listen to me, husband, early tomorrow morning you're to take both the children and give them each a piece of bread. Then lead them into the middle of the forest where it's most dense. After you build a fire for them, go away and leave them there. We can no longer feed them."

"No, wife," the man said. "I don't have the heart to take my own children and abandon them to wild beasts, for they'd soon come and tear them apart in the forest."

"If you don't do that," his wife responded, "we shall all have to starve to death."

She didn't give him any peace until he said yes.

The two children were still awake because of their hunger, and they had heard everything that their mother said to their father. Gretel thought, "Now it's all over for me," and began to weep pitiful tears. But Hansel spoke: "Be quiet, Gretel. Don't get upset. I'll find a way to help us."

Upon saying this, he got up, put on his little jacket, opened the bottom half of the door, and crept outside. The moon was shining very brightly, and the white pebbles glittered in front of the house like pure silver coins. Hansel stooped down to the ground and stuffed his pocket with as many pebbles as he could fit in. Then he went back into the house.

"Don't worry, Gretel. Just sleep quietly." And he lay down again in his bed and fell asleep.

Early the next morning, before the sun had even begun to rise, their mother came and woke the two children.

"Get up, children. We're going into the forest. Here's a piece of bread for each of you. But be smart and don't eat it until noon."

Gretel put the bread under her apron because Hansel had the pebbles in his pocket. Then they all set out together into the forest. After they had walked a while, Hansel stopped still and looked back at the house. He did this time and again until his father said, "Hansel, what are you looking at there and why are you dawdling? Pay attention and march along!"

"Oh, father," said Hansel, "I'm looking at my little white cat that's sitting up on the roof and wants to say good-bye to me."

"You fool," the mother said. "That's not a cat. It's the morning sun shining on the chimney."

But Hansel had not been looking at the cat. Instead, he had been looking at the shiny pebbles from his pocket that he had been dropping on the ground. When they reached the middle of the forest, the father said, "Children, I want you to gather some wood. I'm going to make a fire so you won't get cold."

Hansel and Gretel gathered together some brushwood and built quite a nice little pile. The brushwood was soon kindled, and when the fire was ablaze, the mother said, "Now, children, lie down by the fire and sleep. We're going into the forest to chop wood. When we're finished, we'll come back and get you."

Hansel and Gretel sat by the fire, and when noon came, they kept eating their pieces of bread until evening. But their mother and father did not return. Nobody came to fetch them. When it became pitch dark, Gretel began to weep, but Hansel said, "Just wait awhile until the moon has risen."

And when the full moon had risen, Hansel took Gretel by the hand. The pebbles glittered like newly minted silver coins and showed them the way. They walked the whole night long and arrived back at their father's house at break of day. Their father rejoiced with all his heart when he saw his children again, for he had not liked the idea of abandoning them alone in the forest. Their mother also seemed to be delighted by their return, but secretly she was angry.

Not long after this, there was once again nothing to eat in the house, and one evening Gretel heard her mother say to their father: "The children found their way back one time, and I just let that go, but now there's nothing left in the house except for a half loaf of bread. Tomorrow you must take them farther into the forest so they won't find their way back home again. Otherwise, there's no hope for us."

All this saddened the father, and he thought, "It'd be much better to share your last bite to eat with your children." But since he had given in the first time, he also had to yield a second.

Hansel and Gretel overheard their parents' conversation. Then Hansel got up and intended to gather pebbles once again, but their parents had locked the door. Nevertheless, he comforted Gretel and said, "Just sleep, dear Gretel. The dear Lord will certainly help us."

Early the next morning they each received little pieces of bread, but they were smaller than the last time. On the way into the forest Hansel crumbled the bread in his pocket and stopped as often as he could to throw the crumbs on the ground.

"Hansel, why are you always stopping and looking around?" asked the father. "Keep going!"

"Oh, I'm looking at my little pigeon that's sitting on the roof and wants to say good-bye to me," Hansel answered.

"You fool!" his mother said. "That's not your little pigeon. It's the morning sun shining on the chimney."

Now their mother led the children even deeper into the forest until they came to a spot they had never been to before in their lives. Once again they were to sleep by a large fire, and their parents were to come and fetch them in the evening.

When noon came, Gretel shared her bread with Hansel because he had scattered his along the way. Noon went by and then evening passed, but no one came for the poor children. Hansel comforted Gretel and said, "Just wait until the moon has risen, Gretel. Then I'll see the little bread crumbs that I scattered. They'll show us the way back home."

When the moon rose and Hansel looked for the bread crumbs, they were gone because the many thousands of birds that fly about the forest had found them and gobbled them up. Nevertheless, Hansel believed he could find the way home and pulled Gretel along with him, but they soon lost their way in the great wilderness. They walked the entire night and all the next day as well, from morning till night, until they fell asleep from exhaustion. Then they walked for one more day, but they didn't find their way out of the forest. They were now also very hungry, for they had had nothing to eat except some berries that they had found growing on the ground.

On the third day they continued walking until noon. Then they came to a little house made of bread with cake for a roof and pure sugar for windows.

"Let's sit down and eat until we're full," said Hansel. "I want to eat a piece of the roof. Gretel, you can have part of the window since it's sweet."

Hansel had already eaten a good piece of the roof and Gretel had devoured a couple of small round windows and was about to break off a new one when they heard a shrill voice cry from inside:

"Nibble, nibble, I hear a louse!
Who's that nibbling on my house?"

Hansel and Gretel were so tremendously frightened that they dropped what they had in their hands, and immediately thereafter a small, ancient woman crept out of the door. She shook her head and said, "Well now, dear children, where've you come from? Come inside with me. You'll have a good time."

She took them both by the hand and led them into her little house. Then she served them a good meal of milk and pancakes with sugar and apples and nuts. Afterward she made up two beautiful beds, and when Hansel and Gretel lay down in them, they thought they were in heaven.

The old woman, however, was really a wicked witch on the lookout for children and had built the house made of bread only to lure them to her. As soon as she had any children in her power, she would kill, cook, and eat them. It would be like a feast day for her. Therefore, she was quite happy that Hansel and Gretel had come her way.

Early the next morning, before the children were awake, she got up and looked at the two of them sleeping so sweetly, and she was delighted and thought, "They'll certainly be a tasty meal for you!"

Then she grabbed Hansel and stuck him into a small coop, and when he woke up, he was behind a wire mesh used to lock up chickens, and he couldn't move about. Immediately after, she shook Gretel and yelled, "Get up, you lazybones! Fetch some water, and then go into the kitchen and cook something nice. Your brother's sitting in a chicken coop. I want to fatten him up, and when he's fat enough, I'm going to eat him. But now I want you to feed him."

Gretel was frightened and wept, but she had to do what the witch demanded. So the very best food was cooked for poor Hansel so that he would become fat, while Gretel got nothing but crab shells. Every day the old woman came and called out, "Hansel, stick out your finger so I can feel whether you're fat enough."

However, Hansel stuck out a little bone, and the witch was continually puzzled that Hansel didn't get any fatter.

One evening, after a month had passed, she said to Gretel, "Get a move on and fetch some water! I don't care whether your little brother's fat enough or not. He's going to be slaughtered and boiled tomorrow. In the meantime I want to prepare the dough so that we can also bake."

So Gretel went off with a sad heart and fetched the water in which Hansel was to be boiled. Early the next morning Gretel had to get up, light the fire, and hang up a kettle full of water.

"Make sure that it boils," said the witch. "I'm going to light the fire in the oven and shove the bread inside."

Gretel was standing in the kitchen and wept bloody tears and thought, "It would have been better if the wild animals in the forest had eaten us. Then we would have died together and wouldn't have had to bear this sorrow, and I wouldn't have to boil the water that will be the death of my dear brother. Oh dear God, help us poor children get out of this predicament!"

Then the old woman called: "Gretel, come right away over here to the oven!"

When Gretel came, she said, "Look inside and see if the bread is already nice and brown and well-done. My eyes are weak. I can no longer see so well from a distance, and if you can't see, then sit down on the board, and I'll shove you inside. Then you can get around inside and check everything."

The witch wanted to shut the oven door once Gretel was inside, for she wanted to bake her in the hot oven and eat her, too. This is what the wicked witch had planned and why she had called the girl. But God inspired Gretel, and she said, "I don't know how to do it. First you show it to me. Sit down on the board, and I'll shove you inside."

And so the old woman sat down on the board, and since she was light, Gretel shoved her inside as far as she could, and then she quickly shut the oven door and bolted it with an iron bar. The old woman began to scream and groan in the hot oven, but Gretel ran off, and the witch was miserably burned to death.

Meanwhile, Gretel went straight to Hansel and opened the door to the coop. After Hansel jumped out, they kissed each other and were glad. The entire house was full of jewels and pearls. So they filled their pockets with them. Then they went off and found their way home. Their father rejoiced when he saw them again. He hadn't spent a single happy day since his children had been away. Now he was a rich man. However, the mother had died.

16

HERR FIX-IT-UP

Fix-It-Up had been a soldier for a long time. When the war came to an end, however, and there was nothing but the same old things to do every day, he resigned from the army and decided to become a servant for a great lord. There would be clothes trimmed with gold, a lot to do, and always new things happening. So he set out on his way and came to a foreign court, where he saw a lord taking a walk in the garden. Fix-It-Up did not hesitate. He moved briskly over to the lord and said, "Sir, I'm looking for employment with a great lord. If Your Majesty is himself such a person, it would give me great pleasure to serve you. There's nothing I don't know or can't do. I know just how to carry out orders, no matter how they are given."

"Fine, my son," the lord said. "I'd be pleased to have you. First tell me, what do I desire right now?"

Without answering, Fix-It-Up spun around, rushed away, and returned with a pipe and tobacco.

"Fine, my son. You are hired as my servant, but now I'm going to command you to get Princess Nomini, the most beautiful maiden in the world. I want to have her for my wife."

"All right," said Fix-It-Up. "That's a trifle for me. Your Majesty shall soon have her. Just give me a coach drawn by six horses, a coachman, guards, couriers, servants, and a cook, all in full dress. I myself must have princely garments, and everyone must obey my commands."

Soon they departed. Fix-It-Up, the servant, sat inside the coach, which headed straight toward the beautiful princess's court. When the road came to an end, they drove into a field and soon reached the edge of a large forest filled with many thousands of birds. A boisterous song soared splendidly into the blue air.

"Stop! Stop!" exclaimed Fix-It-Up. "Don't disturb the birds. They are praising their creator and will serve me some other time. Let's go to the left."

So the coachman had to turn and drive around the forest. Soon after, they came to a large field, where close to a thousand million ravens were sitting and crying shrilly for food.

"Stop! Stop!" exclaimed Fix-It-Up. "Untie one of the horses way up front. Lead it into the field and slaughter it so that the ravens can eat. I don't want them to suffer from hunger."

After the ravens had eaten, the journey continued, and they came to a pond with a fish in it that was moaning and groaning: "For God's sake, I have nothing to eat in this terrible swamp. Throw me into a running river, and I'll repay your deed one day."

Before the fish could even finish speaking, Fix-It-Up had exclaimed, "Stop! Stop! Cook, put the fish in your apron. Coachman, drive it to a running river."

Fix-It-Up himself got out and threw the fish into the water, and the fish flapped its tail in joy.

"Now, get the horses going," said Fix-It-Up. "We must arrive at the designated spot by evening."

When he reached the royal residence, he drove straight to the best inn, where the innkeeper and all his people came out and welcomed him in their best manners, thinking that a foreign king had arrived, though it was only a servant. Fix-It-Up had himself announced at the royal court, where he endeavored to make a good impression and court the princess.

"My son," said the king, "many such suitors have already been turned away because they couldn't perform the tasks I assigned them to win my daughter."

"All right," said Fix-It-Up, "set any kind of hard task that you want me to do."

"I've ordered a quarter of a liter of poppy seeds to be sown in a field. If you can gather them so that not one kernel is missing, you shall have the princess for your wife."

"Hoho!" Fix-It-Up thought, "that's not much for me." He then took a measuring cup, a sack, and snow-white sheets, went out to the field, and spread the sheets next to the field where the seeds had been sown. Soon after, those birds whose singing he had left undisturbed in the forest arrived, and they picked up the seeds, kernel after kernel, and carried them to the white sheets. When the birds had picked up all of them, Fix-It-Up poured them into the sack, took the measuring cup under his arm, went to the king, and measured out the poppy seeds for him. Now he thought the princess was already his—but he was wrong.

"One thing more, my son," said the king. "My daughter has recently lost her golden ring. You must return it to me before you can have her."

Fix-It-Up did not get upset. "Let Your Majesty show me the river and bridge where the ring was lost, then I shall soon return it to you."

When Fix-It-Up was brought there, he looked down, and there he saw the fish that he had thrown into the river. It stuck its head out into the air and said, "Wait a moment. I'll dive below. A whale has the ring underneath its fins, and I'll fetch it."

Indeed, the fish soon returned and tossed the ring onto the shore. Fix-It-Up brought it to the king, but the latter replied, "Now, just one more thing. There's a unicorn in the forest, and it's been causing a great deal of damage. If you can kill it, there's nothing more you'll have to do."

Fix-It-Up did not get very upset here either. Instead, he went straight into the forest, where he came across the ravens whom he had once fed.

"Just have a little more patience," they said. "The unicorn is lying down and sleeping, but it's not on the side where you can see its eye. When it turns over, we'll peck out its good eye. Then it'll be blind and run furiously against trees and get itself stuck with its horn. That's when you'll be able to kill it easily."

Soon the beast tossed itself around a few times and lay on its other side. All at once the ravens swooped down and pecked out its good eye. When it felt the pain, it jumped up and ran wildly around the forest. After it got its horn stuck in a thick oak tree, Fix-It-Up jumped out, cut off its head,

and brought it to the king, who could no longer deny him his daughter. She was delivered to Fix-It-Up, who took a seat next to her in the coach. He was in full dress, just as he had come, and immediately drove off and brought the lovely princess to his lord. Fix-It-Up was given a fine reception, and the lord's wedding with the princess was celebrated in great splendor. Then Fix-It-Up was appointed prime minister.

Everyone in the company to whom this tale was told wished to be at the celebration. One person wanted to be chambermaid; the other, wardrobe attendant. Someone wanted to be a chamber servant; another, the cook, and so on.

17

THE WHITE SNAKE

Every day at noon a covered dish was placed on the king's table. Then, after everyone left, the king would eat alone from this dish, and nobody in the entire realm knew what kind of food was in it. One of the servants became curious and wanted to know what the dish contained. On one occasion, after the king had ordered him to take the dish away, he could no longer restrain himself. So he took the dish to his room and uncovered it. As he lifted the cover, he found a white snake lying inside, and once he laid his eyes on it, he felt a great desire to taste some of it. So he cut off a piece and began eating it. No sooner did his tongue touch the flesh of the snake than he understood the language of animals and heard what the birds on the window sill were saying to each other.

On this very same day the queen lost one of her most beautiful rings, and the suspicion fell on him. The king also said that if he was not able to find the thief by morning, he himself would be punished as if he had been the guilty person. The servant became sad and went down into the courtyard, where some ducks were resting in the water. As he was watching them, he heard one of them say, "There's something heavy in my stomach. I ate a ring that the queen has lost."

The servant took the duck and carried it to the cook, "Kill this one. It's fat enough."

So the cook cut off the duck's neck, and when he began cleaning it, the queen's ring was lying in its stomach. The servant brought it to the king, who was astonished and happy. Since he was sorry that he had treated the servant unjustly, he said, "Demand whatever you would like and whatever position of royal honor you would like."

However, the servant declined every offer even though he was young and handsome. His heart was sad, and he didn't want to remain at the court any longer. So he asked only for a horse and for money to travel and see the world. Well, he was provided with everything in the very best way.

The next morning he rode off and came to a pond where three fish were trapped in the reeds and were wailing that they'd have to die if they couldn't get back into the water. So he dismounted, took them out of the reeds, and put them back into the water. Then the fish cried out: "We'll remember you, and one day we'll repay you."

He rode on, and a while later he heard an ant king crying out: "Get away from us! Your enormous beast is trampling us with his large hooves!" The young man looked down to the ground and saw that his horse had stepped on an ant hill. So he turned his horse away, and the ant king called out: "We'll remember you, and one day we'll repay you."

Soon the servant entered a forest where two ravens were throwing their young ones out of their nests. They said that their tiny ones were now big enough and could feed themselves.

The young birds lay on the ground and screamed that they would die from starvation because their wings were still too small, and they couldn't fly yet and search for food. So the young man dismounted, killed his horse with his sword, and threw the horse to the young ravens. They hopped over to the horse, ate their fill, and said, "We'll remember this, and one day we'll repay you."

The young man moved on and came to a large city, where he heard a proclamation that whoever wanted to marry the king's daughter would have to perform a task given by her, and if he didn't complete it successfully, he would forfeit his life. Many princes had already been there and had lost their lives, so there was nobody any more who dared to try. This is why the princess had the proclamation issued again. The servant thought about it and decided to declare himself as a suitor. So he was led out to the sea, where a ring was thrown into it. He was to fetch it, and if he came out of the water without it, he'd be pushed back into the sea and would have to die in the water. As he was standing on the shore, the three fish that he had taken from the reeds and thrown into the water came swimming toward him. One of the fish held a shell in its mouth, and the ring was in the shell. The fish set it down on the beach at the feet of the young man, who was full of joy. So he brought the ring to the king and demanded the princess. However, when the princess heard that he wasn't a prince, she refused to accept him. Instead, she scattered ten sacks full of millet seeds in the grass. He was to pick them all up before sunrise the next day, and every single grain was to be gathered or else he'd lose his life. All at once the ant king came with all his ants whom the young man had protected, and they picked up the millet seeds during the night and poured them back into the sacks. By morning they had finished the task. When the princess saw that the sacks had been filled, she was astonished, and the young man was brought before her. Since he was handsome, she liked him but demanded that he perform a third task: he was to fetch an apple from the Tree of Life. As he stood there and thought about how he might get it, one of the ravens whom he had fed with his horse came and brought the apple in its beak. This is how he became the princess's husband, and, when her father died, he became king of the entire country.

18
THE JOURNEY OF THE STRAW,
THE COAL, AND THE BEAN

A straw, a coal, and a bean came together and wanted to take a great journey. They had already gone through many countries when they reached a brook without a bridge and couldn't cross. Finally, straw came up with a good idea. He laid himself across the brook, and the others were to cross over him, first coal, then bean. Coal took wide steps and slowly crossed the straw, while bean toddled after. When coal got to the middle of straw, however, straw began to burn and burned through and through. Coal fell fizzling into the water and died. Straw broke into two pieces and flowed away. Bean, who was somewhat behind, slipped and fell into the water but managed to help herself a little by swimming. Finally, bean had to drink so much water that she burst and was driven to shore in this condition. Fortunately, a tailor was sitting there. He was resting while taking a hike in the woods. Since he had a needle and thread in his sack, he sewed bean together. Ever since this time all the beans have a seam.

❧

According to another story bean was the first to make it across the straw. She reached the other side safely and looked back at coal on the other side and how he was crossing. In the middle of the way coal burned through straw, fell into the water, and fizzled. When bean saw this, she laughed so hard that she burst. The tailor, who was sitting on the shore, sewed her up but only had black thread. This is why all the beans have a black seam.

19

THE FISHERMAN AND HIS WIFE

Once upon a time there was a fisherman who lived with his wife in a piss pot near the sea. Every day the fisherman went out to fish, and all he did was fish and fish. One day he was sitting with his line and gazing into the clear water. And all he did was sit and sit. Suddenly his line sank deep down to the bottom, and when he pulled it up, he had a large flounder on the line, and the flounder said to him, "Listen here, fisherman, I beg of you, let me live. I'm not a real flounder but an enchanted prince. So what good would it do you to kill me? I certainly wouldn't taste very good. Put me back into the water, and let me go."

"Hold on," said the man. "You don't have to waste your words on me. I would have thrown a talking fish back into the water anyway."

He then put the fish back into the clear water, and the flounder swam to the bottom, leaving behind a long streak of blood. Then the fisherman stood up and returned to the piss pot to be with his wife and told her that he had caught a flounder but since it had been an enchanted prince, he had let him go.

"Didn't you wish for anything?" asked the wife.

"No," said the husband. "What should I have wished for?"

"Ah," said the wife. "Don't you think it's awful that we've got to live in this piss pot? It stinks, and it's disgusting. You should have wished for a little hut. Go back and call him. Tell him we want a little hut. I'm sure he'll give us one."

The husband didn't think that this was the right thing to do, but he went back to the sea anyway, and when he arrived, the sea was green and yellow, and he stood on the shore and said:

"Flounder, flounder, in the sea,
if you're a man, then speak to me.
Though I don't agree with my wife's request,
I've come to ask it nonetheless."

The flounder came swimming up to him and said, "Well, what does she want?"

"Oh," said the man, "my wife, Isabel, thinks I should have wished for something because I caught you. Since she doesn't want to live in a piss pot, she'd like to have a hut."

"Just go home," said the flounder. "She's already got it."

The fisherman went home, and his wife was standing in the doorway of a hut and said to him: "Come inside, husband. Look! Now, isn't this much better?"

There was a stove and a parlor, also a kitchen. Behind the hut was a little yard and garden with all kinds of vegetables and chickens and ducks.

"Oh," said the fisherman, "now we can enjoy ourselves."

"Yes," said the wife, "we're going to enjoy it."

Everything went well for about a week or two, and then the wife said, "Listen, husband, the hut is much too cramped, and the yard and garden are too little. I want a large stone castle. Go back to the flounder and tell him to give us a castle."

"Ah, wife," said the husband. "The flounder has just given us a hut, and I don't want to go back again so soon. The flounder might be unwilling to do anything."

"What do you mean?" said the wife. "He can easily do it, and he'll be glad to do it. Just go back to him!"

So the fisherman left, and his heart grew heavy. When he got to the sea, the water was purple, dark blue, gray, and dense but still calm. Then he stood there and said:

"Flounder, flounder, in the sea,
if you're a man, then speak to me.
Though I don't agree with my wife's request,
I've come to ask it nonetheless."

"What now! What does she want?" the flounder asked.

"Oh," said the fisherman, somewhat distressed. "My wife wants to live in a large stone castle."

"Go home. She's standing in front of the door," the flounder said.

The fisherman went home, and his wife was standing in front of a large palace.

"So, husband," she said, "isn't this beautiful?"

He went inside with her, and there were many servants, and the walls were all bright. The chairs and tables were made of gold. Behind the palace was a huge yard and a park half a mile long with deer and does and rabbits. There was also a stable for cows and horses.

"Oh," said the husband, "now let's live in the beautiful castle and be content."

"We'll have to think about that," said the wife, "and sleep on it."

Then they went to bed.

The next morning the wife woke up. It was just daybreak, and he poked her husband in his side with her elbow and said, "Husband, get up. We must be king and rule this entire country."

"Ah, wife!" said the husband. "Why should we be king? I don't want to be king."

"Well," said the wife, "then I'll be king."

"Oh, wife," said the husband, "where can you be king? The flounder won't want to make you king."

"Husband," said the wife, "go straight to him and tell him I must be king!"

The fisherman went but was very distressed that his wife wanted to be king.

When he got to the sea, it was completely gray and black, and the water was fermenting from below. The fisherman stood there and said:

"Flounder, flounder, in the sea,
if you're a man, then speak to me.
Though I don't agree with my wife's request,
I've come to ask it nonetheless."

"Well, what does she want?" asked the flounder.

"Oh," said the man, "she wants to be king."

"Go back home," said the flounder. "She's already king."

Then the man went home, and as he approached the palace, he saw that there were many soldiers, drums, and trumpets. His wife was sitting on a high throne of gold and diamonds, and she wore a large golden crown. Two rows of ladies-in-waiting were standing on either side of her, each lady a head shorter than the next.

"Oh," said the fisherman, "now you're king, aren't you?"

"Yes," said his wife, "I am king."

After he gazed at her for some time, he said, "Oh, wife, it's wonderful that you're king! Now let's not wish for anything more."

"No, husband," the wife said as she became very restless. "I have too much time on my hands, and I can't stand it anymore. I'm king, but now I also want to be emperor."

"Oh, wife," said the fisherman, "why do you want to be emperor?"

"Husband," she said, "go to the flounder. I want to be emperor!'

"Oh, wife," the husband said. "He can't make you emperor. I don't want to tell that to the flounder."

"I'm king," she said, "and you're just my husband. Go there at once!"

The fisherman went away, but as he was walking, he thought, "This won't turn out well at all. It's outrageous for her to be emperor. The flounder's going to become sick and tired of this in the end." When he got to the sea, it was all black and dense, and a strong wind whipped across the surface and made the water curdle. Then the fisherman stepped forward and said:

"Flounder, flounder, in the sea,
if you're a man, then speak to me.
Though I don't agree with my wife's request,
I've come to ask it nonetheless."

"Well, what does she want?" asked the flounder.

"Oh, flounder," he said. "My wife wants to be emperor."

"Go back home," said the flounder. "She's already emperor."

Then the man went home, and when he arrived, he saw his wife sitting on a very high throne made from a single piece of gold. She was wearing a large crown three yards tall and covered with diamonds and garnets. She was flanked on either side by two rows of bodyguards, each man shorter than the next, beginning with a tremendous giant two miles tall and ending with the tiniest dwarf, who was no bigger than my pinky. There were also many princes and dukes standing before her, and her husband stepped up and said, "Wife, now you're emperor, aren't you?"

"Yes," she said, "I'm emperor."

"Oh," said the fisherman, and he gazed at her for some time, "it's wonderful that you're emperor."

"Husband," she replied. "why are you standing there like that? I'm emperor, but now I also want to be pope."

"Oh, wife," said the husband. "Why do you want to be pope?"

"Husband," she said. "I want to be pope!"

"No, wife," said the fisherman. "The flounder can't make you pope. It won't turn out well."

"Stop talking nonsense, husband!" said the wife. "If he can make me emperor, he can also make me pope. Go there at once!"

So the fisherman went off, but he felt rather queasy. He was trembling, and his knees began to wobble. A strong wind swept across the land. The water rose up in waves, and the waves splashed against the shore. Ships were in distress as they were tossed up and down by the waves. Though there was still a little blue in the middle of the sky, the horizon was completely red, as if a heavy thunderstorm were coming. Then he stepped forward and said:

"Flounder, flounder, in the sea
if you're a man, then speak to me.
Though I don't agree with my wife's request,
I've come to ask it nonetheless."

"Well, what does she want?" asked the flounder.

"Oh," the man said, "she wants to be pope."

"Go back home," said the flounder. "She's already pope."

Then the man went home, and when he arrived, his wife was sitting on a throne two miles high and was wearing three large golden crowns on her head. Numerous bishops and priests were standing around her, and there were two rows of candles on either side of her. The biggest candle was as thick and as large as the highest tower, and the tiniest was a church candle.

"Wife," the man said as he took a good look at her, "are you the pope?"

"Yes," she said, "I'm pope."

"Oh, wife," he said, "Isn't it wonderful that you're pope. You must be satisfied. Now that you're pope, you can't become anything greater."

"I'll think about it," said the wife.

Then they both went to bed, but she wasn't satisfied, and her ambition prevented her from sleeping. She kept thinking of ways she might become greater than she was. When the sun began to rise, she sat at the window and thought, "Aha, I could also make the sun rise!" Then she became quite grim and poked her husband and said, "Husband, go to the flounder. I want to be like God."

The husband was still half asleep, but he was so shocked by what she had said that he fell out of the bed.

"Ah, wife," he said. "Be content and remain pope."

"No," his wife said. "I won't have any peace of mind and won't be able bear it until I can make the sun and moon rise. I want to be like God!"

"Ahh, wife!" the husband said. "The flounder can't do that. He can make you emperor and pope, but he can't make you God."

"Husband," she said and looked ghastly, "I want to be like God. I want you to go to the flounder at once!"

Now his limbs began to tremble, and he was filled with fear. Outside a great storm was raging so much that all the trees and mountains were shaking. The sky was pitch black, and there was thunder and lightning. Black waves rose up in the sea as high as mountains, and they all had crests of white foam on top. Then the fisherman said:

"Flounder, flounder, in the sea,
if you're a man, then speak to me.
Though I don't agree with my wife's request,
I've come to ask it nonetheless."

"Well, what does she want?" the flounder asked.
"Oh," he said, "she wants to be like God."
"Go back home. She's sitting in your piss pot again."
And that's where they are still sitting this very day.

20

A STORY ABOUT A BRAVE TAILOR

I

Once in the little city of Romandia a tailor was sitting and working, and he had an apple lying nearby. There were also many flies around the apple as was usual during the summer time. The tailor became angry, and he took a piece of cloth. Then he hit the flies on the apple and killed seven of them. When the simple-minded tailor saw this, he thought that he had taken care of the situation quite well, and he soon had a beautiful suit of armor made for himself and also had golden letters inscribed that read: *Seven with One Stroke*. Then, dressed in his armor, he went onto the street, and whoever saw him believed that he had killed seven men with one stroke. After that, everyone was very terrified of him.

Now in the same region there was a king whose praise resounded far and wide, and the lazy tailor made his way to king's court, lay down on the grass, and slept. The royal servants, who went in and out of the castle, saw the tailor in the splendid suit of armor and read the inscription. They were very puzzled about what this warrior was doing in the king's courtyard during a time of peace. They thought he was undoubtedly a great lord. The king's councilors, who had also seen the tailor, informed his majesty that this man could be very useful whenever there might be a conflict. The king was very satisfied with their advice and soon summoned the well-armed tailor and asked him whether he wanted to enter his royal service. The tailor answered right away and told his majesty the king that this is why he had come and asked him to tell him where he might be of use to the king. The king immediately accepted him into his service and gave him special lodgings.

Now it didn't take long for the knights to show the good tailor their ill will. They wished the devil would cart him away. But they were afraid that, if ever they had differences, they wouldn't be able to stand up to him because he had killed seven with one stroke. So, they continually thought of ways to get rid of this warrior. Finally, they discussed the situation with one another and agreed that they would all go to the king and ask to be released from his service, and the king granted their wish.

The king was sad to lose all his knights on account of one man, and he wished he had never laid eyes on him. Indeed, he actually wanted to get rid of him, but he didn't dare to discharge him for fear that the tailor might kill him and all his people and take over the his realm. The king pondered the situation for a long time, going back and forth in his mind, until he hit upon a plan. Since he needed such a strong and powerful warrior, he summoned the tailor and offered the following proposal: there were two giants living in a forest in the king's country, and they were causing great damage by robbing, murdering, and burning people. Nobody could get near them because they tore apart anyone who approached. Neither weapons nor anything else helped. However, if the tailor could conquer these two giants and kill them, the king promised him he would receive the king's only daughter for his wife and half the kingdom as dowry. Moreover, one hundred knights were to accompany him and lend him assistance.

The tailor felt good about this proposal, especially since he would become the king's son-in-law, and he replied that he'd like very much to kill the giants, but he didn't need the help of the knights, for he knew quite well how to kill the giants. Then he went to the forest, and after he left the knights at the edge of the woods, he entered and began looking to see if he could find the giants in the distance. After he searched for a long time, he found them sleeping and snoring beneath a tree. The tailor didn't have to think long about what to do. He quickly filled his shirt with stones and climbed up the tree under which they were sleeping. Then he threw one stone after another on the chest of one of the giants until he woke up. The giant became angry with his companion and asked him why he was hitting him. The other giant excused himself as best he could. Then they lay down to sleep again, and the tailor threw a stone at the other giant. He, too, became angry and asked his companion why he was throwing stones at him. They quarreled for a while, but since they were tired, they let it pass, and their eyes closed again. Then the tailor threw a stone at the first giant again with all his might, and the giant couldn't tolerate his companion doing this anymore. So, he hit him violently because he thought that it was his companion who had struck him. Well the other giant didn't like this and stood up. They both became so furious that they ripped trees from the ground and began beating each other to death. Fortunately, they didn't tear up the tree that the tailor was sitting in. When he saw what had happened, he summoned his courage, which he normally didn't have, and climbed cheerfully down the tree. Then he stabbed the giants with his sword a few times to create wounds and left the forest to meet the knights, who asked him whether he had seen the giants.

"Yes," he said. "I've slaughtered the two of them and have left them lying beneath a tree."

The knights doubted very much that he could come away from the giants without being wounded. So they rode into the forest to inspect this miracle and found everything just as the tailor had said it was. While they all felt astonished, they also felt great horror. Indeed, they felt worse than ever. They feared that he might kill them all if he suspected that they were his enemy. So they rode home and told the king about the tailor's deed.

Now the tailor wished to have the king's daughter along with half the realm, but when the king saw that he had killed the giants, he regretted that he had promised his daughter in marriage to the unknown warrior and began thinking of a way to break his promise, for he had no intention of giving his daughter to him. So he said to the tailor that there was a unicorn in the forest that caused great damage by harming fish and people, and if the tailor captured the unicorn, the king would give him his daughter.

The tailor was satisfied with this proposal. So he took some rope, went to the forest, and ordered his escorts to remain outside. He wanted to enter alone, and as soon as he went into the forest, he saw the unicorn charging at him and intent on killing him. However, the tailor was nimble, and he waited until the unicorn was very close before jumping behind a nearby tree. Meanwhile, the unicorn was running at full speed and couldn't turn, so that it thrust its horn into the tree so hard that it became stuck. When the tailor saw this, he went to the unicorn, put the rope around its neck, and tied it to the tree. Then he left the forest and announced his victory over the unicorn. Once the king learned of the tailor's triumph, he became tremendously sad and didn't know what to do, for the tailor continued to desire his daughter. So once again the king demanded that he perform a task and capture a wild boar that was running around in the forest, and if he succeeded, the king would immediately give him his daughter. The king's huntsmen were to lend him a hand. So the tailor went off to the forest with the huntsmen, but he ordered them to stay outside, and they were pleased, for the wild boar had already given them such rough treatment that they had no desire to chase it, and they thanked the tailor very much. Once the tailor entered the forest, the boar charged at him, foaming at the mouth and gnashing its teeth, and sought to trample him to the ground. Fortunately, there was a chapel in the forest where people often rested, and it was nearby. When the tailor saw it, he ran inside and jumped right out again through one of the windows. The boar followed him inside, while the tailor ran around on the outside, slammed the door shut, and locked the boar in the little church. Then he went and announced to the huntsmen that he had captured the boar. In turn, they rode to the king and informed him of the tailor's deed.

It's not clear whether the king liked it or not, and that doesn't matter. He had to give his daughter to the tailor. However, I'm certain that if he had known that the hero was actually a tailor, he would have put a noose around his head instead of giving his daughter to him. As it was, the king had to give his daughter to this stranger but with grave concern. Thereafter, the tailor didn't ask much but just thought about becoming the king's son-in-law. So the wedding took place with little joy, and a king was made out of a tailor.

After he had spent some nights lying next to his bride, the tailor began talking in his sleep and said: "Boy, finish that jerkin and mend the trousers fast, or else I'll give you a whack on your head with my yardstick."

Well, his wife happened to hear all of this, and she went to her father to complain. She begged him to help her get rid of this husband who was nothing but a tailor. The king was cut to the heart when he heard that he had given his only daughter to a tailor. So he consoled her as best he could and told her to leave the door of her bedroom open that night. Then he would post some servants outside, and when the tailor began to talk, they would go inside and do away with him.

The king's daughter was content with this plan. However, the king had a weapons-bearer at his court who was kindly disposed to the tailor, and he had overheard everything. So he went quickly to the young king and informed him about the plot against him and advised him to protect himself as best he could.

The tailor was very grateful and assured his friend that he knew how to take care of this matter. When night arrived, the tailor went to bed with his young queen and pretended to fall asleep, while she secretly got out of bed, went to the door, opened it, and then got back into bed. As soon as the tailor heard this, he began to talk loudly as if he were talking in his sleep and so loudly that the servants outside the door could hear him.

"Boy, finish that jerkin and mend the trousers fast, or else I'll give you a whack on your head with my yardstick! I've slain seven with one stroke, killed two giants, captured a unicorn, and trapped a wild boar. Do you think I'm afraid of those fellows waiting outside my door?"

When the men heard the tailor's words, they fled as if the wild host of hell were after them, and nobody wanted to do anything to him after this. Thus the tailor remained a king for the rest of his life.

II

One summer morning a little tailor was sitting at his table by his window. Just then a peasant woman came down the street and cried out, "Good jam for sale! Good jam for sale!"

The tailor stuck his head out the window and called, "Up here, my dear woman, you're sure to make a good sale with me!"

When the woman came up, he inspected each of the jars and finally bought a quarter of a pound. Afterward he fetched a loaf of bread, cut a full slice for himself, spread it with the jam, and placed it on the table next to him.

"You'll taste good," he said to himself, "but first I want to finish the jacket before I take a bite."

So he began to sew and made big stitches out of joy. Meanwhile, the smell of the sweet jam rose to the flies, and a lot of them flew and landed on the jam.

"Hey, who invited you as guests?" the little tailor said and chased them away. But it didn't take long for the flies to come back in even larger numbers. My little tailor became angry, and he grabbed a piece of cloth from under his worktable.

"Wait, I'll let you have it!" And he whacked them.

When he withdrew the cloth, he counted to see how many flies he had hit, and there were twenty-nine dead ones before his eyes.

"You're quite a man!" he said to himself, and since he was so delighted with himself he cut out a belt and embroidered it with: *Twenty-nine with one stroke!*

"Now you have to go out into the world!" he thought, and so he tied the belt around him and searched his house for something to take with him, but he found only a piece of old cheese, which he put in his pocket. And as he set out on his way, he caught a bird and also stuck it into his pocket.

His way led him up a high mountain, and when he reached the peak, he came across a huge giant who was sitting there, and he said, "How are you, my good fellow? You're gazing at the world, right? Well, I happen to be on my way into the world."

The giant looked at the tailor contemptuously and said, "You're a miserable creature!"

The little tailor responded by opening his coat to show the giant his belt. "You can read for yourself what kind of man you have standing before you!"

The giant read the words *Twenty-nine with one stroke!* and thought that it meant the tailor had slain twenty-nine men. Therefore, he began to show some respect for the little tailor. Nevertheless, he wanted to test him first. So he took a stone in his hand and squeezed it until water began to drip from it.

"You're not as strong as that!"

"I can do that as well," the little tailor said, "if that's all you have to show."

He immediately reached into his pocket, took out the soft cheese, and squeezed it until the liquid ran out.

"That beats yours, doesn't it?" the tailor declared.

The giant was puzzled, and so he picked up a stone and threw it so high that it could barely be seen with the naked eye.

"Now, you do the same!"

"That was a good throw," said the tailor, "but even so, the stone had to return to the ground in the end. Now, I'm going to throw one that won't ever come back."

He reached into his pocket, took out the bird, threw it into the air, and the bird flew away for good.

"How did you like that?"

The giant was astounded. So he decided to join him, and they continued walking together until they came to a cherry tree. The giant seized the top, where the fruit was ripest. He bent it down, handed it to the tailor, and told him to eat some of the fruit. But the little tailor was much too weak to hold on to the treetop, and when the giant let go of it, the tailor was catapulted into the air. After he had come down again, unharmed, the giant said, "What's this? Don't tell me that you're not strong enough to hold on to that twig!"

"That's nothing," the tailor responded. "Do you think that something like that is really difficult for a man who's slain twenty-nine with one stroke? Do you know why I did that? I jumped over the tree because some huntsmen were shooting there in the bushes. Let's see if you can jump over it yourself."

Now the giant believed for sure that there was nobody in the world who could surpass the little tailor in strength and cunning.

[*The rest of this tale is missing.*]

21

CINDERELLA

Once upon a time there was a rich man who lived happily with his wife for a long time, and they had one little girl together. Then the wife became ill, and as she became deathly ill, she called her daughter and said, "Dear child, I must leave you, but when I am up in heaven, I shall look after you. Plant a little tree on my grave, and whenever you wish for something, shake it, and you'll have what you wish. And whenever you are otherwise in a predicament, then I'll send you help. Just stay good and pure."

After she said this, she closed her eyes and died. Her child wept and planted a little tree on her grave and didn't need to water it, for her tears were good enough.

The snow covered the mother's grave like a little white blanket, and by the time the sun had taken it off again and the little tree had become green for the second time, the man had married a second wife. However, the stepmother already had two daughters from her first husband. They had beautiful features but proud, nasty, and wicked hearts. After the wedding had now been celebrated, and all three entered the house, a difficult time began for the poor child.

"What's this terrible and useless thing doing in our rooms?" the step-mother said. "Off with you into the kitchen. Whoever wants to eat bread must first earn it. She can be our maid."

The stepsisters took away her clothes and dressed her in an old gray smock.

"You look good in that!" they said, while mocking her and leading her to the kitchen, where the poor child had to do heavy work: she had to get up before dawn, carry the water into the house, make the fire, cook, and wash. Meanwhile her sisters did everything imaginable to cause her grief and make her look ridiculous. They poured peas and lentils into the ashes of the hearth so she had to sit there the entire day and separate them. In the evening, when she was tired, there was no bed for her, and she had to lie next to the hearth in the ashes. Since she always rummaged in dust and looked dirty, they named her Cinderella.

At a certain time the king decided to organize a magnificent ball that was to last three days, and his son was supposed to choose a bride at this event. The two proud stepsisters were also invited to it.

"Cinderella," they called to her, "Come up here! Comb out our hair, brush our shoes, and fasten our buckles! We're going to see the prince at the ball."

Cinderella worked hard and cleaned and brushed as well as she could. However, the stepsisters continually scolded her, and when they had finished dressing, they asked her in a mocking tone: "Cinderella, wouldn't you like to go to the ball?"

"Oh, yes," Cinderella replied. "But how can I go? I don't have any clothes."

"No," said the eldest daughter. "That's all we'd need for you show up there! If the people heard that you were our sister, we'd be ashamed. You belong in the kitchen where there's a bowl full of lentils. When we return, they must be sorted, and take care that we don't find a bad one among them. Otherwise, you know what will happen to you."

After that the stepsisters left, and Cinderella stood there and looked after them, and when she could no longer see them, she went sadly into the kitchen and shook the lentils on to the hearth, and they formed a very large pile.

"Oh," she sighed and said, "I'll have to sort them until midnight, and I won't be able to shut my eyes no matter how much they may hurt. If my mother knew about this!"

Then she knelt down in the ashes in front of the hearth and wanted to begin sorting. All at once two white pigeons flew through the window and landed next to the lentils on the hearth. They nodded with their little heads and said, "Cinderella, would you like us to help you sort the lentils?"

"Yes," answered Cinderella:

"The good ones for the little pot,
the bad ones for your little crop."

And peck, peck! Peck, peck! They began and ate the bad ones and let the good ones remain. And in a quarter of an hour the lentils were so clean that there was not a bad one among them, and Cinderella could smooth them out in the little pot. Now the pigeons said to her, "Cinderella, if you want to see your sisters dance with the prince, then climb up to the pigeon coop."

Cinderella followed them and climbed to the top of the ladder of the pigeon coop and could see the ballroom from there. Indeed, she could see her sisters dance with the prince, and a thousand chandeliers glittered and glistened before her eyes. And after she had seen enough, she climbed down the ladder. Her heart was heavy, and she laid herself down in the ashes and fell asleep.

The next morning the two sisters went into the kitchen, and when they saw that Cinderella had cleanly sorted the lentils, they were angry because they would have liked to have scolded her. Since they couldn't do that, they began to tell her about the ball and said, "Cinderella, that was so much fun, especially the dance. The prince, who's the most handsome in the world, led us out onto the dance floor, and one of us will become his bride."

"Yes," Cinderella said. "I saw the chandeliers glimmer. That must have been splendid."

"What! How did you manage that?" the eldest sister asked.

"I climbed up to the pigeon coop."

When the sister heard this, she was filled with jealousy, and she immediately ordered the pigeon coop to be torn down.

Now Cinderella had to comb and clean again, and the youngest sister, who had a little sympathy in her heart, said, "Cinderella, when it turns dark, you can go to the ball and look in through the windows."

"No," said the eldest. "That will only make her lazy. Here's a sack of sweet peas, Cinderella. Sort the good from the bad and work hard. If you don't have them sorted cleanly by tomorrow, then I'll spill them all into the ashes, and you'll have to starve until you've fished them out of the ashes."

Cinderella sat down on the hearth in distress and poured the peas out of the sack. Then the pigeons flew into the kitchen once again and asked in a friendly way: "Cinderella, do you want us to sort the peas?"

"Yes."

"The good ones for the little pot,
the bad ones for your little crop."

Peck, peck! Peck, peck! It all went so quickly as if twelve hands were there. And when they were finished, the pigeons said: "Cinderella, do you want to go and dance at the ball?"

"Oh, my God!" she cried out. "But how can I go there in my dirty clothes?"

"Go to the little tree on your mother's grave. Shake it and wish for clothes. However, you must return before midnight."

So, Cinderella went to the grave, shook the little tree, and spoke:

"Shake and wobble, little tree!
Let beautiful clothes fall down to me."

No sooner had she said all this than a splendid dress lay right before her along with pearls, silk stockings, silver slippers, and everything else that belonged to her outfit. Cinderella carried everything into the house, and after she had washed herself and dressed herself, she was as beautiful as a rose washed by the dew. And when she stepped outside, a carriage stood there drawn by six black horses adorned with feathers. There were also servants, dressed in blue and silver, who helped her inside. Then off they galloped to the king's castle.

When the prince saw the carriage come to a halt before the gate, he thought that a strange princess from afar had come traveling to the ball. So he himself went down the stairs, helped Cinderella out of the carriage, and led her into the ballroom. And when the glitter of the four thousand chandeliers fell upon her, she was so beautiful that everyone there was amazed, and the sisters also stood there and were annoyed that some other young lady was more beautiful than they. However, they didn't think in the least that it might be Cinderella, who was presumably at home in the ashes. Now, the prince danced with Cinderella and showed her royal honor. As he danced, he thought to himself, "I'm supposed to choose a bride, and I know she's the only one for me." On the other hand, Cinderella had lived for such a long time in ashes and sadness, and now she was in splendor and joy. But when midnight came, before the clock struck twelve, she stood up and bowed good-bye. Even though the prince begged and begged, she refused to remain any longer. So the prince led her down the stairs. The carriage was below and waiting for her, and it drove off in splendor as it had come.

When Cinderella arrived home, she went once again to the little tree on her mother's grave.

"Shake and wobble, little tree!
Take these clothes back from me."

Then the tree took the clothes, and Cinderella had her gray smock on again. And she returned to the kitchen with it, put some dust on her face, and laid herself down to sleep.

In the morning the sisters came. They looked morose and kept quiet. Then Cinderella said, "You must have had an enjoyable time last night."

"No, a princess was there, and the prince almost always danced with her. Nobody had ever seen her or knew where she came from."

"Was it perhaps that lady who arrived in the splendid carriage pulled by six black horses?" Cinderella asked.

"How do you know this?"

"As I was standing in the entrance to the house, I saw her drive by."

"In the future stay inside working," said the eldest sister, who looked angrily at Cinderella. "What business do you have to stand in the entrance to the house?"

For a third time Cinderella had to dress up the two sisters, and as a reward they gave her a bowl with peas that she was to sort. "And don't you dare to leave your work!" the eldest daughter cried out to her.

Cinderella thought, "If only my pigeons will return!" And her heart beat anxiously until the pigeons came as they had the previous night and said, "Cinderella, do you want us to sort the peas?"

"Yes."

"The good ones for the little pot,
the bad ones for your little crop."

Once more the pigeons pecked the bad ones out, and once they were finished, they said, "Cinderella, shake the little tree. It will throw down even more beautiful clothes. Go to the ball, but take care that you return before midnight."

Cinderella went to her mother's grave:

"Shake and wobble, little tree!
Let beautiful clothes fall down to me."

Then a dress fell down, and it was even more glorious and splendid than the previous one. It was made out of gold and precious gems. In addition there were golden gusseted stockings and gold slippers. And after Cinderella was completely dressed, she glistened really like the sun at midday. A carriage drawn by six white horses that had plumes on their heads stopped in front of the house, and the servants were dressed in red and gold. When Cinderella arrived, the prince was already on the stairs and led her into the ballroom. And if everyone had been astonished by her beauty the day before, they were even more astounded this evening, and the sisters stood in a corner and were pale with envy. If they had known that it was Cinderella, who was supposed to be at home in the ashes, they would have died of envy.

Now the prince wanted to know who the strange princess was, where she came from, and where she drove off to. So he had people stationed on the road, and they were to pay attention to her whereabouts. Moreover, he had the stairs painted with black pitch so that she wouldn't be able to run so fast. Cinderella danced and danced with the prince and was filled with so much joy that she didn't think about midnight. All of a sudden, as she was in the middle of a dance, she heard the clock begin to strike. She was reminded of the pigeons' warning and was terrified. So she rushed to the door and flew down the stairs. However, since they were covered with pitch, one of her golden slippers got caught, and Cinderella didn't stop to take it with her out of fear. Indeed, just as she reached the last step of the stairs, the clock struck twelve. Consequently, the carriage and horses disappeared, and Cinderella stood in her gray smock on the dark road. In the meantime, the prince had rushed after her, and he found the golden slipper on the steps. He pulled it from the pitch and carried it with him, but by the time he made it down the stairs, everything had disappeared. Even the people who had stood guard came and said that they had seen nothing.

Cinderella was glad that nothing worse had happened, and she went home. Once there she turned on her dim oil lamp, hung it in the chimney, and laid herself down in the ashes. It didn't take long before the two sisters also returned and called out: "Cinderella, get up and light the way."

Cinderella yawned and pretended that she had been wakened from her sleep. As she showed them the way, she heard one of the sisters say, "God knows who the presumable princess is. If she were only in her grave! The prince danced just with her alone, and after she had gone, he didn't want to remain, and the entire ball came to an end."

"It was really as if all the lights had suddenly been blown out," the other said.

Meanwhile, the prince was thinking, "If everything else has gone wrong for you, now the slipper will help you find your bride." So he had a proclamation announced and declared that whichever maiden's foot fit the golden slipper was to become his wife. But the slipper was much too small for anyone who tried it on. Indeed, many couldn't even slip their foot into the slipper and couldn't have done so even if the single slipper were two. Finally, it was the turn of the two sisters to take the test. They were glad because they had small beautiful feet and believed that it couldn't go wrong for them and that the prince should have gone to them right away.

"Listen," said the mother secretly. "here's a knife, and if the slipper is still too tight for you, then cut off a piece of your foot. It will hurt a bit. But what does that matter? It will soon pass, and one of you will become queen."

So the eldest sister went into the chamber and tried on the slipper. Her toe slipped inside, but her heel was too large. So, she took the knife and cut off a part of her heel until she could force her foot into the slipper. Then she went out of the chamber to the prince, and when he saw that she had the slipper on her foot, he said that she was to be his bride. Then he led her to his carriage and wanted to drive off. However, when he came to the gate, the pigeons were above and called out:

"Looky, look, look
at the shoe that she took.
There's blood all over, the shoe's too small.
She's not the bride that you met at the ball."

The prince leaned over and saw that blood was spilling out of the slipper, and he realized that he had been deceived. So he brought the false bride back to the house. However, the mother said to her second daughter, "Take the slipper, and if it's too short for you, then cut off one of your toes."

So the sister took the slipper into her chamber, and since her foot was too large, she bit her lips and cut off a large part of her toes. Then she quickly slipped her foot into the slipper and came out of her chamber. Since the prince thought she was the right bride, he wanted to drive off with her. However, when he came to the gate, the pigeons called out again:

"Looky, look, look
at the shoe that she took.
There's blood all over, and the shoe's too small.
She's not the bride you met at the ball."

The prince looked down and saw that the stockings of the bride were colored red and that her blood was streaming out of the slipper. So the prince brought her to her mother and said, "She, too, is not the right bride. But is there another daughter in your house?"

"No," said the mother, "there's just a nasty Cinderella. She sits below in the ashes. I'm sure the slipper won't fit her."

The mother didn't want to have her summoned, but the prince demanded that she do so. Therefore, Cinderella was alerted, and when she heard that the prince was there, she washed her face and hands quickly so that they were fresh and clean. When she entered the room, she curtsied. Then the prince handed her the golden slipper and said, "Try it on! If it fits, you'll become my wife."

So Cinderella took off the heavy shoe from her left foot and put this foot into the golden slipper, and after she pressed a bit, her foot fit as though the slipper had been made for her. And when she stood up, the prince looked at her face and recognized the beautiful princess once again and cried: "This is the right bride!"

The stepmother and the two haughty sisters were horrified and became pale, but the prince led Cinderella away. He helped her into the carriage, and as they drove off through the gate, the pigeons called out:

"Looky, look, look,
there's no blood at all.
The golden shoe's a perfect fit.
She's truly the bride you met at the ball."

22
HOW SOME CHILDREN PLAYED AT SLAUGHTERING

I

In a city named Franecker, located in West Friesland, some young boys and girls between the ages of five and six happened to be playing with one another. They chose one boy to play a butcher, another boy was to be a cook, and a third boy was to be a pig. Then they selected one girl to be a cook and another girl to be her assistant. The assistant was to catch the blood of the pig in a little bowl so they could make sausages. As agreed, the butcher now fell upon the little boy playing the pig, threw him to the ground, and slit his throat open with a knife, while the assistant cook caught the blood in her little bowl.

A councilman was walking nearby and saw this wretched act. He immediately took the butcher boy with him and led him into the house of

the mayor, who instantly summoned the entire council. They deliberated about this incident and didn't know what to do with the boy, for they realized it had all been part of a children's game. One of the councilmen, a wise old man, advised the chief judge to take a beautiful red apple in one hand and a Rhenish gold coin in the other. Then he was to call the boy and stretch out his hands to him. If the boy took the apple, he was to be set free. If he took the gold coin, he was to be killed. The judge took the wise man's advice, and the boy grabbed the apple with a laugh. Thus he was set free without any punishment.

II

There once was a father who slaughtered a pig, and his children saw that. In the afternoon, when they began playing, one child said to the other, "You be the little pig, and I'll be the butcher." He then took a shiny knife and slit his little brother's throat.

Their mother was upstairs in a room bathing another child, and when she heard the cries of her son, she immediately ran downstairs. Upon seeing what had happened, she took the knife out of her son's throat and was so enraged that she stabbed the heart of the other boy, who had been playing the butcher. Then she quickly ran back to the room to tend to her child in the bathtub, but while she had been gone, he had drowned in the tub. Now the woman became so frightened and desperate that she wouldn't allow the neighbors to comfort her and finally hung herself. When her husband came back from the fields and saw everything, he became so despondent that he died soon thereafter.

23

THE LITTLE MOUSE, THE LITTLE
BIRD, AND THE SAUSAGE

Once upon a time a little mouse, a little bird, and a sausage came together and set up house. For a long time they lived together in peace and happiness, and they managed to increase their possessions by a considerable amount. The little bird's job was to fly into the forest every day and bring back wood. The mouse had to carry water, light the fire, and set the table while the sausage did the cooking.

Now, if things go too well for people, they always look for new things! So, one day as the bird was flying about, he came upon another bird, and he boasted and told him about his superb situation. But the other bird called him a poor sap because he had to do most of the work while the other two friends had easy lives. For instance, after the mouse started the fire and carried the water into the house, she generally went to her little room and rested until she was called to set the table. The sausage stayed by the pot and kept an eye on the cooking, and right at mealtime, he slid through the stew or vegetables to make sure everything was salted, seasoned, and ready to eat. As soon as the little bird came home and laid down his bundle, they would sit down at the table, and after finishing the meal, they would sleep soundly until the next morning. Such was their glorious life.

However, the little bird had been disturbed by what the other bird had said the previous day and told his companions that he had been their slave long enough and was no longer going to be taken for a fool. He wanted them to change and try another arrangement. No matter how long the mouse and the sausage vehemently argued against this, the bird dominated and insisted that they try a new way. So they drew lots, and it fell upon the sausage to get the wood; the mouse became cook; and the bird was to fetch water.

What happened?

After the sausage went to fetch the wood, the bird started the fire, and the mouse put the kettle on the stove. Then they waited for the sausage to return home with the wood for the next day. However, the sausage was gone for such a long time that the other two had an uneasy feeling, and the bird flew out a little way to meet him.

Not far from their home, the sausage had encountered a dog. Now this dog had considered the sausage free game and had grabbed him and swallowed him down. The little bird arrived and accused the dog of highway robbery, but it was of no use, for the dog maintained he had found forged letters on the sausage, and therefore, the sausage had had to pay for this with his life.

Now the little bird sadly picked up the wood and carried it back home. He told the mouse what he had seen and heard, and they were very distressed. Nevertheless, they agreed to do the best they could and stay together. Meanwhile, the little bird set the table, and the mouse prepared the meal. She intended to put the finishing touches on it by seasoning it and sliding through the vegetables the way the sausage used to do, but before she even reached the middle of the vegetables, she got stuck and had to pay for it with her life.

When the bird came to serve the meal, there was no cook. He became so upset that he scattered wood all over the place, calling and searching for the mouse. But his cook was no longer to be found. Since the little bird was so distracted, he didn't notice that the wood had caught fire, and the house went up in flames. The bird rushed out to fetch some water, but the bucket slipped and fell into the well, dragging the bird along. Since he couldn't manage to get himself out, he was left to drown.

24
MOTHER HOLLE

A widow had two daughters, one who was beautiful and diligent, the other, ugly and lazy. But she was fonder of the ugly and lazy one, and the other had to do all the work and was just like the Cinderella in the house.

Now, one day the beautiful maiden went out to fetch water, and as she bent over to pull the bucket from the well, she leaned over too much and fell into the water. And when she awoke and came to her senses, she was lying on the ground in a beautiful meadow, where the sun was shining and thousands of flowers were growing. She left the meadow, and soon she came to a baker's oven full of bread, but the bread was yelling, "Oh, take me out! Take me out, or else I'll burn, I've already been baked long enough!"

So she went to the oven and diligently took out everything. After that she moved on and came to a tree full of apples.

"Oh, shake me! Shake me!" the tree exclaimed. "My apples are all ripe."
So she shook the tree until the apples fell like raindrops, and she kept
shaking until they had all fallen to the ground. After that she moved on. At
last she came to a small cottage where an old woman was looking out of a
window. She had such big teeth that the maiden was scared and wanted to
run away. But the old woman cried after her, "Don't be afraid, my dear child!
Stay with me, and if you do all the housework properly, everything will turn
out well for you. You must only make my bed nicely and give it a good shaking so the feathers fly. Then it will snow on earth, for I am Mother Holle."[1]

Since the old woman had spoken so kindly to her, the maiden agreed
to enter her service. She took care of everything to the old woman's satisfaction and always shook the bed so hard that the feathers flew about
like snowflakes. In return, the woman treated her well: she never said an
unkind word to the maiden, and she gave her roasted or boiled meat every
day. After the maiden had spent a long time with Mother Holle, her heart
saddened. Even though everything was a thousand times better there
than at home, she still had a yearning to return. At last she said to Mother
Holle, "I've got a tremendous longing to return home, and even though
everything is wonderful here, I can't stay any longer."

"You're right," Mother Holle responded, "and since you've served me so
faithfully, I myself shall bring you up there again."

She took the maiden by the hand and led her to a large gate. When it
was opened and the maiden was standing beneath the gateway, an enormous shower of gold came pouring down, and all the gold stuck to her so
that she became completely covered with it.

"I want you to have this because you've been so diligent," said Mother
Holle. Thereupon, the gate closed, and the maiden found herself up on
earth. Then she went to her mother, and since she was covered with so
much gold, her mother gave her a warm welcome. Then, when her mother
heard how she had obtained so much wealth, she wanted her other, ugly
and lazy daughter to have the same good fortune. Therefore, this daughter

---

[1] Whenever it snowed in olden days, people in Hessia used to say Mother Holle is making
her bed.

also had to jump down the well. Like her sister, she awoke in the beautiful meadow and walked along the same path. When she came to the oven, the bread cried out again, "Oh, take me out! Take me out, or else I'll burn! I've already been baked long enough!"

But the lazy maiden answered, "Do you think I want to get myself dirty?"

She moved on, and soon she came to the apple tree that cried out, "Oh, shake me! Shake me! My apples are all ripe."

However, the lazy maiden replied, "Are you serious? One of the apples could fall and hit me on my head."

When she came to Mother Holle's cottage, she wasn't afraid because she had already heard about the old woman's big teeth, and she hired herself out to her right away. On the first day she made an effort to work hard and obey Mother Holle when the old woman told her what to do, for the thought of gold was on her mind. On the second day she started loafing, and on the third day she loafed even more. Indeed, she didn't want to get out of bed in the morning, and she did a poor job of making Frau Holle's bed. She certainly didn't shake it hard enough to make the feathers fly. Soon Mother Holle became tired of this and discharged the maiden from her service. The lazy maiden was quite happy to go and now expected the shower of gold. Mother Holle led her to the gate, but as the maiden was standing beneath the gateway, a big kettle of pitch came pouring down over her instead of gold.

"That's a reward for your services," Mother Holle said and closed the gate. The lazy maiden went home covered with pitch, and it stuck to her for as long as she lived.

25
THE THREE RAVENS

Once upon a time there was a mother who had three little sons who were playing cards one day next to the church. And when the sermon was finished, their mother returned home and saw what they had been doing. So she cursed her godless children, and they were immediately turned into three coal-black ravens and flew away.

The three brothers, however, had a little sister who loved them with all her heart, and she grieved so much about their banishment that she no longer had any peace of mind and finally set out to look for them. The only thing that she took with her for the long, long journey was a little stool on which she rested when she became too tired, and she ate nothing the entire time but wild apples and pears. Unfortunately, she couldn't find the three ravens. But one time, when they had flown over her head, one of them had dropped a ring, and when she picked it up, she recognized it as the ring that she had given to her youngest brother one time as a present.

The sister continued her journey, and she went so far, so very far, until she came to the end of the world and went to the sun, which was, however, much too hot and ate small children. So after that she went to the moon, which was, however, much too cold and also mean, and when it saw her, it said, "I smell, I smell human flesh!"

So the maiden left there quickly and went to the stars, which were good to her, and each one sat on a little stool, and the morning star stood up and gave her a gammy leg to help her open the gate to the glass mountain.

"If you don't have this little leg, you won't be able to climb the glass mountain. It's on the glass mountain that you'll find your brothers!"

So the sister took the gammy leg, wrapped it in some cloth, and continued her journey until she came to the glass mountain. However, the gate was closed, and just as she wanted to take the gammy leg from the cloth, she discovered that she had lost it along the way. Since she didn't know what to do, she took a knife, sliced off her pinky, stuck it into the lock, and opened the gate. Then a little dwarf came toward her and said, "My child, what are you looking for here?"

"I'm looking for my brothers, the three ravens."

"The lord ravens are not at home," said the little dwarf. "If you want to wait, then come in."

And the little dwarf brought three little plates and three little mugs, and the sister ate a bit from each little plate and drank a sip from each mug, and she let the little ring fall into the last mug. All of a sudden a whizzing and a buzzing could be heard in the air.

"The lord ravens are flying back home," said the little dwarf.

And the ravens began to speak one after the other:

"Who has eaten from my little plate?"

"Who has drunk from my little mug?"

As the third raven, however, came to his little mug, he found the ring and saw clearly that their little sister had arrived. They recognized her because of the ring, and they were all saved and transformed and were happy to go home.

26

LITTLE RED CAP

Once upon a time there was a sweet little maiden. Whoever laid eyes upon her couldn't help but love her. But it was her grandmother who could never give the child enough. One day she made her a present, a small, red velvet cap, and since it was so becoming and the maiden always wanted to wear it, people only called her Little Red Cap.

One day her mother said to her: "Come, Little Red Cap, take this piece of cake and bottle of wine and bring them to your grandmother. She's sick and weak, and this will strengthen her. Be nice and good and greet her from me. Go directly there and don't stray from the path, otherwise you'll fall and break the glass, and your grandmother will get nothing."

Little Red Cap promised to obey her mother. Well, the grandmother lived out in the forest, half an hour from the village, and as soon as Little Red Cap entered the forest, she encountered the wolf. However, Little Red Cap didn't know what a wicked sort of an animal he was and was not afraid of him.

"Good day, Little Red Cap," he said.

"Thank you kindly, wolf."

"Where are you going so early, Little Red Cap?"

"To grandmother's."

"What are you carrying under your apron?"

"Cake and wine. My grandmother's sick and weak, and yesterday we baked this cake so it will help her get well."

"Where does your grandmother live, Little Red Cap?"

"About a quarter of an hour from here in the forest. Her house is under the three big oak trees. You can tell it by the hazel bushes," said Little Red Cap.

The wolf thought to himself, "What a juicy morsel she'll be for me! Now, how am I going to catch her?" Then he said, "Listen, Little Red Cap, haven't you seen the beautiful flowers growing in the forest? Why don't you look around? I believe you haven't even noticed how lovely the birds are singing. You march along as if you were going straight to school in the village, and yet it's so delightful out here in the woods!"

Little Red Cap looked around and saw that the sun had broken through the trees and that the woods were full of beautiful flowers. So she thought to herself, "If I bring grandmother a bunch of flowers, she'd certainly like that. It's still early, and I'll arrive on time."

So she plunged into the woods to look for flowers. And each time she plucked one, she thought she saw another even prettier flower and ran after it, going deeper and deeper into the forest. But the wolf went straight to the grandmother's house and knocked at the door.

"Who's there?"

"Little Red Cap. I've brought you some cake and wine. Open up."

"Just lift the latch," the grandmother called. "I'm too weak and can't get up."

The wolf lifted the latch, and the door sprang open. Then he went straight to the grandmother's bed and gobbled her up. Next he took her clothes, put them on along with her nightcap, lay down in her bed, and drew the curtains.

Meanwhile, Little Red Cap had been running around and looking for flowers, and only when she had as many as she could carry did she continue on the way to her grandmother. She was puzzled when she found the door open, and as she entered the room, it seemed so strange inside that she thought, "Oh, my God, how frightened I feel today, and usually I like to be at grandmother's." Then she went to the bed and drew back the curtains. There lay her grandmother with her cap pulled down over her face, giving her a strange appearance.

"Oh, grandmother, what big ears you have!"

"The better to hear you with."

"Oh, grandmother, what big eyes you have!"

"The better to see you with."

"Oh, grandmother, what big hands you have!"

"The better to grab you with."

"Oh, grandmother, what a terribly big mouth you have!"

"The better to eat you with!"

No sooner did the wolf say that than he jumped out of bed and gobbled up poor Little Red Cap. After the wolf had the fat chunks in his body, he lay down in bed again, fell asleep, and began to snore very loudly. The huntsman happened to be passing by the house and thought to himself, "The way the old woman's snoring, you'd better see if something's wrong." He went into the room, and when he came to the bed, he saw the wolf lying in it. He had been searching for the wolf a long time and thought that the beast had certainly eaten the grandmother. "Perhaps she can still be saved," he said to himself. "I won't shoot." So he took some scissors and cut open the wolf's belly. After he made a couple of cuts, he saw the little red cap shining forth, and after he made a few more cuts, the girl jumped out and exclaimed, "Oh, how frightened I was! It was so dark in the wolf's body."

Soon the grandmother emerged alive. Little Red Cap quickly fetched some large heavy stones, and they filled the wolf's body with them. When he awoke and tried to run away, the stones were so heavy that he fell down at once and died.

All three were delighted. The huntsman skinned the fur from the wolf. The grandmother ate the cake and drank the wine that Little Red Cap had brought. And Little Red Cap thought to herself: "Never again will you stray from the path by yourself and go into the forest when your mother has forbidden it."

ﻋﻭ

It's also been told that Little Red Cap returned to her grandmother one day to bring some baked goods. Another wolf spoke to her and tried to entice her to leave the path, but this time Little Red Cap was on her guard. She went straight ahead and told her grandmother that she had seen the wolf, that he had wished her good day, but that he had had such a mean look in his eyes that "he would have eaten me if we hadn't been on the open road."

"Come," said the grandmother. "We'll lock the door so he can't get in."

Soon after, the wolf knocked and cried out, "Open up, grandmother. It's Little Red Cap, and I've brought you some baked goods."

But they kept quiet and didn't open the door. So the wicked wolf circled the house several times and finally jumped on top of the roof. He wanted to wait till evening when Little Red Cap would go home. He intended to sneak after her and eat her up in the darkness. But the grandmother realized what he had in mind. In front of the house was a big stone trough, and she said to the child, "Fetch the bucket, Little Red Cap. I cooked sausages yesterday. Get the water they were boiled in and pour it into the trough."

Little Red Cap kept carrying the water until she had filled the big, big trough. Then the smell of sausages reached the nose of the wolf. He sniffed and looked down. Finally, he stretched his neck so far that he could no longer keep his balance on the roof. He began to slip from the roof and fell right into the big trough and drowned. Then Little Red Cap went happily and safely to her home.

27

DEATH AND THE GOOSE BOY

A poor goose boy went walking along the bank of a large, turbulent river while looking after a flock of white geese. When he saw Death come toward him across the water, the boy asked him where he had come from and where he intended to go. Death answered that he had come from the water and wanted to leave the world. The poor goose boy asked Death once more how one could actually leave the world. Death said that one must go across the river into the new world that lay on the other side. The goose boy said he was tired of this life and asked Death to take him across the water. Death said it was not time yet, for there were things Death still had to do.

Not far from there lived a greedy man, who at night kept trying to gather together more and more money and possessions. Death led him to the large river and pushed him in. Since he couldn't swim, he sank to the bottom before he could reach the bank. His cats and dogs that had run after him were also drowned. A few days later Death returned to the goose boy and found him singing cheerfully.

"Do you want to come with me now?" he asked.

The goose boy went willingly and crossed the river with his white geese, which were all turned into white sheep. The goose boy looked at the beautiful country and heard that the shepherds of places like that became kings, and as he was looking around, the arch-shepherds, Abraham, Isaac, and Jacob, came toward him, put a royal crown on his head, and led him to the castle of the shepherds, where he can still be found.

28

THE SINGING BONE

A wild boar was causing great damage throughout the entire country. Nobody dared to go into the forest, where the beast was running around. Whoever had been so bold as to enter the forest and to try to kill the boar had been ripped apart by its tusks. So the king proclaimed that whoever killed the wild boar would receive his only daughter for a wife.

Now, three brothers were living in the realm. The eldest was wily and smart; the second, somewhat intelligent; and the third and youngest, naïve and dumb. They thought of winning the princess and wanted to look for the wild boar and kill it. The two older brothers went out together, while the youngest proceeded alone. As this young man entered the forest, a little man appeared before him. He was holding a heavy lance in his hand and said: "Take this lance and attack the wild boar without fear. You'll easily be able to kill it."

And this is what happened. He struck the boar with the black lance so that it fell to the ground. Then he cheerfully lifted the beast on his shoulders and carried it toward home. Along the way he passed by a house in which his older brothers were enjoying themselves by drinking wine. When they saw him carrying the boar on his back, they called out to him: "Come inside and have a drink with us. You must be tired."

The innocent bumpkin didn't suspect anything evil. So he went inside and told them how he had killed the boar with the lance and was delighted about his good fortune.

In the evening they headed toward their home together, and the two older brothers made a plan to take their brother's life. They let him go ahead of them, and as they approached the city and were on a bridge, they attacked him and beat him to death. Then they buried him deep under the bridge. Afterward the eldest took the boar, carried it to the king, and received the princess for his wife.

It took many years before this deed was revealed, and it happened when a shepherd was crossing the bridge and noticed a little bone lying down below in the sand. Since it was so clean and snow white, he wanted to make a mouthpiece for his horn out of it. So he went down and picked it up. Later he made it into a mouthpiece, and as he set it into the horn and wanted to blow, the little bone began to sing on its own accord:

"Dear shepherd, blowing on my bone,
Hear my song, for I want you to know
My brothers killed me years ago!
They buried me by the brook that flows
and carried off the dead wild boar,
and won the king's lone daughter."

The shepherd immediately took the horn and brought it to the king, and once again it sang the same words. When the king heard the song, he had the ground beneath the bridge dug up, and the skeleton of the dead brother was revealed. The two evil brothers confessed their crime and were thrown into the water. However, the bone of the murdered brother was laid to rest in a beautiful grave in the churchyard.

29

THE DEVIL WITH THE THREE GOLDEN HAIRS

A woodcutter was chopping wood in front of the king's house, while the princess was standing at a window above and observing him. When noon arrived, he sat down in the shadows and wanted to rest. Now the princess was able to see that he was very handsome and fell in love with him. So she had him summoned to her, and as soon as he caught sight of her and saw how beautiful she was, he fell in love with her. Soon they were united in their love for one another, but the king learned that the princess was in love with a woodcutter, and as soon as he knew this, he went to her and said: "You know that you may only wed the man who brings me the three golden hairs from the devil's head, whether he be a prince or a woodcutter."

The king thought that there had never been a prince courageous enough to accomplish this task, and therefore, an inferior man like the woodcutter would certainly not succeed. The princess was distressed because many princes who had tried to fetch the devil's three golden hairs had died. Since there was nothing else she could do, she told the woodcutter what her father had said. However, the woodcutter was not at all depressed by this and said: "I'll certainly succeed. Stay true to me until I return. Early tomorrow I shall set out."

Indeed, the woodcutter began his journey to the devil the next day and soon came to a big city. In front of the gate, a guard asked him what kind of craft he practiced and what he knew.

"I know everything," answered the woodcutter.

"If you know everything," the gatekeeper said, "then make our princess healthy again. No doctor in the world has been able to cure her."

"When I return."

In the second city he was also asked what he knew.

"I know everything."

"Then tell us why our beautiful well at the marketplace has become dry."

"When I return," said the woodcutter, and he refused to be detained.

After a while he came to a fig tree that was rotting, and nearby stood a man who asked him what he knew.

"I know everything,"

"Then tell me why the fig tree is rotting and no longer bearing any fruit."

"When I return."

The woodcutter traveled on and encountered a ferryman who had to transport him across a river, and he asked him what he knew.

"I know everything."

"So tell me when will I be finally relieved and when someone else will transport people across the river?"

"When I return."

After the woodcutter was on the other side, he entered hell. Everything appeared black and sooty. However, the devil was not home. Only his wife was sitting there. The woodcutter said to her, "Good day, Mrs. Devil, I've come here to take three golden hairs that your husband has on his head, and I'd like to know why a princess cannot be cured, why a deep well at a marketplace doesn't have any water, why a fig tree doesn't bear any fruit, and why a ferryman has not been relieved from his work."

The wife was horrified and said, "When the devil comes and finds you here, he'll eat you right away, and you'll never be able to get the three golden hairs. But since you are so young, I feel sorry for you, and I'll see if I can save you."

The woodcutter had to lay down beneath the bed, and no sooner did he do this than the devil came home.

"Good evening, wife," he said and proceeded to take off his clothes. Then he burst out saying, "What's going on in this room? I smell, I smell the flesh of a man. I've got to look around."

"What are you going to smell?" his wife asked. "You've got the sniffles, and the smell of human flesh is still stuffed up in your nose. Don't mess up everything. I've just cleaned the house."

"I won't make any noise. I'm tired this evening, and you won't even begrudge me some little thing to eat."

Upon saying that the devil laid himself down in the bed, and his wife had to lie down beside him. Soon he fell asleep. First he blew, then he snored. At the beginning he did this softly, and then he was so loud that the windows trembled. When his wife saw that he was sound asleep, she grabbed hold of one of the three golden hairs, ripped it out, and threw it to the woodcutter beneath the bed. The devil jumped up: "What are you doing, wife? Why are you tearing out my hair?"

"Oh, I had a nightmare! I must have done it because I was afraid."

"What did you dream about?"

"I dreamed about a princess who was deathly sick, and no doctor in the world could cure her."

"Well, why don't they get rid of the white toad that's sitting under her bed?"

After saying that the devil turned to his other side and fell asleep again. When his wife heard him snoring, she grabbed hold of a second hair, ripped it out, and threw it under the bed. The devil jumped up.

"Hey, what are you doing? Have you gone mad? You've been terrible ripping my hair!"

"Oh, listen my dear husband! I was standing before a large well at a marketplace, and people were yammering because there was no longer any water in it. They asked me if I knew if there was any way to help them. Well, I looked down the well, but it was so deep that I became dizzy. I wanted to stop myself, and then I got entangled in your hair."

"You should have told them that they had to pull out the white stone lying at the bottom of the well, and now leave me in peace with all your dreams!"

He lay down once more and soon began snoring atrociously as before. His wife thought: "I've got to dare once more," and sure enough, she ripped the third golden hair out and threw it down to the woodcutter. The devil leapt into the air and wanted to teach her a nasty lesson, but his wife calmed him down, kissed him, and said, "What horrible dreams! A man showed me a fig tree that was wilting, and he complained that it was no longer bearing any fruit. Then I wanted to shake the tree to see if something would fall off it, and the next thing I knew I was shaking your hair."

"That would have been in vain. There is a mouse gnawing at the roots of the tree. If it's not killed, then the tree will be lost. Once the mouse is dead, the tree will be fresh, regain its health, and bear fresh fruit. So, now stop plaguing me with all your dreams. I want to sleep, and if you wake me one more time, I'll give you a good slap in your face!"

His wife was very much afraid of the devil's anger, but the poor woodcutter had to know one more thing that only the devil knew. So the wife pulled his nose and lifted him up into the air. The devil jumped up as though he were out of his mind and gave her a smack in the face that resounded all over the place. His wife began to weep and said: "Do you want me to fall into the water and drown? The ferryman brought me across the river, and as the barge approached the other side, it bumped into the bank, and I was afraid that I might fall and wanted to grab hold of the anchor which was attached to a chain. That's why I grabbed hold of your nose."

"How come you didn't pay attention? The barge does this all the time."

"The ferryman complained to me that nobody has come to relieve him, and there's no end to his work."

"All he has to do is get the first man who comes to take over the ferrying from him until a third man comes who relieves him. This is the way that he can help himself. But your dreams are really strange. Everything you've told me about the ferryman is true, and everything else as well. Now don't wake me again. Soon it will be morning, and I want to sleep a little more. Otherwise, I'll make you pay if you disturb me."

After the woodcutter had heard everything and the devil was snoring again, he thanked the devil's wife and departed. When he arrived at the barge, the ferryman wanted some information.

"First take me across."

When the woodcutter was on the other side, he said to the ferryman: "The next person who comes and wants to be taken across the river, keep him there until he takes over your job and continues your work until another man comes to relieve him."

Soon thereafter the woodcutter came to the man with the wilted fig tree, and he said to him: "All you have to do is kill the white mouse that's gnawing on the roots. Then your tree will bear fruit again just as it did in the past."

"What do you demand for a reward?" asked the man.

"I want a troop of soldiers," and no sooner did he say this than a troop began marching behind him.

The woodcutter thought that things were going well and arrived in the city where the well at the marketplace had run dry.

"Fetch the white stone that's lying at the bottom of the well."

So someone climbed down and fetched the stone, and no sooner was he above than the well was once again filled with the clearest water.

"How should we reward you?" the mayor asked.

"Give me a regiment of cavalry officers."

And as the woodcutter went through the city gate, a regiment of cavalry officers rode behind him. This was how he entered the other city where the princess whom no doctor could cure was lying on her sick bed.

"All you have to do is kill the white toad that's hiding beneath the princess's bed."

And when that was done, the princess began to recuperate and became healthy and rosy.

"What do you want for a reward?" asked the king.

"Four wagons loaded with gold," said the woodcutter.

Finally, the woodcutter reached home, and behind him were a troop of infantrymen, a regiment of cavalry officers, and four wagons loaded entirely with gold. The three golden hairs of the devil, however, were carried by himself. He ordered his regiments to wait in front of the royal gate. They were to enter quickly if he gave them a signal from the castle. Then he went to the father of his beloved princess and handed him the devil's three golden hairs and asked him to give him the princess for his bride in keeping with the promise he had made. The king was astonished and said that the woodcutter had done quite right with regard to the devil's three golden hairs. Nevertheless, the king stated he would have to think about whether he would give him the princess for his bride. As soon as the woodcutter heard this, he moved to the window and whistled to his companions. All of a sudden the troops of infantrymen and regiments of cavalry officers and four heavily loaded wagons marched and rolled through the gate.

"My king," said the woodcutter, "take a look at my people whom I have brought along with me, and over there is all my wealth in those wagons full of gold. Don't you want to give me the princess?"

The king was terrified and said: "Yes, with all my heart."

Then the woodcutter and the princess were married and lived in bliss.

This is why whoever is not afraid of the devil can tear out his hair and win the entire world.

30
LITTLE LOUSE AND LITTLE FLEA

A little louse and a little flea were living together in a house and were brewing beer in an eggshell when the louse fell in and was scalded. Then the flea began to scream as loud as he could, and the little door to the room asked: "Why are you screaming, little flea?"

"Because little louse has been scalded."

Then the little door began to creak, and a little broom in the corner asked, "Why are you creaking, door?"

"Why shouldn't I creak?
Little louse has just got scalded.
Little flea is weeping."

Then the little broom began to sweep in a frenzy, and when a little cart came driving by, it asked, "Why are you sweeping, broom?"

"Why shouldn't I sweep?
Little louse has just got scalded.
Little flea is weeping.
Little door is creaking."

"Well, then I'm going to race around," said the little cart, and it began racing around furiously, and the little dung heap, which it passed, asked, "Why are you racing around, little cart?"

"Why shouldn't I race around?
Little louse has just got scalded.
Little flea is weeping.
Little door is creaking.
Little broom is sweeping."

"Then I'm going to burn with fury," said the little dung heap, and it began to burn in bright flames. Then a little tree nearby asked, "Why are you burning, little dung heap?"

"Why shouldn't I burn?
Little louse has just got scalded.
Little flea is weeping.
Little door is creaking.
Little broom is sweeping.
Little cart is racing."

"Well, then I'm going to shake myself," said the tree, and it shook itself so hard that all its leaves began to fall. Then a maiden with a water jug came by and asked, "Little tree, why are you shaking?"

"Why shouldn't I shake?
Little louse has just got scalded.
Little flea is weeping.
Little door is creaking.
Little broom is sweeping.
Little cart is racing.
Little dung heap is burning."

"Well, then I'm going to break my little water jug," said the maiden, and as she was breaking it, the little spring from which the water came asked, "Maiden, why are you breaking the little water jug?"

"Why shouldn't I break it?
Little louse has just got scalded.
Little flea is weeping.
Little door is creaking.
Little broom is sweeping.
Little cart is racing.
Little dung heap is burning.
Little tree is shaking."

"Goodness gracious!" said the little spring. "Then I'm going to flow," and it began to flow so violently that they were all drowned in the water—the maiden, the little tree, the little dung heap, the little cart, the little door, the little flea, and the little louse, every last one of them.

31
MAIDEN WITHOUT HANDS

A miller, who was so poor that he had nothing else but his mill and a large apple tree behind it, went into the forest to fetch wood. While there he met an old man who said: "Why are you torturing yourself so much? I'll make you rich if you promise to give me what's behind your mill. In three years I'll come and fetch what's mine."

The miller thought to himself: "That's my apple tree." So, he said, "yes," and signed it away to the man. When the miller returned home, his wife said to him, "Tell me, miller, how did all this wealth suddenly get into our house? All at once I've discovered our chests and boxes are full of money."

"It's from a stranger I met in the forest," he said. "He promised me great wealth if I agreed in writing to give him what's behind our mill."

"Oh, husband!" his wife exclaimed in dread. "This is terrible. That was the devil! He didn't mean the apple tree but our daughter, who was behind the mill sweeping out the yard."

The miller's daughter was a beautiful and pious maiden, and after three years the devil appeared quite early and wanted to fetch her, but she drew a circle around herself and purified herself. Consequently, the devil couldn't get near her, and he said angrily to the miller, "I want you to take all the water away from her so she can't wash herself anymore! Then I'll have power over her."

Since the miller was afraid of the devil, he did as he was told. The next morning the devil came again, but she wept on her hands and washed herself with her tears so that she was completely clean. Once more the devil couldn't get near her and said furiously to the miller, "Chop off her hands so that I can grab hold of her."

The miller was horrified and replied, "How can I chop off the hands of my own dear child! I won't do it!"

"You know what! Then I'll take you instead if you don't do it!"

The father was so terribly scared of him that in his fear he promised to do what the devil commanded. He went to his daughter and said, "My child, if I don't chop off both your hands, the devil will take me away, and in my fear I promised I'd do it. Please forgive me."

"Father," she answered, "do what you want with me."

Then she extended both her hands and let him chop them off. The devil came a third time, but she had wept so long and so much on her stumps that they, too, were all clean. So he lost any claim he had to her.

Now, since the miller had gained so much wealth thanks to his daughter, he promised her he would see to it that she'd live in splendor for the rest of her life. But she didn't want to remain there.

"I want to leave here and shall depend on the kindness of people to provide me with whatever I need."

Then she had her maimed hands bound to her back, and at dawn she set out on her way and walked and walked the entire day until it had become dark and she had reached the king's garden. There was a hole in the hedge of the garden. So she went inside through the hole and found an apple tree that she shook with her body. When the apples fell to the ground, she leaned over and lifted them with her teeth and ate them. She lived this way for two days, but on the third the guards came and saw her. So they seized her and threw her into the prison house, and on the next day she was led before the king and was to be expelled from the country.

"Why?" cried the prince. "It would be better if she looked after the chickens in the courtyard."

So she remained there for some time and looked after the chickens. Meanwhile the prince saw her often and became very fond of her. However, the time came for him to marry, and royal messengers were sent out all over the world to find a beautiful bride for him.

"You don't have to send out messengers to search so far," said the prince. "I know a bride who is very close by."

The old king reflected and tried to think of a maiden, but he wasn't familiar with any young lady in his land who was beautiful and rich.

"You don't intend to marry that maiden who tends the chickens in the courtyard, do you?"

The son explained, however, that he wouldn't marry anyone else but her. Finally the king had to yield to his wish, and soon thereafter, he died. The prince inherited the throne and lived happily with his wife for some time.

Yet at one point the young king had to leave his realm to fight in a war, and during his absence his wife gave birth to a beautiful child. She sent a messenger with a letter to announce the good news. However, on the way the messenger stopped to rest near a brook and fell asleep. Then the devil appeared, for he was still trying to harm the pious queen, and so he exchanged the letter for another one that said the queen had given birth to a changeling. When the king read the letter, he was quite distressed, but he wrote a letter in which he declared that the queen and the child should be protected until his return. The messenger started back with the letter, but he stopped to rest at the same spot and fell asleep. Once again the devil came and put a different letter in his pocket that said they should banish the queen and the child from his land. This was to be done even if all the people at the court wept out of sadness.

"I didn't come here to become queen. I don't have any luck and also don't demand any," the queen declared. "Bind my child and my hands on my back. Then I'll set out into the world."

That evening she reached a fountain in a dense forest where a good old man was sitting.

"Please show me some mercy," she said, "and lift my child to my breast so that I can give him something to drink."

The man did this, whereupon he said to her, "There's a thick tree standing over there. Go over and wrap your maimed arms around it."

When she did this, her hands grew back. Thereupon, the old man pointed to a house.

"Go and live there. Don't leave the house, and don't open the door unless someone asks three times to enter for God's sake."

In the meantime the king returned home and realized how he had been deceived. Consequently, he set out accompanied by a single servant to look for his wife. After a long journey he lost his way one night in the same forest in which the queen was living. However, he didn't know that the queen was so close.

"Over there," his servant said, "there's a little light glimmering in a house. Thank God, we can rest there."

"Not at all," responded the king. "I don't want to rest very long. I want to continue to search for my wife before I can take any rest."

But the servant pleaded and complained so much about being tired that the king agreed out of compassion. When they arrived at the house, the moon was shining, and they saw the queen standing at the window.

"Goodness, that must be our queen," the servant said. "She resembles her very much. But I realize that she can't be the queen because this woman has hands."

The servant requested lodging for the night, but she refused because he didn't ask for God's sake. So he wanted to move on and look for another place to spend the night. Then the king himself stepped forward and cried out, "For God's sake, let me enter!"

"I can't let you enter until you ask me three times for God's sake."

And after the king asked another two times for God's sake, she opened the door. Then his little son came skipping toward him and led the king to his mother, and he recognized her immediately as his beloved wife. The next morning just as they left the house and began traveling together to return to their country, the house vanished right behind them.

32
CLEVER HANS

I

"Where are you going, Hans?" his mother asked.

"To Gretel's," Hans replied.

"Take care, Hans."

"Don't worry. Good-bye, Mother."

Hans arrived at Gretel's place.

"Good day, Gretel."

"Good day, Hans. Have you brought me anything nice?"

"Didn't bring anything. Want something from you."

Gretel gave him a needle.

"Good-bye, Gretel," Hans said.

"Good-bye, Hans."

Hans took the needle, stuck it in the hay wagon, and walked home behind the wagon.

"Good evening, Mother."

"Good evening, Hans. Where have you been?"

"At Gretel's."

"What did you bring her?"

"Didn't bring her a thing. Got something."

"What did Gretel give you?"

"Got a needle."

"Where'd you put the needle, Hans?"

"Stuck it in a hay wagon."

"That was stupid of you. You should have stuck it in your sleeve."

"Doesn't matter. I'll do better next time."

"Where are you going, Hans?"

"To Gretel's, Mother."

"Take care, Hans."

"Don't worry. Good-bye, Mother."

Hans arrived at Gretel's place.

"Good day, Gretel."

"Good day, Hans. Have you brought me anything nice?"

"Didn't bring anything. Want something from you."

Gretel gave Hans a knife.

"Good-bye, Gretel."

"Good-bye, Hans."

Hans took the knife, stuck it in his sleeve, and went home.

"Good evening, Mother."

"Good evening, Hans. Where have you been?"

"At Gretel's."

"What did you bring her?"

"Didn't bring her a thing. Got something."

"What did Gretel give you?"

"Got a knife."

"Where'd you put the knife, Hans?"

"Stuck it in my sleeve."

"That was stupid of you, Hans. You should have put it in your pocket."

"Doesn't matter. I'll do better next time."

"Where are you going, Hans?"

"To Gretel's, Mother."

"Take care, Hans."

"Don't worry. Good-bye, Mother."

Hans arrived at Gretel's place.

"Good day, Gretel."

"Good day, Hans. Have you brought me anything nice?"

"Didn't bring anything. Want something from you."

Gretel gave Hans a kid goat.

"Good-bye, Gretel."

"Good-bye, Hans."

Hans took the goat, tied its legs together, and stuck it in the pocket of his coat. By the time he got home the goat had suffocated.

"Good evening, Mother."

"Good evening, Hans. Where have you been?"

"At Gretel's."

"What did you bring her?"

"Didn't bring her a thing. Got something."

"What did Gretel give you?"

"Got a goat."

"Where'd you put the goat, Hans?"

"Stuck it in my pocket."

"That was stupid of you, Hans. You should have tied the goat to a rope."

"Doesn't matter. I'll do better next time."

"Where are you going, Hans?"

"To Gretel's, Mother."

"Take care, Hans."

"Don't worry. Good-bye, Mother."

Hans arrived at Gretel's place.

"Good day, Gretel."

"Good day, Hans. Have you brought me anything nice?"

"Didn't bring anything. Want something from you."

Gretel gave Hans a piece of bacon.

Hans took the bacon, tied it to a rope, and dragged it along behind him. The dogs came and ate the bacon. By the time Hans arrived home he had the rope in his hand but nothing attached to it anymore.

"Good evening, Mother."

"Good evening, Hans. Where have you been?"

"At Gretel's."

"What did you bring her?"

"Didn't bring her a thing. Got something."

"What did Gretel give you?"

"Got a piece of bacon."

"What have you done with the bacon, Hans?"

"Tied it to a rope. Dragged it home. Dogs got it."

"That was stupid of you, Hans. You should have carried it on your head."

"Doesn't matter. I'll do better next time."

"Where are you going, Hans?"

"To Gretel's, Mother."

"Take care, Hans. "

"Don't worry. Good-bye, Mother."

Hans arrived at Gretel's place.

"Good day, Gretel."

"Good day, Hans. Have you brought me anything nice?"

"Didn't bring anything. Want something from you."

Gretel gave Hans a calf.

"Good-bye, Gretel."

"Good-bye, Hans."

Hans took the calf, set it on his head, and the calf kicked him in his face.

"Good evening, Mother."

"Good evening, Hans. Where have you been?"

"At Gretel's."

"What did you bring her?"

"Didn't bring her a thing. Got something."

"What did Gretel give you?"

"Got a calf."

"What have you done with the calf?"

"Put it on my head. Kicked me in my face."

"That was stupid of you, Hans. you should have led the calf to the stable, and put it in the stall."

"Doesn't matter. I'll do better next time."

"Where are you going, Hans?"

"To Gretel's, Mother."

"Take care, Hans."

"Don't worry. Good-bye, Mother."

Hans arrived at Gretel's place.

"Good day, Gretel."

"Good day, Hans. Have you brought me anything nice?"

"Didn't bring anything. Want something from you."

"I'll come along with you," Gretel said.

Hans took Gretel, put a rope around her, and led her into the stable, tied her to a stall, and threw her some grass. Then he went to his mother.

"Good evening, Mother."

"Good evening, Hans. Where have you been?"

"At Gretel's."

"What did you bring her?"

"Didn't bring her a thing. Got something."

"What did Gretel give you?"

"Got nothing. She came along."

"Where have you left Gretel?"

"Led her by a rope and tied her up in the stall and threw her some grass."

"That was stupid of you, Hans. You should have thrown friendly looks at her with the eyes."

Hans went out into the stable, cut out the eyes of all the cows and sheep, and threw them in Gretel's face. Then Gretel got angry, tore herself loose, and ran away. That was how Hans lost his bride.

II

A very rich widow lived in the valley of Geslingen, and she had an only son who was coarse and had crazy ideas. He was also the greatest fool among all the inhabitants of the valley. Now one time this very same dunce happened to notice the beautiful, attractive, and intelligent daughter of a highly respected and distinguished man in Saarbrücken. The fool took an immediately liking to her. So he implored his mother to arrange a marriage with this young woman. If she didn't, he would smash the oven and the windows and break all the staircases in the house. His mother knew and clearly understood how mad her son was and feared that if she didn't let him court the young maiden right away and didn't give him a great deal of property to boot, he would act like such a boorish ass that he'd be out of control and there would be no reasoning with him. Even though the maiden's parents were wonderful people and of noble lineage, they were also very poor so that, because of their poverty, they were not in a position to look after her according to her social position. Consequently, they were obliged to approve the dunce's courting. But his mother was also afraid that her son was such a big bumbling oaf that the maiden would perhaps reject him. Therefore, she gave him all kinds of lessons so that he would know how to treat the young woman with fine and polite manners and how to be nimble on his feet.

After the maiden had her first meeting with him and talked with him, she gave him a pair of handsome gloves as a gift. They were made out of soft Spanish leather. The fool put them on and started out for home. Suddenly there was a rainstorm, and he kept the gloves on. He didn't care whether they became wet or not. As he was walking along the path, he slipped and fell into the swampy water. When he arrived home, he was covered with mud, and the gloves were nothing but soggy leather. He complained to his mother, and the good old woman scolded him and said, "The next time you should wrap them in a handkerchief and stuff them inside your shirt next to your chest."

Soon thereafter the numbskull showed up again at the maiden's house, and she asked him about the gloves. He told her what had happened, and she laughed and quickly grasped how little wisdom he possessed. Now she gave him another present, and this time it was a hawk. He took it, headed for home, and remembered his mother's words of advice. So he strangled the hawk, wrapped it in his handkerchief, and stuck it inside his shirt. His mother scolded him again and told him he should have carried it carefully in his hand.

The yokel went to the maiden a third time, and she asked him how things were going with the hawk. So he told her what had happened, and she thought to herself, "He's truly a living fool," and realized that he didn't deserve anything precious or splendid. Therefore, she gave him a big hoe with spikes as a gift that he could use while he was plowing the land. Again he took his mother's advice to heart and carried it home high above his head with his hands like a large ladle. His mother was not at all satisfied and told him he should have tied it to a horse and dragged it home.

Finally, the maiden realized that even the Lord would not be able to help the fool, since there wasn't an ounce of brains or wisdom in him, but she didn't know how to get rid of him. So the next time she saw him, she gave him a huge piece of bacon and shoved it into his chest. Of course, he was very satisfied and wanted to go home right away. However, he was afraid that he might lose it and, therefore, tied it to the tail of his horse. Then he mounted the steed and rode home. As he was riding, the dogs came running after him and ripped the bacon from the horse's tail and ate it. When the fool arrived home, the bacon was gone.

It was now completely clear to this mother that her son's wisdom would prevent a marriage. So she decided to drive to the maiden's parents to set the date for the marriage, and before she departed, she had a serious word or two with him and told him to keep the house in order and not to do anything foolish, particularly since she had a goose that was about to hatch some eggs.

Now, as soon as the mother was out of the house, her son disappeared quickly into the cellar, where he got drunk on the wine and lost the plug to the wine barrel. As he hunted for the plug, all the wine spilled and flooded the cellar. Consequently, the bumbler took a sack of flour and shook it all over the wine so that his mother wouldn't see the damage when she returned home. After doing this, he ran up into the house and began eating some wild venison. But the goose that was sitting on her eggs became frightened and shrieked, "*Gaga! Gaga!*"

In turn, the fool became scared and thought the goose had said, "I'm going to tell on him," and he was positive the bird would tell what he had done in the cellar. So he took the goose and chopped its head off. Now he was afraid that the eggs would spoil and that he was really in trouble. But he thought of a solution: he would sit on the eggs until they hatched. However, it would not work unless he was covered with feathers like the goose. Again he thought of a solution: he took off his clothes and smeared his body all over with honey that his mother had recently made. Then he ripped open the quilt of a bed and rolled around in the feathers so that he looked like a hobgoblin. Finally, he sat down on the goose eggs and was completely quiet so that the silly young geese inside would not become afraid. As the numbskull was sitting there, his mother returned and knocked on the door. Since the fool was sitting on the eggs, he didn't want to answer. She knocked again, and he screamed, "*Gaga! Gaga!*" and thought that he was hatching the silly young geese (or fools like himself), and therefore he couldn't speak. Finally, his mother threatened him so much that he crawled out of the nest and opened the door. When she saw him, she thought he was the devil himself and asked him what was going on, and he told her that everything was in top shape. However, his mother was anxious about her dunce because his bride was due to arrive soon. So she said to him that she would gladly forgive him, but he must now control himself, for his bride would soon be there. She advised him to welcome her in a friendly way and to be nice to her and to steadily cast polite eyes upon her.

The fool replied, "Yes, mother, I'll do as you say."

So he wiped off all the feathers, got dressed, and went out into the stable, where he cut out the eyes of all the sheep and stuffed them under his shirt next to his chest. As soon as the bride arrived, he went toward her and cast all the eyes that he had gathered at her face, for he thought this was the way it was to be done.

The good maiden was mortified that he had dirtied and ravaged her like that. It was clear that the fool was a complete boor and that he was totally berserk and might do anything or everything to her that came to his mind. So she turned around, went home, and rejected him.

Well, he remained a fool just as he was before, and he's still hatching young geese to this day. I'm concerned, however, that when the geese wake up, they, too, will become young fools. May the Lord protect us.

33
PUSS IN BOOTS

A miller had three sons, a mill, a donkey, and a cat. The sons had to grind grain, the donkey had to haul the grain and carry away the flour, and the cat had to catch the mice. When the miller died, the three sons divided the inheritance: the oldest received the mill, the second the donkey, and nothing was left for the third but the cat. This made the youngest sad, and he said to himself, "I certainly got the worst part of the bargain. My oldest brother can grind wheat, and my second brother can ride on his donkey. But what can I do with the cat? Once I make a pair of gloves out of his fur, it's all over."

The cat, who had understood everything that he had said, began to speak. "Listen, there's no need to kill me when all you'll get will be a pair of poor gloves from my fur. Have some boots made for me instead. Then I'll be able to go out, mix with people, and help you before you know it."

The miller's son was surprised the cat could speak like that, but since the shoemaker happened to be walking by, he called him inside and had him fit the cat for a pair of boots. When the boots were finished, the cat put them on. After that he took a sack, filled the bottom with grains of wheat, and attached a piece of cord to the top, which he could pull to close it. Then he slung the sack over his back and walked out the door on two legs like a human being.

At that time there was a king ruling the country, and he liked to eat partridges. However, recently the situation had become grave for him because the partridges had become difficult to catch. The whole forest was full of them, but they frightened so easily that none of the huntsmen had been able to get near them. The cat knew this and thought he could do much better than the huntsmen. When he entered the forest, he opened the sack, spread the grains of wheat on the ground, placed the cord in the grass, and strung it out behind a hedge. Then he crawled in back of the hedge, hid himself, and lay in wait. Soon the partridges came running, found the wheat, and hopped into the sack, one after the other. When a good number were inside, the cat pulled the cord. Once the sack was closed tight, he ran over to it and wrung their necks. Then he slung the sack over his back and went straight to the king's castle. The sentry called out, "Stop! Where are you going?"

"To the king," the cat answered curtly.

"Are you crazy? A cat to the king?"

"Oh, let him go," another sentry said. "The king's often very bored. Perhaps the cat will give him some pleasure with his meowing and purring."

When the cat appeared before the king, he bowed and said, "My lord, the Count"—and he uttered a long, distinguished name—"sends you his regards and would like to offer you these partridges, which he recently caught in his traps."

The king was amazed by the beautiful, fat partridges. Indeed, he was so overcome with joy that he commanded the cat to take as much gold from his treasury as he could carry and put it into the sack. "Bring it to your lord and give him my very best thanks for his gift."

Meanwhile, the poor miller's son sat at home by the window, propped his head up with his hand, and wondered why he had given away all he had for the cat's boots when the cat would probably not be able to bring him anything great in return. Suddenly, the cat entered, threw down the sack from his back, opened it, and dumped the gold at the miller's feet.

"Now you've got something for the boots. The king also sends his regards and best of thanks."

The miller's son was happy to have such wealth, even though he didn't understand how everything had happened. However, as the cat was taking off his boots, he told him everything and said, "Surely you have enough money now, but we won't be content with that. Tomorrow I'm going to put on my boots again, and you shall become even richer. Incidentally, I told the king you're a count."

The following day the cat put on his boots, as he said he would, went hunting again, and brought the king a huge catch. So it went every day, and every day the cat brought back gold to the miller's son. At the king's court he became a favorite, so that he was permitted to go and come and wander about the castle wherever he pleased. One day, as the cat was lying by the hearth in the king's kitchen and warming himself, the coachman came and started cursing, "May the devil take the king and princess! I wanted to go to the tavern, have a drink, and play some cards. But now they want me to drive them to the lake so they can go for a walk."

When the cat heard that, he ran home and said to his master, "If you want to be a rich count, come with me to the lake and go for a swim."

The miller didn't know what to say. Nevertheless, he listened to the cat and went with him to the lake, where he undressed and jumped into the water completely naked. Meanwhile, the cat took his clothes, carried them away, and hid them. No sooner had he done it than the king came driving by. Now the cat began to wail in a miserable voice, "Ahh, most gracious king! My lord went for a swim in the lake, and a thief came and stole his clothes that were lying on the bank. Now the count is in the water and can't get out. If he stays in much longer, he'll freeze and die."

When the king heard that, he ordered the coach to stop, and one of his servants had to race back to the castle and fetch some of the king's garments. The count put on the splendid clothes, and since the king had already taken a liking to him because of the partridges that, he believed, had been sent by the count, he asked the young man to sit down next to him in the coach. The princess was not in the least angry about this, for the count was young and handsome and pleased her a great deal.

In the meantime, the cat went on ahead of them and came to a large meadow, where there were over a hundred people making hay.

"Who owns this meadow, my good people?" asked the cat.

"The great sorcerer."

"Listen to me. The king will be driving by, and when he asks who the owner of this meadow is, I want you to answer, 'The count.' If you don't, you'll all be killed."

Then the cat continued on his way and came to a wheat field so enormous that nobody could see over it. There were more than two hundred people standing there and cutting wheat.

"Who owns this wheat, my good people?"

"The sorcerer."

"Listen to me. The king will be driving by, and when he asks who the owner of this wheat is, I want you to answer, 'The count.' If you don't do this, you'll all be killed."

Finally, the cat came to a splendid forest where more than three hundred people were chopping down large oak trees and cutting them into wood.

"Who owns this forest, my good people?"

"The sorcerer."

"Listen to me. The king will be driving by, and when he asks who the owner of this forest is, I want you to answer, 'The count.' If you don't do this, you'll all be killed."

The cat continued on his way, and the people watched him go. Since he looked so unusual and walked in boots like a human being, they were afraid of him. Soon the cat came to the sorcerer's castle, walked boldly inside, and appeared before the sorcerer, who looked at him scornfully and asked him what he wanted. The cat bowed and said, "I've heard that you can turn yourself into a dog, a fox, or even a wolf, but I don't believe that you can turn yourself into an elephant. That seems impossible to me, and this is why I've come: I want to be convinced by my own eyes."

"That's just a trifle for me," the sorcerer said arrogantly, and within seconds he turned himself into an elephant.

"That's great, but can you also turn yourself into a lion?"

"Nothing to it," said the sorcerer, and he suddenly stood before the cat as a lion. The cat pretended to be terrified and cried out, "That's incredible and unheard of! Never in my dreams would I have thought this possible! But you'd top all of this if you could turn yourself into a tiny animal, such as a mouse. I'm convinced that you can do more than any other sorcerer in the world, but that would be too much for you."

The flattery had made the sorcerer quite friendly, and he said, "Oh, no, dear cat, that's not too much at all," and soon he was running around the room as a mouse.

All at once the cat ran after him, caught the mouse in one leap, and ate him up.

While all this was happening, the king had continued driving with the count and princess and had come to the large meadow.

"Who owns the hay?" the king asked.

"The count," the people all cried out, just as the cat had ordered them to do.

"You've got a nice piece of land, count," the king said.

Afterward they came to the large wheat field.

"Who owns that wheat, my good people?"

"The count."

"My! You've got quite a large and beautiful estate!"

Next they came to the forest.

"Who owns these woods, my good people?"

"The count."

The king was even more astounded and said, "You must be a rich man, count. I don't think I have a forest as splendid as yours."

At last they came to the castle. The cat stood on top of the stairs, and when the coach stopped below, he ran down, opened the door, and said, "Your majesty, you've arrived at the castle of my lord, the count. This honor will make him happy for the rest of his life."

The king climbed out of the coach and was amazed by the magnificent building, which was almost larger and more beautiful than his own castle. The count led the princess up the stairs and into the hall, which was flickering with lots of gold and jewels.

The princess became the count's bride, and when the king died, the count become king, and the puss in boots was his prime minster.

34
HANS'S TRINA

Hans's Trina was lazy and didn't want to do any work. She said to herself: "What should I do? Should I eat, sleep, or work?—Ahh! I think I'll eat first!"

After she had stuffed herself fully, she said to herself again: "What should I do? Work or sleep?—Ahh! I think I'll sleep a little first."

Then she lay down and slept, and when she woke up, it was night. So she could no longer go out and work.

One time Hans returned home at noon and found Trina sleeping again in their room. So he took his knife and cut off her dress at the knees. Trina awoke and thought: "It's time now to go to work." However, when she went outside to work and saw that the dress was so short she became frightened and wondered whether she really was Trina and said to herself:

"Am I or am I not Trina?" She didn't know how to answer this question and stood there a while in doubt. Finally, she thought: "You should go home and ask if you are you. They'll know for sure."

So she returned home, knocked at the window, and called inside: "Is Hans's Trina inside?"

Since the others thought she was in her usual place, they answered: "Yes, she's lying down in her room and sleeping."

"Well, then I'm not me," Trina said in delight. So she went off to the village and never returned, and this is how Hans got rid of his Trina.

35
THE SPARROW AND HIS FOUR CHILDREN

A sparrow had four young ones in a swallow's nest. When they were fledged, some bad boys broke up the nest, but fortunately all the young birds escaped in a whirlwind. Then their father became sorry that his sons went off into the world before he was able to warn them about its many dangers or to give them good advice about how to fend for themselves.

In the autumn a great many sparrows came together in a wheat field. It was there that the father came upon his four sons once again, and he joyfully took them home with him.

"Ah, my dear sons, I was terribly concerned about you all summer, especially since you had been carried away by the wind before I could give you my advice. Now, listen to my words, obey your father, and keep this in mind: Little birds must face grave dangers!"

Then he asked his oldest son where he had spent the summer and how he had fed himself.

"I lived in the garden and hunted caterpillars and little worms until the cherries turned ripe."

"Ah, my son," said the father, "such tasty morsels are not bad, but it can be dangerous searching for them. So, from now on, be on your guard, especially when people walk around the gardens carrying long green poles that are hollow inside and have a hole on the top."

"Yes, father," said the son. "And what should I do when a green leaf is stuck over the hole with wax?"

"Where have you seen this?"

"In a merchant's garden," the young bird said.

"Oh, my son," responded the father, "merchants are wily people! If you have been among such worldly folk, you have learned enough of their shrewd ways. But see that you use all this shrewdness well and don't become overconfident."

Then he asked the next son, "Where did you set up your home?"

"At court," said the son.

"Sparrows and silly little birds have no business being in such a place. There is too much gold, velvet and silk, armor and harnesses, sparrow hawks, screech owls, and falcons. Keep to the horse stables, where the oats are winnowed and threshed. Then you may be lucky enough to get your daily piece of bread and eat it in peace."

"Yes, father," said this son, "but what shall I do if the stable boys make traps and set their gins and snares in the straw? Many a bird has gone away limp because of this."

"Where have you seen this?"

"At the court, among the stable boys."

"Oh, my son, those court servants are bad boys! If you have been at court and mixed with the lords and left no feathers behind, you have learned quite a bit and will know how to get by in the world. However, keep your eyes open all around you and above you, for often even the smartest dogs have felt the bite of wolves."

The father now took his third son to account.

"Where did you try your luck?"

"I cast my lot on the highways and country roads, and sometimes I managed to find a grain of wheat or barley."

"Indeed, this is a fine meal," said the father, "but keep on the alert for signs of danger and look around carefully, especially when someone bends over and is about to pick up a stone. Then make sure you take off quickly."

"That's true," said the son. "But what should I do when someone may already be carrying a rock, or a stone from a walk, under his shirt or in his pocket?"

"Where have you seen this?"

"Among the miners, dear father. When they return from work, they generally carry stones with them."

"Miners are workers and resourceful people! If you've been around mining boys, you've seen and learned something.

Fly there if you will, but this you must know:
Mining boys have killed many a sparrow."

Finally, the father came to the youngest son.

"You, my dear little chatterbox, you were always the silliest and weakest. Stay with me. The world is filled with crass and wicked birds that have crooked beaks and long claws. Stick to your own kind and pick up little spiders and caterpillars from the trees or cottages. This way you'll live long and be content."

"My dear Father, he who feeds himself without causing harm to other people will go far, and no sparrow hawk, falcon, eagle, or kite will do him harm if, each morning and evening, he faithfully commends himself and his honestly earned food to merciful God, who is the creator and preserver of all the birds of the forest and village. Likewise, it is He who hears the cries and prayers of the young ravens, for no sparrow or wren shall ever fall to the ground against His will."

"Where have you learned this?"

The son answered: "When the gust of wind tore me from you, I landed in a church. There I picked the flies and spiders from the windows and heard those words during a sermon. Then the Father of all sparrows fed me during the summer and protected me from misfortune and fierce birds."

"Faith, my dear son! If you take refuge in the churches and help clean out the spiders and the buzzing flies, and if you chirp to God like the young ravens and commend yourself to the eternal Creator, you will stay well, even if the entire world be full of wild and malicious birds.

For he who worships God in every way,
who suffers, waits, is meek, and prays,
who keeps his faith and conscience pure,
God will keep him, safe and sure."

36

THE LITTLE MAGIC TABLE, THE GOLDEN
DONKEY, AND THE CLUB IN THE SACK

I

Once upon a time there was a shoemaker who had three sons and a goat. The sons had to help him in his trade, and the goat had to nourish them with her milk. In order for the goat to get good, delicious food every day, the sons took turns and led her out to graze in a meadow. The eldest took her to the churchyard, where the goat jumped about and ate the grass. In the evening, when he led her home, he asked, "Goat, have you had enough?"

The goat answered:

"Oh, my, I'm stuffed!
Enough's enough.
Meh! Meh!"

"Then let's head for home," the son said and led it back to the stable and tied it up. The old shoemaker asked his son whether the goat had received enough to eat. The son answered: "It's really stuffed. It's had enough."

However, the shoemaker wanted to see for himself whether that was true. So he went to the stall in the stable and asked: "Goat, have you had enough?"

The goat replied:

"How can I have eaten enough?
I just jumped over mounds real rough.
Didn't find one blade of grass 'cause the ground was tough.
Meh! Meh!"

When the shoemaker heard this, he was convinced that his son had lied to him. He became furious, jumped up, took his cane from the wall, gave his son a good beating, and sent him away. The next day the second son had to take the goat to a meadow and led it to the very best grass, which the goat completely devoured. In the evening, he asked the goat: "Goat, have you had enough?"

"Oh, my, I'm stuffed!
Enough's enough.
Meh! Meh!"

"Then let's head home," and he took the goat to the stable and told the old man that the goat was full. Once again the father went to the stable and asked, "Goat, have you had enough?"

"How can I have eaten enough?
I just jumped over mounds real rough.
Didn't find one blade of grass 'cause the ground was tough.
Meh! Meh!"

The shoemaker became angry and also gave a good beating to his second son and chased him from the house. Finally, the third son had to take the goat into the meadow. He was on his guard and looked for the very best grass. Indeed, there was nothing left when the goat had finished eating. In the evening the son asked: "Goat, have you had enough?"

"Oh, my, I'm stuffed.
Enough's, enough.
Meh! Meh!"

"Then let's head home," he said and took the goat to the stable and assured his father that the goat was full. But the old man went to the stable again and asked: "Goat, are you full?"

"How can I have eaten enough?
I just jumped over mounds real rough.
Didn't find one blade of grass 'cause the ground was tough.
Meh! Meh!"

So after the father gave his third son a good beating, he chased him from the house.

Now the shoemaker wanted to take the goat out by himself. So he tied it with a rope and led it to the middle of the best grass on the meadow, where the goat ate grass the entire day. In the evening, the shoemaker asked: "Goat, have you had enough?"

"Oh, my, I'm stuffed.
Enough's enough.
Meh! Meh!"

"Well, let's head for home," and he led the goat to the stable. When he tied her up in the stall, he asked once again, "Goat, have you had enough?" Now the goat answered him as usual:

"How can I have eaten enough?
I just jumped over mounds real rough.
Didn't find one blade of grass 'cause the ground was tough.
Meh! Meh!"

When the shoemaker heard this, he realized that he had driven his three sons away even though they had been innocent. Consequently, he became so angry with the nasty goat that he fetched his razor and shaved the goat's head until it was bald and gave it a good whipping.

In the meantime the eldest son had apprenticed himself to a carpenter, and when he had finished his apprenticeship and wanted to begin his travels, the carpenter gave him a little magic table and told him that he only had to say, "Little table, be covered," and it would be covered by a white tablecloth, and on it would be a silver plate with a silver knife and fork, a crystal glass filled with red wine, and all over, the most beautiful dishes of food. Upon receiving this gift, he set out into the world, and wherever he was, in a field, in the forest, or in a tavern, and whenever he set his table down and said, "Little table be covered," he would then have the most splendid meal.

One day he entered an inn where many guests had already gathered. They asked him whether he wanted to eat with them. He answered, "No, but you should all eat with me."

Upon saying this, he set down his little table in the room and said: "Little table, be covered!" And suddenly it stood there covered with the most sumptuous food, and when a dish became empty, a new one appeared immediately in its place, and all the guests were marvelously treated. The innkeeper, however, thought, "If you had such a table, you'd be a rich man," and that evening, as the carpenter was fast asleep and had put his little table in a corner, the innkeeper fetched another one that looked just like it and replaced the genuine one with it. Early the next morning the good fellow got up, lifted the little table onto his back, and didn't notice that it was the wrong one. He went home and said to his father: "Don't worry about anything anymore or concern yourself. I have a little magic table, and we can now live in luxury for the rest of our days."

His father was delighted to hear this and invited all their relatives to their home, and when they had all gathered together, the son set the table in the middle of the room and said: "Little table, be covered!"

But the little table remained as empty as it had been, and the son realized that he had been duped and was ashamed of himself while the relatives left without drinking and eating. Father and son had to resume their usual work.

The second son had gone to a miller, and when he had finished his apprenticeship, the miller gave him the donkey Bricklebrit as a gift. Whenever one said "Bricklebrit" to this donkey. it would begin to spew gold coins from the front and the behind. After he departed, the young man reached the same tavern where his brother's little table had been stolen from him. He let himself be treated like a prince, and when he was given the bill, he went to the donkey in the stable and said: "Bricklebrit!" All at once he had more gold coins than he needed. However, the innkeeper had observed this, and during the night he got up, untied the golden donkey, and replaced it with his animal. So, in the morning the miller's apprentice left with the wrong donkey and didn't realize that he had been deceived. When he returned home to his father, he also declared: "Enjoy life! I have the donkey Bricklebrit, and you can have as much gold as you wish."

So once again his father invited all their relatives, and a large white cloth was spread out in the middle of the room. Then the donkey was brought from the stable and set onto the cloth. The miller said: "Bricklebrit!" but it was in vain. Not a single gold coin appeared. Immediately the son realized that he had been duped. He was ashamed of himself and began to practice his trade to support himself.

The third son had gone to a turner, who gave him a sack with a club in it as a gift when the young man was ready to go off on his travels. Whenever he said, "Club, come out of the sack!" the club would jump out and dance on people's backs and beat them mercilessly. Now the young turner had heard that his brothers had lost their treasures at an inn. Therefore, he went to the same inn and said that his brothers had brought with them a little magic table and the donkey Bricklebrit, but what he was carrying in his sack was much more precious and worth much more. The innkeeper was curious and thought that all good things come in threes, and wanted to steal this treasure during the night. But the turner had placed the sack under his pillow, and when the innkeeper came and tried to pull it out, the young man said: "Club, come out of the sack!"

All at once the club jumped out of the sack, and danced with the innkeeper and beat him so mercilessly that he readily promised to return the little magic table and the donkey Bricklebrit. Once he received them, the youngest son set out for home and brought everything to his father and lived with him and his brothers in happiness and joy.

As for the goat, she had run off to a foxhole. And when the fox came home and looked into his cave, he saw a pair of large fiery eyes glaring at him. He became so frightened that he ran away and encountered the bear, who said: "Brother fox, why are you making such a face?"

"A gruesome beast is sitting in my cave with terrifying fiery eyes."

"Well, then I'll drive it out for you," the bear said and went to the cave. However, when he arrived at the cave and saw the fiery eyes, he, too, was struck by fear and ran off. Now a bee came flying by and asked: "Why are you looking so pale, bear?"

"A gruesome beast is sitting in the fox's cave, and we can't chase it away."

Then the bee said: "I'm nothing but a tiny creature and you don't give me the attention that I deserve, but perhaps I can help you."

So the bee flew into the foxhole and stung the goat on its smooth shaven head so that she jumped up screaming *"Meh! Meh!"* and ran away. And to this day nobody knows whatever happened to the goat.

II

A tailor had three sons whom he wanted to send off into the world one after the other. They were supposed to learn an honest living. Since he didn't want them to leave empty-handed, each was to receive a pancake and a penny.

The eldest set out and encountered a little man who lived in a nutshell. However, he was enormously rich and said to the tailor's son, "If you look after my herd on the mountain and will protect it, you'll receive a good gift from me. However, you must beware of the house at the foot of the mountain. There are a lot of merry things going on there. You can always hear music and shouting and dancing. If you enter that house, then you can forget about working for me."

The tailor's son agreed, drove the herd up the mountain, looked after it diligently, and always kept far away from the house. However, one time on a Sunday, he heard how much fun people were having inside, and he thought, "One time won't hurt." So he went inside, danced, and was delighted. But when he went outside again, it was night, and the entire herd had disappeared. So he went to his master with a heavy heart and confessed to him what he had done. The man in the nutshell was immensely angry. However, since the young man had served him so diligently, and since he had confessed his mistake openly, he gave him a magic table as a gift.

The tailor's son was deeply grateful and set out on the way home to his father. Along the way he stopped at an inn and asked the innkeeper to give him a special room. He told him that he didn't need any food and locked himself in the room. The innkeeper wondered what the strange guest was going to do in the room. So he sneaked upstairs and looked through the keyhole. All at once he saw how the stranger set a small table down in front of him and said, "Little table, cover yourself!" and as soon as he said that, the best food and drink appeared before him. The innkeeper thought that the little table would be better in his hands. So, in the night, when the stranger was fast asleep, he fetched the magic table and replaced it with another that looked the same.

In the morning the tailor's son departed and didn't notice that he had been deceived. When he returned home, he told his father about his good fortune, and the old man was happy and wanted to test the miraculous table right away. But even when his son spoke the words "Little table, cover yourself" a few times, it was to no avail. The table remained empty, and the young man realized that he had been robbed.

Now the second son received his pancake and a penny and went into the world to do better things. He, too, came upon the man in the nutshell and served him faithfully a long time, but he let himself be led astray. He went into the house, had fun, danced, and lost the herd. So he had to take his leave, but the man gave him a donkey. Whenever he said to the animal, "Rattle and shake yourself, spew gold from behind and from the front," gold rained from all sides. The second son set out for home with great pleasure, but he stopped at the inn, and the innkeeper replaced the donkey with a common one, and when the young man returned home and wanted to make his father rich, it was all over, and his good fortune was ruined.

Finally, the third son was equipped with the pancake and penny and went into the world. And he promised to do better. He served the man in the nutshell faithfully, and in order to prevent himself from entering the dangerous house, he stuffed his ears with cotton, and when the year of service had been completed, he delivered the entire herd to the man, and not one animal was missing. Then the little man said: "I must give you a special reward. Here is a satchel. There's a club in it, and as soon as you say, 'Club, get out of the satchel,' it will jump out and cause people a great deal of pain."

The third son set out for home and stopped by the inn and saw the innkeeper who had taken his brothers' gifts. He threw his satchel on the table and spoke about his brothers: "One of them had a little magic table, and the other, a golden donkey. All that's quite good, but it's nothing compared to what I have in this satchel. It's the most valuable thing in the world."

The innkeeper became curious and hoped to get this treasure as well. When night came, the the third son laid himself down in the straw, and he placed the satchel beneath his head. The innkeeper stayed awake and waited until he thought that the third son was fast asleep. Then he went and fetched another satchel and wanted to pull out the satchel from under the young man's head. However, the third son had stayed awake, and when he noticed the innkeeper's hand, he cried out: "Club, get out of the satchel!"

All at once the club jumped out and fell upon the innkeeper and beat him so badly that he fell upon his knees and screamed for mercy. However, the third son refused to let the club stop until the thief returned the little table and the golden donkey. Then he set out for home with the three magic gifts to join his brothers, and from then on they lived with their wealth and in happiness, and the father always said: "I didn't provide them with my pancake and my penny for nothing."

37

THE TABLECLOTH, THE KNAPSACK,
THE CANNON HAT, AND THE HORN

Once there were three brothers from the region of the Black Mountains. Originally, they were very poor and traveled to Spain, where they came to a mountain completely surrounded by silver. The oldest brother took advantage of the situation by gathering as much silver as he could carry and went back home with his booty. The other two continued traveling and came to a mountain where nothing could be seen but gold. One brother said to the other, "What should we do?"

The second took as much gold as he could carry, as his older brother had done, and went home. However, the third wanted to see if he could have even better luck and continued on his way. He walked for three days and then entered an enormous forest. After wandering about for some time, he became tired, hungry, and thirsty and couldn't find his way out of the forest. So he climbed a tall tree to see if he could catch a glimpse of the end of the forest. However, he saw nothing but the tops of trees. His only wish now was to fill his body once more, and he began climbing down the tree. When he got to the bottom, he noticed a table covered with many different dishes underneath the tree. He was delighted by this and ate until he was full. After he had finished eating, he took the tablecloth with him and moved on. Whenever he got hungry or thirsty again, he opened the tablecloth, and whatever he wished for would appear on it.

After a day's journey he encountered a charcoal burner, who was burning coals and cooking potatoes. The charcoal burner invited him to be his guest, but he replied, "No thanks, but I want you to be my guest."

"How's that possible?" the charcoal burner asked. "You don't seem to be carrying anything with you."

"That doesn't matter," he said. "Just sit down over here."

Then he opened his tablecloth, and soon there was everything and anything one could possibly wish for. The charcoal burner enjoyed the meal and wanted to have the tablecloth. After they had eaten everything, he said, "How'd you like to trade with me? I'll give you an old soldier's knapsack for the tablecloth. If you tap it with your hand, a corporal and six men armed from top to bottom will come out each time you tap. They're of no help to me in the forest, but I'd certainly like the tablecloth."

They made the trade: the charcoal burner kept the tablecloth, while the man from the Black Mountains took the knapsack. However, no sooner had the man gone some distance than he tapped the knapsack. and out popped the war heroes.

"What does my master want?"

"I want you to march back and fetch my tablecloth that I left behind with the charcoal burner."

So they returned to the charcoal burner and then brought back the tablecloth. In the evening he came to another charcoal burner, who invited him to supper. He had the same potatoes without grease, but the man from the Black Mountains opened his tablecloth instead and invited him to be his guest. Nobody could have wished for a better meal! When it was over, this charcoal burner also wanted to make a trade. He gave the man a hat for the tablecloth. If the man turned the hat on his head, cannons would fire as if an entire battalion of soldiers and battery were right on the spot.

When the man from the Black Mountains had gone some distance, he tapped the old knapsack again, and the corporal and his six men were ordered to fetch the tablecloth again. Now the man continued his journey in the same forest, and in the evening he came upon a third charcoal burner, who invited him to eat potatoes without grease like the others. Then they negotiated, and the charcoal burner gave the man a little horn for the tablecloth. If the man blew on it, all the cities and villages as well as the fortresses would collapse into heaps of rubble.

The charcoal burner didn't get to keep the tablecloth any longer than the other two, for the corporal and his six men soon came and fetched it. Now, when the man from the Black Mountains had everything together, he returned home and intended to visit his brothers, who had become rich from their gold and silver. When he went to them wearing an old tattered coat they refused to recognize him as their brother. So he immediately tapped his knapsack and had one hundred and fifty men march out and give his brothers a good thrashing on their backs. The entire village came to their aid, but they could do very little in this affair. News of this soon reached the king, who sent a military squad to take the soldiers prisoner, but the man from the Black Mountains kept tapping his knapsack and had an infantry and cavalry march out. They defeated the military squad and forced it to retreat. The following day the king had even more soldiers sent to bring an end to the old guy. However, he kept tapping his knapsack until he had an entire army. In addition, he turned his hat a few times. The cannons fired, and the enemy was defeated and took flight. Finally, peace was made, and he was appointed viceroy and awarded the princess for his bride.

However, the princess was constantly bothered by the fact that she had to take such an old guy for her husband. Her greatest wish was to get rid of him. Every day she tried to discover the source of the power that he used to his advantage. Finally, since he was so devoted to her, he revealed everything to her. She managed to talk him into giving her his knapsack, whereupon she forced him out. Afterward, when soldiers came marching against him, his men were defeated. However, he still had his little hat. So he turned it and had the cannons fired. Once again he defeated the enemy, and peace was made. After this he was deceived again when the princess talked him into giving her his little hat. Now, when the enemy attacked him, he had nothing left but his little horn. So he blew it, and the villages, cities, and all the fortresses collapsed instantly into heaps of rubble. Then he alone was king and blew his horn until he died.

38

MRS. FOX

I

Once upon a time there was an old fox with nine tails. Since he wanted to know how faithful his wife was, he stretched himself out beneath the bench and pretended to be as dead as a door mouse. Then his wife, Mrs. Fox, went upstairs into her room and locked the door. Her maid, the cat, was sitting on the hearth and cooking. When it became known now that the old fox had died, there was a knocking at the door:

"What are you doing, my fine maiden cat?
Are you awake? Where are you at?"

The cat went to the door and opened it. A young fox stood outside.

"I'm not sleeping. I'm awake.
I'm cooking warm beer and a butter cake.

Would the gentlemen like to be my guest?"
"No, thank you. But what is Mrs. Fox doing?"

"Mrs. Fox sits up in her room until it's late
and yammers all about her fate.
She weeps until her eyes are silky red
all because Mr. Fox is dead."

"Well, tell her a young fox is here who'd like to court her."
So the cat went up to the stairs, *trippety-trap*.

She opened the door, *clippety-clap.*

"Mrs. Fox, are you there?"

"Yes, my little cat, I'm here."

"There's a young fox outside who wants to court you."

And Mrs. Fox said to her:

"My child, what's he look like to you?

Does he also have nine so bushy tails like blessed Mr. Fox?"

"Oh, no, he only has one tail."

"Then I don't want him."

So the cat went down the stairs and sent the suitor away. Soon after there was another knocking at the door, and it was another fox that had two tails, and the same thing happened to him that happened to the first fox. Afterward others came with more tails than the previous fox until a suitor came with nine tails. Now Mrs. Fox said to the cat:

"Open the door and gate quite wide
and drag old Mr. Fox outside!"

But when they were just about to hold the wedding, old Mr. Fox reappeared. Within seconds he threw the entire crowd out of the house and chased Mrs. Fox away.

II

Old Mr. Fox died, and a suitor, a wolf, came to the door and knocked:

"Good day, Miss Cat von Kehrewitz.
How come you're sitting there alone
What are you making, it smells so good?"

Cat: "I'm making porridge out of milk and bread
Does the gentleman desire now to be fed?"

Wolf: "No, thanks. Is Mrs. Fox at home?"

Cat: "She sits up in her room until it's late
and yammers all about her hard cruel fate.

She weeps about her misery until her eyes are silky red,
all because Mr. Fox is dead."

Wolf: "If she wants to have another husband now,
tell her I'm here and have her come down."

So the cat ran up the stairs to find her way
through hallway after hallway,
until she came to a very large room packed full of things,
where she knocked on the door with her five golden rings:

"Mrs. Fox are you inside?
If you want a husband right now,
then you should come down, please come down."

Mrs. Fox: "Is the gentleman wearing red pants
and does he have a pointed mouth?"

Cat: "No."

Mrs. Fox: "Then he's of no use to me."

Now the wolf was rejected, and afterward a dog came, and he was treated the same way. Then came a moose, a rabbit, a bear, a lion, and all the animals of the forest. But they were all lacking something that the old fox had possessed, and the cat had to send them all away. Finally, a young fox came.

Mrs. Fox: "Is the gentleman wearing red pants
and does he have a pointed mouth?"

Cat: "Yes."

Mrs. Fox: "Well then, let him come up.
But first clean the room,
and throw Mr. Fox out the window!
He brought many a fat mouse into the house
but ate them alone, the nasty old louse,
he never gave me one to eat in this house."

Now the wedding was held, and they danced, and if they haven't stopped dancing, then they are still dancing.

39

THE ELVES

About the Shoemaker for Whom They Did the Work

A shoemaker had become so poor that he didn't have enough leather left for a single pair of shoes. In the evening he cut out the shoes that he planned to work on the next morning. However, when he got up the next day and was about to sit down to do his work, he saw the two shoes already finished and beautifully made, standing on the table. Soon a customer paid so well that the shoemaker could purchase enough leather for two pairs of shoes, which he cut out that evening. The next morning when he once again wanted to sit down and work, they were already finished, just as the pair had been the other day. Now he was able to purchase enough leather for four pairs of shoes from the money he received from the two pairs. And so it went. Whatever he cut out in the evening was finished by morning, and soon he was a well-to-do man again.

Now one evening right before Christmas after he had cut out many shoes and wanted to go to bed, he said to his wife: "We should stay up one time and see who does our work in the night."

So they lit a candle, hid themselves in the corner of the room behind the clothes that had been hung up there, and watched closely. At midnight two cute little naked men came and sat down at the workbench, took all the cutout pieces of the shoes, and worked so swiftly and nimbly that the shoemaker could not take his eyes off them. Indeed, they were incredibly fast, and he was amazed. They didn't stop until they had finished the work on all the shoes. Then they scampered away, and it wasn't even day yet.

Now the shoemaker's wife said to him: "The little men have made us rich. So we ought to show that we're grateful. I feel sorry for them running around without any clothes and freezing. I want to sew shirts, coats, jackets, and trousers for them, and you should make a pair of shoes for each one of them."

The shoemaker agreed, and when everything was finished, they set all the things out in the evening. They wanted to see what the little men would do and hid themselves again. Then the little ones appeared as usual at midnight. When they saw the clothes lying there, they seemed to be quite pleased. They put the clothes on extremely quickly, and when they were finished, they began to hop, jump, and dance. Finally, they danced right out the door and never returned.

About a Servant Girl Who Acted as Godmother

A poor maiden was industrious and neat and swept the dirt from the door of a large house every day. One morning she found a letter lying in front of the door, and since she couldn't read, she brought it to her employers. The letter was an invitation to the maiden from the elves, who asked her to be godmother to one of their children. The maiden thought about this for a while, but after her employers convinced her that she shouldn't refuse the invitation, she said yes.

Soon after, three elves came and led her to a hollow mountain. Everything was small there and also incredibly dainty and splendid. The mother was lying on a black ebony bed with pearl knobs. The covers were embroidered with gold. The cradle was ivory. The bathtub was made of gold. The maiden performed her duties as godmother and then wanted to depart right after doing this. But the elves asked her to remain with them for another three days. She spent those days with great joy, and when they were over and she wanted to return home, they filled her pockets full of gold and led her back out of the mountain. And when she came to her home, she realized that it wasn't three days she had been gone but one whole year.

About a Woman Whose Child They Had Exchanged

The elves had taken a mother's child from the cradle and replaced the baby with a changeling who had a fat head and glaring eyes and who would do

nothing but eat and drink. In her distress the mother went to her neighbor and asked her for advice. The neighbor told her to carry the changeling into the kitchen, put him down on the hearth, light the fire, and boil water in two egg shells. That would cause the changeling to laugh, and when he laughed, he would lose his power. The woman did everything the neighbor said, and when she put the eggshells filled with water on the fire, the blockheaded changeling said:

"Now I'm as old
as the Wester Wood,
and in all my life I've never seen
eggshells cooked as these have been."

And the changeling had to laugh about this, and as soon as he laughed, a crowd of elves came all at once. They brought the right child with them, placed him down on the hearth, and carried off the changeling.

40
THE ROBBER BRIDEGROOM

A princess was pledged to marry a prince, and he asked her many times to come once and visit him in his castle. But since the way to the castle led through a large forest, she continually refused because she feared she might lose her way. If that was her concern, the prince told her, he would readily help her by tying a ribbon on each tree so that she could easily find her way. Nevertheless, she tried to postpone the trip for some time since she inwardly dreaded it. Finally, she couldn't make any more excuses and had to set out one day on the journey.

It took her the entire day to walk through a long, long forest. When she finally arrived at a large house, everything was quiet inside, and only an old woman sat in front of the door.

"Can you tell me whether the prince, my bridegroom, lives here?"

"It's good, my child, that you have come now," responded the woman, "because the prince is not at home. Before your arrival I had to fetch water and pour it into a large kettle. They want to kill you, and afterward they'll cook and eat you."

Just as she was saying this the prince could be seen returning from a robbery with his villainous band of robbers. Fortunately, the old woman took pity on the princess because of her youth and beauty, and before anyone had noticed her, she said: "Quick, go down into the cellar and hide yourself behind the large barrel!"

No sooner did the princess dash down into the cellar than the robbers also went down there, dragging an old woman whom they had captured. The princess saw clearly that it was her grandmother, for she could see everything that happened from her corner without being noticed. The robbers grabbed hold of the old grandmother, killed her, and pulled off all the rings from her fingers, one after the other. However, the gold ring on one of her fingers wouldn't come off. So one of the robbers took a hatchet and chopped off the finger, but the finger sprang behind the barrel and fell right into the princess's lap. After the robbers had searched in vain for the finger a long time, one of them spoke out: "Has anyone looked behind the large barrel?"

"It's better if we continue searching when there's more light," another said. "Early tomorrow morning we'll continue looking. Then we'll soon find the ring."

Soon thereafter the robbers lay down to sleep in the cellar, and as they were sleeping and snoring, the bride came out from behind the barrel. The robbers were lying there all in a row, and she had to step over the sleeping men until she came to the door. She cautiously entered the rooms in between, and she was constantly afraid that she might wake someone, but fortunately nothing happened, and once she reached the outside door and was in the forest again, she followed the ribbons, for the moon shone brightly up to the time that she managed to reach her home.

She told her father everything that had happened to her, and he immediately gave orders for an entire regiment to surround the castle as soon as the bridegroom was to arrive. The soldiers did as he ordered. Then the bridegroom came the same day and asked right away why the princess had not come to him as she had promised to do.

Then she said: "I had such a dreadful dream. I dreamt I came to a house where an old woman was sitting in front of the door, and she said to me: 'What a good thing it is, my child, that you have come now because nobody is home, and I must tell you, I had to carry water to a large kettle. They want to kill you and then boil and eat you.' And as she was speaking, the robbers came home. Then, before anyone could notice, the old woman said: 'Quick, go down into the cellar and hide behind the large barrel.' No sooner did I hide behind the barrel than the robbers came down the cellar stairs and dragged an old woman with them. Then they grabbed hold of her and murdered her. After they had murdered the old woman, they pulled off all the rings from her fingers, one after another. But they couldn't pull off the gold ring from one of the fingers. So one of the robbers grabbed a hatchet and chopped off the finger, which flew into the air and fell behind the barrel right into my lap, and *here is the finger!*"

Upon saying this, the princess suddenly drew the finger from her pocket.

When the bridegroom heard and saw all this, he became chalk white from fright. He immediately thought of fleeing and jumped through the window. However, there were guards standing beneath the window. They caught the bridegroom and his entire band of robbers. All of them were executed as payment for their villainy.

41
HERR KORBES

Once upon a time there were a little hen and a little rooster who wanted to take a trip together. So the little rooster built a beautiful wagon with four red wheels and hitched four little mice to it. Then the little hen climbed into the wagon along with the little rooster, and this is how they drove off. Soon they came across a cat, who asked: "Where are you going?"

"We're off to see Herr Korbes today.
We're off without delay."

"Take me with you," said the cat.
"Gladly," answered the little rooster. "Sit in the back so you won't fall off in front.

Be sure you take good care,
for I've got clean red wheels down there.
Roll on, you wheels, *high ho!*
Squeak, squeak, you mice, *high ho!*
We're going to see Herr Korbes today.
We're off without delay."

Soon a millstone came, followed by an egg, a duck, a pin, and a sewing needle, who all got into the wagon and rode along. However, when they arrived at Herr Korbes's house, he wasn't there. The little mice pulled the wagon into the barn. The little hen and the little rooster flew up on a perch. The cat settled down on the hearth. The duck took a place by the well sweep. The egg wrapped itself in a towel. The pin stuck itself in a chair cushion. The sewing needle jumped on the bed right into the pillow. And the millstone climbed to the top of the door.

When Herr Korbes came home, he went to the hearth to make a fire, but the cat threw ashes right into his face. He ran quickly into the kitchen to wash the ashes off, but the duck splashed water in his face. As he tried to dry himself with the towel, the egg rolled toward him and broke open so that his eyes became glued shut. Now he wanted to rest and sit down in the chair, but the pin stuck him. This made him very irritated, and so he went and lay down in his bed, but the sewing needle stuck him just as his head hit the pillow. He became so angry and mad that he wanted to run out of the house. Just as he got through the front door, however, the millstone jumped down and killed him.

42

THE GODFATHER

A poor man had so many children that he had already asked everyone in the world to be godfather after he had yet another child. So there was nobody left to ask. He became so distressed that he lay down and fell asleep. Then he dreamt that he was to go outside the town gate and ask the first person he met to be godfather. So that's what the man did. He went out in front of the gate and asked the first man he met to be godfather. The stranger gave him a little bottle of water and said: "With this water you can cure the sick when Death stands at the sick person's head, but when Death stands at the sick person's feet, the patient must die."

Now one day the king's child became sick, and Death stood at the child's head. So the man cured him with the water. The second time that the king's child became sick, the man cured him again because Death was standing at the head. But the third time, Death was standing at the foot of the bed, and the child had to die.

Later the man went to the godfather to tell him about everything. When he climbed the stairs in the house and reached the first landing, he encountered a shovel and a broom quarreling with each other. The man asked where the godfather lived, and the broom replied:

"One flight higher."

When he came to the second landing, he saw a bunch of dead fingers lying there, and asked once again where the godfather lived.

"One flight higher," replied one of the fingers.

On the third landing there was a pile of skulls who told him once again: "One flight higher."

On the fourth landing he saw some fish sizzling in a pan over a fire. They were frying themselves and also told him, "One flight higher."

After he had climbed to the fifth floor, he came to the door of a room and looked through the keyhole. There he saw the godfather, who had a pair of long, long horns. When he opened the door and entered the room, the godfather quickly jumped into the bed and covered himself.

"Godfather," the man said, "when I came to the first landing, a broom and shovel were quarreling."

"How can you be so simple-minded?"said the godfather. "That was the servant and the maid just talking to each other."

"On the second landing I saw dead fingers lying about."

"My goodness, how foolish you are! Those were salsify roots."

"On the third landing there were skulls lying about."

"You stupid man, those were cabbage heads."

"On the fourth landing I saw fish in a pan frying themselves."

Just as he said that, the fish came in and served themselves on a platter.

"And when I came to the fifth landing, I looked through the keyhole and saw that you had long, long horns."

"Now, that's just not true."

43
THE STRANGE FEAST

A blood sausage and a liver sausage had been friends for some time, and the blood sausage invited the liver sausage for a meal at her home. At dinnertime the liver sausage merrily set out for the blood sausage's house. But when she walked through the doorway, she saw all kinds of strange things. There were many steps, and on each of them she found something different. A broom and shovel were fighting with each other, and there was a monkey with a big wound on his head, and more such things.

The liver sausage was very frightened and upset by this. Nevertheless, she took heart, entered the room, and was welcomed in a friendly way by the blood sausage. The liver sausage began to inquire about the strange things on the stairs, but the blood sausage pretended not to hear her or made it seem it was not worth talking about, or she said something about the shovel and the broom such as, "That was probably my maid gossiping with someone on the stairs." And she shifted the topic to something else.

Then the blood sausage said she had to leave the room to go into the kitchen and look after the meal. She wanted to check to see that everything was in order and nothing had fallen into the ashes. The liver sausage began walking back and forth in the room and kept wondering about the strange things until someone appeared—I don't know who it was—and said, "Let me warn you, liver sausage, you're in a bloody murderous trap. You'd better get out of here quickly if you value your life!"

The liver sausage didn't have to think twice about this. She ran out the door as fast as she could. Nor did she stop until she got out of the house and was in the middle of the street. Then she looked around and saw the blood sausage standing high up in the attic window with a long, long knife that was gleaming as though it had just been sharpened. The blood sausage threatened her with it and cried out, "If I had caught you, I would have had you!"

44
GODFATHER DEATH

Once upon a time there was a poor man who already had twelve children when the thirteenth was born. Since he was at his wits' end and in such distress, he ran into the forest, where he encountered our dear Lord, who said to him: "I feel sorry for you, my poor man. I shall stand sponsor to your child at the baptism and take care of him so that he'll live happily on this earth."

Upon saying this, the Lord left him standing there and moved on.

Soon thereafter the poor man encountered Death, who likewise spoke to him and said, "I want to be your godfather and stand sponsor to your child. If he has me as his friend, he will never be in need. I'll make him into a doctor."

"I'm satisfied with what you say," said the man. "You don't make a difference between rich and poor when you fetch them. Tomorrow is Sunday. My son will be baptized. Just show up at the right time."

The next morning Death came and held the child during the baptism. After the child had grown up, Death came once again and took his godson into the forest.

"Now you are to become a doctor, and you only have to pay attention to what I say. When you are called to a sick person and you see me standing at his head, it is a sign that I won't take him. Let him smell the vapors of this bottle and rub the salve on his feet. Then he'll become well again. However, if I stand at his feet, then it's all over, and I'll take him. Don't try to cure him."

Upon saying this, Death gave him the bottle, and the young man became a famous doctor. He only had to take a look at a sick person, and he knew in advance whether the person would become well again or had to die.

One time he was called to the king, who was lying in bed because of a serious illness. When the doctor entered the room, he saw Death standing at the king's feet, and so the vapors of the bottle could not be of any help.

Nevertheless, he had an urge to deceive Death. So, he grabbed hold of the king and turned him around so that Death stood at his head. This change succeeded, and the king became well again. However, when the doctor returned home, Death came to him, gave him some fierce looks, and said, "If you dare trick me another time, I'll twist your head off."

Soon thereafter the king's beautiful daughter became sick, and nobody in the world could help her. The king wept day and night. Finally, he announced that whoever cured her would have her as his reward and marry her. So the doctor came and saw Death standing at the feet of the princess. Since he was completely enchanted by her beauty, however, he forgot all of Death's warnings, turned the princess around, let her smell the vapors of the bottle, and rubbed the soles of her feet with the salve.

No sooner did he return home than Death stood there with a horrible look on his face. Then he seized his godson and carried him to an underground cave, where a thousand candles were burning.

"Take a look!" Death said. "These are the candles of the living, and this light over here that's only burning a little, this is your life. Watch out!"

45
THE WANDERING OF THUMBLING,
THE TAILOR'S SON

A tailor had a son who was small, not much larger than a thumb. Therefore, he was called Thumbling. However, he was filled with courage and said to his father: "Father, I want to go out wandering."

"Fine with me, my son," said the old man, and he took a darning needle and put a lump of sealing wax on it in the light. "Now you'll also have a dagger to take with you on your way."

The little tailor set out into the world, and his first work was with a master tailor, but the food wasn't good enough.

"Mistress," Thumbling said to the master's wife, "if you don't give us better food, I'll take some chalk tomorrow and write 'Too many potatoes, too little meat!' on the house door, and then I shall leave."

"What do you want, you little grasshopper?!" replied the wife, who became angry, grabbed a washcloth, and wanted to beat him with it. However, my little tailor crawled quickly under the thimble, looked out from beneath it, and stuck out his tongue. She picked up the thimble, but Thumbling hopped into a bunch of washcloths, and as the wife began separating the washcloths to search for him, he crawled into a crack in the table.

"Hey! Hey! My lady!" he cried out and raised his head from the crack.

As soon as the tailor's wife tried to hit him, he jumped into the drawers until she finally caught him and chased him out of the house.

Now, the little tailor continued wandering and came to a large forest, where he met a band of robbers, who wanted to steal the king's treasure. When they saw the little tailor, they thought he could be of great help to them. So they spoke to Thumbling and said that he was a good and able fellow and that he should come along with them to the treasure chamber, crawl inside, and throw the money outside to them. Well, Thumbling agreed. So he went to the treasure chamber and examined the door to see if there was a crack in it. Fortunately, he soon found one and wanted to climb through it, but one of the guards said to his companion, "Look at that nasty spider crawling over there! I'm going to stamp on it until I kill it!"

"Hey, leave the spider alone," the other guard said. "It's done nothing to you."

This was how Thumbling fortunately made his way into the treasure chamber. Then he went to the window where the robbers were standing outside, and he threw one coin after another out the window. When the king examined his treasure chamber later, there was so much money missing that nobody could understand how it had been stolen because all the locks had been well protected.

The king called for more guards, who heard something rattling in the coins. They went inside and wanted to grab hold of the thief. But the little tailor sat down in a corner beneath a coin and cried out: "Here I am!"

The guards ran over there, while Thumbling leaped to another corner, and when they were at the first corner, he cried out, "Here I am!"

The guards ran to the next corner, but Thumbling hopped to another corner once again and cried out: "Here I am!"

This way he kept making fools out of them and kept doing this until they became tired and left the chamber. Now Thumbling gradually threw all the coins through the window. He sat himself down on the last one and went flying through the window. The robbers gave him tremendous praise and would have made him their captain if he had wanted that. Then they divided the loot, but Thumbling wouldn't take more than one coin because he couldn't carry more than that.

Afterward he resumed walking, and finally, since he was not having much success with tailoring, he hired himself out as a servant at an inn. However, the maids weren't fond of him because he saw everything they did in secret without their noticing it. Then he reported them afterward. As a result, they wanted very much to play a prank on him.

So, one time, when he went for a walk in the meadow, where a maid was mowing the grass, she mowed him together with the grass and threw the grass and Thumbling to the cows when she returned home. Then the black cow swallowed Thumbling, and he was now cooped up inside the cow and heard that evening that the cow was to be slaughtered. Since his life was in danger, he cried out: "I'm here!"

"Where are you?"

"In the black cow!"

However, the people couldn't understand him, and the cow was slaughtered. Fortunately, he wasn't struck by the blows to the cow and became mixed with the sausage meat. When this meat was about to be chopped up, he cried out: "Don't chop too deeply! Don't chop too deeply! I'm stuck beneath the meat."

Because of all the noise, however, nobody heard him. So Thumbling jumped quickly between the chopping knives avoiding any harm, but he couldn't get completely away and was stuffed into a blood sausage that was hung in the chimney to be smoked until winter when the sausage was to be eaten. Well, when his lodging was eventually sliced open, he jumped out and ran away.

Now the little tailor wandered again. However, a fox came across his path and snatched him.

"Mister fox," Thumbling cried, "you've got me! Let me go!"

"All right," said the fox. "Since there's not very much of you, I'll let you go if you get your father to give me all the hens in the chicken yard."

So Thumbling swore that he'd do this, and the fox carried him to his home and was given all the hens in the chicken yard. Meanwhile, the little tailor brought his father the one coin that he had earned from all his wanderings.

"But why did the fox get all the poor little hens to eat?"

"Oh you fool, a father certainly loves his child more than he does his hens."

46
FITCHER'S BIRD

Once upon a time there was a sorcerer who was a thief, and he used to go begging from house to house in the guise of a beggar. One time a maiden opened the door and gave him a piece of bread. He only had to touch her to force her to jump into his basket. Then he carried her off to his house, where everything was splendid inside, and he gave her whatever she desired.

Some time later he said to her: "I have some business to attend to outside the house, and so I must take a trip. Here is an egg. Take good care of it and carry it with you wherever you go. I'm also giving you a key, and if you value your life, don't go into the room that it opens."

Nevertheless, when he was gone, she went and opened up this room, and as she entered it, she saw a large basin in the middle with dead and butchered people lying in it. She was so tremendously horrified that the egg she was carrying plopped into the basin. To be sure she quickly took it out and wiped the blood off, but the blood reappeared instantly. She wiped and scraped, but she couldn't get rid of the stain.

When the man returned from his journey, he demanded the key and the egg. He looked at both of them, and he realized right away that she had been in the bloody chamber.

"Didn't you pay attention to my instructions?" he said angrily. "Now you'll go back into the bloody chamber against your will."

Upon saying this, he grabbed her, led her to the chamber, chopped her into pieces, and tossed her into the basin with the others.

After some time had passed the man went begging again and captured the second daughter. He took her from the house, and the same thing happened to her. She opened the forbidden door, let the egg fall into the blood, and was chopped to pieces and thrown into the basin.

Now the sorcerer wanted to have the third daughter as well. So he captured her and put her into his basket. After he returned home, he gave her the key and the egg before he set out on his journey. However, the third daughter was smart and cunning. She put the egg into a cupboard and then went into the secret chamber. When she found her sisters in the bloody basin, she looked all over the place for their missing parts and put them all together—head, body, arms, and legs. So the two sisters came back to life. Then their sister led them out of the chamber and hid them.

When the man came home and didn't find any blood stains on the egg, he asked the third sister to become his bride. She said yes, but she told him that before she'd marry him, he had to fill his basket full of gold and carry it to her parents on his back. In the meantime she would make preparations for the wedding. Instead, she stuck her sisters into the basket, covered them with gold, and told them that they were to get help from home.

"Now carry this basket to my parents," she said to the man, "but don't dare to stop and rest along the way. I can see everything from my window."

So the man lifted the basket onto his back and went on his way. It was, however, so heavy that he was almost crushed to death by the weight. At one point he wanted to rest, but one of the sisters immediately cried out from the basket: "I see from my window that you're resting! Get a move on at once!"

He thought that it was his bride who was crying out, and so he immediately continued walking. Whenever he stopped along the way, he heard a voice and had to keep moving.

Back at his place, the bride took a skull, decorated it with jewels and set it on the window case. Then she invited the sorcerer's friends to the wedding, and after that was done, she dipped herself into a barrel of honey, cut open a bed, and rolled around in the feathers so that it was impossible to recognize her because she looked so strange. And this is how she set out on her way. Soon she met some of the wedding guests, who asked:

"Where are you coming from, oh, Fitcher's bird?"
"From Fitze Fitcher's house, haven't you heard?"
"And what may the young bride be doing there?"
"She's swept the whole house from top to bottom.
Just now she's looking straight out of the window."

Soon thereafter she met the bridegroom, who was on his return home:

"Where are you coming from, oh, Fitcher's bird?"
"From Fitze Fitcher's house, haven't you heard?"
"And what may the young bride be doing there?"
"She's swept the whole house from top to bottom.
Just now she's looking straight out of the window."

The bridegroom looked and saw the decorated skull. He thought it was his bride and waved to her. However, once he and his guests were all gathered inside the house, the helpers who were sent by the sisters finally arrived. These people locked all the doors of the house and then they set fire to it. And since nobody could get out, they were all burned to death.

47
THE JUNIPER TREE

All this took place a long time ago, most likely some two thousand years ago. There was a rich man who had a beautiful and pious wife, and they loved each other very much. Though they didn't have any children, they longed to have some. Day and night the wife prayed for a child, but still none came, and everything remained the same.

Now, in the front of the house there was a yard, and in the yard stood a juniper tree. One day during winter the wife was under the tree peeling an apple, and as she was peeling it, she cut her finger, and her blood dripped onto the snow.

"Oh," said the wife, and she heaved a great sigh. While she looked at the blood before her, she became quite sad. "If only I had a child as red as blood and as white as snow!"

Upon saying that, her mood changed, and she became very cheerful, for she felt something might come of it. Then she went home.

After a month the snow vanished. After two months everything turned green. After three months the flowers sprouted from the ground. After four months all the trees in the woods grew more solid, and the green branches became intertwined. The birds began to sing, and their song resounded throughout the forest as the blossoms fell from the trees. Soon the fifth month passed, and when the wife stood under the juniper tree, it smelled so sweetly that her heart leapt for joy. Indeed, she was so overcome by joy that she fell down on her knees. When the sixth month had passed, the fruit was large and firm, and she was quite still. In the seventh month she picked the juniper berries and ate them so avidly that she became sad and sick. After the eighth month passed, she called her husband to her and wept.

"If I die," she said, "bury me under the juniper tree."

After that she was quite content and relieved until the ninth month had passed. Then she had a child as white as snow and as red as blood. When she saw the baby, she was so delighted that she died.

Her husband buried her under the juniper tree, and he began weeping a great deal. After some time he felt much better, but he still wept every now and then. Eventually, he stopped, and after more time passed, he took another wife. With his second wife he had a daughter, while the child from the first wife was a little boy, who was as red as blood and as white as snow. Whenever the woman looked at her daughter, she felt great love for her, but whenever she looked at the little boy, her heart was cut to the quick. She couldn't forget that he would always stand in her way and prevent her daughter from inheriting everything, which was what the woman had in mind. Gradually the devil took hold of her and influenced her feelings toward the boy until she became quite cruel toward him: she pushed him from one place to the next, slapped him here and cuffed him there, so that the poor child lived in constant fear. When he came home from school, he found no peace at all.

One day the woman went up to her room, and her little daughter followed her and said, "Mother, give me an apple."

"Yes, my child," said the woman, and she gave her a beautiful apple from the chest that had a large heavy lid with a big, sharp iron lock.

"Mother," said the little daughter, "shouldn't brother get one too?"

The woman was irritated by that remark, but she said, "Yes, as soon as he comes home from school."

And, when she looked out of the window and saw him coming, the devil took possession of her, and she snatched the apple away from her daughter. "You shan't have one before your brother," she said and threw the apple into the chest and shut it.

Meanwhile the little boy came through the door, and the devil compelled her to be friendly to him and say, "Would you like to have an apple, my son?" Yet, she gave him a fierce look.

"Mother," said the little boy, "How ferocious you look! Yes, give me an apple."

Then she felt compelled to coax him.

"Come over here," she said as she lifted the lid. "Take out an apple for yourself."

And as the little boy leaned over the chest, the devil prompted her, and *crash!* She slammed the lid so hard that his head flew off and fell among the apples. Then she was struck by fear and thought, "How am I going to get out of this?" She went up to her room and straight to her dresser, where she took out a white kerchief from a drawer. She put the boy's head back on his neck and tied the neckerchief around it so nothing could be seen. Then she set him on a chair in front of the door and put the apple in his hand.

Some time later little Marlene came into the kitchen and went up to her mother, who was standing by the fire in front of a pot of hot water, which she was constantly stirring.

"Mother," said Marlene, "brother's sitting by the door and looks very pale. He's got an apple in his hand, and I asked him to give me the apple, but he didn't answer, and I became very scared."

"Go back to him," said the mother, "and if he doesn't answer you, give him a box on the ear."

Little Marlene returned to him and said, "Brother, give me the apple." But he wouldn't respond.

So she gave him a box on the ear, and his head fell off. The little girl was so frightened that she began to cry and howl. Then she ran to her mother and said, "Oh, mother, I've knocked my brother's head off!" And she wept and wept and couldn't be comforted.

"Marlene," said the mother. "What have you done! You're not to open your mouth about this. We don't want anyone to know, and besides there's nothing we can do about it now. So we'll make a stew out of him."

The mother took the little boy and chopped him into pieces. Next she put them into a pot and let them stew. But Marlene stood nearby and wept until all her tears fell into the pot, so it didn't need any salt. When the father came home, he sat down at the table and asked, "Where's my son?'

The mother served a huge portion of the stewed meat, and Marlene wept and couldn't stop.

"Where's my son?"the father asked again.

"Oh," said the mother, "he's gone off into the country to visit his mother's great-uncle. He intends to stay there awhile."

"What's he going to do there? He didn't even say good-bye to me."

"Well, he wanted to go very badly and asked me if he could stay there six weeks. They'll take good care of him."

"Oh, that makes me sad," said the man. "It's not right. He should have said good-bye to me." Then he began to eat and said, "Marlene, what are you crying for? Your brother will come back soon." Without pausing, he said, "Oh, wife, the food tastes great! Give me some more!" The more he ate, the more he wanted. "Give me some more," he said. "I'm not going to share this with you. Somehow I feel as if it were all mine."

As he ate and ate, he threw the bones under the table until he was all done. Meanwhile, Marlene went to her dresser and took out her best silk neckerchief from the bottom drawer, gathered all the bones from beneath the table, tied them up in her silk kerchief, and carried them outside the door. There she wept bitter tears and laid the bones beneath the juniper tree. As she put them there, she suddenly felt relieved and stopped crying. Now the juniper tree began to move. The branches separated and came together again as though they were clapping their hands in joy. At the same time smoke came out of the tree, and in the middle of the smoke there was a flame that seemed to be humming. Then a beautiful bird flew out of the fire and began singing magnificently. He soared high in the air, and after he vanished, the juniper tree was as it was before. Yet the silk kerchief was gone. Marlene was very happy and gay. It was as if her brother were still alive, and she went merrily back into the house, sat down at the table, and ate.

Meanwhile, the bird flew away, landed on the roof of a goldsmith's house, and began to sing:

"My mother, she killed me.
My father, he ate me.
My sister, Marlene, she made sure to see
my bones were gathered secretly,
bound nicely in silk, as neat as can be,
and laid beneath the juniper tree.
Tweet, tweet! What a lovely bird I am!"

The goldsmith was sitting in his workshop making a golden chain. When he heard the bird singing on his roof, he thought the song was very beautiful. Then he stood up, and as he walked across the threshold, he lost a slipper. Still, he kept on going, right into the middle of the street with only one sock and a slipper on. He was also wearing his apron, and in one of his hands he held the golden chain, in the other his tongs. The sun was shining brightly on the street as he walked, and then he stopped to get a look at the bird.

"Bird," he said, "how beautifully you sing! Sing me that song again."

"No," said the bird, "I never sing twice for nothing. Give me the golden chain, and I'll sing it for you again."

"All right," said the goldsmith. "Here's the golden chain. Now sing the song again."

The bird swooped down, grasped the golden chain in his right claw, went up to the goldsmith, and began singing:

"My mother, she killed me.
My father, he ate me.
My sister, Marlene, she made sure to see
my bones were gathered secretly,
bound nicely in silk, as neat as can be,
and laid beneath the juniper tree.
Tweet, tweet! What a lovely bird I am!"

Then the bird flew off to a shoemaker, landed on his roof, and sang:

"My mother, she killed me.
My father, he ate me.
My sister, Marlene, she made sure to see
my bones were gathered secretly,
bound nicely in silk, as neat as can be,
and laid beneath the juniper tree.
Tweet, tweet! What a lovely bird I am!"

When the shoemaker heard the song, he ran to the door in his shirt sleeves and looked up at the roof, keeping his hand over his eyes to protect them from the bright sun.

"Bird," he said, "how beautifully you sing!" Then he called into the house, "Wife, come out here for a second! There's a bird up there. Just look. How beautifully he sings!" Then he called his daughter and her children, and the journeyman, apprentices, and maid. They all came running out into the street and looked at the bird and saw how beautiful he was. He had bright red and green feathers, and his neck appeared to glisten like pure gold, while his eyes sparkled in his head like stars.

"Bird," said the shoemaker, "now sing me that song again."

"No," said the bird. "I never sing twice for nothing. You'll have to give me a present."

"Wife," said the man, "go into the shop. There's a pair of red shoes on the top shelf. Get them for me."

His wife went and fetched the shoes.

"There," said the man. "Now sing the song again."

The bird swooped down, grasped the shoes in his left claw, flew back up on the roof, and sang:

"My mother, she killed me.
My father, he ate me.
My sister, Marlene, she made sure to see
my bones were gathered secretly,
bound nicely in silk, as neat as can be,
and laid beneath the juniper tree.
Tweet, tweet! What a lovely bird I am!"

When the bird finished the song, he flew away. He had the chain in his right claw and the shoes in his left, and he flew far away to a mill. The mill went *clickety-clack, clickety-clack, clickety-clack*. The miller had twenty men sitting in the mill, and they were hewing a stone. Their chisels went click-clack, click-clack, click-clack. And the mill kept going clickety-clack, clickety-clack, clickety-clack. The bird swooped down and landed on a linden tree outside the mill and sang:

"My mother, she killed me."

Then one of the men stopped working.

"My father, he ate me."

Then two more stopped and listened.

"My sister, Marlene, she made sure to see."

Then four more stopped.

"My bones were gathered secretly,
bound nicely in silk, as neat as can be."

Now only eight kept chiseling.

"And laid beneath . . ."

Now only five.

". . . the juniper tree."

Now only one.

"Tweet, tweet! What a lovely bird I am!"

Then the last one also stopped and listened to the final words.

"Bird, how beautifully you sing! Let me hear that, too. Sing your song again for me."

"No," said the bird. I never sing twice for nothing. Give me the millstone, and I'll sing the song again."

"I would if I could," he said. "But the millstone doesn't belong to me alone."

"If he sings again," said the others, "he can have it."

Then the bird swooped down, and all twenty of the miller's men took some wooden beams to lift the stone. "Heave-ho! Heave-ho! Heave-ho!" Then the bird stuck his neck through the hole, put the stone on like a collar, flew back to the tree, and sang:

"My mother, she killed me.
My father, he ate me.
My sister, Marlene, she made sure to see
my bones were gathered secretly,
bound nicely in silk, as neat as can be,
and laid beneath the juniper tree.
Tweet, tweet "What a lovely bird I am!"

After the bird had finished his song, he spread his wings, and in his right claw he had the chain, in his left the shoes, and around his neck the millstone. Then he flew away to his father's house.

The father, mother, and Marlene were sitting at the table in the parlor, and the father said, "Oh, how happy I am! I just feel so wonderful!"

"Not me," said the mother. "I feel scared as if a storm were about to erupt."

Meanwhile, Marlene just sat there and kept weeping. Then the bird flew up, and when he landed on the roof, the father said, "Oh, I'm in such good spirits. The sun's shining so brightly outside, and I feel as though I were going to see an old friend again."

"Not me," said his wife. "I'm so frightened that my teeth are chattering. I feel as if fire were running through my veins."

She tore open her bodice, while Marlene sat in a corner and kept weeping. She had her handkerchief in front of her eyes and wept until it was completely soaked with her tears. The bird swooped down on the juniper tree, where he perched on a branch and began singing:

"My mother, she killed me."

The mother stopped her ears, shut her eyes, and tried not to see or hear anything, but there was a roaring in her ears like a turbulent storm, and her eyes burned and flashed like lightning.

"My father, he ate me."

"Oh, Mother," said the man, "listen to that beautiful bird singing so gloriously! The sun's so warm, and it smells like cinnamon."

"My sister, Marlene, made sure to see."

Then Marlene laid her head on her knees and wept and wept, but the man said, "I'm going outside. I must see the bird close up."

"Oh, don't go!" cried the wife. "I feel as if the whole house were shaking and about to go up in flames!"

Nevertheless, the man went out and looked at the bird.

"My bones were gathered secretly,
bound nicely in silk, as neat as can be,
and laid beneath the juniper tree.
Tweet, tweet! What a lovely bird I am!"

After ending his song, the bird dropped the golden chain, and it fell around the man's neck just right, so that it fit him perfectly. Then he went inside and said, "Look how lovely that bird is! He gave me this beautiful golden chain, and he's just as beautiful as well!"

But the woman was petrified and fell to the floor. Her cap slipped off her head, and the bird sang again:

"My mother, she killed me."

"Oh, I wish I were a thousand feet beneath the earth so I wouldn't have to hear this!"

"My father, he ate me."

Then the woman fell down again as if she were dead.

"My sister, Marlene, she made sure to see."

"Oh," said Marlene, I want to go outside, too, and see if the bird will give me something."
Then she went out.

"My bones were gathered secretly,
bound nicely in silk, as neat as can be."

All at once the bird threw her the shoes.

"And laid them beneath the juniper tree.
Tweet, tweet! What a lovely bird I am!"

Marlene felt cheerful and happy. She put on the new red shoes and danced and skipped back into the house.

"Oh," she said, "I was so sad when I went out, and now I feel so cheerful. That certainly is a splendid bird. He gave me a pair of red shoes as a gift."

"Not me," said the wife, who jumped, and her hair flared up like red-hot flames. "I feel as if the world were coming to an end. Maybe I'd feel better if I went outside."

As she went out the door, *crash!* The bird threw the millstone down on her head, and she was crushed to death. The father and Marlene heard the crash and went outside. Smoke, flames, and fire were rising from the spot, and when it was over, the little brother was standing there. He took his father and Marlene by the hand, and all three were very happy. Then they went into the house, sat down at the table, and ate.

48
OLD SULTAN

A farmer had a faithful dog named Sultan. He was old and couldn't latch onto things with his teeth anymore. So the farmer said to his wife: "I'm going to shoot old Sultan. He's no longer of use to us anymore."

His wife replied, "Don't you do it! We should support the faithful dog in his old age. He's served us well so many years."

"You must be out of your mind!" her husband said. "What are we going to do with him? He doesn't have a tooth left in his head. No thief would be afraid of him anymore. If he's served us well, he's done it because of his hunger, and because he was well fed here. Tomorrow is his last day. End of discussion!"

The dog had overheard everything that they had discussed. Since he had a good friend, the wolf, he went out to see him in the evening and whine about his fate and tell him that his master was going to shoot him the next day.

"Don't worry," the wolf said. "I'm going to give you a good plan: Early tomorrow morning your master will be going out with his wife to make hay, and they'll take their little child with them because nobody will be staying at home. They generally lay the child behind the hedge while they work. Now, you're to lie down next to the child as if you want to rest and guard him. I'll come out of the forest and steal the child. Then you've got to jump up and run after me and chase me away. They'll believe that you rescued their child, and you'll be in their good graces, and they'll give you anything you want for the rest of your life."

The dog liked the plan, and it was carried out just as they had conceived it. The wolf ran off a short distance, and when the dog overtook him, the wolf dropped the child, and the dog brought him back to his master, whereupon the man cried out in a very loud voice: "Well, since our old Sultan has chased away the wolf once again, he's going to stay alive, and we'll support him for the rest of his life. Wife, go home and cook him some bread mush that he can easily swallow. Also, bring him my pillow. He's to have it for his bed as long as he lives."

All of a sudden old Sultan had it so good that he couldn't have wished for a better life. The wolf came to him and was delighted to learn that everything had succeeded so well.

"Now you certainly won't have anything against it and will help me when I steal a fat sheep from your master."

But Sultan was loyal to his master and told him what the wolf had in mind. So the man waited for the wolf in the barn, and when the wolf came and wanted to get a good bite of sheep, the farmer practically skinned him alive. Later the wolf was so outraged that he scolded old Sultan, called him a miserable fellow, and challenged him to a duel to settle things.

They were to take their positions right outside the forest, and each one was to bring a second with him. The wolf was the first one at the place and had brought the wild boar as his second, and old Sultan had only been able to recruit a lame cat and finally set out with her. When the wolf and the boar saw the cat coming toward them, constantly limping, they thought that she was picking up stones to throw at them, and they both became frightened. So the wild boar crawled into some bushes, and the wolf jumped up a tree. When the dog and cat reached the spot, they were both puzzled to find nobody there. However, the boar in the bushes began twitching his ear, and when the cat saw something move, she sprang on top of the boar and bit and scratched him. Consequently, the boar leapt into the air with a loud cry and ran away. As he was running, he yelled out: "Your opponent's sitting up there in the tree!"

So it came to light that the wolf had cowardly retreated, and the only way he could climb down from the tree was by agreeing to a peaceful settlement.

49

THE SIX SWANS

A king went hunting in a vast forest, got lost, and couldn't find his way out. Finally, he came upon a witch and asked her to show him the way out of the forest. However, the witch told him she wouldn't do it. He had to remain there and would lose his life. He could only be saved if he married her daughter. The king cherished his life, and he was so frightened, he said yes. So the witch brought the maiden to him. Though she was young and beautiful, he couldn't look at her without getting the creeps and secretly shuddering. However, he intended to keep his promise. Then the old woman led both of them on the right path out of the forest, and once they were at the king's home, the witch's daughter became his wife.

Now the king still had seven children from his first wife, six boys and a girl, and since he was afraid the stepmother might harm them, he brought them to a castle in the middle of a forest. It lay so well concealed nobody knew the way to it, and he himself would not have found it if a wise woman had not given him a ball of yarn. When he threw the ball before him, the yarn unwound itself and showed him the way.

Since the king loved his children very much, he frequently went to the castle. However, the queen became curious and wanted to know why he was going out into the forest all alone. She interrogated the servants, and they revealed the entire secret. The first thing she did was to use her cunning and acquire the ball of yarn. Then she took seven small shirts and went out into the forest. The ball of yarn showed her the way, and when the six little princes saw her coming from the distance, they were delighted because they thought their father was coming and ran out to her. But all at once she threw a shirt over each one of them, and as soon as they were touched by the shirts, they were turned into swans and flew away over the forest.

Now the queen thought that she had gotten rid of all her stepchildren and returned home. So the maiden, who had remained in her room, was saved. The next day the king went to the castle in the forest, and she told him what had happened and showed him the swan feathers that had fallen down from her six brothers into the courtyard. The king was horrified but couldn't believe that that the queen had done such an evil deed. At the same time, he was worried that the princess might also be stolen away from him. So he wanted to take her with him. However, she was afraid of her stepmother and begged the king to allow her to spend one more night in the castle. Then, during the night, she fled and went deeper into the forest.

She walked the entire day, and toward evening she came to a hut. Once she entered, she found a room with six small beds. Since she was now tired, she lay herself down beneath one of the beds and wanted to spend the night there. Yet at sunset six swans came flying through the window, landed on the floor, and blew on one another until all their feathers were blown off as if some cloth had slipped off them, and there stood her six brothers. She crawled out from beneath the bed, and the brothers were both glad and distressed to see her again.

"You can't stay here," they said. "This is a robbers' den. When they come home from their marauding, they live here. We can take off our swan skins for only a quarter of an hour every evening and assume our human form during this time. Then it's all over. If you want to rescue us, you must sew six little shirts made out of asters, but during this time you're not allowed to speak or laugh. Otherwise all your work will be for naught."

As the brothers were speaking, the quarter of an hour expired, and once again they were transformed into swans. The next morning, however, the maiden gathered asters, perched herself on a branch of a tall tree, and began to sew. She didn't speak a single word or laugh. She just sat there and concentrated on her work.

After she had been there for some time, the king who owned this land went hunting and came to the tree where the maiden was perched. His hunters called to her and told her to come down. But because she was not permitted to answer them, she wanted to satisfy them by throwing them presents. So she threw them her golden necklace. Yet they continued to call out. So she threw them her girdle, and when this didn't work either, she threw down her garters and little by little everything that she had on and could do without until she had nothing left but her little shift. Still all this was not enough for the hunters. They climbed the tree, carried her down, and led her by force to the king, who was astonished by her beauty. He covered her with his cloak, lifted her onto his horse, and brought her to his home. Even though she was mute, he loved her with all his heart, and she became his wife.

Now the king's mother was angry about all of this and spoke ill of the young queen: nobody knew where the wench came from, and she wasn't worthy of the king. When the queen gave birth to her first child, the old mother-in-law took the child away and smeared the queen's mouth with blood while she was asleep. Then she accused the young queen of having eaten her own child and of being a sorceress. However, because of his great love for his wife, the king refused to believe this.

Some time later the queen gave birth to a second prince, and the godless mother-in-law played the same trick and accused the queen of cannibalism again. Since the queen wasn't allowed to talk and had to sit there mute and work on the six little shirts, she couldn't save herself and was sentenced to burn at the stake.

The day came when the sentence was to be carried out. It was exactly the last day of the six years, and she had managed to finish sewing the six shirts. Only the left sleeve of the last shirt was missing. When she was led to the stake, she took the six shirts with her, and when she stood on the pile of wood and the fire was about to be lit, she saw the six swans flying through the air until they descended right near her. So she threw the shirts over them, and as soon as the shirts touched them, the swan skins fell off, and her six brothers stood before her in the flesh. Only the sixth one was missing his left arm; instead, he had a swan's wing on his shoulder. Now she could speak once again and told everyone how her mother-in-law had slandered her in such a wicked way. Consequently, the old woman was tied to the stake and burned to death. However, the young queen lived with the king and her six brothers a long time in great joy.

50

BRIAR ROSE

A king and a queen couldn't have children, and they wanted very much to have one. Then one day, while the queen was bathing, a crab crawled out of the water, came onshore, and said: "Your wish will soon be filled, and you will give birth to a daughter."

Indeed, this is what happened, and the king was so delighted by the birth of the princess that he organized a great feast and also invited the fairies who were living in his realm. Since he had only twelve golden plates, however, there was one fairy who had to be excluded, for there were thirteen in all.

The fairies came to the feast, and at the end of the celebration they gave the child some gifts. One gave virtue; the second, beauty; and the others gave every splendid thing that one could possibly wish for in the world. But, just after the eleventh fairy had announced her gift, the thirteenth appeared, and she was quite angry she had not been invited to the festivities.

"Since you didn't ask me to attend this celebration," she cried out, "I say to you that when your daughter turns fifteen, she will prick herself with a spindle and fall down dead!"

The parents were horrified, but the twelfth fairy hadn't made her wish yet, and she said: "The girl will not die. She will fall into a deep sleep for one hundred years."

The king still hoped to save his dear child and issued an order that all spindles in his entire kingdom were to be banned. Meanwhile, the girl grew up and became marvelously beautiful. On the day she turned fifteen, the king and queen had gone out, and she was left completely alone in the palace. So she wandered all over the place just as she pleased and eventually came to an old tower where she found a narrow staircase. Since she was curious, she climbed the stairs and came to a small door with a yellow key stuck in the lock. When she turned it, the door sprang open, and she found herself in a little room where she saw an old woman spinning flax. She took a great liking to the old woman and joked with her and said she wanted to try spinning one time. So she took the spindle from the old woman's hand, and no sooner did she touch the spindle than she pricked herself and fell down into a deep sleep.

Just at that moment the king returned to the palace with his entire courtly retinue, and everybody and everything began to fall asleep—the horses in the stable, the pigeons on the roof, the dogs in the courtyard, and the flies on the wall. Even the fire flickering in the hearth became quiet and fell asleep. The roast stopped sizzling, and the cook, who was just about to pull the kitchen boy's hair, let him go, and the maid, who was plucking the feathers of a hen, let it drop and fell asleep. And a hedge of thorns sprouted around the entire castle and grew higher and higher until it was impossible to see the castle anymore.

There were princes who heard about the beautiful Briar Rose, and they came and wanted to rescue her, but they couldn't penetrate the hedge. It was as though the thorns clung tightly together like hands, and the princes got stuck there and died miserable deaths. All this continued for many, many years until one day a prince came riding through the country, and an old man told him that people believed that a castle was standing behind the hedge of thorns and that a gorgeous princess was sleeping inside with her entire royal household. His grandfather had told him that many princes had come and had wanted to penetrate the hedge. However, they got stuck hanging in the thorns and had died.

"That doesn't scare me," said the prince. "I'm going to make my way through the hedge and rescue the beautiful princess."

So off he went, and when he came to the hedge of thorns, there was nothing but flowers that separated and made a path for him, and as he went through them, the flowers turned back into thorns. After he reached the castle, the horses were lying asleep in the courtyard, and there was an assortment of hunting dogs. The pigeons were perched on the roof and had tucked their heads beneath their wings. When he entered the palace, the flies were sleeping, as was the fire in the kitchen along with the cook and the maid. The prince continued walking, and he saw the entire royal household with the king and queen lying asleep. Everything was so quiet that he could hear himself breathe.

Finally, he came to the old tower where Briar Rose was lying asleep. The prince was so astounded by her beauty that he leaned over and kissed her. Immediately after the kiss, she woke up, and the king and queen and the entire royal household and the horses and the dogs and the pigeons on the roof and the flies on the walls and the fire woke up. Indeed, the fire flared up and cooked the meat until it began to sizzle again, and the cook gave the kitchen boy a box on the ear, while the maid finished plucking the chicken. Then the wedding of the prince with Briar Rose was celebrated in great splendor, and they lived happily to the end of their days.

Once upon a time a forester went out hunting in the forest, and as he entered it, he heard some cries that sounded like those of a small child. He followed the sounds and eventually came to a tall tree where he saw a little child sitting on the top. The child's mother had fallen asleep with him under the tree, and a hawk had seen the child in her lap. So it had swooped down, carried the child away with its beak, and set him down on top of the tree.

The forester climbed the tree and brought the child down, and thought: "You ought to take him home with you and raise him with your little Lena." So he took the boy home, and the two children grew up together. However, the boy who had been found on top of the tree was called Foundling because he had been carried off by a bird. Foundling and little Lena were very fond of each other. In fact, they loved each other so much that they became sad if they were not constantly within sight of each other.

Now the forester had an old cook, and one evening she took two buckets and began fetching water. But she didn't go to the well simply one time but many times. When little Lena saw this, she asked, "Tell me, old Sanna, why are you fetching so much water?"

"If you promise to keep quiet, I'll let you in on my secret."

Little Lena of course replied that she wouldn't tell a soul. Then the cook said, "Early tomorrow morning, when the forester goes out hunting, I'm going to heat some water over the fire, and when it's boiling, I'm going to throw Foundling in and cook him."

Early the next morning the forester got up to go out hunting, and after he had gone, the children were still in bed. Then little Lena said to Foundling, "If you won't forsake me, I won't forsake you."

"Never ever," said Foundling.

"Well then, I'm going to tell you something important," said little Lena. "Last night old Sanna carried many buckets of water into the house, and I asked her why she was doing that. She said that if I wouldn't tell a soul, she'd let me in on her secret, and I promised her not to tell a living soul. Then she said that early this morning, when my father goes out hunting, she would boil a kettle full of water, throw you in, and cook you. So let's get up quickly, dress ourselves, and run away together."

Then the two children got up, dressed themselves quickly, and ran away. When the water in the kettle began to boil, the cook went into the bedroom to get Foundling and throw him into the kettle. But as she entered the room and went over to the beds, she saw that the two children were gone, and she became greatly alarmed.

"What shall I say when the forester comes home and sees that the children are gone?" she said. "I'd better send some people after them so we get them back."

The cook sent three servants to pursue them and bring them back. But the children were sitting at the edge of the forest and saw the three servants coming from afar.

"If you won't forsake me, I won't forsake you," said little Lena.

"Never ever," said Foundling.

"Then change yourself into a rosebush, and I'll be the rose on it," said little Lena.

When the three servants reached the edge of the forest, they saw nothing but a rosebush with a little rose on it. The children were nowhere to be seen.

"There's nothing we can do here," they said, and they went home, where they told the cook they had seen nothing but a rosebush with a rose on it. Then the cook scolded them. "You blockheads! You should have cut the rosebush in two, plucked the rose, and brought it back with you. Now go quickly and do it!"

So they had to set out once more and look for the children. But when the children saw them coming from afar, little Lena said, "If you won't forsake me, I won't forsake you."

"Never ever," said Foundling.

"Then change yourself into a church, and I'll be the chandelier hanging in it," little Lena said.

When the three servants arrived at the spot, there was nothing but a church and a chandelier inside it.

"What should we do here? Let's go home."

When they got home, the cook asked whether they had found anything. They said no. They'd found nothing but a church with a chandelier inside.

"You fools!" the cook scolded them. "Why didn't you destroy the church and bring back the chandelier?"

This time the old cook herself set out on foot accompanied by the three servants and pursued the children. But the children saw the three servants coming from afar and also the cook, who was waddling behind them.

"Foundling," said little Lena. "If you won't forsake me, I won't forsake you."

"Never ever," said Foundling.

"Then change yourself into a pond," said little Lena, "and I'll be the duck swimming on it."

When the cook arrived and saw the pond, she lay down beside it and began to drink it up. However, the duck quickly swam over, grabbed her head in its beak, and dragged her into the water. The old witch was thus drowned, and the children went home together. They were very happy, and if they haven't died, they're still alive.

52
KING THRUSHBEARD

A king had a daughter who was marvelously beautiful but so proud and haughty that she rejected one suitor after the other out of stubbornness and ridiculed them as well.

Once her father held a great feast and invited all the marriageable young men to the event. They were all lined up according to their rank and class: first came the kings, then the dukes, princes, counts, and barons, and finally the gentry. The king's daughter was led down the line, and she found fault with each one of the suitors there. In particular, she made the most fun of a good king who stood at the head of the line and had a chin that was a bit crooked.

"My goodness!" she exclaimed and laughed. "He's got a chin like a thrush's beak!"

From then on, everyone called him Thrushbeard.

When her father saw how his daughter did nothing but ridicule people, he became furious and swore that she would have to marry the very first beggar who came to his door. A few days later a minstrel appeared and began singing beneath the princess's window. When the king heard him, he ordered him to come up to him immediately. Despite his dirty appearance, his daughter had to accept him as her bridegroom. A minister was summoned right away, and the wedding took place. After the wedding was finished, the king said to his daughter: "It's not fitting for you to stay in my palace any longer since you're a beggar woman. You must now depart with your husband."

The beggar took her away, and as they walked through a huge forest, she asked the beggar:

"Tell me, who might the owner of this beautiful forest be?"
"King Thrushbeard owns the forest and all you can see.
If you had taken him, it would belong to you."
"Alas, poor me! What can I do?
I should have wed King Thrushbeard. If only I knew!"

Soon they crossed a meadow, and she asked again:

"Tell me, who might the owner of this beautiful green meadow be?"
"King Thrushbeard owns the meadow and all you can see.
If you had taken him, it would belong to you."
"Alas, poor me! What can I do?
I should have wed King Thrushbeard. If only I knew!"

Then they came to a large city, and she asked once more:

"Tell me, who might the owner of this beautiful big city be?"
"King Thrushbeard owns the forest and all you can see.
If you had taken him, it would belong to you."
"Alas, poor me! What can I do?
I should have wed King Thrushbeard. If only I knew!"

The minstrel became very grumpy when he heard that she always desired another man and didn't think that he was good enough for her. Finally, they came to a tiny cottage, and she exclaimed:

"Oh, Lord! What a wretched tiny house!
It's not even fit for a little mouse."

The beggar answered, "This house is our house, and we shall live here together."

"Now, make a fire at once and put the water on so you can cook me my meal. I'm very tired."

However, the king's daughter knew nothing about cooking, and the beggar had to lend a hand himself. At first things went reasonably well, and after they had eaten, they went to bed. But the next morning she had to get up very early and work. For a few days they lived miserably until the man finally said: "Wife, we can't go on this way any longer. We're eating everything up and not earning anything. You've got to weave baskets."

He went out and cut some willows and brought them home, and she had to begin to weave baskets. However, the rough willows bruised her hands.

"I see you can't do this work," said the man. "So try spinning. Perhaps you'll be better at that."

She sat down and spun, but her fingers were so soft that the hard thread soon cut her, and blood began to flow.

"You're not fit for any kind of work," said the man who was now very irritated. "I'm going to start a business with earthenware. You're to sit in the marketplace and sell the wares."

On the first occasion everything went well. People gladly bought her pots because she was beautiful, and they paid what she asked. Indeed, many gave her money and didn't even bother to take the pots with them. When everything had been sold, her husband bought a lot of new earthenware. Once again his wife sat down with it at the marketplace and hoped to make a good profit. Suddenly, a drunken hussar came galloping along and rode right over the pots so that they were all smashed to pieces. The woman became terrified, and for the rest of the day she didn't dare to go home. When she finally did, the beggar was nowhere to be seen.

For some time she lived in poverty and in great need. Then a man came and invited her to a wedding. She wanted to take all kinds of leftovers from the wedding and live off them for a while. So she put on her little coat with a pot underneath and stuck a large leather purse with it. The wedding was magnificent and with plenty of good things. She filled the pot with soup and her leather purse with scraps. As she was about to leave with everything, one of the guests demanded that she dance with him. She resisted with all her might, but to no avail. He grabbed hold of her, and she had to go with him. All at once the pot fell so that the soup flowed on the ground, and the many scraps also tumbled out of her purse. When the guests saw all this, they broke out in laughter and ridiculed her.

She was so ashamed that she wished she were a thousand fathoms under the earth. She ran out the door and tried to escape, but a man caught up with her on the stairs and brought her back. When she looked at him, she saw it was King Thrushbeard, and he said: "I and the beggar are the same person, and I was also the hussar who rode over your pots and smashed them to pieces. All this happened to you for your benefit and to punish you because you had ridiculed me some time ago. Now, however, our wedding will be celebrated."

Then her father also appeared with his entire court, and she was cleaned and magnificently dressed, appropriate for her position, and the festive event was her marriage with King Thrushbeard.

53
LITTLE SNOW WHITE

Once upon a time, in the middle of winter, when snowflakes were falling like feathers from the sky, a beautiful queen was sitting and sewing at a window with a black ebony frame. And as she was sewing and looking out the window at the snow, she pricked her finger with the needle, and three drops of blood fell on the snow. The red looked so beautiful on the white snow that she thought to herself, "If only I had a child as white as snow, as red as blood, and as black as the wood of the window frame!" Soon thereafter she gave birth to a little daughter who was as white as snow, as red as blood, and her hair as black as ebony. That's why the child was called Little Snow White.

The queen was the most beautiful woman in the entire land and very proud about her beauty. She also had a mirror, and every morning she stepped in front of it and asked:

"Mirror, mirror, on the wall,
who in this land is fairest of all?"

The mirror would answer:

"You, my queen, are the fairest of all."

And then she knew for certain that there was nobody more beautiful in the entire world. However, Little Snow White grew up, and when she was seven years old, she was so beautiful that her beauty surpassed even that of the queen, and when the queen asked her mirror:

"Mirror, mirror, on the wall,
who in this land is fairest of all?"

The mirror answered:

"You, my queen, may have a beauty quite rare,
but Little Snow White is a thousand times more fair."

When the queen heard the mirror speak this way, she became pale with envy, and from that hour onward, she hated Snow White, and when she looked at her and thought that Little Snow White was to blame that she, the queen, was no longer the most beautiful woman in the world, her heart turned against Little Snow White. Her jealousy kept upsetting her, and so she summoned the huntsman and said: "Take the child out into the forest to a spot far from here. Then stab her to death and bring me back her lungs and liver as proof of your deed. After that I'll cook them with salt and eat them."

The huntsman took Little Snow White and led her out into the forest, but when he drew his hunting knife and was about to stab her, she began to weep and pleaded so much to let her live and promised never to return but to run deeper into the forest, the huntsman was moved to pity, also because she was so beautiful. Anyway, he thought the wild beasts in the forest would soon devour her: "I'm glad that I won't have to kill her." Just then a young boar came dashing by, and the huntsman stabbed it to death. He took out the lungs and liver and brought them to the queen as proof that the child was dead. Then she boiled them in salt, ate them, and thought that she had eaten Little Snow White's lungs and liver.

Meanwhile, Little Snow White was so all alone in the huge forest that she became afraid and began to run and run over sharp stones and through thorn bushes. She ran the entire day. Finally, as the sun was about to set, she came upon a little cottage that belonged to seven dwarfs. However, they were not at home but had gone to the mines. When Little Snow White entered, she found everything tiny, but dainty and neat. There was a little table with a white tablecloth, and on it were seven little plates with seven tiny spoons, seven tiny knives and tiny forks, and seven tiny cups. In a row against the wall stood seven little beds recently covered with sheets. Since she was so hungry and thirsty, Little Snow White ate some vegetables and bread from each of the little plates and had a drop of wine to drink out of each of the tiny cups. And since she was so tired, she wanted to lay down and sleep. So she began trying out the beds, but none of them suited her until she found that the seventh one was just right. So she lay down in it and fell asleep.

When it turned night, the seven dwarfs returned home from their work and lit their seven little candles. Then they saw that someone had been in their house.

The first dwarf said: "Who's been sitting in my chair?"

"Who's eaten off my plate?" said the second.

"Who's eaten some of my bread?" said the third.

"Who's eaten some of my vegetables?" said the fourth.

"Who's been using my little fork?" said the fifth.

"Who's been cutting with my little knife?" said the sixth.

"Who's had something to drink from my little cup?" said the seventh.

Then the first dwarf looked around and said, "Who's been sleeping in my bed?"

Then the second cried out, "Someone's been sleeping in my bed!"

And he was followed by each one of them until the seventh dwarf looked at his bed and saw Little Snow White lying there asleep. The others came running over to him, and they were so astounded that they screamed and fetched their seven little candles to observe Little Snow White.

"Oh, my Lord! Oh, my Lord!" they exclaimed. "How beautiful she is!"

They took great delight in her but didn't wake her up. Instead, they let her sleep in the bed, while the seventh dwarf spent an hour in each one of his companions' beds until the night had passed. When Little Snow White awoke, they asked her who she was and how she had managed to come to their cottage. Then she told them how her mother had wanted to have her killed, how the huntsman had spared her life, and how she had run all day until she had eventually arrived at their cottage.

Then the dwarfs took pity on her and said, "If you'll keep house for us, cook, sew make the beds, wash, and knit, and if you'll keep everything neat and orderly, you can stay with us, and we'll provide you with everything you need. When we come home in the evening, dinner must be ready. During the day we're in the mines and dig for gold. You'll be alone and will have to watch out for the queen and not let anyone enter the cottage."

In the meantime, the queen believed that she was once again the most beautiful woman in the land and stepped before her mirror and asked:

"Mirror, mirror, on the wall,
who in this land is fairest of all?"

The mirror answered:

"You, my queen, may have a beauty quite rare,
but beyond the seven mountains, this I must tell,
Little Snow White is living quite well.
Indeed, she's still a thousand times more fair."

When the queen heard this, she was horrified, for she saw that she had been deceived and that the huntsman had not killed Little Snow White. Since nobody but the seven dwarfs lived in the seven mountains region, the queen knew immediately that Little Snow White was dwelling with them and began once again plotting ways to kill her. As long as the mirror refused to say that she was the most beautiful woman in the land, she would remain upset. Since she couldn't be absolutely certain and didn't trust anyone, she disguised herself as an old peddler woman, painted her face so that nobody could recognize her, and went to the cottage of the seven dwarfs, where she knocked at the door and cried out, "Open up! Open up! I'm the old peddler woman. I've got pretty wares for sale!"

Little Snow White looked out of the window: "What do you have for sale?"

"Stay laces, dear child!" the old woman replied and took out a lace woven from yellow, red, and blue silk. "Do you want it?"

"Well, yes," said Little Snow White and thought, "I can certainly let this good old woman inside. She's honest enough."

So Little Snow White unbolted the door and bought the lace.

"My goodness, you're so sloppily laced up!" said the old woman. "Come, I'll lace you up properly for once."

Little Snow White stood in front of the old woman, who took the lace and tied it around Little Snow White so tightly that she lost her breath and fell down as if dead. Then the queen was satisfied and left.

Not long after nightfall the dwarfs came home, and when they saw their dear Snow White lying on the ground, they were horrified, for she seemed to be dead. They lifted her up, and when they saw that she was laced too tightly, they cut the stay lace in two. At once she began to breathe a little, and after a while she had fully revived.

"That was nobody else but the queen," they said. "She wanted to take your life. Be careful, and don't let anyone else enter the cottage."

Now the queen asked her mirror:

"Mirror, mirror, on the wall,
who in this land is fairest of all?"

The mirror answered:

"You, my queen, may have a beauty quite rare,
But Little Snow White's alive, this I must tell,
She's with the dwarfs and doing quite well.
Indeed, she's still a thousand times more fair."

The queen was so horrified that all her blood rushed to her heart when she realized that Little Snow White was alive once again. So she began thinking day and night how she could put an end to Little Snow White. Finally, she made a poisoned comb, disguised herself in a completely different shape, and went off to the dwarfs' cottage once again. When she knocked on the door, however, Little Snow White called out: "I'm not allowed to let anyone enter!"

The queen then took out the comb, and when Little Snow White saw it shine and that the woman was someone entirely different from the one she had previously met, she opened the door and bought the comb.

"Come," said the peddler woman, "I'll also comb your hair."

But no sooner did the old woman stick the comb in Little Snow White's hair than the maiden fell down and was dead.

"Now you'll remain lying there," the queen said, and her heart had become lighter as she returned home.

However, the dwarfs came just in the nick of time. When they saw what had happened, they pulled the poison comb out of Little Snow White's hair, and she opened her eyes and was alive again. She promised the dwarfs that she would certainly not let anyone inside again.

Now the queen stepped in front of her mirror once more and asked:

"Mirror, mirror, on the wall,
who in this land is fairest of all?"

The mirror answered:

"You, my queen, may have a beauty quite rare,
But Little Snow White's alive, this I must tell,
She's with the dwarfs and doing quite well.
Indeed, she's still a thousand times more fair."

When the queen heard this once again, she trembled and shook with rage. "Little Snow White shall die!" she exclaimed. "Even if it costs me my own life!"

Then she went into a secret chamber where no one was allowed to enter. Once inside she made a deadly poisonous apple. On the outside it looked beautiful with red cheeks. Anyone who saw it would be enticed to take a bite. Thereafter, she disguised herself as a peasant woman, went to the dwarfs' cottage, and knocked on the door. Little Snow White looked and said "I'm not allowed to let anyone inside. The seven dwarfs have strictly forbidden me."

"Well, if you don't want to let me in, I can't force you," answered the peasant woman. "I'll surely get rid of my apples in time. But let me give you one to test."

"No," said Little Snow White. "I'm not allowed to take anything. The dwarfs won't let me."

"You're probably afraid," said the old woman. "Look, I'll cut the apple in two. You eat the beautiful red half."

However, the apple had been made with such cunning that only the red part was poisoned. When Little Snow White saw the peasant woman eating her half, and when her desire to taste the apple grew stronger, she finally let the peasant woman give her the other half through the window. As soon as she took a bite of the apple, she fell to the ground and was dead.

The queen rejoiced, went home, and asked the mirror:

"Mirror, mirror, on the wall,
who in this land is the fairest of all?"

And the mirror answered:

"You, my queen, are now the fairest of all."

"Now I can rest in peace," she said. "Once again I'm the most beautiful in the land, and Snow White will remain dead this time."

When the dwarfs came home from the mines that evening, they found Little Snow White lying on the ground, and she was dead. They unlaced her and tried to find something poisonous in her hair, but nothing helped. They couldn't revive her. So they laid her on a bier, and all seven of them sat down beside it and wept and wept for three whole days. Then they intended to bury her, but she looked more alive than dead, and she still had such pretty red cheeks. So, instead they made a glass coffin and placed her inside so that she could easily be seen. Then they wrote her name on the coffin in gold letters and added the family name. One of the dwarfs remained at home every day to keep watch over her.

So Little Snow White lay in the coffin for a long, long time but did not rot. She was still white as snow and red as blood, and if her eyes could have opened, they would have been black as ebony, for she lay there as if she were sleeping.

Now it happened that a prince came to the dwarfs' cottage one day and wanted to spend the night there. When he entered the room and saw Little Snow White lying in the coffin and the seven little candles casting their light right on her, he couldn't get enough of her beauty. Then he read the golden inscription and saw that she was a princess. So he asked the dwarfs to sell him the coffin with the dead Little Snow White inside. But they wouldn't accept all the gold in the world for it. Then he pleaded with them to give Little Snow White to him as a gift because he couldn't live without gazing upon her, and he would honor her and hold her in high regard as his most beloved in the world. Well, the dwarfs took pity on him and gave him the coffin, and the prince had it carried to his castle. It was then placed in his room, where he himself sat the entire day and couldn't take his eyes off her. And when he had to leave the room and couldn't see Little Snow White, he became sad. Indeed, he couldn't eat a thing unless he was standing near the coffin. However, the servants, who had to carry the coffin from place to place in the castle all the time, became angry about this, and at one time a servant opened the coffin, lifted Little Snow White into the air, and said: "Why must we be plagued with so much work all because of a dead maiden?" On saying this he shoved Little Snow White's back with his hand, and out popped the nasty piece of apple that had been stuck in Little Snow White's throat, and she was once again alive. As soon as this happened, she went to the prince, and when he saw his dear Little Snow White alive, he rejoiced so much that he didn't know what to do. Then they sat down at the dinner table and ate with delight.

The wedding was planned for the next day, and Snow White's godless mother was also invited to attend. When she now stepped before the mirror, she said:

"Mirror, mirror, on the wall,
who in this land is the fairest of all?"

And the mirror replied:

"You, my queen, may have a beauty quite rare,
but Little Snow White is a thousand times more fair."

When she heard this, she was horrified and became so afraid, so very afraid that she didn't know what to do. However, her jealousy drove her so much that she wanted to be seen at the wedding. When she arrived, she saw that Little Snow White was the bride. Iron slippers were then heated over a fire. The queen had to put them on and dance in them, and her feet were miserably burned, but she had to keep dancing in them until she danced herself to death.

54
SIMPLE HANS

Once a king lived happily with his daughter, who was his only child. Then, all of a sudden, she gave birth to a baby, and no one knew who the father was. For a long time the king didn't know what to do. At last he ordered the princess to take the child and go to the church. Once there, a lemon was to be placed in the hands of the child, and the boy was to walk about and offer it to a man. As soon as boy stopped and chose a man, they would know that he was child's father, and he would be declared the princess's husband. Everything was arranged accordingly, and the king also gave orders to allow only highborn people into the church.

However, there was a crooked little hunchback living in the city who was not particularly smart and was therefore called Simple Hans. Well, he managed to push his way into the church among the others without being noticed, and when the child offered the lemon, he handed it to Simple Hans. The princess was mortified, and the king was so upset that he had his daughter, the child, and Simple Hans stuck into a barrel, which was cast into the sea. The barrel soon floated off, and when they were alone

at sea, the princess groaned and said, "You nasty, impudent hunchback! You're to blame for my misfortune! Why did you force your way into the church? My child's of no concern to you."

"That's not true," said Simple Hans. "He does concern me because I once made a wish that you would have a child, and whatever I wish comes true."

"Well, if that's the case, wish us something to eat."

"That's easily done," replied Simple Hans, and he wished for a dish full of potatoes. The princess would have liked to have something better. Nevertheless, she was so hungry that she joined him in eating the potatoes. After they had satisfied their hunger, Simple Hans said, "Now I'll wish us a beautiful ship!"

No sooner had he said this than they were sitting on a splendid ship that contained more than enough to fulfill their desires. The helmsman guided the ship straight toward land, and when they went ashore, Simple Hans said, "Now I want a castle over there!"

Suddenly there was a magnificent castle standing there, along with servants dressed in golden uniforms. They led the princess and her child inside, and when they were in the middle of the main hall, Simple Hans said, "Now I wish to be a young and clever prince!"

All at once his hunchback disappeared, and he was handsome, upright, and kind. Indeed, the princess took such a great liking to him that she became his wife.

For a long time they lived happily together, and then one day the old king went out riding, lost his way, and arrived at their castle. He was puzzled because he had never seen it before and decided to enter. The princess recognized her father immediately, but he did not recognize her, for he thought she had drowned in the sea a long time ago. She treated him with a great deal of hospitality, and when he was about to return home, she secretly slipped a golden cup into his pocket. After he had ridden off, she sent a pair of knights after him. They were ordered to stop him and search him to see if he had stolen the golden cup. When they found it in his pocket, they brought him back. He swore to the princess that he hadn't stolen it and didn't know how it had gotten into his pocket.

"That's why," she said, "one must beware of rushing to judgment." And she revealed to him that she was his daughter. The king rejoiced, and they all lived happily together, and after the king's death, Simple Hans became king.

55

RUMPELSTILTSKIN

Once upon a time there was a miller who was poor, but he had a beautiful daughter. Now, one day he happened to talk to the king and said, "I have a daughter who knows the art of transforming straw into gold."

So the king had the miller's daughter summoned to him right away and ordered her to spin all the straw in a room into gold in one night, and if she couldn't do this, she would die. Then she was locked in the room where she sat and wept. For the life of her, she didn't have the slightest inkling of how to spin straw into gold. All of a sudden a little man entered the room and said, "What will you give me if I spin everything into gold?"

She took off her necklace and gave it to the little man, and he did what he promised. The next morning the king found the entire room filled with gold, but because of this, his heart grew even greedier, and he locked the miller's daughter in another room full of straw that was even larger than the first, and she was to spin it all into gold. Then the little man came again, and she gave him a ring from one of her fingers, and everything was spun into gold.

However, on the third night the king had her locked again in another room that was larger than the other two and filled with straw.

"If you succeed, you shall become my wife," he said.

Then the little man came again and spoke: "I'll do everything for you one more time, but you must promise me your firstborn child that you have with the king."

Out of desperation she promised him what he wanted, and when the king saw once again how the straw had been spun into gold, he took the miller's beautiful daughter for his wife.

Soon thereafter the queen gave birth, and the little man appeared before her and demanded the promised child. However, the queen offered the little man all that she could and all the treasures of the kingdom if he would let her keep her child, but it was all in vain. Then the little man said, "In three days I'll come again to fetch the child. But if you know my name by then, you shall keep your child."

During the first and second nights the queen tried to think of the little man's name, but she wasn't able to come up with a name and became completely depressed. On the third day, however, the king returned home from hunting and told her, "I was out hunting the day before yesterday, and when I went deep into the dark forest, I came upon a small cottage, and in front of the house there was a ridiculous little man, hopping around as if he had only one leg and screeching:

"Today I'll brew, tomorrow I'll bake.
Soon I'll have the queen's namesake.
Oh, how hard it is to play my game,
for Rumpelstiltskin is my name!"

When the queen heard this, she rejoiced, and when the dangerous little man came, he asked, "What's my name, your Highness?" she responded first by guessing,

"Is your name Conrad?"

"No."

"Is your name Henry?"

"No."

"Is your name Rumpelstiltskin?"

"The devil told you that!" the little man screamed, and he ran off full of anger and never returned.

56
SWEETHEART ROLAND

Once upon a time there was a mother who had one daughter of her own and hated her stepdaughter because she was a thousand times more beautiful and better than her own. One time the stepdaughter wore a beautiful apron that the other daughter liked and coveted so much out of envy that she told her mother she wanted the apron and insisted that she get it for her.

"Be quiet, my dear child," said the mother. "You shall have it soon. Your stepsister has long since deserved to die, and tonight, I want you to get into the rear of the bed and push her toward the front. Then I'll come when she's asleep and chop off her head."

But the stepdaughter had been standing in a corner and had overheard everything. So she let the wicked daughter climb into bed first so she could lie down on the far side. But after she fell asleep, the other beautiful sister pushed her toward the front and took her place in the rear of the bed. During the night the old woman crept into the room. She felt around to see if someone was actually lying up front. Then she gripped an axe with both hands and began chopping until she chopped off her own child's head.

After she had left the room, the maiden stood up and went to her sweetheart, whose name was Roland, and knocked at his door.

"Listen!" she cried out. "We must flee in haste. My stepmother killed her own daughter and thinks she actually killed me. When the sun rises and she sees what she's done, I'll be lost. So I've taken her magic wand to help ourselves along the way."

Sweetheart Roland stood up, and before they left, they went first to take the dead head of the stepsister and let three drops of blood drip from it onto the floor, one in front of the bed, one in the kitchen, and one on the stairs. Then they ran off.

The next morning, when the mother got up, she called her daughter: "Come, you'll get the apron now."

But the daughter didn't come.

"Where are you?"

"Here I am! On the stairs sweeping," answered one of the drops of blood.

The old woman went out but saw no one.

"Where are you?"

"Here I am! In the kitchen warming myself," the second drop of blood replied.

The old woman went into the kitchen, but she found no one there.

"Where are you?"

"Here I am! In bed sleeping."

The old woman ran into the room, where she saw her own daughter on her bed swimming in blood. She was horrified and realized that she had been deceived. All at once she burst into anger and rushed to the window. Since she was a witch, she could see quite far into the world, and she spotted her stepdaughter fleeing with her sweetheart. They were already far away. So she put on her seven-league boots, and it didn't take her long before she had overtaken them. However, the maiden knew through the magic wand that they were being followed and turned herself into a lake and her sweetheart Roland into a duck that swam on it. When the stepmother arrived, she sat down on the bank of the lake and threw bread crumbs to lure the duck to shore. But it was all in vain, and by nightfall the old woman had to return home without having accomplished anything.

Meanwhile, the maiden and her sweetheart regained their natural forms and continued on their way. At daybreak, however, the witch pursued them once more. Then the maiden changed herself into a beautiful flower growing in the middle of a briar hedge, and her sweetheart was transformed into a fiddler. When the old woman arrived, she asked the fiddler whether she could pluck the beautiful flower.

"Of course," he answered, "and I'll play a tune while you're doing it."

So she crawled into the hedge to pluck it, and as she reached the middle of the hedge, he began to play a tune, and she was compelled to dance and dance without stopping so that the thorns tore the clothes from her body and scratched her so badly that blood flowed, and she died from the wounds.

Now they were both free, and Roland said to the maiden: "I want to go to my father and arrange for the wedding."

"In the meantime I'll turn myself into a red stone and stay here and wait until you come back."

Roland departed, and the maiden stood in the field as a red stone and waited for her sweetheart a long time, but he didn't return and had forgotten her. When he failed to come back, she grew sad, turned herself into a flower, and thought, "Someone will surely come along and trample me."

But a shepherd found the flower, and since it was so beautiful, he took it with him and tucked it away in a chest. From that time on, amazing things began to happen in the shepherd's cottage. When he got up in the morning, all the work would already be done: the sweeping, dusting, a fire in the hearth. At noon when he came home, the food was cooked, and the table set, the meal served. He couldn't figure out how all this was happening, for he never saw a living soul in his cottage. Though it pleased him very much, he eventually became frightened and went to a wise woman for advice.

She told him that there was magic behind all this, and he should get up very early some morning and watch for anything that moved in the room. Then, if he saw something, he was to quickly throw a white cloth over it. The shepherd did as she told him, and on the following morning, he saw the chest open and the flower come out. Immediately he threw the white cloth over the flower, and suddenly the transformation came to an end and the beautiful maiden, whom her sweetheart Roland had forgotten, stood before him. The shepherd wanted to marry her, but she said, no, because she only wanted to serve him and clean his house. Soon thereafter she heard that Roland was about to hold a wedding and marry another maiden. It was customary at this event for every person who attended it to sing. So the faithful maiden also went, but she didn't want to sing until at last she was compelled to do so. As she began to sing, Roland recognized her right away, jumped up, and said that she was his true bride, and he didn't want anyone else but her. So he married her, and her sorrows came to an end while her joy began to thrive.

57

THE GOLDEN BIRD

A certain king had a pleasure garden, and in this garden there was a tree that bore golden apples. Soon after the apples became ripe, one was found missing the very first night. The king became furious and ordered his gardener to keep watch under the tree every night. So the gardener commanded his eldest son to guard the tree, but he fell asleep at midnight, and the next night another apple was missing. So the gardener had his second son stand guard the following night, but he, too, fell asleep at midnight, and in the morning yet another apple was missing. Now the third son wanted to stand guard, but the gardener wasn't satisfied at first. Finally, he relented, and the third son lay down under the tree and watched and watched, and when the clock struck midnight, the air was filled with noise, and a bird came flying. It was made entirely out of gold, and just as it was about to peck off an apple with its beak, the gardener's son stood up and hurriedly shot an arrow at the bird. However, the arrow didn't harm the bird other than costing it a feather as it quickly flew away. The next morning the golden feather was brought to the king, who immediately assembled his councilors, and everyone declared unanimously that a feather like this was worth more than the entire kingdom.

"One feather alone won't help me," said the king. "I want and must have the entire bird."

So the king's eldest son set out and was certain he'd find the golden bird. After he had gone a short distance, he came to a forest, and on the edge of the forest sat a fox. So the prince grabbed his rifle and took aim. But the fox started speaking: "Don't shoot! I'll give you some good advice if you hold your fire. I already know where you want to go. You want to catch the golden bird. This evening you'll come to a village where you'll see two inns facing each other. One will be brightly lit, with a great deal of merrymaking inside. Don't go into that place. Instead, go into the other inn, even though it looks dismal."

But the son thought, "How can an animal give me sensible advice?" and he took his rifle and pulled the trigger. However, his shot missed the fox, who stretched out his tail and dashed quickly into the forest. Then the eldest son continued his journey, and by evening he arrived at the village where the two inns were standing. In one of them there was singing and dancing, while the other appeared rather dismal and shabby. "I'd certainly be a fool," he thought, "if I were to stay at that dismal-looking inn instead of staying at this beautiful one here." So he went into the cheerful inn, lived to the hilt like a king, and forgot the bird and his home.

After some time had passed and the eldest son still hadn't returned home, the second son set out, and he, too, encountered the fox and received good advice, but when he came to the two inns, he saw his brother at the window of the inn in which there were sounds of carousing. When his brother called out to him, he couldn't resist and wiled his time away in good cheer.

Some more months passed by, and now the youngest son also wanted to set out into the world, but his father refused to let him go. The king was most fond of him and was afraid that he would have a mishap and wouldn't return. However, his son wouldn't leave him in peace so that the king finally permitted his son to depart. At the edge of the forest, he, too, encountered the fox, who gave him the good advice. Since the young prince was good-natured and didn't attempt to harm the animal's life, the fox said: "Climb on my tail, and you'll get there more quickly."

No sooner did the prince sit down on the fox's tail than the fox began to run. And the fox went over sticks and stones so swiftly that the wind whistled through the prince's hair. When they came to the village, the prince got off the tail, followed the fox's good advice, and, without looking around, entered the shabbier inn and spent a quiet night there. The next morning he found the fox on his way once again, and the fox said to him: "If you go straight ahead, you'll eventually come to a castle. In front of this castle there's a whole regiment of soldiers lying on the ground, but don't worry about them, for they'll all be snoring and sleeping. Enter the castle and proceed until you come to a chamber where the golden bird is hanging in a wooden cage. Nearby you'll also find a magnificent golden cage hanging just for decoration. But be careful not to take the bird out of its shabby cage and put it into the good one. Otherwise, you'll be in for trouble."

Upon saying these words, the fox stretched out his tail again, and the prince sat down on it. The fox raced over sticks and stones so swiftly that the wind whistled through the prince's hair. When the young man arrived in front of the castle, everything was as the fox said it would be. He entered the last room, saw the golden bird sitting in its wooden cage and also a golden cage beside it. The three golden apples were lying about the room as well. The prince thought it would be ridiculous to leave the beautiful bird in the plain, ugly cage. So he opened the door, grabbed hold of the bird, and put it into the golden cage. As soon as that happened, the bird uttered a dreadful cry that caused the soldiers to wake up, and soon they took the prince prisoner and led him to the king.

The next morning he was brought before the court, and after he confessed to everything, he was sentenced to death. However, the king said he would spare his life under one condition: the prince had to bring him the golden horse that ran faster than the wind. If he did, he would receive the golden bird as his reward.

The prince set out, but he was depressed and sighed. All of a sudden, however, the fox stood in front of him again and said: "You see, all this happened because you didn't listen to me. However, if you listen to me, I'll give you advice once again, this time how to get the golden horse. First, you must go straight ahead until you come to a castle where the horse is standing in the stable. There will be stable boys lying on the ground out front, but they'll be snoring and sleeping, and you'll be able to lead the golden horse out of its stall with ease. But make sure you put the poor wooden and leather saddle on the horse and not the golden one that's hanging nearby."

Then the youngest son sat down on the fox's tail, and the fox raced over sticks and stones so swiftly that the wind whistled through the prince's hair. Shortly after, everything happened as the fox said it would. The grooms snored and were holding golden saddles in their hands. When he saw the golden horse, he felt sorry for it and thought it would be a shame to put the poor saddle on it. So he decided to give the horse the one that he deserved. Yet, just as he was about to take a good saddle from one of the stable boys, the groom woke up, as did the others. Again he was captured and thrown into prison. The next morning he was sentenced to death again. However, his life would be spared and he would be granted the golden horse and the bird as well if he fetched the marvelously beautiful princess.

So the son sadly set out on his way, and soon the old fox was standing there again.

"Why didn't you listen to me? You'd have the bird and the horse by now. Nevertheless, I'll give you advice one more time. Now go straight out, and toward evening you'll come to a castle. At midnight the princess will go to the bathhouse to bathe herself. You're to go inside and give her a kiss. By doing this you'll be able to take her with you. But don't allow her to take leave of her parents."

The fox stretched out his tail and raced over sticks and stones so swiftly that the wind whistled through the prince's hair. When he arrived at the golden castle, it was just as the fox had said it would be. At night he gave the princess a kiss in the bathhouse, and she was ready to go with him, but she implored him with tears to let her say farewell to her parents. At first he refused, but when she kept on weeping and fell at his feet, he finally gave in. But no sooner did the princess approach her father than he and everyone else in the castle woke up, and the young man was taken prisoner.

The next morning the king said to him: "You may have my daughter only if you remove the mountain that's lying in front of my window and blocking my view. You have one week to perform this task."

This mountain, however, was so huge, so very huge, that it would have taken all the people in the world to carry it away. And after he had worked for seven whole days and saw how little he had accomplished, he became very worried. However, on the evening of the seventh day, the fox appeared and said, "Go lie down and get some sleep. I'll do the job for you."

The next morning, when the young man awoke, the mountain had vanished. So he went cheerfully to the king and told him that the mountain had been removed, and he was now to give him his daughter. So the king had to do this, and the two of them now set out together.

However, the fox came and said: "Now we must have all three—the princess, the horse, and the bird."

"Yes," said the young man. "If you can do all this, but it will be difficult for you."

"If you only listen, things will work out." the fox replied. "Now when you come to the king, who demanded the marvelously beautiful princess, tell him, 'Here she is.' There will be enormous rejoicing. So mount the golden horse that they must give you and shake hands with everyone and say good-bye. Make sure that the beautiful maiden is the last person, and when you have clasped her hand, swing her up to you in one motion and gallop away."

Everything went as planned, and the fox spoke once more to the young man: "Now, as you approach the castle where the golden bird's being kept, I'll remain with the princess before the gate. Then ride into the castle courtyard. They'll see that the golden horse is the right one, and so they'll carry out the golden bird. You remain sitting and tell them you want to see if the bird is the right one. As soon as you have the cage in your hand, you race away."

Everything went well, and as soon as he had the bird, the princess got on the horse again, and they continued to ride through the vast forest. Then the fox came and said he wanted the young man to shoot him dead and cut off his head and paws. However, the young man absolutely refused.

"Well then," said the fox, "at least I'll give you one last piece of advice. Beware of two things: don't buy flesh that's bound for the gallows, and don't sit on the edge of a well."

"That's not so difficult, if that's all there's to it."

So now the young man continued his journey with the beautiful maiden until he finally came to the village where his two brothers had remained. All at once there was a great commotion and uproar. So he asked what was going on and was told that two men were about to be hanged. When he came closer to the scene, he saw that the men were his brothers, who had committed all sorts of terrible acts and had squandered all their possessions.

"Can't they be pardoned in any way?" the young man asked.

"No, unless you're willing to spend your money for these crooks and buy their freedom."

The prince didn't think twice about it and paid what they demanded. His brothers were set free, and he continued the journey in their company.

When they came to the forest where they had first met the fox, it was cool and lovely there, and the two brothers said, "Let's go over to the well and rest awhile. We could also eat and drink."

The young prince said yes, and during their conversation he forgot the fox's warning and sat down on the edge of the well, not suspecting any evildoing. But the two brothers pushed him backward down into the well, took the maiden, the horse, and the bird, and went home to the king.

"We've managed to capture all this, and we've brought you everything."

There was great rejoicing, but the horse refused to eat, the bird didn't sing, and the maiden sat and wept.

Meanwhile, the youngest brother lay down in the well that fortunately was dry, and even though he hadn't broken any of his arms or legs, he couldn't find his way out. Meanwhile the old fox came once again and scolded him for not listening because otherwise this would not have happened. "Nevertheless, I can't help myself and must help you out. Grab my tail and hold on tightly."

Then the fox pulled him up to the top. When they were above, the fox said: "Your brothers have posted guards who are to kill you if you cross the border."

So the prince put on the clothes of a poor man and succeeded in reaching the king's court without being recognized. No sooner was he there than the bird began to sing, the horse began to eat, and the princess stopped weeping. Then the prince appeared before the king and revealed his brothers' crime and how everything had happened. So the brothers were seized and executed, and he received the princess. Later, after his father's death, he became king as well.

Many years later the prince went walking through the forest again and encountered the old fox, who implored him desperately to shoot him dead and cut off his head and paws. This time the prince did it, and no sooner was it done than the fox turned into none other than the brother of the beautiful princess and was finally released from a magic spell.

58

LOYAL GODFATHER SPARROW

Once upon a time there was a deer about to give birth, and she asked the fox to be the godfather. However, the fox invited the sparrow to be godfather as well, and the sparrow also wanted to invite his special good friend the house dog to be godfather. However, the dog's master had tied him up with a rope because the dog had returned home very drunk from a wedding. The sparrow thought that this was not a problem and pecked

and pecked at the rope one thread after the other as long as it took for the dog to be released. Now they went together to the godfathers' banquet and enjoyed themselves very much, because there was plenty to eat and drink there. The dog, however, didn't pay attention and drank too much wine again. When they stood up, his head was so heavy that he could barely stand on his four legs. Nevertheless, he staggered part of the way toward home. Finally, however, he fell over and remained lying in the middle of the road. Just then a carter came and wanted to drive over him with his cart.

"Carter, don't do that," the sparrow cried out, "or you'll pay for it with your life!"

However, the carter didn't listen to him. Instead, he whipped the horses and drove the horses right over the dog so that the wheels broke the dog's bones. The fox and the sparrow dragged the godfather home, and when dog's master saw him, he said: "He's dead," and gave him to the carter to bury.

Now, the carter thought that the dog's skin was still useful. So he loaded the dog onto his cart and drove away. However, the sparrow flew nearby and yelled out: "Carter, you'll pay for this with your life! Carter, you'll pay for this with your life!"

The carter was angry at the little bird because he thought he was being taken for a fool. So he grabbed his axe and tried to hit the sparrow, who flew higher into the air. Instead of hitting the sparrow, the carter hit his horse's head so that the horse fell down dead. The carter had to leave it lying there and drive on with the other two horses. Then the sparrow returned and sat down on the head of another horse.

"Carter, you'll pay for this with your life!"

The carter ran toward the bird and yelled: "I've got you!" but as he tried to hit the sparrow, he struck his horse on the head so that it fell over dead. Now there was only one horse left. The sparrow didn't wait long and sat down on the head of the third horse and cried out: "Carter, you'll pay for this with your life!"

But the carter was now so furious that he didn't think about what he was doing and just swung his axe randomly. Now all his three horses had been beaten to death, and he had to leave the cart standing there. Angry and vitriolic he went home and sat down behind the oven. But the sparrow had flown after him, sat down in front of the window, and cried out: "Carter, you'll pay for this with your life!"

The carter grabbed his axe and smashed the window, but he didn't hit the sparrow. Now the bird hopped inside the house, sat down on top of the oven, and cried out: "Carter, you'll pay for this with your life!"

Crazy and blind with rage he chopped the entire oven to pieces, and as the sparrow flew from one place to another, the carter smashed all the household utensils, mirrors, chairs, benches, table, and the walls of the house. Finally, he grabbed hold of the sparrow and said: "Now I've got you!" He stuck the bird into his mouth and swallowed it whole. However, when the sparrow was in the carter's body, it began to flap its wings, and it fluttered up to the carter's mouth, stuck its head outside, and cried out: "Carter, you'll pay for this with your life!"

Well now the carter gave the axe to his wife and commanded; "Wife, strike the bird in my mouth and kill it!"

But the wife missed her mark, and instead she struck her husband in the head so that he immediately fell down the ground dead, while the sparrow flew out and away.

59
PRINCE SWAN

There was once a maiden all alone in the middle of a large forest. Suddenly, a swan came flying up to her. It had a ball of yarn and said: "I'm not a swan. I'm an enchanted prince, and if you unravel the yarn to which I'm attached, then I'll be released from a spell. But take care that you don't break it in two. Otherwise, I won't be able to return to my kingdom and won't be saved. If you unravel the yarn, you'll become my bride."

The maiden took the yarn, and the swan climbed into the sky. The maiden unraveled the yarn easily, and she unraveled and unraveled the entire day so that the end of the yarn could already be seen. However, just then it unfortunately became caught on a thorn bush and broke in two. The maiden was very distressed and wept. Since it was turning night, and the wind was blowing so loudly in the forest, she became afraid and began to run as fast as she could. And as she was running, she saw a small light and rushed toward it. There she found a house and knocked on the door. A little old woman came out and was astounded to see a maiden standing before her door.

"Oh, my child," she said. "Where are you coming from so late in the night?"

"Please, may I have a place to sleep for the night and also some food?" she asked. "I've lost my way in the forest."

"This is a difficult situation," the old woman replied. "I'd gladly give you what you want, but my husband is a cannibal. If he finds you, he'll eat you. There's no mercy. But if you remain outside, the wild animals will eat you. So I'll see if I can help you get through this."

The old woman let her enter, gave her some food to eat, and then hid her beneath the bed. The cannibal always came home before midnight right after the sun had fully set and left right before sunrise. So it wasn't long before he entered and said: "I smell, I smell human flesh!" And he searched around the room until he reached under the bed and dragged the maiden out. "Now this will make for a good snack!"

But the old woman pleaded and pleaded for the maiden's life until he promised to let her live overnight and to eat her for his breakfast. However, the old woman woke the maiden before sunrise.

"Hurry, and get away before my husband awakes. Here's a golden spinning wheel for you as a gift you're to cherish. My name is *Sun*."

The maiden went away and in the evening she came to another house, and the same thing happened there that happened the previous night. At her departure the second old woman gave her a golden spindle and said: "My name is *Moon*."

On the third evening she came to a third house, where the old woman gave her a golden reel and said: "My name is *Star*."

And she also informed her that even though the yarn hadn't been completely unraveled, enough had been unraveled so that Prince Swan had been able to reach his kingdom where he was the king. In fact, he was already married and lived in great splendor on the glass mountain. Then she said: "You'll reach the mountain this evening, but a dragon and a lion are lying in front and are protecting it. That's why you must take this bread and bacon to pacify them."

And everything happened just as she said. The maiden threw the bread and bacon into the jaws of the monsters, and they let her pass. When she came to the castle gate, however, the guards wouldn't let her enter. So she sat down in front of the gate and began to spin on her little golden wheel. The queen peered down from above and was pleased by the beautiful little wheel. So she went down and asked if she could have it. The maiden told her that she could have it if she could spend the night next to the king's bedroom. The queen agreed, and the maiden was led upstairs to a room. Now everything that was spoken in this room could be heard in the king's bedroom. So when it was night and the king was in his bed, the maiden sang:

> "Doesn't King Swan still think of me?
> His faithful Julianne, his bride to be?
> She's come from afar where she's seen all three,
> Sun, moon, and star, and faced two beasts.
> Won't King Swan now wake up at least?"

But the king didn't hear her because the cunning queen had been afraid of the maiden and had given the king a sleeping potion. So he slept soundly and didn't hear the maiden and all that she had revealed. In the morning, all her efforts had been lost, and the maiden had to return to the gate and sit down and spin with her second spindle, which also pleased the queen. So the maiden gave it to her with the same condition that she would be allowed to spend the night next to the king's bedroom, where she once again sang:

> "Doesn't King Swan still think of me?
> His faithful Julianne, his bride to be?
> She's come from afar where she's seen all three,
> Sun, moon, and star, and faced two beasts.
> Won't King Swan now wake up at least?"

But the king slept soundly due to the sleeping potion, and so the maiden lost her spindle. On the third morning she sat down with her golden reel and kept winding it. The queen wanted this precious object as well and promised the maiden that she could spend another night next to the king's bedroom. However, the maiden had discovered the queen's deception and asked the king's servant to give the king something else to drink that evening. Then she began to sing again:

"Doesn't King Swan still think of me?
His faithful Julianne, his bride to be?
She's come from afar where she's seen all three,
Sun, moon, and star, and faced two beasts.
Won't King Swan now wake up at least?"

Well, the king awoke when he heard her voice, and he recognized her and asked the queen: "If someone loses a key and then finds it again, which key does one keep, the old or the new?"

The queen replied: "Certainly, the old one."

"Well then," he said, "you can no longer be my wife. I've found my first bride again."

The next morning the queen had to return to her father's realm, and the king married his true bride, and they lived happily together until they died.

60

THE GOLDEN EGG

Once upon a time there were a couple of poor broom-makers, and they had a little sister to support. They had just barely enough to lead a miserable life. Every day they had to go into the forest to search for brushwood, and later after they had bound the brooms, the little sister sold them.

One time they went into the forest, and the youngest brother climbed a birch tree and wanted to chop off the branches. All of a sudden he found a nest, and a dark-colored little bird was sitting in it. He could see something glittering between its feathers, and since the little bird didn't fly away and was also not shy, he lifted the bird's wing and found a golden egg. So he took it and climbed down the tree. They were delighted by their discovery and brought it to the goldsmith, who told them that it was genuine gold and gave them money for it.

The next morning they went into the forest again and found another golden egg. The little bird was patient and let them take it just like the first time. All this continued for a long time. Every morning they fetched a golden egg and were soon rich. However, one morning the bird said: "From now on I'm not going to lay any more eggs, but bring me to the goldsmith, and you'll all be fortunate."

The broom-makers did what she said and brought the bird to the goldsmith. When it was alone with him, the bird sang:

"Whoever eats my heart
will soon be king and very smart.
Whoever eats my liver, whether young or old.
Will find each morning a bag full of gold."

When the goldsmith heard that, he called for the two young broom-makers and said: "Let me have the bird, and I'll marry your little sister."

The two young men said yes, and the wedding was soon held. Then the goldsmith said: "For my wedding day I want to eat the bird. So you two roast the bird on a stake and be careful that you don't ruin it. Then bring it to me when it's done."

The goldsmith intended to take out the heart and liver and eat them. The two brothers stood at the fire and turned the spit, and when they kept turning it and the bird was almost done roasting, a little piece fell out.

"Hey," said one of the brothers, "I've got to try that!" and he ate it up. Soon thereafter another little piece fell out.

"That's for me," said the other brother, and he tasted it. They had eaten the little heart and the little liver, and they had no idea how blessed they were by all this.

When the bird had been completely roasted, they carried it to the wedding table. The goldsmith sliced it open and wanted to eat the heart and liver as quickly as possible, but they had both vanished. All at once he became dreadfully angry and screamed: "Who ate the bird's heart and liver?"

The two broom-makers replied: "That must have been us. Two small pieces fell out as we were turning the spit. So we ate them."

"Well, if you've eaten the heart and liver, then you can keep your sister!" And in his rage he chased them all away.—

[*Fragment.*]

61

THE TAILOR WHO SOON BECAME RICH

Once, during the winter, a poor tailor crossed over the field to visit his brother. Along the way he found a frozen thrush. "Whatever's bigger than a louse," the tailor said to himself, "that's what the tailor carries into his house!" So he picked up the thrush and stuck it into his coat. When he reached his brother's house, he decided to look first through the window to see if they were home. All at once he saw a fat parson sitting near his sister-in-law at the table. There was a roast and a bottle of wine sitting on the table. Meanwhile, the tailor's brother was about to return home. He knocked at the door and wanted to enter. From the outside the tailor saw how the woman quickly hid the parson in a crate, stuck the roast into the oven, and shoved the wine into the bed. Now since his brother had entered, the tailor didn't wait any longer. He went into the house and greeted his sister-in-law and his brother. Then he sat down on the crate in which the parson was hiding.

"Wife, I'm hungry. Do you have anything to eat?" the husband asked.

"No, I'm sorry. There's nothing at all in the house today."

But the tailor pulled out his frozen thrush, and the brother cried out, "My! What are you doing with that frozen thrush?"

"Hey! Don't you know that this thrush is worth a lot of money! It can tell your future and your fortune!"

"Well, then let it tell our future and our fortune."

The tailor placed it next to his ear and said: "The thrush told me that there's a dish full of roast meat in the oven."

The husband went to the oven and found the roast meat.

"What else did the thrush say to you?"

"There's a bottle of wine in the bed."

"My! I'd like to have this thrush. Sell it to me."

"You can have it if you give me this crate that I'm sitting on."

The brother wanted to give it to him right away, but his wife said, "No, I'm against it. I'm much too fond of this crate. I'm not going to give it away."

However, her husband said: "What? Are you, dumb or something? What use is this old crate to you?"

So the husband gave his brother the crate for the bird, and the tailor took the crate on a wheelbarrow and began walking on the road. Along the way he said: "I'm going to take the crate and throw it into the water! I'm going to take the crate and throw it into the water!" Finally, the parson began moving inside and said: "You know what's in the crate. Let me out, and I'll give you 50 gold coins."

"All right, I'll do it for that amount."

So he let him out and went home with the money. The people were puzzled as to where he had earned so much money, and he said, "Let me tell you. The skins of animals have become very expensive. So I slaughtered my old cow and received a good deal of money in return."

Since the villagers also wanted to profit from this, they went out and cut the throats of all their oxen, cows, and sheep and carried their fur and skins to the city, where, however, they received precious little money for them because there had suddenly been so many skins and fur for sale. Well, the farmers became infuriated about their loss and threw dirt and some other rubbish at the tailor's door. However, he put everything into his crate, went to a tavern in the city, and asked the tavern keeper whether he might store the crate at his place for a while because it contained many valuable things and the crate wasn't safe at his home. The tavern keeper said he'd gladly do it and let the tailor store the crate at the tavern.

Some time later the tailor returned and asked for his crate, and when he opened it to see whether everything was in it, he saw that it was full of dirt. So he threw a violent fit, cursed the tavern keeper, and threatened to take him to court. In response the tavern keeper, who was concerned about his reputation and was afraid about his credit rating, willingly gave him 100 gold coins. The farmers were once again furious that everything that caused problems for the tailor he managed to turn into profit. So they took the crate and forced him inside. Then they threw the crate into the river and let it float off. The tailor kept quiet for a while until he came to an edge of land that stuck out in the river. Then he cried out very loudly: "No, I'm not going to do it! I won't do it! Even if the whole world wants it to be done!"

A shepherd heard his shouting and asked: "What is it that you don't want to do?"

"Oh," responded the tailor, "there's a king who has a foolish whim and insists that whoever's able to swim down the river in this crate is to marry his only daughter, but I've made up my mind not to do it even if the entire world wants it."

"Listen, is it possible that someone else can replace you in the crate and can get the princess?"

"Oh, yes, that's also possible."

"Then I'll replace you."

So the tailor stepped out of the crate, and the shepherd got in. The tailor closed the crate, and soon after the shepherd went down under in the crate. Meanwhile, the tailor took the shepherd's entire herd of sheep and drove them home.

The farmers wondered how he happened to return. Moreover, they were puzzled that he now had so many sheep. So the tailor explained to them: "I had sunk into the water, deep, deep down! When I got to the bottom, I found this entire herd and took the sheep back up with me."

The farmers wanted to fetch some sheep as well, and they all went together to the river. The sky was completely blue on this day with small white clouds, and consequently, when they looked into the water, they cried out: "We already see the lambs at the bottom!"

"I want to be the first one under," the mayor said. "I'll look around, and if everything's all right, I'll call you."

As he dove into the river, the water rustled and murmured—*plump!* The others thought that he was calling out to them to "Jump!" So they all jumped in one after another. In the end the entire village belonged to the tailor.

BLUEBEARD

There was once a man who lived in a forest with his three sons and beautiful daughter. One day a golden coach drawn by six horses and attended by several servants came driving up to his house. After the coach stopped a king stepped out and asked him if he could have his daughter for his wife. The man was happy that his daughter would benefit from such a stroke of good fortune and immediately said yes. There was nothing objectionable about the suitor except for his beard, which was totally blue and made one shudder somewhat whenever one looked at it. At first the maiden also felt frightened by it and resisted marrying him. But her father kept urging her, and finally she consented. However, her fear was so great that she first went to her brothers, took them aside, and said, "Dear brothers, if you hear me scream, leave everything standing or lying wherever you are, and come to my aid."

The brothers kissed her and promised to do this. "Farewell, dear sister. If we hear your voice, we'll jump on our horses and soon be at your side."

Then she got into the coach, sat down next to Bluebeard, and drove away with him. When she reached his castle, she found everything splendid, and whatever the queen desired was fulfilled. They would have been very happy together if she had only been able to have accustomed herself to the king's blue beard. However, whenever she saw it, she felt frightened.

After some time had passed, he said to her, "I must go on a long journey. Here are the keys to the entire castle. You can open all the rooms and look at everything. But I forbid you to open one particular room, which this little golden key can unlock. If you open it, you will pay for it with your life."

She took the key and promised to obey him. Once he had departed, she opened one door after another and saw so many treasures and magnificent things that she thought they must have been gathered from all over the world. Soon nothing was left but the forbidden room. Since the key was made of gold, she believed that the most precious things were probably kept there. Her curiosity began to gnaw at her, and she certainly would have passed over all the other rooms if she could have only seen what was in this one. At last her desire became so great that she took the key and went to the room. "Who can possibly see when I open it?" she said to herself. "I'll just glance inside." Then she unlocked the room, and when the door opened, a stream of blood flowed toward her, and she saw dead women hanging along all the walls, some only skeletons. Her horror was so tremendous that she immediately slammed the door, but the key popped out of the lock and fell into the blood. Swiftly she picked it up and tried to wipe away the blood, but to no avail. When she wiped the blood away on one side, it appeared on the other. She sat down, rubbed the key throughout the day, and tried everything possible, but nothing helped: the bloodstains could not be erased. Finally, in the evening she stuck it into some hay, which was supposed to be able to absorb blood.

The following day Bluebeard came back, and the first thing he requested was the bunch of keys. Her heart pounded as she brought the keys, and she hoped that he wouldn't notice that the golden one was missing. However, he counted all of them, and when he was finished, he said, "Where's the key to the secret room?"

As he said this, he looked straight into her eyes, causing her to blush red as blood.

"It's upstairs," she answered. "I misplaced it. Tomorrow I'll go and look for it."

"You'd better go now, dear wife. I need it today."

"Oh, I might as well tell you. I lost it in the hay. I'll have to go and search for it first."

"You haven't lost it," Bluebeard said angrily. "You stuck it there so the hay would absorb the bloodstains. It's clear that you've disobeyed my command and entered the room. Now, you'll enter the room whether you want to or not."

Then he ordered her to fetch the key, which was still stained with blood.

"Now, prepare yourself for your death. You shall die today," Bluebeard declared. He fetched his big knife and took her to the threshold of the house.

"Just let me say my prayers before I die," she said.

"All right. Go ahead, but you'd better hurry. I don't have much time to waste."

She ran upstairs and cried out of the window as loud as she could, "Brothers, my dear brothers! Come help me!"

The brothers were sitting in the forest and drinking some cool wine. The youngest said, "I think I heard our sister's voice. Let's go! We must hurry and help her!"

They jumped on their horses and rode like thunder and lightning. Meanwhile, their sister was on her knees, praying in fear.

"Well, are you almost done?" Bluebeard called from below, and she heard him sharpening his knife on the bottom step. She looked out the window but could only see a cloud of dust as if a herd were coming. So she screamed once again, "Brothers, my dear brothers! Come help me!"

And her fear became greater and greater when Bluebeard called, "If you don't come down soon, I'll be up to get you. My knife's been sharpened!'

She looked out the window again and saw her three brothers riding across the field as though they were birds flying through the air. For the third time she screamed desperately and with all her might, "Brothers, my dear brothers! Come help me!"

The youngest brother was already so near that she could hear his voice. "Calm yourself. Another moment, dear sister, and we'll be at your side!"

But Bluebeard cried out, "That's enough praying! I'm not going to wait any longer. If you don't come, I'm going to fetch you."

"Oh, just let me pray for my three dear brothers!"

However, he wouldn't listen to her. Instead, he went upstairs and dragged her down. Then he grabbed her by the hair and was about to plunge the knife into her heart when the three brothers knocked at the door, charged inside, and tore their sister out of his hands. They then drew out their sabers and cut him down. Afterward he was hung up in the bloody chamber next to the women he had killed. Later, the brothers took their dear sister home with them, and all of Bluebeard's treasures belonged to her.

63

THE GOLDEN CHILDREN

Once upon a time there lived a poor man and a poor woman who had nothing but a little hut. The husband was a fisherman, and one day, as he was sitting by the water's edge and had cast out his net, he caught a golden fish, and the fish said: "If you throw me back into the water, I'll turn your little hut into a splendid castle, and in the castle there will be a cupboard. When you open it, there'll be dishes of boiled and roasted meat in them, as much as you desire. But you may not tell anyone in the world how you came by your good fortune, otherwise, you will lose it all."

The fisherman threw the golden fish back into the water, and when he came home, a huge castle was standing where otherwise his hut usually stood, and his wife sat in the middle of a splendid room. The man was very pleased by this, but he also wanted to eat something.

"Wife, give me something to eat," he said. "I'm tremendously hungry."

However, his wife answered:"I don't have a thing and can't find anything in this large castle."

"Just go over there to the cupboard."

When his wife opened the cupboard, she found cake, meat, fruit, and wine.

"What more could my heart desire?" His wife was astonished, and then she said: "Tell me, where in the world has this treasure of riches come from all of a sudden?"

"I'm not allowed to tell you. If I tell you, our good fortune will vanish."

After he said this, his wife became only more curious, and she kept asking him and tormenting him and didn't allow him any peace day and night until he finally revealed to her that everything came from a golden fish. No sooner had he said this than the castle and all the rich treasures vanished, and the fisherman and his wife were sitting once again in the old fishing hut.

Now the man had to resume his work all over again, and he fished and fished until he caught the golden fish once more. The fish promised the fisherman again that, if he let it go free, the fish would give him the beautiful castle again and the cupboard full of boiled and roasted meat but only on condition that he remain silent about who granted this favor. Well, the fisherman held out for a while but eventually his wife tormented him so drastically that he revealed the secret, and in that very moment they sat once again in their shabby hut.

So the husband went fishing again, and he fished and caught the golden fish a third time.

"Listen," said the fish. "Take me home with you and cut me into six pieces. Give two to your wife to eat, two to your horse, and plant two in the ground. You'll reap a blessing by doing this. Your wife will give birth to two golden children, The horse will produce two golden foals. And two golden lilies will grow from the earth."

The fisherman obeyed, and the fish's prophecy came true. Soon the two golden children grew and became strong young men. "Father," they said, "we want to set out into the world. We'll mount our golden horses, and you'll be able to see from the golden lilies how we are doing. If they are fresh, then we are healthy. If they wilt, then we're sick. If they perish, then we shall be dead."

Upon saying this they rode off and came to an inn where there were many people inside, and when the people saw the two golden children on the golden horses, they began to make fun of them. In turn, the young men became angry, and one of them became ashamed, turned around, and rode home. However, the other continued to ride on and came to a forest. But the people outside the forest told him that he shouldn't enter because it was full of robbers, and they would attack him. But the golden boy wouldn't let himself be scared by that and said: "I must and shall go through the forest!"

Then he took a bearskin and covered himself and his horse with it so that nothing more of the gold could be seen, and he then rode into the forest. Soon thereafter he heard something calling out in the bushes: "Here's one!"

Then another voice spoke: "Let him go. What should we do with a bearskin? He's as poor and empty-handed as a church mouse!"

So this is how the golden young man escaped the robbers and rode into a village where he saw a maiden who was so beautiful that he couldn't imagine any other maiden as beautiful as she was in the whole world. So he asked her to marry him, and the maiden said yes, and she would remain true to him for the rest of her life. So they held the wedding and were happy. Then the bride's father came home, and when he saw that his daughter had married a loafer in a bearskin (for he hadn't taken off his bearskin), he became angry and wanted to murder the bridegroom. However, the bride pleaded as best she could and told her father that she loved the man in the bearskin very much, and after all, he was her husband! Finally, the father calmed down, and the next morning he got up and wanted to see his son-in-law one more time, and all at once he saw a splendid, golden young man lying in bed. But the bridegroom had dreamed that he should go hunting after a magnificent stag, and when he awoke, he wanted to go into the forest to hunt this stag. His newlywed wife implored him to stay there and was afraid that something might happen to him. However, he said: "I must and shall go off."

Upon saying this he got up and went into the forest. Soon he saw a proud stag standing before him just as in his dream. But when he took aim and was about to shoot, the stag began to flee. The golden man went after him and followed him over ditches and through bushes the entire day and wasn't tired. Yet, the deer evaded him, and the young man soon found himself in front of a witch's house. He called out and asked whether she had seen the stag. She answered, "yes," while the witch's small dog kept barking at him without stopping. So he became angry and wanted to shoot it. When the witch saw this, she changed the young man into a millstone. And at that very same moment the golden lily perished at the golden youth's home. When the other brother saw this, he mounted his golden steed and raced away and came upon the witch. He threatened her with death unless she restored his brother to his natural form. So the witch had to obey, and the two brothers rode home together, the first one to his bride, and the other to his father. In the meantime, the golden lily revived itself, and if the lilies haven't perished, then both of them are still standing.

64
THE SIMPLETON

The White Dove

There was once a splendid pear tree that stood in front of a king's castle, and each year it produced the most beautiful fruit. However, as soon as the pears became ripe, they were taken that very night, and nobody knew who the thief was.

Now, the king had three sons, and the youngest among them was considered simple-minded and was called Simpleton. The oldest was ordered by the king to guard the tree for one year so that the thief could be caught. He did this and watched every night. Soon, the fruit was in full bloom and was full of fruit, and as the pears began to turn ripe, he kept watch even more diligently. Finally, the pears were completely ripe and were to be picked the next day. However, on the last night, the king's son became drowsy and fell asleep, and when he awoke, every single one of the pears was gone. Only the leaves were left.

Then the king commanded the second son to keep watch for a year. However, he didn't fare any better than his older brother. On the last night he couldn't fend off sleep, and the next morning, all the pears had been picked.

Finally, the king ordered Simpleton to keep watch for a year. Everyone at the king's court laughed about this. Nevertheless, Simpleton kept watch, and in the last night he resisted sleep and saw how a white dove came and carried off the pears one by one. As the dove made off with the last one, Simpleton stood up and followed it to the top of a high mountain, where it disappeared into a crack along the cliffs. Simpleton looked around him, and suddenly a little gray man was standing next to him.

"God bless you," said Simpleton.

"God has already blessed me in this very moment through your words," answered the little gray man. "You have released me from a magic spell. Now, if you climb down the cliff, your fortune will be made."

So Simpleton climbed down the rocks. Many steps led him to the bottom, where he saw the white dove trapped and entangled in a spider's web. When the bird caught sight of him, it ripped through the web, and after the last thread had been torn, a beautiful princess stood before him. Simpleton had also released her from a spell, and she became his wife, and he, a rich king, who ruled his country with wisdom.

The Queen Bee

Once two princes went forth in search of adventure, and after they fell into a wild, decadent way of life, they never returned home again. Their youngest brother, who was called Simpleton, went out to look for them, but when he finally found them, they ridiculed him for thinking that he, so naïve as he was, could make his way in the world when they, who were much more clever, had not been able to succeed.

After a while the three of them traveled together and came to an anthill. The two oldest wanted to smash it and watch the little ants crawl around in fright and carry away their eggs, but Simpleton said, "Leave the little creatures in peace. I won't let you disturb them."

So they continued on their way and came to a lake where a great many ducks were swimming. The two brothers wanted to catch a few and roast them, but Simpleton said again, "Leave the creatures in peace. I won't let you kill them."

Finally, they came to a beehive, and there was so much honey in the hive that it had dripped down the tree trunk. The two older brothers wanted to build a fire beneath it and suffocate the bees to get at the honey. However, Simpleton prevented them again and said, "Leave the creatures in peace. I won't let you burn them."

Soon the three brothers came to a castle, and they saw nothing but stone horses standing in the stables. Not a living soul could be seen. They went through all the halls until they reached the end, where there was a door with three locks hanging on it. In the middle of the door there was a peephole through which one could look into the room, and they saw a little gray man sitting at a table. They called to him once, then twice, but he didn't hear them. Finally, they called a third time, and he got up and came out. However, he didn't say a word. Instead, he just led them to a table richly spread with food, and after they had something to eat and drink, he brought each one to his own bedroom.

The next morning the little gray man went to the oldest brother, beckoned to him, and conducted him to a stone tablet on which were inscribed three tasks that had to be performed if the castle was to be disenchanted. The first task involved gathering one thousand pearls that were lying in the moss of the forest. They belonged to the king's daughter and had to be picked up from the moss before sundown. If one single pearl were to be missing, the seeker would be turned to stone.

The prince went to the moss and searched the entire day, but when the day drew to an end, he had found only a hundred. Consequently, he was turned into stone. The next day the second brother undertook the adventure, but he didn't fare much better than the oldest: he found only two hundred pearls and was turned into stone. Finally, it was Simpleton's turn to search for the pearls in the moss. However, since it was so difficult to find them and everything went so slowly, he sat down on a stone and began to weep. While he was sitting on the stone and weeping, the king of the ants whose life he had once saved came along with five thousand ants, and it didn't take long before the little creatures had gathered the pearls together and stacked them in a pile.

Now, the second task involved fetching the key to the bedroom of the king's daughter from the lake. When Simpleton came to the lake, the ducks whose lives he had once saved came swimming toward him and then dived down to fetch the key from the bottom of the lake.

Next came the third task, which was the hardest. The king had three daughters who lay asleep, and Simpleton had to pick out the youngest and the loveliest. However, they all looked exactly alike, and the only difference between them was that they each had eaten a different kind of sweet before falling asleep: the oldest had eaten a piece of sugar, the second a little syrup, the youngest a spoonful of honey. Just then the queen bee whom Simpleton had protected from the fire came along and tested the lips of all three princesses. At last she settled on the mouth of the princess who had eaten honey, and thus the prince was able to recognize the right daughter. Now the magic spell was broken, and everyone was set free from the deep sleep. All those who had been turned into stone regained their human form. Simpleton married the youngest and loveliest daughter and became king after her father's death, while his two brothers were married to the other two sisters.

The Three Feathers

Once upon a time there was a king who decided to send his three sons off into the world. Whoever would bring him the finest woven linen was to take over the realm after his death. Consequently, he went outside in front of the castle and blew three feathers into the air so that they would know in what direction they should go, and he told each one to follow the flight of his feather.

One feather flew to the west and was followed by the eldest son. The next to the east was followed by the second son. However, the third feather flew and fell on a stone not far from the palace. So the third son, the Simpleton, had to remain behind. His two brothers made fun of him and said that he should search for the linen beneath the stone.

Meanwhile Simpleton sat down on the stone and wept, and as he swayed back and forth, the stone slid away, and beneath it was a marble slab with a ring on top. Simpleton lifted the slab and discovered some stairs that led below. So he went down and came to a subterranean vault, where he found a maiden sitting and weaving flax. She asked him why his eyes were so wet from tears, and he revealed his sorrows to her and told her that he had to find the finest woven linen and had not been able to set out and search for it. Then the maiden reeled off her yarn, and all at once he saw the most splendid woven linen, and she told him to bring it up to his father.

When he came up from the ground, he had already been gone for a long time, and his brothers had just returned and thought that they had surely brought the finest woven linen back to their father. However, after each one of them showed their linen, Simpleton's turned out to be much finer, and the realm would have been his, but the two brothers were not satisfied and insisted that their father set another condition. So the king demanded the most beautiful carpet and once again blew three feathers into the air, and the third fell on the stone again. So Simpleton was prevented from setting out while the others went to the east and the west.

Simpleton lifted the stone and went down to the vault again and found the maiden weaving a marvelously beautiful carpet out of blazing colors, and when she was done, she said: "I made this for you. Carry it up to your father. No one in the world will have such a magnificent carpet."

So he appeared before his father and once again surpassed his brothers, who had brought the most beautiful carpets from many different countries. And they insisted again that their father set another condition as to who would inherit the realm, and the king now demanded that they must bring the most beautiful woman back home. The feathers were blown once more, and Simpleton's landed on the stone. So he went beneath the ground and complained to the maiden how his father had once more set a difficult condition. But the maiden said that she would gladly help him. All he had to do was to go farther into the vault, and he would find the most beautiful woman in the world.

Simpleton went down the vault and came to a room glimmering and flickering with gold and jewels, but instead of a beautiful woman, there was a nasty frog sitting in the middle. The frog called out to him: "Embrace me, and immerse yourself!"

But he didn't want to do this. So the frog called out a second time: "Embrace me, and immerse yourself!"

So Simpleton grabbed hold of the frog and carried it above to a pond where he jumped into the water with the frog. However, no sooner did they touch the water than he held the most beautiful woman in his arms. Then they climbed out of the water, and he brought her to his father, and she was a thousand times more beautiful than the women whom the other princes had brought with them. Once again the realm would have belonged to Simpleton, but the two brothers made a racket and demanded that whoever's beautiful woman could jump up to the ring that was hanging in the middle of the hall should inherit the realm. The eldest son's woman could jump only halfway; the second son's woman jumped a bit higher; but the third son's woman jumped right up to the ring. So the two elder brothers finally had to agree that Simpleton would inherit the realm after their father's death, and when the father died, Simpleton became king and ruled with wisdom for a long time.

The Golden Goose

Once upon a time there was a man who had three sons. However, the youngest was a simpleton. One day the eldest son said: "Father, I want to go into the forest and chop wood."

"Let it be," the father said. "Otherwise you'll come home with a bandaged arm."

But the son didn't pay attention to his father and thought he knew how to take care of himself. He put some cake in his pocket and went into the forest, where he met a little old gray man who said: "I'm so hungry. Give me a piece of the cake that you have in your pocket."

However, the clever son responded: "Why should I give you a piece of my cake? Then I'll have nothing for myself. Get out of here!"

The son went off with his axe and began to chop down a tree. It didn't take long, however, for him to make a slip with the axe, and he cut himself in the arm. So he had to go home and have his arm bandaged. This was all because of the little old gray man.

Some time later the second son went into the forest, where the little man asked him for a piece of cake, too. He also refused and consequently struck himself in the leg so that he had to be carried back home. Finally, Simpleton went out into the forest, and the little man spoke to him just as he had to the others and asked for a piece of cake.

"You can have the entire thing," said Simpleton and gave it to him.

Then the little man spoke: "Chop this tree down, and you'll find something."

Simpleton began hacking away, and when the tree fell, a golden goose was sitting there. He took the bird with him and went to an inn, where he wanted to spend the night. He didn't want to stay in the large room. Rather, he wanted a room for himself alone. Once there he set the goose down in the middle of the room. The innkeeper's daughters had seen the goose and were curious and would have liked to have had a feather from the goose. Then the eldest daughter said: "I'll go upstairs, and if I don't return soon, then come after me."

Upon saying this she went to the goose, but no sooner did she touch the feather than she found herself attached to the goose. Now, since she didn't come back downstairs, the second sister went to look after her, and as soon as she saw the goose, she couldn't resist the desire to pluck a feather. The eldest sister tried her best to warn her not to do this, but nothing helped. Her sister grabbed hold of the goose and was soon attached to the feather. Now, after the third daughter had waited long enough below, she finally went upstairs, and her sisters called out to her and warned her for heaven's sake not to come near the goose. However, she didn't listen to them and was set on having one of the feathers and got stuck to it.

The next morning Simpleton took the goose in his arm and went off. The three daughters were tightly attached to the goose and had to follow him. When they came to a field, they met the parson, who cried out at them: "Phooey! Naughty girls! What are you doing running after this young fellow, in public no less? Shame on you!"

Upon saying this he grabbed one of the girls by the hand and tried to yank her away. However, as soon as he touched her, he became stuck to her and now had to run along behind them.

Shortly after this happened, the sexton came and cried out: "Hey, parson, where are you off to in such a hurry? We still have a christening today!"

The sexton ran up to him, grabbed him by the arm, and became attached. As the five of them marched one after the other after Simpleton, two farmers with their hoes came from the field. The parson called them over to help detach themselves, but no sooner did they touch the sexton than they got stuck, and so now there were seven who ran after Simpleton with the goose.

Soon he came to a city ruled by a king who had a daughter so serious that nobody could get her to laugh. Consequently, the king issued a decree declaring that whoever made the princess laugh would have her for his bride. When Simpleton heard this, he went to the king's daughter and took along the goose with the group of people attached to the bird. As soon as the princess saw this parade, she began to laugh boisterously and couldn't stop. Therefore, Simpleton demanded to have her for his bride, but the king made all kinds of excuses and said Simpleton would first have to bring him a man who could drink up all the wine in a cellar. So Simpleton went into the forest to the spot where he had chopped down the tree, and he saw a man sitting there with a sad face. So Simpleton asked him what had caused him to have such a heavy heart.

"Oh! I'm so thirsty and can't get enough to drink. I've already emptied a barrel of wine, but that's only a like a drop on a hot stone!"

"Well, I can help you," Simpleton said. "Come with me. You'll be able to drink until you are full."

Simpleton led him to the king's cellar, and the man set to work on the large barrels. He drank and drank until his lips began to hurt him, and before the day was over, he had drunk up everything in the cellar.

Now Simpleton demanded his bride, but the king was annoyed that a common fellow whom everyone called Simpleton should carry off his daughter, and so he set a new condition: Simpleton had to produce a man who could eat a mountain of bread. So Simpleton returned to the forest, and there was a man sitting at the spot of the tree that he had cut down, and this man was tightening a belt around his waist and making an awful face.

"I've eaten an oven full of coarse bread, but what good is that when I'm still enormously hungry? I don't feel a thing in my body and must tighten my belt if I'm not to die of hunger."

As soon as Simpleton heard this, he was cheerful and said: "Get up and come with me. You'll eat until you're full."

Simpleton led the man to the king, who had all the flour of the entire kingdom gathered and baked into an enormous mountain, but the man from the forest took a place in front of it, and he caused the entire mountain to vanish in a day and a night. Once again, Simpleton asked for his bride, but the king sought a way out again and demanded a ship that could sail on water and on land. If he produced this ship, then he could have the princess right away. So Simpleton went into the forest once more and met the little gray man to whom he had given his cake.

"I've drunken and eaten for you," the little man said, "and now I'll give you the ship. I'm giving you all this because you were so kind and took pity on me."

So he gave Simpleton the ship that sailed on land and on water, and when the king saw this, he could no longer prevent him from marrying his daughter. Then the wedding was celebrated, and Simpleton inherited the realm and lived a long time happily with his wife.

65
ALL FUR

Once upon a time there was a king who had the most beautiful wife in the world, and her hair was pure gold. They had a daughter together, and she was just as beautiful as her mother, and her hair was just as golden. One day the queen became sick, and when she felt she was about to die, she called the king to her and made a request: if after her death he wanted to marry again, he should only take someone who was as beautiful as she was and who had golden hair like hers. Once the king promised her that, she died.

For a long time the king was so distressed that didn't think about a second wife. Finally, his councilors urged him to remarry. So messengers were sent to all the princesses in the world, but none of them were as beautiful as the dead queen. Nor could they find such golden hair anywhere in the world.

Now one day the king cast his eyes on his daughter, and when he saw that her features were very similar to those of her mother and that she also had such golden hair, he thought, "Since you won't find anyone as beautiful in the world, you must marry your daughter." And right then he felt such a great love for her that he immediately informed his councilors and the princess of his decision.

The councilors wanted to talk him out of it, but it was in vain. The princess was totally horrified about his godless intention. However, since she was smart, she told the king that he first had to provide her with three dresses, one as golden as the sun, one as white as the moon, and one as bright as the stars and then a cloak made of a thousand kinds of pelts and furs, and each animal in the kingdom had to contribute a piece of its skin to it.

The king had such a passionate desire for her that everyone in his realm was ordered to work. His huntsmen had to catch all the animals and take a piece of their skin. Thus a cloak was made from their fur, and it didn't take long before the king brought the princess what she had demanded.

Now the princess said that she would marry him the next day. However, during the night, she collected the gifts that she had received from her fiancé from another kingdom: a golden ring, a little golden spinning wheel, and a little golden reel, and the three dresses, all of which she put into a nutshell. Then she blackened her face and hands with soot, put on the cloak made of all kinds of fur, and departed. She walked the whole night until she reached a great forest, where she was safe. Since she was tired, she climbed into a hollow tree and fell asleep.

She continued to sleep until it became broad daylight. As it so happened, the king, her bridegroom,[2] was out hunting in the forest. When his dogs came to the tree, they started to sniff and run around it. The king sent his huntsmen to see what kind of animal was hiding in the tree. When they returned to him, they said that there was a strange animal lying in it, and they had never seen anything like it in their lives. Its skin was made up of a thousand different kinds of fur, and it was lying there asleep. Then the king ordered them to catch it and tie it on the back of the wagon. The huntsmen did this, and as they pulled it from the tree, they saw it was a maiden. Then they tied her on the back of the wagon and drove home with her.

"All Fur," they said, "you'll do well to work in the kitchen. You can carry wood and water and sweep up the ashes."

Then they gave her a little stall beneath the steps.

"You can live and sleep there."

So she had to work in the kitchen, where she helped the cook, plucked the chickens, tended the fire, sorted the vegetables, and did all the dirty work. Since she did everything so diligently, the cook was good to her and sometimes called All Fur to him in the evening and gave her some of the leftovers to eat. Before the king went to bed, she had to go upstairs and pull off his boots, and as soon as she would pull one off, he would always throw it at her head. And so All Fur led a miserable life for a long time. Ah, you beautiful maiden, what shall become of you?

At one time a ball was held in the castle, and All Fur thought, "perhaps now I could see my dear bridegroom once again." So she went to the cook and asked him to allow her to go upstairs for a while to see the splendor from the doorway.

[2] Evidently the princess had never met her fiancé (bridegroom).

"Go ahead," said the cook, "but you can't stay longer than half an hour. You've got to sweep up the ashes tonight."

So All Fur took her little oil lamp, went into her little stall, and washed the soot off her so that her beauty came to light again like flowers in springtime. Then she took off the fur cloak, opened the nut, and took out the dress that shone like the sun. When she was fully dressed, she went upstairs, and everyone made way for her, for they believed that she was nothing less than a distinguished princess who had just come into the ballroom. The king immediately offered her his hand and led her forth to dance. And as he was dancing with her, he thought, "this unknown princess resembles my dear bride," and the longer he gazed at her, the more she resembled her so that he was almost certain it was her. When the dance ended, he wanted to ask her. However, as she finished the dance, she curtsied and disappeared before the king could begin to speak. Then he asked the guards, but nobody had seen the princess leave the castle. She had quickly run to her little stall, taken off her dress, blackened her face and hands, and put on the fur cloak once again. Then she went into the kitchen and started to sweep up the ashes.

"Let it be until morning," the cook said. "I want to go upstairs and take a look at the dance. Make a soup for the king, but don't let any hairs fall in, otherwise you'll get nothing more to eat."

All Fur cooked a bread soup for the king, and then at the end, she slipped the golden ring that the king had given to her as a present into the soup. When the ball came to an end, the king had his bread soup brought to him, and it tasted so good that he was convinced that he had never eaten one so good. However, when he had finished, he found the ring at the bottom of the bowl. As he looked at it carefully, he saw that it was his wedding ring and was puzzled.[3]

He couldn't grasp how the ring came to be there, and so he had the cook summoned, and the cook became angry with All Fur.

"You must have certainly let a hair fall into the soup. If that's true, you'll get a beating!"

[3] This was the ring that he had sent to her as a gift.

However, when the cook went upstairs, the king asked him who had cooked the soup because it had been better than usual. So the cook had to confess that All Fur had made it, and the king ordered him to send All Fur up to him. When she came, the king said: "Who are you and what are you doing in my castle? Where did you get the ring that was in the soup?"

Then she replied:

"I'm nothing but a poor child whose mother and father are dead
I am nothing and am good for nothing except for having boots
    thrown at my head.
I also know nothing about the ring."

Upon saying that she ran away.

Some time later there was another ball, and once again All Fur asked the cook's permission to go upstairs. The cook allowed her but only for half an hour, and then she was to return and cook the bread soup for the king. So, All Fur went to her little stall, washed herself clean, took out the dress as silvery as the moon and cleaner and more sparkling than fallen snow. When she appeared upstairs, the dance had already begun. The king offered his hand to her again and danced with her. He no longer doubted that she was his bride, for nobody in the world except her had such golden hair. However, when the dance was over, the princess had already departed once again, and despite all his efforts, the king couldn't find her, and he hadn't even spoken a single word with her.

Indeed, she was All Fur again with blackened hands and face. She stood in the kitchen and cooked the bread soup for the king while the cook went upstairs to watch the dance. When the soup was done, she put the golden spinning wheel into the bowl. The king ate the soup, and it seemed even better this time. When he found the golden spinning wheel at the bottom, he was even more astounded because he had at one time sent it to his bride as a present. The cook was summoned, and then All Fur, but once again she replied that she knew nothing about it, and that she was only there to have boots thrown at her head.

When the king held a ball for the third time, he hoped his bride would come again, and he wanted to make sure to hold on to her. All

Fur asked the cook again to let her go upstairs, but he scolded her and said: "You're a witch. You always put something in the soup and can cook it better than I do."

However, since she pleaded so passionately and promised to behave herself, he let her go upstairs again for half an hour. Thereupon she put on the dress that sparkled as bright as the stars in the night and went upstairs and danced with the king. He thought he had never seen her more beautiful. As they were dancing, however, he slipped a ring onto her finger and ordered the dance to last for a very long time. Nevertheless, he couldn't hold onto her, nor could he speak a single word to her, for when the dance was over, she mingled with the people so quickly that she vanished before he turned around.

All Fur ran to her little stall, and since she had been away longer than half an hour, she undressed quickly. In her hurry she couldn't blacken herself completely so that a finger remained white. When she went into the kitchen, the cook was already upstairs, and she quickly cooked the bread soup and put the golden reel into it.

Just as he had found the ring and the golden spinning wheel, the king also found the reel. Now he knew for sure that his bride was nearby, for nobody else could have possessed the presents. All Fur was summoned and wanted once again to avoid the king and run away. However, as she tried to run off, the king caught sight of the white finger on her hand and held her tight. He found the ring that he had slipped onto her finger and tore off her fur cloak. Then her golden hair toppled down, and she was his dearly beloved bride. Now the cook was richly rewarded, and the king held the wedding and they lived happily until their death.

66

HURLEBURLEBUTZ

Once a king got lost during a hunt, and suddenly a little white dwarf appeared before him.

"Your majesty," he said, "if you give me your youngest daughter, I'll show you how to get out of the forest."

The king consented out of fear, and the dwarf helped him find his way. As he took leave of the king, he cried out: "I'll be coming to fetch my bride in a week."

When the king reached home, he was sad about his promise because his youngest daughter was his favorite. His daughters noticed how sad he was and wanted to know what the cause of his worry was. Finally, he had to tell them that he had promised the youngest of them to a little white dwarf in the forest and that the dwarf would be coming to fetch her in a week. However, they told him to cheer up, for they would lead the dwarf on a wild goose chase.

When the day came for the dwarf's arrival, they dressed a cowherd's daughter in their clothes and sat her down in their room.

"If someone comes to fetch you, you're to go with him!" they ordered, and they themselves left the house.

No sooner had they left than a fox entered the castle and said to the maiden, "Sit down on my furry tail, Hurleburlebutz! Off to the forest!"

The maiden sat down on the fox's tail, and he carried her out into the forest. When they came to a beautiful clearing, where the sun was shining very bright and warm, the fox said, "Get off and take the lice out of my hair!"

The maiden followed his orders, and the fox laid his head on her lap so she could louse him. While she was doing this, the maiden said, "When I was in the forest yesterday about this time, it was more beautiful!"

"What were you doing in the forest?" the fox asked.

"Oh, I was tending the cows with my father."

"So, you're not the princess! Sit down on my furry tail, Hurleburlebutz! Back to the castle!"

The fox carried her back and said to the king, "You've deceived me. That was a cowherd's daughter. I'll come again in a week and fetch your daughter."

At the end of the week the princesses dressed a gooseherd's daughter in splendid garments, sat her down, and went away. Then the fox came again and said, "Sit down on my furry tail, Hurleburlebutz! Off to the forest!"

When they arrived at a sunny spot in the forest, the fox said once more, "Get off and take the lice out of my hair!"

As the maiden was lousing the fox, she sighed and said, "I wonder where my geese are now?"

"What do you know about geese?"

"Oh, I take them to the meadow every day with my father."

"So, you're not the king's daughter! Sit down on my furry tail, Hurleburlebutz! Back to the castle!"

The fox carried her back and said to the king, "You've deceived me again. That was the gooseherd's daughter. I'm going to come again in a week, and if you don't give me your daughter, you'll be in for trouble."

The king became frightened, and when the fox returned, he gave him the princess.

"Sit down on my furry tail, Hurleburlebutz! Off to the forest!"

She had to ride on the fox's tail, and when they got to a sunny place, he said to her, "Get off and take the lice out of my hair!"

However, when he laid his head in her lap, the princess began to cry and said, "I'm a king's daughter, and yet I must louse a fox! If I were sitting at home now, I'd be looking at the flowers in my garden!"

Then the fox knew that he had the right bride and turned himself into the little white dwarf. He was now her husband, and she had to live with him in a little hut and cook and sew for him. This lasted a good long time, and the dwarf did everything he could to please her.

One day the dwarf said to her, "I've got to go away, but three white doves will soon come flying here. When they swoop down to the ground, catch the middle one. Once you've got it, cut off its head right away. But pay attention and make sure you've got the middle dove, or else there'll be a disaster."

The dwarf departed, and it didn't take long for the three white doves to come flying toward her. The princess paid close attention and grabbed the middle one. Then she took a knife and cut off its head. No sooner was the dove lying on the ground than a handsome young prince stood before her and said, "A fairy cast a spell over me causing me to lose my human form for seven years. Then I was to fly by my wife as a dove between two other doves, and she would have to catch me and cut off my head. If she didn't catch me, or if she caught another and I flew by, then everything would be lost, and I would never be saved. That's why I asked you to pay attention, for I'm the white dwarf, and you're my wife."

The princess was delighted, and together they went to her father. When he died, they inherited the kingdom.

67

THE KING WITH THE LION

A young prince sat with his bride-to-be and said: "I'm going to give you a ring and my picture and want you to carry these things to remember me and to remain true to me. My father is deathly ill and has asked me to come to him. He wants to see me one more time before he dies and I become king. So I want you to go home now."

Upon saying this the prince rode off and found his father on his death-bed. Right before he died, he asked his son to marry a particular princess after his death. The prince was so depressed and loved his father so much that, without thinking about it, he said yes, and right after that the king closed his eyes and died.

After he was acclaimed king and the mourning period ended, he had to keep his word and asked permission to court the other princess who had been promised to him. Meanwhile, the first bride had heard that the prince was courting another princess, and she grieved so much that she almost died. Her father asked her why she was so sad and told her all she had to do was to ask him for what she wanted and her wish would be granted. So the princess reflected for a moment, and then she asked for eleven young women who completely resembled her in size as well as in stature. So the king had his men search for the eleven young women throughout his entire kingdom, and when they were all together, she dressed herself in hunter's clothes and had the eleven dressed the same way so that all twelve of them were completely alike. Shortly thereafter, she rode to the king, her former bridegroom, and requested a position for herself and the others as hunters. The king didn't recognize her, but because they were such handsome people, he gladly granted the request and welcomed them to his court.

Now the king had a lion, and nothing could be kept from him. This lion knew all the secrets of the court. One evening the lion said to the king: "You believe you've employed twelve hunters, but they're actually twelve young women."

The king refused to believe him, but the lion added: "Have peas spread out in your anteroom one time. Men have a heavy step, and if they walk over the peas, none of the peas will move. But women, they skip and shuffle, and the peas roll beneath their feet."

The king liked this plan, but one of the king's servants loved the hunters and had overheard all this. So he ran to the young women and said: "The lion thinks that you're women and wants to have peas spread out in the anteroom to test you."

Consequently, the princess ordered her eleven young ladies to use all their might and step firmly on the peas. When it turned morning and the peas were all spread out, the king summoned the twelve hunters, but they had such a firm and strong gait that not one single pea moved.

That evening the king reproached the lion and accused him of lying. In response the lion said: "They covered up who they really are. Now, just have twelve spinning wheels set up in the anteroom, and they'll show how pleased they are. No man would ever do that."

The king followed the lion's advice once more and had the spinning wheels set up in the room. However, the servant revealed to the hunters what was happening so that the princess ordered the young ladies once more not to look at the spinning wheels at all. So that's what they did, and the king refused to believe the lion any more. He became more and more fond of the hunters, and when he went out hunting, they had to go along with him.

One time, when they were out in the forest, news arrived that the prince's bride was coming and that she would soon be there. When the prince's real bride heard this, she fainted. The king thought that something had happened to his dear hunter. He ran over and wanted to help him. As he took off his glove, he noticed that she was wearing the ring that he had given to his first bride, and moreover, when he saw the picture that she was carrying in her necklace, he recognized her and immediately notified the other bride to return to her realm because he already had a wife, and when one recovers an old key, one doesn't need a new one. Soon after, the wedding was celebrated, and it was clear that the lion had not lied, and he once again found favor in the king's eyes.

68

THE SUMMER AND THE WINTER GARDEN

A merchant wanted to go to a fair and asked his three daughters what he should bring back for them. The eldest said: "A beautiful dress."

The second: "A pair of pretty shoes."

The third: "A rose."

But it was difficult to find a rose because it was midwinter. However, since the youngest was the most beautiful daughter and was so extremely fond of flowers, the father replied that he would see whether he could find a rose and would make every effort to do so.

When the merchant was returning home after the fair, he carried a splendid dress for the eldest and a pair of beautiful shoes for the second daughter, but he hadn't been able to obtain a rose for the youngest daughter. Each time he had entered a garden and had asked for roses, the people had made fun of him and asked him whether he really believed that roses grew in snow. He was very sorry about that, and as he was pondering whether there might be something that he could bring home for his favorite child, he reached a castle, and there was a garden on one side in which it was half summer and half winter. On one side the most beautiful small and large flowers were blooming, and on the other side, everything was bare and deep snow lay on the ground. The man got off his horse, and since he noticed an entire hedge full of roses on the summer side, he was glad and went over there. Then he plucked a rose, got on his horse, and began riding away. He had ridden only a short distance when he heard something running behind him and panting. So he turned around and saw a large black beast that shouted: "Return my rose to me, or I'll kill you! Return my rose to me, or I'll kill you!"

The man replied: "Please, let me keep the rose. I'm supposed to bring it to my daughter. She is the most beautiful maiden in the world."

"If you like. But in exchange, I want you to give me your beautiful daughter as my wife."

In order to get rid of the beast, the man said, yes, and thought he wouldn't come come and demand his daughter, but the beast yelled after him: "I'm coming to fetch my bride in one week."

Now the merchant brought each one of his daughters what she had wished. All of them were delighted, and the youngest daughter was the most pleased by the rose. After a week had passed, the three sisters were sitting at the dinner table when all of a sudden someone with heavy footsteps came up the stairs and knocked at the door.

"Open up! Open up!" he yelled.

So they opened the door, but they were truly horrified when a large black beast entered.

"Since my bride didn't come and the time is up, I've come to fetch her myself!"

Upon saying that he went up to the youngest daughter and grabbed her. She began to scream, but that didn't help at all. She had to go off with him, and when her father came home, he found that his dearest child had been kidnapped.

Meanwhile the black beast carried the beautiful maiden into his castle, which was quite wonderful and beautiful. There were musicians, who had begun playing, and below was the garden that was half summer and half winter. And the beast did everything to make her feel comfortable, and one could read from her eyes how pleased she was. They ate together, and she had to ladle out the food for him, otherwise he wouldn't eat. The beast thought she was precious, and eventually she became very fond of the beast.

One day she said to him: "I've become very anxious, and I don't know why, but I feel as though my father were ill, or that perhaps one of my sisters is sick. Couldn't I see them just one time?"

So the beast led her to a mirror and said: "Look into the mirror," and when she looked into the mirror, it was as if she were at home. She saw her room and her father, who was really sick from heartbreak. Indeed, he felt guilty that a wild beast had kidnapped his daughter and had probably been devoured by him. If he had known how well she was, he wouldn't have been so depressed. She also saw her two sisters at the father's bedside, and they were weeping. All this troubled her heart, and she asked the beast whether he might let her return home for several days.

"Go to your father, but promise me that you'll return within a week."

She promised him, and as she was leaving, he called after her: "Don't stay any longer than one week."

When she returned home, her father rejoiced that he was able to see her one more time, but the illness and the sorrow had eaten away at his heart too much. Consequently, he couldn't regain his health and died after a couple of days. So his daughter couldn't think of anything else due to her grief, and before her father was buried, she went to his corpse and wept with her sisters, and they consoled each other. Finally, when she thought about her dear beast once again, more than a week had gone by. All of a sudden she became really anxious, and she felt as if he were also sick, and she immediately set out and went directly to his castle. When she arrived there once again, the castle was completely silent and sad. The musicians weren't playing, and everything was draped in black. The garden was now completely winter and covered by snow. And when she went to look for the beast, he was gone. She searched all over the place but couldn't find him. Now she was doubly distressed and didn't know how to console herself. Sadly she went into the garden and saw a heap of cabbage heads. The ones at the top were already old and rotten. She spread them around, and when she had turned over a few, she saw her dear beast, who had been lying under them, and he was dead. Quickly she fetched some water and continually poured water on him. All of a sudden, he jumped up and was suddenly changed into a handsome prince. A wedding was held, and the musicians immediately began playing. The summer side of the garden became splendid again, the black drapes were torn down, and they lived there happily ever after.

69

JORINDA AND JORINGEL

Once upon a time there was an old castle in the middle of a great, dense forest. An old woman lived there all by herself; and she was a powerful sorceress. During the day she turned herself into a cat or a night owl, but in the evening she would return to her normal human form. She had the ability to lure game and birds, which she would slaughter and then cook or roast. If any man came within a hundred steps of the castle, she would cast a spell over him, so that he wouldn't be able to move from the spot until she broke the spell. If an innocent maiden came within her magic circle, she would change her into a bird and stuff her into a wicker basket. Then she would carry the basket up to a room in her castle where she had well over seven thousand baskets with rare birds of this kind.

Now, once there was a maiden named Jorinda, who was more beautiful than any other maiden in the kingdom. She was betrothed to a handsome youth named Joringel. During the time before their marriage, they took great pleasure in each other's company. One day they went for a walk in the forest so they could be alone and talk intimately with one another.

"Be careful," Joringel said, "that you don't go too close to the castle."

At dusk the sun shone brightly through the tree trunks and cast its light on the dark green of the forest. The turtledoves were singing mournfully in the old beech trees, and at times Jonrinda wept. Then she sat down in the sunshine and sighed, and Joringel sighed too. They became very sad as if they were doomed to die, and when they looked around them, they became confused and didn't know how to get home. The sun was still shining half above and half behind the mountains. When Joringel looked through the bushes and saw the wall of the old castle not very far away, he became so alarmed that he was nearly frightened to death, while Jorinda sang:

"Oh, my bird, with your ring of red,
sitting and singing your tale of woe!
You tell us now that the poor dove is dead.
You sing your tale of woe—*oh-oh, oh-oh!*"

Just then, as Joringel looked at Jorinda, she was turned into a nightingale singing "*oh-oh, oh-oh!*"

A night owl with glowing eyes flew around her three times, and each time it cried, "*To-whoo! To-whoo! To-whoo!*"

Joringel couldn't budge. He stood there like a stone unable to weep, to talk, or to move hand or foot. When the sun was about to set, the owl flew into a bush and then immediately returned as a haggard old woman, yellow and scrawny, with large red eyes and a crooked nose that almost touched her chin with its tip. She muttered something to herself, caught the nightingale, and carried it away in her hand. Joringel was still unable to speak, nor could he move from the spot. The nightingale was gone. Soon the woman came back and said with a muffled voice, "Greetings, Zachiel. When the moon shines into the basket, let him loose, Zachiel, just at the right moment."

Then Joringel was set free, and he fell on his knees before the woman and begged her to give Jorinda back to him, but she said he would never get her back again and went away. Joringel shouted. He wept, he moaned, but it was all in vain. "Oh, now what's to become of me?"

Joringel went off and eventually came to a strange village, where he tended sheep for a long time. He often went around and around the castle and always kept his distance. Finally, he dreamed one night that he had found a flower as red as blood, and in the middle of it was a pearl. He plucked the flower and went with it to the castle: everything that he touched with the flower was released from the magic spell. He also dreamed that he managed to regain his Jorinda with the flower.

When he awoke the next morning, he began searching all over the mountains and valleys for the flower in his dream. He searched for nine days, and early on the ninth day he found a flower as red as blood. In its middle was a large dewdrop as big as the finest pearl. He carried this flower day and night until he reached the castle. When he came to within a hundred steps of the castle, he didn't become spellbound but was able to get to the gate. Overjoyed by that, Joringel touched the gate with the flower, and it sprang open. So he entered, crossed the courtyard, and listened for the sound of birds. Finally, he heard them and went toward the room where the sorceress was feeding the birds in their seven thousand baskets. When she saw Joringel, she became angry, very angry. She began berating him and spitting poison and gall at him, but she could only come within two feet of him, and he paid no attention to her. Instead, he went and examined the baskets with the birds. Since there were hundreds of nightingales, he didn't know how he'd be able to find his Jorinda again. While he was examining the baskets, he noticed that the old woman had stealthily picked up one of them and was heading toward the door. Quick as a flash he ran over and touched the basket with the flower, and immediately thereafter, he touched the old woman as well. Now she could no longer use her magic, and consequently Jorinda appeared before him. She threw her arms around his neck and was just as beautiful as before. After Joringel had turned all the other birds into young women, he went home with his Jorinda, and they lived together in happiness for a long time.

70

OKERLO

A queen put her child out to sea in a golden cradle and let it float away. However, the cradle didn't sink but drifted to an island inhabited only by cannibals. When the cradle drifted toward the shore, a cannibal's wife happened to be standing there. Upon seeing the child, who was a beautiful baby girl, she decided to raise her and later give her to her son, who would wed her one day. But she had a great deal of trouble hiding the maiden carefully from her husband, Old Okerlo, for if he had laid his eyes on her, he would have eaten her up, skin and bones.

When the maiden had grown up, she was to be married to the young Okerlo, but she couldn't stand him and cried all day long. Once when she was sitting on the shore, a young, handsome prince came swimming up to her. When it was clear they each took a liking to the other, they exchanged vows. Just then the old cannibal's wife came, and she got tremendously angry at finding the prince with her son's bride. So she grabbed hold of him and said, "Just wait! We'll roast you at my son's wedding."

The young prince, the maiden, and Okerlo's three children had to sleep together in one room. When night came, Old Okerlo began craving human flesh and said, "Wife, I don't feel like waiting until the wedding. I want the prince right now!"

However, the maiden had heard everything through the wall, and she got up quickly, took off the golden crown from one of Okerlo's children, and put it on the prince's head. When the old cannibal's wife came in, it was dark. So she had to feel their heads and took the boy who wasn't wearing a crown and brought him to her husband, who immediately devoured him.

Meanwhile, the maiden became terribly frightened, for she thought, "As soon as day breaks, everything will be revealed, and we'll be in for trouble." So, she got up quietly and fetched seven-mile boots, a magic wand, and a cake with a bean that provided answers for everything. After that she departed with the prince. They were wearing the seven-mile boots, and with each step they took, they went a mile. Sometimes they asked the bean, "Bean, are you there?"

"Yes," the bean said. "I'm here, but you'd better hurry. The old cannibal's wife is coming after you in some other seven-mile boots that were left behind!"

The maiden took the magic wand and turned herself into a swan and the prince into a pond for the swan to swim on. The cannibal's wife came and tried to lure the swan to the bank, but she didn't succeed and went home in a bad mood. The maiden and the prince continued on their way.

"Bean, are you there?"

"Yes," the bean said. "I'm here, but the old woman's coming again. The cannibal explained to her how you duped her."

The princess took the wand and changed herself and the prince into a cloud of dust. Okerlo's wife couldn't penetrate it and again had to return empty-handed, while the maiden and the prince continued on their way.

"Bean, are you there?"

"Yes, I'm here, but I see Okerlo's wife coming once more, and she's taking tremendous steps!"

The maiden took the magic wand for the third time and turned herself into a rosebush and the prince into a bee. The old cannibal's wife came and didn't recognize them because of their changed forms. So she went home.

But now the maiden and the prince couldn't regain their human forms because the maiden, in her fear, had thrown the magic wand too far away. Yet their journey had taken them such a long distance that the rosebush now stood in a garden that belonged to the maiden's mother. The bee sat on the rose, and he would sting anyone who tried to pluck it. One day the

queen herself happened to be walking in the garden and saw the beautiful flower. She was so amazed by it that she wanted to pluck it. But the little bee came and stung her hand so hard that she had to let go of the rose. Yet she had managed to rip the flower a little, and suddenly she saw blood gushing from the stem. Then she summoned a fairy to break the enchantment of the flower and the bee, and the queen then recognized her daughter again and was very happy and delighted. Now a great wedding was held, and a large number of guests were invited. They came in magnificent array, while thousands of candles flickered in the hall. Music was played, and everyone danced until dawn.

"Were you also at the wedding?"

"Of course I was there. My hairdo was made of butter, and as I was exposed to the sun, it melted and was muddled. My dress was made from a spider's web, and as I went through some thorn bushes, they ripped it off my body. My slippers were made of glass, and as I stepped on a stone, they broke in two."

71

PRINCESS MOUSESKIN

A king had three daughters, and he wanted to know which one loved him most. So he summoned them to him and began asking. The oldest daughter said she loved him more than the whole kingdom. The second said she loved him more than all the jewels and pearls in the world. But the third said she loved him more than salt. The king was furious that she compared her love for him to such a meager thing. Consequently, he handed her over to a servant and ordered him to take her into the forest and to kill her.

When they reached the forest, the princess begged the servant to spare her life. Since he was devoted to her, he wouldn't have killed her anyway. Indeed, he said he would go with her and do her bidding. But the princess demanded nothing except a garment made out of mouseskin. When he fetched it for her, she wrapped herself in the skin and went straight to a neighboring kingdom. Once there she pretended to be a man and asked the king to employ her. The king consented, and she was to be his personal servant. In the evening, whenever she pulled off his boots, he always tossed them at her head. One time he asked her where she came from.

"From the country where one doesn't toss boots at people's heads."

Her remark made the king suspicious. Finally, the other servants brought him a ring that Mouseskin had lost. It was so precious that they thought she had stolen it. The king called Mouseskin to him and asked how she had obtained the ring. Mouseskin could no longer conceal her true identity. She unwrapped the mouseskin, and her golden hair streamed down. As she stepped out of the skin, he could see that she was beautiful, indeed so beautiful that he immediately took off his crown, put it on her head, and declared her to be his wife.

When the wedding was celebrated, Mouseskin's father was also invited to attend. He believed that his daughter had died a long time ago and didn't recognize her. However, at the dinner table all the dishes put before him were unsalted, and he became irritated and said, "I'd rather die than eat such food!"

No sooner had he uttered those words than the queen said to him, "Well, now you say you can't live without salt, but when I said I loved you more than salt, you wanted to have me killed."

All at once, he recognized his daughter, kissed her, and begged her forgiveness. Now that he had found her again, she was more dear to him than his kingdom and all the jewels in the world.

72

THE PEAR REFUSED TO FALL

The master went to shake the pear, but the pear refused to fall.
The master sent the servant out to shake the pear and make it fall.
But the servant did not shake at all,
the pear refused to fall.

The master sent the guard dog out
to bite the servant with his snout.
But the dog did not bite at all,
the servant did not shake at all,
the pear refused to fall.

The master sent the big stick out
to hit the dog right on his snout.
But the stick did not hit at all,
the dog did not bite at all,
the servant did not shake at all,
the pear refused to fall.

The master sent the fire out
to burn the stick down to a crisp.
But the fire did not burn at all,
the stick did not hit at all,
the dog did not bite at all,
the servant did not shake at all,
the pear refused to fall.

The master sent the water out
to snuff the little fire out.
But the water did not snuff at all,
the fire did not burn at all,
the stick did not hit at all,
the dog did not bite at all,
the servant did not shake at all,
the pear refused to fall.

The master sent the little calf out
to lap the water up.
But the calf did not lap at all,
the water did not snuff at all,
the fire did not burn at all,

the stick did not hit at all,
the dog did not bite at all,
the servant did not shake at all,
the pear refused to fall.

The master sent the butcher out
to kill the little calf.
But the butcher did not kill at all,
the calf did not lap at all,
the water did not snuff at all,
the fire did not burn at all,
the stick did not hit at all,
the dog did not bite at all,
the servant did not shake at all,
the pear refused to fall.

The master sent the henchman out
to go and hang the butcher.
Now the butcher wants to kill the calf,
the calf wants the water to lap,
the water wants the fire to snuff,
the fire wants the stick to burn,
the stick wants the dog to hit,
the dog wants the servant to bite,
the servant wants the pear to shake,
and the pear is ready to fall.

73
THE CASTLE OF MURDER

Once upon a time there was a shoemaker who had three daughters. One day when the shoemaker was out, a well-dressed nobleman came with a splendid carriage and servants, and he appeared to be very rich. He fell in love with one of the beautiful daughters, who thought herself fortunate to have found such a rich gentleman, and she gladly agreed to ride off with him. As they were on their way, it turned dark, and he asked her:

"The moon's shining very bright.
My horses are dashing into the night.
Sweet love, are you having any doubts?"

"No, why should I have any doubts? I'm well taken care of by you," but indeed she did feel a certain uneasiness. When they were in a large forest, she asked him if they would soon be there.

"Yes," he said. "Do you see the light in the distance? That's my castle."

At last they arrived, and everything was very beautiful. The next day he said to her that he had to leave her for a few days because he had to take care of some important and urgent business. However, he wanted to leave all the keys with her so she could see the whole castle and what treasures she, as mistress, now possessed. When he was gone, she went through the entire castle and found that everything was beautiful. She was completely satisfied until she came to the cellar, where an old woman was sitting and scraping out intestines.

"My goodness, granny, what are you doing there?"

"I'm scraping intestines, my child. Tomorrow I'll be scraping yours, too!"

The maiden was so terrified by her words that she dropped the key she was holding into a basin of blood, and she couldn't wash the blood off the key.

"Now your death is certain," said the old woman, "because my master will be able to see you were in the chamber, and no one is allowed to enter here except him and me."

(One must indeed know that this was the way her two sisters had lost their lives before her.)

Just then a hay wagon began to drive away and leave the castle. The old woman told her the only way she could save herself was by hiding under the hay and driving off in the wagon. And this is what the maiden did. In the meantime, the nobleman returned home and asked where the maiden was.

"Oh," said the old woman, "since I had no more work for today, and since she was due to be slaughtered tomorrow, I decided to kill her. Here's a lock of her hair. The dogs ate up the heart, the warm blood, and all the rest. I'm scraping out the intestines."

The nobleman was glad that she was dead. Meanwhile, she arrived in the hay wagon at a nearby castle, where the hay was supposed to be delivered. She climbed out of the hay and told everything she knew. Then she was asked to remain, and after some time had passed, the lord of this castle invited all the gentry of the surrounding region to a great feast. Since the nobleman from the castle of murder had also been invited, the maiden changed her features and clothes so she wouldn't be recognized.

Once they were all there, everyone had to tell a tale. When it was the maiden's turn, she told the particular story that concerned the nobleman and made his heart tremble with fear, and he wanted to force his way out. However, the lord of the castle had planned ahead of time to have the authorities ready to take our fine count to prison. His castle was destroyed, and all the treasures were given to the maiden for her own. Afterward she married the lord's son in the house where she had been so well received, and they lived together many, many years.

74
JOHANNES WATERSPRING
AND CASPAR WATERSPRING

A king insisted his daughter was not to marry and had a house built for her in the most secluded part of a forest. She had to live there with her ladies in waiting, and no other human being was allowed to see her. Near the house in the woods, however, there was a spring with marvelous qualities, and when the princess drank from it, she consequently gave birth to two princes. They were identical twins and named after the spring—Johannes Waterspring and Caspar Waterspring.

Their grandfather, the old king, had them instructed in hunting, and as they grew older, they became big and handsome young men. When the day arrived for them to set out into the world, each received a silver star, a horse, and a dog to take on the journey. Once they came to a forest, they immediately saw two hares and wanted to shoot them, but the hares asked for mercy and said that they would like to serve them and that they could be useful and help them whenever they were in danger. The two brothers let themselves be persuaded and took them along as servants.

Soon after they came upon two bears, and when they took aim at them, these animals also cried out for mercy and promised to serve them faithfully. So the retinue was increased, and now they came to a crossroad, where they said, "We've got to separate here, and one of us should go to the right, and the other should head off to the left."

Before doing this, each of them stuck a knife in a tree at the crossroad so that they could determine by the rust whether the other was faring well and whether he was still alive. Then they took leave from another, kissed one another, and rode off.

Johannes Waterspring came to a city that was quite still and sad because the princess was to be sacrificed to a dragon that was devastating the entire country and could be pacified only by this sacrifice. It was announced that whoever wanted to risk his life and kill the dragon would receive the princess for his bride. However, nobody had volunteered. They had also tried to trick the monster by sending out the princess's chambermaid, but the dragon realized what was happening right away and did not take the bait.

Johannes Waterspring thought, "You must try your luck. Perhaps you'll succeed." And so he set out with his company and headed toward the dragon's nest. The battle was fierce: the dragon spewed forth fire and flames and ignited all the grass around them so that Johannes Waterspring certainly would have suffocated if the hare, dog, and bear had not stamped out and subdued the fire. Finally, the dragon succumbed, and Johannes Waterspring cut off its seven heads and then sliced its seven tongues, which he stuck into his sack. Now, however, he was so tired that he lay down right at that spot and fell asleep. While he was sleeping, the princess's coachman arrived, and when he saw the man lying there and the seven heads next to him, he thought, "You've got to take advantage of this. So he stabbed Johannes Waterspring to death and took the seven heads with him. He carried everything to the king and said he had killed the monster. Indeed, he had brought the seven heads as evidence, and the princess became his bride.

In the meantime Johannes Waterspring's animals had set up camp nearby after the battle and had also slept. When they returned to their master, they found him dead. As they were looking, they saw how the ants, whose mound had been stamped on during the battle, were spreading the sap from an oak tree on their dead ones, and these ants immediately came back to life. So the bear went and fetched some of the sap, and he spread it on Johannes Waterspring. Shortly thereafter Johannes was completely well and healthy and thought about the princess for whom he had fought. So he rushed to the city, where her marriage to the coachman was being celebrated, and the people were saying that the coachman had killed the seven-headed dragon. Johannes Waterspring's dog and bear ran into the castle where the princess tied some roast meat and wine around their necks and ordered her servants to follow the animals and to invite their owner to the wedding. So now Johannes Waterspring showed up at the wedding just as the platter with the seven dragon heads was being displayed. These were the heads that coachman had brought with him, but now Johann Waterspring pulled out the seven tongues from his sack and placed them next to the heads. Consequently, he was declared the real dragon slayer and became the princess's husband, while the coachman was banished.

Not long thereafter Johannes went out hunting and followed a deer with silver antlers. He hunted the deer for a long time but could not catch it. Finally, he met an old woman, who turned him and his dog, horse, and bear into stone.

Meanwhile Caspar Waterspring returned to the tree in which he and his brother had stuck their knives and saw that his brother's knife had rusted. He immediately decided to search for his twin and rode off. Soon he came to the city where his brother's wife was living. She thought he was her real husband because he looked just like him and was delighted by his return and insisted that he stay with her. But Caspar Waterspring continued traveling until he found his brother and animals, all turned into stone. Soon after he forced the old woman to break the magic spell, and then the brothers rode toward their home. Along the way, they agreed that the first one to be embraced by the princess should be her husband. Well, it turned out to be Johannes Waterspring.

75
THE BIRD PHOENIX

One day a rich man went for a walk along the river. All at once he saw a small casket swimming by. He grabbed hold of the casket, and when he opened the cover, he saw a small child lying inside. So he took the child home and had him raised in his house. However, the rich man disliked the boy, and one time he took the boy with him in boat on the river. Once the boat was in the middle of the river, he swam to shore, and left the child alone in the boat. The boat continued floating down the river until it passed the mill, and the miller saw the child. The miller took pity on the child, fetched him from the boat, and raised him in his house.

One day the rich man happened to come by, recognized the child, and carried him away. Soon thereafter he gave the young man a letter to bring to his wife, and the letter read: "As soon as you read this letter, you are to kill the person who delivered it."

However, as the young man was traveling through the forest, he met an old man who said to him: "Show me the letter that you're carrying in your hand."

The old man took the letter, turned it around once, and gave it back to the young man. Now the letter read: "You are immediately to offer our daughter as wife to the young man delivering this letter."

And this is what happened, and when the rich man heard about this, he became furious and said: "Well, this wedding's not going to happen so quickly. Before I give you my daughter, you must bring me three feathers from the bird Phoenix."

So, the young man set out on his way to the bird Phoenix and met the old man again on the same spot in the forest.

"Keep walking for the entire day," he said. "In the evening you'll come to a tree. Two doves will be sitting on it, and they'll tell you how to proceed."

That evening, when the young man came to the tree, two doves were sitting on it. One of the doves said: "Whoever searches for the bird Phoenix must walk the entire day. In the evening he'll come to a gate that's locked."

Then the second dove said: "There is a gold key that lies underneath this tree, and it will open the gate."

The young man found the key and later used it to open the gate. Two men were sitting there, and one of them said: "Whoever searches for the bird Phoenix must travel a great distance over the high mountain, and then he'll finally come to a castle."

On the evening of the third day he finally reached the castle, where a wise little lady sat and said: "What do you want here?"

"Oh, I'd like to get three feathers from the bird Phoenix."

"Your life is in danger," she said. "If the bird Phoenix becomes aware of your presence, he'll eat you up skin and hair. Nevertheless, I'll see if I can help you get the three feathers. He comes here every day, and I must comb him with a narrow comb. So now quick, get under the table."

After he did this, young man was then covered completely by a cloth.

Meanwhile the bird Phoenix came home, sat down at the table, and said: "I smell, I smell human flesh!"

"Oh, what! You see, don't you, that nobody's here!"

"Comb me now!" the bird Phoenix responded.

The wise little lady combed the bird Phoenix, and as she was doing this, he fell asleep. When he was sound asleep, she grabbed a feather, pulled it out, and threw it beneath the table. All at once he woke up: "Why are you tearing my hair like that? I dreamed that a human came and pulled out one of my feathers."

She calmed him down, and so it went, two more times. When the young man had the three feathers, he set out for home and was now able to obtain his bride.

76

THE CARNATION

A long time ago there lived a king who never wanted to marry. Now one day he stood at a window and watched some people entering the church. Among them was a maiden who was so beautiful that he immediately abandoned his resolution. So he had the maiden summoned to him and chose her for his wife. After one year had passed, she gave birth to a prince, and the king didn't know whom to ask to be the godfather. Finally, he said: "The first man I meet, no matter who it is, I'll ask him to be the godfather."

He went out, and the first person he met was a poor old man, and he asked him to be the godfather. The poor man agreed but requested that he be the only one to carry the child into the church, that the church was to be locked, and that nobody be allowed to observe the ceremony. All this was granted. However, the king had an evil, curious gardener, and when the old man carried the child into the church, he sneaked after him and hid himself among the benches. Soon he watched the old man carrying the child before the altar and blessing him. The old man seemed to be someone who understood secret powers, and he gave the child the gift of realizing everything he wished for.

The evil gardener immediately thought how advantageous it would be for him if he had the child. So one day when the queen went for a walk and carried the child in her arm, the gardener tore it away from her, smeared her mouth with the blood of a slaughtered chicken, and accused her of killing and eating her child in the garden. So the king had her thrown into prison, while the gardener sent the child far away to a forester in the woods. He was supposed to raise the child, and it was there that the prince learned all about hunting. Moreover, the forester had a beautiful daughter by the name of Lisa, and the two young children became very fond of one another. Lisa revealed to him that he was a prince, and that he had the power to realize every wish he made.

After some time had passed, the gardener came to the forester, and when the prince saw him, he immediately wished the gardener to become a poodle, and his dear Lisa, a carnation. He stuck her on himself, and the poodle had to run alongside the prince. Then he went to his father's court, where he entered the royal service as hunter, and soon he became the king's favorite hunter because he could shoot any kind of animal in the forest. All the prince had to do was to wish, and the animals came running to him. Despite all the services he rendered the king, the prince did not ask to be compensated. He only asked for a room for himself that he kept locked, and he insisted on taking care of meals for himself. All this seemed strange to his fellow hunters, especially his refusal to receive wages, so that one of his comrades followed him and looked through the keyhole. All at once he saw the new hunter sitting at a table next to a beautiful maiden, who was his dear Lisa, whom he changed into her natural form whenever he was in the room. She kept him company whenever they were alone, and whenever he went out, she became a carnation again and stood in a glass of water.

The hunters thought that he must have a great amount of wealth and broke into his room when the prince went out hunting. However, they found absolutely nothing, only the carnation on the window sill. Since the flower was so beautiful, they brought it to the king, who became so very fond of it that he demanded it from the hunter. However, the young hunter refused to give it to him, even for all the money in the world, because the flower was his beautiful Lisa. Finally, when the king insisted on having it, the hunter revealed everything that had happened and that he was his son. When the king heard this, he rejoiced with all his heart. The queen was released from the prison, and the faithful Lisa became the prince's wife. The godless gardener was compelled to remain a poodle for the rest of his life and was often kicked by the servants when he lay underneath the table.

77
THE CARPENTER AND THE TURNER

A carpenter and a turner wanted to see who could make the best piece of work. The carpenter made a dish that could swim by itself, while the turner made wings that he could use to fly. Everyone said that the carpenter's masterpiece was better. So the turner took his wings, put them on, and flew out of the country. He flew the entire day until he came to another country, where a prince saw him flying and asked to borrow the pair of wings. Since the prince promised to pay him well, the turner gave him the wings, and the prince flew to another kingdom. There he saw a tower illuminated by many lights. He decided to swoop down to the ground and find out what the occasion was. When he learned that the most beautiful princess in the world lived there, he became very curious. In the evening he flew through an open window and was able to be with the princess but not for very long, for they were betrayed, and the prince and princess were sentenced to die at the stake.

However, the prince had taken his wings with him, and as the flames flared, he tied the wings on and flew with the princess to his homeland, where he descended to the ground. Since everyone had been sad during his absence, he revealed his true identity and was elected king.

After some time had passed, the father of the maiden who had been carried away by the prince made it known that whoever brought back his daughter would receive half his kingdom. When the prince learned about this, he gathered together an army and brought the princess to her father, who was forced to keep his promise.

78
THE OLD GRANDFATHER AND THE GRANDSON

Once upon a time there was an old man who could barely walk. His knees trembled, and he didn't hear or see much. Moreover, he had lost all his teeth. When he sat at the dinner table, he could barely hold the spoon. He spilled the soup on his napkin, and the food continued to flow from his mouth. His son and his son's wife felt disgusted by this, and therefore, the grandfather finally had to take a place behind the oven in the corner of the room. They gave him his food in a clay bowl. In addition, it was never full, and he would look morosely over to the table, his eyes filled with tears. One time his trembling hands could not gasp the bowl tightly enough, and it fell to the ground and broke. The young wife scolded him, while he said nothing and only sighed. So they bought a wooden bowl for a penny, and now he had to eat out of it.

One time, as they were sitting at the dinner table, the little four-year-old grandson collected small wooden sticks on the floor.

"What are you doing there?" his father asked.

"Oh," the child answered, "I'm making a little trough so mother and father can eat out of it when I'm older and bigger."

Then the husband and wife looked at each other for a while. Finally, they burst into tears and immediately brought the old grandfather to the table. From then on they let him eat with them and also said nothing whenever he happened to spill a few things.

79
THE WATER NIXIE

A little brother and a little sister were playing near a well, and as they were playing, they both fell into the water. A water nixie was there and said: "Now I've got you, and now be good children and work nice and hard for me!"

Then she gave the maiden some dirty, tangled flax to spin and also a hollow bucket to fetch water. The young boy had to chop down a tree with a blunt axe, and all they got to eat were dumplings as hard as rocks. Eventually, the children lost their patience, and one Sunday, they waited until the nixie was in church and then ran away. After the church service was over, the nixie saw that the chickens had fled the coop, and she set out after them as fast as she could. The children saw her coming from afar, and the maiden threw a brush behind her. The brush changed into a huge mountain of bristles with thousands and thousands of thorns. The nixie had great difficulty in climbing over them. When the children saw her, the boy threw a comb behind him that changed into a huge mountain with thousands and thousands of spikes, but the nixie was able to grab hold of them and climb over the mountain. Now the maiden threw a mirror behind her that formed a glass mountain that was so very, very slippery that the nixie couldn't climb over it. So she thought: "I'd better go home and fetch my axe and split the mountain in two." However, by the time she had returned and had smashed the glass, the children had long since made their escape, and the water nixie had to return to tread water in her well.

80
THE DEATH OF LITTLE HEN

Some time ago little hen went with little rooster to the nut mountain. They enjoyed themselves and ate nuts together. One time, however, little hen found such a large nut that she wasn't able to swallow the kernel, and it got stuck so firmly in her throat that she feared she might choke to death.

"Little rooster!" she screamed. "Please run as fast as you can and fetch me some water, otherwise I'll choke to death."

Little rooster ran as fast as he could to the well and said: "Well, you must give me some water. Little hen's lying on the nut mountain, and she's about to choke to death!"

"First run to the bride," the well answered, "and get some red silk for me."

"So little rooster ran to the bride and said, "Bride, I need some red silk from you. The silk is for the well, who'll give me some water to take to little hen, who's lying on the nut mountain, where she's swallowed a large kernel and is about to choke to death."

The bride answered: "First run and fetch me my wreath that got caught on the branch of a willow."

So little rooster ran to the willow, pulled the wreath from the branch, and brought it back to the bride. In return the bride gave him some red silk, and little rooster brought it to the well, who gave him water in exchange. Then little rooster brought the water to little hen, but by the time he had reached her, she had choked to death and lay there motionless and dead. Little rooster became so sad that he uttered a loud cry, and all the animals came and mourned for her. Six mice built a little wagon that was to carry little hen to her grave. When the wagon was finished, the mice harnessed themselves to it, and the little rooster was to drive the wagon. Along the way they encountered the fox, who asked: "Where are you going, little rooster?"

"I'm off to bury my little hen."

"May I ride with you?"

"Yes, but since you're so heavy, take a seat in the back.
If you sat up front, my horses would fall, and the wagon would crack."

So the fox sat down in the back. Then the wolf, the bear, the stag, the lion, and all the animals in the forest took a seat in the back. Thus they continued their journey until they came to a brook.

"How shall we get across?" asked little rooster.

A straw was lying near the brook and said: "I'll lay myself across the book. Then you can drive over me."

However, as soon as the six mice touched the bridge, the straw slipped and fell into the water, and the six mice went tumbling after and drowned. So the situation was just as bad as it had been before, but a piece of hot coal came along and said: "I'm large enough. I'll lay myself across, and you can drive over me."

Then the piece of coal also laid itself across the water, but unfortunately it grazed the surface a little. Soon it started hissing, and before long it was extinguished and died. When a stone saw that, it took pity on little rooster and offered its help. It lay down across the water, and now little rooster himself pulled the wagon across. When he reached the other side and was already on land with dead little hen, he wanted to help the others in the back out of the wagon, but there were too many of them, and the wagon slipped backward, causing everyone to fall into the water and drown. So little rooster was all alone with dead little hen, and he dug a grave for her. Then he laid her in it and made a mound on top. Afterward he sat down on the ground and grieved until he, too, died, And then everyone was dead.

81
THE BLACKSMITH AND THE DEVIL

Once upon a time there was a blacksmith who enjoyed life: he squandered his money and carried on many lawsuits. After a few years, he didn't have a single cent left in his pouch.

"Why should I torture myself any longer in this world?" he thought. So he went into the forest with the intention of hanging himself from a tree. Just as he was about to stick his head into the noose, a man with a long white beard came out from behind a tree carrying a large book in his hand.

"Listen, blacksmith," he said. "Write your name down in this large book, and for ten long years you'll have a good life. But after that you'll be mine, and I'll come and fetch you."

"Who are you?" asked the blacksmith.

"I'm the devil."

"What can you do?"

"I can make myself as tall as a fir tree and as small as a mouse."

"Then show me. Seeing is believing," said the blacksmith.

Thereupon the devil made himself as tall as a fir tree and as small as a mouse.

"That's good," said the blacksmith. "Give me the book, and I'll write down my name."

After the blacksmith had signed his name, the devil said, "Now, just go home, and you'll find chests and boxes filled to the brim, and since you've not made much of a fuss, I'll also visit you once during this time."

The blacksmith went home, where he found all his pockets, boxes, and chests filled with gold coins, and no matter how much he took, they never became empty or even reduced in the least.

So he began his merry life once again, invited his comrades to join him, and was the happiest fellow in the world. After a few years had passed, the devil stopped by one day, as he had promised, to see how things were going. On his departure he gave the blacksmith a leather sack and told him that whoever jumped into this sack would not be able to get out again until the blacksmith himself took him out. Indeed, the blacksmith had a great deal of fun with it. When the ten years were over, however, the devil returned and said to him, "Your time is up, and now you are mine. Get ready for your trip."

"All right," said the blacksmith, who swung his leather sack over his back and went away with the devil.

When they came to the place in the forest where the blacksmith had wanted to hang himself, he said to the devil, "I want to make sure that you're really the devil. Make yourself as large as a fir tree and as small as a mouse again."

The devil was prepared and performed his feat. But just as he changed himself into a mouse, the blacksmith grabbed him and stuck him into the sack. Then the blacksmith cut off a stick from a nearby tree, threw the sack to the ground, and began beating the devil, who screamed pitifully and ran back and forth in the sack. Yet, it was all in vain: he couldn't get out.

Finally, the blacksmith said, "I'll let you go if you give me the sheet from your large book on which I wrote my name."

The devil refused at first, but eventually he gave in. The sheet was ripped out of the book, and the devil returned home to hell, annoyed that he had let himself be duped and beaten as well. Meanwhile, the blacksmith went home to his smithy and continued to live happily as long as it was God's will. Finally, he became sick, and when he realized death was near, he ordered two long nails and a hammer to be put into his coffin. This was done just as he had instructed, and after he died, he approached the heaven's gate and knocked. However, Saint Peter refused to open the gate because the blacksmith had lived in league with the devil. When the blacksmith heard this, he turned around and went to hell. But the devil wouldn't let him enter, for he had no desire to have the blacksmith in hell, where he would only make a spectacle of himself.

Now the blacksmith was angry and began to make a lot of noise in front of hell's gate. A little demon became curious and wanted to see what the blacksmith was doing. So he opened the gate a little and looked out. Quickly the blacksmith grabbed him by the nose and nailed him solidly to the gate of hell with one of the nails he had with him. The little demon began to screech like a wildcat, so that another demon was drawn to the gate. He, too, stuck his head out, and the blacksmith was alert: he grabbed this one by the ear and nailed him to the gate next to the first little demon. Now both of them began to let out such terrible cries that the old devil himself came running. When he saw the two little demons nailed solidly to the gate, he became so terribly angry that he wept and jumped about. Then he ran up to heaven to see the dear Lord. Once there he told the Lord that He had to admit the blacksmith into heaven. There was nothing anyone could do to stop the blacksmith, the devil said. So the blacksmith would continue to nail all the demons by their noses and ears, and he the devil would no longer be master in hell. Well, the dear Lord and Saint Peter quickly realized that if they wanted to get rid of the devil, then they would have to let the blacksmith enter heaven. So now the blacksmith sits in heaven nicely and peacefully, but I don't know how the two little demons were able to free themselves.

Once upon a time there was a rich king who was so rich that he believed his wealth would last forever. Therefore, he wallowed in luxury and gambled on a golden board with silver dice. All this continued for some time until he squandered his wealth and was forced to mortgage his cities and castles one after the other. Finally, nothing was left except an old castle in the forest. He moved there with his queen and three daughters, and their lives were miserable: they had only potatoes to eat for their daily meal.

One day the king decided to go hunting to see if he could perhaps shoot a hare. After filling his pocket full of potatoes, he went off to a nearby forest that nobody dared enter because terrible stories had been told about what one might encounter there, such as bears that ate people, eagles that hacked out eyes, and wolves, lions, and all kinds of cruel beasts. However, the king was not in the least afraid and went straight into the forest. At first he didn't see anything except huge and mighty trees, and everything was quiet beneath them. After he had walked around for a while, he became hungry and sat down underneath a tree to eat his potatoes. All of a sudden a bear came out of the thicket, trotted straight toward him, and growled, "How dare you sit under my honey tree! You'll pay for this!"

The king was horrified and handed the bear his potatoes to appease him. But the bear began to speak and said, "I don't want your potatoes. I'm going to eat you yourself. But, if you give me your oldest daughter, you can you save yourself! If you do this, I'll give you a hundred pounds of gold in the bargain."

Since the king was afraid of being eaten, he said, "You shall have her. Just let me go in peace."

The bear showed him the way out of the forest and growled after him, "In a week's time I'll come and fetch my bride."

As he went home, the king felt more at ease and was convinced that the bear would not be able to crawl through a keyhole. So from then on everything at the castle was to be shut tight. He ordered all the gates to be locked, the drawbridges to be lifted, and told his daughter not to worry.

But just to be on the safe side and to protect his daughter from the bear bridegroom, he gave her a little room under the pinnacle high up in the castle. She was to hide there until the week was over.

Early on the seventh morning, however, when everyone was still asleep, a splendid coach drawn by six horses came driving up to the castle. It was surrounded by numerous knights clad in gold, and as soon as the coach was in front, the drawbridges dropped down by themselves, and the locks sprung open without keys. The coach drove into the courtyard, and a young, handsome prince stepped out. When the king was wakened by the noise and looked out the window, he saw the prince had already fetched his oldest daughter from the locked room and was lifting her into the coach. He could just call after her:

"Farewell, my maiden dear.
I see you're off to wed the bear."

She waved to him with her little white handkerchief from the coach, and then they sped off into the magic forest as if the coach were harnessed to the wind. The king felt very bad about having given his daughter to a bear. He was so sad that he and the queen wept for three days. But on the fourth day, after he had done enough weeping, he realized that he couldn't change what had happened and went down into the courtyard. There he found a chest made out of smooth wood, which was very difficult to lift. Immediately he remembered what the bear had promised him. So he opened it and found a hundred pounds of glittering and glistening gold.

When the king saw the gold, he felt consoled. He reacquired his cities and kingdom and began leading his former life of luxury once more. Soon after, he was obliged to mortgage everything all over again, and he retreated to his castle in the forest and had nothing to eat but potatoes. Yet the king still had a falcon, and one day the king took it hunting with him and went out into the field to get something better to eat. The falcon soared high into the sky and flew in the direction of the dark magic forest, which the king no longer dared enter. Right after the falcon flew into the woods, an eagle shot out and pursued the falcon, which returned to the king, who tried to fend off the eagle with his spear. But the eagle grabbed the spear and broke it like a reed. Then the eagle crushed the falcon with one claw and dug into the king's shoulder with the other.

"Why have you disturbed my kingdom in the sky?" the eagle cried out. "Either you give me your second daughter for my wife, or you shall die!"

"All right," the king said. "You shall have my second daughter, but what will you give me for her?"

"Two hundred pounds of gold," the eagle said. "In seven weeks I'll come to fetch her."

Then the eagle let him go and flew off into the forest. The king felt bad about having also sold his second daughter to a wild beast and didn't dare tell her anything about it. Six weeks passed, and in the seventh the princess went out one day on the lawn in front of the castle to water the linseed. All at once a splendid parade of handsome knights came riding up, and at their head was the handsomest knight of all, who dismounted and cried out:

"Up you go, my maiden dear.
Come wed the eagle. No need to fear!"

And before she could answer him, he had already lifted her onto his horse and raced off with her into the forest, flying like a bird. Farewell! Farewell!

The king and queen waited a long time for the princess to come back to the castle, but no matter how long they waited, she didn't return. Then the king finally revealed that he had promised her to an eagle when he had once been in trouble, and the eagle must have fetched her. After the king got over his sadness somewhat, he remembered the eagle's promise, went down to the lawn, and found two golden eggs, each weighing one hundred pounds. "Money is a sign of piety," thought the king, and he dismissed all gloomy thoughts from his mind. He resumed his merrymaking once more and lived luxuriously until he ran through the two hundred pounds of gold. Then the king returned to the castle in the forest, and the last of the princesses had to boil the potatoes.

The king didn't want to hunt any more hares in the forest or any more birds in the sky, but he did desire to eat some fish. So the princess had to weave a net, which he took with him to a pond not far from the castle. A small boat was there, and he got in and threw the net into the water. On his very first try he caught a bunch of beautiful flounders with red speckles, but when he wanted to row ashore with his catch, the boat wouldn't budge, and he couldn't get it to move, no matter how much he tried. All of a sudden an enormous whale came puffing up to him and cried out, "Who said you could catch the subjects of my realm and take them away with you? This will cost you your life!"

As the whale said this, he opened his jaws as if he were going to swallow the king and the little boat as well. When the king saw his terrible jaws, he completely lost his courage and recalled that he had a third daughter.

"Spare my life," he cried out, "and you shall have my third daughter!"

"That's fine with me," roared the whale. "I'll also give you something for her. I don't have gold. That's not good enough for me. But the floor of my sea is plastered with precious pearls. I'll give you three sacks full of them. In the seventh month I'll come and fetch my bride."

Then he dived down into the water, while the king rowed ashore and brought the flounders home. Yet, when they were baked, he refused to eat any of them, and when he looked at his daughter, the only one left and the most beautiful and loveliest of them all, he felt as if a thousand knives were cutting his heart. Six months passed, and the queen and princess didn't know what was wrong with the king, for he didn't smile once during all that time. In the seventh month the princess was in the courtyard in front of a man-made well and drew a glass of water. Suddenly a coach with six white horses and men clad entirely in silver came driving up. A prince stepped out of the coach, and he was more handsome than any other prince she had ever seen in her life. He asked her for a glass of water, and when she handed it to him, he embraced her and lifted her into the coach. Then they drove back through the gate over the field toward the pond.

"Farewell, you maiden dear.
You're bound to wed the whale down there."

The queen stood at the window and watched the coach as it moved off in the distance. When she was unable to find her daughter, her heart

was saddened, and she called her and looked for her everywhere. But the daughter was nowhere to be seen or heard. When the queen was certain the princess could not be found, she began to weep, and now the king revealed to her that a whale must have fetched their daughter, for he had been forced to promise their daughter to him. Indeed, that was the reason he had been so sad. The king wanted to comfort his wife and told her about the great treasure they would now get for the princess. However, the queen didn't want to hear anything about it and said her only child was more dear to her than all the treasures of the world.

During the time that the whale prince had carried off the princess, his servants had carried three tremendous sacks into the castle, which the king found at the door. When he opened them, he found they were full of big, beautiful, and precious pearls, just as large as the fattest peas imaginable. All of a sudden he was rich again and richer than he had ever been before. He reacquired his cities and castles, but this time he didn't resume his luxurious way of living. Instead, he became quiet and thrifty. Whenever he thought about what had happened to his three dear daughters with the wild beasts and that perhaps they had already been eaten up, he lost all zest for life.

Meanwhile, the queen couldn't be consoled and wept more tears for her daughters than all the pearls the whale had given them. Finally, she became more calm and peaceful, and after some time she was happy again, for she gave birth to a handsome baby boy. Since God had given them the child so unexpectedly, he was named Reinald the Miracle Child. The boy grew big and strong, and the queen often told him about his three sisters, who were being held prisoners by three beasts in the magic forest. When he turned sixteen, he demanded some armor and a sword from the king, and when he received all this, he decided to embark on an adventure. So he blessed his parents and set forth.

He went straight toward the magic forest and had only one thing on his mind—to search for his sisters. At first he wandered around in the great forest for a long time without encountering a human being or a beast. But after three days he saw a young woman sitting in front of a cave and playing with a young bear cub, while another very young one was lying on her lap.

Reinald thought she must surely be his oldest sister. So he left his horse behind him and approached her.

"Dearest sister," he said, "I'm your brother Reinald, and I've come to visit you."

The princess looked at him, and since he resembled her father very strongly, she didn't doubt his words, but she was frightened and said, "Oh, dearest brother, hurry and run away as fast as you can if you value your life. When my husband the bear comes home and finds you here, he'll show you no mercy and will eat you up."

But Reinald said, "I'm not afraid, and I won't leave you until I know how you are and what things are like for you."

When the princess saw that he was resolute, she led him into the dark cave that was like the dwelling of a bear. On one side was a heap of leaves and hay on which the old bear and his cubs slept, and on the other side was a magnificent bed with red covers trimmed with gold. That belonged to the princess. She told him to crawl under the bed and handed him something to eat. It didn't take long before the bear came home.

"I smell, I smell the flesh of a human being," he said and wanted to stick his hand under the bed.

But the princess cried out, "Be quiet! Who would ever come here?"

"I found a horse in the forest and ate it," he growled, and his nose was still bloody from eating the horse. "Where there's a horse, there's a man, and I smell him."

Again he wanted to look under the bed, but she gave him such a kick in the side that he did a somersault, went back to his place, put his paw in his mouth, and fell asleep.

Every seventh day the bear was restored to his natural form. He became a handsome prince; his cave, a splendid castle; the animals in the forest, his servants. It was on such a day that he had fetched the princess. Beautiful young women had come to meet her from the castle. There had been a glorious festival, and she had gone to sleep full of joy, but when she had awakened, she had found herself lying in the bear's dark cave, and her husband had been turned into a bear growling at her feet. Only the bed and everything she had touched had remained in its natural condition and hadn't been changed. Thus she lived six days in suffering, but on the seventh she was comforted. She didn't grow old because only one day a week counted in her life, and she was content with her existence. She had given her husband two sons, who also became bears for six days and regained their human form on the seventh day. She stuffed their straw bed with the most delicious food all the time, including cake and fruit, and they lived off this food the entire week. Moreover, the bear obeyed her and did whatever she wanted.

When Reinald awoke, he lay in a silken bed. Servants waited on him and dressed him in the finest clothes, for his visit fell right on the seventh day. His sister entered with the two handsome princes and his brother-in-law the bear. They were glad about his arrival. Everything was magnificent and glorious, and the entire day was filled with pleasurable and joyous things. But, in the evening the princess said, "Dear brother, now it's time for you to depart. At daybreak my husband will become a bear again, and if he finds you here tomorrow, he won't be able to control his natural instincts and will eat you up."

Then the bear prince came and gave him three bear hairs and said, "Whenever you're in trouble, just rub these hairs, and I'll come to your aid."

Then they kissed each other and said farewell. Reinald climbed into a carriage drawn by six horses and drove off. He went over hill and valley, up and down mountains, through deserts and forests, shrubs and hedges without stopping to rest until the sky began turning grey at dusk. Then Reinald suddenly lay on the ground, and the horses and carriage disappeared. At sunrise he saw six ants galloping away, drawing a nutshell behind them.

Reinald realized he was still in the magic forest and wanted to search for his second sister. Again he wandered about aimlessly and lonely for three days without accomplishing anything. But on the fourth day he heard a big eagle come swooping down to settle in a nest. Reinald hid in the bushes and waited for the eagle to fly away. After seven hours it soared into the air again. Then Reinald emerged from the bushes, went over to the tree, and cried out, "Dearest sister, are you up above? If so, let me hear your voice. I'm Reinald, your brother, and I've come to visit you!"

Then he heard a voice calling down to him, "If you're Reinald, my dearest brother, whom I've never seen, come up to me."

Reinald wanted to climb the tree, but the trunk was too thick and slippery. He tried three times in vain. Suddenly a silken rope ladder dropped down, and he climbed it until he reached the eagle's nest, which was strong and secure like a platform on a linden tree. His sister sat under a canopy made out of rose-colored silk, and an eagle's egg was lying on her lap. She was keeping it warm in order to hatch it. They kissed each other and rejoiced, but after a while the princess said, "Now, hurry and see to it that you get out of here, dearest brother. If the eagle, my husband, sees you, he'll hack your eyes out and devour your heart as he's already done with three of your servants, who were looking for you in the forest."

"No," said Reinald. "I'm staying here until your husband is transformed."

"That will happen but only in six weeks. If you can hold out that long, go and hide in the tree. It's hollow on the inside, and I'll drop food down to you every day."

Reinald crawled into the tree, and the princess let food down to him every day. Whenever the eagle flew away, he climbed up to her. After six weeks the eagle was transformed, and once more Reinald awoke in a bed that was like the one at his brother-in-law the bear's place. Only here it was more splendid, and he lived with the eagle prince in great joy. On the seventh evening they said their farewells. The eagle gave him three eagle feathers and said, "If you're in trouble, rub them, and I'll come to your aid."

Then he gave him servants to show him the way out of the forest. But when morning came, they suddenly disappeared, and Reinald was all alone on top of a high rocky cliff in a terrible wilderness. He looked around him, and in the distance he saw the reflection of a large lake, which glistened from the sun's rays. He thought of his third sister, who might be there. So he began to climb down the cliff and work his way through the bushes and between the rocks. He needed three days to do this, and he often lost sight of the lake, but on the fourth day he succeeded in getting there. Once he was on the bank, he called out, "Dearest sister, if you're in the water, let me hear your voice. I'm Reinald, your brother, and I've come to visit you."

But no one answered, and everything was very quiet. He threw bread crumbs into the water and said to the fish, "Dear fish, go to my sister and tell her that Reinald the Wonder Child is here and wants to see her."

But the red-speckled flounders snapped up the bread and didn't listen to his words. Then he saw a little boat and immediately took off his armor. He kept only his sword in his hand as he jumped into the boat and rowed off. After he had gone a long way, he saw a chimney made of rock crystal jutting out of the water, and there was a pleasant smell rising up from it. Reinald rowed toward it and was convinced that his sister was living down below. So he climbed on top of the chimney and slid down. The princess was greatly startled when she suddenly saw a pair of wriggling legs followed shortly by a whole man, who identified himself as her brother. She rejoiced with all her heart, but then she turned sad and said, "The whale has heard that you've wanted to visit me, and he's declared that if you come while he's a whale, he'll not be able to control his desire to eat you up. Moreover, he'll break my crystal house, and I'll also perish in the flood of water."

"Can't you hide me until the time comes when the magic loses its power?"

"Oh, no. How can I do that? Don't you see that the walls are all made out of crystal, and you can see through them?"

Nevertheless, she thought and thought, and finally she remembered the room where the wood was kept. She arranged the wood in such a careful way that nobody could see anything from the outside, and it was there that she hid the Wonder Child. Soon after, the whale came, and the princess trembled like an aspen leaf. He swam around the crystal house a few times, and when he saw a little piece of Reinald's clothing sticking out of the wood, he beat his tail, snorted ferociously, and if he had seen more, he would surely have destroyed the house. He came once a day and swam around it until the magic stopped in the seventh month. Suddenly Reinald found himself in a castle right in the middle of an island, and the castle surpassed even the splendor of the eagle's castle. Now he lived with his sister and brother-in-law for a whole month in the lap of luxury. When the time was over, the whale gave him three scales and said, "When you're in trouble, rub them, and I'll come to your aid."

The whale brought him to the bank, where his armor was still lying on the ground. The Wonder Child moved around in the wilderness for seven more days, and he slept seven nights under the open skies. Then he caught sight of a castle with a steel gate that had a mighty lock on it. In front of the gate was a black bull with flashing eyes. It was guarding the entrance, and Reinald attacked it. He gave the bull a powerful blow on its neck, but the neck was made of steel, and the sword broke as if it were glass. He tried to use his lance, but it broke like a piece of straw. Then the bull grabbed him with its horns and threw him into the air so that he got caught in the branches of a tree. In his desperation Reinald remembered the three bear's hairs and rubbed them in his hand. All at once the bear appeared and fought with the bull. He tore the bull to pieces, but a bird came out of the bull's stomach, flew high into the air, and rushed off. But Reinald rubbed the three eagle's feathers, and suddenly a mighty eagle came flying through the air and pursued the bird, which flew directly toward a pond. The eagle dived at the bird and mangled it, but Reinald saw the bird drop a golden egg into the water. Now he rubbed the three fish scales in his hand, and immediately a whale came swimming up, swallowed the egg, and spat it out onto the shore. Reinald picked it up and cracked it open with a stone. There he found a little key that fit the steel gate. As soon as he just touched the gate with the key, the gate sprang open by itself, and he entered. All the bars on the other doors slid off by themselves, and he went through seven doors into seven splendid and brightly lit rooms. In the last room a maiden was lying asleep on a bed. She was so beautiful that he was completely dazzled by her. He sought to wake her, but it was in vain. Her sleep was so deep that she seemed to be dead. In his rage he struck a black slate standing next to the bed. At that very moment the maiden awoke but fell right back to sleep. Now he took the slate and threw it onto the stone floor so that it shattered into a thousand pieces. No sooner did this happen than the maiden opened her eyes wide, and the magic spell was broken. She turned out to be the sister of Reinald's three brothers-in-law. Because she had rejected the love of a godless sorcerer, he had sentenced her to a deathlike sleep and changed her brothers into animals. They were to remain that way so long as the black slate remained untouched.

Reinald led the maiden out of the castle, and as they passed through the gate, his brothers-in-law came riding up from three different directions. They had been released from the magic spell, and with them came their wives and children. Indeed, the eagle's bride had hatched the egg and carried a beautiful baby girl in her arms. Now all of them traveled to the old king and queen. The Miracle Child brought his three sisters home. Soon he married the beautiful maiden, and their wedding provided great joy and pleasure to everyone,

Now the cat's run home, for my tale is done.

83

THE POOR MAIDEN

Once upon a time there was a poor little maiden. Her mother and father had died, and she no longer had a house in which she could live, and a bed in which she could sleep. She had nothing more in the world than the clothes on her back, and she carried a small piece of bread in her hand that someone who had taken pity on her had given to her. Despite all this, the maiden was good and pious.

As she set out on her way, she encountered a poor man who asked her so desperately for something to eat that she gave him the piece of bread. Then she continued on her way and met a child who said to her: "My head is freezing. Please give me something that I can tie around it."

So the maiden took off her cap and gave it to the child. And after she had walked a bit farther, she came across another child without a bodice. So she gave him hers. Further on she met another child who asked her for a little dress, and she took off her own dress and gave it to her. Finally she came to a forest, and it had already become dark. Then, yet another child came and asked for her undershirt, and the pious maiden thought: "It's pitch black. You can certainly give away your undershirt," and so she gave it to the child. All of a sudden the stars fell from heaven and turned into pure shining hard coins, and even though she had given away her undershirt, she had another one on her made from the finest linen. So she gathered the coins in the undershirt and became rich for the rest of her life.

84
THE MOTHER-IN-LAW

Once there lived a king and a queen, and the queen had a terribly evil mother-in-law. One day the king went to war, and the old queen had her daughter-in-law locked up in a damp cellar along with her two little sons. After some time had passed, the mother-in-law said to herself, "I'd really like to eat one of the children."

So she called her cook and ordered him to go down into the cellar, take one of the little sons, slaughter him, and cook him.

"What kind of sauce would you like?" asked the cook.

"A brown one," said the old queen.

The cook then went down into the cellar and said, "Ah, your highness, the old queen wants me to slaughter and cook one of your sons this evening."

The young queen was deeply distressed and said, "Well, why don't we take a pig? Cook it the way she wants, and say that it was my child."

The cook did just that and served the pig in a brown sauce to the old queen as though it were a child. Indeed, she ate it with great relish. Soon thereafter the old queen thought, "the child's meat tasted so tender that I'd like to have the second as well." So, she called the cook and ordered him to go down into the cellar and slaughter the second son.

"What kind of a sauce should I cook him in?"

"Oh, in a white one," said the old queen.

The cook went down into the cellar and said, "Ah, the old queen has ordered me now to slaughter your second little son and cook him, too."

"Take a suckling pig," the young queen said, "and cook it exactly as she likes it."

The cook did just that and set it in front of the old queen in a white sauce, and she devoured it with even greater relish than before.

Finally, the old queen thought, "Now that the children are in my body I'd like to eat the young queen as well." The old queen called the cook and ordered him to cook the young queen.

[*Fragment: The cook slaughters a doe the third time. However, the young queen has trouble preventing her children from screaming. She doesn't want the old queen to hear them and realize they are still alive, and so on.*]

85
FRAGMENTS

Snowflower

A young princess was called Snowflower because she was white like snow and was born during the winter. One day her mother became sick, and the princess went out to pluck herbs that might heal her. As she went by a big tree, a swarm of bees flew out and covered her entire body from head to foot. But they didn't sting or hurt her. Instead, they carried honey to her lips, and her entire body glowed through and through with beauty.

The Princess with the Louse

Once upon a time there was a princess who was so clean, indeed, the cleanest in the entire world, that nobody ever saw the least bit of dirt or stain on her. However, one time a louse was found sitting on her head, and this was regarded as such a true miracle that nobody wanted to kill the louse. Instead, people decided to nourish it with milk so that it would grow. So, this is indeed what happened, and the louse grew until it was finally as large as a calf. When the louse died later, the princess ordered it to be skinned, and a dress was to be made out of its fur. Soon thereafter a man came to court the princess, and she demanded that he was first to guess the animal that had provided the fur for her dress before she would marry him. Since he couldn't do this, and nor could other suitors, they all had to leave the palace. Finally, a handsome prince came who was able to solve the riddle in the following way.—

Prince Johannes

This is a tale about his melancholy and nostalgic wanderings, about his flight with the spirit, about the red castle, about his numerous trials and tribulations until he was finally allowed to glimpse the beautiful princess of the sun.

The Good Cloth

Two daughters of a seamstress inherited a good old cloth, and whenever anything was wrapped in it, the cloth turned the object into gold. This cloth provided them with enough to live on, and they also did some sewing to earn a little extra money. One sister was very smart, the other very stupid. One day the oldest went to church, and a Jew came down the street calling, "Beautiful new cloth for sale! Beautiful cloth to trade for old cloth! Anyone want to trade?"

When the stupid sister heard that, she ran out to him and traded the good old cloth for a new cloth. This was exactly what the Jew had wanted, for he knew all about the power of the old cloth. When the older sister came home, she said, "We're doing poorly with our sewing. I've got to get some money. Where's our cloth?"

"It's good that I've done what I've done," said the stupid sister. "While you were gone, I made a trade for a brand-new cloth."

[*After this the Jew is turned into a dog, the two maidens into hens. Eventually, the hens regain their human form and beat the dog to death.*]

86
THE FOX AND THE GEESE

Once the fox came to a meadow where there was a flock of nice, plump geese. Then he laughed and said, "Ho, I've come just at the right moment. You're sitting there together so nicely that all I have to do is eat you up one by one."

The geese began cackling in fright and jumped up. They screamed for mercy and begged piteously for their lives. However, the fox said: "No mercy! You've got to die."

Finally, one of the geese plucked up her courage and said, "Well, if we poor geese must surrender our innocent young lives, then show us some mercy by granting us one last prayer so that we won't have to die with our sins. After that we'll line up in a row so that you'll continually be able to pick out the fattest among us."

"All right," said the fox. "That's a fair and pious request. I'll wait until you're done."

So the first goose began a good long prayer and kept saying, "*Ga! Ga!*" Since she refused to end her prayer, the second didn't wait for her turn and also began saying, "*Ga! Ga!*" (And when they all will have finished praying, the tale will be continued to be told, but in the meantime they're still saying their prayers.)

VOLUME II

PREFACE TO VOLUME II

Despite the strong and pressing demands of time, we produced this additional collection of household tales faster and more easily than the first. In part this was due to the fact that, by itself, our collection had gained friends who supported it, and in part because those who would have liked to have supported it earlier saw now clearly what we had intended and how we had intended to work. Moreover, we were finally favored by that sort of luck that appears to be coincidence but is actually the result of the usual diligent perseverance of collectors: after one first becomes accustomed to paying attention to similar kinds of things, one then encounters them more frequently than one might otherwise expect. Indeed, this is generally the case with folk customs, certain qualities, sayings, and jokes.

We are especially grateful for the kindness of friends from the duchies of Paderborn and Münster, who provided the tales in Low German. Their familiarity with this dialect is particularly beneficial with regard to the internal integrity of the tales. In these regions, traditionally famous for their German freedom, the tales have been preserved in many places as an almost regular Sunday pastime. In the mountains the shepherds told their own stories, also known in the Harz region and probably in other large mountainous areas, about the Emperor Redbeard, who lives there with his treasures, and also about the race of giants (the Hühnen) and how they throw their hammers to each other from mountain tops that are many miles apart from one other. We are thinking about publishing these tales elsewhere. Indeed, this region is still rich in traditional customs and songs.

One of our lucky coincidences involved making the acquaintance of a peasant woman from the village of Zwehrn near Kassel. It was through her that we received a considerable number of the tales published here that can be called genuinely Hessian and are also supplements to the first volume. This woman, still active and not much over fifty years old, is called Viehmann, and she has a firmly set and pleasant face with bright, clear eyes and had probably been beautiful in her youth. She has retained these old stories firmly in her memory, a gift that she says is not granted to everyone. Indeed, many people can't even retain any tales, while she narrates in a manner that is thoughtful, steady, and unusually lively. Moreover, she takes great pleasure in it. At the beginning she speaks very freely, and then, if one wishes, she will repeat the tale slowly so that, with a little practice, one can copy down what she says. In this way we were able to retain much of what she said literally, and the story's true essence will be easily recognized. Whoever believes that the transcription of such storytelling results in easy falsification, carelessness in the preservation of the tales, and, therefore, the impossibility of recording long narratives as a rule, ought to hear how exactly she always repeats each tale and how eager she is to get it right. She never changes anything when she retells a story and corrects mistakes as soon as she notices them even right in the middle of the telling. The attachment to tradition is much stronger among people who resolutely follow the same way of life than we who have a fondness for change can understand. This is exactly the reason why such storytelling that has been put to test has a certain insistent intimacy and an internal efficiency that other things do not easily attain, even though they can seem more lustrous on the outside. The epic source of folk narratives resembles the color green that one finds throughout nature in many different shades; it satisfies and soothes without ever causing fatigue.

The essential value of these tales is indeed to be held in great esteem, for they shed a new and particular light on our ancient heroic poetry in a way that nobody has ever managed to bring about. Briar Rose, who is pricked by a spindle that puts her to sleep, is actually Brunhilde, pricked by a thorn that puts her to sleep, not the one in the *Niberlungenlied*, but the one in the Old Norse tradition. Snow White slumbers in a glowing vivid red color, as did Snäfridr, the most beautiful woman of all, while Harald the Fair-Haired sits at her coffin for three years, similar to the faithful dwarfs, who keep watch and protect the living-dead maiden. However, the piece of apple in her mouth is a magic sleeping tablet or apple. The tale about the golden feather, which the bird drops and thus causes the king to send out his men all over the world to search for it, is nothing other than the tale of King Mark in *Tristan*, to whom a bird brings the golden hair of a princess, for whom he now begins to yearn. We understand much better why Loki remains stuck to a gigantic eagle through reading the tale about the golden goose in which young women and men stick to the goose when they touch it. Who doesn't recognize Sigurd's own story depicted in the character of the evil goldsmith, the talking bird, and the eating of the heart? The present volume conveys other enormous and outstanding episodes about Sigurd and his youth that are partly in the songs about him that we know, and these episodes help us in the difficult task of interpreting the incident about the treasure that is to be divided. Nothing is more valuable and at the same time more certain than that which flows from two sources that were separated early on and later join each other in their own riverbed. There is nothing but primeval German mythos buried in these folk tales that was thought to have been lost, and we are firmly convinced that if one were now to begin searching in all the blessed parts of our fatherland, this research would lead to neglected treasures that would transform themselves into incredible treasures and would help found the scientific study of the origins of our poetry. It is exactly the same with the numerous dialects of our language in which the majority of the words and peculiarities that have long been considered extinct continue to live without being recognized.

Our collection was not merely intended to serve the history of poetry but also to bring out the poetry itself that lives in it and make it effective: enabling it to bring pleasure wherever it can and also therefore, enabling it to become an actual educational primer. Objections have been raised against this last point because this or that might be embarrassing and would be unsuitable for children or offensive (when the tales might touch on certain situations and relations—even the mentioning of the bad things that the devil does) and that parents might not want to put the book into the hands of children. That concern might be legitimate in certain cases, and then one can easily make selections. On the whole it is certainly not necessary. Nature itself provides our best evidence, for it has allowed these and those flowers and leaves to grow in their own colors and shapes. If they are not beneficial for any person or personal needs, something that the flowers and leaves are unaware of, then that person can walk right by them, but the individual cannot demand that they be colored and cut according to his or her needs. Or, in other words, rain and dew provide a benefit for everything on earth. Whoever is afraid to put plants outside because they might be too delicate and could be harmed and would rather water them inside cannot demand to put an end to the rain and the dew. Everything that is natural can also become beneficial. And that is what our aim should be. Incidentally, we are not aware of a single salutary and powerful book that has edified the people in which such dubious matters don't appear to a great extent, even if we place the Bible at the top of the list. Making the right use of a book doesn't result in finding evil, but rather, as an appealing saying puts it, evidence of our hearts. Children read the stars without fear, while others, according to folk belief, insult angels by doing this.

Once again we have published diverse versions of the tales along with all kinds of relevant notes in the appendix.[1] Those readers who feel indifferent about such things will find it easier to skip over them than we would have found to omit them. They belong to the book insofar as it is a contribution to the history of German folk literature. All the variants seem more noteworthy to us than they do to those who see in them nothing more than alterations or distortions of a once extant primeval prototype. In contrast, we think they are perhaps only attempts to approach the actual spirit of the prototype in many different inexhaustible ways. The repetitions of single sentences, features, and introductory passages are to be regarded as epic lines that reoccur continually as soon as the tone is struck that sets them off, and actually they should not be understood in any other way. Everything that has been collected here from oral transmission (perhaps with the exception of "Puss in Boots") is purely German in its origins as well as in its development and has not been borrowed from any place, as one can easily prove on the basis of externals if one wanted to dispute this for individual cases. The reasons that are usually brought forth to argue that the tales have been borrowed from Italian, French, or Oriental books, which are not read by the people, especially if they live in the country, are exactly like those attempts to prove the tales stem from recent literature in which soldiers, apprentices, cannons, tobacco pipes, and other new things appear. But these things, just like the words of our contemporary language, are exactly the things that were reshaped by the lips of storytellers, and one can certainly rely on the fact that the storytellers in the sixteenth century used country troopers and shotguns instead of soldiers and cannons in their tales just as the magic helmet was used in the age of chivalry and knights, not the hat that makes people invisible.

We suspended the translation of *The Pentamerone*, initially promised for this volume, as well as the selection of those tales from the *Gesta Romanorum*, because we wanted to make space for our indigenous tales.

Kassel, September 30, 1814

Note

1. These notes are in the section "Notes to Volumes I and II" in this book.

I
THE POOR MAN AND THE RICH MAN

In olden times, when the dear Lord himself was still wandering the earth among mortals, he happened to grow tired one evening, and night descended before he could reach an inn. Then he saw two houses right in front of him, just opposite one another. One house was large and beautiful and belonged to a rich man, and the other was small and shabby and belonged to a poor man. Our dear Lord thought, "I'm sure I won't be a burden to the rich man," and he knocked at the door. All at once the rich man opened the window and asked what he wanted.

"A night's lodging."

The rich man examined the traveler from head to toe, and since the dear Lord was dressed very simply and didn't look like he had much money in his pockets, the rich man shook his head and said, "I can't put you up. My rooms are full of seeds. If I were to put up all the people who knocked at my door, then I'd soon have to go out begging for myself. Look for a place somewhere else."

With that he slammed the window shut and left the dear Lord standing there. So the dear Lord turned around and went across the street to the small house. No sooner had he knocked than the poor man already had the door open and asked the traveler to enter and spend the night in his house.

"It's already dark," he said, "and you won't be able to go much farther tonight."

The Lord was pleased to hear that, and he entered the house. The poor man's wife welcomed him by shaking his hand. She told him to make himself feel at home and to feel free to use anything they had, even though they didn't have much. Whatever they had, he could gladly have. Then she put potatoes on the fire, and while they were cooking, she milked the goat so that they would at least have a little milk with the meal. When the table had been set, the dear Lord sat down and ate with them, and he enjoyed the meager repast because there were grateful faces around him. When they had eaten and it was time to go to bed, the wife whispered to her husband, "Listen, dear husband, let's make up a bed of straw for ourselves tonight so that the poor traveler can sleep in our bed and rest. He's been traveling the whole day and is probably very tired."

"That's wonderful," he answered. "I'll go and offer it to him."

And he went to the dear Lord and told him that, if he did not mind, he could sleep in their bed and give his limbs a proper rest.

The dear Lord didn't want to take the old couple's bed, but they insisted until he finally took their bed and lay down in it. Meanwhile, they made a bed of straw for themselves and lay on the ground. The next morning they were up before daybreak and cooked a pitiful breakfast for their guest. When the sun began to shine through the little window and the dear Lord stood up, he ate with them again and prepared to continue his journey. As he was standing in the doorway, however, he turned around and said, "Because you are so kind and good, I'm going to grant you three wishes, and they shall indeed be fulfilled."

"There's nothing I want more than eternal salvation," said the man, "and also that we stay healthy and get our meager daily bread as long as we wish. As for the third thing, I don't know what to wish."

"Don't you want to wish for a new house in place of this old one?" asked the dear Lord.

"Oh, yes," said the man. "I'd certainly be pleased if I could have that as well."

Right before his departure the dear Lord fulfilled their wishes, turned the old house into a new one, and departed.

When the rich man got up, it was broad daylight. As he looked out his window toward the other side of the road, he saw a beautiful new house. His eyes popped wide open, and he called his wife and said: "Take a look. How did that happen? Just yesterday there was a dumpy house standing there, and today there's this new beautiful one. Run over and find out what happened."

So his wife went over and asked the poor man, who told her, "Last night a traveler came by looking for a night's lodging, and right before his departure this morning he granted us three wishes, eternal salvation, good health and our meager daily bread for the rest of our lives, and a beautiful new house in place of our old shack."

After the rich man's wife heard this, she hurried back and told her husband what had happened. Then the man said, "I'd like to tear myself in two and beat myself to a pulp. If I had only known! The stranger came to our house first, but I turned him away."

"Hurry," said his wife, "and get on your horse. The man hasn't got far. You must catch up to him and get him to grant you three wishes, too."

Now the rich man mounted his horse and managed to catch up with the dear Lord. He used sweet talk with the dear Lord and begged him not to take it amiss that he had not let him into his house right away, for he had gone to look for the door key, but the stranger had disappeared in the meantime. The rich man assured him that, if he passed by again, he would find a place to stay at his house.

"Very well," said the dear Lord. "If I come back again, I shall stay with you."

Then the rich man asked him whether he also could have three wishes, like his neighbor. The Lord said yes, but that they would not turn out well for him, and it might be best if he refrained from wishing for anything. The rich man disagreed and asserted that he'd be able to choose something good if he knew for certain that the wishes would be fulfilled.

"Just ride home," said the dear Lord. "The three wishes you make shall be fulfilled."

Now the rich man had what he wanted. So he rode home and began to ponder what he should wish for. As he was thus steeped in thought, he let the reins drop, and the horse began jumping so much that his thoughts were continually disturbed and he couldn't collect them. He was so annoyed by the horse that he lost his patience and said: "I wish you'd break your neck!"

As soon as he had uttered those words, *boom!*—he was thrown to the ground, and the horse lay dead and didn't move anymore. Thus the first wish had been fulfilled. Since the rich man was greedy, however, he didn't want to leave the saddle behind. So he cut it off, swung it over his back, and proceeded on foot. Despite all this, he consoled himself that he had two wishes left. As he went walking through the sand under the blazing noonday sun, he became hot and surly. The saddle rested heavily on his back, and he was having a great deal of trouble thinking of a wish. Whenever he thought he had found the right wish, it would seem to him afterward to be too little and modest. At one point he began thinking about how easy his wife had it at home, where she was probably in a cool room and enjoying a fine meal. Just the thought of that irritated him so much that, before he knew it, he blurted out, "I wish she were sitting on this saddle at home and couldn't get off, instead of my carrying it on my back!"

And just as the last word left his lips the saddle vanished from his back, and he realized that his second wish had been fulfilled. He became so hot now that he began to run. He was looking forward to sitting down alone in his room where he would think of something great for his last wish. However, when he arrived home and opened the door to the living room, his wife was sitting on the saddle in the middle of the room. Since she couldn't get off, she was screaming and complaining.

"You should be happy," he said. "I'm going to get you all the riches in the world with my wish. Just stay where you are."

However, she yelled at him, "What good are all the riches in the world to me if I have to sit on this saddle. You wished me up here, and now you'd better get me off!"

Whether he liked it or not, he had to use the third wish to help her get rid of the saddle and climb down off of it. His wish was fulfilled at once, and so he got nothing from the wishes but irritation, wasted effort, and a lost horse. On the other hand, the poor people spent their lives happily, peacefully, and devoutly until they reached their blissful end.

2

THE SINGING, SPRINGING LARK

Once upon a time there was a man about to go on a long journey, and upon his departure he asked his three daughters what he should bring back to them. The oldest wanted pearls, the second diamonds, but the third said, "Dear father, I'd like to have a singing, springing lark."

"Yes," said the father. "If I can get one, you shall have it." So he kissed all three daughters and departed.

Now, by the time he was ready for his return journey, he had purchased pearls and diamonds for the two oldest daughters, but even though he had looked all over, he had not been able to find the singing, springing lark for his youngest. He was particularly sorry about that because she was his favorite. In the meantime, his way took him through a forest, in the middle of which he discovered a magnificent castle. Near the castle was a tree, and way on top of this tree he saw a lark singing and springing about.

"Well, you've come just at the right time!" he said, quite pleased, and he ordered his servant to climb the tree and catch the little bird. But when the servant went over to the tree, a lion jumped out from under it, shook himself, and roared so ferociously that the leaves on the trees trembled.

"If anyone tries to steal my singing, springing lark," he cried, "I'll eat him up!"

"I didn't know the bird belonged to you," said the man. "Can I buy my way out of this?"

"No!" said the lion. "There's nothing that can save you unless you promise to give me the first thing you meet when you get home. If you agree, then I'll not only grant you your life, but I'll also give you the bird for your daughter."

However, the man refused and said, "That could be my youngest daughter. She loves me most of all and always runs to meet me when I return home."

But the servant was very frightened and remarked, "It could also be a cat or a dog."

The man let himself be persuaded, took the singing, springing lark with a sad heart, and promised the lion he would give him the first thing that he encountered when he reached his house.

When he now rode home, the first thing that he met was none other than his youngest and dearest daughter. Indeed, she came running up to him, threw her arms around him, and kissed him. As soon as she saw that he had brought her a singing, springing lark, she was even more overcome by joy. But her father could not rejoice and began to weep.

"Alas, dearest child!" he said. "I've had to pay a high price for this bird. To get it I had to promise you to a wild lion, and when he gets you, he'll tear you to pieces and eat you up."

Then he went on to tell her how everything had happened and begged her not to go there, no matter what the consequences might be. Yet she consoled him and said, "Dearest father, since you've made a promise, you must keep it. I'll go there, and once I've made the lion nice and tame, I'll be back here safe and sound."

The next morning she had her father show her the way. Then she took leave of him and walked calmly into the forest.

Now, the lion was actually an enchanted prince. During the day he and his men were lions, and during the night they assumed their true human forms. When she arrived there, she was welcomed in a friendly way, and the wedding was celebrated. As soon as night came, the lion became a handsome man, and so they stayed awake at night and slept during the day, and they lived happily together for a long time.

One day the prince came to her and said, "Tomorrow there will be a celebration at your father's house because your oldest sister is to be married. If it would give you pleasure to attend, my lions will escort you there."

She replied that, yes, she would very much like to see her father again, and she went there accompanied by the lions. There was great rejoicing when she arrived, for they had all believed that she had been torn to pieces by the lion and had long been dead. But she told them how well off she was and stayed with them just as long as the wedding celebration lasted. Then she went back to the forest.

When the second daughter was about to be married, she was again invited to the wedding, but on this occasion she said to the lion, "This time I don't want to go without you. You must come with me."

However, the lion didn't want to attend the wedding and said it would be too dangerous for him because if a ray of light were to fall upon him, he would be changed into a dove and have to fly about with the doves for seven years.

But she wouldn't leave him in peace and said that she'd be sure to take good care of him and protect him from the light. So they went off together and also took their small child with them. Once there she had a hall built for him so strong and thick that not a single ray of light could penetrate it. That was the place where he was to sit when the wedding candles were lit. However, its door was made out of green wood, and it split and developed a crack that nobody saw.

Now the wedding was celebrated in splendor, but when the wedding procession with all the candles and torches came back from church and passed by the prince's hall, a very, very thin ray fell upon the prince, and he was instantly transformed into a dove. When his wife entered the hall to look for him, she could only find a white dove sitting there, and he said to her, "For seven years I shall have to fly about the world, but for every seven steps you take I shall leave a drop of red blood and a white feather to show you the way. And, if you follow the traces, you'll be able to rescue me."

Then the dove flew out the door, and she followed him. At every seventh step she took, a little drop of blood and a little white feather would fall and show her the way. Thus she went farther and farther into the wide world and never looked about or stopped until the seven years were almost up. She was looking forward to that and thought they would soon be free. But they were still quite far from their goal.

Once, as she was moving along, she failed to find any more little feathers or little drops of blood, and when she raised her head, the dove had also vanished. "I won't be able to get help from a mortal," she thought, and so she climbed up to the sun and said to her, "You shine into every nook and cranny. Is there any chance that you've seen a white dove flying around?"

"No," said the sun, "I haven't, but I'll give you a little casket. Just open it when your need is greatest."

She thanked the sun and continued on her way until the moon began to shine in the evening. "You shine the whole night through and on all fields and woods. Have you seen a white dove flying around?"

"No," said the moon, "I haven't, but I'll give you an egg. Just crack it open when your need is greatest."

She thanked the moon and went farther until the Night Wind stirred and started to blow. "You blow over every tree and under every leaf. Have you seen a white dove flying around?"

"No," said the Night Wind, "I haven't, but I'll ask the three other winds. Perhaps they've seen one."

The East Wind and the West Wind came and reported they had not seen a thing, but the South Wind said, "I've seen the white dove. It's flown to the Red Sea and has become a lion again, for the seven years are over. Right now the lion's in the midst of a battle with a dragon, which is really an enchanted princess."

Then the Night Wind said to her, "Here's what I would advise you to do: Go to the Red Sea, where you'll find some tall reeds growing along the shore. Then count them until you come to the eleventh one, which you're to cut off and use to strike the dragon. That done, the lion will be able to conquer the dragon, and both will regain their human forms. After that, look around, and you'll see the griffin sitting by the Red Sea. Get on his back with the prince, and the griffin will carry you home across the sea. Now, here's a nut for you. When you cross over the middle of the sea, let it drop. A nut tree will instantly sprout out of the water, and the griffin will be able to rest on it. If he can't rest there, he won't be strong enough to carry you both across the sea. So if you forget to drop the nut into the sea, he'll let you fall into the water."

She went there and found everything as the Night Wind had said. She counted the reeds by the sea, cut off the eleventh, and struck the dragon with it. Consequently, the lion defeated the dragon, and both immediately regained their human forms. But when the princess, who had previously been a dragon, was set free from the magic spell, she picked the prince up in her arms, got on the griffin, and carried him off with her. So the poor maiden, who had journeyed so far, stood alone and forsaken again. However, she said, "I'll keep going as far as the wind blows and so long as the cock crows until I find him."

And off she went and wandered a long, long way until she came to the castle where the two were living together. Then she heard that their wedding celebration was soon to take place. "God will come to my aid," she remarked as she opened the little casket that the sun had given her. There she found a dress as radiant as the sun itself. She took it out, put it on, and went up to the castle. Everyone at the court and the bride herself stared at her. The bride liked the dress so much she thought it would be nice to have it for her wedding and asked if she could buy it.

"Not for money or property," she answered, "but for flesh and blood."

The bride asked her what she meant by that, and she responded, "Let me sleep one night in the prince's room."

The bride didn't want to let her, but she also wanted the dress very badly. Finally, she agreed, but the bridegroom's servant was ordered to give him a sleeping potion. That night when the prince was asleep, the maiden was led into his room, where she sat down on his bed and said, "I've followed you for seven years. I went to the sun, the moon, and the four winds to find out where you were. I helped you conquer the dragon. Are you going to forget me forever?"

But the prince slept so soundly that it seemed to him as if the wind were merely whispering in the firs. When morning came, she was led out of the castle again and had to give up her golden dress.

Since her ploy had not been of much use, she was quite sad and went out to a meadow, where she sat down and wept. But as she was sitting there, she remembered the egg that the moon had given her. She cracked it open, and a hen with twelve chicks jumped out, all in gold. The peeping chicks scampered about and then crawled under the mother hen's wings. There was not a lovelier sight to see in the world. Shortly after that she stood up and drove them ahead of her over the meadow until they came within sight of the bride, who saw them from her window. She liked the little chicks so much that she came right down and asked if she could buy them.

"Not for money or possessions, but for flesh and blood. Let me sleep another night in the prince's room."

The bride agreed and wanted to trick her as she had done the night before. But when the prince went to bed, he asked the servant what had caused all the murmuring and rustling during the night, and the servant told him everything: that he had been compelled to give him a sleeping potion because a poor girl had secretly slept in his room, and that he was supposed to give him another one that night.

"Dump the drink by the side of my bed," said the prince.

That night the maiden was led into the room again, and when she began to talk about her sad plight, he immediately recognized his dear wife by her voice, jumped up, and exclaimed, "Now I'm really free from the spell! It was like a dream. The princess had cast a spell over me and made me forget you, but God has helped me just in time."

That night they left the castle in secret, for they were afraid of the princess's father, who was a sorcerer. They got on the griffin, who carried them over the Red Sea, and when they were in the middle, she let the nut drop. Immediately a big nut tree sprouted, and the griffin was able to rest there. Then he carried them home, where they found their child, who had grown tall and handsome. From then on they lived happily until their death.

3

THE GOOSE GIRL

There once was an old queen whose husband had been dead for many years, and she had a beautiful daughter. When the daughter grew up, she was betrothed to a prince who lived far away. When the time came for her to be married, and the princess had to get ready to depart for the distant kingdom, the old queen packed up a great many precious items and ornaments: gold and silver, goblets and jewels. In short, everything that suited a royal dowry, for she loved her child with all her heart. She also gave her a chambermaid, who was to accompany her and deliver her safely into the hands of her bridegroom. Each received a horse for the journey, but the princess's horse was named Falada and could speak. When the hour of departure arrived, the old mother went into her bedroom, took a small knife, and cut her finger to make it bleed. Then she placed a white handkerchief underneath her finger, let three drops of blood fall on it, and gave it to her daughter.

"My dear child," she said, "take good care of these three drops, for they will help you on your journey when you're in need."

After they had bid each other a sad farewell, the princess stuck the handkerchief into her bosom, mounted her horse, and began her journey to her bridegroom. After riding an hour, she felt very thirsty and called to her chambermaid, "Get down and fetch some water from the brook with my goblet that you brought along for me. I'd like to have something to drink."

"Hey, if you're thirsty," said the chambermaid, "get down yourself. Just lie down by the water and drink. I don't like being your servant."

Since the princess was very thirsty, she dismounted, bent over the brook, and drank some water, but she was not allowed to drink out of the golden goblet.

"Oh, God!" she said.

Then the three drops of blood responded, "Ah, if your mother knew, her heart would break in two!"

But the princess was quite humble. She said nothing and got back on her horse. They continued riding a few miles further. The day was warm and the sun so sticky and hot that she soon she got thirsty again. When they came to a stream, she called to her chambermaid once more. "Get down and bring me something to drink from my golden cup," for she had long since forgotten the servant's nasty words.

"If you want to drink," the chambermaid said even more haughtily than before, "drink by yourself. I don't like being your servant."

Since she was very thirsty, the princess dismounted, lay down next to the running water, and wept.

"Oh, God!" she said.

Once again the drops of blood responded, "Ah, if your mother knew, her heart would break in two!"

As she was leaning over the bank and drinking the water, her handkerchief with the three drops of blood fell out of her bosom and floated downstream without her ever noticing it, so great was her fear. But the chambermaid had seen it and was delighted because she knew that now she could have power over the princess. Without the three drops of blood, the princess had become weak. So, as she was about to get back on the horse named Falada, the chambermaid said, "Falada belongs to me. Yours is the nag!"

The princess had to put up with all that. Moreover, the chambermaid ordered her to take off her royal garments and to put on the maid's shabby clothes. Finally, she had to swear under open skies that she would never tell a soul at the royal court what the chambermaid had done. If the princess hadn't given her word, she would have been killed on the spot. But Falada saw all this and took good note of it.

Now the chambermaid mounted Falada, and the true bride had to get on the wretched nag. Thus they continued their journey until they finally arrived at the royal castle. There was great rejoicing when they entered the courtyard, and the prince ran to meet them. He lifted the chambermaid from her horse, thinking that she was his bride. Then he led her up the stairs, while the true princess was left standing below. Meanwhile, the old king peered out a window, and when he saw her standing in the courtyard, he was struck by her fine, delicate, and beautiful features. He went straight to the royal suite and asked the bride about the girl she had brought with her, the one standing below in the courtyard, and who she was.

"Oh, I picked her up along the way to keep me company. Just give her something to keep her busy."

But the old king had no work for her and could only respond, "I have a little boy who tends the geese. Perhaps she could help him."

The boy's name was Little Conrad, and the true bride had to help him tend the geese.

Shortly after, the false bride said to the young king, "Dearest husband, I'd like you to do me a favor."

"I'd be glad to," he answered.

"Well then, let me summon the knacker. I want him to cut off the head of the horse that carried me here because it gave me nothing but trouble along the way."

However, she actually was afraid the horse would reveal what she had done to the princess. When all the preparations had been made and faithful Falada was about to die, word reached the ears of the true princess, and she secretly promised the knacker a gold coin if he would render her a small service. There was a big dark gateway through which she had to pass every morning and evening with the geese, and she wanted him to nail Falada's head on the wall under the dark gateway, where she could always see it. The knacker promised to do it, and when he cut off the horse's head, he nailed it firmly onto the wall under the dark gateway.

Early the next morning, when she and Conrad drove the geese out through the gateway, she said in passing:

"Oh, poor Falada, I see you hanging there."

Then the head answered:

"Dear princess, is that you really there?
Oh, if your mother knew,
her heart would break in two!"

She walked out of the city in silence, and they drove the geese into the fields. When she reached the meadow, she sat down and undid her hair, which was as pure as gold. Little Conrad liked the way her hair glistened so much that he tried to pull out a few strands. Then she said:

"Blow, wind, oh, blow with all your might!
Blow Little Conrad's cap out of sight,
make him chase it everywhere
till I've braided all my hair
and fixed it so that it's all right."

Then a gust of wind came and blew off Little Conrad's cap into the fields, and he had to run after it. By the time he returned with it, she had finished combing and putting her hair up, and he couldn't get a single strand of it. Little Conrad became so angry that he wouldn't speak to her after that. Thus they tended the geese until evening, when they set out on their way home.

The next morning, when they drove the geese through the dark gateway, the maiden said:

"Oh, poor Falada, I see you hanging there."

Then Falada responded:

"Dear princess, is that you really there?
Oh, if your mother knew,
her heart would break in two!"

Once she was in the field again, she sat down in the meadow and began to comb out her hair. Little Conrad ran up and tried to grab it, but she quickly said:

"Blow, wind, oh, blow with all your might!
Blow Little Conrad's cap out of sight,
and make him chase it everywhere
till I've braided all my hair
and fixed it so that it's all right."

The wind blew and whisked the cap off his head and drove it far off so that Conrad had to run after it. When he came back, she had long since put up her hair, and he couldn't get a single strand. Thus they tended the geese until evening. However, upon returning that evening, Little Conrad went to the old king and said, "I don't want to tend the geese with that girl anymore."

"Why not?" asked the old king.

"Well, she torments me the whole day long."

Immediately the old king ordered him to tell him what she did, and Conrad said, "In the morning, when we pass through the dark gateway, there's a horse's head on the wall, and she always says:

'Oh, poor Falada, I see you hanging there.'

And the head answers:

'Dear princess, is that you really there?
Oh, if your mother knew,
her heart would break in two!'"

And thus Little Conrad went on to tell the king what happened out on the meadow, and how he had had to run after his cap.

The old king ordered him to drive the geese out again the next day, and when morning came, the old king hid himself behind the dark gateway and heard her speak to Falada's head. Then he followed her into the fields and hid behind some bushes in the meadow. Soon he saw with his own eyes how the goose girl and the goose boy led the geese to the meadow, and how she sat down after a while and undid her hair that glistened radiantly. Before long, she said:

"Blow, wind, oh, blow with all your might!
Blow Little Conrad's cap out of sight,
and make him chase it everywhere
until I've braided all my hair
and fixed it so that it's all right."

Then a gust of wind came and carried Little Conrad's cap away, so that he had to run far, and the maiden calmly combed and braided her hair. All this was observed by the old king. He then went home unnoticed, and when the goose girl came back that evening, he called her aside and asked her why she did all those things.

"I'm not allowed to tell you, nor am I allowed to bemoan my plight to anyone. Such is the oath I swore under the open skies. Otherwise, I would have been killed."

Although he kept on insisting and would give her no peace, she wouldn't talk. Then he said, "If you don't want to tell me anything, then you certainly may let the iron stove over there listen to your sorrows."

"All right," said the maiden, "I'll do that."

Upon saying that, she crawled into the iron stove and poured her heart out and told it what had happened to her and how she had been betrayed by the wicked chambermaid.

Now the oven had a hole on top, and the old king overheard what she said and listened to every word she uttered about her fate. He immediately intended to make everything good and had her dressed in royal garments, and it was like a miracle to see how beautiful she really was. The old king called his son and revealed to him that he had the wrong bride, who was nothing but a chambermaid. The true bride, however, was standing there before him, the former goose girl. The young king was delighted and ecstatic when he saw how beautiful and virtuous she was. Now a great feast was prepared, and all their friends and the entire court were invited to attend. At the head of the table sat the bridegroom, with the princess at one side and the chambermaid at the other, but the chambermaid was so distracted that she could no longer recognize the princess, who was dressed in a dazzling manner. After they finished eating and drinking and were all in high spirits, the old king gave the chambermaid a riddle to solve: what punishment did a woman deserve who deceived her lord in such and such a way? Whereupon he told her the whole story and concluded by asking, "How would you sentence her?"

"She deserves nothing better," said the false bride, "than to be stripped completely naked and put inside a barrel studded with sharp nails. Then two white horses should be harnessed to the barrel and made to drag her through the streets until she's dead."

"You're the woman," said the old king, "and you've pronounced your own sentence. All this shall happen to you."

After the sentence had been carried out, the young king married his true bride, and they both reigned over their kingdom in peace and bliss.

4

THE YOUNG GIANT

A farmer had a son no bigger than the size of a thumb and the son didn't become any bigger or even grow so much as a hair's breadth in the coming years. One day, when the farmer was preparing to go out to the field to do some plowing, the little fellow said, "Father, I want to go with you."

"No," said the father. "You'd better stay here. You're of no use to me out there, and you could get lost."

Thumbling began to weep, and if his father was going to have his peace and quiet, he had to take the boy with him. So his father stuck him in his pocket, and once he was out on the field, he pulled him out and set him down in a freshly plowed furrow. As the boy was sitting there, a big giant came over the hill.

"Do you see the big bogeyman over there?" said the father, who just wanted to scare the little fellow so he would behave. "He's coming to get you."

Now the giant had long legs, and after only a few steps, he reached the furrow, picked up Thumbling, and carried him away. The father stood

there so petrified with fright that he couldn't utter a sound. He was certain his child was now lost to him, and he would never set eyes on him again for the rest of his life.

Meanwhile, the giant took the boy and let him suckle at his breast, and Thumbling grew and became big and strong like most giants. When two years had passed, the old giant took him into the woods to test him.

"Pull out that willow tree," he said.

By now the boy had become so strong that he tore up a young tree right out of the ground, roots and all. But the giant thought he must do better than that. So he took him home again and suckled him for two more years. When he tested him once more, the boy tore out a much larger tree. Yet, it still wasn't enough for the giant, who suckled him another two years, and when he then took him into the woods, he said, "Now, rip out a decent-sized tree!"

All at once, the boy tore up the thickest possible oak tree right out of the ground so that it cracked in two, and this was mere child's play for him.

When the giant saw what he had done, he said. "That's enough now. You've learned all you need to know," and he took him back to the field where he had found him.

His father was plowing there as the young giant came over to him and said, "Look, father, look at what's become of me. I'm your son!"

The farmer was frightened and said, "No, you're not my son. Go away from me."

"Of course I'm your son! Let me do your work. I can plow just as well as you can, or even better."

"No, you're not my son. You can't plow. I don't want you. Go away from me!"

However, since the farmer was afraid of the big man, he let go of the plow, stepped aside, and sat down at the edge of the. field. Then the young man grabbed the plow and merely pressed his hand on it, but his grip was so powerful that the plow sank deep into the earth. The farmer couldn't bear to watch all that, and so he called over to him. "If you're so set on plowing, then you've got to learn not to press down so hard. Otherwise, you'll ruin the field."

Then the young man unharnessed the horses and began pulling the plow himself. "Just go home, father," he said, "and have mother cook me a large dish of food. In the meantime, I'll plow the field for you."

The farmer went home and told his wife to cook the food, and the young man plowed the field, two whole acres, all by himself. After that he harnessed himself to the harrow and harrowed the field with two harrows at the same time. When he was finished, he went into the woods and pulled up two oak trees, put them on his shoulders, and attached a harrow at each end of a tree and a horse at each end of the other tree. Then he carried everything to his parents' house as if it were a bundle of straw. When he reached the barnyard, his mother didn't recognize him and asked, "Who's that horrible big man?"

"That's our son," the farmer said.

"No," she said, "that can't be our son. We never had one that large. Our son was a tiny thing." Then she yelled at him, "Go away! We don't want you!"

The young man didn't respond but led the horses into the stable and gave them oats and hay and put things in order. After he had finished, he went into the kitchen, sat down on a bench, and said, "Mother, I'd like to eat now. Is supper almost ready?"

"Yes," she replied and didn't dare to contradict him. She brought him two tremendous bowls of food that would have lasted her and her husband a week. However, the young man finished everything by himself and then asked whether she could give him something more.

"No," she said, "that's all we have."

"That was really just a nibble. I've got to have more."

So she went out and put a large pig's trough full of food on the fire. When it was ready, she carried it in.

"At last, a little more," he said and gobbled up everything that was in it. But that was still not enough.

"Father," he said, "I can tell I'll never get enough to eat here. So, if you'll get me an iron staff strong enough that I can't break it across my knees, I'll go away again."

The farmer was happy to hear that. He hitched two horses to his wagon and went to the blacksmith, who gave him a staff so big and thick that the two horses could barely pull it. The young man laid it across his knees, and *crack!* he broke it in two, as if it were a beanstalk, and threw it away. His father hitched four horses to his wagon and fetched another staff, one so large and thick that the four horses could barely pull it. Once again his son snapped it across his knees and threw it away.

"Father," he said, "this one's no use to me. You've got to harness some more horses and fetch a stronger staff."

Then his father hitched up eight horses to his wagon and brought back a staff so large and thick that the eight horses could barely pull it. When his son took it in his hand, he immediately broke off a piece from the top and said, "Father, I see that you can't get the kind of staff I need. So I won't stay here any longer."

The young man went away, and he began passing himself off as a journeyman blacksmith. Soon he came to a village that had a blacksmith among its inhabitants. He was a miserly man who never gave anyone a thing and kept everything for himself. The young man went to the smithy and asked him whether he could use a journeyman.

"Yes," said the blacksmith, who looked him over and thought, "That's a sturdy fellow. He'll certainly be good at hammering, and he's sure to earn his keep." Then he asked, "How much do you want for your wages?"

"None at all," he answered. "But every two weeks when the other journeymen receive their wages, I shall give you two blows that you must be able to withstand."

The miser voiced great satisfaction with the terms because he thought he could save money this way. The next morning the strange journeyman was supposed to hammer first, and when the master brought out the red-hot bar and the journeyman dealt the blow, the iron flew all over in pieces, and the anvil sank so deep into the ground that they couldn't get it out again. The miser became furious and said, "That's all! I can't use you anymore. You hammer much too roughly. What do I owe you for the one blow?"

"I'll give you just a tiny tap, that's all," said the journeyman, and he lifted his foot and gave the miser such a kick that he flew over four stacks of hay. Then the journeyman picked out the thickest iron staff he could find in the smithy, used it as a walking stick, and went on his way. After he had been traveling for a while, he came to a large farming estate and asked the bailiff if he needed a foreman.

"Yes," said the bailiff, he could use one. He remarked that he looked like a sturdy and able fellow and asked him what he would like for a year's wages. Again the journeyman answered that he didn't want to be paid, but that the bailiff would have to withstand three blows that he would give him at the end of every year. The bailiff was satisfied with that, for he, too, was a miser. The next morning the hired workers got up early because they were supposed to drive to the forest and cut wood, but the young man was still in bed. One of the workers called to him, "Hey, it's time to get up! We're going to the forest, and you've got to come with us."

"Not yet," he replied in a rude and surly voice. "You all go. I'll get there and back before the rest of you anyway."

Then the workers went to the bailiff and told him that the foreman was still in bed and wouldn't drive to the forest with them. The bailiff told them to wake him again and order him to hitch up the horses. But the foreman answered just as he had before, "You all go. I'll get there and back before the rest of you anyway."

So he remained in bed another two hours, and when he finally managed to get up, he fetched two bushels of peas from the loft, cooked himself a porridge, and took his own sweet time in eating it. After that was done, he went out and hitched up the horses and drove to the forest. Near the forest was a ravine through which he had to drive. When he drove through it, he stopped the horses, got out, walked behind the wagon, and took some trees and bushes to build a large barricade that would prevent horses from getting through the ravine. When he arrived at the forest, the others were just leaving with their loaded wagons and heading home.

"Drive on," he said to them. "I'll still get home before you."

But he only drove a short way into the forest, where he immediately ripped out two of the biggest trees from the ground, threw them into his wagon, and turned back. When he reached the barricade, the others were still standing around, since they had been prevented from getting through.

"You see," he said. "If you had stayed with me, you'd have made it home just as quickly, and you'd have had another hour's sleep."

He wanted to drive on, but his horses couldn't work their way through the barricade. So he unharnessed them, set them on top of the wagon, took hold of the shafts, and whisked everything through as easily as if the wagon were loaded with feathers. Once he was on the other side, he said to the workers, "You see, I got through faster than you."

And he drove on, while the others had to stay where they were. At the barnyard he grabbed hold of one of the trees, lifted it by his hand, showed it to the bailiff, and said, "How do you like this nice cord of wood?"

The bailiff said to his wife, "He's a good man, our foreman, even if he does sleep long. He still makes it home sooner than the others."

So the young man served the bailiff for a year, and when it was over and the other workers received their wages, it was time for him to collect his pay as well. However, the bailiff was afraid of the blows he had coming to him. He begged the foreman to forgo everything and said that, in return, he would make him bailiff and take over the job as foreman himself.

"No," said the young man. "I don't want to be bailiff. I'm the foreman and want to stay foreman. And I intend to dole out what we agreed upon."

The bailiff offered to give him whatever he wanted, but it did no good. The foreman rejected everything he proposed, and the bailiff didn't know what to do except to ask him for a two-week period of grace. He needed time to think of a way out of his situation. The foreman granted him an extension, and now the bailiff summoned all his clerks together. He asked them to think up a way to help him and to advise him. After they had deliberated a long time, they finally said that the foreman had to be killed. The bailiff was to have large millstones brought to the courtyard. Then he was to order the foreman to climb down into the well and clean it out. When the foreman was down below, they would roll the millstones to the well. and heave them on his head. The bailiff liked the idea, and everything was prepared: the millstones were brought to the courtyard. Once the foreman was standing below, they rolled the millstones to the well and threw them down. All at once there was a big splash high into the air. They were convinced they had broken his skull. However, he called up to them, "Chase the chickens away from the well! They're scratching around in the sand and throwing grains into my eyes so that I can't see."

So the bailiff yelled, "Shoo! Shoo!" as if he were scaring the chickens away. When the foreman had finished his work, he climbed up and said, "Just look at what a fine necklace I've got on now!" but he meant the millstone that he was wearing around his neck.

Now the foreman wanted to receive his pay, but the bailiff requested another two weeks' grace to think up a new plan. The clerks met again and advised him to send the foreman to the haunted mill to grind grain at night since nobody had ever emerged alive from it the next morning. The bailiff liked the proposal and called the foreman to him that very same evening. He ordered him to carry eight bushels of grain to the mill and grind it that night because they needed it right away. So the foreman went to the loft and put two bushels in his right pocket and two in his left. He carried the other four in a sack that he slung over his shoulder so that half was on his back and half on his chest. And off he went to the haunted mill. The miller told him he could easily grind the grain during the day, but not at night, because the mill was haunted, and anyone who had gone in there at night had not returned alive in the morning.

"Don't worry, I'll manage," said the foreman. "Why don't you go and get some sleep." Then he went into the mill and poured the grain into the hopper. Toward eleven o'clock he went into the miller's room and sat down on a bench. After he had been sitting there awhile, the door suddenly opened, and an enormous table came in. Next he saw wine, roast meat, and all sorts of good food appear on the table by themselves, but nobody carried these things in. After that the chairs slid to the table, but nobody came. All at once he saw fingers handling knives and forks and putting food on the plates; otherwise he didn't see a thing. Since he was hungry and saw all this food, he sat down at the table, and enjoyed the meal. When he had eaten his fill and the fingers had also emptied their plates, he distinctly heard all the lights being suddenly snuffed out, and when it was pitch dark, he felt something like a smack in the face. Then he said, "If anything like that happens again, I'm going to strike back."

When he received a second smack in the face, he struck back, and so it went the whole night. He took nothing without paying it back generously, with interest, and kept himself busy by smacking anything that came near him. At daybreak, however, everything stopped. When the miller got up, he went by to see how the foreman was, and he was amazed to find him alive.

"I got some smacks in the face," the foreman said, "but I also gave some in return and ate a full meal."

The miller was happy and said that the mill was now released from its curse, and he wanted to give the foreman a good deal of money as a reward.

"I don't want money," said the foreman, "I already have enough."

Then he took the flour on his back, went home, and told the bailiff he had done his job and now wanted to be paid the wages they had agreed upon. When the bailiff heard that, he really became upset. He paced up and down the room, and beads of sweat ran down his forehead. So he opened the window to get some fresh air, but before he knew it, the foreman had given him such a kick that he went flying through the window out into the sky. He flew and flew until he was completely out of sight. Then the foreman said to the bailiff's wife that she'd have to take the other blow.

"No, no!" she exclaimed. "I won't be able to stand it," and she opened the other window because beads of sweat were running down her face also. Then he gave her a kick too, and she went flying out the window. Since she was lighter than her husband, she soared much higher.

Her husband called out to her, "Come over here!"

But she replied, "No, you come over here to me! I can't make it over to you."

So they floated in the air, and neither could get to the other. Whether they are still floating, I don't know, but I do know that the young giant took his iron staff and continued on his way.

5

THE GNOME

Once upon a time there was a rich king who had three daughters. Every day they went walking in the palace garden, where the king, who loved trees, had planted many different kinds, but he was most fond of one particular tree, which he protected by placing it under a spell: Whoever picked one of its apples would be sent a hundred fathoms underground.

When harvest time came, the apples on that tree became as red as blood. Every day the three daughters looked under the tree to see if the wind had blown an apple to the ground, but they never found one. Gradually the tree became so full and its branches so heavy that it seemed the tree would collapse. By then the youngest sister had such a craving for an apple from this tree that she said to her sisters, "Our father loves us far too much to put a curse on us. I believe he cast the spell mainly with strangers in mind."

Upon saying that, she plucked a nice plump apple, ran to her sisters, and said: "Just taste it, dear sisters! I've never tasted anything so delicious in all my life."

Then the two other princesses also took a bite of the apple, and suddenly all three sank deep down into the earth, leaving no trace whatsoever behind them.

At noon the king wanted to call them to the dining table, but they were nowhere to be found. He looked all around the castle and garden but couldn't find them. Finally, he became so distressed that he made it known throughout the country that whoever brought his daughters back could have one of them for his wife. As a result, more men than you can imagine went out searching for them all over the kingdom, for the princesses were known to be beautiful and kind to all. Indeed, they were loved by everyone in the country.

Among the searchers were three huntsmen who had spent a week looking for them and had eventually come to a large castle. When they went inside, they found beautiful rooms, and in one of the rooms the table was set with delicious dishes that were still steaming hot, but there was not a living soul to be seen or heard in the whole castle. At last they were so hungry that they sat down and ate up all the food Then they agreed to stay in the castle and drew lots to see which one would remain there while the other two continued to look for the princesses. The lot fell to the oldest, and the next day he stayed in the castle while the two youngest went out searching. At noon a tiny gnome came and asked for a piece of bread. The huntsman took a loaf of bread that he found there and cut off a slice. As he was handing it to the little man, the gnome let it drop and asked him to kindly pick up the piece for him. As the huntsman was bending over, the gnome took a stick, grabbed him by his hair, and gave him a good beating. The next day the second huntsman stayed home, and he fared no better. When the other two returned in the evening, the oldest asked him, "Well, how did things go?

"Very badly."

So the two eldest brothers confided in each other about their plight and didn't tell the youngest anything about it because they didn't like him. They always called him Stupid Hans, because he was not particularly worldly-wise.

On the third day the youngest stayed home, and again the gnome came to fetch a piece of bread. When the huntsman handed him a piece, the gnome let it drop again and asked him to kindly pick it up for him.

"What?" cried the huntsman. "Can't you pick the bread up yourself? If you won't make the effort to take better care of your daily bread, then you really don't deserve to eat it."

Then the gnome got very angry and ordered him to do it. But the young huntsman acted swiftly: he grabbed the gnome and thrashed him soundly. The gnome shrieked loudly and said, "Stop! Stop! Let me go, and I'll tell you where the king's daughters are."

When he heard that, he stopped thrashing him. The gnome told the huntsman that he came from beneath the earth, where there were more than a dozen other gnomes like him, and if the huntsman would go with him, he would show him where the king's daughters were. Then the gnome pointed to a deep well without any water in it and told him to beware of his companions, for they were not to be trusted, and that he would have to save the king's daughters by himself. To be sure, his brothers wanted to rescue the king's daughters too, but they didn't want to exert themselves or take any risks. The best way would be to take a large basket, get into it with his hunting knife and a bell, and then have himself lowered down into the well. There he would find three rooms, and in each one he would see a princess picking the lice from a many-headed dragon. In each room he would have to cut the dragon's heads off.

After the gnome had told him all that, he disappeared, and toward evening, the other two huntsman returned and asked him how his day went.

"So far, so good," he said, and he told them that he hadn't seen anyone until noon, when a tiny gnome had come and asked for a piece of bread. After he had handed it to him, the gnome had dropped it and asked him to pick it up. When he refused, the dwarf began to spit at him. They had a quarrel, and he gave the gnome a beating. Afterward the little fellow told him where the king's daughters were.

Upon hearing that, the two brothers became so livid that they turned green with envy. The next morning they went to the well together and drew lots to see who would be the first to get into the basket. The lot fell to the eldest again, and he had to get into the basket and take the bell with him.

"If I ring," he said, "you must pull me up quickly."

When he was just a little way down, he rang the bell, and they pulled him up again. Then the second brother got in and did the very same thing. Finally, it was the youngest brother's turn, and he let himself be lowered all the way to the bottom.

After he got out of the basket, he took his hunting knife, went to the first door, and listened. When he heard the dragon snoring loudly, he opened the door slowly and saw one of the king's daughters picking lice from the nine dragon's heads in her lap. So he took his hunting knife and cut off all nine heads. The princess jumped up, threw her arms around him, and kissed him many times. Then she took her necklace of pure gold and hung it around his neck. After that he went to the second princess, who was picking lice from a seven-headed dragon, and he rescued her as well. Finally, he went to the youngest, who had a four-headed dragon to louse, and he set her free too. Now they were all enormously happy and couldn't stop hugging and kissing him. Soon thereafter he rang the bell very loudly so his brothers who were above could hear. One after the other, he put the princesses into the basket and had them pulled up. When his turn came, he remembered the gnome saying that his brothers were not to be trusted. So he took a big stone that was lying there and put it into the basket. When the basket was about midway up, the wicked brothers cut the rope so that the basket with the stone inside fell to the ground. Since they thought that he was now dead, they ran off with the king's three daughters and made them promise to tell their father that they were the ones who had rescued them. Afterward the two of them went to the king and asked to marry his daughters.

In the meantime, the youngest huntsman had become depressed and just walked around the three rooms, for he thought he was doomed to die. Then he saw a flute hanging on the wall and said, "Why are you hanging there? This is no place for merrymaking!" He looked at the dragon heads, too, and said, "You can't help me either." He paced up and down the floor so much that he wore the ground down so that it became smooth. At last he had an idea: he took the flute from the wall and played a tune on it. Suddenly many gnomes appeared, and with each note he played, another would emerge, and he kept on playing until the room was full of them. They asked him what he desired, and he said that he would like to return to the top of the earth again and see the light of day. Then they each grabbed a strand of his hair and flew up to earth with him. When he was above, he went straight to the king's castle, where one of the princesses was to be married. Soon thereafter he found the room in which the king was sitting with his three daughters. When the princesses saw him, they fainted. The king got very angry and immediately had him taken to prison. He thought the huntsman had harmed his daughters, but when the princesses regained consciousness, they pleaded a great deal with the king to release him. When the king asked them why, they said they were not allowed to tell him the reason. However, their father said they should tell it to the stove. Meanwhile, he left the room, listened at the door, and heard everything. Shortly after, he had the two older brothers hanged on the gallows and gave the youngest daughter to the young huntsman for his wife.

When the wedding took place, I was wearing a pair of glass shoes and stumbled over a stone. The stone said, *Clink!* and my slippers broke in two.

6

THE KING OF THE GOLDEN MOUNTAIN

A merchant had two children, a boy and a girl, who were still infants and couldn't walk. About this time the merchant had invested his entire fortune in richly laden ships that he sent out to sea. Just when he thought he was about to make a lot of money through this venture, he received news that the ships had sunk. So now, instead of being a rich man, he was a poor one and had nothing left but a field outside the city. In order to take his mind off his troubles somewhat, he went into his field, and as he was pacing back and forth, a little black man suddenly stood beside him and asked him why he was so sad and what was troubling his heart.

"If you could help me," said the merchant, "I'd certainly tell you."

"Who knows?" answered the little black man. "Just tell me. Perhaps I can help you."

Then the merchant told him that he had lost his whole fortune at sea and had nothing left but the field.

"Don't worry," said the little black man. "You shall have as much money as you want if you promise in twelve years from now to bring me the first thing that brushes against your leg when you return home. And you must bring it to this spot."

The merchant thought, "That's not much to ask. What else can that be but my dog?" Of course, he didn't think of his little boy, and therefore, he said yes. Then he gave the little black man a signed and sealed agreement and went home.

When he returned to his house, his little boy was so happy to see him that he held himself up by some benches, toddled over to his father, and grabbed him around the legs. The father was horrified, for he remembered the agreement, and he knew now what he had signed away. Still, he thought the little man might have been playing a joke on him since he didn't find any money. One month later, however, when he went up into his attic to gather some old tinware to sell, he saw a huge pile of money lying on the floor. Once he saw the money, he was delighted and was able to purchase things again and became an even greater merchant than before and trusted in God to make him a good man. In the meantime, his son grew and learned how to use his brains wisely. As he neared his twelfth birthday, however, the merchant became so worried that one could see the anxiety written on his face. One day his son asked him what was bothering him, and the father didn't want to tell him. But the son persisted until his father finally revealed everything to him: how without thinking he had promised him to a little black man and received a lot of money in return, and how he had given the little man a signed and sealed agreement to deliver him on his twelfth birthday.

"Oh, father," said the son. "Don't be discouraged. Everything will turn out well. The black man has no power over me."

The son had himself blessed by the priest, and when the hour arrived, he went out to the field with his father. There he drew a circle and stepped inside it with his father. The little black man came then and said to the old man, "Have you brought what you promised me?"

The father kept quiet, but the son said, "What do you want here?"

"I've come to discuss matters with your father, not with you."

"You deceived my father and led him astray," replied the son. "Give me back the agreement."

"No," said the little black man, "I won't give up my rights."

They talked for a long time until it was finally agreed that, since the son no longer belonged to his father, nor did he belong to his arch-enemy, he was to get into a little boat and drift downstream on the river. His father was to shove the boat off with his foot, and the son's fate was to be decided by the river. The boy said farewell to his father, got into the little boat, and the father had to shove it off with his own foot. The little boat capsized with the bottom up and the top face down. Since the father believed his son had drowned, he went home and mourned for him.

However, the boat didn't sink but continued to drift calmly downstream with the boy safely inside. Finally, it touched down upon an unknown shore and stood still. The boy went ashore, saw a beautiful castle in the distance, and went toward it. When he entered, he realized it was enchanted. He went through all the rooms, but they were empty except for the last chamber, where he encountered a snake. Now, this snake was an enchanted princess, who was delighted to see him and said, "Have you come at last, my savior? I've been waiting now twelve years for you. This kingdom is enchanted, and you must release it from the magic spell. Tonight twelve black men wearing chains will come and ask you what you're doing here. You must keep quiet and refuse to answer them. Let them do whatever they want with you: they will torture you, beat you, and stab you. Let them do that, just don't talk. At midnight they must go away. The second night twelve other men will come, and the third night there will be twenty-four, who will chop off your head. But at midnight their power will be gone, and if you have held out until then and have not uttered a single word, I shall be saved and shall come to you carrying the Water of Life. I'll rub some on you, and you'll be alive again and as healthy as you were before."

"I shall gladly release you from the spell," the young man said, and everything happened just as she had said: the black men could not force a word out of him, and on the third night the snake turned into a beautiful princess who came with the Water of Life and brought him back to life. Then she embraced him and kissed him, and there was joy and jubilation throughout the castle. Soon thereafter they celebrated their wedding, and he was king of the Golden Mountain.

From then on they lived happily together, and the queen gave birth to a handsome boy. After eight years had passed, the king's thoughts turned to his father. His heart went out to him, and he wished he could see him again. But the queen didn't want to let him go and said, "I can tell that this will bring me bad luck."

Still, he gave her no peace until she consented to let him go. Upon his departure she gave him a wishing ring and said, "Take this ring and put it on your finger. With it you can transport yourself immediately to wherever you want to go. But you must promise me never to use it to wish me away from here to your father's place."

He promised her, put the ring on his finger, and wished that he was home, outside the city where his father lived. All at once he found himself outside the city. When he reached the city gate, the sentries wouldn't let him enter because he was wearing such strange and rich clothes. So he climbed a hill where a shepherd was tending his flock. He exchanged clothes with him, put on the shepherd's old coat, and then went into the city without being disturbed. After he got to his father's house, he revealed his identity, but his father wouldn't believe he was his son and said that, to be sure, he had had a son, but this son had long since been dead. Nevertheless, the father offered the man a plate of food since he saw he was a poor, needy shepherd.

"I'm truly your son," said the shepherd to his parents. "Don't you remember any birthmarks you'd recognize me by?"

"Yes," said his mother, "our son had a raspberry mark under his right arm."

He pulled up his shirt, and when they saw the raspberry mark, they no longer doubted that he was their son. Then he told them that he was king of the Golden Mountain and that he had a princess as his wife and a handsome seven-year-old son.

"Now that can't possibly be true," said his father. "What kind of a king would run around in a tattered shepherd's coat?"

Immediately the son got angry, and not thinking of his promise, he turned his ring and wished both his wife and son there, and within seconds they were with him. But the queen wept and accused him of breaking his promise and making her unhappy. Since she was there, however, and couldn't do anything about it, she had to accept her situation, but there was evil on her mind.

Shortly thereafter her husband led her outside the city to the field and showed her the spot on the riverbank where the little boat had been shoved off. Then he said, "I'm tired now. Sit down next to me. I'd like to sleep a little on your lap."

He laid his head on her lap, and she loused him a bit until he fell asleep. While he was sleeping, she took the ring off his finger and drew her foot out from under him, leaving only her slipper behind. Finally, she took her child in her arms and wished herself back in her kingdom. When he awoke, he was lying there all alone. His wife and child were gone, and the ring as well. Only the slipper, as a token, had been left behind. "You can't go back home again to your parents," he said to himself. "They'd only say you were a sorcerer. You'd better pack up and get back to your kingdom."

So he went on his way and finally came to a mountain where three giants were standing and quarreling about how best to divide their father's inheritance. When they saw him riding by, they called to him and said that since little people were clever, they wanted him to divide the inheritance among them. This inheritance consisted of three things: First, a sword that chopped off everyone's head except that of the person who held it and said, "All heads off except mine!" Then the heads would lie on the ground. Second, a cloak that made one invisible if one put it on. Third, a pair of boots that carried the person who wore them to any spot he wished in a matter of seconds.

The king told them that they had to give him the three objects so that he could test them to see if they were in good condition. They handed him the cloak, and when he had put it on his shoulders, he wished to become a fly, and he was immediately turned into a fly.

"The cloak is good," he said. "Now give me the sword."

"No," they said. "We won't give it to you. If you say, 'All heads off except mine!' we'd lose our heads, and you alone would keep yours."

Nevertheless, they gave it to him on condition that he try it out on a tree. He did that, and the sword was also good. Now he wanted to have the boots, but they said, "No, we won't give them away. If you put them on and wish yourself on top of the mountain, then we would stand here below with nothing."

"Oh, no," he said, "I'd never do anything like that."

So they gave him the boots as well. But when he had all three objects, he wished himself to be on top of the Golden Mountain, and he was immediately there. Moreover, the giants had vanished, and this was the way their inheritance was divided.

When the king now drew near the castle, he heard cries of joy and the sounds of fiddles and flutes. The people at the court told him that his wife was celebrating her wedding with another man. So he put on the cloak and turned himself into a fly. Then he went into the castle and took a place behind his wife, and nobody saw him. When they put a piece of meat on her plate, he snatched it and ate it. And when they gave her a glass of wine, he snatched it and drank it. They kept giving her food and wine, but she would always end up with nothing because her plate and glass would vanish immediately. She became so ashamed that she left the table, went into her chamber, and began weeping, while he stayed behind her all the time.

"Has the devil got me in his power?" she said out loud to herself. "Perhaps my savior never came!"

Then he gave her a couple of rough smacks in the face and said, "Your savior came! Now he's got you in his power, you faithless thing! Did I deserve to be treated the way you treated me?"

After saying this he went into the hall and announced that the wedding was over and that he had returned. But he was mocked by the kings, princes, and ministers who were assembled there. Since he wanted to make short work of them, he asked them to leave or else. Upon hearing that, they tried to take him prisoner, but he took out his sword and said, "All heads off except mine!"

All at once they all lay there in blood, and he was once again king of the Golden Mountain.

7

THE RAVEN

Once upon a time there was a queen who had a daughter, and she was so little that she had to be carried in her mother's arms. One day the child became restless, and no matter what the mother said, she wouldn't keep quiet. The mother became impatient, and as she looked at the ravens flying around outside the castle, she opened the window and said, "I wish you were a raven and would fly away! Then I'd have my peace and quiet."

No sooner had she said those words than the child was changed into a raven and flew from her arm out through the window. The bird flew far away, and nobody could follow her. She headed for a dark forest, where she stayed for a long time.

Some time later, a man was making his way through this forest when he heard the raven calling. He went toward the voice, and as he came closer, the raven said, "I am a king's daughter by birth and have been cursed by a spell. However, you can set me free."

"How can I do this?" he asked.

"Go into the house over there," she said. "There's an old woman sitting inside. She'll offer you something to eat and drink and tell you to enjoy the meal, but you're not to touch a thing. You're not to drink, because if you drink anything, you'll fall asleep and won't be able to release me from the spell. In the garden behind the house there's a big pile of tanbark. You're to stand on it and wait for me. I shall come three days in a row at two o'clock in the afternoon with a carriage. But if you aren't awake, I won't be set free."

The man said he'd do everything, but the raven said, "Oh, I can already tell you won't set me free. You'll take something from the old woman."

Again the man promised her he wouldn't touch the food or the drink. However, once he was inside the house, the old woman went over to him and said, "How worn-out you are! Come and refresh yourself. Have something to eat and drink."

"No," said the man. "I don't want to eat or drink."

But she wouldn't leave him in peace and kept saying, "Well, if you don't want to eat, just take a sip from the glass. One little sip won't hurt."

Finally, he let himself be persuaded and drank. Toward two in the afternoon he went outside into the garden and climbed onto the pile of tanbark to wait for the raven. As he stood there, he suddenly felt so tired that he couldn't help himself and had to lie down and rest a little. He didn't want to fall asleep, but no sooner had he stretched himself out than his eyes closed by themselves, and he fell asleep. He slept so soundly that nothing in the world could have wakened him. At two o'clock the raven came driving up in a carriage with four white horses, but she was already in full mourning and said, "I already know he's asleep."

When she drove into the garden, he was indeed fast asleep. She climbed out of the carriage, went over to him, and shook him and called him, but he didn't wake up. She continued to cry out until he finally awoke from his sleep, and she said: "I see that you can't set me free, but I shall come again tomorrow. I'll be driving in a carriage drawn by four brown horses. You are not to take anything at all from the old woman, neither food nor drink."

He replied, "I won't. Certainly not."

However, she said: "I know already that you'll take something."

At noon the next day the old woman came to him again and asked him why he wasn't eating and drinking, and he replied: "I don't want anything to eat or drink."

However, she placed the food and drink in front of him so that he could smell everything, and she convinced him to drink once more. Toward two o'clock he went into the garden and climbed onto the pile of tanbark to wait for the raven. Then he felt so tired that his limbs could no longer support him. Since he couldn't help himself, he lay down to sleep a little. When the raven drove up in her carriage drawn by four brown stallions, she was in full mourning again and said, "I know already he's sleeping."

When she went over to him, he lay fast asleep and couldn't be wakened. She climbed out of the carriage, shook him, and tried to wake him. It was more difficult than the day before until he finally awoke.

"I certainly see," said the raven, "that you can't free me. Tomorrow at two o'clock I shall come once more, but it will be the last time. My horses will be black, and I shall be dressed all in black. You are not to take anything from the old woman, nothing to eat or drink."

"Certainly not," he said.

"Oh, I know for sure that you'll take something!" she replied.

The next day the old woman asked him what the matter was and why he wasn't eating or drinking.

"I don't want to eat or drink," he replied.

In spite of this, she said he should taste how good all the food was just one time, otherwise he would die from hunger. So he let himself be persuaded and drank something again. When the time came, he went outside into the garden and climbed onto the pile of tanbark to wait for the princess. But he became so tired that he couldn't keep standing and lay down and slept like a log. At two o'clock the raven came, and her carriage was drawn by four black horses. The carriage and everything else were also black, and she was already in full mourning. "I know he's asleep," she said, "and he won't be able to set me free."

When she went over to him, he was lying there sound asleep. She shook him and called him, but she couldn't wake him up. So she put a loaf of bread beside him. No matter how much he took from the bread, it would always replenish itself. Then she placed a piece of meat next to him. No matter how much he took from the meat, it would always replenish itself. The third thing she placed next to him was a bottle of wine. No matter how much wine he drank, it would always replenish itself. After that she drew a golden ring from her finger and placed it on his finger. Her name was engraved on it. Finally, she left him a letter on the ground in which she explained that the things she had given him would never run out, and she concluded her letter by saying: "I clearly see that you can't set me free in a place like this. But if you still want to save me, then come to the golden castle of Mount Stromberg. You can do it. I know that for sure." And after she had given him all those things, she climbed back into her carriage and drove off to the golden castle of Mount Stromberg.

When the man woke and saw that he had slept, he was terribly sad and said, "I'm sure she's been here, and I haven't set her free." Then he noticed the things lying beside him, and he read the letter that explained everything that had happened. So he stood up and set out for the golden castle of Mount Stromberg, even though he didn't know where it was. After he had wandered about the world for a long time, he finally came to a dark forest and continued wandering for fourteen days and realized he couldn't find his way out. When it turned evening, he was so tired that he lay down beneath a bush and fell asleep. The next day he moved on, and in the evening, as he was about to lie down beneath another bush when he heard such a moaning and groaning that he was unable to sleep. When the hour came for people to light their lamps, he saw a light glimmering in the distance, got up, and went toward it. Shortly after, he came to a house that appeared to be very small because a big giant was standing in front of it. "Whether you go inside or stay here," he thought to himself, "the giant will put an end to your life. So, you might as well do it." So he stepped toward the door, and when the giant saw him, he said, "It's good that you've come. I haven't had a thing to eat for a long time. So I'm going to gobble you up for supper."

"Let things be," said the man. "If you want something to eat, I've got something with me."

"If that's true," said the giant, "you can rest easy. I wanted to eat you only because I had nothing else."

They both went inside and sat down at the dinner table, and the man took out the bread, wine, and meat that never ran out. And they ate until they were full. After supper the man asked him, "Can you tell me where to find the golden castle of Mount Stromberg?"

The giant said, "I'll look it up on my map. It shows all the cities, villages, and houses."

He took out a map that he kept in the room and looked for the castle, but it wasn't on it. "Don't worry," he said. "I've got even larger maps in the closet upstairs. We can look for it on them."

They looked at the maps, but couldn't find the castle. Now, the man wanted to move on, but the giant begged him to stay a few more days until his brother returned. He had gone out to fetch some food. He also had good maps. They could try again with his maps and find the castle for sure. So the man waited until the brother came back. Well, the brother said he didn't know for certain, but he believed that the Castle of Stromberg was on his map. Then the three of them ate once again until they were quite full. Afterward the second giant went to his room and said, "Now I'll take a look at my map." But the castle wasn't on it. Then he said he had another map upstairs in a room full of maps. It had to be on one of them. When he brought the maps downstairs, they began searching again, and finally they found the Castle of Stromberg. However, it was thousands of miles away.

"How will I ever get there?" asked the man.

"I've got two hours to spare," said the giant. "I'll carry you as far as I can, but then I must return home and nurse our child."

So he carried the man until he was about a hundred hours' walk away from the castle and said, "You can go the rest of the way by yourself."

"Yes, indeed," said the man. "I can certainly do that."

As they were about to separate, the man said, "Let's first eat once more until we're full."

After they did that, the giant took his leave and went home, while the man went on day and night until he finally came to the golden castle of Mount Stromberg. But the castle was up on a glass mountain, and he saw the enchanted maiden driving around the castle. He wanted to climb up to her, but he continually slipped on the glass and became very distressed and said to himself: "It's best if I build a little hut for myself. I've got plenty to eat and drink." So he built a hut for himself and stayed there for one solid year and watched the princess every day drive around on top of the mountain, but he couldn't climb up to her.

One day he saw three giants fighting with each other and called out to them, "God be with you!"

They stopped fighting, listened to see where the cry came from, and then resumed fighting when they couldn't see anyone. It was dangerous just to be near them, but again the man called out, "God be with you!"

Again they stopped, looked around, and resumed their fighting when they couldn't see anyone. Finally, the man called out for a third time, "God be with you!" and this time he thought to himself, "You'd better go see what these three are up to." So he went out to them and asked them why they were fighting. One of them said he had found a stick, and that whenever he struck a door with it, the door would spring open. The second said he had found a cloak and that whenever he hung it over his shoulders, he would be invisible. The third said he had caught a horse and that one could ride it anywhere, even up the glass mountain. Then the man said, "I'll make an exchange with you. I'll take those three things, and to be honest, I don't have any money, but I do have other things that are worth more than money. First, however, I must test your things to see whether you've told me the truth."

They let him sit on the horse, put the cloak over his shoulders, and handed him the stick. As soon as he had all three objects, they could no longer see him. So he gave them all a good beating and cried out, "Now, are you satisfied?"

The man rode up the glass mountain, and when he got to the top, he found the castle door was closed. So he struck the gate with the stick, and it immediately sprang open. He entered and went up the stairs until he came to a hall. There sat the princess, and she had a goblet filled with wine in front of her. However, she couldn't see him because he was wearing the cloak. When he went over to her, he pulled off the ring that she had given him and threw it into the goblet so that it rang out.

"That's my ring!" she exclaimed. "Well then, the man who's going to set me free must be here somewhere."

She had her servants search all over the castle, but they couldn't find him. Indeed, he had gone outside, mounted the horse, and thrown off the cloak. When they finally saw him out by the gate, they screamed for joy. So he dismounted and took the princess in his arms. She kissed him and said, "Now you've finally set me free."

Soon thereafter they held the wedding and lived happily together.

8

THE CLEVER FARMER'S DAUGHTER

Once upon a time there was a poor farmer who had only a small house and one daughter but no land. One day the daughter said, "I think we should ask the king for a little piece of farming land."

When the king learned about their poverty, he gave them a small field, which the farmer and his daughter cleared so they could sow a little wheat and plant some kind of fruit. After they had almost finished their work, they found a mortar of pure gold on the ground.

"Listen," said the farmer to his daughter, "since the king was so gracious as to give us this field, we ought to give him this mortar in return."

But the daughter didn't agree and said, "Father, if we give the mortar without the pestle, then we'll have to find the pestle as well. I think we'd be better off if we kept quiet about the whole thing."

However, the farmer didn't listen to her. He took the mortar, carried it to the king, and said that he had found it on the heath. Now he wanted to offer it to the king in his honor. The king took the mortar and asked the farmer if he had found anything else.

"No," replied the farmer.

Then the king asked him about the pestle and told him to bring it to him. The farmer replied that they hadn't found the pestle, but that was like talking to the wind. He was thrown into prison, where he was to stay until he produced the pestle. The servants brought him bread and water every day, the usual fare in prison, and every day they heard the farmer sighing, "Oh, if only I had listened to my daughter! Oh, if only I had listened to my daughter!"

Finally, the servants went to the king and told him how the prisoner kept crying, "Oh, if only I had listened to my daughter!" and how he refused to eat and drink. The king ordered the servants to bring the prisoner before him, and he asked the farmer to tell him why he kept sighing, "Oh, if only I had listened to my daughter!"

"What did your daughter tell you?"

"Well, she told me not to bring you the mortar; otherwise, I'd have to bring you the pestle as well."

"If you have such a clever daughter, I want to see her."

So she had to appear before the king, who asked her if she really was so clever and said that he wanted to give her a riddle to solve, and that if she solved it, he would marry her. She replied right away that she would solve it. Then the king said, "Come to me, not dressed, not naked, not on horse, not by carriage, not on the road, not off the road, and if you do, I'll marry you."

The farmer's daughter went home and got undressed until she was completely naked, so that she was not dressed. Next she took a large fishnet and wrapped it completely around her so that she was not naked. Then she took some money, leased a donkey, and tied the fishnet to its tail. The donkey had to drag her along so that she neither rode nor drove. And, since the donkey had to drag her along the wagon tracks, only her big toes could touch the ground so that she was neither on the road nor off it. Thus, when she appeared before the king this way, he said she had solved the riddle and had fulfilled all the conditions. He released her father from the prison, took her as his wife, and ordered her to look after all the royal possessions.

Now, some years went by, and one day, when the king was out reviewing his troops, a group of farmers happened to stop in front of his castle. They had been selling wood, and some of the wagons were drawn by horses, others by oxen. One of the farmers had three horses, and his mare gave birth to a foal that ran away and lay down between two oxen hitched to another farmer's wagon. When the two farmers came together, they started bickering, throwing things at each other, and making a lot of noise. The farmer with the oxen wanted to keep the foal and claimed that the oxen had given birth to it. The other said no, his horse had given birth to it, and the foal was his. The quarrel was taken before the king, and he declared that wherever the foal had laid itself down, there it should stay. So the farmer with the oxen got the foal, even though it didn't belong to him. The other farmer went away, wept, and grieved over his foal. However, since he had heard that the queen came from a poor farmer's family and was compassionate, he went to her and asked whether she could help him get his foal back.

"Yes," she said. "But you must promise not to tell that I've helped you. Now, here's what you have to do: Early tomorrow morning when the king goes out to review his guard, you're to place yourself in the middle of the road where he has to pass. Bring a large fishnet with you and pretend to fish with it. You're to keep fishing and shaking the net out as though it were full."

Then the queen also told him what to answer the king when he questioned him.

The next day the farmer got up and went fishing on dry land. When the king rode by and saw that, he sent his messenger to ask the foolish man what he was doing.

"I'm fishing," he replied.

When the messenger asked how he could fish without water, the farmer answered, "If two oxen can manage to give birth to a foal, then I can manage to catch a fish on dry land."

The messenger brought the farmer's answer back to the king, who summoned the farmer and said he knew that the farmer had not thought up the answer himself. The king wanted to know who had helped him with the answer, and he'd better confess right away. But the farmer refused to talk and kept repeating, may God help him if he hadn't thought up the answer himself. So they laid him down on a bundle of straw, beat and tortured him until he confessed that the queen had given him the idea.

When the king returned home, he said to his wife, "Why did you dupe me? I no longer want you for my wife. Your time is up! Go back to the farmhouse where you came from."

However, he granted her one last request: she could take the dearest and best thing that she could think of with her, and that was to be her parting gift.

"Very well, dear husband," she said. "Your wish is my command."

Then she embraced him, kissed him, and asked him to drink to her departure. He agreed, and she ordered a strong sleeping potion before saying farewell. The king took a big swig, but she only drank a little. Soon he fell into a deep sleep, and when she saw that, she called a servant, took a beautiful white linen sheet, and wrapped him in it. Other servants had to carry the king outside and put him into a carriage. Then she drove him to her house and put him to bed. He slept a whole day and night, and when he woke up, he looked around him and said, "My God! Where am I?"

He called his servants, but nobody was there. Finally, his wife came to the bed and said, "Dear king, you ordered me to take the dearest and best thing with me from the castle. Since you are the dearest and best thing I know, I took you with me."

"Dear wife," the king replied, "you shall be mine, and I shall be yours forever."

Then he took her back with him to the royal castle and married her again. And I am sure that they are still living together even today.

9

THE GENIE IN THE GLASS

A man paid for his son to study, and after the boy had successfully attended a few schools, the father couldn't support him anymore. So he told him to come home and said: "You know that I've run out of money. I can't give you anything anymore."

"Dear father," said the son, "don't worry. If that's the way it is, I'll stay and travel with you and earn some money from carpentry."

Indeed, the father was a day laborer and earned his living as a carpenter.

"My son," the father said, "that will be difficult for you to do because I only have one axe and can't buy one for you."

"Well," the son answered, "Go to our neighbor, and ask him to lend you one."

So the father borrowed an axe for his son, and they went into the forest to work. After they had worked until noon, the father said: "Now we'll rest a bit and eat our lunch. Then we'll be refreshed when we return to our work."

The student took his lunch in his hand and said to his father that he wanted to go around and search for birds' nests.

"Don't be foolish!" the father said. "Why do you want to run around in the forest like that? Stay with me. Otherwise, you'll get tired and won't be able to do much work anymore."

However, the son walked about in the forest, ate his bread, and looked for birds' nests. When he came to a large, dangerous oak tree, he searched all around. All of a sudden he heard a voice coming from the roots of the tree. It was crying out in quite a muffled tone: "Let me out! Let me out!"

He listened for it and called: "Where are you?"

Once again the voice cried: "Let me out! Let me out!"

"Yes, but I don't see anything," the student said. "Where are you?"

"I'm over here in the roots of the oak tree."

So the student began to search and found a glass bottle in the hollow of the tree, and the voice was coming from there. When he held the bottle against the light, he could see a shape in it like a frog, and the shape cried out: "Pull out the cork!"

The student did this, and as he pulled out the cork, an enormous man came out and said: "Do you know what reward you've earned by letting me out?"

"No," the student said.

"Well then, I'll tell you. I must break your neck for doing this."

"No, you can't do this to me," the student answered. "You should have told me sooner. Then I wouldn't have let you out. We've got to ask more people about this before you do anything."

"Forget about more people! You must receive the reward you deserve. Do you think people had pity for me when I was stuck in the bottle? No, they were punishing me! Do you know what my name is?"

"No," the student replied. "I don't know."

"I'm the all-powerful Mercurius," the genie said. "I've got to break your neck."

"No, that's not the right way to go about things." the student said. "Take it easy. First you must prove whether you can get back into the bottle; otherwise I won't believe that you ever came out of it. When I see that, I'll surrender to you and be your prisoner."

The genie agreed and returned though the opening and down the neck of the bottle. As soon as he was inside, the student took the cork that he had pulled out and shoved it back into the top of the bottle. He had easily duped the genie, and now the genie pleaded with the student to let him out and set him free.

"No," said the student. "I can't free anyone who seeks to put an end to my life, and I'll never ever let you out again."

"I'll give you as much money as you'll need for the rest of your life," the genie replied.

"You'd only deceive me like you did the first time," the student said.

"No," stated the genie. "I won't do anything to you."

The student was eventually persuaded by the genie, and he pulled the cork out again.

After the genie climbed out, he said: "Now I'll reward you. Here's a special bandage made of plaster. If you rub this on a wound with one end, the wound will be healed, and if you rub it on steel or iron with the other end, it will be turned into silver."

The student wanted to try out the bandage right away, and he made a tiny scratch on a tree and rubbed it with the bandage. All at once it was healed. So the student thanked the genie, and the genie thanked the student for releasing him from the bottle, and they took leave of one another.

The student returned to his father, who had resumed working and scolded his son for staying away so long. "Didn't I say that you'd do nothing?"

"I'll make up for it," the student replied.

"Well," said the father, "there's no way to make up for lost time."

"Father, what do you want me to do first?"

"Chop down that tree."

So the student took out his plaster and rubbed his axe with it. After he had struck the tree two times, the axe was worn down and the blade was no longer sharp enough because it was entirely made of silver.

"Look, father," said the son. "What kind of axe did you give me? It's now completely bent."

"Oh, what have you done now?" the father said and had become even angrier. "Now I'll have to pay for the axe. Your help will be my undoing."

"Don't be angry, father," said the son. "I'll certainly pay for the axe."

"Yes, you numbskull, how are you going to pay for it? You have nothing but what I give you. Your head's full of hazy ideas from studying. You don't understand the first thing about using an axe."

The son wanted to persuade his father to call it a day, but the father told him to go away. However, the student wouldn't leave him in peace and said he wouldn't go home until his father came with him. The son took the axe with him, and the father, who was an old man, couldn't see that it had become silver. When they reached home, the father said: "Now see if you can sell the axe somewhere."

So the student took the axe, brought it to a goldsmith in the city, and asked him how much he'd pay for it. As soon as the goldsmith saw the axe, he said that he wasn't rich enough to pay for it and didn't have enough money on hand. Then the student told him to give him what he had, and he would wait until the goldsmith could borrow more money to pay for it. So the goldsmith gave him three hundred gold coins, and the student borrowed another hundred. Then the student went home with the money to his father and said: "I've got money, so now go to the neighbor and ask him how much he wants for the axe."

"I already know," the father said. "he wants a gold coin and a penny."

"Well then," the student replied. "Give him two gold coins and twelve pennies. That's more than double what he wants, and it's enough."

Then the student gave his father a hundred gold coins and declared that he'd never want for money and told him the entire story of what had happened. Meanwhile, the student took the other three hundred gold coins and went to finish his studies. Afterward he could heal all kinds of wounds and became the most famous doctor in the world.

10

THE THREE LITTLE BIRDS

More than a thousand years ago there were many minor kings in this country, and one of them lived on the mountain called Köterberg. He was very fond of hunting, and one day, when he left his castle and went down the mountain with his huntsmen, he came upon three maidens tending their cows. When they saw the king with his men, the oldest pointed at the king and called to the other two, "Hallo, hallo! If I can't have that man over there, I don't want any at all."

Then the second responded from the other side of the mountain and pointed at the fellow walking on the king's right. "Hallo, hallo! If I can't have that man over there, I don't want any at all."

Finally, the youngest pointed at the fellow on the king's left and called out, "Hallo! Hallo! If I can't have that man over there, I don't want any at all."

The two men were the king's ministers, and the king had heard what the maidens had said. After he returned from the hunt, he summoned the three maidens and asked them what they had said the day before on the mountain. They refused to answer, but the king asked the oldest if she would take him for her husband. She said yes, and her two sisters also married the two ministers, for the maidens were all beautiful and had fine features, especially the queen, who had hair like flax.

The two sisters didn't bear any children, and once when the king had to take a trip, he asked them to stay with the queen and cheer her up, for she was with child. While he was away, she gave birth to a little boy who had a bright red star as a birthmark. But the two sisters decided to throw the pretty baby boy into the river. After they had thrown him into the water—I think it was the Weser—a little bird flew up in the air and sang:

"Get ready for your death.
I'll see what I can do.
Get ready for the wreath.
Brave boy, can that be you?"

When the two sisters heard the song, they feared for their lives and ran off. Later the king returned home, and they told him the queen had given birth to a dog, and the king responded, "Whatever God does is always for the best."

However, a fisherman lived by the river, and he fished the little boy out of the river while he was still alive. Since his wife had not given birth to any children, they fed and cared for him.

After a year had passed, the king went on another journey, and the queen gave birth to a second boy during his absence. The two wicked sisters again took the baby away and threw him into the river. Then the little bird flew up into the air once more and sang:

"Get ready for your death.
I'll see what I can do.
Get ready for the wreath.
Brave boy, can that be you?"

When the king came home, the sisters told him the queen had again given birth to a dog, and he responded as before, "Whatever God does is always for the best."

However, the fisherman fetched this baby out of the water, too, and fed and cared for him.

Once again the king went on a journey, and the queen gave birth to a little girl, whom the wicked sisters also threw into the river. Then the little bird flew up into the air once more and sang:

"Get ready for your death.
I'll see what I can do.
Get ready for the wreath.
Brave girl, can that be you?"

When the king came back home, the sisters told him the queen had given birth to a cat. This time the king became so angry that he had his wife thrown into prison, where she was forced to stay for many years.

In the meantime, the children grew up, and one day the oldest went out fishing with some other boys, but they didn't want him around and said, "You foundling, go your own way!"

The boy was very upset when he heard that and asked the old fisherman whether it was true. Then the fisherman told him how he had been out fishing one day and had found him in the water. The boy then said he wanted to go out and search for his father. The fisherman begged him to remain, but there was no holding him back. At last the fisherman gave in, and the boy went forth. He walked for many days until he came to a large and mighty river, where he found an old woman standing and fishing.

"Good day, grandma," said the boy.

"Why, thank you kindly."

"You'll be fishing here a long time before you catch any fish."

"And you'll be searching a long time before you find your father. How are you going to get across the river?"

"God only knows."

Then the old woman picked him up and carried him across on her back. Once he was on the other side, he continued his search for his father a long time, but he couldn't find him.

When a year had gone by, the second boy went out looking for his brother. He, too, came to the river, and the same thing happened to him as with his brother. Now only the daughter was left alone at home, and she grieved so much for her brothers that finally the fisherman had to let her go, too. Soon she also came to the large river and said to the old woman, "Good day, grandma."

"Why, thank you kindly."

"May God help you with your fishing."

When the old woman heard that, she treated the girl in a friendly way. She carried her across the river, gave her a stick, and said, "Now, my daughter, just keep going straight ahead, and when you come to a big black dog, you must be quiet. Don't be afraid or laugh or stop to look at it. Then you'll come to a large open castle. You must drop the stick on the threshold and go right through the castle and out the other side, where you'll see an old well. A big tree will be growing from the well, and a cage with a bird inside will be hanging on the tree. Take the cage down and get a glass of water from the well. Then carry both things back the same way you came. When you come to the threshold, pick up the stick, and when you come to the dog again, hit it in the face with the stick, but see to it that you don't miss. Then come back here to me."

The girl found everything just as the woman had said, and on her way back from the castle she met her two brothers, who had been searching half the world for each other. They went on together to the spot where the black dog was lying. Then she hit it on the face, and it turned into a handsome prince, who accompanied them to the river. The old woman was still standing there and was happy to see them. She carried all four of them across the river, and then she departed because she had now been released from a magic spell.

The others traveled back to the old fisherman, and they were all glad to have found each other again. Once inside the house, they hung the birdcage on the wall. But the second son was still restless. So he took a bow and went hunting. When he became tired, he took out his flute and began playing a little tune. The king, who also was out hunting, heard the music and went toward it. When he saw the boy, he said, "Who's given you permission to hunt here?"

"Nobody."

"Who're your parents?'

"I'm the fisherman's son."

"But he doesn't have any children."

"If you think I'm lying, come along with me."

The king did so and asked the fisherman, who told him all that had happened. Suddenly, the little bird in the cage began to sing:

"Oh, king of noble blood,
your children are back for good.
But their mother sits in prison
with nothing much to live on.
Her sisters are the wicked ones,
who took your daughter and sons
and left them to the river's fate,
but all were saved by the fisherman
before it was much too late."

When they heard the song, they were all astounded. The king took the little bird, the fisherman, and the three children with him to his castle, where the prison gate was opened and his wife released. However, she had become very sick and was haggard. So her daughter gave her a drink of water from the well, and she regained her health. But the two wicked sisters were burned to death, and the daughter married the prince.

II

THE WATER OF LIFE

Once upon a time there was a king who became sick, and nobody believed he would survive. He had three sons who were very saddened by this, and they went down into the palace garden, where they wept. All of a sudden they met an old man who asked them why they were so depressed, and they told him that their father was so sick that he would probably die. Nothing seemed to help.

"I know of a remedy," the old man said. "It's the Water of Life. If he drinks it, he'll regain his health. But it's difficult to find."

"Well, I'll find it," said the oldest, and he went to the sick king and requested permission to leave and search for the Water of Life, for that was the only cure for his illness."

"No," said the king. "The danger is much too great. I'd rather die instead!"

But the son pleaded so long that finally the king had to give his consent. Deep down the prince felt, "If I bring him the water, I'll become my father's favorite and shall inherit the kingdom."

So he set out and, after he had been riding for some time, he encountered a dwarf, who called to him and said, "Where are you going in such haste?"

"You twerp," the prince said contemptuously, "that's none of your business!" And he rode on.

But the little dwarf became furious and put a curse on him. Meanwhile, the prince found himself traveling through a mountain gorge, and the farther he rode, the more the mountains closed together, until the way became so narrow that he couldn't proceed. Nor could he turn his horse or get out of his saddle. He remained confined there.

Meanwhile the sick king waited and waited for the prince, but he didn't return. Then the second son said, "Father, let me go and search for the

Water of Life," and he thought to himself, "If my brother's dead, then the kingdom will fall to me."

At first the king didn't want to let him go either, but finally he gave in. So the prince set out on the same road that his brother had taken and met the dwarf, who stopped him and asked where he was going in such haste.

"You twerp," said the prince, "that's none of your business!" And he rode off with great arrogance.

But the dwarf put a curse on the prince, and he ended up in a mountain gorge, where he couldn't go forward or backward. Indeed, that's what happens to arrogant people.

Now, when the second son also failed to return, the youngest offered to set forth and fetch the water, and eventually the king had to let him go, too. After he met the dwarf and was asked where he was going in such haste, he stopped and answered, "I'm looking for the Water of Life because my sick father is on the brink of death."

"Do you know where to find it?"

"No," said the prince.

"Well, I'll tell you because you've spoken to me in such a polite way. It's gushing from a fountain in the courtyard of an enchanted castle. You won't make your way there unless I give you an iron wand and two loaves of bread. You're to knock three times on the castle gate with the iron wand, then it will spring open. Inside are two lions lying on the ground. They'll open their jaws, but if you throw a loaf of bread to each of them, they'll be quiet. Then you must hurry and fetch some of the Water of Life before the clock strikes twelve. Otherwise, the gate will slam shut, and you will be locked in."

The prince thanked him, took the wand and the bread, and went on his way. When he arrived there, everything was just as the dwarf had said. After the third knock the gate sprang open, and when he had calmed the lions with the bread, he entered the castle and went into a big beautiful hall, where he found spellbound princes sitting all around. He took the rings from their fingers and also grabbed a sword and loaf of bread that were lying on the floor. Then he moved on to the next room, where he encountered a beautiful princess, who was delighted to see him. She kissed him and told him that he had set her free and could have her entire kingdom as reward. If he would return in a year's time, their wedding would be celebrated. Then she also told him where to find the fountain with the Water of Life, but that he had to hurry and draw the water before the clock struck twelve.

So he went on and finally came to a room with a beautiful, freshly made bed, and since he was tired, he wanted to rest a little. Once he lay down, however, he fell asleep. When he awoke, the clock was striking a quarter to twelve, and he jumped up in a fright, ran to the fountain, and drew some water in a cup that happened to be lying on the ledge. Then he rushed outside, and just as he was running through the iron gate, the clock struck twelve, and the gate slammed so hard that it took off a piece of his heel.

Nevertheless, he was happy that he had found the Water of Life, and on his way home he passed the dwarf again. When the little man saw the sword and the bread, he said, "You've managed to obtain some valuable things. With the sword you'll be able to defeat whole armies, and the bread will always replenish itself."

Then the prince thought, "I don't want to return home to my father without my brothers," and so he said, "Dear dwarf, could you tell me where my two brothers are? They went out looking for the Water of Life before me and never came back."

"They're trapped between two mountains," said the dwarf. "I put them there with a magic spell because they were so arrogant."

Then the prince pleaded until finally the dwarf decided to release them but not without a warning. "Beware of them," he said. "They have evil hearts."

When he was reunited with his brothers, he was happy and told them all that had happened: how he found the Water of Life and was now bringing back a cupful to their father, how he had rescued the beautiful princess and was going to marry her after waiting a year, and how he would receive a vast kingdom after their marriage. Once he told all this, they rode on together and came to a country plagued by war and famine. The king was already convinced that he would soon perish because the situation was so desperate. But the prince went to him and gave him the bread, which he used to feed his people and satisfy their hunger. After that the prince also gave him the sword, which he used to defeat the enemy armies, and he was then able to live in peace and quiet. So the prince took back the loaf of bread and the sword, and the brothers rode on. Meanwhile, they passed through two other countries plagued by famine and war, and on each occasion the prince gave the king his bread and sword. In this way he was able to help save three kingdoms.

Later on they boarded a ship and sailed across the sea. During the trip the two older brothers began talking with one another and said: "The youngest found the Water of Life, and we are empty-handed. So our father will give him the kingdom that is ours by right, and our brother will deprive us of our happiness."

Overcome by desire for revenge, they planned to put an end to their brother's life. So they waited until he was sound asleep and then poured the Water of Life from his cup into their own and replaced it with bitter saltwater. When they arrived home, the youngest brought the cup to the sick king and told him to drink it and he would get well. No sooner did the king drink the bitter saltwater than he became sicker than ever. And as he began to moan the two oldest brothers came and accused the youngest of wanting to poison the king, while they, on the other hand, had brought the true Water of Life, and they handed it to their father.

As soon as he drank some, he felt his sickness on the wane and became as strong and healthy as in the days of his youth. After that the two older brothers went to the youngest and belittled him. "Oh, we know you found the Water of Life," they said, "but we're the ones who've received the reward for all your trouble. You should have been smarter and kept your eyes open. We took the water from you when you fell asleep at sea, and in a year's time one of us will fetch the beautiful princess. Still, you'd better not expose us. Father will not believe you anyway, and if you breathe a single word about it, your life will be worth nothing. If you keep quiet, we'll let you live."

The old king was angry at his youngest son because he believed that his son had wanted to take his life. So he summoned his ministers and ordered them to sentence his son to be shot in secret. So, one day, as the prince went out hunting, suspecting no danger, one of the king's huntsmen had to accompany him. When they were all alone out in the forest, the huntsman looked so sad that the prince asked him, "Dear hunter, what's the matter?"

"I can't say," answered the huntsman, "and yet I should."

"Tell me," said the prince. "Whatever it is, I'll forgive you."

"Ah," said the huntsman. "The king has ordered me to kill you."

The prince was taken aback by this news and said, "Dear huntsman, let me live. I'll give you my royal garments, and you give me your common ones in exchange."

"I'll gladly do that," said the huntsman. "I couldn't have shot you anyway."

They exchanged clothes, and the huntsman went home, while the prince went deeper into the forest. After a while three wagons loaded with gold and jewels arrived at the king's castle for his youngest son. They had been sent by the three kings who had defeated their enemies with the prince's sword and who had nourished their people with his bread. The wagons were an expression of their gratitude, and when the old king saw that, he began to think, "Perhaps my son was innocent?" And he said to the people at his court, "If only he were still alive! Now I regret that I ordered him to be killed."

"Then I did the right thing," said the huntsman. "I couldn't bring myself to shoot him," and he told the king what had happened. The king was glad and made it known in all the surrounding kingdoms that his son should return and would be restored to favor.

In the meantime, the princess had decided to build a glittering gold road that would lead up to her castle. She told her guards that whoever came riding to her straight up the middle of the road would be the right man and they should let him enter. However, whoever rode up on the side of the road would not be the right man, and they were not to let him enter.

When the year of waiting was almost up, the oldest son thought he would get an early start and pass himself off as her savior. Then he would get her for his wife and the kingdom as well. So he rode forth, and when he came to the castle and saw the beautiful road, he thought, "It would be a terrible shame if you rode on it." So he turned off to the right and rode along the side. But when he got to the castle gate, the guards told him that he was not the right man and he had better go away. Soon thereafter the second prince set out, and when he came to the gold road and his horse set its hoof down on it, he thought, "It would be a terrible shame if you damaged the road." He turned to the left and rode along the side. However, when he reached the gate, the guards told him he had better go away, for he was not the right man.

When the year was completely over, the third son prepared to ride out of the forest and hoped to forget his sorrows in the company of his beloved. As he set out he kept thinking about her and wishing he were already with her. When he arrived at the gold road, he didn't even notice it, and his horse rode right down the middle of it. Once he reached the gate, it opened, and the princess welcomed him with joy. She pronounced him her savior and lord of the realm, and they celebrated their wedding in great bliss. When it was over, she told him his father had sent for him, and had pardoned him. So he rode home and explained to his father how his brothers had deceived him and why he had kept quiet about it. The old king wanted to punish them, but they had fled on a ship and never returned as long as they lived.

12

DOCTOR KNOW-IT-ALL

Once upon a time there was a poor farmer named Crab, who drove a cord of wood into town with his two oxen and sold the wood to a doctor for two gold coins. When the farmer went inside to get his money, the doctor was just about to sit down to dinner, and the farmer admired the fine food and drink at the doctor's table. His heart yearned for something like that, and he thought how nice it would be if he were a doctor. He lingered there awhile and finally asked if it were possible for someone like him to become a doctor.

"Of course," said the doctor. "There's not much to it. First, buy yourself an ABC book. The kind with the picture of a rooster in it. Second, you must get cash for your wagon and two oxen and purchase some clothes and other things that doctors tend to need. Third, you must have a sign painted with the words *I am Doctor Know-It-All* and nail it above your front door."

The farmer did everything he was told, and when he had doctored for some time but not very long, a rich and mighty nobleman was robbed of some money, and he heard about Doctor Know-It-All, who was living in such and such a village and would probably know what had become of the money. So the nobleman had his carriage prepared, drove out to the village, and inquired at the farmer's house whether he was Doctor Know-It-All.

Yes, that was he, the farmer responded. Then the nobleman requested that he return with him and help him get back his stolen money. The farmer agreed, but added that Greta, his wife, had to come along too. The nobleman gave his approval, offered them both a seat in his carriage, and they drove off together. When they came to the nobleman's mansion, the table was already set, and Doctor Know-It-All was to eat with the lord, but he wanted his wife, Greta, to eat with them, too. So they all sat down together at the table.

Now, when the first servant arrived with a dish of delicious food, the farmer nudged his wife and said, "Greta, that was the first," and he meant that that was the man with the first course. But the servant thought he meant "That's the first thief," and since he really was the thief, he got scared and went out to tell his accomplices, "The doctor knows everything. There's trouble ahead. He said I was the first."

The second servant didn't even want to go in, but he had no choice. When he entered with his dish, the farmer nudged his wife and said, "Greta, that's the second."

This servant too got scared and hurried out. The third fared no better. Again the farmer said, "Greta, that's the third."

The fourth had to carry in a covered dish, and the nobleman asked the doctor to demonstrate his skill and guess what lay under the cover. Crabs were being served, and when the farmer looked at the covered dish, he had no idea what to say. Finally, he blurted out: "Poor me, poor *Crab*!"

When the nobleman heard that, he exclaimed, "There, he knows! I'm sure he must also know who has the money."

The servant was frightened to death and winked at the doctor to step outside for a moment. When he got outside, all four servants confessed to him that they had stolen the money. They proposed that he take charge of it and offered a large sum in addition if he would not expose them. Otherwise, they would soon be dangling from the gallows. Then they led him to the place where they had hidden the money. The doctor was satisfied, went back inside, sat down at the table, and said, "Sir, now I intend to look in my book to see where the money's been hidden."

In the meantime, the fifth servant had crawled into the stove to see if he could hear what else the doctor knew. As the doctor sat there at the table, he opened his ABC book and turned the pages back and forth looking for the rooster. Since he couldn't find it right away, he said, "I know you're there. I'm bound to find you."

The servant in the stove thought that the doctor was talking about him, and he jumped out of the stove in fright and said, "That man knows everything!"

Then Doctor Know-It-All showed the nobleman where the money was, but he didn't reveal who had stolen it. As a reward he received money from both sides and became a famous man.

13

THE FROG PRINCE

Once upon a time there was a king who had three daughters, and in his courtyard there was a well with beautiful clear water. On a hot summer's day the eldest daughter went down to the well and scooped out a glass full of water. However, when she looked at it and held it up to the sun, she saw that the water was murky. She found this very unusual and wanted to scoop out another glass when a frog stirred in the water, stuck his head up high, and finally jumped on to the edge of the well, where he spoke:

"If you'll be my sweetheart, my dear,
I'll give you water clearer than clear."

"Oh, who'd ever want to be a nasty frog's sweetheart?" she cried out and ran away.

Then she told her sisters that there was an odd frog down at the well that made the water murky. The second sister became curious, and so she went down to the well and scooped a glass of water for herself, but it was just as murky as her sister's glass so that she wasn't able to drink it. Once again, however, the frog was on the edge of the well and said:

"If you'll be my sweetheart, my dear,
I'll give you water clearer than clear."

"Do you think that would suit me?" the princess replied and ran away.

Finally, the third sister went, and things were no better. But when the frog spoke,

"If you'll be my sweetheart, my dear,
I'll give you water clearer than clear,"

she replied, "Yes, why not? I'll be your sweetheart. Get me some clean water."

However, she thought, "That won't do any harm. I can speak to him just as I please. A dumb frog can never become my sweetheart."

Meanwhile the frog had jumped back into the water, and when she scooped up some water a second time, it was so clear that the sun neatly gleamed with joy in the glass. Then she drank and quenched her thirst and also brought her sisters some of the water.

"Why were you so simple-minded and afraid of the frog," she said to them, and afterward the princess didn't think anything more about it and went happily to bed. However, after she had been lying there for a while and couldn't fall asleep, she suddenly heard some scratching on the door and then some singing:

"Open up! Open up!
Princess, youngest daughter,
don't you remember, what you said
when I sat on the well on the water's edge?

You wanted to be my sweetheart, my dear,
and I gave you water clearer than clear."

"Oh, that's my sweetheart, the frog," the princess said, "and since I gave him my word, I'll open the door."

So she got out of bed, opened the door a little, and then lay back down in the bed. The frog hopped after her and jumped on the bed down by her feet and remained there. When the night was over and morning dawned, the frog sprang off the bed and went out through the door. The next evening, when the princess was once again lying in bed, there was some scratching and singing at the door once more. The princess opened the door, and the frog lay in the bed at her feet until it turned day. On the third evening the frog came just like he had done the previous evenings.

"This is the last time that I'll open the door to you," the princess said to him. "In the future there will be no more of this."

Then the frog jumped and crawled under her pillow, and the princess fell asleep. When she woke up the next morning, she thought the frog would hop off again. Instead, she saw a handsome young prince standing before her, and he told her that he had been the bewitched frog and that she had saved him because she had promised to be his sweetheart. Then the two of them went to the king, who gave them his blessing, and a wedding was held. Meanwhile, the two other sisters were angry with themselves because they had not taken the frog to be their sweetheart.

14
THE DEVIL'S SOOTY BROTHER

A discharged soldier had nothing to live on and no longer knew what to do with his life. So he went out into the forest, and after walking for a while, he met a little man who was actually the devil himself.

"What's the matter?" the little man said to him. You look so gloomy."

"I'm hungry and have no money," said the soldier.

"If you hire yourself out to me and will be my servant," the devil said, "you'll have enough for the rest of your life. But you've got to serve me seven years, and after that you'll be free. There's just one other thing I've got to tell you: you're not allowed to wash yourself, comb your hair, trim your beard, cut your nails or hair, or wipe your eyes."

"If that's the way it must be, let's get on with it," the soldier said, and he went away with the little man, who led him straight to hell and told him what his chores were: he was to tend the fires under the kettles in which the damned souls were sitting, sweep the house clean and carry the dirt out the door, and keep everything in order. However, he was never to peek into the kettles, or things would go badly for him.

"I understand," said the soldier. "I'll take good care of everything."

So the old devil set out again on his travels, and the soldier began carrying out his duties. He put fuel on the fires, swept the floor, and took the dirt outside. When the old devil returned, he was satisfied and went off again. Now, for the first time, the soldier took a good look around hell. There were kettles all about, and they were boiling and bubbling with tremendous fires under each one of them. He would have given his life to know what was in them if the devil had not strictly forbidden it. Finally, however, he could no longer restrain himself. He lifted the lid of the first kettle a little and looked inside, only to see his old sergeant sitting there.

"Aha, you crumb!" he said. "Fancy meeting you here! You used to step on me, but now I've got you under my foot."

He let the lid drop quickly, stirred the fire, and added fresh wood. After that he moved to the second kettle, lifted the lid a little, and peeked inside. There sat his lieutenant.

"Aha, you crumb!" he said. "Fancy meeting you here! You used to step on me, but now I've got you under my foot."

He shut the lid again and added a log to the fire to make it really good and hot for him. Now he wanted to see who was sitting in the third kettle, and it turned out to be his general.

"Aha, you crumb! Fancy meeting you here! You used to step on me, but now, I've got you under my foot."

He took out a bellows and pumped it until the fire of hell was blazing hot under him. And so it was that he served out his seven years in hell. He never washed, combed his hair, trimmed his beard, cut his nails, or wiped his eyes. The seven years passed so quickly that he was convinced that only six months had gone by. When his time was completely up, the devil came and said, "Well, Hans, what've you been doing all this time?"

"I've tended the fires under the kettles, and I've swept and carried the dirt out the door."

"But you also peeked into the kettles. Well, you're just lucky that you added more wood to the fire; otherwise, you would have forfeited your life. Now your time is up. Do you want to go back home?"

"Yes," said the soldier. "I'd like to see how my father's doing."

"All right, if you want to get your proper reward, you must go and fill your knapsack with the dirt you've swept up and take it home with you. And you must also go unwashed and uncombed, with long hair on your head and a long beard, with uncut nails, and with bleary eyes. And if anyone asks you where you come from, you've got to say 'From hell.' And if anyone asks you who you are, you're to say 'I'm the devil's sooty brother, who's my king as well.'"

The soldier said nothing. Indeed, he carried out the devil's instructions, but he was not at all satisfied with the reward

As soon as he returned to the world and was out in the forest again, he took the knapsack and wanted to shake it out. But when he opened it, he discovered that the dirt had turned into pure gold. When he saw that, he was delighted and went into the city. An innkeeper was standing in front of his inn as Hans approached, and when he caught sight of Hans, the innkeeper was terrified because the soldier looked so dreadful, even more frightening than a scarecrow. He called out to him and asked, "Where are you coming from?"

"From hell."

"Who are you?"

"The devil's sooty brother, who's my king as well."

The innkeeper did not want to let him inside, but when Hans showed him the gold, he went and unlatched the door himself. Then Hans ordered the best room and insisted on the finest service. He ate and drank his fill but did not wash or comb his hair as the devil had instructed. Finally, he lay down to sleep, but the innkeeper could not get the knapsack of gold out of his mind. Just the thought of it left him no peace. So he crept into the room during the night and stole it.

When Hans got up the next morning and went to pay the innkeeper before leaving, his knapsack was gone. However, he wasted no words and thought, "It's not your fault that this happened," and he turned around and went straight back to hell, where he complained about his misfortune to the devil and asked for help.

"Sit down," said the devil. "I'm going to wash and comb your hair, trim your beard, cut your hair and nails, and wash out your eyes."

When he was finished with the soldier, he gave him a knapsack full of dirt again and said, "Go there and tell the innkeeper to give you back your gold; otherwise, I'll come and fetch him, and he'll have to tend the fires in your place."

Hans went back up and said to the innkeeper. "You stole my money, and if you don't give it back, you'll go to hell in my place and you'll look just as awful as I did."

The innkeeper gave him back the money and even more besides. Then he begged him to be quiet about what had happened.

Now Hans was a rich man and set out on his way home to his father. He bought himself a pair of rough linen overalls and wandered here and there playing music, for he had learned that from the devil in hell. Once he happened to play before an old king in a certain country, and the king was so pleased that he promised Hans his oldest daughter in marriage. However, when she heard that she was supposed to wed a commoner in white overalls, she said, "Before I do something like this, I'll drown myself in the deepest lake."

So the king gave Hans his youngest daughter, who was willing to marry him out of love for her father. So the devil's sooty brother got the king's daughter, and when the old king died, he got the whole kingdom as well.

THE DEVIL IN THE GREEN COAT

There were once three brothers, and the two eldest used to push the youngest around, and when they decided to go out into the world, they said to him: "We don't need you. You can go off wandering by yourself."

Then they left him, and he had to set off all alone. When he came to a large meadow, he was very hungry and sat down beneath a ring of trees and began to weep. All of a sudden he heard a roar, and when he looked up, the devil came toward him. He was dressed in a green coat and had a cloven foot.

"What's the matter?" he spoke. "Why are you weeping?"

Then the young man told him his troubles and said: "My brothers have driven me away from them."

"Well, I'm willing to help you," replied the devil. "If you put this green coat on, you'll see that it has pockets that are always full of money. You just have to dig into the pockets whenever you like. But in exchange for the coat I demand that you don't wash yourself for seven years, that you don't comb your hair, and that you don't pray. If you die during the seven years, then you are mine. If, however, you live, then you'll be free. In addition, you'll be rich for the rest of your life."

The young man's troubles were so great that they drove him to accept the devil's bargain. So the devil took off the green coat, and the young man put it on. As soon as he stuck his hand in a pocket, he had a handful of money.

Now he set out into the world with the green coat, and the first year was good. He could pay for anything he liked with his money, and he was still regarded as a human being for the most part. Things became worse in the second year. His hair had grown so long that nobody could recognize him and nobody would give him lodging for the night because he looked so atrocious. The more time passed, the worse it became. However, he gave poor people a lot of money so that they would pray for him and request that he wouldn't die during the seven years and fall in the devil's hands.

At a certain point in the fourth year he came to an inn, and the inn-keeper wouldn't let him stay there. However, he took out a heap of money and was willing to pay in advance so that the innkeeper gave him a room. That evening he heard a loud moaning in the neighboring room, and so he went next door and saw an old man sitting there. He was crying and com-plaining about something and told the young man to go away because he wouldn't be able to help him. The young man asked him, however, what was troubling him. The old man told him that he didn't have any money and that he owed the innkeeper a great deal. And now he was being detained until he paid his debt. Then the young man in the green coat said: "If that's all it is, I've got plenty of money. I'll pay, and you'll be freed of your debts."

Now the old man had three beautiful daughters and told him to come along with him, and he would give him one of the daughters for his reward. So the young man went with him, and when they arrived at the old man's home and the eldest daughter saw him, she screamed and cried that she would never marry such a hideous man who didn't have human traits and looked like a bear. The second daughter immediately ran off and preferred to set out into the wide world than marry the young man. However, the youngest said, "Dear father, since you've promised him and he's helped you get out of trouble, I shall obey you."

So the young man in the green coat took a ring from his finger and broke it in two. Then he gave her one half and kept the other for himself. He wrote his name in her half and her name in his half and told her to keep her half in a safe place. Afterward he stayed a little while longer with her until he said, "Now I must take my leave. I shall be gone three years. Be true to me during this time. Then I'll return, and we'll celebrate our wedding. If I don't return in three years, you'll be free, and I shall be dead. However, pray for me and ask God to protect me."

Now, during the three years, the two older sisters made a great deal of fun of the youngest and said that she couldn't get a real man and would have to marry a bear. However, the youngest daughter kept quiet and thought, "I must obey my father no matter what."

In the meantime the young man in the green coat traveled about the world and often stuck his hand into a pocket to buy the most beautiful things he saw for his bride. He didn't do anything evil. Indeed, he only did good deeds wherever he could and gave poor people money so that they would pray for him. So God showed him mercy, and the three years flew by and he was healthy and alive. Now that the time was over, he went back to the meadow and sat down under the ring of trees. Once again there was a tremendous roar, and the devil arrived. He grumbled and viciously threw the young man's old coat at him and demanded the green one in return. Well, the young man was glad to take off the green coat and handed it to the devil.

He was now free and rich for the rest of his life. So he went home, cleaned himself, and moved on to visit his bride. When he came to the door, the father met him. The young man greeted him and said he was the bridegroom, but the father didn't recognize him and wouldn't believe him. When the young man went over to the bride, she, too, wouldn't believe him. Finally, he asked whether she still had her half of the ring. She said, yes, and went to fetch it. Then he took out his half and held it next to hers, and they matched. Now they knew that he was definitely the bridegroom. And when she saw that he was a handsome man, she was very happy and fond of him, and they held the wedding. However, since the two sisters had passed up their chance for happiness, they became so furious that one of them drowned herself on the wedding day, and the other hanged herself.

That evening something knocked and banged on the door, and when the bridegroom went and opened it, the devil was standing there in his green coat and said, "You see! Now I've got two souls instead of just yours!"

16

THE WREN AND THE BEAR

Once, during summertime, as the bear and the wolf were walking through the forest, the bear heard a bird singing a beautiful song and said, "Brother wolf, what kind of bird can sing as beautifully as that?"

"That's the king of the birds," said the wolf. "We must bow down before him."

However, it was nothing but the wren, popularly known as the fence king.

"If that's the case," said the bear, "I'd like very much to see his royal palace. Please take me there."

"You can't go there just like that," said the wolf. "You'll have to wait until the queen comes."

Soon thereafter the queen arrived carrying some food in her bill, and the king as well, and they began feeding their young ones. The bear wanted to run in right after them, but the wolf held him by his sleeve and said, "No, you've got to wait until His Majesty and Her Highness have gone away again."

So they took note of the place where the nest was and trotted off. However, the bear could not rest until he saw the royal palace, and after a short while, he went back to it. The king and queen had already flown away, and he looked inside and saw five or six young birds lying there.

"Is that the royal palace?" exclaimed the bear. "It's a miserable palace. And you're not royal children in the least. You're a disgrace!"

When the young wrens heard that, they were tremendously angry and cried out, "No, we're not! Our parents are honorable people. Bear, you're going to pay for your remarks!"

The bear and the wolf became frightened. They turned around, went back to their dens, and sat. But the young wrens kept crying and shrieking, and when their parents returned with food, they said, "We're not going to touch so much as a fly's leg until you establish whether we're a disgrace or not. The bear was just here, and he insulted us."

"Calm down," said the old king. "I'll settle this matter."

He flew away with the queen to the bear's den and called inside, "Hey, you grumbly old bear, why did you insult my children? You'll pay for this. We'll have to settle this matter in a bloody war!"

So war was declared against the bear, who summoned all the four-legged animals: the ox, donkey, steer, stag, deer, and all those beasts that walk upon the earth. To counter this, the wren summoned everything that flies: not only the big and small birds, but also the gnats, hornets, bees, and flies had to come too.

When the time came for the war to begin, the wren sent out scouts to discover who the commanding general of the enemy forces was. The gnat was the wiliest of them all and roamed out into the forest, where the enemy had assembled. Then he hid under a leaf on the tree where the password was to be given out. The bear was standing right there, and he called the fox to him and said, "Fox, you're the most sly of all the animals. I want you to be our general and to lead us."

"Fine," said the fox. "But what shall we use as signals?"

Since nobody had any ideas, the fox said, "I've got a nice long bushy tail that looks almost like a red plume. If I lift up my tail, that will mean everything's all right, and you should charge. But, if I let it droop, then run for your lives."

Once the gnat heard that, he flew back to the wren and reported everything down to the last detail. At daybreak, when the battle was to commence, the four-legged animals came thundering with such a clatter that the earth began to tremble. The wren and his army also came flying through the air. They buzzed, shrieked, and swarmed so much that everyone in the surrounding area was frightened to death. As both sides attacked, the wren sent the hornet out with instructions to dive under the fox's tail and to sting him with all his might. Now, when the fox felt the first sting, he twitched and lifted a leg, but he stood his ground and kept holding up his tail. With the second sting, he had to lower his tail momentarily. But by the third sting he could no longer stand the pain and had to howl and tuck his tail between his legs. When the other animals saw that, they thought all was lost and began to run, each to his own den. And so the birds won the battle.

The king and queen flew home to their children and called, "Children, rejoice! Eat and drink to your heart's content. We've won the war."

But the young wrens said, "We're not going to eat a thing until the bear comes to our nest to beg our pardon and say that we're a credit to the family."

Then the wren flew to the bear's den and cried out, "Hey, you grumbly bear, I want you to go to my nest and ask my children for pardon. You'd better tell them they're a credit to the family; otherwise, your ribs will be broken to pieces."

On hearing this, the bear became extremely frightened, and he crawled to the nest, where he apologized. Now the young wrens were finally satisfied, so they sat down together and ate, drank, and made merry till late in the night.

17
THE SWEET PORRIDGE

Once upon a time there was a poor but pious girl who lived alone with her mother. When they had nothing left to eat, the girl went out into the forest, where she met an old woman who already knew about her troubles and gave her a small pot. She instructed the girl to say to it "Little pot, cook," for it would then make a good, sweet millet porridge. And the girl was to say "Little pot, stop!" to make it stop cooking.

The girl brought the pot home to her mother, and it put an end to their poverty and hunger. From then on they ate sweet porridge as often as they liked. One day, when the girl had gone out, the mother said, "Little pot, cook," and it began cooking. After she had eaten her fill, she wanted the pot to stop, but she had forgotten the right words. So the pot continued to cook, and the porridge ran over the rim and proceeded to fill the kitchen and the whole house, then the next house and the street, as if it wanted to feed the entire world. The situation was desperate, and nobody knew what to do. Finally, when only one house was left standing without any porridge in it, the girl returned home and merely said, "Little pot, stop!" It stopped cooking, and whoever sought to go back into the town had to eat his way through.

18
THE FAITHFUL ANIMALS

Once upon a time there was a man who didn't have much money, and he went out into the wide world with the little money that he had left. He arrived at a village, where some young boys had gathered together and were making noise and yelling.

"What's going on?" the man asked.

"Oh, we've got a mouse," they answered, "and we're making it dance for us. Just look at the funny way the mouse toddles!"

But the man felt sorry for the poor little animal, and he said, "Let the mouse go, boys, and I'll give you some money if you do."

So he gave them money, and they let the mouse go. The poor animal ran into a hole as fast as it could. The man went off and came to another village. There some boys had a monkey, who was being forced to dance and do somersaults. The boys were laughing at the monkey and wouldn't leave it in peace. Once again the man gave them money to let the monkey go. Afterward the man came to a third village, where some boys had a bear on a chain. The bear had to stand on its hind legs and dance, and when it growled, the boys laughed at it even more. The man bought the bear's freedom as well, and the bear was happy to run on his four feet again and dashed off.

Now the man had given away the last of his money and didn't have a red cent left in his pocket. So he said to himself, "The king has a great deal of money in his treasure chamber, and he doesn't need it all. You can't let yourself die of hunger. You might as well go and take some, and if you make money later, you can replace what you take."

Well, he managed to get into the treasure chamber and take some money. However, as he was creeping out, he was caught by the king's men. They accused him of being a thief and took him to the court. Since he had committed a crime, he was sentenced to be put into a box, and the box was cast off into water. The lid of the box was full of holes so that air could get inside. In addition, he had been given a jug of water and a loaf of bread. As he was floating on the water in a state of fright, he heard some fumbling with the lock and then some gnawing and puffing. All of a sudden, the lock sprang open, the lid popped up, and there stood the mouse, the monkey, and the bear, who had opened the box. Since he had helped them, they wanted to repay him. However, they didn't know what step to take next and began discussing the matter with one another. While they were doing this, a white stone that looked like a round egg came rolling into the water.

"It's come just at the right moment," said the bear. "That's a magic stone. Whoever possesses it can wish for whatever he desires."

The man fetched the stone from the water, and when he held it in his hand, he wished for a castle with a garden and stables. No sooner had he uttered the wish than he sat in a castle with a garden and stables. Everything was so beautiful and splendid that he couldn't get over his amazement. After some time passed, several merchants came his way.

"Just look!" they exclaimed. "What a glorious castle! The last time we came by here, there was nothing but mere sand."

Since they were curious, they went inside and asked the man how he had managed to build everything so swiftly.

"It wasn't I who did it," he said. "It was my magic stone."

"What kind of a stone is it?" they asked.

The man went to fetch it and showed it to the merchants. They wanted very much to buy it and asked him to sell it in exchange for all their beautiful wares. The man took a fancy to the wares, and since the heart can be fickle and yearn for new things, he let himself be fooled and thought the beautiful wares were more valuable than his magic stone. So he gave it away, and no sooner did it leave his hands than his good fortune disappeared, and he sat once more in the locked box on the river with nothing but a jug of water and a loaf of bread. When the faithful animals—the mouse, the monkey, and the bear—saw his misfortune, they came again and wanted to help him, but this time they couldn't get the lock open because it was much stronger than the first one.

"We've got to get the magic stone back," said the bear, "or else everything we try will be useless."

Since the merchants were still living in the castle, the animals went there together. As they were approaching it, the bear said, "Mouse, go through the keyhole and tell us what to do. You're small, and nobody will notice you."

The mouse agreed but came back and said, "There's nothing we can do. I looked inside, but the stone is hanging on a red ribbon under the mirror, and all around it are cats with fiery eyes. They're stationed there to guard it."

Then the bear and monkey said, "Go back inside and wait until their master is lying asleep in his bed. Then slip through the hole, crawl on top of his bed, pinch his nose, and bite off some of his hair."

The mouse crawled back inside and did what the others told him to do. The master woke up and rubbed his nose in great annoyance.

"The cats are useless!" he said. "The mice go right by them and bite the hair off my head."

So he chased the cats away, and the mouse won the day. When the master went to sleep the following night, the mouse crept inside, and she nibbled and gnawed on the red ribbon on which the stone was hanging until the ribbon split in two and the stone fell to the ground. Then the mouse dragged it to the house door. However, this was hard work for the mouse, and she said to the monkey, who was keeping a lookout, "Pull it out with your paw."

This was easy for the monkey, and after he took the stone in his hand, they all returned to the river.

"How are we going to get to the box?" the monkey asked.

"We'll deal with that soon enough," said the bear. "I'll get into the water and swim. Monkey, you get on my back. Hold on to me tightly and put the stone in your mouth. Mouse, you can sit in my right ear."

So they did what he said and swam down the river. After they had gone some distance, the bear felt that it was too quiet and wanted to talk.

"Listen, monkey," he said. "I think we're good comrades. What do you think?"

However, the monkey kept quiet and didn't reply.

"Is that the way to behave?" said the bear. "Won't you give your comrade an answer? You're some lousy fellow if you don't!"

Now the monkey could no longer keep silent. He let the stone fall into the water and cried out, "You stupid fellow! How could I answer you with the stone in my mouth? Now it's lost, and you're to blame."

"Let's not quarrel," said the bear. "We'll think of something."

They discussed the situation and then called together the frogs, the toads, and all the animals that lived in the water and said, "A powerful enemy intends to attack you. Go and collect all the stones you can find, and we'll build a wall to protect you."

The animals were frightened and brought stones from all over the place. Finally, a fat, old croaker of a frog emerged from the bottom carrying the magic stone with the red ribbon in his mouth. Now the bear was happy. He relieved the frog of his burden, told the animals that everything was all right, and sent them home with a quick farewell. Then the three swam down the river to the man in the box, opened the lid with the help of the stone, and arrived just at the right moment, for the man had consumed the bread and had drunk the water and was already half dead. As soon as he held the magic stone in his hands once again, he wished to regain his good health and to be transported to his beautiful castle with the garden and stables. Then he lived there in happiness, and the three animals stayed with him and had a good life for the rest of their years.

19
TALES ABOUT TOADS

I

A child sat on the ground in front of the house door and had a little bowl with milk and bread nearby and ate. A toad came crawling and dipped its little head into the bowl and ate with the boy. The next day it came again and did this every day for some time. The child took delight in this, and when he saw, however, that the toad would only drink the milk and leave the bread lying there, the child took his little spoon, hit the toad a little on its head, and said: "You thing you, eat the bread too."

In the meantime the boy had become handsome and big, and his mother stood right behind him and saw the toad. Then she ran over to them and beat the toad to death. From that time on the child became emaciated and finally died.

II

A little orphan girl was sitting on the city wall and spinning when she saw a toad come toward her. So she spread out a blue silk neckerchief next to her that toads like to walk on very much. As soon as the toad caught sight of the kerchief, it turned back, but it soon returned carrying a tiny golden crown. It laid the crown on the kerchief and went away again. The girl picked up the crown in her hands. It glittered and was made out of delicately spun gold. The toad soon came back a second time, but when it didn't see the crown anymore, it crawled to the wall and began hitting its head against the wall out of grief. The toad continued doing this until its strength gave out, and it finally lay there dead. If the little girl had left the crown lying on the kerchief, the toad would probably have brought even more of its treasures out of the hole.

III

"*Hoo-hoo, hoo-hoo*," called the toad.

"Come out," said the child,

The toad came out, and the child asked about his little sister. "Have you seen Little Red Stocking by any chance?"

"No," the toad said. "I haven't seen her either. How about you? *Hoo-hoo, hoo-hoo, hoo-hoo*."

20
THE POOR MILLER'S APPRENTICE
AND THE CAT

Once there were three young men who worked in a mill owned by an old miller who lived there without wife or children. After the men had worked for him for some years, he said to them: "Go out and see who can bring back the best horse. The winner will get my mill."

Now, the third of the hired hands was just an apprentice, and the other two thought he was a simpleton and didn't deserve the mill. He, in fact, didn't even want it, but he set out with the other two workers, and when they came to a village, the two men said to simple Hans, "You might as well stop here. You'll never get a horse as long as you live."

But Hans went on with them, and when night came, they arrived at a cave and lay down to sleep inside. The two clever ones waited until Hans fell asleep. Then they got up and made off, while Hans continued sleeping. They thought that they had made a smart move, but just wait, fortune is not about to shine on them!

When the sun rose and Hans woke up, he was lying in the deep cave; he looked all around and cried, "Oh, God, where am I?"

Then he got up and crawled out of the cave. He went into the forest and began thinking, "How shall I ever get a horse?" While he was walking along and pondering his situation, he met a little multicolored cat, and she spoke to him in a friendly way.

"Where are you going, Hans?"

"Oh, you can't help me."

"I know quite well what you're looking for," said the cat. "You want a fine horse. Come with me and be my faithful servant for seven years. After that I'll give you the finest-looking horse you'll ever see in your life."

Then she took him with her to her enchanted castle, where he had to serve her. He chopped wood every day, and she gave him a silver axe, a silver wedge and saw, and a copper mallet for this chore. So he chopped firewood, stayed with the cat, and had plenty to eat and to drink. He saw nobody except the multicolored cat.

One day she said to him: "Go and mow my meadow and dry out the grass."

She gave him a silver scythe and a golden whetstone and told him to return everything to her in proper condition when he was finished. Hans did as he was told, and when he was finished with the work, he brought in the hay and returned the scythe and whetstone. Then he asked whether he could have his payment.

"No," said the cat. "First you must do one more thing for me. Here, now take this wood made of silver, an axe, a square, and everything you need, all in silver. I want you to build me a small cottage."

So Hans built the cottage, and when it was finished, he pointed out that he had completed his task and still didn't have a horse. Indeed, even though it felt like only six months, the seven years had passed. So the cat asked whether he would like to see her horses.

"Yes," said Hans.

Then she went to her cottage and opened the door: twelve proud horses were standing there, and their coats were so sparkling bright and shiny that his heart jumped with joy. The cat gave Hans something to eat and drink and said, "It's time for you to go home, but I'm not going to give you your horse now. I'll bring it with me in three days' time."

The cat showed Hans the way to the mill, and he set out. However, she hadn't given him any new clothes, so he had to keep wearing the old tattered overalls he had been wearing all these years, and they had become much too short all over for him. When he reached home, the two other hired men were there already. Of course, each of them had brought a horse with him, but one horse was blind, and the other lame.

"Hans," they asked, "where's your horse?"

"I'm expecting it in three days."

They laughed and said, "Where in the world could you ever get a horse? We can't wait to see your fine creature!"

Hans went into the miller's house, but the miller told him he was too ragged and disheveled to sit at the table. If anyone happened by, he would disgrace them. So they gave him a little food outside. When they went to sleep in the evening, the other two hired men refused to give him a bed. Finally, he had to crawl into the goose house, where he lay down on some hard straw. When he awoke the next morning, the three days were already up, and a coach drawn by six horses arrived at the mill. My, how the horses glistened in the sunlight! It was a beautiful sight, and a servant had brought a seventh horse, which was intended for the poor miller's apprentice. Then a gorgeous princess stepped out of the coach and went into the mill. This princess was none other than the little multicolored cat whom Hans had served for seven years. She asked the miller where the apprentice was.

"We couldn't let him sleep in the mill," said the miller. "He was too ragged and dirty. So he's lying in the goose house."

The princess had him fetched immediately, and when they got him out, he had to hold his overalls together in order not to expose himself.

The servant unpacked a bundle of splendid clothes and then washed him and dressed him. When Hans was ready, no king could have looked more handsome. After this the maiden demanded to see the horses that the other hired men had brought: one was blind and the other lame. Then she ordered her servant to bring the seventh horse. When the miller saw it, he said he had never seen a horse like it in his yard.

"It's for the apprentice," she said.

"Then he must have the mill," said the miller.

But the princess said that he could keep his mill, and he could have the horse, too. She took her faithful Hans by the hand, led him into the coach, and drove off with him. First they went to the small cottage that he had built for her with the silver tools, but it had become a huge castle, and everything in it was made of silver and gold. Afterward she married him, and he was rich, so rich that he had more than enough money for the rest of his life.

So remember, don't ever let anyone tell you that simpletons can never amount to anything.

21

THE CROWS

An honest and diligent soldier had earned and saved some money because he had been diligent and had not squandered his earnings in the taverns as the other soldiers had. It so happened that two of his comrades were quite devious and wanted to get at his money, and so they pretended to be very friendly with him. One day they said to him, "Listen, why should we stay here in this city? We're locked in as though we were prisoners. Besides, someone such as you could really earn something decent and live happily if you were in your own country."

They kept talking to him like this until finally he agreed to leave with them. However, the other two only intended to steal his money. After they had gone part of the way, the two soldiers said, "We must turn right over there if we want to get to the border."

"No," he replied. "That leads straight back into the city. We've got to keep to our left."

"What!" the other two exclaimed. "You always want to have the last word in everything!"

Then they rushed at him and began hitting him until he fell down, and they took the money out of his pocket. But that wasn't enough. They poked his eyes out, dragged him to the gallows, and tied him up tightly. After that they left him behind and went back to the city with his stolen money.

The poor blind man wasn't aware that he had been left in such a terrible place. He groped about and could feel that he was sitting beneath a beam of wood. Since he thought it was a cross, he said, "Well, at least it was good of them to tie me up under a cross. God is with me." And he began praying to God. When it was almost night, he heard the fluttering of wings, which turned out to be three crows landing on the beam. After that he heard one of them say, "Sister, what good news have you brought? Oh, if only the people knew what we know! The king's daughter is sick, and the old king has promised to give her to anyone who can cure her. But no one can do it, for she'll only get well again if the toad in the pond over there is burned to ashes and she drinks the ashes with some water."

Then the second crow said, "Oh, if only the people knew what we know! A dew will fall from heaven tonight, and it will have such miraculous and healing powers that the blind will be able to regain their sight if they rub their eyes with it."

Finally, the third crow said, "Oh, if only the people knew what we know! The toad can only help one person, and the dew can only help a few. Meanwhile, there's a great emergency in the city. All the wells are dried out, and nobody knows that if the people removed the square stone in the marketplace and dug beneath that spot, the most beautiful water would gush forth."

After the three crows had finished talking, the blind man heard the fluttering of wings again, and they flew away. Gradually he was able to untie himself, and then he stooped down, pulled out a few blades of grass, and rubbed his eyes with the dew that had fallen on them. All at once he regained his sight. The moon and the stars were in the sky, and he saw that he was standing next to the gallows. After that he looked for some earthenware to gather as much of the precious dew as he could find. When this was done, he went to the pond, dug into the water, grabbed hold of the toad, and burned it to ashes. Next he carried the ashes to the king's court and had the king's daughter take some. When she was restored to health, he demanded her for his wife as the king had promised. However, the king didn't take a liking to him because he was dressed so poorly, and he said that whoever wanted to have his daughter would first have to provide water for the city. In this way the king hoped to get rid of him. But the soldier went to the city and ordered the people to remove the square stone from the marketplace and to dig beneath the spot for water. No sooner had they dug than they hit upon a spring, and a mighty jet of water shot forth. Now the king could no longer refuse to give his daughter to him. After the wedding, they lived together in a happy marriage.

One day, when the soldier was taking a walk through the fields, he met his former comrades who had treated him so disgracefully. They didn't recognize him, but he knew them right away and went up to them.

"Look," he said. "I'm your former comrade whose eyes you poked out so cruelly. But fortunately the dear Lord has allowed me to prosper."

They fell to his feet and begged for mercy. Since he had a kind heart, he took pity on them and brought them back to his palace. He gave them food and clothes and afterward told them what had happened and how he had gained such honor. When the two heard all that, they were restless and eager to spend a night beneath the gallows to see if they could perhaps hear something good as well. So they went and sat under the gallows. Soon they heard the fluttering of wings above their heads, and the three crows arrived. One of them said to the others, "Listen, sisters, someone must have overheard us, for the king's daughter is healthy, the toad is gone from the pond, a blind man has regained his sight, and they've dug a fresh well in the city. Come, let's look for the eavesdropper and punish him."

When they swooped down from the beam, they found the two soldiers, and before the men could defend themselves, the crows sat on their heads and hacked out their eyes, and they kept hacking their faces until they were dead and then left them lying beneath the gallows. After a few days, when the soldiers had not returned, their former comrade thought, "Where could the two be wandering about?" He went out to look for them but found nothing except their bones, which he took away from the gallows and buried in a grave.

22

HANS MY HEDGEHOG

Once there was a rich farmer, and he and his wife didn't have any children. When he went into town with the other farmers, they often made fun of him and asked why he had no children. One day he finally got angry, and when he went home, he said, "I want to have a child, even if it's a hedgehog."

Then his wife gave birth to a child whose upper half was hedgehog and bottom half, human. When she saw the child, she was horrified and said, "You see how you cursed us!"

"There's nothing we can do about it now," said her husband. "The boy must be christened, but we'll never find a godfather for him."

"There's only one name I can think of for him," said the wife, "and that's Hans My Hedgehog."

After he was christened, the pastor said, "He won't be able to sleep in a regular bed because of his quills."

Consequently, they gathered together some straw, spread it on the floor behind the stove, and laid Hans My Hedgehog on it. His mother couldn't nurse him because he might have stuck her with his quills. So he lay behind the stove for eight years, and eventually his father got tired of him and wished he might die, but he didn't die. He just kept lying there.

One day there was a fair in town, and the farmer decided to go to it and asked his wife if she wanted anything.

"Some meat and a few rolls," she said. "That's all we need for the house."

Then he asked the maid, and she wanted a pair of slippers and hand-sewn stockings. Finally, he went and asked his son, "Hans My Hedgehog, what would you like to have?"

"Father," he said, "just bring me back some bagpipes."

When the farmer returned home, he gave his wife the meat and rolls he had bought. Then he handed the maid the slippers and hand-sewn stockings. Finally, he went behind the stove and gave Hans My Hedge-hog his bagpipes. Upon receiving the bagpipes, he said, "Father, please go to the blacksmith and have him shoe my rooster. Then I'll ride away and never come back."

The father was happy at the idea of getting rid of him and had his rooster shod. When the rooster was ready, Hans My Hedgehog mounted it and rode away, taking some donkeys and pigs with him, which he wanted to tend out in the forest. Once he reached the forest, he had the rooster fly him up into a tall tree, where he sat and tended the donkeys and pigs. Indeed, he sat there for many years until the herd was very large, and he never sent word to his father about his whereabouts.

As he sat in the tree he played his bagpipes and made some beautiful music. One day a king, who had lost his way in the forest, came riding by. When he heard the music, he was so astonished that he sent his servant to look around and see where the music was coming from. The servant looked around, but all he could see was a small animal, sitting up in a tree, that seemed to be a rooster with a hedgehog sitting on top of it playing music. The king told the servant to ask the creature why he was sitting there and whether he knew the way back to the king's country. Hans My Hedgehog climbed down from the tree and said he would show him the way if the king would promise in writing to give him the first thing he met at the castle courtyard when he returned home.

"No danger in that," thought the king. "Hans My Hedgehog can't understand writing, so I can write whatever I want." The king took pen and ink and wrote something down, and after he had done this, Hans My Hedgehog showed him the way, and the king arrived home safely. When his daughter saw him coming from afar, she was so overcome with joy that she ran out to meet him and kissed him. Then he thought of Hans My Hedgehog and explained to her what had happened: he had been forced to make a promise in writing to a strange creature who had demanded to have the first thing the king met upon returning home. This creature had been sitting on a rooster as though it were a horse and had been playing beautiful music. The king told his daughter that he had, however, writ-ten down that Hans My Hedgehog was not to get what he demanded.

Anyway, it made no difference because he couldn't read. The princess was happy to hear that and said it was a good thing since she would never have gone with him anyway.

Hans My Hedgehog continued tending his donkeys and pigs. He was always cheerful sitting there perched in his tree, playing his bagpipes. Now it happened that another king came driving by with his servants and couriers. He too had lost his way, and the forest was so large that he didn't know how to get back home. He too heard the beautiful music from afar and told a courier to go and see what it was. So the courier went to the tree and saw the rooster sitting there with Hans My Hedgehog on its back, and the courier asked him what he was doing up there.

"I'm tending my donkeys and pigs, but what can I do for you?"

The courier asked him whether he could show them the way out of the forest since they were lost and couldn't make it back to their kingdom. Hans My Hedgehog climbed down from the tree with his rooster and told the old king that he would show him the way if the king would give him the first thing that met him when he returned home to his royal castle. The king agreed and put it in writing that Hans My Hedgehog was to have what he demanded. When that was done, Hans My Hedgehog rode ahead of him on the rooster and showed the way. The king reached his kingdom safely, and as he entered the castle courtyard, there was great rejoicing. His only daughter, who was very beautiful, ran toward him and embraced him. She was very happy to see her old father again and asked him what in the world had kept him so long. He told her he had lost his way and would not have made it back at all had it not been for a strange creature, half human, half hedgehog, who had helped him find his way out of the forest. The creature had been sitting astride a rooster up in a tall tree and had been playing beautiful music. In return for his aid the king had promised to give him the first thing that met him at the castle courtyard. Now he was very sorry that it had happened to be her. However, out of love for her old father, the princess promised him that she would go with Hans My Hedgehog whenever he came.

In the meantime, Hans My Hedgehog kept tending his pigs, and the pigs had more pigs, and eventually there were so many that the entire forest was full of them. Then Hans My Hedgehog sent word to his father to clear out all the pigsties in the village, for he was coming with such a huge herd of pigs that anyone who wanted to slaughter one could have his pick. On hearing this, his father was distressed, for he had believed that Hans My Hedgehog had long been dead. Nevertheless, Hans My Hedgehog mounted his rooster, drove his pigs ahead of him into the village, and ordered the slaughtering to begin. *Whew!* There was such chopping and butchering that the noise could be heard for miles around. Afterward Hans My Hedgehog said, "Father, have the blacksmith shoe my rooster one more time. Then I'll ride away and never return as long as I live."

So his father had the rooster shod and was glad that Hans My Hedgehog didn't want to return again. Now, when Hans My Hedgehog departed, he set out for the country of the first king whom he had helped, but the king had given his men orders to stop anyone who was riding on a rooster and playing bagpipes from entering the castle. If necessary, they were to use their guns, spears, or swords to stop him. So when Hans My Hedgehog came riding, they attacked him with their bayonets, but he put spurs to his rooster, and the bird rose in the air, flew over the gate, and landed on the ledge of the king's window. He called to the king to keep his promise and give him the princess; otherwise, he would take his life and his daughter's as well. Then the king implored his daughter with the best words he could use to go with Hans My Hedgehog to save their lives. So she dressed herself all in white, and her father gave her a coach with six horses, splendid servants, money, and property. She got into the coach and was followed by Hans My Hedgehog, with his bagpipes and his rooster by his side. They then said good-bye and drove away, and the king thought that was the last be would ever see of his daughter, but things happened much differently from how he thought they would. When they had gone a little way from the city, Hans My Hedgehog took off the princess's beautiful clothes and stuck her with his quills until she was covered with blood.

"This is what you get for being so deceitful!" he said. "Go away. I don't want you."

Then he chased her home, and she lived in disgrace for the rest of her life.

Meanwhile, Hans My Hedgehog took his bagpipes, got on his rooster, and continued his journey toward the second kingdom, which belonged to the other king whom he had led out of the forest. However, this king had ordered his men to present arms, to allow Hans My Hedgehog to enter, and to greet him by shouting "Long may he live!" After that they were to escort him into the royal palace. When the king's daughter saw him, she was frightened because he looked so strange. However, she thought there was nothing she could do, for she had promised her father to go with him. Therefore, she welcomed Hans My Hedgehog and had to go with him to the royal table, where she sat next to him. Then they ate and drank. When evening came and it was time to go to bed, she was very much afraid of his quills, but he said not to fear because he had no intention of harming her. Then he told the old king to have four men stand watch in front of the bedroom door and to make a big fire, for when he got inside and prepared to go to bed, he would slip out of his hedgehog's skin and leave it in front of the bed. The men were then to rush in quickly, throw the skin on the fire, and stand there until it was completely extinguished.

When the clock struck eleven, he went into the room, stripped off the hedgehog's skin, and left it on the floor in front of the bed. Right after this the men came, picked up the skin, and threw it into the fire. When the fire had consumed it, he was set free and lay in bed just like a human being, but he was pitch black, as if he had been burned. The king sent for his doctor, who rubbed him with special ointments and balms, and gradually, he became white and turned into a handsome young man. When the princess saw that, she was very happy. The next morning they got up in a joyful mood and had a fine meal. Then the wedding was held, and Hans My Hedgehog was given the kingdom by the old king.

After some years had passed, the young king took his wife and drove to visit his father, and he told the old man that he was his son. The father, however, said he had no son, though he once had one, but he had been born with quills like a hedgehog and had gone off into the world. Then Hans My Hedgehog revealed himself to his father, and the old man rejoiced and went back with him to his kingdom.

23

THE LITTLE SHROUD

A mother had a little boy of seven who was handsome, and she loved him more than anything in the world. But, all of a sudden, he died. The mother couldn't stop grieving and wept day and night. Not long after the boy was buried, he began to appear at night in places where he had formerly sat and played when he had been alive. Then, whenever his mother wept, he would weep too, and when morning came, he would disappear. Since his mother wouldn't stop her weeping, he came one night clad in the little white shroud that he had worn in his coffin and with a wreath on his head. He sat down at her feet on the bed and said, "Oh, Mother, please stop weeping. Otherwise, I won't be able to get to sleep in my coffin. My little shroud is all wet from the tears you've been shedding on it."

Upon hearing this, his mother became frightened and stopped weeping. The next night, the child came again with a light in his hand and said, "You see, now my shroud is almost dry, and I can rest in my grave."

Then his mother commended her grief to the dear Lord and bore it silently and patiently. The child never returned after that but slept in his little bed beneath the ground.

24

THE JEW IN THE THORNBUSH

A farmer had a hard-working and faithful servant, who served him for three years without receiving any wages. Finally, it occurred to the servant that he really didn't want to work for nothing, and he went to his master and said: "I've served you honestly and tirelessly for a long time. That's why I trust you'll now want to give me what's due to me, in keeping with God's commandments."

However, the farmer was a sleazy man and knew that the servant was simple-minded. So he took three pennies and gave him a penny for each year. That's how the servant was paid. Meanwhile, he believed that all this was a fortune and thought, "Why should I put up with drudgery anymore? I can now take care of myself and be free and have a merry time in the world." So he stuck his huge amount of money in a sack and began traveling cheerfully over hill and dale.

When he came to a field, skipping and singing, a little man appeared and asked him why he was so merry.

"Oh, why should I be gloomy? I'm healthy, and I've got an enormous amount of money and don't need to worry. I've saved all that I earned from working for my master three years, and it's all mine!"

"How much is your treasure?" asked the little man.

"Three whole pennies," answered the servant.

"I'm a poor man. Give me your three pennies."

Now since the servant had a kind heart and took pity on the little man, he gave him the money.

Then the man said: "Because you have a pure heart, you are to be granted three wishes, one for each penny. Now you may have what your heart desires."

The servant was satisfied with this and thought, "I prefer things to money," and he said: "First, I wish for a fowling gun that hits everything I aim at; second I wish for a fiddle that will make everyone dance when I play it; third I want people always to do what I request."

The little man said, "All your wishes are granted," and he immediately gave him the fiddle and the gun and went off on his way.

Well, if the servant had been happy before, he thought that he was now ten times happier, and he had not gone very far when he encountered an old Jew. A tree was standing there, and a small lark was sitting on top of the highest branch and sang and sang.

"It's a miracle of God that such a little bird can sing like that!" said the Jew. "I'd give anything to have it."

"Well, if that's all you want, the bird will soon come down to us," said the servant. Then he took aim with his gun and shot the lark between the eyes so that it fell down from the tree.

"Go and pick it up," he said to the Jew.

However, the bird had fallen into some thornbushes that were under the tree. The Jew crawled into the bushes, and when he was stuck in the middle of the bushes, the servant took out his fiddle and began playing. Then the Jew started to dance and couldn't stop. Instead, he jumped even higher with more force. Meanwhile, the thorns ripped his clothes so that they hung in shreds on him, and he was scratched and wounded, causing his entire body began to bleed. .

"For God's sake!" the Jew screamed. "Stop playing your fiddle. What crime have I done to deserve this?"

"You've skinned enough people," thought the servant, "so you're just getting the justice that you deserve." And he played a new jig. Meanwhile the Jew began pleading and making promises and said he'd give him money if he stopped. At first, however, the servant didn't think the Jew offered him enough and drove him to dance even more until the Jew promised him a hundred solid gold coins that he was carrying in his bag and that he had just obtained by cheating a good Christian. When the servant saw all that money, he said: "Well, given this condition, yes, I'll stop." So he took the bag and stopped playing his fiddle. Then he calmly and happily went on his way.

Meanwhile the Jew broke out of the thornbush. He was half naked and miserable and began contemplating how he'd avenge himself. He cursed the fellow and wished evil things would happen to him. Finally, he ran to a judge and complained that, without being at fault, he had been robbed of his money by a scoundrel and that he had been beaten mercilessly, and the fellow who had done this was carrying a gun on his back, and a fiddle was hanging from his shoulder. So the judge sent out some couriers and officers who were supposed to track down the servant and see where they could find him. Soon the young man was discovered and brought before the court.

The Jew accused the servant of robbing his money, but the servant said: "You gave the money to me so that I'd stop playing my fiddle."

The judge made short matter of all this and sentenced the servant to hang on the gallows. Well, soon he stood on the platform of the gallows with the noose around his neck, and he said, "Judge, please grant me one last request."

"As long as you don't ask me to spare your life."

"It's not about my life. I'd like to play my fiddle just one last time."

The Jew started screaming: "For God's sake, don't let him do this! Don't let him do this!"

But the judge declared: "I'm going to allow him to do this one last time, and let's leave it at that."

Also, since he had such talent, nobody at the marketplace wanted to refuse or have his request denied.

"For God's sake," the Jew shouted. "Tie me up!"

Then the servant took the fiddle and stroked it with the bow. Everyone started to shake and sway—the judge, the clerk, and the officers. Nobody could tie up the Jew. Now the servant stroked the fiddle a second time, and the hangman let go of the rope and began to dance himself, and when the servant really started fiddling, everyone danced together—the judge and the Jew at the head of all the people who had come to the marketplace to watch. At the beginning it was quite merry, but since the fiddling and dancing didn't end, they all screamed miserably and pleaded with the servant to stop. However, he refused to do it unless the judge granted him his life and also promised to let him have the hundred gold coins. In addition he yelled to the Jew: "You swindler, confess and tell us where you got the money from, otherwise I'll keep playing the fiddle for you only."

"I stole it, I stole it!" he screamed so that everyone heard him. "And you earned it honestly."

So the servant stopped playing the fiddle, and the scoundrel was hung in his place on the gallows.

25

THE EXPERT HUNTSMAN

Once upon a time there was a young fellow, and after he had learned the locksmith's trade, he told his father that he had to go out into the world and try his luck.

"Yes," said his father. "I'm satisfied with your decision," and he gave him money for his journey.

So the young man wandered about looking for work. After some time he found that he was not very successful as a locksmith. Moreover, the trade no longer suited him, for he had a craving to become a huntsman. Then one day during his travels he met a huntsman clad in green, who asked him where he came from and where he was going. The young man told him he was a locksmith but no longer liked the trade and wanted to become a huntsman, and he asked whether the man could take him on as an apprentice.

"Yes, I can if you want to come along with me."

The young fellow went with him, hired himself out for several years, and learned the craft of hunting. After his apprenticeship had ended, he wanted to try his luck elsewhere. The only wage he received from the huntsman was an air gun, but it was made in such a special way that it never missed when fired.

The young huntsman set off and soon came to a very large forest that was impossible to cross in one day. When evening came, he climbed a high tree to keep himself safe from wild animals. Toward midnight he thought he saw the glimmer of a small light in the distance. He looked through the branches at the spot and took note of where the light was coming from. Then he removed his hat and threw it toward the light so that he would have a marker to point him in the direction he wanted to go. After he climbed down, he went after his hat, put it on again, and proceeded straight ahead. The farther he went, the larger the light grew, and when he got up close to it, he saw a tremendous fire with three giants sitting around and eating, with large pieces of meat in their mouths that they had roasted on the fire. Then the huntsman took his gun and shot a piece of meat away from the first giant's mouth just as he was about to bite into it. He did this also to the second giant. Then the giants said to one another, "Anyone who can shoot a piece of meat from our mouths must be a real sharpshooter. We'd certainly like him to join us if he wants to."

But the huntsman now shot a piece of meat from the third giant's mouth, and the giants shouted, "Who are you? Come over to us. Sit down and eat with us."

So now, the young fellow joined the giants and told them he was an expert huntsman, and that whatever he took aim at with his gun he was sure to hit. After hearing this, the giants told him things would go well for him if he came along with them. There was a large river at the other end of the forest, they explained, and on the other side of the river was a tower, and in the tower there was a beautiful princess, whom they intended to kidnap.

"All right," said the huntsman. "I'll get her for you soon enough."

"But wait, there's something else," the giants continued. "There's a little dog that starts barking as soon as anyone approaches, and when it barks, everyone at the royal court wakes up. That's why we can't get in. Do you think you can shoot the little dog?"

"Certainly," he said. "That's just trifling sport for me."

Soon after that the huntsman got on a boat and sailed over the river, and as soon as he landed, the little dog came running and was about to bark when the huntsman took out his air gun and shot it dead. When the giants saw that, they rejoiced, thinking that they had the princess for sure, but the huntsman wanted first to check on things at the castle and told them to stay outside until he called them. So he went into the castle, where everyone was asleep, and it was dead quiet. When he opened the door to the first room, he saw a saber of pure silver hanging on the wall. It had a gold star on it, and the king's name was inscribed on the handle. Nearby on a table lay a sealed letter, which he opened, and it said that whoever had possession of the saber could kill anything he encountered. So he took the saber from the wall, went to the entrance, and called the giants to come in. However, he told them he couldn't get the door to open completely and that they had to crawl through a hole. So the first giant came and crawled inside, and as soon as his head appeared, the huntsman took the saber and sliced off his head and shoved his body completely inside. Then he called the second giant and sliced his head off, too, and shoved him inside. Finally, he called the third giant and told him that they already had the princess. So he came crawling inside, and he fared no better than the two other giants. This was how the huntsman saved the princess from the giants.

After this he closed the hole and went on to explore the castle. Next he came to the room where the princess was lying asleep. She was so beautiful that he stopped in his tracks, gazed at her, and held his breath. He looked around some more and saw a pair of slippers underneath her bed. Her father's name and a star were on the right slipper, and on the left, her own name and a star. She was also wearing a large, silk neckerchief embroidered with gold. Her father's name was on the right side, and her own on the left, all in gold letters. The huntsman took a pair of scissors, cut off the right corner of the neckerchief, and slipped it into his knapsack. He also put in the right slipper with the king's name on it. The maiden kept sleeping, all wrapped up in her nightgown. Then he cut off a piece of the gown as well, without touching her, and put it into his knapsack with the rest of the articles. After that he went away and let her sleep undisturbed. When he came to the place where the giants were lying, he cut out all three of their tongues from their heads and stuck them in his knapsack. Finally, he decided to take everything home and show it all to his father.

When the king woke up in the castle, he saw the three giants lying there dead. Then he went into his daughter's bedchamber, woke her up, and asked her who could have possibly come and killed the giants.

"Dear father," she said, "I don't know. I was asleep."

When she got up and wanted to put on her slippers, the right one was missing, and when she looked at her neckerchief the right corner had been cut off and was missing. Then she glanced down at her nightgown and saw that a piece had been taken out of it. The king ordered the entire court to assemble, all the soldiers and everyone who was there, and he asked who had killed the giants.

Now, the king had an ugly, one-eyed captain, who claimed that he had done it. Thereupon the old king announced that he was entitled to wed his daughter since he had saved her. But the maiden said, "Dear father, I'd rather leave home and go as far away from here as my legs will carry me than marry him."

Since she refused to marry the captain, the king commanded her to take off her royal garments, put on peasant clothes, and leave the court. He ordered her, furthermore, to go to a potter and start selling pottery. So she took off her royal garments, went to a potter, and borrowed a stock of his earthenware. She promised to pay him back if she sold everything by evening. Then the king told her to go sit by the roadside and sell the earthenware. In the meantime, he ordered some farmers to drive their wagons over her wares and crush everything into a thousand pieces. When the princess set out her wares along the road, the wagons came and smashed everything to pieces. She burst into tears and said, "Oh, Lord, how am I going to pay the potter now?"

This was the way that the king wanted to force her to marry the captain. However, she went back to the potter and asked him if he would lend her some more earthenware. He told her no, not until she paid for the stock that he had already given her. So she went to her father and screamed and told him she wanted to go far away from there.

He answered that she was to go into the forest where he was going to have a cottage built for her. She was to stay there for the rest of her life and cook for anyone who came along. But she was not allowed to accept money for this.

When the cottage was finished, a sign was hung outside the door, and on it was written "Today for nothing, tomorrow for money." She lived there a long time, and news spread throughout the world that a maiden was living there who cooked for nothing, just as the sign said on the door. Word of this also reached the huntsman, and he thought, "That's something for you. After all, you're poor and have no money." So he took his air gun and knapsack, in which he had put all the tokens he had taken from the castle, went into the forest, and found the cottage with the sign, "Today for nothing, tomorrow for money." Now, he was still wearing the saber with which he had cut off the heads of the giants, and he carried it into the cottage with him. He asked to have something to eat and was delighted to see the beautiful maiden, who was as pretty as a picture. She asked him where he had come from and where he was going, and he replied, "I'm just traveling about the world."

Then she asked him where he had got the saber, for her father's name was on it. In response, he inquired whether she was the king's daughter.

"Yes," she answered.

"With this saber," he said, "I cut off the heads of three giants," and as proof he took the tongues out of his knapsack. Then he also showed her the slipper, the corner of her neckerchief, and the piece of nightgown. All at once she was overcome with joy, for she realized that he was the one who had saved her. Then they went to the old king together, and she led her father into her room and told him that the huntsman was the one who had saved her. When the old king saw the proof, all his doubts vanished, and he said he was glad and that the huntsman was entitled to marry the princess, and the princess was tremendously happy.

So now they dressed up the huntsman as a foreign lord, and the king had a banquet prepared. When they went to the table, the captain came and sat on the left side of the princess and the huntsman, on the right. The captain thought that the huntsman was a foreign lord who had come for a visit. When they had finished eating and drinking, the old king said to the captain that he wanted him to solve a riddle: how would it be possible if someone said he had killed three giants but couldn't find their tongues when asked to look for them?

"They probably never had any tongues," said the captain.

"Not so," replied the king. "Every creature has a tongue," and he asked the captain what a person deserved if he were to deceive a king.

"He should be torn to pieces," the captain replied.

The king told him he had pronounced his own sentence. The captain was thrown into prison and subsequently torn into four pieces. The princess, though, was wed to the huntsman, and he returned home to fetch his father and mother, who came to live happily with their son, and after the old king's death he inherited the kingdom.

26
THE FLESHING FLAIL FROM HEAVEN

A farmer once set out to plow with a pair of oxen. When he got to his field, the horns of both oxen began to grow. They grew and grew, and by the time he was ready to go home, the horns were so big that the oxen would not fit through the farm gate. Fortunately, a butcher happened to come along at that moment and was willing to take them over. They agreed that the farmer would bring a measure of turnip seeds to the butcher, and the butcher was to pay one Brabant gold coin for each seed. That's what I call a good bargain!

Now, the farmer went home, got the measure of turnip seeds, and carried them in a sack. However, along the way one little seed fell out of the sack. The butcher paid him the price agreed upon. Now, as the farmer was on his way back home, the seed had grown into a tree that reached all the way to heaven.

"Oh," thought the farmer, "you can't let an opportunity like this pass you by. You've got to go up and see for yourself what the angels are doing there." So he climbed up and saw the angels threshing oats. He watched them doing this, and while he was watching, he noticed that the tree he was standing on had begun to wobble. He looked down and saw that somebody was chopping it down. "It'd be terrible," he thought, "if you were to fall all the way down." Given his desperate situation, he could think of nothing better to do than to twist a rope out of the oat chaff that lay there in heaps. After that he grabbed a hoe and a fleshing flail that were lying around there in heaven, and he let himself down by the rope. However, when he landed on earth, he landed in a deep, deep hole, so he was lucky to have taken the hoe because he was able to hack out steps for himself. He climbed the steps and took the flail with him because he wanted to have proof if anyone ever doubted his story.

27
THE CHILDREN OF THE TWO KINGS

Once upon a time there was a king who had a little boy, and according to the constellation of the stars, it was predicted that he would be killed by a stag when he turned sixteen. One day, when he had reached that age, the huntsmen went out hunting with him in the forest, but the prince got separated from them. Suddenly, he saw a big stag and kept trying to shoot it, without much success. Finally, the stag ran away and led him on a chase until they were out of the forest. All at once a big, lanky man was standing there instead of the stag and said, "Well, it's a good thing I've got you now. I wore out six pair of glass skates chasing after you and could never catch you."

He took the prince with him and dragged him across a large lake toward a big royal castle. Once there the prince had to sit down at a table and eat something with the man. After they had eaten together, the king said, "I've got three daughters and want you to watch over the oldest one for me from nine in the evening until six in the morning. Each time the clock strikes the hour, I shall come and call you. If you don't answer me, you will be put to death in the morning. However, if you answer you shall have my daughter for your wife."

When the young people went up to the bedchamber, there was a stone statue of Saint Christopher standing there, and the king's daughter said to him, "My father will come at nine o'clock and every hour until the clock strikes six. If he asks anything, I want you to answer him in place of the prince."

The stone Saint Christopher nodded his head very fast, then more and more slowly until he finally came to a stop. Meanwhile, the prince lay down on the threshold and fell asleep. The next morning the king said to the young prince, "You've done well, but I can't give you my daughter. Now, I want you to watch over my second daughter. Then I'll consider giving you my oldest daughter for your wife. I shall come every hour on the hour, and when I call, you must answer me. If you don't answer, your blood will flow."

The prince went with the second daughter up to the bedchamber, where there was a stone statue of Saint Christopher, much larger than the first, and the king's daughter said to him, "If my father asks a question, I want you to answer."

The big stone Saint Christopher nodded his head very fast, then more and more slowly until he came to a stop. The prince lay down on the threshold, put his hand under his head, and went to sleep. The next morning the king said to him, "You've done well, but I can't give you my daughter. Now, I want you to watch over my youngest daughter. Then I'll consider giving you the second for your wife. I shall come every hour, and when I call, answer me. If you don't answer me when I call, your blood will flow."

Again the prince went with the youngest daughter up to the chamber, and there stood a Saint Christopher, much bigger and taller than the other two. The king's daughter said to him, "When my father calls, I want you to answer."

The big, tall Saint Christopher nodded his head for a good hour before he came to a stop, and the prince lay down on threshold and fell asleep. The next morning the king said, "Indeed, you kept watch very well, but I can't give you my daughter yet. Now, I've got a large forest, and if you cut it down for me between six this morning and six this evening, I'll consider giving her to you."

The king gave him a glass axe, a glass wedge, and a glass pickaxe. When the prince reached the forest, he began chopping right away, and the axe broke in two. Then he took the wedge and began hitting it with the pickaxe, but it splintered into tiny pieces the size of grains of sand. This made the prince very downcast, for he thought he would now have to die. So he sat down and wept.

At noon the king said, "One of you girls must bring him something to eat."

"No," said the oldest, "we won't bring him anything. Let the one he watched over last take him something."

So the youngest daughter had to go and bring him something to eat. When she reached the forest, she asked him how everything was going.

"Oh," he said, "things are going very badly."

She told him to come over to her and have a little something to eat.

"No," he responded. "I can't, for soon I must die, and I don't want to eat anymore."

She spoke kindly to him and implored him to try. So, he went over to her and ate something. After he had eaten, she said, "Now I'll louse you a little, and then you'll feel much better."

When she loused him, he became so tired that he fell asleep. Then she took her kerchief, made a knot in it, and struck the ground three times.

"Workers, come out!" she cried.

Suddenly numerous gnomes appeared from beneath the earth and told the princess they would carry out her commands.

"In three hours' time," she said, "this great forest must be cut down, and the wood stacked in piles."

The gnomes went and called all their relatives to come out and help them with the work. Then they started, and within three hours everything was finished, and they went and reported to the king's daughter. Once again she took out her white kerchief and said, "Workers, go home!" And they all vanished on the spot.

When the prince woke up, he was very happy, and she said, "When the clock strikes six, you're to go home."

He did as she told him, and the king asked him, "Have you cut down the whole forest?"

"Yes," said the prince.

When they were sitting at the table, the king said, "I can't give you my daughter for your wife yet. You must first do something else."

The prince asked what he had to do.

"I have a very large pond," said the king. "You must go there tomorrow morning and clean it out so that it glistens like a mirror, and there must be all kinds of fish in it."

The next morning the king gave him a glass scoop and said, "You must be finished with the pond by six o'clock."

The prince departed, and when he reached the pond, he stuck the scoop into the muck, and the end broke off. Then he tried a pickaxe, but it broke as well, and he became discouraged. At noon the youngest daughter brought him something to eat and asked him how everything was going. The prince said that things were going very badly, and he was bound to lose his head. "All the tools fell apart on me again."

"Oh," she said, "you should come and eat something first, then you'll feel much better."

"No," he said, "I can't eat. I feel too sad."

But she spoke so kindly to him that he finally went and ate something. Once again she loused him, and he fell asleep. She took her kerchief once more, tied a knot in it, and struck the ground three times with it. "Workers, come out!" she cried.

Suddenly numerous gnomes appeared and asked her what she desired.

"In three hours' time the pond must be all cleaned up and must shine so brightly that you can see your own reflection in it. Then you must fill it with all kinds of fish."

The gnomes went off and called all their relatives to come and help them. They finished everything in two hours, returned to the king's daughter, and reported, "We've done what you commanded."

Once again she took her kerchief and struck the ground three times. "Workers, go home!" And they all vanished on the spot.

When the prince woke up, the pond was finished, and just as the king's daughter was about to leave him, she told him to go home at six o'clock. When he got there, the king asked, "Have you finished the pond?"

"Yes," said the prince. "Everything's fine."

When they were sitting at the table again, the king said, "Indeed, you finished the pond, but I can't give you my daughter yet. You must first do one more thing."

"What's that?" asked the prince.

"I've got a big mountain with nothing on it but thornbushes. I want them all cut down, and then you must build the most magnificent castle imaginable, and all the proper furnishings must be in it."

When the prince got up the next morning, the king gave him a glass axe and glass drill to take with him and told him that he had to be finished by six o'clock. As the prince began to chop the first thornbush with the axe, it broke into little pieces that flew all around him, and the drill also turned out to be useless. Then he became very dejected and waited to see if his beloved would come again and help him out of this desperate situation. At noon she came and brought him something to eat. He went to meet her and told her everything that had happened. Then he ate something, let her louse him, and fell asleep. Once again she took her kerchief and struck the ground with it three times. "Workers, come out!" she cried.

Numerous gnomes again appeared and asked her what she desired.

"In three hours' time," she said, "you must cut down all the thornbushes and build the most magnificent castle imaginable on the mountain, and all the proper furnishings must be in it."

They went off and called all their relatives to come and help them, and when the time was up, everything was finished. Then they went and reported to the king's daughter, whereupon she took the kerchief and struck the ground three times with it. "Workers, go home!" she said, and they all vanished on the spot.

When the prince woke up and saw everything, he was as happy as a lark. Since the clock had just struck six, they went home together, and the king asked, "Is the castle finished now?"

"Yes," said the prince.

When they were sitting at the table, the king said, "I can't give you my youngest daughter until the two oldest are married."

The prince and the king's daughter were very sad, and the prince didn't know what to do. Then one night he went to the king's daughter, and they ran away together. After they had gone a short distance, the daughter looked around and saw her father pursuing them. "Oh," she said, "what shall we do? My father's after us, and he'll soon catch up. Wait, I'll turn you into a rosebush and myself into a rose, and I'll protect myself by hiding in the middle of the bush."

When the father reached the spot, there was a rosebush with a rose standing there. When he tried to pluck the rose, the thorns pricked his fingers, so he had to return home. His wife asked him why he hadn't brought back the couple. He told her that he had almost caught them, but then had lost sight of them and had found only a rosebush and a rose where he had thought they were.

"If you had only plucked the rose," the queen said, "the bush would have come along."

So he went away again to fetch the rose. In the meantime, the two had made their way far over some fields, and the king had to run after them. Once again the daughter looked around and saw her father coming after them. "Oh," she said, "what shall we do now? Wait, I'll turn you into a church and myself into a pastor. Then I'll stand in the pulpit and preach."

When the king reached the spot, a church was standing there, and a pastor was preaching in the pulpit. So he listened to the sermon and returned home. The queen asked him why he had failed to bring back the couple with him, and he replied, "I ran after them a long time, and just as I thought I had caught up with them, I came upon a church with a pastor preaching in the pulpit."

"You should have taken the pastor with you," said his wife. "The church would have come along. It's no use sending you anymore. I'll have to go myself."

After she had gone a long way and saw the two from afar, the king's daughter looked around and saw her mother coming. "We've run out of luck now," she said. "My mother herself is coming. Wait, I'll turn you into a pond and myself into a fish."

When the mother reached the spot, there was a large pond, and a fish was leaping about in the middle of it. The fish stuck its head out of the water, looked around, and was as merry as could be. The mother tried very hard to catch the fish, but she was unable to land it. Then she got so angry that she drank the entire pond dry just to catch the fish. However, she became so sick that she had to spit out the water, and she vomited the entire pond out again. "It's plain to me that I'm helpless against you." So she made her peace and asked them to return with her, which they did. Now, the queen gave her daughter three walnuts and said, "These will help you in your greatest need."

Then the young couple set off again. After they had walked for ten hours, they had approached the castle where the prince came from, and nearby was a village. When they arrived in the village, the prince said, "Stay here, my dearest. I'll go up to the castle first and then come back to fetch you with a carriage and servants."

When he got to the castle, everyone was happy to see him again. He told them he had a bride, who was now in the village, and he wanted to go fetch her in a carriage. They harnessed the carriage right away, and several servants climbed on the back. Just as the prince was about to get in, his mother gave him a kiss, and he forgot everything that had happened and everything he wanted to do. His mother then ordered them to unharness the carriage, and they all went back into the castle. Meanwhile, the king's daughter sat in the village and waited and waited. She thought the prince would come and fetch her, but no one came. Finally, she hired herself out at the mill that belonged to the castle. She had to sit by the river every afternoon and wash the pots and jars. Once the queen came out of the castle and took a walk along the river. When she saw the beautiful maiden, she said, "What a lovely girl! She's quite appealing!" Then everyone around her took a look, but nobody recognized her.

The king's daughter served the miller as maid honestly and faithfully for a long time. Meanwhile, the queen had found a wife for her son, and she came from a country far away. When the bride arrived, they were to be married right away, and crowds of people gathered to see the event, and the maid asked the miller if she might go and watch too.

"Go right along," said the miller.

Before she left, she cracked open one of the three walnuts and found a beautiful dress inside. She put it on, wore it to the church, and stood near the altar. All at once the bride and bridegroom arrived and sat down in front of the altar. When the pastor was about to bless them, the bride looked to one side and saw the maid dressed as a lady standing there. Then she stood up and said that she wouldn't marry until she had a dress as beautiful as the lady's. So they returned home and sent servants to ask the lady if she would sell the dress. No, she told them, she wouldn't sell it, but they might be able to earn it. They asked her what they would have to do, and she said that they could have the dress if she could sleep outside the prince's door that night. They said, yes, she could do that, but the servants were ordered to give the prince a sleeping potion.

The king's daughter lay down on the threshold and whimpered all night: she had had the forest cut down for him, she had had the pond cleaned up for him, she had had the castle built for him, she had turned him into a rosebush, then a church, and finally a pond, and yet, he had forgotten her so quickly. The prince didn't hear a thing, but her cries woke the servants, who listened but didn't know what to make of it all.

When they got up the next morning, the bride put on the dress and went to the church with the bridegroom. Meanwhile, the beautiful maid opened the second walnut, and she found a dress more splendid than the first, put it on, and wore it to the church, where she stood near the altar. Then everything happened as on the previous day. Once again the maid lay down in front of the prince's door during the night, but this time the servants didn't give the prince a sleeping potion but something to keep him awake, and he went to bed. The miller's maid whimpered once more, as she had before, and told him about all the things she had done for him. The prince heard it all and became very sad, for he remembered everything that had happened. He wanted to go to her right then and there, but his mother had locked the door. However, the next morning he went straight to his beloved and told her what had happened and begged her not to be angry with him for having forgotten her for so long. Then the king's daughter opened the third walnut and found a dress that was even more beautiful than the other two. She put it on and went to the church with her bridegroom. Groups of children gathered around them and gave them flowers and placed colored ribbons at their feet. After they were blessed at the wedding, they had a merry celebration, but the false mother and false bride had to leave.

And the lips are still warm on the last person who told this tale.

28
THE CLEVER LITTLE TAILOR

Once upon a time there was a princess who was extremely proud. Whenever a suitor appeared before her, she gave him a riddle to solve, and if he couldn't solve it, she would ridicule him and send him away. Indeed, she let it be known that whoever was able to solve her riddle would be allowed to marry her, no matter who the person might be.

After some time had passed, three tailors happened to meet. The two oldest thought that, because they had sewn many a fine stitch and had got them all right, they were sure to win the princess and would hit upon the right answer. The third tailor was a useless little thing, who knew next to nothing about his craft. So the other two tailors said to him, "You'd be better off staying at home. You won't get very far with your dense head."

However, the little tailor refused to let himself be confused and said that he had his mind set on it and knew how to take care of himself. So he sallied forth as if he owned the world.

Together the three of them announced themselves to the princess and asked her to give them the riddle. They told her that the right people had finally come, for they all had such fine minds that one could thread a needle with each one of them. So the princess said, "I have two kinds of hair on my head. What are the colors?"

"If that's all there's to it," said the first tailor, "one's black, and the other's white, just like the cloth they call pepper and salt."

"Wrong," said the princess. "Let the second try."

"Well, if it's not black and white," said the second tailor, "then it's got to be brown and red, like my father's frock coat."

"Wrong," said the princess. "Let the third try. I can tell by his face that he thinks he knows the answer."

The little tailor stepped forward boldly and said, "The princess has silver and golden hair on her head, and those are the two colors."

When the princess heard that, she turned pale and nearly fainted from fright, for the little tailor had guessed right, and she had been firmly convinced that nobody in the world would ever solve the riddle. When her heart began to beat again, she said, "You haven't won me yet, for you must do one more thing. Down in the stable there's a bear, and you must spend the night with him. If you're still alive when I get up in the morning, then I'll marry you."

She thought that she'd get rid of the tailor this way because the bear had never let anyone that he had got his paws on survive. But the little tailor was not about to let himself be frightened by this. Indeed, he was delighted and said, "I'll manage to complete this task as well."

When evening came, the little tailor was taken down to the bear, who immediately headed straight for the little fellow to give him a big welcome with his paws.

"Easy does it, easy does it," said the little tailor. "I'll calm you down soon enough."

Then, as though he had nothing in the world to worry about, he casually took some walnuts out of his pocket and began cracking them open with his teeth and eating the kernels. When the bear saw this, he began craving some nuts too. So the little tailor reached into his pocket and gave him a handful. However, these were not nuts but small stones. The bear put them into his mouth and could not crack any of them open, no matter how much he tried.

"Good gracious," thought the bear. "What a stupid oaf I am! I can't even crack open nuts." And he said to the little tailor, "Will you crack open some nuts for me?"

"What kind of a fellow are you anyway?" asked the little tailor. "You have such a big mouth, and yet you can't even crack open little nuts."

Then he took the stones and stealthily substituted a nut for them and cracked it in two in his mouth.

"I've got to try this thing once more," said the bear. "When I see you do it, I can't imagine why I can't do it, too."

Once again the little tailor gave him plain stones, and the bear worked at it and bit with all his might. God help the little tailor, if he had managed to bite it open!

After that was over, the little tailor took out a violin from under his coat and played a little tune. When the bear heard the music, he couldn't help but dance, and after he had danced for a while, he was so delighted that he said to the little tailor, "Is it hard to learn how to play the fiddle?"

"It's child's play. Watch me. I place the fingers of my left hand down here and move the bow with my right. Then you can have a merry old time—*whoop-de-doo* and away we go!"

"I'd like to learn how to play the fiddle," said the bear. "Then I could dance as much as I liked. What do you think about that? Will you give me lessons?"

"Gladly," said the little tailor, "if you have talent for it. But show me your paws. They're tremendously long. I'll have to cut your nails a bit."

So he went and fetched a vise, and the bear put his paws into it. Then the tailor tightened the vise and said, "Now wait until I return with the scissors," and he let the bear growl as long as he liked, while the tailor lay down on a bundle of straw in the corner and fell asleep.

That night, when the princess heard the bear's tremendous growling, she thought that he had made an end of the tailor and was growling out of joy. The next morning she got up feeling quite at ease and happy, but when she glanced out the window toward the stable, she saw the little tailor standing outside, looking as cheerful and fresh as a fish in water. After this she couldn't break her agreement because she had given her promise in public. The king summoned a coach, and she had to drive to church with the little tailor to get married. When the couple climbed into the coach, the other two tailors, who were false-hearted and begrudged the little tailor his luck, went to the stable and set the bear free. Now, the bear ran after the coach in a great rage, and the princess heard him panting and growling. In her fright she cried out, "Ah, the bear's after us and wants to get you!"

The little tailor, alert as ever, immediately stood on his head, stuck his feet out the window, and shouted, "You see the vise? If you don't go away, then you'll soon be back in it!"

When the bear saw that, he turned and ran away. Our little tailor drove calmly to the church and was married to the princess. Thereafter, he lived as happily as a lark with her, and whoever doesn't believe me must give me a gold coin.

29
THE BRIGHT SUN WILL BRING IT TO LIGHT

A journeyman tailor was traveling around and practicing his trade. However, at one time he couldn't find any work and became so poverty-stricken that he didn't have a single cent left for food. Just at this point in his travels he met a Jew, who, he thought, probably had a lot of money with him. So he abandoned God, went straight toward the Jew, and said, "Give me your money, or I'll kill you."

"Spare my life!" said the Jew. "I don't have much money, just eight pennies."

"You've got more money than that! Out with it!" the tailor responded.

Then he used force and beat the Jew until he was nearly dead. Just as the Jew was on the point of death, he uttered his last words, "The bright sun will bring it to light!"

Upon saying this, he died.

The tailor searched the man's pockets for money but couldn't find anything more than the eight pennies that the Jew had told him about. So he picked him up, carried him behind a bush, and continued on his travels, practicing his craft along the way. After he had been traveling a long time, he came to a place where he began working for a master tailor who had a beautiful daughter. He fell in love with her, married her, and they had a good and happy marriage.

Some time later, after they already had two children, the father-in-law and the mother-in-law died, and the young couple had the house to themselves. One morning, as the man sat at the table in front of a window, his wife brought him some coffee. He poured it into the cup and was about to drink it when the sun shone upon coffee and cast a reflection on the wall so that little rings flickered here and there. The tailor looked up and said, "Ah, the sun wants very much to bring it to light, but it can't."

"Good gracious, my dear husband!" said his wife. "What's that? What do you mean by that?"

"I can't tell you," he answered.

But she said, "If you really love me, you must tell me." and she spoke very sweetly, swore she would never tell a soul about it, and gave him no peace.

So he told her how, many years ago, he had been traveling around in rags and without money, when he had met a Jew and had killed him. Then the Jew had said in his death throes, "The bright sun will bring it to light!" Now the sun wanted to bring it to light and had cast its reflection on the wall, where it made rings. But it was not able to bring it to light.

After telling her this, he implored her not to tell anybody; otherwise he would lose his life. She promised him not to, but after he sat down to work, she went to her neighbor, told her the story in confidence, making her promise not to tell a soul about it. Yet after three days had passed, the whole city knew the story, and the tailor was brought before the court and convicted.

So, after all, the bright sun did manage to bring it to light.

30
THE BLUE LIGHT

Once upon a time there was a king who had a soldier as servant. When the soldier became very old, the king sent him away without giving him anything for his service. Now the soldier had no idea how he was to eke out an existence and went off sadly and walked until he reached a forest in the evening. After he went farther, he saw a light, and as he approached it, he came upon a small house that was owned by a witch. He asked for a night's lodging and a little food and drink. At first she refused him, but finally she said: "All right, I'll be merciful, but you must dig my garden tomorrow morning."

The soldier promised to do it and was given a place to sleep. The next morning he hoed the witch's garden and worked until evening, when the witch wanted to send him on his way, but he said, "I'm so tired. Let me stay another night."

She didn't want to let him, but finally she gave in. So the next day he was to chop up a cartload of wood into small pieces, and indeed, the soldier chopped the wood into logs, and by the end of the day he had worn himself out so much that once again he couldn't depart and asked for lodging for a third night. In exchange for the lodging, the witch demanded that he fetch the blue light from her well the following day. So the next morning the witch led him to a well and tied a long rope around him and lowered him down the well. When he reached the bottom, he found the blue light and made a signal to the witch so that she would pull him up. Indeed, she pulled him up, but just as he reached the edge of the well, she reached down with her hand and wanted to take the blue light from him and then let him fall back down. However, he sensed her evil intentions and said: "No, you don't. I won't give you the light until both my feet are firmly on the ground."

The witch became furious, and she shoved him with the light down the well and went away. The soldier was now quite sad down in the moist dark quagmire, for he thought his fate was sealed. He reached into his pocket for his pipe, which was half full, and thought: "I might as well smoke it to the end as my last pleasure." So he lit it with the blue light and began to smoke. As the smoke floated around a bit, a little black man appeared and asked: "Master, what do you command? I must do anything you demand."

"Then first help me out of this well."

The little man took him by the hand and led him up above, and they took the blue light with them. When they were back above ground, the soldier said: "Now go and beat the old witch to death for me."

After the little man did this, he showed the soldier the witch's treasures and gold, and the soldier loaded them in a sack and took everything with him. Then the little man said, "If you need me, just light your pipe with the blue light."

The soldier returned to the city and stopped at the best inn where he had fine clothes made for himself and had a room furnished in a splendid way. When it was ready, the soldier called the little man and said: "The king sent me away and let me starve because I could no longer serve him well. Now bring the king's daughter to me here tonight. She will have to wait on me and do what I command."

"That's dangerous," the little man said, but he did what the soldier demanded anyway. He went and fetched the sleeping princess from her bed and brought her to the soldier. Then she had to obey and do what he said. In the morning when the cock crowed, the little black man had to bring her back again. When she got up, she told her father: "I had a strange dream this past night, and it seemed to me that I had been taken away and had become a soldier's maid and had to wait on him."

"Fill your pockets full of peas," replied the king, "and make a hole in it. The dream could be true. Then the peas will fall out and leave a trail on the street."

So she did this, but the little man had overheard what the king had advised her to do. When evening came and the soldier said that the little man should bring the king's daughter to him again, the little man spread peas all over the city so that the few peas that fell out of her pocket could leave no trace. The next morning the people of the city had to pick up and sort all the peas. Once again, the king's daughter told her father what had happened to her, and he answered: "Keep one shoe on, and hide the other secretly wherever you are."

The little black man heard the plan, and that night, when the soldier demanded that he bring him the king's daughter, the little man said: "I can no longer help you. You're going to have some bad luck if you're exposed."

However, the soldier insisted on having his will done

"Well then, after I've returned her to the king, make sure you get yourself out of here right away and through the city gate."

So the king's daughter kept one of her shoes on and hid the other in the soldier's bed. The next morning, when she was once again with her father, he had the entire city searched and the shoe was found in the soldier's room. To be sure, the soldier had already rushed out of the city, but he was soon overtaken and thrown into a sturdy prison. Now he was chained and tied up with rope, and due to the frantic flight, his most valuable things, the blue light and the pipe, had remained behind, and the only thing he had with him was a gold coin. As he was now standing sadly at the window of his prison, he saw one of his comrades passing by. So he called out to him and said: "If you get me the little bundle that I left in my room at the inn. I'll give you a gold coin."

So his comrade went there and brought back the blue light and the pipe in exchange for the gold coin. The prisoner lit his pipe right away and summoned the little black man who said to him: "Have no fear. Go wherever they take you, and let them do what they want. Just remember to take the blue light with you."

The next day the soldier was interrogated and sentenced to hang on the gallows. As he was being led out to be executed, he asked the king to grant him one last favor.

"What kind of a favor?" asked the king.

"I'd like to smoke my pipe along the way."

"You can smoke three pipes if you like," answered the king.

Then the soldier took out his pipe and lit it with the blue light. All at once the little black man was there.

"Beat everyone here to death," the soldier said, "and tear the king into three pieces."

Well the little man began and beat all the people around him to death. The king kneeled and pleaded for mercy, and to save his life he gave the soldier the kingdom and his daughter for his wife.

31

THE STUBBORN CHILD

Once upon a time there was a stubborn child who never did what his mother told him to do. Therefore, the dear Lord did not look kindly upon him, and he became sick. No doctor could cure him, and in a short time he lay on his deathbed. When he was being lowered into his grave and was covered over with dirt, one of his little arms suddenly emerged and reached up into the air. They pushed it back down and covered the dirt with fresh dirt, but that didn't help. The little arm kept popping out. So the child's mother had to go to the grave herself and smack the little arm with a switch. After she did that, the arm withdrew, and then, for the first time, the child had peace beneath the earth.

32

THE THREE ARMY SURGEONS

Three army surgeons who were traveling around the world thought that they had learned all there was to know about their profession. One day they came to an inn, where they wanted to spend the night, and the innkeeper asked them where they were coming from and where they were heading.

"We're traveling about the world and practicing our profession."

"Well, show me what you can do," said the innkeeper.

Then the first surgeon said he would cut off his own hand and put it back on again in the morning. The second said he would tear out his heart and put it back in place in the morning. The third said he would poke out his eyes and put them back in their sockets in the morning. Indeed, they had a salve that immediately healed any wound when they rubbed it on, and they carried the salve in a little flask that they kept with them all the time. So each one cut a different organ from his body: the hand, the heart, and the eyes. Then they put them on a plate and gave them to the innkeeper, who handed the plate to the maid, who was to put it in the cupboard for safekeeping.

Unknown to everyone, however, the maid had a sweetheart, who was a soldier, and when the innkeeper, the three surgeons, and everyone in the house were asleep, the soldier came and wanted something to eat. The maid opened the cupboard and brought him some food, but she was so enraptured that she forgot to shut the cupboard door. She sat down at the table next to her sweetheart and began chatting away. In her bliss she couldn't imagine anything going wrong, but the cat came creeping inside, found the cupboard open, and carried off the hand, heart, and eyes of the three surgeons. After the soldier had eaten and the maid was about to clear away the dishes and shut the cupboard, she noticed that the plate given to her by the innkeeper was empty. Filled with dread, she said to her sweetheart, "Oh, poor me! What am I to do! The hand's gone. The heart and eyes are also gone. They'll make me pay for this tomorrow!"

"Calm down," he said. "I'll help you out of this mess. Just give me a sharp knife. There's a thief hanging on the gallows outside. I'll go and cut off his hand. Which hand was it?"

"The right one."

The maid gave him a sharp knife, and he went to the gallows, cut off the right hand from the poor sinner, and brought it to the maid. Then he grabbed a cat and poked its eyes out. Now only the heart was missing.

"Haven't you just slaughtered a pig? Isn't the meat in the cellar?"

"Yes," said the maid.

"Well, that's perfect," said the soldier, who went and brought back the pig's heart.

The maid put everything together on the plate and placed it back in the cupboard. After her lover departed, she calmly went to bed. In the morning, when the surgeons got up, they told the maid to fetch the plate with the hand, heart, and eyes. She brought it to them from the cupboard, and the first surgeon took the thief's hand and rubbed salve on it. Immediately the hand grew back on him. The second took the cat's eyes and put them into his sockets. The third put the pig's heart back into place. As the innkeeper stood and watched all this, he marveled at their skill and said that he had never seen anything like it before. Indeed, he was going to praise and recommend them to everyone he met. Then they paid the bill and continued on their journey.

As they walked along, the surgeon with the pig's heart kept leaving the other two to sniff around in corners the way pigs do. The others tried to hold him back by his coattails, but that didn't help. He broke loose and ran to all those spots that were most infested with garbage. The second surgeon also began acting in a strange way. He kept rubbing his eyes and said to the third one, "My friend, what's going on? These aren't my eyes. I can't see a thing. Please lead me; otherwise, I'll fall."

So they proceeded with difficulty till evening, when they came to another inn. They entered the main room, where a rich man was sitting at a table and counting his money. The surgeon with the thief's hand walked around him, and his hand began twitching. Finally, when the gentleman turned his head, the surgeon reached into the pile and took a handful of money. One of his companions saw him do this and said, "Friend, what are you doing? You know it's not proper to steal. Shame on you!"

"Oh, no!" he exclaimed. "I can't stop myself. My hand keeps twitching, and I've got to grab things whether I like it or not."

Afterward they went to bed, and their room was so dark that it was impossible to see one's hand before one's face. Suddenly the surgeon with the cat's eyes woke up, then roused the others, and said, "Brothers, look! Do you see the little white mice running around?"

The other two sat up in their beds, but they couldn't see a thing. So he said, "Something's wrong with us. We didn't get our own organs back. The innkeeper cheated us, and we've got to return."

The next morning the three surgeons made their way back to the inn and told the innkeeper that they weren't given their right organs. One had got a thief's hand; the second, cat's eyes; and the third, a pig's heart. The innkeeper said that it must have been the maid's fault and went to call her. However, she had seen the three surgeons coming and had run out the back door and never returned. The three surgeons told the innkeeper then that he had better give them lots of money; otherwise, they would burn his house down. So he gave them what he had on hand and whatever else he could raise, and the three departed. The money lasted them the rest of their lives, but they would have preferred to have had their own organs restored to them.

33
THE LAZY ONE AND THE INDUSTRIOUS ONE

Once upon a time there were two journeymen who traveled together, and they swore they would always stick together. However, when they reached a large city, one of them began living loosely and forgot his promise. He left the other, went off by himself, and wandered here and there. Most of all he loved to be at the places where he could find the most excitement. The other journeyman remained committed to his job in the city, worked industriously, and then continued his travels.

One night he passed by the gallows without realizing it, but he saw a man lying asleep on the ground. He was shabby and destitute, and since the stars were so bright, the journeyman recognized him as his former companion. So he laid himself down next to him, covered him with his coat, and fell asleep. However, he was soon wakened by two voices. They were ravens sitting on top of the gallows.

One said, "God provides!"

The other, "Act according to the situation!"

After those words were spoken, one of the ravens fell exhausted to the ground. The other went and sat next to him until it was day. Then he fetched some worms and water, revived him with that, and woke him from the dead.

When the two journeymen saw all this, they were astounded and asked the one raven why the other was so miserable and sick. Then the sick raven said, "It was because I didn't want to do anything, for I believe that all my food will be provided for by heaven."

The two journeymen took the ravens with them to the next village. One of the birds was cheerful and searched for his food. He bathed himself every morning and cleansed himself with his beak. However, the other stayed around the house, was bad-tempered, and always looked shaggy. After a while the landlord's daughter, who was a beautiful maiden, became very fond of the industrious raven. She picked him up from the floor and petted him with her hand, and then one day she pressed him to her face and gave him a kiss out of sheer delight. The bird fell to the ground, rolled over, fluttered, and turned into a handsome man. Then he revealed that the other raven was his brother and that they had both insulted their father, who had put a curse on them by saying, "Fly around as ravens until a beautiful maiden kisses you of her own free will."

So one of the brothers was released from the spell, but nobody wanted to kiss the one who was idle, and he died as a raven.

The journeyman who had been living loosely took a lesson from this, and he became industrious and proper and took good care of his companion.

34
THE THREE JOURNEYMEN

There were once three journeymen who had agreed to stay together during their travels and to always work in the same city. Yet, after a while their masters couldn't pay them, and eventually they had nothing to live on and were reduced to rags.

"What shall we do?" one of them said. "We can't stay here any longer. Let's set out on our travels again. Then, if we don't find any work in the next city we come to, we'll part ways. But, before we do that, let's arrange with the innkeeper that we write to him about our whereabouts so that each of us can get news of the others through him. Then we can separate."

His companions thought that this was the best solution. While they were still conversing with one another, a richly clad gentleman came upon them and asked them who they were.

"We're journeymen and are looking for work. We've been together until now, but since we can't find any work, we're going to part ways."

"There's no need for that," said the man. "If you'll do what I tell you, you'll have more than enough money and work. In fact, you'll become respected gentlemen and will be able to drive around in carriages."

"Just as long as we won't be endangering our souls and salvation, we'll do whatever you want," said one of them.

"No," responded the man. "I won't make any claims on your souls."

However, one of the other journeymen had been looking at the man's feet, and when he caught sight of a horse's hoof and a human foot, he didn't want to have anything to do with him.

But the devil said, "You have nothing to fear. I'm not interested in your souls but in someone else's, and he's already half mine and his time is about to run out."

Since they now felt safe, they agreed to the devil's proposal, and he told them what he wanted them to do. The first journeyman was to answer every question with "*All three of us.*" The second, with "*For money.*" The third, with "*That's all right.*" These answers were to be given one after the other, but the men were not allowed to say anything else. If they didn't follow the devil's instructions, then all their money would disappear immediately, but as long as they followed them, their pockets would always be full.

At the outset the devil gave them as much money as they could carry and told them to stop at such and such an inn in the next city. When they got there, the innkeeper went over to them and asked, "What do you want to eat?"

The first one answered, "All three of us."

"Yes," said the innkeeper. "That's what I assume."

"For money," said the second.

"Obviously," said the innkeeper.

"And that's all right," said the third.

"Of course it's all right," said the innkeeper.

They received something good to eat and drink, and the service was good. After the meal they had to pay, and the innkeeper brought the bill to one of them.

"All three of us," said the first.

"For money," said the second.

"And that's all right," said the third.

"Of course it's all right," said the innkeeper. "All three of you must pay. I can't serve anyone without money."

Then they paid him but gave him much more money than he had charged. The other guests at the inn observed this and said, "Those fellows must be crazy."

"That's exactly what they are," said the innkeeper. "They're not particularly smart in the head."

The journeymen stayed at the inn for some time, and they said nothing but "All three of us," "For money," and "That's all right." However, they watched and knew everything that happened there.

One day a great merchant happened to enter the inn. He was carrying a lot of money with him and said, "Innkeeper, I want you to keep my money for me. Those three crazy journeymen are here, and they might steal it from me."

The innkeeper took the money bag, and as he carried it up to the room, he felt it was heavy with gold. So he gave the three journeymen a room downstairs, while the merchant was to have a special room upstairs. At midnight, when the innkeeper thought they were all sleeping, he and his wife took an axe and went and beat the merchant to death. After the murder they went back to bed. The next morning there was a great commotion: the merchant lay dead in bed, swimming in blood. All the guests gathered together quickly, and the innkeeper said, "The three crazy journeymen did this."

The guests confirmed this and said, "It couldn't have been anyone else."

The innkeeper summoned the journeymen and said to them, "Did you kill the merchant?"

"All three of us," said the first one.

"For money," said the second.

"And that's all right," said the third.

"You've all heard it now," said the innkeeper. "They themselves have confessed."

The journeymen were taken to the prison and were to be put on trial. When they saw that things were getting serious, they became afraid, but the devil came that night and said, "Just hold out one more day and don't throw away your good luck. Not a hair on your heads will be touched."

The next morning they were brought before the court, and the judge asked, "Are you the murderers?"

"All three of us."

"Why did you kill him?"

"For money."

"You villains!" said the judge. "Didn't you dread committing such a sin?"

"That's all right."

"They've confessed and are still unrepentant as well," said the judge. "Execute them right away."

So they were conducted outside, and the innkeeper was obliged to join the group of witnesses. The executioner's assistants took hold of the journeymen and led them up onto the scaffold, where the executioner was waiting for them with a bare sword. Just then a coach drawn by four blood-red foxes appeared, and it was moving so rapidly that sparks flew from the pavement. Someone was waving a white cloth from the window, and the executioner said, "Pardon is coming."

"Pardon! Pardon!" was also the cry from the coach. Then the devil, dressed in splendid fashion as a distinguished gentleman, stepped out of the coach and said, "You three are innocent, and you may now tell us what you saw and heard."

Then the oldest said, "We didn't kill the merchant. The murderer is standing among us," and he pointed to the innkeeper. "If you want proof, go into his cellar, where you'll find other bodies hanging. He's killed those people as well."

So the judge sent the executioner's assistants to the cellar, and they found everything exactly as the journeyman had said. When they reported this to the judge, he ordered the executioner to cut off the innkeeper's head on the scaffold. Then the devil said to the three journeymen, "Now I have the soul that I wanted. You're all free and shall have money for the rest of your lives."

35
THE HEAVENLY WEDDING

Once there was a peasant boy who heard a priest talking in church. "Whoever desires to enter the kingdom of heaven must always walk a straight path."

So the boy set upon his way and went straight along, always straight ahead without turning, over hill and valley. Finally, his way led into a large city and then into the middle of a church, where a holy service was being performed. When he saw all the magnificent pomp, he thought that he had now reached heaven. So he sat down and rejoiced with all his heart. When the holy service was over, and the sexton told him to leave, he answered, "No, I'm never going to leave. I'm happy now that I've finally made it to heaven."

The sexton then went to the priest and told him that there was a boy who didn't want to leave the church because he thought he was in heaven.

"If this is what he believes," the priest said, "then let him stay."

Later he went to the boy and asked him if he would like to do some work.

"Yes," the little fellow answered. He was used to working, but he never wanted to leave heaven again. So he remained in the church, and when he observed how the people went up the image of the Virgin Mary with the blessed child Jesus carved in wood and how they knelt down and prayed, he thought, "That's our dear Lord," and he said, "Listen, dear Lord, you're much too thin! The people are certainly letting you starve. I'll bring you half my food every day."

From then on he brought the image of mother and child half of his food every day, and the image began to enjoy the meals. After a few weeks the people noticed that the mother and child in the image had put on weight and that they had become fat and strong, and they were quite surprised. The priest couldn't understand it either. So he remained in the church and followed the little boy and saw how he shared his meal with the Virgin Mary and how she also accepted it.

After some time the boy became sick and couldn't leave his bed for a week. But when he could get out of bed again, the first thing he did was to bring his food to the Blessed Virgin. The priest followed him and heard him say, "Dear God, please don't think wrong of me for not having brought you anything for such a long time, but I was sick and couldn't get up."

Then the image answered him by saying, "I've seen your good intentions, and that's enough for me. Next Sunday I want you to come with me to the wedding."

The boy was glad about this and told the priest, who asked him to go to the image and inquire whether the priest could also come along.

"No," replied the image. "You alone."

The priest wanted to prepare the boy first by giving him holy communion. The boy was happy to do this, and on the next Sunday, when he partook of the holy communion, he fell down dead, and thus he went to the eternal wedding.

36
THE LONG NOSE

Once there were three old discharged soldiers who were so old that they could no longer eat even milk pudding. The king sent them away and didn't give them a pension. Consequently, they had nothing to live on and had to go begging. One day they began walking through a large forest and were unable to reach the end. When night arrived, two of them lay down to sleep, and the third kept watch so that the wild animals wouldn't tear them to pieces. After the two soldiers had fallen asleep and while the third was standing guard, a little dwarf in a red outfit appeared and cried out, "Who's there?"

"Good friends," said the soldier.

"What kind of good friends?"

"Three old discharged soldiers who have nothing to live on."

The dwarf then called him over, saying that he wanted to give him something. If the soldier took care of it, the dwarf explained, he would have enough to live on for the rest of his life. So the soldier went over to him, and the dwarf gave him an old cloak that would grant every wish made by the person wearing it. But the soldier was not to tell his comrades about it until daylight. When day finally came and they woke up, he told them what had happened. They continued to walk deeper into the forest until the second night. When they lay down to sleep, the second soldier had to keep watch and stood guard over the others. Then the red dwarf came and cried out, "Who's there?"

"Good friends."

"What kind of good friends?"

"Three old discharged soldiers."

Then the dwarf gave him an old little pouch that would always remain full of money no matter how much he took from it. However, he was not to tell his comrades about it until daylight. Once again they continued their walk through the forest for a third day, and that night the third soldier had to keep watch. The red dwarf came to him too and cried out, "Who's there?"

"Good friends."

"What kind of good friends?"

"Three old discharged soldiers."

The red dwarf gave him a horn, and whenever anyone blew it, all the soldiers from all over would gather together. The next morning, when each one now had a gift, the first soldier put on the cloak and wished that they were out of the forest. Immediately they were outside. They then went into an inn and ordered food and drink, the best that the innkeeper could provide. When they had finished, the soldier with the little pouch paid everything and was very generous to the innkeeper.

Soon they became tired from traveling, and the soldier with the pouch said to the one with the cloak, "I'd like you to wish for a castle for us. We've got money enough. Now we can live like kings."

So the soldier with the cloak wished for a castle, and quick as a wink it was standing there with everything that went with a castle. After they had lived there for some time, he wished for a coach with three white horses. They wanted to travel from one kingdom to the next and pass themselves off as three princes. So they drove off with a great retinue of servants, who looked quite regal, and went to a king who had only one daughter. When they arrived, they had themselves announced. Immediately, they were asked to dinner and to spend the night there. They had a merry old time, and after they had eaten and drunk, they began to play cards, which was the princess's favorite game. She played with the soldier who had the pouch, and she saw that no matter how much she won, his pouch never became empty, and she realized that it must be some sort of a magical thing. So she said to him then that since he had become so warm from playing, he should have something to drink. She gave him a glass but put a sleeping potion into the wine. No sooner had he drunk the wine than he fell asleep, and she took his pouch. Then she went into her chamber and sewed another pouch that looked just like the old one. Finally, she stuck some money inside it and put it back in place of the old one.

The next morning the three soldiers resumed their journey, and when the one with the pouch spent the little money that was left and reached inside the pouch for some more, he found it was empty and remained empty. Then he exclaimed, "That deceitful princess has switched my pouch. Now we're poor people!"

But the soldier with the cloak said, "Don't get gray hairs over this. I'll have it back in no time."

He put on the cloak and wished himself to be transported to the princess's chamber. Within seconds he was there, and she was sitting and counting money, which she continually took from the pouch. When she saw him, she screamed that a robber was there. And she screamed so loudly that the entire court came running and tried to catch him. Hastily he jumped through a window and left the cloak hanging there, so that this, too, was lost.

When the three soldiers came together again, they had nothing left but the horn. The soldier with the horn said, "I'll get help now. Let's start a war!"

And he blew together so many hussar and cavalry regiments that they were impossible to count. Next he sent a messenger to the king to let him know that if the king didn't return the pouch and the cloak, not a single stone from his castle would be left standing. The king tried to persuade

his daughter to return the cloak and pouch before they suffered a great misfortune. But she wouldn't listen to him and said that she wanted to try something first. So she disguised herself as a poor maiden, carried a basket on her arm, and went out to the soldiers' camp to sell all kinds of drinks. Her chambermaid had to go along with her. When the princess reached the middle of the camp, she began to sing, and her voice was so beautiful that all the soldiers ran out of their tents, and the one with the horn ran out too and listened. When the princess saw him, she gave her chambermaid a signal to crawl into his tent, where the chambermaid took the horn and ran back with it to the castle. Then the princess also went home and now had everything. Once again the three comrades had to go begging. So they moved on, and the one who had possessed the pouch said, "You know, we can't stay together anymore. You two go in that direction, and I'll take this path."

He set out alone and entered a forest, and since he was tired, he lay down beneath a tree to sleep awhile. When he awoke and looked up, he became aware that he had been sleeping under a beautiful apple tree with splendid apples hanging from the branches. Out of hunger he took one, ate it, and then another. Suddenly his nose began to grow and grow and became so long that he could no longer stand up. His nose grew through the forest and sixty miles beyond. Meanwhile, his comrades were traveling about in the world and looking for him because they felt it was better to be together. However, they had been unable to find him. Suddenly, one of them tripped over something and stepped on it. He thought, "My, what was that?" Then it moved, and he saw that it was a nose. The two soldiers decided to follow the nose, and eventually they reached their comrade in the forest. He was lying there and couldn't stir nor budge. So they took a pole and wrapped the nose around it. They wanted to lift it in the air and carry him away, but the nose was too heavy. Then they looked in the forest for a donkey, and they set their friend and the long nose on two poles and had the donkey carry him away in this manner. They dragged him a short distance, but they found him so heavy that they had to rest. While they were resting, they saw a tree nearby with beautiful pears hanging from the branches. Then the little red dwarf came out from behind the tree and said to the soldier with the long nose that, if he ate one of the beautiful pears, the nose would fall off. So he ate a pear, and right away the long nose fell off, and his nose was exactly the size it had been before. Thereupon the dwarf said, "Break off some apples and pears and make some powder out of them. Whenever you give someone the apple powder, the nose will grow, and whenever you give someone the pear powder, the nose will fall off again. Now, go as a doctor and give the princess some of the apples and also the powder. Then her nose will grow even twenty times longer than yours. But brace yourself for anything that might happen!"

So the soldier took some of the apples and went to the king's court, where he at first pretended to be a gardener's helper. He said he had special apples that couldn't be found anywhere in the region, and when the princess heard about this, she asked her father if she could buy some of the apples. The king replied, "Buy as many as you wish."

So she bought the apples and ate one. It tasted so good that she was convinced that she had never tasted an apple like it in her entire life. Then she ate another one, and once she did this, the gardener's helper departed, and her nose began to grow. It grew so tremendously that she couldn't get up out of her chair and fell over. Her nose grew sixty yards around the table, sixty around the closet, and a hundred yards through the window and around the castle and another twenty miles out toward the city. There she lay. She couldn't stir nor budge, and none of the doctors could help her. The old king issued a proclamation that any man who could help his daughter would receive a great deal of money.

The old soldier had waited for this moment and announced himself as a doctor. He promised to save her with God's help. Thereupon he gave her powder from the apples, and her nose began to grow once more and became even longer. That evening he gave her powder from the pears, and the nose became somewhat smaller, but not much. The next day he gave her powder from the apples again in order to scare her soundly and punish her. The nose grew again, but not more than had fallen off the day before. Finally, he said to her, "Your Royal Highness, you must have stolen something at one time. If you don't give it up, there'll be no help for you."

"I don't know what you're talking about," she said.

"You must," he responded. "Otherwise, my powder won't help, and if you don't give up what you've stolen, you'll die from the long nose."

Then the old king said, "Give up the pouch, the cloak, and the horn that you've stolen. Otherwise, your nose will never become small again."

So the chambermaid had to fetch all three things and put them down. Now the doctor gave the princess powder from the pears. Her nose fell off, and two hundred and fifty men had to come and chop the nose into pieces. Meanwhile, the soldier went away with the pouch, the cloak, and the horn and returned to his comrades. Then they wished to be back in their castle, where they are probably still sitting and keeping house.

37
THE OLD WOMAN IN THE FOREST

There was once a poor servant girl who went traveling with her masters through a large forest, and as they were passing through the middle of it, some robbers came and murdered all the people they could find. Everyone was killed except the maiden, who had jumped from the carriage in her fright and hidden behind a tree. After the robbers departed with their booty, she came out of her hiding place and burst into bitter tears. "What am I to do?" she said. "Oh, poor me, I'll never find my way out of the forest. I don't see a single house. I'm bound to starve to death."

She walked about searching for a way out of the forest but couldn't find one. When evening came, she sat down beneath a tree, commended herself to God, and planned to remain there no matter what might happen. But after she had been sitting there awhile, a white dove came flying to her with a little golden key in its beak. It put the key in her hand and said, "Do you see that large tree over there? You'll find a little lock on it, and if you open it with this key, you'll find plenty of food inside and won't have to suffer from hunger anymore."

So the maiden went to the tree, opened it, and found milk in a small bowl and white bread to dip into it, so she could eat to her heart's content. When she was full, she said, "Now's the time when the chickens at home usually go to roost. I'm so tired I wish I could also lie down in my bed!"

Then the dove flew by again, carrying another little golden key in its beak, and said, "Open the tree over there, and you'll find a bed."

She opened it and found a lovely soft bed. Then she prayed to the dear Lord to protect her during the night, lay down, and fell asleep. In the morning the dove came a third time with another little key and said, "Open that tree over there, and you'll find some clothes."

When she opened it, she found clothes lined with jewels and gold, more splendid than those of a princess. Thus she lived for some time, and the dove came every day and took care of everything she needed, and it was a good, quiet life.

However, one day the dove came and said, "Would you do a favor for me?"

"Gladly, with all my heart," said the maiden.

"I'm going to lead you to a small cottage," said the dove. "You are to go inside, where you'll find an old woman seated right next to the hearth. She'll say good day to you, but you're not to answer her, no matter what she does. Go past her to the right, where you'll come upon a door. Open it, and you'll find a room where there will be a lot of different kinds of rings lying on a table. You'll see magnificent ones with glistening stones, but you're to leave them alone. Pick out a simple one that will be lying among them and bring it to me as fast as you can."

The maiden went to the cottage and through the door. There sat the old woman who glared at her and said, "Good day, my child."

But the maiden didn't answer her and proceeded toward the door.

"Where are you going?" cried the old woman, who grabbed her skirt and tried to hold on to her. "This is my house. Nobody's allowed to go in there if I don't want them to."

But the maiden kept quiet, broke away from the woman, and went straight into the room. There she saw a large number of rings lying on a table, glistening and glimmering before her eyes. She tossed them about and looked for the simple one but couldn't find it. While she was look-ing for the ring, she noticed the old woman slinking by with a birdcage in her hand. The woman was about to make off with it, but the maiden went up to her and took the cage out of her hand. When she lifted it up and looked inside, she saw a bird with a simple ring in its beak. She was glad and ran out of the house with it. She thought the white dove would come and fetch the ring now, but it didn't appear. So she leaned against a tree, intending to wait for the dove. As she was standing there the tree seemed to become soft and flexible, and it lowered its branches. Suddenly the branches wrapped themselves around her and were two arms. When she looked around her, she saw that the tree had turned into a handsome man, who embraced her and kissed her affectionately.

"You've saved me and set me free from the power of the old woman," he said. "She's a wicked witch, and she had turned me into a tree. For a few hours every day I was a white dove. As long as she possessed the ring, I couldn't regain my human form."

His servants and horses had also been released from the magic spell that had also caused them to be changed into trees, and they were now standing beside him. Then they all traveled to his kingdom, for he was a prince, and the couple got married and lived a happy life.

38
THE THREE BROTHERS

There was once a man who had three sons, and he owned nothing but the house in which he lived. Now each of his sons hoped very much to inherit the house after his death. Since the father cared for them equally, he didn't want to hurt their feelings, nor did he want to sell the house because it had belonged to generations of his ancestors. Otherwise, he would have divided the money from a sale and shared it among his sons. Finally, he had an idea and said to his sons, "Go out into the world, and see what you can make of yourselves. Learn a skill, and when you return, whichever one of you puts on the best performance of his talents shall get the house."

The sons were satisfied with this proposal. The oldest decided he wanted to become a blacksmith; the second, a barber; and the third, a fencing master. Then they agreed on a time when they would all return home, and finally they set upon their way. It so happened that each of them found a good master, and each learned something decent and useful.

The blacksmith had to shoe the king's horses and thought, "Now you'll certainly get the house." The barber shaved only distinguished gentlemen and believed that the house was already his. The fencing master received many cuts but gritted his teeth and didn't let himself become discouraged, for he thought to himself, "If you're afraid of a cut, you'll never get the house."

When the appointed time arrived, they went back home, but they didn't know how to show off their talents in the best way. So they sat down together and discussed the matter, and while they were sitting there, a hare came running across the field in their direction. "Oh," said the barber, "that's just what I needed."

He took a bowl and soap and worked up a lather until the hare was close by. Then he lathered it on the run and shaved a little beard for the hare, also on the run. In the process he neither cut the hare nor hurt it in any way.

"I like that," said the father. "Unless your brothers do something extraordinary, the house is yours."

Before long a man came riding by in a carriage at full speed.

"Now you'll see what I can do, father," said the blacksmith, who rushed after the carriage, ripped the four shoes from the horse, which continued to gallop, and put on four new ones, also at full speed.

"You're a remarkable fellow!" said the father. "You do your things just as well as your brother. Now I don't know who should get the house."

Then the third son said, "Father, let me show you what I can do."

And since it had begun to rain, he took his sword, swung it over his head, and made crosscuts, so that not a drop of rain fell on him. When it began to rain harder and then finally so hard that it was pouring cats and dogs, he swung the sword faster and faster and remained as dry as if he were sitting safely under cover. When the father saw that, he was astonished and said, "That's truly the best performance. The house is yours."

The other two brothers accepted the decision, as they had promised to do, and since they cared for each other so much, all three of them stayed in the house together and practiced their crafts. Indeed, they had learned their skills so well and were so talented that they earned a great deal of money. They lived happily together in this way until their old age, and when one of them fell sick and died, the other two grieved so much that they too soon fell sick and died. Since they had all been so skillful and had cared so much for each other, they were all buried in the same grave.

39
THE DEVIL AND HIS GRANDMOTHER

There once was a great war, and the king, who had many soldiers, paid his men so poorly that they couldn't live off their wages. Three of his soldiers got together, therefore, and planned to desert. Two began talking, and one said to the other, "If we're caught, they'll hang us on the gallows. So what do you think we should do?"

"There's a large wheat field over there," the other said. "If we hide in it, nobody will ever find us. The army won't enter the field."

So they crept into the wheat field and sat there for two nights and two days and almost died from hunger because they couldn't go out into the open. Finally, they said, "What's the sense of deserting if we have to die a miserable death?"

Just then a fiery dragon came flying above the wheat field and asked: "What are you three doing there in the wheat field?"

"We're three soldiers," they said, "and we've deserted the army because we couldn't live off our pay anymore. Now we'll die of hunger because the army is all around us, and we can't find a way to escape."

"Well, if you'll serve me for seven years," said the dragon, "I'll take you right through the middle of the army in a way that nobody will catch you."

"We don't have a choice," they replied. "So we'll accept your offer."

Then the dragon grabbed them with his claws, took them under his wings, and carried them through the sky to safety. Afterward he set them down on the ground again. The dragon, however, was none other than the devil, and he gave them a little whip, and all they had to do was to crack it, and they'd have as much money as they wanted.

"With this whip you'll be able to live like great lords, keep horses, and drive around in carriages. But at the end of seven years, you'll be mine."

Upon saying this, he took out a book, and they all had to sign their names to the agreement.

"But," he added, "before you're finally mine, I'll give you a riddle, and if you solve it, you'll be free, and I'll have no power over you."

Then the dragon flew away, and the three soldiers began their journey with their little whip. They always had plenty of money, ordered the finest clothes to be made for them, and traveled about the world. Wherever they were, they lived joyous and splendid lives. They drove around with horses and a carriage and ate and drank well. The time went by quickly, and as the seven years were drawing to an end, two of them became extremely anxious, but the third took it lightly and said, "Brothers, don't be afraid. Perhaps we can solve the riddle."

When they were all together, an old woman came along and asked them why they were so sad.

"Oh, what's it to you? You can't help us."

"Who knows," she answered. "Just tell me your troubles."

So they told her that they had been the devil's servants for almost seven years, and he had supplied them with money as though it were water. However, they had signed their lives over to him and would become his if they couldn't solve a riddle after the seven years were up.

"If you want some help," the old woman said, "then one of you must go into the forest, where he'll find a cliff that's caved in and looks like a little house."

"That won't save us," thought the two sad ones, and they remained outside the forest, while the cheerful one set out on his way and found everything just as the old woman had said. Inside he found an ancient woman sitting there. She was the devil's grandmother and asked him where he had come from and what he wanted. He told her everything that had happened, and since she found him very appealing, she took pity on him and lifted a large stone.

"You're to sit quietly down there. When the dragon comes, I'll ask him about the riddle."

At midnight the dragon came flying home and wanted his dinner. The grandmother set the table and brought food and drink. This made him happy, and they ate and drank together. During their conversation she asked him how his day had been and how many souls he had captured.

"I've still got three soldiers lined up. They'll soon be mine," he said.

"Oh, three soldiers," she said. "They're tough. They might still get away from you."

"They're mine for sure," responded the devil scornfully. "I'm going to ask them a riddle they'll never be able to solve."

"What kind of a riddle?" she asked.

"Let me tell you: There's a dead monkey lying in the great North Sea. That will be their roast. A whale's rib will be their silver spoon, and an old horse's hoof will be their wine glass."

When the devil had gone to bed, the old grandmother lifted up the stone and let the soldier out.

"Did you pay close attention to everything?"

"Yes," he said and had to leave by a different way so that the devil wouldn't notice him. So he went quickly through a window and rushed back to his companions. Once there he told them what he had heard, and now they could solve what no living soul had ever solved. Indeed, they were all so cheerful and in such good spirits that they took the whip and snapped it so that they had plenty of money. When the seven years were completely up, the devil came with the book, showed them their signatures, and said, "Now I'm going to take you with me to hell, where you'll be given a meal. However, if you can guess what kind of a roast you're going to have, you'll be free and may keep the little whip."

Then the first soldier began to talk. "In the great North Sea there's a dead monkey. That will probably be the roast."

The devil was annoyed and went "*Hm! Hm! Hm!*" and asked the second soldier, "What will be your spoon?"

"The rib of a whale will be our silver spoon."

The devil made a face, muttered "*Hm! Hm! Hm!*" again, and asked the third soldier, "Do you know what your wine glass will be?"

"An old horse's hoof will be our wine glass."

At that the devil flew away and abandoned them. He no longer had power over them, but the three soldiers kept the little whip. Indeed, they whipped up as much money they wanted whenever they wanted money and lived happily until the end of their days.

40

FAITHFUL FERDINAND AND
UNFAITHFUL FERDINAND

Once upon a time there lived a man and a woman who didn't have any children while they were rich, but when they became poor, they had a little boy. Since nobody was willing to stand as godfather for their child, the father said that he would go to the next village to see if he could find one. Along the way he met a beggar, who asked him where he was going. The father told him that he was going to see if he could find a godfather for his son, since nobody was willing to act as godfather in his village because he was so poor.

"Oh," said the beggar. "You're poor, and I'm poor. So I might as well be your godfather. But I'm so poor that I won't be able to give your child anything. Go home and tell the midwife to bring the child to the church."

When they all arrived at the church, the beggar was already inside, and he named the child Faithful Ferdinand. As he was about to leave the church, the beggar said, "Go home now. I can't give you anything, and I don't want you to give me anything either."

However, he gave the midwife a key and told her to give it to the father when she reached the house. He was to keep it until the boy became fourteen. At that time the boy was to go out to the heath, where he would find a castle. The key would fit the castle door, and everything inside would belong to him.

When the boy was seven and had grown nice and strong, he went to play with some other boys. Their godfathers had given them all presents, one more wonderful than the next, but Faithful Ferdinand had nothing to talk about. He burst into tears and ran home to his father.

"Didn't I get anything at all from my godfather?" he asked.

"Oh, yes," said the father. "You received a key. If there's a castle on the heath, you're to go there and open it."

So he went to the heath, but there was no sign of a castle. When seven more years passed and he was fourteen, he went to the heath again, and this time a castle was standing there. When he opened it, there was only a horse inside, a white horse, and the boy was so excited to have a horse that he mounted it and galloped home to his father. "Now that I've got a white horse," he said, "I'm going to travel about."

So he set out, and as he was riding along, he found a pen along the way. At first he wanted to pick it up, but then he thought to himself, "Oh, you'd better leave it there. You're bound to find a pen where you're going if you need one." But just as he was about to ride away, a voice called out from behind him, "Faithful Ferdinand, take it with you."

He looked around but couldn't see anyone. Then he went back and picked it up. After he rode on for a while, he came to a sea, where he discovered a fish lying on the shore and gasping for air.

"Wait, my little fish," he said, "and I'll help you back into the water."

He grabbed the fish by the tail and threw it back into the water. Then the fish stuck its head out of the sea and said, "Since you helped me out of the mud, I'm going to give you a flute. Whenever you're in trouble, just play it, and I'll come to your aid. And if you ever drop something into the water, just play it, and I'll get it out for you."

Now Faithful Ferdinand continued on his way, and he came across a man, who asked him where he was going.

"Just to the next town."

"What's your name?"

"Faithful Ferdinand."

"What do you know about that? We have almost the same name. I'm called Unfaithful Ferdinand."

The two of them traveled to the next town together, but there was trouble ahead: Unfaithful Ferdinand knew everything that anyone thought and wanted to do. He knew all this because he practiced all kinds of black magic. Now, at the inn where they decided to stay, there was a fine maiden who had an honest face and nice manners. She fell in love with Faithful Ferdinand, for he was very handsome, and she asked him where he was going. He told her that he was just traveling about, and she said that he really should stay right there because the king of that country wanted to hire a servant or a forerunner, and he could work in the king's employ. He responded that he couldn't just go to someone out of the blue and offer his services. Then the maiden said, "Oh, I'll take care of that."

She went straight to the king and told him that she knew of a fine servant for him. The king was glad to hear this and had Faithful Ferdinand summoned. When the king wanted to make him a servant Faithful Ferdinand asked to be a forerunner because he wanted to be with his horse. So the king made him a forerunner.

When Unfaithful Ferdinand learned about this, he said to the maiden, "What's going on? You can't just help him and forget about me!"

"Oh," said the maiden. "I'll help you too," and she thought, "I'd better keep on his good side, for he's not to be trusted." So she went to the king again and said that she had a servant for him, and the king was pleased.

Now, whenever Unfaithful Ferdinand dressed the king in the morning, his Majesty would always complain, "Oh, if only my beloved could be here with me!" Since Unfaithful Ferdinand kept a grudge against Faithful Ferdinand, and since he also kept hearing the king lament, he finally said, "You have the forerunner, don't you? Well, why don't you send him to find her, and if he doesn't bring her back, have him beheaded."

So the king summoned Faithful Ferdinand and told him that his beloved was in such and such a place, and Faithful Ferdinand was to bring her to him, and if he didn't succeed, he would have to die. Faithful Ferdinand went straight to his white horse, who was kept in the stable, and began to sigh and moan, "Oh, what an unlucky person I am!"

Then he heard a voice behind him. "Faithful Ferdinand, why are you crying?"

He turned around, and since he didn't see anyone near him, he continued to moan. "Oh, my dear little white horse, I must leave you now. I'm going to my doom."

Then he heard the voice again. "Faithful Ferdinand, why are you crying?"

Suddenly he realized for the first time that it was his horse asking the question. "Is it you, my little white horse? Can you talk?" And he continued, "I've got to go to such and such a place and fetch the king's bride. Can you tell me how to do it?"

"Go to the king," the white horse replied, "and tell him that if he'll give you what you need, you'll get her, and you'll need a shipload of meat and a shipload of bread to succeed. There are huge giants in the sea, and if you don't bring them meat, they'll tear you to pieces, and there are huge birds who'll peck your eyes out if you don't bring them bread."

So the king ordered all the butchers in the land to slaughter animals and all the bakers to bake bread until the ships were loaded. When they were full, the white horse said to Faithful Ferdinand, "Now, I want you to climb up on my back and go aboard the ship with me. When the giants come, you're to say:

'Easy does it, my dear giants,
don't think that I've forgotten you,
for I've brought you meat to chew.'

And when the birds come, you're to say:

'Easy does it, my nice dear birds,
don't think that I've forgotten you,
for I've brought you bread to chew.'

Then they won't do anything to you, and when you come to the castle, the giants will help you. Just take a few of them with you and go up into the castle, where you'll find the princess lying asleep, but you mustn't wake her. Have the giants pick her up with the bed and carry her to the ship."

Then everything happened the way the little white horse said it would. Faithful Ferdinand gave the giants and birds the meat and bread he had brought with him. In return, the giants willingly carried the princess in her bed to the king. When she arrived at the king's palace, she told him that she couldn't live without her private papers that were still in her castle. So Faithful Ferdinand was summoned again, at the instigation of Unfaithful Ferdinand, and the king commanded him to fetch the papers from the castle; otherwise, he would have to die.

So Faithful Ferdinand went out into the stable, where he began moaning and said, "Oh, my dear little white horse, I must go away again. What shall we do?"

The white horse told him to have the ships fully loaded as before, and everything happened as it had the first time: the giants and birds ate their fill of the meat and bread and were appeased. When they reached the castle, the horse told Faithful Ferdinand to go into the princess's bedroom, where he would find the papers lying on the table. So he went in and got them. When they were on the sea again, he let his pen drop into the water, and at that the horse said, "Now I can't help you."

But Faithful Ferdinand remembered the flute, and he began to play. Soon the fish came with the pen in its mouth and gave it to him. Afterward Faithful Ferdinand brought the papers to the palace, where the wedding was then held.

The queen, however, couldn't stand the king because he didn't have a nose. On the other hand, she loved Faithful Ferdinand very much. One day, when all the noblemen of the court were gathered together, the queen said she knew some tricks. She said, in fact, that she could cut off a head and put it back on, and she wanted a volunteer to demonstrate her skill. Nobody wanted to be first, but upon Unfaithful Ferdinand's prompting, Faithful Ferdinand felt obliged to volunteer. The queen cut off his head and put it back on again, and it healed immediately. Only a red thread appeared around his neck, where she had cut him.

"My child," the king said to her, "where did you learn that?"

"Oh," she replied, "Shall I try it out on you too?"

"Oh, yes," he said.

Then the queen cut off his head, but she didn't put it back on again. Rather, she pretended she couldn't get it on because it wouldn't stick properly. So the king was buried, and she married Faithful Ferdinand.

Afterward Faithful Ferdinand continued to ride his white horse, and once when he got on it, the horse told him to head for another heath he knew and to gallop around it three times. When Faithful Ferdinand did this, the white horse stood up on its hind legs and turned into a prince.

41

THE IRON STOVE

In the days when wishing still helped, an old witch cast a spell over a prince so that he had to sit in a big iron stove in the forest. He spent many years there, and nobody was able to rescue him. One day a princess got lost in that forest and couldn't find the way back to her father's kingdom. She wandered about for nine days and finally came to the iron stove. As she stood in front of it, she heard a voice from inside that asked, "Where do you come from and where are you going?"

"I've lost the way to my father's kingdom," she answered, "and I can't get back home."

Then the voice from the iron stove said, "I'll help you get home again quickly if you'll promise to do what I ask. My father is a greater king than yours, and I want to marry you."

She was frightened by this and thought, "Dear Lord, what shall I do with an iron stove!" But, she wanted so very much to return home to her father that she promised to do what he asked.

Then he said, "I want you to come back with a knife and scrape a hole in the iron," and he gave her an escort who walked beside her without saying a word and brought her home in two hours.

Now, there was great rejoicing in the castle when the princess returned, and the old king embraced and kissed her. Yet, she was very sad and said, "Dear father, you can't imagine what happened to me! I'd never have been able to escape from the large, wild forest if I hadn't come across an iron stove, but I had to promise it that I'd return there to rescue and marry it."

The old king was so horrified by this that he almost fainted, for she was his only daughter. After some deliberation, they decided to send the miller's beautiful daughter in her place. They led the maiden into the forest, gave her a knife, and told her to scrape away at the iron stove. She scraped for twenty-four hours but couldn't make the slightest dent. At daybreak a voice called out from the iron stove, "It seems to me that it's dawn outside."

"It seems so to me, too," she answered. "I think I hear the clattering of my father's mill."

"So, you're a miller's daughter! Then get out of here at once, and tell them to send the king's daughter."

She returned to the castle and told the old king that the man in the stove didn't want her, he wanted his daughter. The old king was horrified, and his daughter began to weep. However, they still had the swineherd's daughter, who was even more beautiful than the miller's daughter. They agreed to give her a nice sum of money to go to the iron stove in place of the king's daughter. So she was taken into the forest, and she too had to scrape for twenty-four hours, but she couldn't get anything off. At daybreak a voice cried out from the stove, "It seems to me that it's dawn outside."

"It seems so to me, too," she answered. "I think I hear my father blowing his horn."

"So, you're a swineherd's daughter! Get out of here at once, and have them send the king's daughter. Tell her that bad things will happen to her the way I promised, and if she doesn't come, the whole kingdom will collapse and be demolished, and not one stone will be left standing."

When the king's daughter heard that, she began to cry. But there was nothing she could do: she had to keep her promise. So she took leave of her father, put a knife in her pocket, and went to the iron stove in the forest. When she got there, she started scraping, and the iron gave way. After two hours she had managed to scrape a small hole. When she looked inside, she saw oh such a handsome prince glimmering in gold and jewels that her heart was swept away! She continued her scraping until she had made a hole large enough for him to crawl through.

"You are mine," he said, "and I am yours. You're my bride and have set me free."

Now, she requested permission to see her father one more time before leaving with him, and the prince granted it, but she was not to say more than three words to her father, and then she was to return to the prince. So she went home, but she spoke more than three words, whereupon the iron stove vanished immediately and was carried far away over glass mountains and sharp swords. Yet the prince had been released and was no longer locked up in the stove.

After this happened, the princess said good-bye to her father and took some money with her, though not much, and went back into the large forest to look for the iron stove, which was not to be found. For nine days she searched, until her hunger became so great that she didn't know what to do since she had nothing more to live on. When evening came, she climbed a small tree and sat down. She planned to spend the night there because she was afraid of the wild animals. Then, at midnight, she saw a little light in the distance and thought, "Oh, I think I'd be safe there." She climbed down the tree and went toward the light, praying along the way. Finally, she came to an old cottage with a great deal of grass growing around it and a small pile of wood in front. "Oh, where have you landed?" she thought. She looked through the window and saw nothing but small fat toads, and yet there was also a nicely covered table with wine and a roast, and the plates and cups were made of silver. So she summoned her courage and knocked on the door. The fat toad replied at once:

"Maiden, maiden, green and small,
hop to it, hoptoad, and don't you fall.
Hoptoad's dog,
hop back and forth,
and quickly see who's at the door."

Then a small toad went to the door and opened it. When the princess entered, they all welcomed her and made her sit down while they asked, "Where have you come from? Where are you going?"

She told them everything that had happened to her and how she had disobeyed the prince's command not to say more than three words, which had caused the stove along with the prince to disappear, and now she intended to search over hill and valley until she found him. Then the fat old toad said:

"Maiden, maiden, green and small,
hop to it, hoptoad, and don't you fall.

Hoptoad's dog,
hop back and forth and do it sprightly.
Fetch me the box as quick as can be."

After the small toad left and then came back with the box, they gave her food and drink and took her to a nicely made bed that was like silk and velvet. She lay down on it and slept with God's blessing. When morning came, she got up, and the old toad gave her three needles from the box, which she was to take with her. She would need them because she had to cross over a high glass mountain, three sharp swords, and a great lake. If she could manage to do all that, then she would regain her beloved. The toad also gave her three objects that she was to guard very carefully—namely, three big needles, a plow wheel, and three nuts. Upon receiving them, she departed, and when she came to the glass mountain, which was very slick, she stuck the three needles first beneath her feet and then ahead of them, and this was the way she managed to get over it. When she was on the other side, she hid them in a place that she marked carefully. Next she came to the three sharp swords, and she seated herself on the plow wheel and rolled over them. Finally, she came to the great lake, and after crossing it, she arrived at a large, beautiful castle. She went inside and sought work as if she were a poor maiden who wanted to hire herself out. She knew, in fact, that the prince whom she had rescued from the iron stove in the big forest was in this castle. So the princess was taken on as a kitchen maid at low wages. The prince, in the meantime, had already found another maiden whom he wanted to marry, for he thought that the princess had long since died.

That evening, after she had finished washing up and was through with her work, the kitchen maid searched in her pocket and found the three nuts the old toad had given her. She bit one open and was going to eat the kernel when—lo and behold!—she discovered a splendid royal dress inside. When the bride heard about it, she came and asked if she could buy the dress. Indeed, she said that it was not fit for a servant girl. But the kitchen maid replied that she wouldn't sell it, rather the bride could have it if she would allow the maid to sleep one night in the bridegroom's chamber. The bride consented because she didn't have a dress that beautiful.

When evening came, she said to her bridegroom, "That silly kitchen maid wants to sleep in your room."

"If you don't mind," he said, "neither do I."

Nonetheless, the bride gave him a glass of wine with a sleeping potion in it. Then the bridegroom and the kitchen maid went into the chamber to sleep, but he slept so soundly that she couldn't wake him, which made her weep the entire night: "I rescued you from the wild forest and the iron stove," she lamented. "I searched for you and went across a glass mountain, three sharp swords, and a great lake until I found you. And now you won't listen to me."

The servants outside the bedroom door heard her weeping the entire night and told their master the next day. When the kitchen maid had finished washing up that evening, she bit open the second nut, and there was another dress, even more beautiful than the first one. The bride saw it and wanted to buy this one, too, but the kitchen maid didn't want money. She requested instead to sleep in the bridegroom's chamber again However, the bride gave the prince another sleeping potion, and he slept so soundly that he couldn't hear a thing. The kitchen maid wept the entire night and lamented: "I rescued you from the wild forest and the iron stove. I searched for you and went across a glass mountain, three sharp swords, and a great lake until I found you. And now you won't listen to me."

The servants outside the bedroom door heard her weep the entire night and told their master about this in the morning. When the kitchen maid had finished washing up the third night and bit open the third nut, she found a dress lined with pure gold that was even more beautiful than the other two. When the bride saw it, she wanted to have it, but the kitchen maid would give it to her only if she was granted permission to sleep in the bridegroom's chamber a third night. This time, however, the bridegroom was alert and didn't drink the sleeping potion. When the kitchen maid began to weep and lament, "Dearest love, I rescued you from the cruel wild forest and the iron stove," the prince jumped up and said, "You are the true bride! You are mine, and I am yours."

That very night he got into a carriage with her, and they took away the false bride's dresses so that she couldn't get up. When they came to the great lake, they sailed across it, and when they came to the three sharp swords, they sat down on the plow wheel, and when they came to the glass mountain, they stuck the three needles into it. At last they arrived at the old cottage, but when they entered, it became a large castle. The toads were released from a magic spell and turned out to be princes and princesses, and they were all very happy. Then the wedding was celebrated, and the prince and the princess remained in the castle, which was larger than the castle of the king's daughter. However, since the king complained of being left alone, they traveled to him and brought him back to their castle. Now they had two kingdoms and lived a happily married life.

42
THE LAZY SPINNER

A man and his wife lived in a village, and the wife was so lazy that she never wanted to do any work. Whenever her husband gave her something to spin, she never finished it, and whatever she did spin, she didn't wind it, but left it tangled on the bobbin. If her husband scolded her, she used her quick tongue and said, "How can I wind the yarn if I don't have a reel? You go into the forest first and fetch me one."

"If that's the problem," her husband replied, "then I'll go into the forest and get some wood for a reel."

Upon hearing this, his wife became anxious because she'd have to wind the yarn and start spinning again if he found the wood to make a reel. So she gave the matter some thought and came up with a good idea. She secretly followed her husband into the forest, and just as he climbed up a tree to choose and cut the wood, she crawled into some bushes below him, where he couldn't see her, and cried out:

"He who chops wood for reels shall die.
She who winds yarn shall be ruined all her life."

The husband listened, laid down his axe for a moment, and wondered what all this could possibly mean. "Oh, well," he said, "I must have been hearing things. No need to get frightened. It's nothing."

So he took his axe again and was about to begin chopping when he heard the voice from below once more:

"He who chops wood for reels shall die.
She who winds yarn shall be ruined all her life."

He stopped again, and in his fear and terror, he tried to grasp what was happening. After some time had passed, his courage returned. He reached for his axe a third time and was about to chop when he heard the voice cry out loudly for a third time:

"He who chops wood for reels shall die.
She who winds yarn shall be ruined all her life."

This was too much for him, and he lost all desire to chop the wood. He quickly climbed down the tree and made his way home. His wife ran as fast as she could via the byways to get home before he did. When he entered the living room, she acted innocent, as if nothing had happened, and said, "Well, did you bring me a nice piece of wood for a reel?"

"No," he said, "I've realized that it makes no sense to wind," and he told her what he had encountered in the forest, and from then on he left her in peace.

Yet some time later the husband began complaining again about the messy condition of the house. "Wife," he said, "it's a disgrace the way you just leave your spun wool on the bobbin."

"You know what?" she said. "Since we haven't managed to get a reel, you go up to the loft, and I'll stand here below. Then I'll throw the yarn up to you, and you throw it back down to me. That way we'll have a skein."

"Yes, that'll work," said her husband. So they did this, and when they were finished, he said, "We've got the yarn skeined, and now it needs to be boiled as well."

His wife became uneasy again and said, "Yes, indeed, we'll boil it first thing tomorrow morning," but she was really thinking up a new trick. Early the next morning she got up, made the fire, and set the kettle on it, but instead of putting the yarn in the kettle, she put in a clump of wool and let it boil. After this she went to her husband, who was still lying in bed, and said to him, "I've got to go out awhile. So I want you to get up and look after the yarn that's in the kettle on the fire. Make sure you do this right away, and watch things closely, for if the cock crows and you're not taking care, the yarn will become wool."

The husband agreed since he certainly didn't want anything to go wrong. He got up as fast as he could and went into the kitchen. But when he reached the kettle and looked inside, he was horrified to discover nothing but a clump of wool. Then the husband was as quiet as a mouse, for he thought that he had done something wrong and was to blame. In the future he left his wife in peace when it came to yarn and spinning.

43
THE LION AND THE FROG

There once lived a king and a queen, and they had a son and a daughter who loved each other dearly. The prince went hunting very often and sometimes remained in the forest a long time. However, one day he didn't return. His sister almost wept herself blind because of this. Finally, when she could no longer stand it, she went into the forest to search for her brother. After she had gone a long way, she was too tired to go any farther, and when she looked around her, a lion was standing nearby. He seemed friendly and very kind. So she sat down on his back, and the lion carried her away. As they went, he kept stroking her with his tail and cooling her cheeks.

After they had traveled a good distance, they came to a cave, and the lion carried her inside. She didn't get frightened, nor did she want to jump off the lion's back because he was so friendly. They went deeper into the cave, where it became darker and darker until it was eventually pitch black. Nevertheless, they proceeded for a while until they reached daylight again and were in a beautiful garden. Everything was fresh and glistened in the sun, and in the middle of the garden was a magnificent palace. When they came to the gate, the lion stopped, and the princess climbed down from his back. Then the lion began to speak and said, "You shall live in the beautiful house and serve me, and if you carry out all my orders, you shall see your brother again."

So the princess served the lion and obeyed all his commands. One day she went for a walk in the garden, where it was very beautiful, but she was still sad because she was alone and forsaken by the world. As she walked here and there she became aware of a pond, and in the middle of the pond was a small island with a tent on it. Underneath the tent she saw a frog, who was as green as grass and had a rose leaf on his head instead of a crown. The frog looked at her and said, "Why are you so sad?"

"Ah," she replied. "Why shouldn't I be sad?" And she told him about her troubles.

Then the frog said to her in a very friendly way, "If you need anything, just come to me, and I'll lend you a helping hand."

"But how shall I pay you back?"

"You don't have to pay me back," said the frog. "Just bring me a fresh rose leaf every day for my crown."

The princess returned to the palace and was somewhat comforted. Whenever the lion demanded something, she ran to the pond, and the frog hopped here and there and soon brought her what she needed. After a while, the lion said, "This evening I'd like to eat a gnat pie, but it must be prepared very well."

The princess wondered how she could ever get something like that. It seemed impossible for her. She ran out and told her woes to the frog. But the frog said, "Don't worry. I'll make sure that you have a gnat pie."

He sat down, opened his mouth to the left and right, and when he snapped it shut, he had caught as many gnats as he needed. Then he hopped here and there, gathered together some wood shavings, and built a fire. When it began burning, he kneaded the dough for the pie and put it over the coals. After two hours, the pie was finished, and one could not have wished for anything better. Then he said to the maiden, "I won't give you the pie until you promise me that, when the lion is asleep, you'll cut off his head with the sword that's hidden behind his bed."

"No," she said. "I won't do it. The lion's always been good to me."

"If you don't do it, you'll never see your brother again," said the frog. "Besides, you won't be harming the lion."

So she summoned her courage, took the pie, and brought it to the lion.

"That looks delicious," the lion said, and after sniffing it, he began to eat it right away and ate it all up. When he was finished, he felt tired and wanted to sleep a little. So he said to the princess, "Come and sit down beside me and scratch behind my ears a bit until I fall asleep."

She sat down beside him, scratched him with her left hand, and with her right hand she reached for the sword that was lying behind the bed. After he had fallen asleep, she drew out the sword, closed her eyes, and chopped off the lion's head with one blow. But when she looked again, the lion had disappeared, and her dear brother stood next to her. He kissed her affectionately and said, "You've released me from the spell, for I was the lion and had been cursed to remain so until a maiden's hand would chop off my head out of love for me as a lion."

They went together into the garden to thank the frog, but when they got there, they saw that he was hopping all around and gathering together wood shavings to build a fire. When the fire was burning brightly, he hopped into it himself, and it burned a little more until it finally went out and a beautiful maiden was standing there. This was the prince's sweetheart, who had also been cast under a magic spell. Now they all returned home to the old king and queen, and a great wedding was held. Whoever attended did not go home with an empty stomach,

44
THE SOLDIER AND THE CARPENTER

Two carpenters lived in a city in which their houses touched one other. Each carpenter had a son, and their children were always together and played with one another. That's why they were called Little Knife and Little Fork, which likewise are always placed side by side on the table. When they grew up, they refused to be separated. Since one was courageous and the other timid, one became a soldier, and the other learned carpentry. As the time came for the carpenter to go on his travels as a journeyman, the soldier didn't want to be left behind, and so they set out together.

When they reached a city, the carpenter went to work for a master craftsman, and since the soldier wanted to remain there, too, he hired himself out as a servant in the same house. Everything would have gone well, but the soldier had no desire to work. He just loafed about, and it didn't take long for the master to send him packing. Out of loyalty to his companion the carpenter decided not to stay. He handed his resignation to the master and departed with the soldier. And that's how things continued to go. If they had work, it didn't last long because the soldier was lazy and would be sent away, and the carpenter didn't want to stay without him.

One day they arrived in a large city, but when the soldier refused to lift a finger, he was dismissed the very first evening, and they had to leave that night. Now their way took them to the edge of a large mysterious forest, and the timid carpenter said, "I'm not going to enter. I'm sure there are witches and ghosts jumping all over the place."

But the soldier replied, "Oh, nonsense! I'm not yet afraid of things like that!"

The soldier went ahead, and since the timid carpenter didn't want to be separated from him, he went along. In a short time they lost their way and wandered in darkness through the trees. Finally, they saw a light and headed in that direction until they came to a beautiful castle that was brightly lit. In front of the castle was a black dog, and nearby was a red swan on a pond. When they entered the castle, however, they didn't encounter a living creature until they went into the kitchen, where they found a gray cat standing by a pot on the fire and cooking. They moved on and found many splendid rooms that were all empty, but in one of them there was a table amply covered with food and drink. Since they were both very hungry, they went over to the table and enjoyed a fine meal. Afterward the soldier said, "Now that we're finished and full, we're entitled to some sleep!"

When he opened a room, he found two beautiful beds. So they lay down in them, but just as they were about to fall asleep, it occurred to the timid carpenter that they had not said their prayers. As he got up, he saw a cupboard on the wall. He opened it, and inside there was a crucifix with two prayer books. He immediately woke the soldier and got him up. Then they knelt down and said their prayers and fell asleep once more in peace.

The next morning the soldier felt such a violent blow that he jumped into the air.

"Hey, why are you hitting me?" he yelled at his companion, who had also received a blow and replied, "I didn't hit you. Why did *you* hit me?"

Then the soldier said, "It's probably a signal that we should get up."

When they left the room, breakfast was already on the table. But the timid carpenter said, "Before we touch it, let's first look for some people."

"All right," said the soldier. "I agree. Anyway, since the cat prepared and cooked the meal, I've lost my desire to eat it."

So they went from the bottom of the castle to the top but couldn't find a soul. Finally, the soldier said, "Let's go search down in the cellar, too."

When they went down the stairs, they saw an old woman sitting in front of the first cellar. They began speaking to her and said, "Good day! Did you cook that good meal for us?"

"Yes, children, did it taste all right?"

They went farther and came to a second cellar, where a young boy of fourteen was sitting. They greeted him, too, but he didn't answer them. Finally, they moved on to the third cellar, where a maiden of twelve was sitting, and she, too, didn't answer their greeting. Then they continued walking through all the cellars but didn't find anyone else. When they returned, the maiden had already stood up from her seat, and they said to her, "Do you want to go upstairs with us?"

But she asked, "Is the *red swan* still on the pond up there?"

"Yes, we saw it at the entrance."

"That's sad. Then I can't go upstairs with you."

The young boy was also standing when they came to him, and they asked him: "Do you want to come upstairs with us?"

But he said, "Is the *black dog* still in the courtyard?"

"Yes, we saw him at the entrance."

"That's sad. Then I can't go upstairs with you."

When they came to the old woman, she had also stood up.

"Granny," they said. "Do you want to come upstairs with us?"

"Is the *gray cat* still upstairs in the kitchen?"

"Yes, she's sitting at the hearth by a pot and cooking."

"That's sad. Unless you kill the red swan, the black dog, and the gray cat, we can't leave the cellar."

When the two companions went upstairs and into the kitchen again, they wanted to pet the cat, but her fiery eyes began to flash, and she looked very wild. Now, there was still a small room left that they hadn't explored, and when they opened it, they discovered that it was completely empty except for a bow and arrow, a sword, and iron tongs, which were hanging on the wall. Written over the bow and arrow were the words, "This will kill the red swan." Over the sword, "This will chop off the black dog's head." Over the tongs, "This will pinch off the gray cat's head."

"Ah," said the timid carpenter. "Let's get out of here!"

But the soldier replied, "No, let's go after the animals."

So they took the weapons off the wall and went into the kitchen, where the three animals, the swan, the dog, and the cat, were standing together as if they had something evil in mind. When the timid carpenter saw them, he ran away. The soldier followed and tried to give his companion courage, but the carpenter wanted something to eat first. After he had eaten, he said, "I saw some suits of armor in a room, and I want to put one on first."

When he was in the room, he looked for a way to escape and said, "We'd be better off if we climbed through that window. Those animals are not our concern!"

However, when he went over to the window, he found strong iron bars in front of it. Now he no longer had a way out and went over to the suits of armor. He tried to put one on, but they were all too heavy. Then the soldier said, "Stop this! Let's go the way we are."

"All right," said the other, "but I wish there were three of us."

Just as he uttered those words a white dove began flapping its wings on the outside of a window and bumped up against it. The soldier opened the window, and as soon as the dove hopped inside, a handsome young man stood before them and said, "I'll lend you support and help you."

The young man picked up the bow and arrow, but the timid carpenter told him that he was taking the best part of the bargain with the bow and arrow because he'd be in a good position after he took a shot to run wherever he wanted. On the other hand, the carpenter and the soldier would have to get physically closer to the enchanted animals to use their weapons. Upon hearing this, the young man exchanged the bow and arrow for the sword.

Now all three went into the kitchen, where the animals were still together. The young man cut off the dog's head, the soldier grabbed the gray cat with the tongs, and the timid carpenter stood behind and shot the red swan dead. After the three animals had been killed, the old woman and her two children came running from the cellar all at once and let out a great cry, "You've killed our dearest friends! You're traitors!"

They charged at the men and wanted to murder them. But the three men overpowered them and killed them with their weapons. Once they were dead, the men suddenly began to hear all around them strange murmuring sounds that came out of all the corners. Then the timid carpenter said, "Let's bury the three bodies. After all, they were Christians. We know this from the crucifix."

So they carried the bodies out into the courtyard, dug three graves, and laid them down inside. While they were working, however, the murmuring in the castle increased. It became louder and louder, and when they were finished with their work, they heard real voices among the murmurs, and one called out, "Who are you? Who are you?"

Since the handsome young man had disappeared, they became afraid and ran away. After they had gone off a little way, the soldier said, "Hey, we shouldn't have run away. Let's go back and see what's there."

"No," the other said. "I want nothing to do with those bewitched creatures. I want to go to the city and earn an honest living."

But the soldier gave him no peace until he went back with him. When they got to the front of the castle, everything was full of life. Horses dashed through the courtyard, and servants ran back and forth. They pretended to be two poor journeymen and asked for a little something to eat. One of the people said, "Yes, just come inside. Everyone will be helped today."

They were led into a beautiful room and were given food and wine. Afterward they were asked whether they had seen two young men coming from the castle.

"No," they said.

But when someone saw that they had blood on their hands, he asked where the blood came from.

"I cut my finger," replied the soldier.

However, a servant went and told his master, who came himself to see who they were. Indeed, it was the handsome young man who had come to their aid, and when he laid eyes on them, he cried out, "These are the two who saved the castle!"

He welcomed them with great joy and told them how everything had happened. "A housekeeper was living in the castle with her two children. However, she was really a witch, and one time, when her masters scolded her, she replied by doing some evil and transformed all living things in the castle into stone. There were three other servants who also knew something about magic, and she had no real power over them and could only turn them into animals. They did their mischief upstairs in the castle, and since she was afraid of them, she fled into the cellar with her children. She had only limited power over me as well. So she changed me into a white dove but only as long as I was outside the castle. Inside I could be myself. When you two came into the castle, you were supposed to kill the animals so she would be free. As a reward she wanted to kill you, but God had things turn out better. The castle is no longer enchanted, and the very moment that the wicked witch and her children were killed, the people who had been turned into stone became alive again, and the murmuring sounds you heard were the words these people first spoke upon being freed."

The young man then led the two companions to the lord of the castle, who gave them his two beautiful daughters, and they lived happily ever after as great knights until the end of their days.

45
PRETTY KATRINELYA AND PIF-PAF-POLTREE

"Good day, Father Berry-Tea."

"Why, thank you, Pif-Paf-Poltree."

"Could I have your daughter for my wife?"

"Oh, yes, if Mother Milk-Cow, Brother High-and-Mighty, Sister Dear-Cheese, and Pretty Katrinelya are willing, then you can have her."

"Then where can I find Mother Milk-Cow?"

"In the barn milking the cow."

"Good day, Mother Milk-Cow."

"Why, thank you, Pif-Paf-Poltree."

"Could I have your daughter for my wife?"

"Oh, yes, if Father Berry-Tea, Brother High-and-Mighty, Sister Dear-Cheese, and Pretty Katrinelya are willing, then you can have her."

"Then where can I find Brother High-and-Mighty?"

"In the shed chopping up all the wood he can see."

"Good day, Brother High-and-Mighty."

"Why, thank you, Pif-Paf-Poltree."

"Could I have your sister for my wife?"

"Oh, yes, if Father Berry-Tea, Mother Milk-Cow, Sister Dear-Cheese, and Pretty Katrinelya are willing, then you can have her."

"Then where can I find Sister Dear-Cheese?"

"Weeding in the garden, if you please."

"Good day, Sister Dear-Cheese."

"Why, thank you, Pif-Paf-Poltree.

"Could I have your sister for my wife?"

"Oh, yes, if Father Berry-Tea, Mother Milk-Cow, Brother High-and-Mighty, and Pretty Katrinelya are willing, then you can have her."

"Then where can I find Pretty Katrinelya?"

"Counting out her pennies in the parlor."

"Good day, Pretty Katrinelya."

"Why, thank you, Pif-Paf-Poltree."

"Do you want to be my bride?"

"Oh, yes, if Father Berry-Tea, Mother Milk-Cow, Brother High-and-Mighty, and Sister Dear-Cheese are willing, then I'll be your bride."

"Pretty Katrinelya, how much dowry do you have?"

"Fourteen pennies in cash, three and a half coins that are owed to me, half a pound of dried fruits, a handful of pretzels, and a handful of roots.

As you can surely see,
that makes for a fine dowry.

Now, Pif-Paf-Poltree, what is it that do you do? Are you a tailor?"
"Much better than that."
"A shoemaker?"
"Much better than that."
"A farmer?"
"Much better than that."
"A carpenter?"
"Much better than that."
"A blacksmith?"
"Much better than that."
"A miller?"
"Much better than that."
"Perhaps you're a broom-maker?"
"Yes, that's what I am. Isn't that a wonderful way to earn a living?"

46

THE FOX AND THE HORSE

A farmer had a faithful horse that had grown old and could no longer do his work. So his master didn't want to feed him anymore and said, "You're of no more use to me now, but I won't abandon you entirely. Show me that you're still strong enough to bring me a lion, then I'll keep you. But for now, get out of my stable!"

And he chased the horse out into the open field. The horse was sad about this and went into the forest to seek a little shelter from the weather. There he met the fox, who asked, "Why are you hanging your head and moping about all by yourself?"

"Ah," answered the horse, "greed and loyalty can't live side by side in the same house. My master has forgotten how much work I've done for him over the years, and since I can no longer plow properly, he won't feed me and has chased me away."

"Without a word of consolation?" asked the fox.

"The consolation was meager. He told me that if I was still strong enough to bring him a lion, he would keep me, but he knows full well that I can't do that."

"Well, I'm going to help you," said the fox. "Just lie down, stretch yourself out, and don't move. Pretend you're dead."

The horse did what the fox commanded, while the fox went to the lion, whose den was not far away, and said, "There's a dead horse lying out there. If you want a great meal, come along with me."

The lion went with him, and when they were at the horse's side, the fox said, "It's not so comfortable for you here. You know what I'll do? I'll tie the horse to you by his tail so you can drag him and eat him in peace and quiet."

The lion liked the idea, assumed a position for the fox to attach the horse to him, and kept still. However, the fox bound the lion's legs together with the horse's tail, and he tied and twisted it so tightly and firmly that the lion wouldn't have been able to tear himself loose even if he had used all his might. When the fox finally finished his work, he tapped the horse on his shoulder and said, "Pull, horse, pull!"

All at once the horse jumped up and dragged the lion with him. The lion began to roar so loudly that all the birds in the forest flew away out of fright, but the horse let him roar and pulled and dragged him over the fields to his master's door. When his master saw that, he reconsidered everything in a better light and said to the horse, "You shall stay here with me and shall be treated well."

And he gave him all he wanted to eat until the day of the horse's death.

47
THE WORN-OUT DANCING SHOES

Once upon a time there was a king who had twelve daughters, one more beautiful than the other. They slept together in a large room, where their beds stood side by side, and in the evening, when they went to sleep, the king shut and locked the door. However, every morning, their shoes were worn out from dancing, and nobody knew where they had been and how it kept happening. So the king issued a proclamation that whoever could find out where his daughters danced during the night could choose one of them for his wife and be king after his death. But anyone who came and failed to uncover everything after three days and nights would lose his life.

Not long after this proclamation a prince came and was well received. In the evening he was conducted to a room adjoining the bedchamber of the king's daughters. His bed was set up there, and he was told to watch and find out where they went dancing. And, just to make sure they couldn't do anything in secret or go out anywhere else, the door of their room that led to his was kept open. However, the prince fell asleep, and when he awoke the next morning, all twelve of them had been to a dance, for their shoes were standing there with holes in the soles. The same thing happened the second and third nights, and his head was cut off. After that there were many who came to try their luck, but they all left their lives behind them.

Now, it so happened that a poor soldier, who had been wounded and could no longer serve in the army, traveled toward the city where the king lived. Along the way he met an old woman, who asked him where he was going.

"I really don't know myself," he said, "but I'd certainly like to find out where the king's daughters go dancing and where they wear out their shoes so I could become king."

"Oh, that's not so difficult," said the old woman. "Just don't drink the wine that's brought to you in the evening, and then pretend that you've fallen asleep." She also gave him a little cloak and added, "When you put this cloak on, you'll be invisible, and you'll be able to follow all twelve of them."

After receiving such good advice, the soldier now became serious about the entire matter and plucked up his courage to present himself in front of the king as a suitor. He was welcomed just as cordially as the others had been and was given royal garments to put on. In the evening, at bedtime, he was led to the antechamber, and as he was preparing to go to bed the oldest daughter brought him a beaker of wine, but he had tied a sponge underneath his chin and let the wine run into it and didn't drink a single drop. Then he lay down, and after lying there a little while, he began to snore as if in a very deep sleep.

When the princesses heard his snoring, they laughed, and the oldest said: "He, too, could have saved his life."

After this they stood up, opened the closets, chests, and boxes, and took out splendid clothes. They groomed themselves in front of their mirrors and hurried about, eager to attend the dance. But the youngest said, "I don't know. You're all happy, yet I have a strange feeling. I'm sure that something bad is going to happen to us."

"You're a silly goose," said the oldest. "You're always afraid. Have you forgotten how many princes have already tried in vain? I didn't really need to give the soldier a sleeping potion. He'd never have awakened, even without it."

When they were all ready, they first took a look at the soldier, but he had shut his eyes tight, and since he neither moved nor stirred, they thought they were definitely safe. So the oldest went to her bed and knocked on it. Immediately it sank into the ground, and a trap door opened. The soldier watched them climb down through the opening, one after another, with the oldest in the lead. Since there was no time to lose, he got up, put on his little cloak, and climbed down after the youngest. Halfway down the stairs he stepped on her dress slightly, causing her to become terrified and cry out, "What's that? Who's holding my dress?"

"Don't be so stupid," said the oldest. "You've just caught it on a hook."

They went all the way down, and when they were at the bottom, they stood in the middle of a marvelous avenue of trees whose leaves were all made of silver and glittered and glimmered. "I'd better take a piece of evidence with me," the soldier thought, and broke off a branch, but the tree cracked and made a tremendous sound. Again the youngest cried out, "Something's wrong! Didn't you hear the noise? That never happened before."

But the oldest said, "That was just a burst of joy because we'll soon be setting our princes free from the curse."

Then they came to another avenue of trees, where all the leaves were made of gold, and finally to one where all the leaves were made of pure diamond. The soldier broke off branches from each kind, and each time there was a cracking sound that caused the youngest sister to be terrified. But the oldest maintained that they were just bursts of joy. They went on and came to a large lake with twelve boats on it, and in each boat sat a handsome prince. They had been waiting for the twelve princesses, and each one took a princess in his boat, while the soldier went aboard with the youngest princess. Then her prince said, "I don't understand it, but the boat is much heavier today. I'll have to row with all my might to get it moving."

"It's probably due to the warm weather," said the youngest. "I feel quite hot, too."

On the other side of the lake stood a beautiful, brightly lit palace, and sounds of merry music with drums and trumpets could be heard from it. They rowed over there, entered the palace, and each prince danced with his princess. The soldier danced invisibly as well, and whenever a princess went to drink a beaker of wine, he would drain it dry before it could reach her lips. The youngest sister was terribly anxious about this, too, but the oldest continued to quiet her down. They danced until three in the morning, when all the shoes were worn through and they had to stop. The princes rowed them back across the lake, and this time the soldier sat in the first boat with the oldest sister. The princesses took leave of their princes on the bank and promised to return the following night. When they reached the stairs, the soldier ran ahead of them and got into bed, and by the time the twelve princesses came tripping slowly and wearily up the stairs, he was again snoring so loudly that they said, "Well, we're certainly safe from him."

Then they took off their beautiful clothes, put them away, placed the worn-out shoes under their beds, and lay down to sleep. The next morning the soldier decided not to say anything but rather to follow and observe their strange life for the next two nights. Everything happened just as it had on the first night: they danced each time until their shoes were worn out. However, the third time he took a beaker with him for evidence. When the time came for him to give his answer, he took along the three branches and beaker and went before the king. The twelve princesses stood behind the door and listened to what he would say. When the king asked, "Where have my daughters spent the night wearing out their shoes," he answered, "With twelve princes in an underground palace." Then he told him everything and produced the evidence.

Immediately thereafter the king summoned his daughters and asked them whether the soldier had told the truth. When they saw that they had been exposed and that denying would not help, they had to confess everything. Finally, the king asked the soldier which princess he would like for his wife.

"I'm no longer so young," he answered, "so I'll take the oldest."

The wedding was held that same day, and the king promised to make him his successor to the kingdom after his death. The princes, however, were compelled to remain under a curse for as many nights as they had danced with the princesses.

48
THE SIX SERVANTS

An old queen, who was a sorceress, had a daughter, who was the most beautiful maiden under the sun. Whenever a suitor came to court her daughter, he would be given a task to perform, and if he failed, he had to kneel down, and his head would be cut off without mercy.

Now it so happened that there was a prince who wanted to court her, but his father refused to let him go and said: "No, if you go there, you won't return."

Then the son withdrew to his bed and became deathly ill for seven years. When the king saw that he might die, he said: "Go there. Perhaps you'll be fortunate."

As soon as he heard this, his son became well again. He got up from his bed and went on his way. As he was making his way across a forest, he saw a man lying on the ground. This man was enormously fat and actually seemed to be a small mountain. He called the prince over to him and asked him whether he wanted to have him as his servant.

"What can I do with such a fat man like you? How did you become so fat?"

"Oh, this is nothing. When I really want to expand, I'm three thousand times as fat."

"Well then, come with me," said the prince.

The two of them went farther and found another man, who was lying on the ground with his ear glued to the grass.

"What are you doing there?" asked the prince.

"Oh, I'm listening. I can hear the grass grow and everything that's happening in the world. That's why I'm called the listener."

"Tell me what's happening right now at the old queen's palace?"

"A suitor's having his head cut off. I hear the swishing of a sword."

"Come with me," the prince said, and the three continued on their way. All at once they came upon a man who was lying on the ground and was so very long that they had to go a good distance from his feet to reach his head.

"How come you're so long?" asked the prince.

"Oh," responded the tall man, "when I really stretch out my limbs, I'm three thousand times as long, taller than the highest mountain on earth."

"Come with me," said the prince.

So the four of them continued on their way and came across a blindfolded man sitting beside the road.

"Why are you wearing a blindfold?" the prince asked.

"Oh," the man responded, "I shatter whatever I gaze upon with my eyes. That's why I don't dare take off the blindfold."

"Come with me," the prince said.

So the five of them continued on their way and came upon a man lying on the ground basking under the hot sun, but he was freezing and shivered so much that his entire body was shaking.

"How can you be freezing this way in the sunshine?" asked the prince.

"Ah," answered the man, "the hotter it is, the more I freeze, and the colder it is, the hotter I am. In the middle of ice, I can't stand the heat, and in the middle of hot flames, I can't stand the cold."

"Come with me," said the prince, and the six of them continued on their way and came across a man standing there and looking around and over all the mountains.

"What are you looking at?" asked the prince.

"I have such sharp eyes," the man said, "that I can see over all the forests and fields, valleys and mountains, and throughout the whole world."

"Come with me," said the prince, "I can still use someone like you."

Now the seven of them entered the city where the beautiful and dangerous maiden lived, and the prince appeared before the old queen and told her that he wanted to court her daughter.

"All right," she said. "I'll give you three tasks. If you perform each one, then the princess is yours. For your first task you must bring back a ring that I dropped in the Red Sea."

"I shall perform this task," the prince said, and he summoned his servant, Sharp Eyes, who looked into the bottom of the sea and saw the ring lying next to a stone. Then Fat Man came and set his mouth down at sea level and let the waves roll into his mouth until he had swallowed the entire sea that became as dry as a meadow. Then Tall Man bent over a bit and fetched the ring with his hand. So the prince brought it to the old woman, who was astonished and said: "Yes, that's the right ring. You've performed the first task, but now you must perform the second. Do you see the three hundred oxen grazing on the meadow in front of my castle? You must devour them, skin and bones, hair and horns. Then, down in my cellar there are three hundred barrels of wine that you must drink up as well and may only invite one guest to eat and drink with you. If one trace of hair is left from the oxen or one little drop from the wine, then your life will be forfeited to me."

The prince replied: "I'll perform this task," and he took Fat Man as his guest. Well, he ate the three hundred oxen without leaving a single hair and proceeded to drink the wine right out of the barrels without the use of a glass.

When the old sorceress saw that, she was astounded and said to the prince, "No one has ever gotten this far, but there's still one task left." And she thought to herself, "I'll get you yet with my magic spell." Then she said aloud: "Tonight I'm going to bring my daughter into your room, and you're to put your arms around her. While you sit there with her, be sure not to fall asleep. I shall come at midnight, and if she's no longer in your arms, you'll forfeit your life."

"This task is easy," the prince thought. "I'll certainly be able to keep my eyes open. However, it's best to be cautious."

So when the beautiful maiden was brought to him in the evening, he summoned all his servants, and Tall Man had to embrace them with his arms while Fat Man had to block the door so that no living soul could enter. So they sat there, and the beautiful maiden didn't utter a word. However, the moon shone through the window on her face so that the prince could gaze at her marvelous beauty. They all kept watch together until eleven o'clock. Then the sorceress cast a spell on their eyes, and they fell into a slumber that they were unable ward off. So they slept soundly until a quarter of twelve. When they awoke, the maiden was gone and had been carried away by the old woman.

The prince and the servants moaned and groaned, but Listener said: "Be quiet!" And as he listened, he said: "She's being kept in a rock three hundred miles from here and is lamenting her fate."

Then Tall Man said: "I want to help."

All at once he lifted the blindfolded man Exploder onto his back, and in no time they were in front of the enchanted rock. As soon as Tall Man took off the blindfold, Exploder needed only to look around, and he shattered the rock into a thousand pieces. Tall Man lifted the maiden from the rock with his arms and carried her back in a split second. Just as the clock struck twelve, the old woman came, thinking that the prince would certainly be alone and deep in sleep. But there he was, in good spirits and with her daughter wrapped in his arms. Now, to be sure, the old woman had to keep quiet, but she was suffering, and the princess was also annoyed that someone like the prince was supposed to have won her. The next morning the sorceress had three hundred cords of wood gathered together and said to the prince that, even though he had performed the task, he couldn't have her daughter for his wife until someone was ready to sit in the middle of the woodpile and withstand the fire. She was convinced that none of his servants would let himself be burned for the prince's sake and that the prince would have to sacrifice himself on the woodpile out of love for her. Then the princess would be rid of him. But when the servants heard this, they said: "We've all done something with the exception of Frosty."

So they picked Frosty up and placed him in the middle of the pile of wood and set fire to it. Once the fire got going, it burned for three days, and when it was extinguished, Frosty stood in the middle of the ashes trembling like an aspen leaf and said, "Never in my life have I endured such a frost, and if it had lasted much longer, I'd have been frozen stiff."

Now the beautiful maiden had to marry the prince. Still, when they drove to the church, the old woman said, "I'll never give in," and she sent her soldiers to massacre them and to bring back her daughter. However, Listener had his ears perked and had heard everything that the old woman had said. Then he told Fat Man, who spat on the ground once or twice and formed a huge lake that stopped the soldiers.

When the soldiers didn't return, the old woman sent her knights in armor, but Listener heard the rattling of the armor and undid the blindfold of Exploder, who took a piercing look at the enemy, and they shattered like glass. Thus the prince and his bride could continue on their way undisturbed, and after the couple had been wed and blessed in church, the six servants took their leave and set out to seek their fortune in the world.

Half an hour from the prince's castle was a village, and, outside the village a swineherd was tending his pigs. When the prince and his wife arrived there, he said to her, "Do you know who I really am? I'm not the son of a king but a swineherd, and the man with the pigs over there is my father. You and I must now get to work and help my father look after the pigs."

The prince took lodgings at the inn and secretly told the innkeeper and his wife to take away his wife's royal clothes during the night. When she awoke the next morning, she had nothing to put on, and the innkeeper's wife gave her an old dress and a pair of woolen stockings. At the same time the woman acted as if she were giving the princess a grand gift. So the princess believed that the prince really was a swineherd and tended the pigs with him.

"I've deserved this because of my pride," she remarked.

All this lasted a week, by which time she could no longer stand it. Her feet had become all sore. Then some people came and asked her whether she knew who her husband was.

"Yes," she answered. "He's a swineherd, and he's gone out to do a little trading with ribbons."

Then they asked her to go with them, and they brought her up to the castle.

When they entered the hall, the prince was standing there in his royal attire, but she didn't recognize him until he embraced and kissed her and said, "I suffered a great deal for you, and it was only right that you should also suffer for me."

Now the wedding was truly celebrated, and the person who has told this tale would have liked to have been there, too.

49

THE WHITE BRIDE AND THE BLACK BRIDE

A woman was walking with her daughter and stepdaughter over the fields to cut fodder when the dear Lord came toward them in the guise of a poor man and asked, "Which is the way to the village?"

"Oh," said the mother, "look for the way yourself."

And her daughter added, "If you're worried about not finding it, then take a signpost with you."

However, the stepdaughter said, "Poor man, I'll show you the way. Come with me."

Since the mother and daughter had infuriated the dear Lord, he turned his back on them and cursed them so that they became black as night and ugly as sin. But God was gracious to the poor stepdaughter and went with her to the village. When they drew close to the village, he blessed her and said, "Choose three things for yourself, and I'll grant them to you."

The maiden said, "I'd like to be as beautiful and pure as the sun," and in no time she was as white and beautiful as the day.

"Then I'd like to have a money purse that is never empty," and the dear Lord gave her that as well but said, "Don't forget the best thing of all."

And she replied, "For my third wish, I want to live in the eternal kingdom of heaven after my death."

This wish was also granted, and then the Lord separated from her.

When the stepmother arrived home with her daughter and discovered that they were both as black as coal and ugly, while the stepdaughter was white and beautiful, her heart turned even more evil, and she could think of nothing but how she might harm her stepdaughter. However, the stepdaughter had a brother named Reginer, whom she loved very much, and she told him everything that had happened. One day Reginer said to her, "Dear sister, I want to paint your picture so that I may always see you before my eyes. My love for you is so great that I want to see you constantly."

"All right," she said, "but I beg of you not to let anyone else see the picture."

So he painted a portrait of his sister and hung it in his room, which was in the royal castle because he served the king as coachman. Every day he stood in front of the portrait and thanked God for his dear sister's good fortune.

Now it happened that the king's wife had just died, and she had been so beautiful that the king was greatly distressed because her equal couldn't be found anywhere. The court servants had noticed, however, that the coachman stood in front of a beautiful portrait every day, and since they envied him, they reported it to the king, who ordered the portrait to be brought to him. When he saw how the portrait resembled his wife in each and every way and was even more beautiful, he fell desperately in love with it. Consequently, he summoned the coachman and asked him whose portrait it was. The coachman said that it was his sister, and the king decided to marry no other woman but her. So he gave the coachman a carriage and horses and magnificent golden clothes and sent him to fetch his chosen bride.

When Reginer arrived with the news, his sister rejoiced, but the black maiden was jealous of her good fortune and became terribly annoyed. "What's the good of all your clever and artful ways," she said to her mother, "if you can't bring about such good luck for me?"

"Be quiet," said the old woman. "I'll soon make things turn your way."

And through her witchcraft she clouded the eyes of the coachman so that he became half blind, and she stopped up the ears of the white maiden so that she became half deaf. After this had been done, they climbed into the carriage, first the bride in her splendid royal garments, then the stepmother with her daughter, while Reginer sat on the box to drive. When they had gone some distance, the coachman cried out:

"Cover yourself, my sister dear,
don't let the rain get you too wet.
Don't let the wind blow dust on you.
Take care, for you must look your very best
when you appear at your king's request."

The bride asked, "What's my dear brother saying?"

"Ah," replied the old woman. "He said you should take off your golden dress and give it to your sister."

Then she took it off and put it on her sister, who gave her a shabby gray gown in return. They continued on their way, and after a while the brother called out again:

"Cover yourself, my sister dear,
don't let the rain get you too wet.
Don't let the wind blow dust on you.
Take care, for you must look your very best
when you appear at your king's request."

The bride asked, "What's my dear brother saying?"

"Ah," replied the old woman. "He said you should take off your golden bonnet and give it to your sister."

Then she took off the bonnet, put it on the black maiden, and sat with her hair uncovered. They continued on their way, and after a while her brother called out once more:

"Cover yourself, my sister dear,
don't let the rain get you too wet.
Don't let the wind blow dust on you.
Take care, for you must look your very best
when you appear at your king's request."

The bride asked, "What's my brother saying?"

"Ah," replied the old woman. "He said you should take a look out of the carriage."

Just then they happened to be crossing a bridge over a deep river. When the bride stood up and leaned out the window of the carriage, the other two pushed her out, and she fell into the middle of the water. At the very instant that she sank out of sight, a snow white duck arose out of the smooth glittering water and swam down the river. Since the brother hadn't noticed a thing, he kept driving until they reached the court. Then he brought the black maiden to the king as his sister and really thought it was her because his eyes were so clouded and he could only go by the glimmer of the golden clothes. When the king saw how abysmally ugly his intended bride was, he became furious and ordered the coachman to be thrown into a pit full of adders and snakes. Meanwhile, the old witch knew how to charm the king and deceive him through witchcraft so that he allowed her and her daughter to stay. Indeed, the daughter gradually appeared quite nice to him, and thus he actually married her.

One evening, while the black bride was sitting on the king's lap, a white duck swam up the drain to the kitchen and said to the kitchen boy:

"Light a fire, little boy, make it quick,
I need some warmth and can't get sick."

The kitchen boy did as he was asked and lit a fire on the hearth. Then the duck came and sat down next to the fire, shook herself, and cleaned her feathers with her beak. While she sat there and made herself comfortable, she asked,

"What's my brother Reginer doing?"
The kitchen boy answered:

"With snakes and adders in a pit,
that's where he's been forced to sit."

Then she asked,
"What's the black witch doing in the house?"
The kitchen boy answered:

"She's nice and warm, so very warm,
for the king has got her in his arms."

The duck said, "God have mercy!" and swam back down the drain.

The next evening she came again and asked the same questions, and on the third evening as well. The kitchen boy's heart couldn't bear this any longer. So he went to the king and revealed everything to him. Then the king went to the kitchen on the following evening, and when the duck stuck her head out through the drain, he took his sword and cut her head off by the neck. All at once she turned into a most beautiful maiden and looked exactly like the portrait that her brother had made of her. The king rejoiced, and since she was standing there soaking wet, he had fine clothes brought to her, which she put on. Then she told him how she had been thrown into the river. Her first request was to have her brother taken out of the snake pit, and this was done immediately. Then the king went into the room where the old witch sat and asked, "What kind of punishment does a woman deserve if she does something like the following?"

As he recalled all the past events, the black woman was so distracted that she didn't realize what was going on and said, "She deserves to be stripped naked and put into a barrel studded with nails. Then a horse should be hitched to the barrel and sent running out into the world."

This is what happened to her and her black daughter, while the king married the beautiful white bride and rewarded the faithful brother by making him a rich and respected man.

50

THE WILD MAN

Once upon a time there was a wild man who was under a spell, and he went into the gardens and wheat fields of the peasants and destroyed everything. The peasants complained to their lord and told him that they could no longer pay their rent. So the lord summoned all the huntsmen and announced that whoever caught the wild beast would receive a great reward. Then an old huntsman arrived and said he would catch the beast. He took a bottle of brandy, a bottle of wine, and a bottle of beer and set the bottles on the bank of a river, where the beast went every day. After doing that the huntsman hid behind a tree. Soon the beast came and drank up all the bottles. He licked his mouth and looked around to make sure everything was all right. Since he was drunk, he lay down and fell asleep. The huntsman went over to him and tied his hands and feet. Then he woke the wild man and said, "You, wild man, come with me, and you'll get such things to drink every day."

The huntsman took the wild man to the royal castle, and they put him into a cage. The lord then visited the other noblemen and invited them to see what kind of beast he had caught. Meanwhile, one of his sons was playing with a ball, and he let it fall into the cage.

"Wild man," said the child, "throw the ball back out to me."

"You've got to fetch the ball yourself," said the wild man.

"All right," said the child. "But I don't have the key."

"Then see to it that you fetch it from your mother's pocket."

The boy stole the key, opened the cage, and the wild man ran out.

"Oh, wild man!" the boy began to scream. "You've got to stay here, or else I'll get a beating!"

The wild man picked up the boy and carried him on his back into the wilderness. So the wild man disappeared, and the child was lost.

The wild man dressed the boy in a coarse jacket and sent him to the gardener at the emperor's court, where he was to ask whether they could use a gardener's helper. The gardener said yes, but the boy was so grimy and crusty that the others wouldn't sleep near him. The boy replied that he would sleep in the straw. Then early each morning he went into the garden, and the wild man came to him and said, "Now wash yourself, now comb your hair."

And the wild man made the garden so beautiful that even the gardener himself couldn't do any better. The princess saw the handsome boy every morning, and she told the gardener to have his little assistant bring her a bunch of flowers. When the boy came, she asked him about his home and family, and he replied that he didn't know them. Then she gave him a roast chicken full of gold coins. When he got back to the gardener, he gave him the money and said, "What should I do with it? You can use it."

Later he was ordered to bring the princess another bunch of flowers, and she gave him a duck full of gold coins, which he also gave to the gardener. On a third occasion she gave him a goose full of ducats, which the young man again passed on to the gardener. The princess thought that he

had money, and yet he had nothing. They got married in secret, and her parents became angry and made her work in the brewery, and she also had to support herself by spinning. The young man would go into the kitchen and help the cook prepare the roast, and sometimes he stole a piece of meat and brought it to his wife.

Soon there was a mighty war in England, and the emperor and all the great armies had to travel there. The young man said he wanted to go there, too, and asked whether they had a horse in the stables for him. They told him that they had one that ran on three legs that would be good enough for him. So he mounted the horse, and the horse went off, *clippety-clop*. Then the wild man approached him, and he opened a large mountain in which there was a regiment of a thousand soldiers and officers. The young man put on some fine clothes and was given a magnificent horse. Then he set out for the war in England with all his men. The emperor welcomed him in a friendly way and asked him to lend his support. The young man defeated everyone and won the battle, whereupon the emperor extended his thanks to him and asked him where his army came from.

"Don't ask me that," he replied. "I can't tell you."

Then he rode off with his army and left England. The wild man approached him again and took all the men back into the mountain. The young man mounted his three-legged horse and went back home.

"Here comes our hobbley-hop again with his three-legged horse!" the people cried out, and they asked, "Were you lying behind the hedge and sleeping?"

"Well," he said, "if I hadn't been in England, things wouldn't have gone well for the emperor!"

"Boy," they said, "be quiet, or else the gardener will really let you have it!"

The second time, everything happened as it had before, and the third time, the young man won the whole battle, but he was wounded in the arm. The emperor took his kerchief, wrapped the wound, and tried to make the boy stay with him.

"No, I'm not going to stay with you. It's of no concern to you who I am."

Once again the wild man approached the young man and took all his men back into the mountain. The young man mounted his three-legged horse once more and went back home. The people began laughing and said, "Here comes our hobbley-hop again. Where were you lying asleep this time?"

"Truthfully, I wasn't sleeping," he said. "England is totally defeated, and there's finally peace."

Now, the emperor talked about the handsome knight who provided support, and the young man said to the emperor, "If I hadn't been with you, it wouldn't have turned out so well."

The emperor wanted to give him a beating, but the young man said, "Stop! If you don't believe me, let me show you my arm."

When he revealed his arm and the emperor saw the wound, he was amazed and said, "Perhaps you are the Lord Himself or an angel whom God has sent to me," and he asked his pardon for treating him so cruelly and gave him a whole kingdom.

Now, the wild man was released from the magic spell and stood there as a great king and told his entire story. The mountain turned into a royal castle, and the young man went there with his wife, and they lived in the castle happily until the end of their days.

51
THE THREE BLACK PRINCESSES

East India was besieged by an enemy that would not withdraw until it first received a ransom of six hundred gold coins. So it was announced in public that whoever could provide the money would become mayor. There was at that time a poor fisherman who was fishing at sea with his son. The enemy came, took the son prisoner, and gave the fisherman six hundred gold coins for him. The father then went and gave the money to the lords of the city. The enemy departed, and the fisherman became mayor. Thereafter it was proclaimed that whoever did not address him as "Lord Mayor" would be hanged on the gallows.

The son escaped from the enemy and made his way to a large forest on a high mountain. The mountain opened, and he went into a large enchanted castle, where all the chairs, tables, and benches were draped in black. Then three princesses appeared. They were clad entirely in black but had a little white on their faces. They told him not to be afraid, for they wouldn't harm him, and he could rescue them. He replied that he would gladly do so if only he knew how. They told him he was not to speak to them for one whole year, nor was he to look at them. If he wanted anything, he just had to ask for it, and if they were permitted to answer his questions, they would do so.

After he had been there for a long time, he said that he would like to go and see his father. They told him that he could go, but he was to take a purse of money with him, put on certain clothes, and return in a week. Then he was lifted into the sky, and before he knew it, he was in East India. However, his father was no longer in the fishing hut, so the son asked some people where the poor fisherman was. They told him that he must not call him that or he would be taken to the gallows. Then he went to his father and said, "Fisherman, how did you get here?"

"You mustn't call me that," the father replied. "If the lords of the city hear you say that, you'll be taken to the gallows."

However, he wouldn't stop saying it and was taken to the gallows. When he got there, he said, "My lords, grant me permission to go to the fishing hut."

Once there, he put on his old fisherman garb, and then he returned to the lords and said, "Don't you see now that I'm the poor fisherman's son? This was the way I dressed when I earned a living for my mother and father."

They recognized him then and apologized and took him home with them. The son told them everything that had happened, how he got to the forest on a high mountain, how the mountain had opened, and how he had entered an enchanted life where everything was black and where three young princesses had come to him, all in black except for a little white on their faces, and how the princesses had told him not to be afraid, and that he could save them. His mother warned him this might not be a good thing to do and told him to take a consecrated candle with him and to let some of its hot wax drop on their faces.

The son returned to the castle and was so fearful that he let the wax drop on their faces while they slept, and they all turned half white. The three princesses jumped up and cried, "You cursed dog, our blood shall cry out for vengeance! There is no man born now anywhere nor ever will be who can save us. But we still have three brothers bound by seven chains, and they will tear you to pieces."

All at once there was a shrieking throughout the castle, and he jumped out a window and broke his leg. The castle sank back into the earth, the mountain closed, and nobody knows where the castle once stood.

52
KNOIST AND HIS THREE SONS

Between Werrel and Soist there lived a man named Knoist, and he had three sons. One was blind, the other was lame, and the third was stark naked. Once they were walking across a field and saw a hare. The blind one shot it. The lame one caught it, and the naked one stuck it into his pocket. Then they came to a tremendously large lake with three boats on it. One boat leaked, the other sank, and the third had no bottom to it. They went aboard the boat with no bottom. Then they came to a tremendously large forest, where they saw a tremendously large tree. In the tree was a tremendously large chapel, and in the chapel was a hornbeam sexton and a boxwood pastor, who dispensed holy water with cudgels.

Blessed is he who gets away
when the holy water comes his way.

53
THE MAIDEN FROM BRAKEL

Once there was a maiden from Brakel who went to Saint Anne's Chapel at the foot of the Hinnenberg. Since she wanted a husband and thought that nobody else was in the chapel, she sang:

"Holy Saint Anne,
please help me get my man.
Oh, you know him, I'm sure.

He lives down by the Suttmer Gate;
his hair is yellow and very pure.
Oh, you know him well. I'm very sure."

The sexton was standing behind the altar and heard her. So he called out in a shrill voice, "You won't get him, you won't get him!"

The maiden thought that it was the child Mary standing beside Mother Anne who had spoken. Hence, the maiden became angry and replied, "*Tra-la-la,* you stupid brat! Hold your tongue and let your mother speak."

54
THE DOMESTIC SERVANTS

"Where are you going?"

"To Woelpe."

"I'm going to Woelpe, you're going to Woelpe. So then, let's go together."

"Do you also have a husband? What's his name?"

"Chain."

"My husband's named Chain, yours is Chain. I'm going to Woelpe, you're going to Woelpe. So then, let's go together."

"Do you also have a child? What's he called?"

"Scab."

"My child's called Scab. Yours is Scab. My husband's Chain. Yours is Chain. I'm going to Woelpe. You're going to Woelpe. So then, let's go together."

"Do you also have a cradle? What's your cradle called?"

"Hippodeige."

"My cradle's called Hippodeige. Yours is Hippodeige. My child's Scab. Yours is Scab. My husband's Chain. Yours is Chain. You're going to Woelpe. I'm going to Woelpe. So then, let's go together."

"Do you also have a servant? What's your servant called?"

"Do-It-Right."

"My servant's Do-It-Right. Your servant's Do-It-Right. My cradle's Hippodeige, yours is Hippodeige. My child's Scab, yours is Scab. My husband's Chain, your husband's Chain. I'm going to Woelpe, you're going to Woelpe. So then, let's go together."

55

LITTLE LAMB AND LITTLE FISH

Once upon a time there was a little brother and a little sister who loved each other with all their hearts. However, their real mother was dead, and they had a stepmother who wasn't good to them and secretly did all she could to hurt them. It happened that one day the two of them were playing with other children in a meadow in front of the house, and in the meadow was a pond that bordered on one side of the house. The children ran around it, caught each other, and played a counting-out game:

> "Eenie, meenie, let me live,
> my little bird to you I'll give.
> The bird will pick up straw for me.
> The straw I'll give the cow to eat.
> The cow will make me lots of milk.
> I'll give the baker all the milk,
> who'll bake my cat a cake so nice,
> and then the cat will catch some mice.
> The mice I'll hang and let them smoke
> before I take one big slice!"

As they played this game they stood in a circle, and when the word *slice* landed on one of them, he had to run away, and the others ran after him until they caught him. While they were merrily running around, the stepmother watched from the window and became annoyed. Since she understood witchcraft, she cast a spell on the brother and sister and turned the little brother into a fish and the little sister into a lamb. The little fish swam about in the pond and was sad. The little lamb ran about in the meadow and was so distressed that she ate nothing. She wouldn't even touch a blade of grass.

A long time passed, and strangers came as guests to the castle. The treacherous stepmother thought, "Now's the time." So she called the cook and said to him, "Go and fetch the lamb from the meadow and slaughter it. Otherwise, we'll have nothing for the guests."

The cook went to the meadow, got the little lamb, led her to the kitchen, and tied her feet. The lamb bore all this patiently. As the cook took his knife and began to sharpen it on the doorstep in order to kill the lamb, she noticed a little fish swimming back and forth in the water in front of the gutter and looking up at her. It was her little brother, for when he had seen the cook leading the little lamb away, he had swum along in the pond up to the house. Then the little lamb called to him:

"Oh, brother in the pond so deep,
my heart is torn, and I must weep.
The cook's about to take his knife
and bring an end to my short life."

The little fish answered:

"Oh, sister way up high,
you make me sad and want to cry,
while in this pond I swim and sigh."

When the cook heard that the little lamb could speak and was uttering such sad words to the little fish down in the pond, he became frightened and thought, "The lamb must not be a real one but one that the wicked woman in the house cursed." Then the cook said, "Don't worry. I won't slaughter you."

So he took another animal and prepared it for the guests. Then he brought the little lamb to a kind peasant woman and told her everything he had seen and heard. The woman happened to have been the wet nurse of the little girl and guessed at once who the lamb was and went with her to a wise woman. There the wise woman pronounced a blessing over the little lamb and the little fish so that they soon regained their human forms. Afterward she took both of them to a little cottage in a large forest, where they lived by themselves but were content and happy.

SESAME MOUNTAIN

There once were two brothers, one rich and the other poor. The rich one, however, gave nothing to the poor brother, who barely supported himself by dealing in grain. Things often went so badly for him that his wife and children would have to go without food.

One day, as he was going through the forest with his wheelbarrow, he noticed a large, bare mountain off to the side. Since he had never seen it before, he stopped in amazement and gazed at it. While he was standing there, twelve big and wild-looking men came toward him. Since he thought that they might be robbers, he pushed his wheelbarrow into the bushes, climbed a tree, and waited to see what would happen. The twelve men went up to the mountain and cried, "Sesame Mountain, Sesame Mountain, open up."

Immediately, the bare mountain opened in the middle, and the twelve men entered. Once they were inside, the mountain closed. After a short while, however, it opened up again, and the men came out carrying heavy sacks on their backs. After they were all out in the open, they said, "Sesame Mountain, Sesame Mountain, close up."

Then the mountain closed, and there was no longer a single trace of an entrance. The twelve men departed, and when they were completely out of sight, the poor man climbed down from the tree, curious to know what secret things might be hidden in the mountain. So he went up to the mountain and said, "Sesame Mountain, Sesame Mountain, open up," and the mountain opened before him. Then he entered, and the entire mountain was a cavern filled with silver and gold, and in the back there were large piles of pearls and glistening jewels heaped on top of each other like grain. The poor man didn't know what to do or whether he should take any of the treasure. Finally, he filled his pockets with gold, but he left the pearls and jewels lying there.

When he came out again, he repeated the words "Sesame Mountain, Sesame Mountain, close up." Then the mountain closed, and he went home with his wheelbarrow. Now his worries disappeared, and he could buy bread and even wine for his wife and children. He lived happily and honestly, gave to the poor, and was kind to everyone. However, when he ran out money, he went to his brother, borrowed a bushel measure, and fetched more gold. But he refrained from touching any of the great treasures. When he needed some more gold a third time, he borrowed the bushel measure from his brother once again. But the rich man had long been jealous of his brother's good fortune and the beautiful way he had built his house. Indeed, he had been puzzled by his brother's sudden wealth and wondered why he needed a bushel measure. So he thought of a way to trick him and covered the bottom of the measure with sticky wax. When the measure was returned to him, there was a gold coin stuck to it. So he immediately went to his brother and asked him, "What have you been doing with the measure?"

"I've been measuring wheat and barley," said the brother.

Then the rich brother showed him the gold coin and threatened to take him to court about this unless he told him the truth. So the poor brother revealed to him how everything had happened. Consequently, the rich brother had a wagon hitched up at once and drove to the mountain with the idea of taking greater advantage of this wonderful opportunity than his brother had by fetching quite different treasures. When he arrived at the mountain, he cried out, "Sesame Mountain, Sesame Mountain, open up." The mountain opened, and he went inside, where he found all the treasures in front of him. For a long time he couldn't make up his mind what to grab first. Finally, he took as many jewels as he could carry, and when he was about to leave with his load of jewels, his heart and mind became so occupied by the treasure that he forgot the name of the mountain and called out, "Simelei Mountain, Simelei Mountain, open up." But that was not the right name, and the mountain didn't budge and remained closed. Then he became frightened, but the more he tried to recall the name, the more confused his thoughts became, and the treasures were of no use to him at all. That evening the mountain opened up, and the twelve robbers entered. When they saw him, they laughed and cried out, "Well, we've finally caught our little bird! Did you think we hadn't noticed that you had slipped in here three times? Maybe we weren't able to catch you then, but you won't escape us now."

The rich man screamed, "It wasn't me, it was my brother!"

But no matter what he said, no matter how he pleaded for his life, they wouldn't listen, and they cut off his head.

57
THE CHILDREN OF FAMINE

Once upon a time there was a woman with two daughters, and they had become so poor that they no longer had even a piece of bread to put in their mouths. Their hunger became so great that their mother became unhinged and desperate. Indeed, she said to her children, "I've got to kill you so I can have something to eat!"

"Oh, dear mother," said one daughter, "spare me, and I'll go out and see if I can get something without begging."

So the girl went out and came back carrying a little piece of bread, which they shared with one another. But it was not enough to still their hunger. Therefore, the mother spoke to the other daughter, "Now it's your turn to die."

"Oh, dear Mother," she answered, "spare me and I'll go and get something to eat from somewhere else without anyone noticing me."

This daughter, too, went away and came back carrying two little pieces of bread. They shared it with one another, but it was not enough to still their hunger. Therefore, when a few hours had gone by, their mother said to them once more, "You've got to die or else we'll waste away."

"Dear mother," they responded, "we'll lie down and sleep, and we won't get up again until the Judgment Day arrives."

So they lay down and fell into a deep sleep, and no one could wake them from it. Meanwhile, their mother departed, and nobody knows where she went.

58
THE LITTLE DONKEY

There once lived a king and queen who were rich and had everything they desired except children. The queen lamented day and night because of this, saying, "I'm like a field on which nothing grows."

Finally, God fulfilled her wishes. However, when the baby was born, it didn't look like a human child but like a young little donkey. When the mother saw it, she really began to lament and screamed that she would rather have had no child at all than to have had a donkey, and she ordered the donkey to be thrown into the water so the fish could eat him up.

But the king said, "No. Since God has given him to us, then he shall be my son and heir. After my death he shall sit on the royal throne and wear the royal crown."

So the little donkey was brought up at court. As he got bigger, his ears also grew quite high and straight. Otherwise, he had a cheerful disposition, was frisky, played, and was especially fond of music. At one time he went to a famous minstrel and said, "Teach me your art so that I can play the lute as well as you."

"Ah, my dear young lord," answered the minstrel, "this will be difficult for you. Your fingers aren't really made for it. They are much too big, and I'm afraid you'd break the strings."

Yet the little donkey would not be dissuaded, for he was determined to learn how to play the lute. Since he was diligent and persistent, he eventually learned how to play as well as the master himself.

One day the young lord was in a contemplative mood and went out for a walk. He came to a spring and looked at his little donkey figure reflected in the water, which was as clear as a mirror. He was so distressed by the sight that he decided to go out into the world and to take only one trusted companion with him. So they wandered here and there and finally came to a country ruled by an old king who had just one daughter, who was exceedingly beautiful. The little donkey said, "This is where we shall stay awhile," and he knocked on the gate and cried out: "There's a guest out here! Open up and let him in."

When the gate didn't open, he sat down, took his lute, and began playing a lovely tune with his two forefeet. The keeper's eyes opened in astonishment, and he ran to the king and said, "There's a little donkey sitting outside the gate. It's playing the lute like a great expert."

"Then let the musician come in," said the king.

When the little donkey entered, however, everyone began to laugh at the lute player. He was directed to sit down with the servants, but he refused and said, "I'm not a common barnyard donkey. I'm of noble birth."

"If this is what you are," they said, "then sit down with the knights."

"No," he said. "I'll sit with the king."

The king laughed, showed his good humor, and said: "Indeed, let it be the way you want, little donkey. Come here to me." And soon after, he asked, "Little donkey, how do you like my daughter?"

The little donkey turned his head, looked at her, nodded, and said, "Exceptionally well. I've never seen anyone so beautiful as she is."

"Well, you shall sit next to her," said the king.

"That's fine with me," said the donkey, and sat down next to her, ate and drank, and showed that he could conduct himself in a courteous and proper manner.

After the noble animal had spent quite some time at the court, he thought, "What's the use of all this? I've got to go home." He lowered his head sadly, went before the king, and asked his permission to depart. However, the king had taken a great liking to him and said, "My little donkey, what's the matter with you? You look as sour as a jug of vinegar. Stay with me. I'll give you anything you demand. Do you want gold?"

"No," said the donkey and shook his head.

"Do you want some fine, valuable things?"

"No."

"Do you want half my kingdom?"

"Ah, no."

"If only I knew what would make you happy," said the king. "Do you want my beautiful daughter for your wife?"

"Oh, yes," said the donkey. "I'd be delighted to have her for my wife," and suddenly he was quite cheerful and in good spirits, for that was exactly what he had desired.

Soon a huge and splendid wedding was held, and that night, when the bride and bridegroom were led to their bedchamber, the king wanted to know whether the donkey would conduct himself in a nice and polite manner, and he ordered a servant to hide himself in their room. When the two were inside, the bridegroom bolted the door and looked around. Once he was convinced that they were completely alone, he threw off the donkey skin, and all at once he stood there as a handsome young prince.

"Now you see who I am," he said, "and you also see that I'm worthy of you."

The bride was happy, gave him a kiss, and loved him with all her heart. When morning came, he jumped up, put on his donkey skin again, and nobody would have guessed what lay beneath it.

Soon the old king came along.

"Goodness!" he cried. "The donkey's already wide awake." Then, turning to his daughter, he said, "You probably regret that you weren't wed to a real man, don't you?"

"Oh, no, father, I love him as if he were the handsomest man in the world, and I want to keep him for the rest of my life."

The king was puzzled by this, but then the servant, who had concealed himself, came to him and told him everything.

"I don't believe it," said the king.

"Well, keep tonight's watch yourself, and then you shall see it with your own eyes. My advice to you, your Majesty, is to take his skin away from him and throw it into a fire. Then he'll certainly have to reveal himself in his true form."

"That's good advice," said the king, and that night, while they were sleeping, he crept into their room, and when he came to their bed, he saw a noble-looking young man resting in the moonlight and the skin lying discarded on the ground. So he took it away and ordered a tremendous fire to be made outside. Then he threw the skin into the fire and remained there until it was entirely burned to ashes. Since he wanted to see what the young man would do when he discovered the theft, he stayed awake the whole night and lay in wait. When the young man had slept his fill, he got up with the first rays of the sun and wanted to put on his donkey skin, but he couldn't find it anywhere. So he was horrified and overcome by sadness and dread. "Now I must find some way to flee," he said.

However, when he left the room, the king was standing there and said, "My son, why are you in such a hurry? What do you intend to do? Stay here. You're such a handsome man, and I don't want you to leave. I'll give you half my kingdom now, and after my death you'll get all of it."

"Well," said the young man, "since I wish everything that began well to end well, I'll stay with you."

Then the old man gave him half the kingdom, and when he died a year later, the young man had all of it. After the death of his own father, he received yet another kingdom and lived in happiness and wealth.

59
THE UNGRATEFUL SON

Once a man and his wife were sitting by the entrance to their house. They had a roasted chicken in front of them and were about to eat it when the man saw his father coming toward them. So the man quickly grabbed the chicken and hid it because he didn't want to give him any. The old man came, had a drink, and went away. As the son reached to put the roasted chicken back on the table, he found that it had turned into a large toad, which then sprang onto his face, sat right on it, and wouldn't leave him. If anyone tried to take it off, the toad would look at the person viciously as if it wanted to spring right into his face, too. So nobody dared touch it. And the ungrateful son had to feed the toad every day, otherwise, it would have eaten away part of his face. Thus the son wandered aimlessly all over the world.

60
THE TURNIP

Once upon a time there were two brothers, both of whom served as soldiers. One was rich; the other, poor. Since the poor brother wanted to improve his circumstances, he left the army and became a farmer. He dug and hoed his little piece of ground and planted turnip seeds. As the turnips began to grow, one became large and strong and noticeably fatter than the others. It seemed as if it would not stop growing at all. Soon it was called the queen of all turnips because nobody had ever seen one like it, nor will anybody ever see one like it again. At last it became so large that it filled an entire wagon by itself, and two oxen were needed to pull it. The farmer had no idea what to do with the turnip, nor did he know whether it would bring him luck or misfortune. Finally, he thought, "If I sell it, I won't get anything worth much. And, if I eat it, you might as well eat the small turnips, which are just as good. The best thing would be to bring it to the king. That way I can honor him with a gift."

So he loaded the turnip on his wagon, hitched up two oxen, brought it to court, and gave it to the king.

"What kind of a rarity do we have here?" asked the king. "I've seen many strange things in my life, but I've never seen such a monstrosity as this. What kind of a seed did it grow from? Or do you have a green thumb and are lady fortune's favorite son?"

"Oh, no," the farmer replied. "I'm not fortune's favorite son. I'm just a poor soldier who gave up the army life because I could no longer support myself. Now I've taken up farming. You probably know my brother, your Majesty. He's rich, but nobody pays attention to me because I have nothing."

Then the king took pity on him and said, "You shall be relieved of your poverty and shall receive such gifts from me that will make you the equal of your brother."

So he gave him a great deal of gold, fields, meadows, and herds, and made him so terribly rich that his brother's wealth could no longer match his at all. When the brother heard what he had acquired with a single turnip, he became jealous and pondered ways to get fortune to smile on him, too. However, he wanted to do everything in a more clever way. So he took gold and horses and brought them to the king, for he was firmly convinced that the king would give him a much larger present in return. After all, if his brother had obtained so much for a turnip, he would certainly get many more beautiful things.

The king accepted his gifts and said that he could think of nothing better or rarer to give him than the large turnip. So the rich brother had the turnip loaded on his wagon and driven to his home. Once there he didn't know how to vent his anger and frustration. Finally, some evil thoughts came to him, and he decided to kill his brother. He hired murderers and showed them a place where they were to ambush his brother. Afterward he went to his brother and said, "Dear brother, I know where to find a secret treasure. Let's dig it up and divide it among us."

The brother liked the idea and went with him without suspecting a thing. However, when they went outside, the murderers fell upon him, tied him up, and were about to hang him from a tree when they heard loud singing and hoofbeats in the distance. They became frightened for their lives and hastily shoved their prisoner head over heels into a sack. Then they hoisted it up on a branch and fled. However, the brother went to work and made a hole in the sack through which he could poke his head. Then who should happen upon the way but a wandering scholar, a young fellow, riding along the road through the forest and singing a merry song. When the man up in the tree noticed that someone was passing below, he cried out, "Welcome! You've come just at the right time."

The scholar looked all around him but couldn't detect where the voice was coming from. Finally, he said, "Who's calling me?"

The man in the tree answered from above, "Lift your head. I'm sitting up here in the sack of wisdom, where I've learned great things in only a short time. Compared to this, all schools are like a bag of hot wind. Soon I shall have learned all there is to know. Then I'll climb down from the tree and be wiser than all other human beings. I understand the stars and the signs of the zodiac; the movements of the wind, the sand, and the sea; the cures for sickness; and the power of herbs, birds, and stones. If you would spend some time in the sack just once, then you'd know the glorious feeling that flows from the sack of wisdom."

When the scholar heard all this, he was astounded and said, "Blessed be this hour in which I have found you! Would it be possible for me to get into the sack for a little while?"

The man in the tree answered as if he didn't like this idea. "I'll let you do it for a short time if you pay me and speak sweetly, but you'll have to wait another hour because there's still something more that I have to learn."

The student waited a little while, but he became impatient and begged to be let in because his thirst for knowledge was so overwhelming. After he waited a while, the man in the tree pretended to relent and said, "In order for me to leave the house of wisdom, you must lower the sack by the rope. Then you may climb in."

So the scholar lowered the sack, untied it, and set the man free. Next he cried out, "Now pull me up quickly," and he sought to get into the sack feet first.

"Stop!" said the other. "That's not the way."

He grabbed the scholar's head and shoved him upside down into the sack. After that he tied the sack and hoisted the disciple of wisdom up the tree by the rope. Then he swung him back and forth in the air and said, "How's it going, my dear fellow? You see, I'm sure you already feel wisdom coming and are getting valuable experience. Sit there nice and quiet until you get wiser."

Upon saying this, he mounted the scholar's horse and rode away.

61
THE REJUVENATED LITTLE OLD MAN

At the time that our Lord still walked on the earth, he was with Saint Peter and stopped one evening at the house of a blacksmith and received lodging for the night. Now, it happened that a poor beggar, suffering greatly from old age and illness, entered this house and asked for alms from the blacksmith. Saint Peter took pity on him and said, "Lord and Master, may it please you, cure him of his sufferings so he can earn his own living."

Then the Lord said gently to the blacksmith, "Lend me your forge, and put some coals on the fire. I want to make this sick old man young again."

The blacksmith was quite willing, and Saint Peter pumped the bellows, and when the fire sparkled and was in full blaze, the Lord took the little old man and shoved him into the forge, right in the middle of the glowing fire, so that he became as red as a rosebush and praised God in a loud voice. Afterward the Lord stepped over to the water tub and dunked the glowing little man in it so that he was completely covered by the water, and when he was nice and properly cooled off, the Lord gave him his blessing. Then, lo and behold, the little man jumped out of the tub and was sound, upright, and fit as a young man of twenty.

The blacksmith, who had watched everything closely and carefully, invited everyone to supper. His old, half-blind, hunchbacked mother-in-law now went over to the rejuvenated man and asked him earnestly whether the fire had burned him badly. He answered that he had never felt better and that the flames had been like the cool morning dew.

The young man's words kept ringing in the ears of the old woman all night, and early the next morning, after the Lord had thanked the blacksmith and had gone on his way, it occurred to the blacksmith that he could make his mother-in-law young since he had watched everything very carefully, and it had involved the skills of a blacksmith. Therefore, he called his mother-in-law to see whether she wanted to walk sprightly again like a girl of eighteen.

Well, since everything had turned out so well for the young man, she said, "With all my heart."

So the blacksmith made a big fire and shoved the old woman into the forge. She wriggled this way and that and cried bloody murder.

"Sit still! Why are you crying and jumping around? I haven't pumped the bellows enough yet," cried the blacksmith.

Upon saying this, he pumped the bellows again until all her rags caught fire. The old woman wouldn't stop shrieking, and the blacksmith thought, "This isn't working out quite right." So he pulled her out and threw her into the water tub. Then she screamed so loudly that the blacksmith's wife and daughter-in-law heard it upstairs in the house. They both ran downstairs and saw the old woman, who was lying doubled-up in pain and howling and groaning. Her wrinkled and shriveled face had lost its shape.

At the sight of this the two women, who were both with child, became so upset that they gave birth that very night to two babies who were not shaped like human beings but like apes. They ran off into the forest, and it is from them that we have the race of apes.

62

THE ANIMALS OF THE LORD AND THE DEVIL

The Lord God had created all the animals and had selected the wolves for his dogs. However, he had forgotten to create the goat. Then the devil got ready to create as well and made goats with fine long tails. Yet, when they went out to graze, they usually caught their tails in the briar bushes, and the devil always had to go to the trouble of disentangling them from the bushes. Finally, he became so fed up that he went and bit off the tail of each goat, as you can still see today by their stumps.

Now he could let them graze alone. But it happened that the Lord God saw how they soon took to gnawing away at the fruit trees. Then they damaged the precious vines and spoiled other tender plants. He became so disturbed by this that, out of kindness and mercy, he set his wolves upon them, and they soon tore apart the goats that went there. When the devil learned of this, he appeared before the Lord and said, "Your creatures have torn mine apart."

The Lord replied, "Why did you create them to do damage?"

"I couldn't help it," said the devil. "Just as my own inclinations tend toward destruction, my own creatures can have no other nature but this. So now you'll have to pay me compensation."

"I'll pay you as soon as the oak leaves fall. Come to me then, and your money will be ready."

After the oak leaves had fallen, the devil came and demanded his due. But the Lord said, "In the Church at Constantinople there's a tall oak tree that still has all its leaves."

The devil departed, cursing in rage, and began to search for the oak tree. He wandered about in the wilderness for six months before he found it, and when he returned, all the other oak trees were covered with green leaves again. So he had to forget about his compensation. In his anger he poked out the eyes of the remaining goats and replaced them with his own.

This is why all goats have devil's eyes and bitten-off tails, and why the devil likes to appear in their shape.

63
THE BEAM

Once upon a time there was a magician who stood in the middle of a large crowd of people and performed marvelous tricks. Among other things, he made a rooster appear, lift a heavy beam, and carry it as though it were as light as a feather. However, there was a girl who had just found a four-leaf clover, and it made her so clever that she could see through any kind of deception. Consequently, she saw that the beam was nothing but a straw, and she cried out, "Don't you people see that the rooster's carrying a mere piece of straw and not a beam?"

As soon as she said this, the magic vanished, and the people saw what was what and chased the magician away, with scorn and contempt. However, he was filled with rage and said, "I'll get my revenge."

Time passed, and the girl was about to be married. She got dressed up and marched through the fields in a large procession to the village where the church was. All at once, the procession came to a brook overflowing its banks, and there was no bridge or plank to cross it. The bride, however, was quick to react. She lifted her skirts and started to wade. When she got to the middle of the water, a man, who was standing nearby, called to her. It was the magician, and he began mocking her. "Hey! What's the matter with your eyes? You don't think that this is actually a brook, do you?"

Her eyes flew wide open, and she saw that she was standing in the middle of a field of blue flax in full bloom with her skirts raised high. Then everyone else saw this too, and they chased her away with their jeers and laughter.

64
THE OLD BEGGAR WOMAN

Once upon a time there was an old woman. Of course, you've seen old women go begging before. Well, this woman begged, too, and whenever she got something, she said, "May God reward you."

Now, this beggar woman went up to a door where a friendly young rascal was warming himself inside by a fire. As she stood shivering at the door, the youngster spoke kindly to the old woman, "Come in, grandma, and warm yourself."

She entered but went too close to the fire so that her old rags began to burn without her noticing it. The youngster stood there and watched. He should have put out the fire, don't you think? Don't you think so? And even if there was no water at hand, he should have wept out all the water in his body through his eyes. That would have made for two nice streams of water, and with that he could have extinguished the fire.

65
THE THREE LAZY SONS

A king had three sons, and since he loved them equally, he didn't know which to choose to be king after his death. When the time of his death drew near, he summoned them to his bedside and said, "Dear children, I've been contemplating something for a while, and now I want to reveal it to you: I've decided that the laziest among you shall become king after me."

"Well then, father," said the oldest, "the kingdom belongs to me, for I'm so lazy that when I'm lying on my back and want to sleep and a drop of rain falls on my eyes, I won't even shut them so I can fall asleep."

The second said, "Father, the kingdom belongs to me, for I'm so lazy that, when I'm sitting by the fire to warm myself, I'd sooner let my heels be burned than draw back my feet."

The third said, "Father, the kingdom is mine, for I'm so lazy that, if I were about to be hanged and the noose were already around my neck and someone handed me a sharp knife to cut the rope, I'd rather let myself be hanged than lift my hand to cut the rope."

When the father heard that, he said, "You've outdone the others and shall be king."

66
SAINT SOLICITOUS

Once upon a time there was a pious maiden who swore to God she wouldn't marry. Since she was so remarkably beautiful, her father wouldn't accept this and tried to force her to marry. Confronted with this predicament, the maiden implored God to let her grow a beard, and this happened right away. But the king was so enraged that he had her crucified, and she became a saint.

Now, it so happened that a very poor minstrel went into the church where her statue was kept. He knelt down in front of it, and the saint was glad that the minstrel was the first one to recognize her innocence. Consequently, the statue, which was adorned with golden slippers, let one slipper drop to the ground so the pilgrim could have it. He bowed in gratitude and took the gift.

Soon the people in the church became aware that the golden slipper was missing, and questions were asked all around until finally the slipper was found on the poor fiddler. He was now condemned as a wicked thief and led to the gallows to be hanged. The procession went by the church where the statue was standing, and the fiddler requested permission to go inside, pour out his heart to his benefactress with his fiddle, and say his last farewell. His request was granted, but no sooner had he moved his bow than—behold!—the statue let the other golden slipper drop to the ground and thus demonstrated that he had not committed the theft. So the irons and rope were taken off the fiddler, who went merrily on his way. From then on the holy saint was called Solicitous.

67
THE TALE ABOUT THE LAND OF COCKAIGNE

In the days of the land of Cockaigne I went and saw Rome and the Lateran hanging from a small silk thread. There was also a man without feet who outran a fast horse, and a keen-edged sword that sliced a bridge in two.

Then I saw a young ass with a silver nose chasing after two quick hares, and a large linden tree grew hotcakes. I saw a scrawny old goat carrying a hundred cartloads of fat on its body and sixty loads of salt. Now, haven't I lied enough? Then I saw a plow tilling the ground without horse or ox, and a one-year-old child threw four millstones from Regensburg to Trier and from Trier to Strasbourg, and a hawk swam across the Rhine, which he had a perfect right to do. Then I heard some fish make such a noise together that their clamor reached all the way to heaven, and sweet honey flowed like water from a deep valley to the top of a high mountain. All this was quite strange. Then there were two crows mowing a meadow, and I saw two gnats building a bridge, while two doves tore a wolf to pieces. Two children gave birth to two goats, and two frogs threshed grain together. Then I saw two mice consecrating a bishop and two cats scratching out a bear's tongue. Then a snail came and killed two wild lions. There was also a barber who shaved a woman's beard off, and two sucking babes who told their mother to keep quiet. Then I saw two greyhounds dragging a mill out of the water, and an old, worn-out horse stood there and said that it was all right. And in the courtyard there were four horses threshing grain with all their might, and two goats were heating the stove, and a red cow shoved the bread into the oven. Then a chicken crowed, "*Cock-a-doodle doo!* The tale is done, *cock-a-doodle-doo!*"

68

THE TALL TALE FROM DITMARSH

I want to tell you something. I saw two roasted chickens flying swiftly with their breasts turned toward heaven, their backs toward hell. An anvil and a millstone swam across the Rhine very slowly and softly, and a frog sat on the ice and ate a plowshare at Pentecost. There were three fellows on crutches and stilts who wanted to catch a hare. One was deaf, the second blind, the third dumb, and the fourth couldn't move his feet. Do you want to know how they did it? Well, first the blind one saw the hare trotting over the field. Then the dumb one called to the lame one, and the lame one caught the hare by the collar. There were some men who wanted to sail on land. They set their sails in the wind and sailed across the wide fields. As they sailed over a high mountain, they were miserably drowned. A crab chased a hare, making it flee, and high on a roof was a cow who had climbed on top of it. In that country the flies are as large as the goats here.

69
A TALE WITH A RIDDLE

Three women were turned into flowers that stood in a field. However, one of them was permitted to spend the night in her own home. Once, as dawn drew near and she had to return to her companions in the field to become a flower again, she said to her husband, "If you come and pick me this morning, I'll be set free, and I'll be able to stay with you forever."

And this is exactly what happened.

Now the question is how her husband was able to recognize her, for the three flowers were all the same without any distinguishing mark. Answer: Since she had spent the night in her house and not in the field, the dew had not fallen on her as it had on the other two. This is how her husband was able to recognize her.

70
THE GOLDEN KEY

During winter, when the snow was once very deep, a poor boy had to go outside and gather wood on a sled. After he had finally collected enough wood and had piled it on his sled, he decided not to go home right away because he was freezing so much. Instead, he thought he would make a fire to warm himself up a bit. So he began scraping the snow away, and as he cleared the ground, he discovered a golden key. "Where there's a key," he thought, "there must also be a lock." So he dug farther into the ground and found a little iron casket. "If only the key will fit!" he thought, for

there were bound to be wonderful and precious things in the casket. He searched but couldn't find a keyhole. Finally, he found a very tiny one and tried the key, which fit perfectly. So he turned the key around once, and now we must wait until he unlocks the casket completely. That's when we'll see what's lying inside.

LIST OF CONTRIBUTORS AND INFORMANTS

Wherever possible the dates and professions of the contributors have been indicated.

Achim von Arnim (1781–1831), important romantic novelist and short-story writer and close friend of the Grimms, who provided a contact to the Berlin publisher of the first edition of *Kinder- und Hausmärchen*.

Clemens Brentano (1778–1842), romantic poet and writer of fairy tales, who encouraged the Grimms to collect numerous folk tales published in the first edition. The Grimms sent him a manuscript of approximately fifty-four tales in 1810 that they used and edited in the first edition of 1812/15. Brentano left the manuscript in the Ölenberg Monastery in Alsace, and it was first discovered in 1920.

Maria Anna ("Jenny") von Droste-Hülshoff (1795–1859), member of the Bökendorfer Circle. She and her younger sister, Annette von Droste-Hülshoff, one of the finest poets of the nineteenth century, were close friends of the von Haxthausen family. They were very familiar with all kinds of folk tales, and Jenny, who was very attached to Wilhelm, sent him numerous tales.

Johanna Christiane Fulda (1785–?), one of the sisters in the Wild family, who contributed a couple of tales to the collection.

Georg August Friedrich Goldmann (1785–1855), a personal friend and minister in Hannover, who sent the Grimms several different versions of tales from Hannover.

Anne Grant, author of *Essays on the Superstitions of the Highlanders of Scotland* (1811).

Albert Ludwig Grimm (1786–1872), writer of fairy tales, teacher, and author of *Kindermährchen* (1808). No relation to the Brothers Grimm.

Ferdinand Grimm (1788–1845), the fourth of the five Grimm brothers, who often assisted the Grimms in their research and contributed one tale to the first edition.

He was considered the black sheep of the family, held various positions, and published some books of popular literature.

Georg Philipp Harsdörffer (1607–58), Baroque writer and poet, who published *Der grosse Schau-Platz jämmerlicher Mord-Geschichten* in 1649.

Hassenpflug family, a magistrate's family in Kassel with a Huguenot background, very close friends of the Grimms. Dorothea Grimm married Ludwig Hassenpflug, and the Hassenpflugs as a group provided numerous tales for the Grimms, many of which stemmed from the French literary and oral tradition.

Marie Hassenpflug (1788–1856).

Jeanette Hassenpflug (1791–1860).

Amalie Hassenpflug (1800–1871).

Von Haxthausen family, whose estate in Westphalia became the meeting place for the Bökendorfer Circle. Contact was first made with the von Haxthausen family when Jacob made the acquaintance of Werner von Haxthausen in 1808. A warm friendship developed between the Brothers Grimm and most of the Haxthausens in the ensuing years. Most of the members of the family had a vast knowledge of folk literature. Ludowine and Anna von Haxthausen sent many dialect tales to the Grimms that were never published in any of the editions. These tales were found in the posthumous papers of the Grimms. The von Haxthausen sisters were intent on fulfilling the Grimms' principle of fidelity to the spoken word.

Marianne von Haxthausen (1755–1829).

August von Haxthausen (1792–1866).

Ludowine von Haxthausen (1795–1872).

Anna von Haxthausen (1800–1877).

Ludovica Jordis-Brentano (1787–1854), a sister of the German romantic writer Clemens Brentano. She lived in Frankfurt am Main and provided the Grimms with two tales.

Johann Heinrich Jung-Stilling (1740–1817), whose significant autobiography *Heinrich Stillingsjugend* (1777) and *Heinrich Stillings Junglingsjahre* (1778) contained tales that the Grimms used in their collection.

Friedrich Kind (1768–1843), German poet and librettist, who wrote the libretto for Carl Maria Weber's opera, *Der Freischütz*.

Fräulein de Kinsky, a young woman from Holland, who contributed one tale to the first edition.

Heinrich von Kleist (1777–1811), writer, poet, dramatist, and journalist, who published a version of "Wie Kinder Schlachtens mit einander gespielt haben," in the *Abendblatt* (October 13, 1810).

Johann Friedrich Krause (1747–1828), a retired soldier who lived near Kassel and exchanged his tales with the Grimms for leggings.

Friederike Mannel (1783–1833), daughter of a minister in Allendorf, who sent several fine tales through letters to Wilhelm Grimm.

Martin Montanus (1537–66), writer and dramatist, who published *Wegkürzer*, a collection of comic anecdotes in 1557.

Johann Karl Augustus Musäus (1735–87), writer and author of one of the first significant collections containing adapted legends and folk tales, *Volksmährchen der Deutschen* (1782–87).

Johannes Pauli (1455–ca. 1530), a Franciscan writer and author of *Schimpf und Ernst* (1522).

Johannes Praetorius (1630–80), author of *Wünschelruthe* (1667) and *Der abentheurliche Glückstopf* (1669).

Charlotte R. Ramus (1793–1858) and Julia K. Ramus (1792–1862), daughters of Charles François Ramus, head of the French reform evangelical church in Kassel and friends of the Grimms in Kassel. They belonged to the circle of friends that provided the Grimms with numerous tales; they also put the Grimms in contact with Dorothea Viehmann.

Philipp Otto Runge (1777–1810), famous romantic painter, who lived in Hamburg. He provided two dialect tales.

Friedrich Schulz (1762–98), author of *Kleine Romane* (1788–90). A popular writer whose full name was Joachim Christoph Friedrich Schulz, and his story, "Rapunzel," was published in volume 5 of *Kleine Romane* in 1790.

Hans Sachs (1494–1576), leader of the Nürnberg Meistersinger and prolific author of folk dramas, tales, and anecdotes.

Johann Balthasar Schupp (1610–61), satirical writer and author of *Fabul-Hanß* (1660).

Ferdinand Siebert (1791–1847), teacher and pastor in the nearby city of Treysa. He studied with the Grimms at the University of Marburg and later contributed several tales to the Grimms' collection.

Andreas Strobl (1641–1706), author of *Ovum paschale oder neugefärbte Oster-Ayr* (1700).

Dorothea Viehmann (1755–1815), wife of a village tailor in Zwehren near Kassel. The Grimms considered her to be the exemplary "peasant" storyteller.

Anton Viethen and Johann Albert Fabricius (1668–1736), authors of *Beschreibung und Geschichte des Landes Dithmarschen* (1733).

Paul Wigand (1786–1866), close friend of the Brothers Grimm, who studied with them in Kassel. Aside from "The Three Spinners," Wigand contributed nineteen legends to the Grimms' *Deutsche Sagen* (1816–18).

Wild family, a pharmacist's family in Kassel, who were all very close to the Grimm family. Wilhelm eventually married Henriette Dorothea (Dortchen) Wild, who supplied the brothers with numerous tales.

Dorothea Catharina Wild, mother (1752–1813).
Lisette Wild (1782–1858).
Johanna Christiane (Fulda) Wild (1785–?).
Margarete Marianne (Gretchen) Wild (1787–1819).
Marie Elisabeth (Mie, or Mimi) Wild (1794–1867).
Henriette Dorothea (Dortchen) Wild (1795–1867).

Martin Zeiler (1589–1661), Baroque writer, who published a version of "Wie Kinder Schlachtens mit einander gespielt haben" in *Miscellen* (1661).

NOTES TO VOLUMES I AND II

Since there is a fair amount of extraneous material in the Grimms' scholarly notes, I have summarized what I consider to be the most substantial information and translated the variants to the tales. In addition, I have provided the names of the sources for each tale wherever possible. For readers interested in learning more about the Grimms' informants and sources, I recommend the following books.

Rölleke, Heinz. *"Wo das Wünschen noch geholfen hat."* *Gesammelte Aufsätze zu den "Kinder- und Hausmärchen" der Brüder Grimm*. Bonn: Bouvier, 1985.

———. *Die Märchen der Brüder Grimm: Quellen und Studien*. Trier: Wissenschaftlicher Verlag Trier, 2000.

———, ed. *Es war einmal . . . Die wahren Märchen der Brüder Grimm und wer sie ihnen erzählte*. Illustr. Albert Schindehütte. Frankfurt am Main: Eichorn, 2011.

Uther, Hans-Jörg. *Handbuch zu den "Kinder- und Hausmärchen der Brüder Grimm: Entstehung—Wirkung—Interpretation*. Berlin: Walter de Gruyter, 2008.

———. "Die Brüder Grimm als Sammler von Märchen und Sagen." In *Die Grimms— Kultur und Politik*. Ed. Bernd Heidenreich and Ewald Grothe. 2nd rev. ed. Frankfurt am Main: Societäts-Verlag, 2008. 81–137.

Volume I

1. The Frog King, or Iron Henry (Der Froschkönig oder der eiserne Heinrich). Source: Wild family.

There is a handwritten moralistic version that predates the 1812 story and can be found in the Ölenberg Manuscript of 1810. It was changed and edited by Wilhelm Grimm for the first edition of 1812. The Grimms considered this tale to be one of the oldest and most beautiful in German-speaking regions, and it was often given the title

"Iron Henry," named after the faithful servant. The Grimms refer to various versions from the Middle Ages and Renaissance in which a loyal servant binds his heart with iron straps so that it will not break when he learns his master has been cast under a spell. More important for the Grimms, however, was a Scottish version by John Bellenden in the book *Complayant of Scotland* (1548), published in 1801 by John Leyden. The Grimms included Leyden's comment to "The Well at the World's End" in their note because Leyden claimed to have heard fragments in various songs and folk tales. It reads as follows:

> According to the popular tale a lady is sent by her stepmother to draw water from the well of the worlds end. She arrives at the well, after encountering many dangers; but soon perceives that her adventures have not reached a conclusion. A frog emerges from the well, and before it suffers her to draw water, obliges her to betroth herself to the monster, under the penalty of being torn to pieces. The lady returns safe; but at midnight the frog-lover appears at the door, and demands entrance, according to promise to the great consternation of the lady and her nurse.

> "open the door, my hinny, my hart,
> open the door, mine ain wee thing;
> and mind the words that you and I spak
> down in the meadow, at the well-spring!"

> the frog is admitted, and addresses her:

> "take me up on your knee, my dearie,
> take me up on your knee, my dearie,
> and mind the words that you and I spak
> at the cauld well sae weary."

> the frog is finally disenchanted and appears as a prince in his original form.

In general, the Grimms were already very familiar with the Scottish and Celtic oral tradition of folk tales in 1812 and continued to give examples of these tales in their notes up through 1857.

2. The Companionship of the Cat and Mouse (Katz und Maus in Gesellschaft). Source: Margarete Marianne Wild.

The Grimms cite another tale in their notes about the Little Rooster and the Little Hen, who find a jewel in a dung heap. They sell it to a jeweler, who gives them a pot of fat in exchange, and the pot is placed in a cupboard. Gradually, the Little Hen eats the fat until the pot has been emptied. When the Little Rooster discovers this, he becomes so furious that he pecks the Little Hen to death. Afterward, the Little Rooster regrets killing the Little Hen, and so he buries her in a mound of dirt. But his grief is so unbearable that he eventually dies from it.

3. The Virgin Mary's Child (Marienkind). Source: Margarete Marianne Wild.

The Grimms cite similarities to the legend about Saint Ottilie—in particular, how the story was recounted in Benedikte Naubert's *Neue Volksmährchen der Deutschen* (*New German Tales*, 1789–93). In addition, they discuss the motif of the forbidden door, which one can find in numerous tales such as "Bluebeard" and "The Little Shroud" or in Giambattista Basile's "Marchetta." Finally, they provide an interesting variant, which reads as follows:

A poor man cannot provide for his children and goes into the forest where he intends to hang himself. All at once a black coach drawn by four black horses arrives, and a lady dressed in black climbs out of the coach and tells him that he will find a sack with money in a bush in front of his house. In exchange for this money he is to give her whatever is hidden in the house. The man agrees and finds the money. However, that which is hidden is the child in his wife's body. And when the child is born, the lady comes and wants to fetch the baby. But since the mother pleads so much with her, the lady permits her to keep the child until she turns twelve. Then, however, she takes the maiden away to a black castle, where everything is splendid. The young girl is allowed to go wherever she wants and enter all the rooms except for one particular chamber. The maiden obeys for four years, but then she can no longer resist the torment of curiosity and looks through a crack in the door. She sees four ladies dressed in black, who are absorbed in reading books. At that moment her foster mother appears and frightens her. She takes the maiden and says to her: "I must banish you. What do you prefer to lose most of all?" "Speech," the maiden answers. Then the lady slaps her on her mouth so that blood gushes forth, and the lady drives the maiden away. The young girl must spend the night beneath a tree, and in the morning a prince finds her, takes her with him, and marries the beautiful mute maiden against his mother's wishes. When she gives birth to her first child, the wicked mother-in-law throws the baby into a river, splashes blood on the sick young queen, and claims that the queen had eaten her own child. This happens with two more children, and the inno- cent young queen, who cannot defend herself, is to be burned at the stake. She is already standing in the fire when suddenly the black coach comes, and the lady steps out. She goes directly into the flames, which die down. Finally, she walks up to the young queen and slaps her on the mouth, thereby returning the power of speech to her. The three other ladies dressed in black bring the queen's three children, whom they had saved from the river. The mother-in-law's treachery is revealed, and she is stuck into a barrel filled with snakes and poisonous vipers. Then she is rolled down a hill in the barrel.

4. Good Bowling and Card Playing (Gut Kegel- und Kartenspiel). Source: Based on a ballad in Philippine Engelhard's *Spukenmährchen* (Ghost Tales, 1782).

This unusual story was replaced by "A Tale about the Boy Who Went Forth to Learn What Fear Was" in the 1819 edition.

5. The Wolf and the Seven Kids (Der Wolf und die sieben jungen Geißlein). Source: Hassenpflug family.

The Grimms note that this tale has deep roots in France, and they cite Jean de La Fontaine's fables, published between 1668 and 1694 as well as Gilles Corrozet's earlier version "Le loup, la chevre et le chevreau," in *Les fables du très ancien Esope, mises en rithme françoise* (1542), in which the wolf is never allowed to gain entrance into the house of the goats. However, the Grimms explain that this animal tale is much older and can be found in Ulrich Bonner's *Edelstein* (ca. 1350). In addition, they trace the origins of the tale to the great tradition of fables in the Greco-Roman period.

6. The Nightingale and the Blindworm (Von der Nachtigall und der Blindschleiche). Source: Thomas Philippe-Légier, *Mémoires de l'Académie celtique* (1808).

The Grimms translated this animal tale and later omitted it from their collection because of its French origins.

7. The Stolen Pennies (Von dem gestohlenen Heller). Source: Margarete Marianne Wild.

8. The Hand with the Knife (Die Hand mit dem Messer). Source: Anne Grant of Laggan, *Essays on the Superstitions of the Highlanders of Scotland* (1811).

Jacob Grimm translated and adapted one of Grant's folk tales (songs) and quotes her: "One of these (stories) that I have heard sung by children at a very early age, and that is just to them the Babes in the wood, I can never forget. The affecting simplicity of the tune, the strange wild imagery and the marks of remote antiquity in the little narrative, gave it the greatest interest to me, who delight in tracing back poetry to its infancy."

9. The Twelve Brothers (Die zwölf Brüder). Source: Julia and Charlotte Ramus.

The Grimms cite Giambattista Basile's "Li sette palommielle" (The Seven Little Doves) in *Il Pentamerone* (1632–34).

10. Riffraff (Das Lumpengesindel). Source: August von Haxthausen.

11. Little Brother and Little Sister (Brüderchen und Schwesterchen). Source: Marie Hassenpflug.

The Grimms relate that they also knew a fragmentary version:

One day a brother and sister go into the forest, and since the sun is so hot and the trail so long, the brother becomes thirsty. Brother and sister search for water and arrive at a spring where there is a sign that reads: "Whoever drinks from me will become a tiger if he is a man, or a lamb if she is a woman." Immediately the maiden says: "Oh, dear brother, don't drink from this spring, otherwise you'll become a tiger and tear me to pieces." The brother responds by saying that he will wait until they reach the next spring even though he is suffering from thirst. However, when they come to the next spring, there is another sign that reads: "Whoever drinks from me will become a wolf." Once again the maiden says: "Dear, oh dear brother, don't drink, otherwise you'll eat me." And the brother replies: "Once more I shall control my thirst, but I can't do this for much longer." And they come to a third spring where there is a sign that reads: "Whoever drinks from me will become a golden deer if it is a man. If it is a maiden, she will become full grown and beautiful." All at once the brother leans over and drinks and is changed into a golden deer. The maiden also drinks and becomes even more beautiful and all grown-up. Then she ties a rope around the deer and leads him away. The king sees the wonderful deer and has him captured. The maiden stays with him and is overheard one time by the king as she is speaking with the deer. He learns that she is the sister of the golden deer. Then the king marries her. However, the king's mother is jealous and wants to ruin her life. She transforms the maiden so that she becomes ugly and has her killed, and she also has the deer slaughtered by a butcher. However, the maiden's innocence is revealed. The mother-in-law is placed into a barrel with sharp knives and rolled down a hill.

12. Rapunzel (Rapunzel). Source: Friedrich Schulz, "Rapunzel," in *Kleine Romane* (1790).

This tale was edited by Jacob Grimm, and there may be some influence by Giambattista Basile's "Petrosinella" (*Il Pentamerone*, 1634), which the Grimms mention in their note. The Grimms believed that Schulz's tale derived from the oral tradition. However, it is clear that he may have taken some motifs from the French writer Mlle de la Force's "Persinette" in *Les contes des contes* (1698).

13. The Three Little Men in the Forest (Die drei Männlein im Walde). Source: Henriette Dorothea Wild.

The Grimms also refer to a similar motif of three little men in an anonymous Danish song.

14. Nasty Flax Spinning (Von dem bösen Flachsspinnen. Source: Jeanette Hassenpflug.

The literary source was a tale in Johannes Praetorius's *Der abentheuerliche Glücks-topf* (1669). The Grimms summarized Praetorius's tale in their notes this way:

A mother cannot motivate her daughter to spin, and because of this she often slaps her. One time a man sees the mother slapping her daughter and asks why she is doing this. The mother answers: "Oh, I can't stop her from spinning. She spins more flax than I can produce." The man says: "Well then, let me marry her. I'll certainly be satisfied with her untiring hard work, even if there's not much of a dowry." The mother is very glad to do this and is content, and the bridegroom brings his bride immediately to a large supply of flax. The maiden is horrified by this, but she accepts the supply of flax and brings it into her chamber, where she ponders what she should do. At that moment three old women pass by her window: one whose behind is so wide that she can't fit through the door to the room, the second has a gigantic nose, the third has a thick thumb. They offer the maiden their services and promise to spin the flax for her only if the bride doesn't show that she is ashamed of them on her wedding day and pretends that they are her aunts and allows them to sit at her table. The maiden agrees to the conditions. The women spin the flax, and the bridegroom praises the bride. When the day of the wedding arrives, the three repulsive women are also present. The bride honors them and calls them her aunts. The bridegroom is astonished and asks how she could have struck up a friendship with such horrible women. "Oh," says the bride, "all three of them have become the way they are through spinning. One of them developed a big rear through sitting. The second licked her lips so much that they wasted away. That's why her nose sticks out so much. The third turned the spindle much too much with her thumb." Upon hearing this the bridegroom becomes gloomy and says to his bride that she is not to spin anymore thread for the rest of her life to prevent her from becoming a monster like the three women.

The Grimms also remark that they knew a similar oral tale that was told in Corvey.

15. Hansel and Gretel (Hänsel und Gretel). Source: Based on various anonymous stories from Hesse and possibly an oral tale told by Henriette Dorothea Wild.

However, it is clear from their note that the Grimms were also aware of two literary tales: Giambattista Basile's "Ninnillo and Nennella," *Pentamerone* (1634), and Charles Perrault's "Le Petit Poucet," *Histoires ou contes du temps passé* (1697).

16. Herr Fix-It-Up (Herr Fix und Fertig). Source: Johann Friedrich Krause.

The Grimms discuss a similar tale, Giovan Francesco Straparola's "Livoret," *Le piacevoli Notti* (1550).

17. The White Snake (Die weiße Schlange). Source: Hassenpflug family.

The Grimms wrote in their note that "the tales about talking birds that give advice to humans and announce their fate are too numerous to be dealt with here. Humans learn the language of the birds generally in two ways: (1) through eating the heart of a dragon, for example, Siegfried; or (2) through eating the heart of a white snake as depicted here and in a strange Hanoverian tale from Seeburg that we shall publish elsewhere. Another appropriate version that completely belongs here is an old Nordic tale about Kraka and her two sons, Roller and Erich."

18. The Journey of the Straw, the Coal, and the Bean (Strohhalm, Kohle und Bohne auf der Reise). Source: From Kassel, perhaps Dorothea Catharina Wild.

The Grimms mention a medieval Latin poem from a manuscript in Strasbourg. In this story a mouse and a piece of coal travel together on a pilgrimage to confess their sins in a church. When they cross a little brook, the coal falls into the water, hisses, and expires. They also allude to Aesop's fable about the thorn bush, diver, and bat.

19. The Fisherman and His Wife (Von den Fischer und siine Fru). Source: Philipp Otto Runge's tale written in a Pomeranian dialect.

The Grimms were also aware of and influenced by other versions in the works of Johann Gustav Gottlieb Büsching, Albert Ludwig Grimm, and Karl Philipp Conz. They summarize a version that was popular in Hesse as follows:

> The tale concerns the little man Dominé (also called Hans Dudeldee) and his little wife Dinderlindé. Dominé complains about his misfortune and goes out to the sea, where a little fish sticks its head out of the water.
> "What's the matter with you my little man Dominé?"
> "Oh, it really hurts to live in a piss pot."
> "Well, then wish for something else."
> "First I've got to tell all this to my wife."
> So he goes home.
> "Wish us a better house," says Dinderlindé.
> When he returns to the sea, Dominé cries out:
> "Little fish, little fish in the sea!"
> "What do you want little man Dominé?"
> Now the wishing begins, and there are many. First the house, then a garden, an ox and a cow, fields, and so on. Then all the treasures of the world. When they have wished for everything possible, the little man says: "Now I'd like to be the dear lord God himself and my wife the mother of God."
> Then the little fish sticks its head out of the water and cries out:
>
> "If you want to be the dear lord God,
> Go back and live once more in your piss pot."

The Grimms note that the motif of the wife who pushes her husband to higher honors and ranks is certainly ancient—Eve, and from the Etruscan Tanaquil (Livius) up to Lady Macbeth.

20. A Story about a Brave Tailor (Von einem tapfern Schneider). Source: The first version was taken from Martin Montanus's *Wegkürzer* (1557), and the second fragmentary tale is an oral tale from the Hassenpflug family.

The Grimms knew several other versions, and they printed the complete text of a Dutch tale, "Van kleyn Kobisje," in their note.

21. Cinderella (Aschenputtel). Source: This tale was obtained orally from a female patient in the Elisabeth-Hospital in Marburg and written down by the wife of the director of the hospital.

The Grimms note that the tale is among the most popular tales in Europe and was told everywhere. They spend a goodly amount of time discussing the different ways that Cinderella (dirty common girl) was referred to in dialect tales (Aschenpößel,

Asken pel, Askenpüster, Askenböel, Askenbüek, Aschen pöselken, Sudelsödelken, and Aschenpuddel) and in High German tales (Aschenpuddel, Aschenbrödel, and Aescherling). In the second part of the note, there are references to Giambattista Basile's "Cenerentola" (1634), Charles Perrault's "Cendrillon" (1697), and Madame d'Aulnoy's "Finette Cendron" (1698), as well as Polish and Slavic versions. Clearly, the Grimms were familiar with numerous versions that influenced the changes that they made in their tale over the years.

22. How Some Children Played at Slaughtering (Wie Kinder Schlachtens mit einander gespielt haben). Source: The first tale is from Heinrich von Kleist, *Abendblatt* (October 13, 1810); the second, from Martin Zeiler, *Miscellen* (1661).

23. The Little Mouse, the Little Bird, and the Sausage (Von dem Mäuschen, Vögelchen und der Bratwurst). Source: Clemens Brentano in *Badische Wochenschrift* (July 11, 1806).

24. Mother Holle (Frau Holle). Source: Henriette Dorothea Wild.

The Grimms begin their note by relating another version with which they were familiar:

Once upon a time there was a woman who only loved her own daughter and didn't love her stepdaughter. One day she sat both daughters down at the edge of a well, where they were to spin. Then she said, "If either of you lets her distaff drop down the well, I'll throw you into the water." After that she tied her daughter's distaff to her firmly and tied her stepdaughter's distaff loosely. No sooner did the stepdaughter begin to spin than her distaff fell into the water. The stepmother was merciless and threw her into the water. The maiden fell deep down into the well's water and came to a gorgeous garden and entered a house where nobody was to be found. As she entered the kitchen, the soup was about to boil over, the roast meat about to burn, and the cake about to turn black in the oven. She quickly took the kettle of soup away from the fire; she poured some water onto the roast meat; and she took out the cake and set it right. Even though she was very hungry, she didn't touch a thing except for some crumbs that fell onto the floor while she was setting the cake right. Soon thereafter a nixie came into the kitchen. Her hair was terrible, and it certainly had not been combed for over a year. So the nixie demanded that the maiden comb her hair, but she was not to pluck one strand of her hair nor pull a single hair. The maiden was able to perform all this and finish the combing with great skill. Now the nixie told her that she would have liked to have kept her there, but she couldn't because the maiden had eaten some crumbs. However, she gave her a ring as a gift and some other things. If the maiden turned the ring during the night, the nixie would come to her aid. Now, the other daughter was thrown down the well to the nixie. However, she did everything the opposite way and didn't control her hunger. Consequently, she was sent back home with poor presents.

According to the Grimms, Benedikte Naubert published a very good version of this tale in *Neue Volksmährchen der Deutschen* (*New German Tales*, 1789–93). They also cite Gabrielle-Suzanne de Villeneuve's tale, "The Water Nymphs or the Water Nixies," which had served as the basis for one of the Grimms' tales ("Murmelthier," or marmot) in their Ölenberg Manuscript. The Grimms remark that

> Ciron, who is called Marmotte, must do the dirtiest work—she must look after the sheep and, while doing this, she must bring home a certain amount of spun thread. The maiden frequently sits down at the edge of a well, and one day she wants to wash her face and falls into the well. When she regains consciousness, she finds herself in a crystal ball in the hands of a beautiful lady of the well. She must comb this lady's hair, and as a reward she receives a precious dress. Whenever she shakes her hair and combs it, glistening flowers fall, and she will find help when she needs it. Then the lady gives the maiden a shepherd's staff, which protects her from wolves and robbers; a spindle and a distaff that spin by themselves; and finally a tame beaver, which can be sent off to do many different chores. When Marmotte returns home with these gifts in the evening, the other daughter is sent to gain the same gifts. She jumps down into the well and winds up in muddy water, and because she is so spiteful, stinking canes and reeds grow on her head, and whenever she tears one out, many more replace it. Only Marmotte can comb out the ugly things from her stepsister's hair, but then they return after twenty-four hours, and Marmotte must comb them out again.

Marmotte has other adventures following this, and other tales are used to show her in danger, but she is always saved by magic things, and her dilemmas are all fortunately resolved.

The Grimms remark that similar versions can be found in a collection of tales in Braunschweig and also in Giambattista's *Pentamerone*.

25. The Three Ravens (Die drei Raben). Source: Hassenpflug family and Clemens Brentano.

The Grimms discuss various medieval versions and Arthurian romances with a focus on the motifs of the glass mountain and the end of the world. They begin their note with a summary of key incidents pertaining to the plot of tales with the glass mountain:

> There was once an enchanted princess who could only be released from the magic spell if somebody climbed the glass mountain, the place to which she had been banished. At one time a young journeyman arrived at an inn to have his lunch, and he was served a cooked chicken. He carefully collected all the chicken bones, stuck them in a sack, and went to the glass mountain. When he arrived at the mountain, he took a little bone and stuck it into the mountain and climbed up on it. Then he

took another bone, and one bone after another, using them as spikes to climb the mountain until he was about to reach the top when he ran out of the little chicken bones. So he sliced off his little pinky and stuck it into the glass mountain. This is how he finally reached the top and rescued the princess.

The Grimms point to other episodes like this in old Nordic literature and Arthurian stories as well as a rabbinical myth about Shamir. They close their note with a tale that stems from Plutarch and Menander and that can be compared to an Aesopian fable:

One time the moon said to his mother: "The nights are so cold, and I am freezing. Make a warm coat for me!"

So she took his measurements, and he ran off. However, when he returned, he had become so big that the little coat didn't fit him at all. Consequently, his mother began to separate the thread and let out the coat, but all this work was taking too long for the moon, and he went off again. Meanwhile his mother worked hard on the coat and often sat up late at night and sewed in the light of the stars. After the moon had run about a great deal, he returned. Due to all the running, he had lost a good deal of weight and had become slight and pale. The coat was now much too wide for him, and the sleeves hung loosely over his knees. His mother became angry because he had made a fool out of her, and she forbade him from returning home anymore. This is why the poor mischief maker must run around naked and pale in the sky until somebody comes and buys him a little coat.

26. Little Red Cap (Rothkäppchen). Source: Johanna (Jeanette) Hassenpflug and Marie Hassenpflug.

The Grimms mention the versions of Charles Perrault and Ludwig Tieck. They wonder why they had not come across other versions.

27. Death and the Goose Boy (Der Tod und der Gänshirt). Source: Georg Harsdörffer, *Der grosse Schau-Platz jämmerlicher Mord-Geschichten* (1649).

28. The Singing Bone (Der singende Knochen). Source: Henriette Dorothea Wild and/or Johanna Christiane Fulda.

The Grimms note that there is an old Scottish song in which the motif of the talking bone is key. A harpist makes a harp from the breastbone of a drowned sister. The harp plays by itself and expresses grief about the death of the sister.

29. The Devil with the Three Golden Hairs (Von dem Teufel mit drei goldenen Haaren). Source: Amalie Hassenpflug.

The Grimms also mention Johann Gustav Gottlieb Büsching's version, "Märchen vom Pompanz," in *Volks-Sagen, Märchen und Legenden* (1812). However, they reprimand him for stating that his tale emanated from an oral tradition. They point to ways he changed and added elements from a French book. They also claim that their version is closer to the oral tradition and more pure.

30. Little Louse and Little Flea (Läuschen und Flöhchen). Source: Dorothea Catharina Wild.

31. Maiden without Hands (Mädchen ohne Hände). Source: Marie Hassenpflug.

The Grimms note the significance of the fifteenth-century legends of *La belle Hélene de Constantinople*, which were often published in chapbooks. They also cite Giambattista Basile's "La Penta mamomozza" ("The Maiden without Hands") in *Il Pentamerone* (1634).

32. Clever Hans (Der gescheidte Hans). Source: The first version was provided by the Hassenpflug family; the second version was taken from Martin Montanus, *Gartengesllschaft* (1557).

The Grimms also mention Giambattista Basile's "Vardiello," *Il Pentamerone* (1634).

33. Puss in Boots (Der gestiefelte Kater). Source: Jeanette Hassenpflug.

The Grimms also refer to Giovan Francesco Straparola, "Constantino Fortunato" in *Le Piacevoli Notti* (1550/53); Giambattista Basile, "Cagliuso" in *Il Pentamerone* (1634–36); Charles Perrault, "The Master Cat, or Puss in Boots" ("Le Maître chat ou Le Chat botté") in *Histoires ou contes du temps passé* (1697); and Ludwig Tieck's drama, *Der gestiefelte Kater* (1697).

34. Hans's Trina (Hansens Trine). Source: Unknown.

35. The Sparrow and His Four Children (Der Sperling und seine vier Kinder). Source: Johann Balthasar Schupp, *Fabul-Hanß* (1660).

36. The Little Magic Table, the Golden Donkey, and the Club in the Sack (Von dem Tischchen deck dich, dem Goldesel und dem Knüppel in dem Sack). Source: Johanna Isabella Hassenpflug and Henriette Dorothea Wild.

The Grimms mention a similar tale in Giambattista Basile's *Il Pentamerone* (1634–36).

37. The Tablecloth, the Knapsack, the Cannon Hat, and the Horn (Von der Serviette, dem Tornister, dem Kanonenhütlein und dem Horn). Source: Johann Friedrich Krause.

The Grimms provide a summary of a Danish tale, "Historie om tre fattige Skraedere, der ved Pillegrimsrejse kom til stor Vaerdighed og Vekstand," published in a Copenhagen newspaper, *Lykkens flyvende Fane*. The story reads as follows:

Three poor tailors who are not earning much from their profession take leave of their wives and children and set out into the world to see if they can have better luck. They come to a mountain in the desert where a magician is living. The mountain is green in summer and winter, full of flowers and fruit. At noon and midnight everything turns into the finest silver. The oldest tailor fills a bundle and all his pockets with the most beautiful silver flowers and fruit, goes home, throws his needle and iron beneath the table, and becomes a rich merchant. The two other tailors think that they can return to the mountain whenever they want, and they decide to continue to wander and seek their fortune elsewhere. They come to a large iron gate that opens up by itself after they have knocked three times. They enter a garden where there are three trees full of golden apples hanging from the branches. The second tailor picks off as many apples as his rucksack can carry and goes home. There he turns to commerce and becomes an even greater merchant than the first tailor so that everyone believes that the rich Jew in Hamburg is his relative. The third tailor was of the opinion that the garden with the gold apples would always be there for him and decides to go farther to seek his fortune. He wanders about the desert, and when he tries to find the silver mountain and the garden again, he can't find them. Finally, he comes to a huge hill and hears someone playing a pipe. He goes toward the sounds and finds an old witch who is piping in front of a herd of geese that beat their wings and dance as prompted by the sounds of the witch's pipe. For ninety-four years she had been struggling with death on this hill and can't die until the geese trample her to death or a Christian comes who beats her to death with some weapons. As soon as she hears the tailor's steps and sees that he is nearby, she asks him whether he is a Christian and whether he will beat her to death with the club that is standing by her side. The tailor refuses to do this until she tells him that he will find a cloth beneath her head that will provide him with the most delicious food if he just wishes with a few words. So the tailor bashes the witch's skull. Afterward he searches and finds the cloth. Then he immediately packs it into his bundle and sets out for home. A soldier on horseback encounters him and asks him for a piece of bread. The tailor says: "If you give me your weapons, I'll share my food with you." The rider, who had exhausted all his powder and lead in the war, does this gladly. The tailor spreads out his cloth and treats the hungry soldier to food. The rider likes the cloth, and he offers the tailor his magical ammunition pouch in exchange for the cloth. If one knocks on one side of the pouch, a hundred thousand infantrymen and cavalry men appear. If one knocks on the other side of the pouch, all kinds of musicians appear. The tailor agrees to the swap, but after he has the ammunition pouch, he orders ten cavalrymen to pursue the rider and to take back the cloth. Now the tailor returns home, and his wife is surprised that he has earned very little during his wanderings. Pretending not to have gained much, he goes to his former comrades, who generously support him so that he can live off this support with his wife and child for a while. One time, however, he invites his friends to lunch and asks them not to be so proud as to refuse or to spurn him. They reproach him and tell him not to make a feast and waste all that he has. Nevertheless, they promise to come. When they arrive at the appointed time, they find that only the tailor's wife is at home, and she isn't even aware that her husband had invited guests. Indeed, she fears that her husband is somewhat confused. Finally, the tailor comes home and tells his wife to quickly clean the room. He greets his guests and apologizes, for he knows that things are better in their homes, but he wanted to see whether they might have become too proud to come to his house because of their wealth. They sit down at the table, but there are no settings. Then the tailor spreads out his cloth, says some words, and within seconds the cloth is filled with the most delicious food imaginable. "Ha! Ha!" the others think, he's not as bad off as he's pretended. And they assure him of their love and friendship until death. Their host says, "It's not necessary to assure me." As he says this, he knocks on one side of the ammunition pouch. All of a sudden musicians appear and begin to play unusual music. Then he knocks on the other side of the pouch and commands the artillery and a hundred thousand soldiers who set up a rampart and guns and cannons on top. And as the three tailors drink and toast one another, the soldiers fire the cannons. The prince lives four miles from there, and he hears the thunder and believes that the enemy forces have come. So he sends his trumpeter to find out what is happening, and the soldier returns with the news that a tailor is celebrating his birthday and is having fun with his good friends. The prince himself travels to the tailor's house. The tailor treats him to the feast on his cloth, and the prince likes it. The prince offers him lands and a generous allowance for the cloth, but the tailor doesn't want to give him the cloth. He tells the prince that he prefers to keep the cloth because it relieves him of his worries, hard work, and frustration. The prince is brief. He takes the cloth by force and goes off. However, the tailor puts on his ammunition pouch and sets off to the prince's court with it and requests his cloth. Instead, however, he gets a good beating. Then the tailor runs to the rampart of the castle and calls for twenty thousand men to march to the castle. They set up and point their guns and cannons toward the castle and fire. Consequently, the prince has the cloth brought out and humbly asks for the shooting and firing to stop. So the tailor now commands his soldiers return to their quarters. Afterward he goes home and lives in delight with the two other tailors.

38. Mrs. Fox (Von der Frau Füchsin). Source: Based on a tale remembered by Jacob Grimm.
39. The Elves (Von den Wichtelmännern" Source: Henriette Dorothea Wild provided all three tales.

> About the Shoemaker for Whom They Did the Work (Von dem Schuster, dem sie die Arbeit gemacht).
> About a Servant Girl Who Acted as Godmother (Von einem Dienstmädchen, das Gevatter bei ihnen gestanden).
> About a Woman Whose Child They Had Exchanged (Von einer Frau, der sie das Kind vertauscht haben).

40. The Robber Bridegroom (Der Räuberbräutigam). Source: Marie Hassenpflug.
41. Herr Korbes (Herr Korbes). Source: Johanna Isabella Hassenpflug.

42. The Godfather (Der Herr Gevatter). Source: Amalie Hassenpflug.

The Grimms note that the motif of the witch's horns led them to recall another tale which has the following plot:

A witch had a young maiden living with her and trusted her with all the keys in the house, but she forbade her to enter one particular room (as in "Bluebeard"). However, due to her curiosity, the maiden opened the door one day and saw the witch sitting there with two very large horns on her head. The witch became furious and locked the maiden in a very high tower. There was no door to the tower in which she was imprisoned. When the witch brought her food, the maiden had to let down her long hair from the window, and the witch used the hair, which was twenty yards long, to climb up to the window. (From this point on, the tale is similar to "Rapunzel.")

43. The Strange Feast (Die wunderliche Gasterei). Source: Amalie Hassenpflug.
44. Godfather Death (Der Gevatter Tod). Source: Marie Elisabeth Wild.

The Grimms point to the significance of older versions for the development of this tale type. They cite versions from the sixteenth century and one by Johannes Praetorius from the seventeenth century. Most important is their discussion of Jacob Ayer's Shrovetide play, *Der Baur mit seiem Gevatter Tod* (1620).

45. The Wandering of Thumbling, the Tailor's Son (Des Schneiders Daumerling Wanderschaft). Source: Marie Hassenpflug.

The Grimms note that this tale is related to a Danish version, "Svend Tommling," published in a folk book in 1796 by Nyerup, Iris, and Hebe. In this story a man, no bigger than a thumb, wants to marry a woman five feet five inches tall. He was born into the world with a hat and dagger on his side. He knows how to use a plow and is captured by a landowner, who keeps him in his snuffbox . "Tommling" hops out of the snuffbox and falls upon a pig, which becomes his saddlehorse.

The Grimms write that Benjamin Tabart published another version in his English series of fairy tales in 1809. It was called "The Life and Adventures of Tom Thumb," and the Grimms summarized it as follows:

The son of a tailor, this figure is simply Tom Thumb and as such undertakes many adventures and has fine qualities. When his mother goes to milk the cow and it is a windy day, she ties Tom with a thread on a thistle so that he won't blow away. However, the cow eats the thistle. This is only one of the many adventures Tom experiences. What makes this story so mythical and even more remarkable is that "Tom Thumb" seems to be connected to other English and Scottish tales about Tamerlane, Tomlin, and even to Thomas, the mythical poet.

46. Fitcher's Bird (Fitchers Vogel). Source: Friederike Mannel and Henriette Dorothea Wild.

47. The Juniper Tree (Van den Machandel-Boom). Source: Philipp Otto Runge and Daniel Runge.

The Grimms note two different verses sung by the bird, one of which stems from Goethe's *Faust*. In addition they discuss motifs such as the evil stepmother, the gathering of the bones, and the resurrection of the son who was murdered. In this regard they make connections with the myths of Osris, Orpheus, and the legend of Adalbert.

48. Old Sultan (Der alte Sultan). Source: Johann Friedrich Krause.

49. The Six Swans (Die sechs Schwäne). Source: Henriette Dorothea Wild.

The Grimms consider this tale type as having ancient roots that extend back to the Greco-Roman myths; similar motifs can be found in French and Nordic oral traditions. They cite a tale, "Die sieben Schwäne," from the anonymous *Feen-Mährchen* (1801), in which the sister is supposed to sit seven years in a tree without speaking. Each year, after she is married to the prince, she is to finish sewing a shirt and never to shed a tear. But when she gives birth to her third child and the baby is taken away from her, she sheds a tear. Consequently, when she is saved by her seven brothers, the last one is missing an eye.

50. Briar Rose (Dornröschen). Source: Marie Hassenpflug.

The Grimms refer to Charles Perrault's "La Belle au bois dormant," *Histoires ou contes du temps passé* (1697), and to Giambattista Basile's "Sole, Luna e Talia," *Il Pentamerone* (1634). They also allude to Siegfried's rescue of Brünhilde when he penetrates a wall of flames.

51. The Foundling (Vom Fundevogel). Source: Friederike Mannel.

52. King Thrushbeard (König Droßelbart). Source: Hassenpflug family and Henriette Dorothea Wild.

The Grimms explain that the name "Droßelbart" is otherwise "Bröselbart" (Crumbbeard) because breadcrumbs often hang on a man's beard after eating, and this is what offends the princess. Other names, Drossel, Drussel, and Rüssel, are associated with the mouth, nose, or lips. In one version cited by the Grimms, the princess announces that she will wed the man who can solve the riddle about a stretched animal skin without a head and feet, and she wants to know what animal the skin comes from and the gender. Bröselbart knows the secret answer—a female wolf—but he purposely guesses the wrong answer. Later, he returns as a beggar and provides the right answer. The Grimms allude to another version Giambattista Basile's "La Soperbia castecata" in *Il Pentamerone* (1634).

53. Little Snow White (Sneewittchen [Schneeweißchen]). Source: Ferdinand Grimm and Marie Hassenpflug.

The Grimms provide several different versions or summaries of other tales in their note:

a. A count and a countess drove by three mounds of white snow, and the count said: "I wish we had a little girl as white as this snow." Soon thereafter they went by three graves with red blood, and the count spoke again: "I wish we had a little girl with cheeks as red as this blood." Finally, three black ravens flew above them, and he wished for a girl "with hair as black as these ravens." As they continued traveling for some time, they came upon a girl as white as snow, as red as blood, and with hair as black as the ravens, and that was Snow White. The count had her take a seat in the coach right away and was very fond of her, while the countess did not take to her kindly at all. She only thought of how she might get rid of the girl. Finally, she let her glove fall out of the coach and ordered Snow White to go and look for it. As the girl did this, the coachman was ordered to drive on quickly. Now Snow White was alone and came to the dwarfs, and so on.

b. In another version, the queen travels into the forest and asks Little Snow White to pick some roses from the flowers standing along the side of the road and to make a bouquet. While Little Snow White is picking the flowers, the queen drives off and leaves her alone.

c. In the third version, a king loses his wife with whom he had an only daughter, Little Snow White. Then he takes a second wife with whom he has three daughters. The queen hates the stepdaughter because she is so wonderfully beautiful and treats her badly whenever she can. In the forest seven dwarfs live in a cave and kill any maiden who comes near them. The queen knows this, and since she herself doesn't exactly want to kill the maiden, she hopes to get rid of her by driving her out to the cave, where she tells her: "Go inside and wait there for me until I return." Then she departs while Little Snow White rests in the cave and doesn't suspect anything. The dwarfs come, and initially, they want to kill her, but because she is so beautiful, they let her live, and in exchange for their mercy they say that she should keep house for them.

Now Little Snow White had owned a dog called Mirror, and after she had left the castle, he lies there sadly beneath a bench, and the queen asks him:

"Mirror, Mirror, lying on the mat,
Look all over, look in our land,
Who's the most beautiful in Engelland?"

The dog answers: "Little Snow White is more beautiful in the cave of the seven dwarfs than the queen her majesty with her three daughters." All at once the queen realizes that Little Snow White is still alive and makes a poisoned lace for a corset. She takes it with her to the cave, calls Little Snow White and tells her to open up. Little Snow White doesn't want to do this because the seven dwarfs have forbidden her not to let anyone enter the cave, even her stepmother, because the queen wants to bring about her ruin. However, the queen tells Little Snow White that she doesn't have her daughters anymore because a knight had kidnapped them. So she wants to live with Little Snow White and help her clean. Little Snow White takes pity on her and lets her enter. Then she ties the corset with the poisoned lace around Little Snow White so that she falls down dead to the ground. At this point the queen leaves the cave. Soon after the seven dwarfs come, take a knife, and cut the lace in two, and Little Snow White is revived. At the castle the queen asks Mirror lying beneath the bench who's the most beautiful in Engelland, and the dog gives her the same answer he gave before. So she makes a poisoned ribbon, travels to the cave, and talks to Little Snow White in such a persuasive way so that the maiden lets the queen enter again. And, once again, the queen ties the ribbon in Little Snow White's hair, and she falls down dead. But the seven dwarfs return and see what has happened. They cut the ribbon from her hair, and Little Snow White is revived. For the third time the queen asks the dog the same question and receives the same answer. So now she travels to the cave with a poisoned apple. Despite the fact that the dwarfs have warned her very much, Little Snow White is moved by the queen's pleas, opens the door, takes a bite of the apple, and falls down dead. This time, when the dwarfs arrive, they can't help her. Mirror, lying beneath the bench, tells the queen that she is the most beautiful. Meanwhile, the seven dwarfs build a silver coffin, lay Little Snow White inside, and place it beneath a tree in front of their cave. A prince comes by and asks the dwarfs to give him the coffin. So he takes it with him, and once he is home, he has Little Snow White set on a bed and cleaned as if she were alive, and he loves her more than anything in the world. A servant must always keep watch over her, and one time he becomes angry because of this: "Why should we treat a dead maiden as if she were alive?!" He hits her on her back, and a piece of the apple flies out of her mouth, and Little Snow White is alive again.

The Grimms compare this version with Johann Karl August Musäus's "Richilde" in *Volksmährchen der Deutschen* (1782).

54. Simple Hans (Hans Dumm). Source: Hassenpflug sisters.

The Grimms point to parallels with Giovan Francesco Straparola's "Pietro Pazzo," *Le piacevoli notti* (1550), and Giambattista Basile's "Pervonto," *Il Pentamerone* (1634).

55. Rumpelstiltskin (Rumpelstilzchen). Source: Hassenpflug family and Henriette Dorothea Wild.

The Grimms report that the name *Rumpelstilzchen* is derived from a game in Johann Fischart's game index in his translation of *Gargantua*, which appeared in German under the title *Geschichtklitterung* (1575).

The Grimms remark that the "Rumpelstilzchen" story itself begins differently from their version, and they provide a brief summary:

A little maiden was given a bunch of straw, which she was supposed to spin into flax, but she could only spin gold thread out of it, and not one single thread of flax came out of her wheel. She became sad and sat down on the roof and spun and spun three days, but she could spin nothing but gold thread. All at once a little man came and said: I'll help you out of your predicament. A young prince will be coming by and will marry you, but you must promise to give me your firstborn child, and so on. In addition, the little man is discovered in a different way. One of the queen's maids goes into the forest during the night. She sees the little man riding on a cooking spoon around a fire, and so on. At the end of the tale the little man flies out of the window on a cooking spoon.

The Grimms mention that "Rumpelstilzchen" reminds them of a Nordic story about Fenia and Menia, who could grind everything that one wanted, and King Frode, who had them grind peace and gold.

In another summary that the Grimms provide, a woman walks by a garden in which there are beautiful cherries hanging from a tree. She has a craving to eat some and climbs into the garden and eats some. But a black man emerges from the earth, and she must promise her firstborn baby to him because of her theft. When the child is born, he pushes his way through all the guards that the husband had ordered to protect his wife, and the man will only let the woman keep her child if she guesses his name. Now the husband follows him and sees how the black man climbs into a cave that has cooking spoons hung all around it and hears that the man is called *Fleder Flitz*.

The Grimms also cite the important French tale "L'Histoire de Ricdin-Ricdon," in Marie-Jean L'Héritier de Villandon's *La Tour ténébreuse et les jours lumineux* (1705).

56. Sweetheart Roland (Der liebste Roland). Source: Henriette Dorothea Wild or Johanna Christiane Fulda.

According to the Grimms, there is another version in which the two lovers stick a bean in a cake that is lying on the stove and is baking. When the stepmother awakes and calls her daughter, the bean answers every question for the daughter and says that the daughter is in the kitchen and is cooking. The bean does this just as long as the cake is still baking. When the cake is done, the bean becomes quiet. Its power is gone, and the mother becomes aware of what has been happening and finds her dead daughter.

57. The Golden Bird (Vom goldenen Vogel). Source: This tale was obtained orally from an elderly female patient in the Elisabeth-Hospital in Marburg and written down by Wilhelm Grimm.

The Grimms indicate that the beginning of the tale is quite often different, and older versions often begin this way:

A king was sick, or had become blind, and nothing in the world could help him. But then he heard (or dreamed) about a bird Phoenix living in a distant country, and this bird's whistling (or song) could heal him. So the king's sons set out one after the other to find the bird, and the various versions of this tale differ in the depiction of the adventures and how the third son survives and brings the bird to his father.

The Grimms believed that this tale type was ancient and could be traced back to the biblical story about Joseph, the medieval *Saga af Artus Fagra* (fourteenth-century Icelandic work), *The Thousand and One Nights*, and *Das Buch des Ritters Herr Johannsen von Montevilla* (1488) by Jean Mandeville and Otto de Demeringen. Many other versions can be found in northern Europe.

58. Loyal Godfather Sparrow (Vom treuen Gevatter Sperling). Source: Margarete Marianne Wild.

59. Prince Swan (Prinz Schwan). Source: Margarete Marianne Wild.

The Grimms state that this tale is similar to one about the three belts in the anonymous *Feen-Mährchen* (1801), and they summarize it as follows:

> The queen receives three belts from a fairy, who tirelessly gives her help as an old wicked witch. As long as these belts are not broken in two, the queen can believe in the love and faithfulness of her absent husband. When two of the belts break, the queen disguises herself as a pilgrim and searches for her husband. As she walks through a large forest, three golden nuts fall to her feet one after the other. She picks them up and takes them with her. She meets up with a miller and poses as his cousin and uses a false name. Then she finds the king, and without recognizing the queen, he falls in love with her. She shows that she has affection for him, but when he wants to embrace her, the third belt breaks. She is horrified and asks him to close the doors of the house because she cannot stand the sound of their constant slamming. However, as soon as he closes one door, another springs open, and it continues this way throughout the night. The king can do nothing but close the doors, and because of this he becomes irritated and doesn't return. Instead, he marries a princess to whom he had become engaged. Now the queen opens her first golden nut and finds the most splendid sewing stuff in a casket. Then she takes the casket and goes to the castle and sits down across from the princess's windows and begins to sew. The princess sees her and takes a great liking to the sewing stuff. She bargains for the sewing stuff, and in exchange she must let the queen spend the first night in the king's bedchamber. The next day the queen opens the second nut and finds a precious spindle inside. Then she spins with the spindle before the princess and exchanges it for the permission to spend the second night in the king's bedchamber. Finally, the queen exchanges the jewelry in the third box to spend the third night in the king's bedchamber. After the wedding with the princess takes place the next day, the queen is led to the king, and she reveals to him that she is his wife. On the third morning the king summons the princess, the queen, and all the councilors and relates how he had lost the key to a golden padlock and then had found it again. Then he asks the princess, his new wife, whether he should use the new key to the padlock or the old one. She advises him to use the old one, and by doing this, she passes a sentence on herself and must separate from the king.

60. The Golden Egg (Das Goldei). Source: Henriette Dorothea Wild.

The Grimms discuss another version from a collection of tales from Erfurt and summarize this tale as follows:

The bird that lays a golden egg every morning flees Prince Gunild. A farmer captures the bird, and the farmer gives the bird to a goldsmith, who reads on the bird's wings: "Whoever eats my head will find a thousand gold coins under his pillow every day. Whoever eats my heart will become king in Akindilla one day." The goldsmith gives the bird to Ynkas, his nephew, to roast so that the goldsmith can eat the bird. However, Ynkas accidentally eats the head and heart of the bird and must flee the angry and deceived goldsmith, who threatens him. In the course of the action, the bird's prediction is fulfilled.

61. The Tailor Who Soon Became Rich (Von dem Schneider, der bald reich wurde). Source: Hassenpflug family.

According to another tale, the man is called Mr. Hands, whom the farmers hate because he is so smart. Out of jealousy they shut him in a baking oven. However, he takes the debris and ashes in a sack to a refined lady and asks her to keep the sack for him. He tells her that there are herbs, cinnamon, pepper, and little nails inside. Later he comes to fetch the sack and leads her astray by crying out that she had robbed the contents of the sack. In this way he compels her to pay him 300 gold coins. The farmers see him counting his money and ask him how he had earned it. He tells them that he got it out of the debris and ashes of baking oven. So all the farmers smash their baking ovens to pieces and carry the debris and ashes into the city to sell. However, they are treated badly. Now the farmers want to kill Mr. Hands out of revenge. But he puts on his mother's clothes, and in this way he escapes them, and his mother is beaten to death. Then he puts his mother into a barrel and rolls her to a doctor and lets her stand there a while. When he returns, he accuses the doctor of having killed her and manages to extort a certain sum of money. He tells the farmers that he received the money for causing his mother's death. So the farmers beat their own mothers to death. Afterward there is the incident with the shepherd who trades places with him in the cask and drowns. At the end the farmers imitate him and jump into the water.

In another tale published by Johann Gustav Gottlieb Büsching in *Volks-Sagen, Märchen und Legenden* (1812), Kibitz lets the farmer beat his wife to death and then puts her next to a basket full of fruit in a market. When a servant wants to buy some fruit from her for his employer and she doesn't answer him, he pushes her into the water. As compensation, Kibitz receives the coach in which the servant had traveled to the market and everything else that belongs to it.

The Grimms discuss another similar version about Rutschki or the citizen of Quarkenquatsch in a 1794 folk book published in Erfurt. They also note the important tale "The Priest Scarpafico" in Giovan Francesco Straparola's *Le piacevoli notti* (1550).

62. Bluebeard (Blaubart). Source: Hassenpflug family.

The Grimms mention that the incident in which the anxious wife sticks the key in hay to rub off the blood can be attributed to a folk belief that hay can really absorb blood from another object.

Among the many similar tales the Grimms note are Charles Perrault's "La Barbe bleue" in *Histoires ou contes du temps passé* (1697); Giovan Francesco Straparola's "Galeotto" in *Le piacevoli notti* (1550); and Ludwig Tieck's stories, "Ritter Blaubart" (1797) and "Die sieben Weiber des Blaubart" (1797) and his play *Der Blaubart* (1797).

63. The Golden Children (Goldkinder). Source: Friederike Mannel.

The Grimms relate this tale to "Vom Johannes-Wassersprung und Casper-Wassersprung," and they also draw parallels with Giovan Francesco Straparola's "Cesarin," *Le piacevoli notti*, and Giambattista Basile's "Lo mercante" and "La cerva fatatam," *Il Pentamerone* (1634)

64. The Simpleton (Von dem Dummling).

The White Dove (Die weiße Taube). Source: Margarete Marianne Wild.

The Grimms note similarities with a Danish tale, "Historie om trende Bödre."

The Queen Bee (Die Bienenkönigin). Source: Albert Ludwig Grimm.

The Grimms draw parallels with their own tale, "Herr Fix und Fertig."

The Three Feathers (Die drei Federn).

The Grimms note differences in several other tales they knew, especially with regard to the tasks that the three sons must perform. In one tale the father gives each one of the three sons an apple, and whoever throws the apple the farthest will obtain the king's realm. The youngest son throws his apple the farthest, but because he is so simple, the father doesn't want to grant him the realm and demands twenty crates of canvas in a nutshell. The oldest son travels to Holland; the second to Silesia, where there is supposed to be very fine canvas. The third son, the simpleton, goes into the forest. A nutshell falls from a tree, and he finds linen in it. After this the king demands a dog that can jump through a wedding ring, then three yards of yarn that can go through the eye of a needle. The simpleton is able to procure all these items.

In another tale the son who can bring the most beautiful smell will win the kingdom.

Simpleton reaches a house where a cat is sitting in front of the door and asks: "Why are you so sad?"

"Oh, you can't help me!"

"Hey, listen up! Tell me what you need."

Then the cat obtains the best smell for him.

The Grimms also refer to a version in the *Feen-Mährchen* (1801).

The Golden Goose (Die goldene Gans). Source: Hassenpflug family.

65. All Fur (Allerleirauh). Source: Henriette Dorothea Wild and Carl Nehrlich, *Schilly* (1798).

The Grimms allude to Charles Perrault's "Peau d'Ane," *Histoires ou contes du temps passé* (1697), and their own version, "Princess Mouseskin."

66. Hurleburlebutz (Hurleburlebutz). Source: Jeanette Hassenpflug.

The Grimms summarize a tale in *Feen-Mährchen* as follows:

A princess is so proud of her beauty and so arrogant that she mocks all her suitors and depicts them as animals and wants all her wishes to be fulfilled. One time she dreams about a singing, clinging little tree, and her father must set out to find it for her. Fortunately, he finds it, but as he is tearing it out of the ground, a terrifying lion jumps out of the earth. As a consequence the father must promise to give him the first thing that he encounters when he returns home. Indeed, it is the proud princess, who hears the singing, clinging tree as her father approaches. The king is horrified and tells her that she is to be delivered to a lion, but she is not very much worried about this because she has a washerwoman put on her clothes and take her place. After three days the lion comes and says to the washerwoman, "Get on my back," and he carries her off into the forest. The maiden weeps when she sees a river and says, "Who will now help my mother with the washing?" The lion realizes that he has been deceived. He carries the maiden back and then leaves. After three days he returns to find a shepherd's daughter dressed in the princess's clothes. "Get on my back," the lion says and carries her off. When she comes to a bright meadow, the maiden sighs: "Oh, who'll console my Hans when I can't lay with him in the meadow!" The lion goes back once more and brings the false bride to the king and threatens the king. Then he runs directly to the princess, who gets on his back and is carried away. He takes her to a cave, where she must do lowly work for eleven sick animals and heal their festering wounds. She gradually becomes remorseful about her previous arrogance and also cures the lion who becomes wounded. She atones for all her sins, and all of a sudden she finds herself once again in her father's splendid castle. Meanwhile, the lion has become a handsome young man and her bridegroom.

In addition to this version, the Grimms recall two short episodes from other oral tales.

67. The King with the Lion (Der Konig mit dem Löwen). Source: Jeanette Hassenpflug.

The Grimms point out that the forgetting of the first fiancée also occurs in "Prince Swan," "Sweetheart Roland," and "All Fur." There are also three tales in Giambattista Basile's *Il Pentamerone* (1634) in which this incident occurs.

68. The Summer and the Winter Garden (Von dem Sommer- und Wintergarten). Source: Ferdinand Siebert.

The Grimms cite Apuleius's "Psyche and Cupid" in *The Golden Ass* (second century) as the ancient source and then briefly summarize the plot of the tale in Gabrielle-Suzanne de Villeneuve's *Contes marins ou la jeune americaine* (1740). In this version the beast is a dragon. They also summarize a tale from a Leipzig collection of stories:

> The youngest daughter asks her father for a branch from an oak tree that has a twig with three acorns as he leaves on a journey. The father gets lost in a forest and comes upon a splendid castle, which is completely empty. However, he finds everything set out in the best manner. During the night a bear comes and brings a twig with three acorns and demands to have his daughter. At first the father refuses but eventually gives in. Yet, when the father returns home, he locks all the doors of his home. Nevertheless, the bear enters two times at midnight and demands to have the bride. On the third night the suitcases are packed by themselves, and three acorns are on them. The daughter herself is dressed as a bride, and her hair has been curled. She doesn't even know this. The bear stands next to her and puts a golden ring with three acorns on her finger with his paw. Then he carries her off to his castle. When she is there, she sees her father and sisters in a mirror but doesn't return home. After she gives birth to a child and three years pass, the magic spell is broken, and the bear is transformed into a handsome young man.

The Grimms assert that only the beginning of this tale is good and genuine while the ending seems very contrived.

69. Jorinda und Joringel (Jorinde and Joringel). Source: Johann Heinrich Jung-Stilling, *Heinrich Stillings Jugend* (1777).

70. Okerlo (Der Okerlo). Source: Jeanette Hassenpflug.

The Grimms summarize a short incident from *Feen-Mährchen* (1801). The clear source of this tale is Marie-Catherine d'Aulnoy's "L'oranger e l'abaille" in *Contes nouveaux ou les Fées à la Mode* (1697).

71. Princess Mouseskin (Prinzessin Mäusehaut). Source: Wild family.

The Grimms indicate that the major source is Charles Perrault's "Peau d'ane" in *Histoires ou contes du temps passé* (1697).

72. The Pear Refused to Fall (Das Birnli will nit fallen). Source: From an oral tale in Switzerland.

The Grimms refer to a Jewish folk song and quote a few refrains in their summary.

73. The Castle of Murder (Das Mordschloß). Source: Fräulein de Kinsky.

The Grimms translated this from Fräulein de Kinsky, and they printed the tale in Dutch in their note.

74. Johannes Waterspring and Caspar Waterspring (Von Johannes-Wassersprung und Caspar-Wassersprung). Source: Friederike Mannel.

75. The Bird Phoenix (Vogel Phönix). Source: Marie Hassenpflug.

76. The Carnation (Die Nelke). Source: Hassenpflug family.

77. The Carpenter and the Turner (Vom Schreiner und Drechsler). Source: Friederike Mannel.
78. The Old Grandfather and the Grandson (Der alte Großvater und der Enkel). Source: Johann Heinrich Jung-Stilling, *Heinrich Stillings Jugend* (1777).

The Grimms summarize an old minnesang that they obtained from Achim von Arnim's codex.

An old king cedes his throne and realm to his son, who is, however, to support the king until his death. The son gets married, and his young queen complains about the coughing of the old king. The son has the father sleep under a flight of stairs on some straw, where he must live for many years not much better than a dog. His grandson grows up and brings his grandfather food and something to drink every day. One time the grandfather is freezing and asks for a blanket from one of the horses, The grandson goes into the stable, takes a good blanket, cuts it in two because he is upset about the way his grandfather is being treated. His father asks him why he's done this, and he responds: "I'm going to bring one half of the blanket to grandfather, and the other half I'm going to save so that I can cover you when you get old."

The Grimms also summarize an old French version:

A son disowns his old father because of his wife's complaints. The father asks for some warm clothes, and the son refuses to give him any. Then the father asks for a blanket from a horse because his heart is trembling from the cold. The son tells his own son to go into the stable with the old man and to give him a blanket. So the grandson cuts the blanket in two while his grandfather scolds him and reports him to his son for doing this. But the grandson defends his actions by telling his father that he did this to save the other half for him when the time will come to drive the father out of the house. As a consequence the father takes all this to heart and honors his father by taking him back into the house.

The Grimms also recall another similar short version that appeared in Johannes Pauli's *Schimpf und Ernst* (1522).
79. The Water Nixie (Die Wassernix). Source: Marie Hassenpflug.
80. The Death of Little Hen (Von dem Tod des Hühnchens). Source: Oral tale from Hesse.

The Grimms remark that there is a similar tale, "Erschreckliche Geschichte von Hühnchen und Hänchen," in Clemens Brentano's and Achim von Arnim's *Des Knaben Wunderhorn* (1805).
81. The Blacksmith and the Devil (Der Schmidt und der Teufel). Source: Marie Hassenpflug.

The Grimms state that this tale has been popular throughout Europe. They note various versions from the eighteenth century and discuss its German and French origins. Here is a 1772 variant about a blacksmith from Jüterbock:

The pious blacksmith from Jüterbock wore a black and white jacket, and one night he gladly and cheerfully provided lodging to a holy man. The next day, before the holy man's departure, he permitted the blacksmith three wishes. So the blacksmith asked (1) that his favorite chair near the oven be endowed with the power to retain each and every uninvited guest on the chair until the blacksmith lets him go; (2) that his apple tree in the garden be endowed with the power to retain anyone who climbs the tree; (3) that the sack he used for coal be able to retain anyone inside until the blacksmith lets the person go free.

After some time passes, death comes and sits down on the favorite chair where he is detained. Death must grant the blacksmith another ten years of life before the blacksmith will let him go. After the ten years pass, death returns and climbs the apple tree. He can't get down, and the blacksmith calls his apprentices, who give death a terrible beating with poles. This time the blacksmith won't let him down until he grants him eternal life. Death agrees sadly and departs, his arms and legs lame from the beating he received. As he is making his way through a forest, he encounters the devil and spills his heart out and tells him what he has suffered. The devil mocks him and declares that he can get the better of the blacksmith. However, the blacksmith refuses to give the devil lodging for the night. That is, he won't open the door, and the devil must enter through the keyhole, which is easily done by the devil. But the blacksmith has the coal sack ready, and once the devil enters through the keyhole and falls into the sack, the blacksmith ties it up. Then he has his apprentices pound the sack on the anvil. After they have beaten and hammered the poor devil to their hearts' content, the blacksmith lets him go, but the devil must slip through the keyhole the way he had entered.

In another 1806 version collected by Johannes Falk in *Grotesken*, there is a similar tale about the blacksmith from Apolda:

In this version the Lord is traveling with St. Peter, and they spend the night in the blacksmith's home. The next day the Lord grants the blacksmith three wishes, which are: (1) whoever sticks his hand into the sack of nails will not be able to take it out until the sack falls apart; (2) whoever climbs his apple tree must stay above in the tree until the tree collapses; (3) whoever sits on his easy chair cannot stand up until the chair falls apart. Eventually three wicked angels come and want to take him away. However, the blacksmith leads them into all the traps that he had wished for so that the angels must give up their attempt to take him with them. However, death finally comes and forces the blacksmith to go with him. But he is granted one favor and is allowed to have his hammer placed in the coffin with him. When the blacksmith approaches heaven's gate, St. Peter won't open up, and so the blacksmith goes to heaven, where he makes a key. Then he promises to do all kinds of work in heaven and make himself useful, such as making hoofs for St. George's horse. Finally, St. Peter lets him enter through heaven's gate.

The third variant collected by the Grimms has the title, "Histoire nouvelle et divertissement du bon homme Misère," and though printed in France, the Grimms believe it to be of Italian origin:

In this tale Peter and Paul arrive in a village during bad weather. They encounter a washerwoman who thanks heaven that the rain isn't wine but water. They knock on the door of a rich man who refuses to give them lodging. So they go to poor Misery, who takes them in. Then they grant him one wish that pertains to his pear tree that a thief has been robbing. Anyone who climbs the tree gets stuck there. The thief is caught, as are even other people who climb the tree out of curiosity when they hear the terrible cries of the thief and want to free him. Finally, death arrives, and Misery asks death to lend him his sickle so that he can cut down the most beautiful pears to take with him. Death won't let anyone take the sickle out of his hands, and so, like a good soldier, he takes charge of climbing the pear tree himself to cut off the pears. So Misery won't let him come down until death promises him to leave him in peace until the day of judgment. And this is why misery continues to exist in the world.

The Grimms conclude the note by stating that there is another oral version that relates how misery dies and arrives at the gate of heaven, but St. Peter won't let him enter because he had not requested a better wish such as admission to heaven. So misery goes to hell, but the devil won't allow him to enter because misery had made a fool out of him. Consequently, misery must return to earth, and this is why the world is still full of misery.

There are a few other versions that the Grimms mention, indicating how widespread the tale was in Europe.

82. The Three Sisters (Die drei Schwestern). Source: Johann August Musäus, "Die Bücher der Chronika der drey Schwestern," *Volksmährchen der Deutschen* (1782–87).

The Grimms point to other similar tales in Giambattista Basile's "Li tre'rri anemale," *Il Pentamerone* (1634), and some Scottish and English ballads.

83. The Poor Maiden (Das arme Mädchen). Source: Unknown.

84. The Mother-in-Law (Die Schwiegermutter). Source: Probably Charles Perrault's "La belle au bois dormant," *Histoires ou contes du temps passé* (1697).

The Grimms also mention Giambattista Basile's "Sole, Luna e Talia," *Il Pentamerone* (1634).

85. Fragments (Fragmente).

Snowflower (Schneeblume). Source: Based on a French oral tale and published as a poem, "Perceneige" in *Thibaut ou la nassance du comte de champagne* (1811).

The Princess with the Louse (Prinzessin mit der Laus). Source: Marie Hassenpflug. The Grimms also cite Giambattista's "La Polece," *Il Pentamerone* (1634).
Prince Johannes (Vom Prinz Johannes). Source: Taken from the monthly magazine, *Erheiterungen* (1812).
The Grimms prose version is based on a poem by Karl Graß, a painter and poet.
The Good Cloth (Der gute Lappen). Source: Probably the Hassenpflug family.

86. The Fox and the Geese (Der Fuchs und die Gänse). Source: Von Haxthausen family.
This tale without an end was purposely chosen by the Grimms to demonstrate the endlessness of storytelling, and it also provocatively indicates how weaker animals can outsmart the stronger ones.

Volume II

1. The Poor Man and the Rich Man (Der Arme und der Reiche). Source: Ferdinand Siebert.
The Grimms note that this tale is based on the ancient story of Philemon and Baucis in Ovid's *Metamorphosis*. They discuss how the moralistic theme of the punishment of the rich because of their greed and arrogance and the reward of the poor because of their generosity and humility can be found in many different European tales. Among the authors they cite is Benedikte Naubert and her *Neue Volksmährchen der Deutschen* (1789).
2. The Singing, Springing Lark (Das singende, springende Löweneckerchen). Source: Henriette Dorothea Wild.
The Grimms trace the origins of this tale to "Cupid and Psyche" in Apuleius's *The Golden Ass* (second century) and note its similarity to their own tale "Von dem Sommer- und Wintergarten" and to "Vom singenden, klingenden Bäumchen" in the anonymous *Feen-Mährchen* (1801).
3. The Goose Girl (Die Gänsemagd). Source: Dorothea Viehmann.
The Grimms discuss the motif of talking horses as well as the Nordic derivation of names in the tale. They also cite Giambattista Basile's "Le doje pizzelle," *Il Pentamerone* (1634).
4. The Young Giant (Von einem jungen Riesen). Source: Georg August Friedrich Goldmann.
At the beginning of this note the Grimms discuss the significance of the giant in the Nordic oral and literary tradition. In particular there are many references to tales about Siegfried and Thor as well as to Sampson (Bible), Scharmack (Bohemia), and Gargantua. They also summarize another Hessian version, "Kürdchen Bingeling."

Kürdchen Bingeling drank from his mother's breast for seven years. This is why he became so tremendously big and why he could eat so much and could never be satisfied. Meanwhile, he tormented and made fools of all the people he encountered, Consequently, everyone in the community comes together to capture and kill him. He becomes aware of this and sets himself down beneath the gate (similar to Gargantua) so that nobody can come through without chopping and shoveling. Then he goes calmly on his way to another village. He is the same rascal as before, so the entire community decides to rise up against him and capture him. Since there is no gate that he can use as a barricade, he jumps into a well. Now all the villagers stand around the well and consult with each other about their next move. Finally, they decide to throw a millstone down on his head. With great effort they bring a large rock to the well and roll it down. Just as they think he is dead, his head suddenly emerges from the well through the hole in the millstone, which is now hanging from his shoulders so that he cries out: "Oh what a beautiful collar I now have!" When the villagers see this, they begin consulting with one another again and they decide to send for the large bell from the church tower. Then they throw it on him and are sure that they have hit their target (similar to Scharmack). When they are certain that he is lying down in the well and is dead, the villagers leave. All at once, however, he springs out of the well wearing the bell on his head, and he cries out joyfully: "Oh, what a beautiful little cap I've got!" And he runs off.

5. The Gnome (Dat Erdmänneken). Source: Ludowine von Haxthausen and Fernandine von Haxthausen.

The Grimms state that there is another version from Cologne that differs somewhat from "The Gnome":

A powerful king has three beautiful daughters. One day during a splendid celebration, they take a walk in the garden, and they fail to return from the walk in the evening. When they don't appear the next day, the king orders a search throughout the entire realm, but nobody can find them. Then he announces that whoever finds them could have one of his daughters for his wife. In addition, whoever succeeds would receive enough wealth to live on for the rest of his life. Many men set out to find the daughters, but none succeed. Finally, three knights depart and declare that they won't rest until they are successful. They end up in a large forest, where they continue riding, hungry and thirsty. Finally, at nightfall they see a little light in the distance that leads them to a magnificent castle that is apparently empty. Since they are so hungry, they look for food, and one of them finds a piece of meat that is raw. Then the youngest says: "Why don't you two go off and look for something to drink while I roast this meat?" So he sticks the piece of meat on a spit, and while it is sizzling, a little gnome with a long white beard that reaches his knees suddenly appears next to him. His hands and feet are shivering. "Let me warm my hands and feet by the fire, and I'll keep turning the spit and pour butter on the meat." The knight lets him do this, and the gnome turns the roast nimbly, but whenever the knight isn't looking, he sticks his finger in the frying pan and licks the warm brew. The knight catches him doing this a couple of times and tells him to stop, but the tiny thing can't resist and is constantly trying to dip his fingers into the frying pan. Then the knight becomes furious and grabs the gnome by the beard and ruffles him so hard that he screams bloody murder and runs off. Meanwhile, the other two knights come back with some wine that they had found in the cellar, and now they eat and drink together. The next morning they continue searching the castle and find a deep hole. That's where the king's daughters must be hidden, they say to each other, and they draw lots to see which one of them would be let down by a rope while the other two hold on to the rope. The youngest, who had encountered the gnome, draws the lot. It takes a long time before he reaches the ground, where it is completely dark. All at once a door opens, and the gnome, whose beard he had pulled, comes and says: "I should actually pay you back for the wicked thing you did to me, but I pity you. I am the king of the gnomes, and I'll lead you out of this cave because if you stay here one moment longer, you will die."

The knight answers: "Even if am to die right here and now, I won't leave until I know where the king's daughters have been concealed."

"They are guarded by three dragons in this underground cave," the gnome responds. "The eldest sits in the first part of the cave with a three-headed dragon next to her. Every day at noon the dragon lays its heads in her lap, and she must louse the dragon until it falls asleep. A basket is hanging in front of the door with a flute, cane, and sword in it along with the three crowns of the king's daughters. First, you must take this basket and carry it off to a safe place. Then you must take the sword, go back to the room, and slice off the dragon's three heads, but you must slice them off all at once. If you fail to do this, the other heads will awake, and nothing can save you."

Then the gnome gives him a bell and tells him that if he pulls on it, the gnome will rush to help him. So after the knight rescues the first princess, he rescues the second, who has a seven-headed dragon guarding her, and the third, who has a nine-headed dragon guarding her. Then he leads them to the bucket in which he had been let down from the top of the hole. There he calls out to his companions and tells them that they should begin pulling the bucket up. So the two knights pull up the princesses one after the other. When they are above, the two disloyal knights throw the rope down the hole so that the young knight's life will end in a disaster. However, the young knight rings the bell given to him by the gnome. As soon as the gnome arrives, he tells him to blow the flute. Once the knight does this, thousands of gnomes appear from everywhere. Then the king of the gnomes orders them to build stairs for the knight, and he also tells the knight to take the cane out of the basket when he reaches the top and to strike the earth with it. So the little gnomes get to work and build the stairs, and once the knight climbs to the top, he strikes the ground with the cane, and all the gnomes disappear.

The Grimms conclude the summary of the tale by relating it to other tales in which the hero rescues princesses from a dragon, is betrayed, and then reclaims the glory.
6. The King of the Golden Mountain (Der König vom goldenen Berg). Source: Based on a story told to the Grimms by a soldier.

The Grimms relate this tale to motifs in other Germanic and Nordic stories, especially those dealing with Chriemhilde, Brunhilde, and Siegfried in the *Nibelungenlied*.
7. The Raven (Die Rabe). Source: Georg August Friedrich Goldmann.

The Grimms trace several motifs such as the quarrel of the giants and the sleeping potion to old Germanic and Nordic tales.
8. The Clever Farmer's Daughter (Die kluge Bauemtochter). Source: Dorothea Viehmann.

The Grimms draw parallels with the medieval story *Auslag-Sage* and discuss the widespread use of riddles in tales. In particular, they relate the riddle in "The Clever Farmer's Daughter" to one in Johannes Pauli's *Schimpf und Ernst* (1522).
9. The Genie in the Glass (Der Geist im Glas). Source: A tailor from Paderbörn.

The Grimms note the direct relationship to "The Fisherman and the Demon" and "Aladdin and the Magic Lamp" in *The Thousand and One Nights*.
10. The Three Little Birds (De drei Vügelkens). Source: Ludowine von Haxthausen and a shepherd, whom Wilhelm Grimm met in the countryside of Wesphalia near Corvey.

After describing how Wilhelm met a shepherd in August of 1813 while visiting friends in Corvey and how the shepherd provided several tales in dialect, the Grimms point to the significance of Antoine Galland's "Histoire de deux soeurs jalouses de leur cadette," *Les Milles et une nuit* (1712–17). This tale of "The Two Sisters Who Envied Their Younger Sister" was told to Galland in Paris by a Maronite Christian Arab from Aleppo named Youhenna Diab or Hanna Diab. There was no Arabic manuscript for this tale, and Galland created it from memory after listening to Diab and may have introduced elements from the European tales he knew. The Grimms also refer to Giovan Francesco Straparola's "Ancilotto Re di Prouino," *Le piacevoli notti* (1550). The tale was widespread in Europe in both oral and literary traditions.
11. The Water of Life (Das Wasser des Lebens). Source: A combination of tales from Hesse and Paderborn. The tale from Padernborn was provided by the von Haxthausen family.

The Grimms discuss similarities between this tale and others in their collection such as "Bird Phoenix" and "The Three Little Birds" as well as the Arabian and Italian tales mentioned in the previous note.

12. Doctor Know-It-All (Doctor Allwissend). Source: Dorothea Viehmann.

The Grimms note that there is also a very good Low German dialect version that they were not able to completely record.

13. The Frog Prince (Der Froschprinz). Source: Probably the Wild family.

The Grimms remark that the first version of "The Frog Prince," which incorporates the closing anecdote about Iron Henry, is unusual but worth keeping because it is exceptional. They note that these tales are all related to Apuleius's "Cupid and Psyche" in *The Golden Ass*.

14. The Devil's Sooty Brother (Des Teufels rußiger Bruder). Source: Dorothea Viehmann.

The Grimms cite a story about Bearskin in Johann Jakob Christoph Grimmelhausen's *Simplicisimus* (1670) as a major influence on this tale type. They claim that this tale that generally involved a pact with the devil was widespread throughout Europe, and both their friends Clemens Brentano and Achim von Arnim used key motifs from the Bearskin story in their own literary tales.

15. The Devil in the Green Coat (Der Teufel Grünrock). Source: Von Haxthausen family.

The Grimms regard this tale as basically a variant of "The Devil's Sooty Brother."

16. The Wren and the Bear (Der Zaunkönig und der Bär). Source: Dorothea Viehmann.

The Grimms believe that this tale belongs to the medieval cycle of tales about Renard the Fox, and like many other animals tales of this kind, the major theme is how the weaker animals use their brains to get the better of the larger more powerful animals.

17. The Sweet Porridge (Vom süßen Brei). Source: Henriette Dorothea Wild.

The Grimms explain that the word *Brei* ("porridge") was like the word *Brot* ("bread") and generally indicated food in general. The importance of porridge had a great deal to do with the wish and need for food, especially among lower-class people.

18. The Faithful Animals (Die treuen Thiere). Source: Ferdinand Siebert.

The Grimms remark that the animals in this tale are nothing but transformed heroes and people.

19. Tales about Toads (Mährchen von der Unke). Source: The first two tales were provided by Henriette Dorothea Wild and Lisette Wild and were said to be commonly heard in Hesse and neighboring regions. The third tale was a version from Berlin.

They summarize a tale from the *Gesta Romanorum* (thirteenth/fourteenth century) that they believe served as a model for tales of this type:

A knight becomes poor and is sad about this. He catches a viper that had been living in the corner of his room for some time. Then the viper says to him: "Give me milk every day and set it down yourself next to me, and I'll make you rich."

So the knight brings milk to the viper every day, and soon he becomes rich again. However, the knight's dumb wife advises him to kill the viper because of the treasures that they would probably find in its nest. So the knight carries a dish of milk with one hand and a hammer with the other and brings the milk to the viper, which crawls out of its hole to lick the milk. As the viper is drinking the milk, the knight lifts the hammer to kill the viper but misses his mark. Instead he deals the dish a tremendous blow. So the viper immediately scatters away. From that day onward the knight begins to lose weight and to lose his property, in contrast to the way he had previously expanded his wealth and body. He repeatedly asks the viper to forgive him, but the viper says: "Do you think that I've forgotten the blow that you dealt the dish that was intended for my head? There will be no peace between us." So the knight remains impoverished for the rest of his life.

20. The Poor Miller's Apprentice and the Cat (Der arme Müllerbursch und das Kätzchen). Source: Dorothea Viehmann.
21. The Crows (Die Krähen). Source: August von Haxthausen, who wrote down the tale as told to him by a soldier from Mecklenburg.

The Grimms summarize a similar tale in Johannes Pauli's *Schimpf und Ernst* (1522):

A servant is tied to a tree by his master, and during the night wicked ghosts gather there and talk, and as they talk, they reveal that a certain herb growing under the tree has the power to restore sight to blind people. After he restores his own sight, the servant restores the sight of a rich man's daughter. Consequently, he is given a good deal of property and weds the daughter. His previous master also wants to obtain such wealth. He goes to the tree, but the ghosts peck out his eyes.

The Grimms also draw parallels with "Die wahrsagenden Vögel" in *Feen-Mährchdren* (1801) and with a tale in Christoph Helwig's *Jüdische Historien oder thalmüdischerabbinische wunderbarliche Legenden* (1612).
22. Hans My Hedgehog (Hans mein Igel). Source: Dorothea Viehmann.

The Grimms cite Giovan Francesco Straparola's "Il re porco," *Le piacevoli notti* (1550) as an important source, and they draw parallels with other beast/bridegroom tales in their collection that have donkeys and lions seeking brides. At one point they state: "People who implore God too impetuously to bless them with children are often punished with deformed creatures as animals. When the parents, however, have been humbled, the deformed creatures are transformed into human beings."
23. The Little Shroud (Das Todtenhemdchen). Source: Ferdinand Grimm.

The Grimms note that the belief that tears wept for a dead person and that fall on the corpse in the grave disturb the dead person's peace appears in the second "Helge-lied" and also in the Danish folk song about the knight Aage and the maiden Else.

24. The Jew in the Thornbush (Der Jud' im Dorn). Source: Old printed versions mixed with oral stories from Hesse and Paderborn (Von Haxthausen family).

The Grimms cite the following stories as influencing the development of their tale: Albert Dietrich, *Historia von einem Bauernknecht und München, welcher in der Dornhecken hat müssen tanzen* (1618), and Jakob Ayer's Shrovetide play, *Fritz Dolla mit seiner gewünschten Geige* (1620). Interestingly, there is no Jew in these stories. Instead, there is a thieving monk, and the tales are somewhat anti-Catholic. At the same time, there were other seventeenth-century folk versions in Czechoslovakia in which the Jew plays a negative role.

25. The Expert Huntsman (Der gelernte Jager). Source: Dorothea Viehmann.

26. The Fleshing Flail from Heaven (Der Dresschpflegel vom Himmel). Source: Von Haxthausen family.

The Grimms trace this story to the tall tales told by the famous raconteur, Hieronymous Karl Friederich Baron von Münchhausen (1720–97). Some of his preposterous tales were printed in the *Vademeum für lustige Leute* (1781–83), and in 1885, Rudolf Erich Raspe published an English edition of Münchhausen's tales under the title *Baron Munchausen's Narrative of His Marvelous Travels and Campaigns in Russia*.

27. The Children of the Two Kings (De beiden Künnigeskinner). Source: Ludowine von Haxthausen.

The Grimms point to similarities in "The Singing, Springing Lark," "Prince Swan," "Sweetheart Roland," and "Okerlo."

28. The Clever Little Tailor (Vom klugen Schneiderlein). Source: Ferdinand Siebert.

29. The Bright Sun Will Bring It to Light (Die klare Sonne bringt's an den Tag). Source: Dorothea Viehmann.

The Grimms note that in this story, "a profound, marvelous bourgeois motif is articulated. Nobody saw the murder, no human eye except for the sun (God), the heavenly eye. There are other stories about the sun and how it covers itself and doesn't want to view a murder is about to take place." Then they close their note with a remarkable proverb: "Nothing can be so finely woven that the sun can't eventually expose it."

30. The Blue Light (Das blaue Licht). Source: Told by a soldier to August von Haxthausen.

31. The Stubborn Child (Von einem eigensinnigen Kinde). Source: From the Hessian oral tradition.

The Grimms state that this is a simple didactic story for children similar to "The Old Grandfather and the Grandson." Furthermore, they explain that the hand that sticks itself out of the grave was a widespread superstition and pertained to thieves as well as sinners tied to trees. They also recall another similar short version that appeared in Johannes Pauli's *Schimpf und Ernst* (1522).

32. The Three Army Surgeons (Die drei Feldscherer). Source: Dorothea Viehmann. The Grimms summarize a similar tale from the *Gesta Romanurum* (ca. fourteenth century):

> In order to settle an argument, two talented doctors decide to compete with each other and use each other to demonstrate their skills. Whoever loses the competition must serve as the assistant to the other. The first doctor takes out the eyes of the other doctor with the help of an ointment and without causing any damage or pain. After he lays the eyes out on a table, he puts them easily back into the other doctor's sockets. Now the second doctor wants to perform the same trick. He uses his ointment to take out the eyes of the first doctor and lays them out on a table. However, as he is preparing to put the eyes back into the sockets, a raven comes flying through a window, carries away one of the eyes, and eats it. The doctor who performed this operation is desperate because if he can't replace the eye, he will have to become the other doctor's assistant. So he looks around himself and notices a goat. Quickly he cuts out one of the goat's eyes and places it into the socket of his companion as the missing eye. Afterward he asks his companion how he feels, the other doctor says that he didn't experience any pain or damage, but one of his eyes constantly looks over to the bushes and trees (just as goats generally search for leaves) and the other eye keeps looking down.

33. The Lazy One and the Industrious One (Der Faule und der Fleißige). Source: Ferdinand Siebert.

34. The Three Journeymen (Die drei Handwerksburschen). Source: Dorothea Viehmann and Georg August Friedrich Goldmann.

35. The Heavenly Wedding (Die himmlische Hochzeit). Source: An anonymous tale from Mecklenburg combined with a tale from Ludowine von Haxthausen.

The Grimms comment that this tale borders on being a legend and yet retains a childlike quality. The innocent belief in the words of God leads to a misunderstanding and yet to salvation.

36. The Long Nose (Die lange Nase). Source: Dorothea Viehmann.

The Grimms note that this tale can be traced back to the sixteenth century, and in particular, to *Fortunatus* (ca. 1509). They also allude to the *Gesta Romanorum* (1473) as a possible source.

37. The Old Woman in the Forest (Die Alte im Wald). Source: Von Haxthausen family.

The Grimms state that this tale is similar to "Jorinda and Jorungel" and that the old woman is like the witch in "Hansel and Gretel."

38. The Three Brothers (Die drei Brüder). Source: Ferdinand Siebert.

The Grimms explain that this preposterous or tall tale is old and widespread. One of the first examples of this story can be found in *La nouvelle Fabrique des excellens traicts de vérités* (1579) by Philippe d'Alcripe (Picard).

39. The Devil and His Grandmother (Der Teufel und seine Großmutter). Source: Dorothea Viehmann.

The Grimms point to similarities with "The Devil with the Three Golden Hairs" and "Rumpelstiltskin." They also state that "the entire tale has something Nordic in its essence. The devil appears as an awkward, outwitted idiot. The riddle is clearly Nordic. In addition the motif of the old woman's hiding the human creature who has just arrived at the devil's home is an old motif.

40. Faithful Ferdinand and Unfaithful Ferdinand (Ferenand getrü und Ferenand ungetrü). Source: Von Haxthausen family.

The Grimms think that this tale seems to be incomplete and that it would have been more convincing if the horse would have turned into a prince at the end. They also point to a similarity with "Godfather Death."

41. The Iron Stove (Der Eisen-Ofen). Source: Dorothea Viehmann.

This tale is clearly related to other stories in the beast/bridegroom cycle, and the Grimms point to the similarities with "Prince Swan," "The Singing, Springing Lark," and "The Two King's Children" in their own collection and to Giambattista Basile's "Pintosmauto" in *Il Pentamerone* (1634). In addition the Grimms explain that the dark and fiery oven in which the prince is confined is undoubtedly hell or the underworld where Death dwells. In addition the word *Eisenofern* means "ancient and antiquated" and does not have so much to do with iron but is related more with the word *Eitofan*, or place of fire or fireplace.

42. The Lazy Spinner (Die faule Spinnerin). Source: Dorothea Viehmann.

The Grimms point to similarities with "Nasty Flax Spinning" in the first volume of their collection and to Giambattista Basile's "Le sette cotennine," *Il Pentamerone* (1634), as well as to a tale in Johannes Pauli's *Schimpf und Ernst* (1535).

43. The Lion and the Frog (Der Löwe und der Frosch). Source: Ludovica Jordis-Brentano.

44. The Soldier and the Carpenter (Der Soldat und der Schreiner). Source: Von Haxthausen family.

The Grimms comment that there are many good and marvelous things in this tale, but the tale as a whole seems to have suffered somewhat partly because of gaps and partly because of confusion.

45. Pretty Katrinelya and Pif-Paf-Poltree (Die schöne Katrinelje und Pif, Paf, Poltrie). Source: Von Haxthausen family.

46. The Fox and the Horse (Der Fuchs und das Pferd). Source: Maria Anna ("Jenny") von Droste-Hülshoff.

The Grimms note that this tale is related to the medieval cycle of Renard the Fox and similar to "Old Sultan" in the first volume of their collection.

47. The Worn-out Dancing Shoes (Die zertanzten Schuhe). Source: Maria Anna ("Jenny") von Droste-Hülshoff.

The Grimms remark that the penalty for not discovering what the princesses do during the evening is death, as in the story about Turandot.

48. The Six Servants (Die sechs Diener). Source: Von Haxthausen family.

The Grimms note that there is a similar tale written by Hieronymous Karl Friederich Baron von Münchhausen (1720–97). Some of his preposterous tales were printed in the *Vademeum für lustige Leute* (1781–83), and in 1885, Rudolf Erich Raspe published an English edition of Münchhausen's tales under the title *Baron Munchausen's Narrative of His Marvelous Travels and Campaigns in Russia*. They also mention Thor and his servant Thialfi, Giambattista Basile's tales "Lo 'gnorante" and "Lo Polece," *Il Pentamerone* (1634), as well as an anonymous Hessian version that they consider insignificant.

49. The White Bride and the Black Bride (Die weiße und schwarze Braut). Source: Von Haxthausen family and an anonymous tale from Mecklenburg.

The basis for this tale is "Die goldene Ente. Ein Nationalmärchen des Altertums," which appeared in *Sagen der böhmischen Vorzeit* (1808), and which Jacob Grimm had written down in an abbreviated form. It was included in the Ölenberg Manuscript of 1810.

50. The Wild Man (De wilde Mann). Source: A dialect tale written down by Maria Anna ("Jenny") von Droste-Hülshoff.

The Grimms interpret this version as a kind of male "Cinderella" tale.

51. The Three Black Princesses (De drei schwatten Princessinnen). Source: A dialect tale written down by Maria Anna ("Jenny") von Droste-Hülshoff.

The Grimms note that the magic in this particular tale leads to ruin and destruction and not to the expected salvation.

52. Knoist and His Three Sons (Knoist un sine dre Söhne). Source: A dialect tale provided by one of August von Haxthausen's sisters.

The Grimms note that Werrel and Soist were destinations for pilgrimages in Westphalia.

53. The Maiden from Brakel (Dat Mäken von Brakel). Source: A dialect tale provided by the von Haxthausen family.

The Grimms explain that St. Anne is the patron saint of Brakel, and her church right outside the city of Brakel.

54. The Domestic Servants (Das Hausgesinde). Source: Von Haxthausen family.

Although the Grimms classify this nonsense story a tale, it is more a children's game that can be traced back to the early eighteenth century. There is a very similar version of the Grimms' story in *Alle Arten von Scherz- und Pfänderspielen* (1750).

55. Little Lamb and Little Fish (Das Lämmchen und Fischchen). Source: Marianne von Haxthausen.

56. Sesame Mountain (Simeliberg). Source: Ludowine von Haxthausen.

The Grimms found it remarkable that this tale, told in the regions near Münster and the Harz forest and based on "Ali Baba and the Forty Thieves" from *The Thousand*

and One Nights, had made its way in one form or another to Germany. They cite a version from Johann Karl Christoph Nachtigal's *Volcks-Sagen. Nacherzählt von Otmar* (1800) that might have been a source. It was reproduced in Johann Gustav Gottlieb Büsching's *Volks-Sagen, Märchen und Legenden* (1812). What was also unusual, according to the Grimms, is that the name of the mountain, *Sesame*, was similar to the names of German mountains Semsi, Semeli, and Simeli.

57. The Children of Famine (Die Kinder in Hungersnoth). Source: Johannes Praetorius, *Der abentheuerliche Glückstopf* (1669).

58. The Little Donkey (Das Eselein). Source: Jacob Grimm's translation of a medieval Latin text, "Asinarius," in a Strasbourg manuscript.

The Grimms draw parallels with other tales dealing with donkeys in their collection as well as beast/bridegroom stories such as "Hans My Hedgehog."

59. The Ungrateful Son (Der undankbare Sohn). Source: Johannes Pauli, *Schimpf und Ernst* (1552).

The Grimms indicate that this tale was widespread in the medieval period, and they refer to a version by Thomas of Cantimpré from the thirteenth century, probably *Bonum universale de Apibus* (1257–63).

60. The Turnip (Die Rube). Source: Jacob Grimm's translation of a medieval Latin poem, "Raparius," in a Strasbourg fifteenth-century manuscript.

The Grimms believe that the poem was probably written down in the fourteenth century and was based on an oral tale from Alsace.

61. The Rejuvenated Little Old Man (Das junggeglühte Männlein). Source: Based on a farce in verse by Hans Sachs, "Der affen ursprung," (1536).

The Grimms note that the tale reminded them of Greek stories about Medea, Aeson, and Pelias.

62. The Animals of the Lord and the Devil (Des Herrn und des Teufels Gethier). Source: Based on a 1557 tale by Hans Sachs.

The wolves as God's dogs have a remarkable similarity to Nordic gods' dogs that were also wolves.

63. The Beam (Der Hahnenbalken). Source: Based on a poem, "Der Hanenbalken" (1812), written by Friedrich Kind and published in the magazine *Taschenbuch zum geselligen Vergnügen*.

64. The Old Beggar Woman (Die alte Bettelfrau). Source: Johann Heinrich Jung-Stilling, *Heinrich Stillings Jugend* (1777).

The Grimms draw a parallel with the fiery death of Odin.

65. The Three Lazy Sons (Die drei Faulen). Source: *Gesta Romanorum* (thirteenth/fourteenth century) and Johannes Pauli, *Schimpf und Ernst* (1522).

66. Saint Solicitous (Die heilige Frau Kummerniß). Source: A legend by Andreas Strobl, *Ovum paschale oder Neugefärbte Oster-Ayr* (1700).

Strobl's version was based on an exemplar in Benignus Kybler's *Wunder-Spiegel* (1678).

67. The Tale about the Land of Cockaigne (Das Märchen vom Schlauaffenland). Source: A medieval tale in verse, "Sô ist diz von lügenen," transcribed by Wilhelm Grimm from a fourteenth-century collection of old German poems. The Grimms draw parallels to other similar tales such as a farce in Hans Sachs's poems and to Johann Fischart's translation of *Gargantua* (1575).

68. The Tall Tale from Ditmarsh (Das Dietmarsische Lügen-Märchen). Source: A dancing song, "Von eiteln unmöglichen Dingen," in Anton Viethen's and Johann Albert Fabricius's *Beschreibung und Geschichte des Landes Dithmarschen* (1733).

69. A Tale with a Riddle (Räthsel-Märchen). Source: *Rätersch-Büchlein* (sixteenth century), *Straßburger Rätselbuch* (sixteenth century, and *Rätersch-Büchlein* (seventeenth century).

70. The Golden Key (Der goldene Schlüssel). Source: Marie Hassenpflug.

This tale was slightly modified over the years, but it always remained the last story throughout the Grimms' seven editions. Its placement was significant for the Grimms. Just as some version of "The Frog King" always opened the Grimms' collection, "The Golden Key" was always the final tale because it signified the never-ending quality of folk tales that, they believed, would continue to evolve and change throughout time.

INDEX OF TALES